THE CASE OF THE MISSING SERVANT

Private detective Vish Puri is portly, persistent and Punjabi. He cuts a swathe through Delhi's swindlers, cheats and murderers. His crack team of operatives include: Tubelight, a heavy sleeper who takes time to flicker on in the morning, but is skilled at cracking locks and ignitions; Flush, proud owner of the first flush toilet in his village, and an electronics and computer whizz; and Facecream, the beautiful undercover specialist, who can be anything from a street sweeper to the bait in an irresistible honey trap. The team must draw on all their skills to clear the name of an honest public litigator, accused of murdering his servant girl. Can she be found? Will it be another successful outcome for the Most Private Investigators?

TARQUIN HALL

THE CASE OF THE MISSING SERVANT

from the files of Vish Puri, India's 'Most Private Investigator'

Complete and Unabridged

CHARNWOOD
Leicester

First published in Great Britain in 2009 by
Hutchinson, London

First Charnwood Edition
published 2010
by arrangement with
Hutchinson
The Random House Group Limited, London

The moral right of the author has been asserted

This is a work of fiction. Names and characters
are the product of the author's imagination and
any resemblance to actual persons, living or dead,
is entirely coincidental.

British Library CIP Data

Hall, Tarquin.
    The case of the missing servant.
    1. Private investigators- -India- -Delhi- -Fiction.
    2. Gurus- -India- -Delhi- -Fiction. 3. Delhi (India)- -
    Social life and customs- -Fiction. 4. Detective and
    mystery stories. 5. Large type books.
    I. Title
    823.9′2–dc22

    ISBN 978–1–84782–953–5

Published by
F. A. Thorpe (Publishing)
Anstey, Leicestershire

Set by Words & Graphics Ltd.
Anstey, Leicestershire
Printed and bound in Great Britain by
T. J. International Ltd., Padstow, Cornwall

This book is printed on acid-free paper

This book is dedicated to the memory of
Grandpa Briggs

1

Vish Puri, founder and managing director of Most Private Investigators Ltd. sat alone in a room in a guesthouse in Defence Colony, south Delhi, devouring a dozen green chilli *pakoras* from a greasy takeaway box.

Puri was supposed to be keeping off the fried foods and Indian desserts he so loved. Dr Mohan had 'intimated' to him at his last check-up that he could no longer afford to indulge himself with the usual Punjabi staples.

'Blood pressure is up, so chance of heart attack and diabetes is there. Don't do obesity,' he'd advised.

Puri considered the doctor's stern warning as he sank his teeth into another hot, crispy pakora and his taste buds thrilled to the tang of salty batter, fiery chilli and the tangy, red chutney in which he had drowned the illicit snack. He derived a perverse sense of satisfaction from defying Dr Mohan's orders.

Still, the fifty-one-year-old detective shuddered to think what his wife would say if she found out he was eating between meals — especially 'outside' food that had not been prepared by her own hands (or at least by one of the servants).

Keeping this in mind, he was careful not to get any incriminating grease spots on his clothes. And once he had finished his snack and disposed of the takeaway box, he washed the chutney off his hands and checked beneath his manicured nails and between his teeth for any tell-tale residue. Finally he popped some *sonf* into his mouth to freshen his breath.

All the while, Puri kept an eye on the house across the way and the street below.

By Delhi standards, it was a quiet and exceptionally clean residential street. Defence Colony's elitist, upper middle-class residences — army officers, doctors, engineers, *babus* and the occasional *press-wallah* — had ensured that their gated community remained free of industry, commerce and the usual human detritus. Residents could take a walk through the well-swept streets or idle in the communal gardens without fear of being hassled by disfigured beggars . . . or having to negotiate their way around arc welders soldering lengths of metal on the pavements . . . or halal butchers slaughtering chickens.

Most of the families in Defence Colony were Punjabi and had arrived in New Delhi as refugees following the catastrophic partition of the Indian subcontinent in 1947. As their affluence and numbers had grown over the decades, they had built cubist cement villas surrounded by high perimeter walls and imposing wrought iron gates.

Each of these mini-fiefdoms employed an entire company of servants. The residents of number 76, D Block, the house that Puri was watching, retained the services of no fewer than seven full-time people — two drivers, a cook, a

2

cleaner-cum-laundry-maid, a bearer and two security guards. Three of these employees were 'live-in' and shared the *barsaati* on the roof. The overnight security guard slept in the sentry box positioned outside the front gate, though strictly speaking, he really wasn't meant to.

The family also relied on a part-time dishwasher, a sweeper, a gardener and the local pressing-wallah who had a stand under the neem tree down the street where he applied a heavy iron filled with hot coals to a dizzying assortment of garments, including silk saris, cotton *salwars* and denim jeans.

From the vantage point in the room Puri had rented, he could see the dark-skinned cleaner-cum-laundry-maid on the roof of number 76, hanging underwear on the washing line. The *mali* was on the first-floor balcony watering the potted plants. The sweeper was using up gallons of precious water hosing down the marble forecourt. And, out in the street, the cook was inspecting the green chillis being sold by a local costermonger who pushed a wooden cart through the neighbourhood, periodically calling out, '*Subzi-wallah!*'

Puri had positioned two of his best undercover operatives, Tubelight and Flush, down in the street.

These were not their real names, of course. Being Punjabi, the detective had nicknames for most of his employees, relatives and close friends. For example, he called his wife Rumpi; his new driver, Handbrake; and the office boy, who was extraordinarily lazy, Door Stop.

3

Tubelight was so-named because he was a heavy sleeper and took a while to flicker into life in the morning. The forty-three-year-old hailed from a clan of hereditary thieves, and therefore had been highly adept at cracking locks, safes and ignitions since childhood.

As for Flush, he had a flush toilet in his home, a first for anyone in his remote village in the state of Haryana. An electronics and computer whiz, during his career with Indian intelligence he had once managed to place a microscopic bug inside the Pakistani ambassador's dentures.

The other member of the team, Facecream, was waiting a few miles away and would play a crucial part in the operation later that evening. A beautiful and feisty Nepali woman who had run away from home as a teenager to join the Maoists, but became disillusioned with the cause and escaped to India, she often worked undercover — one day posing as a street sweeper; the next as irresistible bait in a honeytrap.

Puri himself was known by various names.

His father had always addressed him by his full name, Vishwas, which the detective had later shortened to Vish because it rhymes with 'wish' (and 'Vish Puri' could be taken to mean 'granter of wishes'). But the rest of his family and friends knew him as Chubby, an affectionate rather than a derisive sobriquet — although as Dr Mohan had pointed out so indelicately, he did need to lose about thirty pounds.

Puri insisted on being called Boss by his employees, which helped remind them who was

4

in charge. In India, it was important to keep a strong chain of command; people were used to hierarchy and they responded to authority. As he was fond of saying, 'You can't have every Johnny thinking he's a Nelson, no?'

The detective reached for his walkie-talkie and spoke into it.

'What's that Charlie up to, over?' he said.

'Still doing timepass, Boss,' replied Flush. There was a pause before he remembered to add the requisite 'over.'

Flush, who was thirty-two, skinny and wore thick, milk-bottle-bottom glasses, was sitting in the back of Puri's Hindustan Ambassador monitoring the bugs the team had planted inside the target's home earlier, as well as all incoming and outgoing phone calls. Meanwhile, Tubelight, who was middle aged with henna-dyed hair and blind in one eye, was disguised as an autorickshaw-wallah in oily clothes and rubber *chappals*. Crouched on his haunches on the side of the street among a group of *bidi*-smoking local drivers, he was gambling at cards.

Puri, a self-confessed master of disguise, had not changed into anything unusual for today's operation, though seeing him for the first time, you might have been forgiven for thinking this was not the case. His military moustache, first grown when he was a recruit in the army, was waxed and curled at the ends. He was wearing one of his trademark tweed Sandown caps, imported from Bates of Jermyn Street in Piccadilly, and a pair of prescription aviator sunglasses.

Now that it was November and the intense heat of summer had subsided, he had also opted for his new grey safari suit. It had been made for him, as all his shirts and suits were, by Mr M. A. Pathan of Connaught Place, whose grandfather had often dressed Muhammad Ali Jinnah, founder of Pakistan.

'A *pukka* Savile Row finish if ever I saw one,' said the detective to himself, admiring the cut in a mirror in the empty room. 'Really tip top.'

The suit was indeed perfectly tailored for his short, tubby frame. The silver buttons with the stag emblems were especially fetching.

Puri sat down in his canvas chair and waited. It was only a matter of time before Ramesh Goel made his move. Everything the detective had learned about the young man suggested that he would not be able to resist temptation.

The two had come face to face on Day One of the operation when Puri had entered number 76, the Goel family residence, disguised as a telephone repairman. That encounter, however brief, had told the detective all he needed to know. Ramesh Goel, who had spiky hair and walked with a swagger, lacked moral fibre. It was the same with so many young, middle-class people these days. Infidelity was rife, divorce rates were on the up, elderly parents were being abused and abandoned in old people's homes, sons no longer understood their responsibilities to their parents or society as a whole.

'Many thousands of males and females are working in call centres and IT sector side by side and they are becoming attached and going in for one-night stands,' Puri had written in his latest letter to the *Times of India*, which the honourable editor had seen fit to publish. 'In this environment, in which males and females are thrust together without proper family supervision or moral code, peer group pressure is at the highest level. Even young females are going in for pre-marital affairs, extramarital affairs — even extra, extramarital affairs. So much infidelity is there that many marriages are getting over.'

American influence was to blame with its emphasis on materialism, individuality and lack of family values.

'A fellow is no longer happy serving society. *Dharma*, duty, has been ejected out of the window. Now the average male wants five-star living: Omega watch, Italian hotel food, Dubai holiday, luxury apartment, a fancy girl on the side,' Puri had written. 'All of a sudden, young Indians are adopting the habits of *goras*, white people.'

Sixty years after Gandhi-ji sent them packing, Mother India was, being conquered by outsiders again.

'Boss, Flush this side, over.' The voice broke into the detective's private lament.

'Boss this side, over,' replied the detective.

'Mouse made contact, Boss. Leaving shortly, over.' 'Mouse' was code for Goel.

The detective made his way as quickly as he could down into the street and, a little short of breath after his exertion on the stairs, joined Flush in the back of the waiting Ambassador.

7

Tubelight folded his hand of cards, made a hasty apology to the other drivers, collected up his winnings (nearly sixty rupees; not bad for an hour's work), and revved up the three-wheeler he had rented for the day from his cousin Bhagat.

A few minutes later, the gates to the Goel residence swung open and a red Indica hatchback pulled out. The vehicle turned right. Tubelight waited five seconds and then followed. Puri's Ambassador, with Handbrake at the wheel, was not far behind.

The team kept a safe distance as Goel sped along the old Ring Road. There was little doubt in the detective's mind where his mark was heading.

'This Charlie might be having *Angrezi* education, but he is like a moth to Vish Puri's flame,' he said with a grin.

Flush, who held his employer in high regard and had learned to tolerate his boastfulness, replied, 'Yes Boss.'

The Ambassador and the *auto* took turns tailing the Indica through the streets of south Delhi, the rush hour traffic helping the team remain inconspicuous. Cars, motorcycles, scooters, cyclists, bicycle rickshaws, trucks, hand-pushed carts, bullock carts, sacred cows and the occasional unroadworthy hybrid vehicle that defied description vied for space on the road. Like bumper cars at a fair-ground, vehicles cut across one another, drivers inching into any space that presented itself, making four and a half lanes out of three. Horns blared constantly, a clamour as jarring as a primary school brass band. Loudest of all were the Blueline buses. Driven by *charas*-smoking maniacs who were given financial incentives for picking up the most passengers, even if they ended up killing or maiming some of them. 'Bloody *goondas*,' Puri called them. But he knew that the harshest penalty these men would ever face was a few hours in a police station drinking *chai*. Politicians and babus owned all the buses and had the police in their pockets. The going rate for expunging the record of a 'manslaughter' charge was about three thousand rupees.

The detective watched one of these battered Blueline buses lumbering through the traffic like an old wounded war elephant, its sides scarred by previous battles. Faces peered down from the scratched windows — some with curiosity, others with envy and perhaps contempt — into the plush interiors of the many thousands of new luxury sedans on Delhi's roads. For the have-nots, here was a glimpse of the lifestyle that hundreds of thousands of the nouveau riches had adopted. For Puri, the scene was a reminder of the widening economic disparity in Indian society.

'Mouse is turning right, Boss,' said Hand-brake.

Puri nodded. 'Tubelight, keep ahead of him,' he said into his walkie-talkie. 'We'll keep back, over.'

Goel's Indica passed over the new spaghetti junction of 'overbridges' in front of the All India Institute of Medical Sciences and continued in the direction of Sarojini Nagar. Had it not been for the occasional ancient tomb or monument — echoes of Delhi's previous incarnations, now jammed between all the concrete and reflective glass — Puri would not have recognised the place.

In his childhood, Delhi had been slow-moving and provincial. But in the past ten years Puri had watched the city race off in all directions, spreading east and south, with more roads, cars, malls and apartment blocks springing up each day. The dizzying prosperity attracted millions of uneducated and unskilled villagers into the capital from impoverished states across north India. With the population explosion — now 16 million and rising — came a dramatic increase in crime. The vast conglomeration of Old Delhi, New Delhi and its many suburbs had been officially renamed the National Capital Region — or the 'National Crime Region', as most newspapers wrote mockingly.

For Puri, this meant more work. Most Private Investigators Ltd. had never been busier. Still, the business was not all welcome. There were days when the detective found his natural optimism waning. Sometimes he would battle home through the honking gridlock wondering if perhaps he should turn his hand to social work.

His dear wife, Rumpi, always reminded Puri that India was making great progress and talked him out of throwing in the towel. She would point out that he was already doing the public a service. His current investigation was but one example. He was on the brink of saving a young woman from a terrible fate and bringing an

10

unscrupulous individual to account.

Yes, it would not be long now before Ramesh Goel was brought to book. Puri would have him in another ten minutes or so.

The detective made sure Handbrake remained three cars behind the Indica on the last leg of his journey down Africa Avenue to Safdarjung Enclave. Predictably, the young man turned into A Block.

Unbeknownst to Goel, as he pulled up outside A 2/12 — 'Boss, he's at A-two-oblique-twelve, over' — he was being filmed with a long lens from a nearby vantage point. It made no difference that he was wearing a baseball cap, sunglasses and a dark raincoat in an effort to disguise himself. Nor that he was using the alias Romey Butter.

Vish Puri had got his man.

2

The detective was not looking forward to the conclusion of the Ramesh Goel case. It rarely gave him any satisfaction to convey bad news to a client, especially such a successful and powerful man as Sanjay Singla.

'But what to do?' Puri said to Elizabeth Rani, his loyal secretary, who had worked for him since Most Private Investigators had opened above Bahri Sons bookshop in Khan Market in south Delhi, in 1988.

'I tell you, Madam Rani, it's a good thing Sanjay Singla came to me,' he added. 'Just think of the bother I've saved him. That bloody Ramesh Goel would have made off with a fortune! A most slippery fellow if ever I met one. Undoubtedly!'

Elizabeth Rani, a stolid widow whose husband had been killed in a traffic accident in 1987 leaving her with three children to provide for, did not have a head for mysteries, intrigue or conspiracies, and often found herself lost in all the ins and outs of his many investigations — especially given that Puri was usually working on two or three at a time. Her job required her to keep Boss's diary, answer the phones, manage the files and make sure Door Stop, the office boy, didn't steal the milk and sugar.

Unofficially, it was also Elizabeth Rani's remit to listen patiently to Puri's expositions and, from

12

time to time, give his ego a gentle massage.

'Such a good job you have done, sir,' she said, placing the Ramesh Goel file on Puri's desk. 'My sincerest compliments.'

The detective grinned from his executive swivel chair.

'You are too kind, Madam Rani!' he answered. 'But as usual, you are correct. I don't mind admitting this operation was first class. Conceived and carried out with the utmost professionalism and secrecy. Another successful outcome for Most Private Investigators!'

Elizabeth Rani waited patiently until he had finished congratulating himself before giving Puri his messages.

'Sir, a certain Ajay Kasliwal called saying he wishes to consult on a most urgent matter. He proposes to meet at the Gym tonight at seven o'clock. Shall I confirm?'

'He gave any reference?'

'He's knowing Bunty Bannerjee.'

A smile came over the detective's face at the mention of his old friend and *batchmate* at the military academy.

'Most certainly I'll see him,' he said. 'Tell Kasliwal I'll reach at seven come rain or shine.'

Elizabeth Rani withdrew from the office and sat down behind her desk in reception.

Her tea mug was halfway to her lips when she heard a knock at the door. Apart from the various clients coming into Most Private Investigators Ltd., there was a small army of wallahs, or people charged with specific tasks vital to the rhythm of everyday Indian life. Ms

13

Rani found the lime and chilli woman at the door and remembered it was Monday. For three rupees per week, the woman would come and hang a fresh string of three green chillies and a lime above the door of each business in the market to ward off evil spirits. Ms Rani was also in charge of paying the local *hijras* during the festival season when they approached all the businesses in the market and demanded *bakshish*; and ensured that the local brass plaque polisher kept the sign on the wall next to the doorbell shiny. It read:

MOST PRIVATE INVESTIGATORS LTD.
VISH PURI, MANAGING DIRECTOR, CHIEF
OFFICER AND WINNER OF ONE
INTERNATIONAL AND SIX NATIONAL
AWARDS
'CONFIDENTIALITY IS OUR WATCHWORD'

Meanwhile, Puri turned his attention to the evidence he had compiled against Ramesh Goel and, having satisfied himself that everything was in order, prepared for the imminent arrival of his client, Sanjay Singla.

Reaching into his drawer for his face mirror, he inspected his moustache, curling the ends between his fingers. His Sandown cap, which he only ever took off in the privacy of his bedroom, also required adjustment. Next, he glanced around the room to check that everything was exactly as it should be.

There was nothing fancy about the small office. Unlike the new breed of young detectives with their leather couches, pine veneer desks and glass partitions, Puri remained faithful to the furniture and décor dating back to his agency's opening in the late 1980s (he liked to think that it spoke of experience, old-fashioned reliability and a certain rare character).

He kept a number of artefacts pertaining to some of his most celebrated cases on display. Amongst them was a truncheon presented to him by the Gendarmerie Nationale in recognition of his invaluable help in locating the French ambassador's wife (and for being so discreet about her dalliance with the embassy cook). But pride of place on the wall behind his antique desk belonged to the Super Sleuth plaque presented to him in 1999 by the World Federation of Detectives for solving The Case of the Missing Polo Elephant.

The room's focal point, however, was the shrine in the far corner. Two portraits hung above it, both of them draped in strings of fresh marigolds. The first was a likeness of Puri's guru, the philosopher-statesman, Chanakya, who lived 300 years before Christ and founded the arts of espionage and investigation. The second was a photograph of the detective's late father, Om Chander Puri, posing in his police uniform on the day in 1963 when he was made a detective.

Puri was staring up at the portrait of his Papa-ji and musing over some of the invaluable lessons his father had taught him when Elizabeth Rani's voice came over the intercom.

'Sir, Singla-ji has come.'

Without replying, the detective pressed a

buzzer under his desk; this activated the security lock on his door and it swung open. A moment later, his client strode into his office — tall, confident, reeking of Aramis.

Puri met his visitor halfway, shaking him by the hand. '*Namashkar*, sir,' he said. 'So kind of you to come. Please take a seat.'

Puri sounded obsequious, but he was not in the least bit intimidated at having such a distinguished man in his office. The deference he showed his client was purely out of respect for hierarchy. Singla was at least five years his senior and one of the richest industrialists in the country.

Private detectives on the other hand were not held in great esteem in Indian society, ranking little higher than security guards. Partly this was because many were con men and blackmail artists who were prepared to sell their aunties for a few thousand rupees. Mostly it was because the private investigation business was not a traditional career like medicine or engineering and people did not have an appreciation — or respect — for the tremendous skills that the job required. So Singla talked to Puri as he might to a middle manager.

'Tell me,' he said in a booming voice, adjusting his French cuffs.

The detective chose not to begin immediately. 'Some chai, sir?'

Singla made a gesture with his hands as if he was brushing away a fly.

'Some water?'

'Nothing,' he said impatiently. 'Let us come to

the point. No delay. What you have found? Nothing bad, I hope. I like this young man, Puri, and I pride myself on being an excellent judge of character. Ramesh reminds me of myself when I was a young man. A real go-getter.'

Singla had made it clear to Puri during their first meeting a fortnight earlier that he had reservations about commissioning an investigation. 'This spying business is a dirty game,' he'd said.

But in the interest of his daughter, he'd agreed to make use of the detective's services. After all, Singla did not really know Ramesh Goel. Nor Goel's family.

How could he?

Up until two months ago, they — the Singlas and the Goels — had never met. And in India, marriage was always about much more than the union between a boy and a girl. It was also about two families coming together.

In the old days, there would have been no need for Puri's services. Families got to know one another within the social framework of their own communities. When necessary, they did their own detective work. Mothers and aunties would ask neighbours and friends about prospective brides and grooms, and their families' standing and reputation. Priests would also make introductions and match horoscopes.

Today, well-off Indians living in cities could no longer rely on those time-honoured systems. Many no longer knew their neighbours. Their homes were the walled villas of Jor Bagh and Golf Links, or posh apartment blocks in Greater

17

Kailash. Their social lives revolved around the office, business functions and society weddings.

And yet the arranged marriage remained sacrosanct. Even among the wealthiest Delhi families, few parents gave their blessing to a 'love marriage', even when the couples belonged to the same religion and caste. It was still considered utterly disrespectful for a child to find his or her own mate. After all, only a parent had the wisdom and foresight necessary for such a vital and delicate task. Increasingly, Indians living in major towns and cities relied on newspaper ads and internet websites to find spouses for their children.

The Singlas' advertisement in the *Indian Express* had read as follows:

SOUTH DELHI HIGH STATUS AGRAWAL
BUSINESS FAMILY
SEEKS ALLIANCE FOR THEIR HOMELY, SLIM,
SWEET-NATURED, VEGETARIAN AND CUL-
TURED DAUGHTER. 5'1".50 KG. WHEATISH
COMPLEXION. MBA FROM USA.
NON-MANGLIK. DOB: JULY '83 (LOOKS
MUCH YOUNGER). ENGAGED IN BUSINESS
BUT NOT INCLINEDTO PROFESSIONAL
CAREER. BOY MAIN CONSIDERATION.
LOOKING FOR PROFESSIONALLY QUALIFIED
DOCTOR/INDUSTRIALIST BOY FROM DELHI
OR OVERSEAS.
PLS SEND BIODATA, PHOTO, HOROSCOPE.
CALL IN
CONFIDENCE.

18

Ramesh Goel's parents had seen the advertisement and applied, providing a detailed personal history and a head-shot of their son.

At twenty-nine, he ticked all the boxes. He was an Agrawal and Cambridge-educated. His family was not fabulously wealthy (Goel's father was a doctor), but for the Singlas, caste and social status were the main concern.

From the start, their daughter, Vimi, liked the look of Ramesh Goel. When she was shown his headshot, she cooed, 'So handsome, no?' Soon after, the two families had tea at the Singlas' mansion in Sundar Nagar. The rendezvous was a success. The parents got along and provided their consent for Vimi and Ramesh to spend time together unchaperoned. The two went out on a couple of dates, once to a restaurant, a few days later to a bowling alley. The following week, they agreed to marry. Subsequently, astrologers were consulted and a date and time was set for the wedding.

But with less than a month before the big day, Sanjay Singla, acting on the advice of a sensible friend, decided to have Goel screened. That was where Puri had come into the picture.

During their initial meeting at Singla's office, the detective had done his best to assure the industrialist that he was doing the right thing.

'You would not invite a stranger into your house. Why invite any Tom, Dick or Harry into your family?' he'd said.

The detective had told Singla about some of the cases he had handled in the past. Only recently, he'd run a standard background check on a Non-Resident Indian living in London who was betrothed to a Chandigarh businessman's daughter and discovered that he was a charlatan. Neelesh Anand of Woodford was not, as he claimed, the owner of the Empress of India on the Romford Road, but a second-order *balti* cook!

As Puri had put it to Singla: 'Had I not unmasked this bloody goonda then he would have made off with the dowry and never been heard of again, leaving the female in disgrace.'

By disgrace he'd meant married, childless and living back at home with her parents — or worse: on her own.

Of course, the Anand case had been a straightforward investigation, a simple matter of calling up his old friend, retired Scotland Yard inspector Ian Masters, and asking him to head down to Upton Park in east London for a curry. Most pre-matrimonial cases that came Puri's way — there were so many now, he was having to turn them away — were simple.

The Goel investigation, however, had been far more involved. Singla had been persuaded to commission the Pre-Matrimonial Five-Star Comprehensive Service, the most expensive package Most Private Investigators provided. Even Ramesh Goel's parents' financial dealings and records had been scrutinised by forensic accountants.

The file now lying on Puri's desk was testimony to the long hours that had gone into the case. It was thick with bank statements, phone records and credit card bills, all acquired through less than legitimate channels.

There was nothing in the family's financial dealings to raise suspicion. It was the photographic evidence that proved so damning.

Puri laid a series of pictures on the desk for his client to see. Together they told a story. Two nights ago, Goel had gone to a five-star hotel nightclub with a couple of male friends. On the dance floor, he had bumped into Facecream, who'd been dressed in a short leather skirt, a skimpy top and high heels. The two had danced together and, afterwards, Goel had offered to buy her a drink, introducing himself as Romey Butter. At first she'd refused, but Goel had insisted.

'Come on, baby, I'll get your engine running,' he'd told her.

The two had downed a couple of tequila slammers and danced again, this time intimately. At the end of the evening, Facecream, going under the name Candy, had given Goel her phone number.

'On the coming night, he set out for the female's apartment at two oblique twelve, A Block, Safdarjung Enclave,' Puri told Singla. 'Inside, he consumed two *pegs* of whisky and got frisky with the female. He said — and I quote — 'Wanna see my big thing, baby?' Then he got down his trousers. Unfortunately for him, the female, Candy, had dissolved one knockout drug in his drink and, forthwith, he succumbed, passing out.'

An hour later, Goel awoke naked and in bed, convinced that he had made love to Candy, who

21

assured him that he was 'the best she'd ever had'.

Lying next to her, Goel confessed that he was getting married at the end of the month. He called his fiancée, Vimi Singla, a 'stupid bitch' and a 'dumb brat' and proposed that Candy become his mistress.

'He said, 'I'll soon be rich, baby. I'll get you whatever you want.''

The detective handed the last photograph to his client. It showed Goel leaving Candy's apartment with a big grin on his face.

'Sir, there is more,' said Puri. 'We have done background checking into Goel's qualifications. It is true he attended Cambridge. Three years he spent there. But he never so much as saw one university lecture. Actually, he attended Cambridge Polytechnic and concerned himself with drink and chasing females.'

The detective paused for breath.

'Sir,' he continued, 'as I intimated to you previously, my job is gathering facts and presenting evidence. That is all. I'm a most private investigator in every sense. Confidentiality is my watchword. Rest assured our dealings will remain in the strictest confidence.'

Puri sat back in his chair and waited for Singla's reaction. It came a moment later, not in English, but Hindi.

'*Saala, maaderchod!*'

With that, the industrialist gathered up the photographs and roughly shoved them back into their file. 'Send me your bill, Puri,' he said over his shoulder as he headed for the door.

'Certainly, sir. And if I can ever be . . . '

But the industrialist was gone.

No doubt he was heading home to call off the wedding.

From everything Puri had read in the society pages, his client would be out of pocket by *crores* and *crores*. No doubt the Umaid Bhavan Palace in Jodhpur was already paid for. So, too, Céline Dion and the Swarovski crystal fountains.

The detective heaved a sigh. Next time he hoped the Singla family would consult with Most Private Investigators before they sent out four thousand gold-leaf embossed invitations.

3

The rubber soles of Puri's new shoes squeaked on the marble floors of the Gymkhana Club reception. The noise caused Sunil, the *incharge*, to look up from behind the front desk. He was holding a phone to his ear and murmuring mechanically into it, '*Ji* madam, o-kay madam, no problem madam.' He gave the detective a weary nod, placing the palm of one hand over the receiver.

'Sir. One gentle man is waiting your kind attention,' he said in a hushed voice.

It was not unusual for a prospective client to ask to meet Puri at the club. The prominent members of society who came to him often guarded their privacy and preferred not to be seen coming and going from the detective's offices.

'Mr Ajay Kasliwal is it?' asked Puri.

'Yes, sir. Thirty minutes back only he reached.'

The detective acknowledged this information with a nod and turned to look at the noticeboard. The club secretary, Col. P. V. S. Gill (Retd.), had posted a new announcement. It was typed on the club's headed paper and, in no fewer than five places, blemished with whitener.

NOTICE
THE DIFFERENCE BETWEEN A SHIRT AND
A BUSH SHIRT IS CLARIFIED AS UNDER:

UNLIKE A SHIRT THE DESIGN OF THE UPPER PORTION OF THE BUSH SHIRT IS LIKE THAT OF A SAFARI.

This made instant sense to Puri (as he believed it should to anyone coming to the club wearing bush shirts or indeed safaris) and his eyes turned to the next notice, a reminder from the under-secretary that *ayahs* were not permitted on the tennis courts. The chief librarian had also posted a note appealing for funds to replace the club's copy of the collected works of Rabindranath Tagore, which had 'most unfortunately and due to unforeseen and regrettable circumstance' been 'totally destroyed' by rats.

Next, the detective cast a quick eye over the dinner menu. It was Monday, which meant mulligatawny soup or Russian salad for starters; a choice of egg curry, cabbage bake with French Frie or Shepard's Pie for mains; and the usual tutti-frutti ice-cream or mango trifle for dessert.

The thought of Shepard's Pie followed by tutti-frutti icecream stirred the detective's appetite and he regretted not having come over to the club for lunch. As per Dr Mohan's instructions, Rumpi was packing his *tiffin* with only weak *daal*, rice and chopped salad these days.

Finally, Puri turned to the list of new applicants for club membership. He read each name in turn. Most he recognised: the sons and daughters of existing members. The others he jotted down in his notebook.

As a favour to Col. P. V. S. Gill (Retd.), Puri

ran background checks on anyone applying for membership not already known in the right Delhi circles. Usually this meant making a couple of discreet phone calls, a service Puri gladly provided the Gym for free. Standards had to be kept up, after all. Recently, a number of Johnny-come-lately types had made applications. Just last month, a liquor *crorepati*, a multimillionaire, had asked to join. Puri had been right to flag him. Only yesterday, the man had been featured in the social pages of the *Hindustan Times* for buying the country's first Ferrari.

The detective slipped his notebook back into the inner pocket of his safari suit and made his way out of reception.

Usually he reached the bar by cutting through the ballroom. This route avoided the main office, which was the domain of Mrs Col. P. V. S. Gill (Retd.). A bossy, impossible woman who ran the club while her husband played cards in the Rummy Room, she regarded Puri as an upstart. He was, after all, the son of a lowly policeman from west Delhi who had only gained entry to the hallowed establishment through Rumpi, whose father, a retired colonel, had made him a member.

Unfortunately, the ballroom was being decorated — a dozen paint-splattered decorators working on bamboo scaffolds bound with rope, were applying lashings of the only colour used on every exterior and interior wall of the Gym: brilliant white — and so Puri was left with no choice but to take the corridor that led past Mrs Gill's door.

He proceeded slowly, painfully aware of his new squeaking shoes, specially made for him to account for the shortness of his left leg. He passed the Bridge Room and the ladies' cloakroom and a row of prints of English country scenes depicting tall, upright gentlemen in top hats and tails.

As he passed Mrs Gill's office, he went on tiptoe, but the door immediately swung open as if she had been lying in wait.

'What is all this squeaking, Mr Puri?' she screeched, her flabby midriff bulging from the folds of her garish *sari*. 'Making quite a racket.'

'My new shoes I'm afraid, madam,' he said.

Mrs Gill looked down at the offending footwear disapprovingly.

'Mr Puri, there are strict rules governing footwear,' she said. 'Rule number twenty-nine paragraph D is most specific! Hard shoes are to be worn at all times.'

'They are orthopaedic shoes, madam,' he explained.

'What nonsense!' Mrs Gill said. 'Hard shoes only!'

She pulled back into her office, closing the door behind her.

Puri continued down the corridor, resolved not to wear his new shoes in the club again. Such Punjabi women were not to be tangled with; in his experience they could be more fearsome adversaries than Bombay's crime bosses.

'Imagine spending sixty years with such a woman,' he mumbled to himself. 'One can only imagine what the colonel did in his past life to

27

deserve such a fate.'

The detective pushed open the door to the bar and stepped into the relative quiet he so cherished. This was the only truly civilised spot left in Delhi, a place where a gentleman could enjoy a quiet peg or two amongst distinguished company — even if some of his fellow members barely acknowledged him.

Judge Suri was sitting in the far corner in his favourite chair, smoking his pipe and reading the *Indian Journal of International Law*. Puri recognised Shonal Ganguly, professor of history at Delhi University, sitting with his wife. Next to the fireplace slouched L.K. George, the former industrialist who had given away his family fortune to the League for the Protection of Cows and their Progeny, and now lived in a crumbling Lutyens bungalow on Racecourse Road. Propping up the bar stood Major-General Duleep Singh along with his eldest son, a surgeon and resident of Maryland visiting from the USA.

Apart from the waiters, the only other person in the room was a distinguished-looking gentleman sitting on his own at one of the little round tables near the French windows with an empty glass in front of him. Puri guessed this must be his guest because his brow was deeply furrowed with worry, a feature prospective clients often shared.

'Sir, your good name please?' asked the detective, approaching the stranger.

'Ajay Kasliwal,' he answered, standing up and offering his hand. Despite the bar's cool temperature, his palm was moist. 'Vish Puri, is it? Well, I'm certainly glad to meet you. Bunty Bannerjee put me on to you. Said you were to be found here most evenings. He sends his best wishes by the way.'

'Most kind of you,' replied the detective. 'How is the old devil? It's been such a very long time!'

'Very good, very good. No complaints. In and out of trouble,' replied Kasliwal with a jovial chuckle.

'Everyone is well?'

'World class! Flourishing, in fact!'

'And Bunty's factory? Thriving, is it?'

'Thriving, absolutely thriving.'

Puri gestured for Kasliwal to take his seat. He sank back into the armchair and his weight caused it to wheeze air like an old bellows.

'You'll join me?' asked the detective.

'Please,' sighed Kasliwal.

The detective snapped his fingers and an elderly waiter who had been working at the club for some forty years approached the table. He was hard of hearing so the detective had to shout his order.

'Bring two Royal Challenge and soda! Two portion chilli cheese toast!'

The waiter nodded, picked up Kasliwal's empty glass and methodically wiped the surface of the table. This provided Puri with an opportunity to study his guest up close.

Kasliwal, who was in his late forties, had an air of privilege about him. His manicured finger-nails, contact lenses, and well-groomed salt-and-pepper hair, swept back from his forehead, indicated that he spent a good deal of time tending to his appearance. His gold watch, two thick gold rings and the gold pen glinting from his shirt pocket left others in no doubt of his wealth and status. There was an intellectual gravitas about the man too. In his thoughtful eyes, Puri perceived a certain striving.

'*Accha*,' said Kasliwal, once the waiter had finally withdrawn. He leaned forward in his armchair. The furrows on his brow deepened. 'Firstly, Puri-ji please understand one thing. I'm not a man to panic easily. Not at all.'

He spoke English with a strong accent and 'not at all' was rolled into one as 'naataataall'.

'Believe me, I've faced many obstacles and challenges in my life. This I can say with utmost confidence. Also, I'm one man who prides himself on honesty. That much is well known. Ask anyone. They will tell you that Ajay Kasliwal is one hundred and fifty per cent honest!'

He went on:

'Puri-ji I understand you are a man of integrity and discretion, also. That is why I've come. Frankly, I'm facing a serious situation. A crisis. It can be my ruin actually. That's why I've *air-dashed* here to see you.'

'You are a lawyer residing in Jaipur, is it?' interrupted Puri.

Kasliwal looked taken aback. 'That's correct,' he said. 'But, how . . . Ah, Bunty told you I suppose.'

Puri enjoyed impressing prospective clients with his deductions, despite the simplicity of his observations.

'I've not spoken with Bunty, actually,' he said,

30

plainly. 'But from your Law Society of India monogrammed tie and type of briefcase, I deducted you are a man of the Bar. As to your home town, traces of red Rajasthani sand are on your shoes. Also, you mentioned air-dashing to Delhi. You arrived here thirty minutes back. So should be you came by the five o'clock flight from Jaipur.'

'Amazing!' exclaimed Kasliwal, with a clap of his hands. 'Bunty said you were a gifted fellow, but never would I have believed!'

The lawyer edged even closer, looking from side to side to make sure no one could overhear their conversation. The waiters were at a safe distance behind the bar. None of the other members appeared to be paying Puri and his guest any attention.

'Yesterday I was paid a visit by the cops,' he said. 'Someone has lodged an FIR against me.'

Kasliwal handed Puri a copy of the 'First Information Report'. The detective read it carefully.

'You're ordered to produce one female named Mary within seven days, is it?' he noted once he'd finished, passing back the document. 'Who is she exactly?'

Before Kasliwal could answer, the waiter returned with their drinks and snacks. Slowly, he placed them on the table one by one and then presented Puri with the bill. The club did not accept cash so all purchases made at the bar or in the restaurant had to be signed for. This system produced piles of paperwork, which kept at least four clerks employed in the club's accounts department. Puri had to sign one bill for the drinks he'd ordered, another for the double Scotch Kasliwal had downed earlier, and another for the food. Naturally, the guest book required a signature as well.

It was several minutes before Kasliwal was able to answer Puri's last question.

'Mary was a maidservant in the house — did cleaning, laundry and all,' he said.

'And where is she now?'

'I'm not having the foggiest! That's the problem! She left two, maybe three months back. Just disappeared one night. I wasn't home at the time. I had work to attend to.'

Puri tucked into a slice of chilli cheese toast as he listened.

'My wife says Mary stole some household items and ran away. But a rumour has circulated that, well . . . ' Kasliwal took a swig of his whisky to fortify his nerves. 'There's no truth in it. You know how people talk, Puri-ji.'

'Most certainly I do. India is one giant rumour mill, actually. Tell me what all they're saying?'

There was a pause.

'That I got Mary pregnant and did away with her,' admitted Kasliwal.

'By God,' intoned the detective.

'This has been the complaint made against me and, as you know, in case of FIRs, the police are obliged to investigate.'

There was a silence while Puri finished his slice of chilli cheese toast, retrieved his notebook from his inside pocket and then pulled out one of the four pens he kept tucked into the breast pocket of his safari suit. After jotting down a few details, he asked: 'Any body has been discovered?'

'No, thank heavens!' exclaimed Kasliwal. 'The police searched my house and grounds and some media persons have been on the doorstep asking questions.'

'Sounds like someone's trying to ruin your good name, is it?' asked the detective.

'That's it! You've hit the nail on the head, Puri-ji! That's exactly what they're trying to do!'

The lawyer went on to explain that in the past few years he had launched a number of public litigation cases in the Rajasthan High Court. This was something many honest lawyers and individuals were doing across India: working through the legal system to bring inept local and national authorities to account.

'I've had some success tackling the water mafia. I've managed to stop a lot of the illegal water drilling in the driest parts of the state,' he explained. 'But with so much corruption in the judiciary itself, it's been a tough innings. So earlier this year, I decided to take on the judges themselves. I've launched a public litigation case calling for them to declare their assets.'

Puri sipped his whisky. Out of the corner of one eye he registered Major-General Duleep Singh and his eldest son leaving the bar.

'Must have made a few enemies along the way,' he said.

'At first they tried to buy me, but I'm not a bowler to do ball tampering. I turned them down flat. To hell with them. So now they're gunning for me. They've seized on this missing servant to muddy my name.'

'It seems there's no hard evidence against you, so surely you've got nothing to worry — ' said the detective.

'Come on Puri-ji, this is India!' interrupted Kasliwal. 'They can tie me up in knots for years to come.'

Puri nodded; he knew what a long, drawn-out court case did to a family. The similarities between the Indian legal system and the Court of Chancery as described in Dickens's *Bleak House* were startling.

'The circumstances are certainly unusual,' he said, eventually. 'What is it you want from me?'

'Puri-ji, I'm begging you, for God's sake, find this bloody Mary!'

'You have her full name?' he asked.

Kasliwal shrugged. 'She was there for two months. I believe she was a tribal.'

'You have a photograph, personal possessions, copy of ID?'

'Nothing.'

Puri's tone became measured. 'She was a verified domestic, registered with the cops at least?'

Kasliwal shook his head.

'Sir, allow me to understand,' said Puri. 'It is your suggestion I locate one tribal-type girl called Mary with no second name, no idea where she is coming from, no idea where she is alighting?'

'That is correct.'

'Sir, with respect, I think you must be some kind of joker.'

'I can assure you that while I'm enjoying a

good joke, I am no joker,' objected Kasliwal. 'Such an accomplished private investigator as yourself should have no difficulty in such a matter. It's a straightforward thing, after all.'

Puri's eyes bulged with incredulity.

'It is certainly not straightforward locating one missing female in a population of one billion plus personages,' he said. 'It will take time and resources and *all* of my considerable skills. Looking in Yellow Pages will not suffice.'

Puri explained that he worked on a day rate and would require two weeks in advance, plus expenses. The total amount caused Kasliwal to gag on his Scotch.

'So much? Surely you can do better than that, Puri-ji! We can reach some accommodation. Funds are a bit tight these days, you know.'

'I don't work for farthings and I don't do negotiation,' said the detective, munching on another piece of chilli cheese toast. 'My fee is final.'

Kasliwal thought for a moment and, with a grave sigh, drew a chequebook from the inside pocket of his jacket.

'Sir, rest assured I will find this female by hook or crook,' said Puri. 'If I fail, then I will return my fee minus expenses.'

The detective drained his glass. 'There is one other thing,' he added.

The lawyer, who was bent over the table writing a cheque, looked up.

'Cash, banker's draft or electronic transfer only,' insisted Puri with a smile.

4

Puri woke the next morning to the sound of water dribbling into an empty bucket in the bathroom. This was his anomalous alarm, a signal that it was 6.30, the hour when Sector Four received its daily supply of water and each household filled up buckets, tanks and all manner of receptacles to carry them through the day.

Puri sat up and glanced over at the single bed next to his. It came as no surprise to find it empty. Hardly a day had gone by during the past twenty-six years when Rumpi had not risen at five. Even during the months when she was heavily pregnant with each of their three daughters, Puri's devoted wife had insisted on getting up at the crack of dawn to oversee the running of the house. No doubt she was downstairs now churning fresh butter for his *double-roti*. Or she was in the second bedroom rubbing mustard oil into her long, auburn hair.

The detective reached for the light switch, which, like the radio alarm and world clock, was fitted into the astonishingly shiny imitation mahogany headboard. The side lamp did not come on, which prompted him to glance over at the electric mosquito repellent plugged into the far wall to see if its red light was glowing. It was off. Sector Four was experiencing more *load shedding*.

Muttering a curse, Puri reached for his flashlight, switched it on and slipped out of bed. His monogrammed slippers — 'VP' — were lying next to one another on the floor where he had carefully positioned them the night before. He wriggled his feet inside their furry lining and reached for his silk dressing gown. His collection of fourteen Sandown caps were arranged on a shelf inside one of the fitted cupboards. He chose the tartan one, pulling it snug over his head. Then he surveyed himself in the mirror, gave the silk handkerchief protruding from the breast pocket of his dressing gown a tug and, pleased with what he saw, walked out into the hallway.

The beam of his flashlight fell on the marble floor, partially illuminating the large silver-plated Ganesh idol and the gilded legs of the hallway table, which supported a vase of plastic sunflowers. Puri walked to the top of the stairs where the sound of giggling from the kitchen caused him to pause.

Listening intently, the detective was able to make out the voice of his new houseboy, Sweetu, who was in the kitchen joking around with Monica and Malika rather than attending to his morning duties. The detective couldn't quite make out what Sweetu was saying, so he crept over to the door of his private study. This was the one room of the house which no one, save Rumpi (who cleaned it every Friday), was allowed to enter. There were only two keys in existence: one hung on his key chain; the other was hidden in a secret compartment built into

37

the shrine in the *puja* room.

Like his office, Puri's study was simply furnished. In one corner stood a fireproof safe containing his private papers, various important files, a selection of fake passports and IDs and his Last Will and Testament. The bottom half of the safe also contained 100,000 rupees in cash, some of his wife's gold and diamond jewellery (the rest she kept in a bank vault), and a loaded .32 IOF pistol — a copy of the .32 Colt pistol made by the Indian Ordnance Factory.

Puri sat at his desk and pulled open one of the drawers. Inside lay a battery-operated receiver set to the frequency of the bug he had concealed in the kitchen. He switched it on, pushed the mono earpiece into his left ear, adjusted the volume and sat back in his chair to listen.

Rumpi frowned upon his practice of listening in on the servants, but Puri made it a policy to monitor all new recruits at home and at the office. He himself relied on servants as primary sources of intelligence and often planted his own operatives inside other people's households. As a man who fiercely guarded his privacy and had a number of dangerous enemies and unscrupulous competitors, he needed to be sure that his own staff were not spying on him or unwittingly passing on details about his private affairs to interested parties.

Furthermore, Puri was well aware of just how lazy servants could be. Village types like Sweetu were often under the illusion that city people did not work for a living and saw no reason why they should behave any differently. Living in a modern house in comparative luxury could give them delusions of grandeur. The boy before Sweetu had had the audacity to seduce a part-time cleaner on Puri's bed. The detective had come home unannounced one afternoon when Rumpi was away visiting her sister and found them at it.

Puri spent ten minutes listening in on the conversation in the kitchen. The talk was mostly about the latest Shahrukh Khan film, a *double-role*. It all sounded harmless enough, as gossip went. But it was obvious that Sweetu was keeping the girls from their duties and shirking his own. The detective decided to put a stop to it and reprimand the boy. Switching off the receiver and locking the study door behind him, he walked to the top of the stairs.

'Sweetu!' he bellowed.

The sound of *Sahib*'s voice brought the boy scuttling from the kitchen into the hallway below.

'Good morning, sir,' he stammered, awkwardly,

'Why are you being idle?' demanded Puri in Hindi. 'You are not employed to discuss Shahrukh's double-roles!'

'Sir, I — '

'No argument. Where is my bed tea?'

'Sir, power cut — '

'Tell Malika to bring it to the roof. And', he added in English, 'don't do chitter chatter!'

Puri headed upstairs, satisfied with the manner in which he had handled Sweetu. The boy was young, only fifteen, and an orphan.

What he needed was discipline. But Puri was never one to abuse, exploit or treat his servants badly, as he had known so many other people do. He believed in looking after the interests of all his employees, providing they were hard-working and loyal. In Sweetu's case, Puri had arranged for the boy to attend school two afternoons a week so that he would learn to read and write and acquire a skill. And in a few years' time, the detective would also help him find a suitable wife.

Had not Chanakya taught that it was the duty of the privileged to help the underprivileged?

Puri climbed the stairs and stepped out on to the flat roof of the house. The sun was climbing into what should have been a clear, azure sky. But as was so often the case these days, a brown pall of dust and pollution blanketed Delhi, smothering the city like some Vedic plague.

The family had hoped to escape the smog when they moved to Gurgaon nine years earlier.

When Puri bought his plot of land, it had lain many miles from the southern outskirts of the capital. It had taken over two years to build his and Rumpi's dream house — a white, four-bedroom Spanish-style villa with orange-tiled awnings, which they'd furnished from top to bottom in Punjabi baroque.

On the roof, Puri had established a garden of potted plants, tending to them every morning at dawn.

In those days, the vistas in all directions had been breath-taking, the sun shimmering off mustard fields and casting long shadows over clutches of mud huts. Goat herders and their flocks wove along time-worn tracks that dissected the complex patchwork of land. Farmers drove oxen and wooden ploughs, kicking up dust in their wake. Barefoot women in bright reds and oranges walked from the hand pump to their homes, brimming brass pots balanced on their heads.

Away from the drone of Delhi traffic and the roar of jets making their approach into Indira Gandhi International Airport, Puri had been greeted by peacock calls and the laughter of boys washing at the nearby village pump. When the wind was right, he had also been treated to the smell of *chappatis* cooking over dung fires and the scent of jasmine, wafting over the exterior wall.

Little had Puri known that in building a new home in Gurgaon, he had become a trendsetter. His move from Punjabi Bagh, northwest Delhi, coincided with the explosion of India's service industries in the wake of the liberalisation of the economy. In the late 1990s, Gurgaon became Delhi's southern extension, and was made available for major 'development'. First, a few reflective glass buildings appeared along the main road to Rajasthan. Then, one by one, the local farmers sold up and their little fields disappeared under the tracks of bulldozers and dump trucks.

In their place came Florida-style gated communities with names like Fantasy Island Estates. They boasted their own schools, medical facilities, shops, fitness centres and mega-malls.

41

Concrete superstructures shot up to the horizon like great splinters of bone forced from the body of the earth. Built by armies of sinewy labourers who crawled like ants along frames of bamboo scaffolding, these were the apartment blocks for the 24/7 call centre and software development workforce.

LUXURY IS A PLACE CALLED PARADISE and DISCOVER A VENETIAN PALACE LIFESTYLE read the plethora of hoardings that invited India's newly affluent to share in the dream.

All this was built on the backs of India's 'underprivileged classes', who were working for slave wages. They had arrived in Gurgaon in their tens of thousands from across the country. But neither the local authorities nor the private contractors provided them with housing, so most had built shacks on the building sites alongside the machinery and brick factories. Before long, shanty towns of corrugated iron and open sewers spread across an undeveloped no man's land.

The Puris now found themselves living between five hundred homes built on a grid of streets with names like A3; and a slum with a population of labourers and carrion that was growing exponentially. To the north, the view was marred by towering pylons and, beyond them, a row of biosphere-like office blocks bristling with satellite dishes.

The smog, too, had caught up with them. The new four-lane highway to Delhi had encouraged more traffic, poisoning the air with diesel fumes. Legions of trucks stirred dust into the atmosphere.

These days, the detective found himself

struggling to keep his beloved plants clean. Each morning, he came up on to the roof armed with a spray gun and gave each of them a bath; and each morning he found them coated in a new deposit of grime.

Puri had just got round to tending to his favourite ficus tree when Malika arrived with his bed tea and biscuits. She laid the tray on the garden table.

'*Namaste*, sir,' she said shyly.

'Good morning.'

He was always happy to see Malika, who had been with the family for six years. She was a bright, cheerful, hardworking girl, despite having an alcoholic husband, a tyrant of a mother-in-law and two children to care for.

'How are you doing?' asked Malika, who was keen to try out her English, which she picked up from watching American soap operas on Star TV.

'I am very well, thank you,' said Puri. 'How are you?'

'Fine,' she answered, but started giggling, blushed and then fled downstairs.

The detective smiled to himself and drank some of his tea before returning to the job at hand. He finished bathing his ficus and then made his way over to the roof's east side where, on the ledge, he was growing six chilli plants. He had nurtured each of them from seed (they had been sent to him by a friend in Assam and came from one of the hottest chillis Puri had ever tasted), and was pleased to see that after many weeks of tender care and watering, they were bearing fruit.

He sprayed the leaves of the first plant and was lovingly wiping them clean when, suddenly, the flowerpot shattered into pieces. A split second later, a bullet whizzed by Puri's ear and punctured the water tank on the platform behind him.

With some difficulty, given his bulk, he managed to prostrate himself on the roof. A third bullet smashed into another of his chilli plants, showering him with broken pottery and earth. The detective heard a fourth and fifth round hit the side of the house as he remained flat on his front, conscious of the pounding in his chest and the shortness of his breath.

A sixth bullet whizzed overhead, puncturing the tank for a second time. Water began to stream out, soaking Puri's silk dressing gown.

He decided to crawl over to the stairwell. If he could get down to his study and retrieve his pistol from the safe, then he could go after the shooter. It crossed his mind that he would need to put on some shoes as well; his monogrammed slippers would get ruined.

But as he reached the door, it suddenly flew open, knocking him squarely on the head. Puri's vision doubled for a moment, and then went solidly black.

5

Puri came round to find Rumpi kneeling by his side holding some smelling salts under his nose. Nearby, Malika and Monica stood looking down at him with concerned expressions. In the doorway of the stairwell hovered an anxious Sweetu, wringing his hands.

'Sir, sir, sir, so sorry, sir. I didn't mean to, sir! I heard shots, sir, so I came running and then . . . I didn't know you were there, sir! Sir, please don't die . . . '

Puri's head was spinning and he felt nauseous. It took what seemed like several minutes until he could focus his thoughts and then he whispered to Rumpi:

'For God's sake, tell the boy to shut up and go away.'

Rumpi complied, assuring Sweetu that 'sir' was going to be fine and that he should get back to work.

After seeking further reassurance that his life was still worth living, the houseboy did as he was told and returned downstairs.

The girls soon followed him to the kitchen, leaving Rumpi to apply an ice pack to the bump on Puri's forehead.

'Thank heavens you're all right, Chubby,' she said tenderly. 'I thought you'd been shot.'

'Had I not reacted with lightning reflexes and thrown myself on the ground, most certainly I'd be lying here permanently,' he said. 'Just I was crawling over to the door when that . . . that fool burst in. Otherwise I would have caught the shooter. Undoubtedly!'

'Oh please, Chubby, it wasn't the boy's fault,' chided Rumpi gently. 'He was only trying to help. Now tell me how you're feeling?'

'Much better, thank you, my dear. A nice cup of chai and I'll be right as rain.'

Slowly, the detective pushed himself up into the sitting position, taking the ice pack from Rumpi and holding it on his forehead.

'Tell me, anyone saw the shooter?' he asked.

'I don't believe so,' answered Rumpi. 'I was in the toilet and the others were downstairs. I heard the shots and the next thing I knew Sweetu was shouting you'd been shot and we all came running.'

'You called the police, is it?'

'I've tried several times, Chubby. But I keep getting a message: 'This number does not exist.' You want I should try again?'

'Yes please, my dear. An official report should be made. Most probably the cops have been negligible in paying the phone bill. Last I heard, they were some years behind so the lines were cut off. If you can't get through, send that Sweetu to the station. Tell him to say that some goonda tried putting Vish Puri in the cremation ground, but very much failed in his duty.'

* * *

The police — an officer and four constables — arrived an hour later. After stomping around

46

on the roof, they concluded that the would-be killer had positioned himself in the vacant plot behind the house.

Their search of the area yielded nothing of value and, predictably, they turned their full attention on the servants.

'Nine times out of ten, it's the help,' the officer told Puri.

The questions put to Monica, Malika and Sweetu were accusatory and misleading, and after all three had answered them in turn and professed their innocence, the policeman told Puri he strongly suspected an 'inside job'. Sweetu was his 'chief suspect'.

'You think he's dangerous, is it?' asked Puri, playing along.

'I'd like to take him down to the station and get the truth out of him,' replied the officer.

The detective pretended to give this suggestion some thought and then said: 'Actually, I'd prefer to have him here. That way I can keep an eye on him and he'll lead me to the hit man.'

Puri showed the cops to the door and, after watching them drive away and pausing for a moment to contemplate their crass stupidity, headed up on to the roof.

A careful inspection of the holes in the water tank and the pits made by the two bullets that had impacted on the exterior wall indicated that the hit man had positioned himself on top of the half-constructed building that stood a few feet to the east of the Puris' home.

Five minutes later, the detective was standing in the spot behind a half-built wall from where his assailant had shot at him.

There, on the ground, amidst some broken bits of brick and lumps of dried concrete, he found six empty slugs and a few cigarette butts. These he scooped up one by one, wrapping them carefully in his handkerchief, and then returned to ground level.

From a number of boot impressions left in the earth, which matched those visible in the dust on the top of the building, he determined that the hit man had entered the site through an open back gate and could easily have come and gone without anyone seeing him.

Puri spent a fruitless hour asking the neighbours and their servants if they had noticed anything unusual that morning and then returned home.

Once seated on the big blue leather couch in the sitting room, he wrote down everything he knew so far.

1. Hit man waiting 15 mins. at least, smoker.
2. Hit man expecting subject.
3. Hit man uses country-made weapon.
4. Hit man is man — size nine boots.

Next, Puri turned to his Most Usual Suspects file, which he'd retrieved from the safe in his study.

It contained up-to-date information on all the individuals with a strong motive for having him murdered and whom he judged to be a grave threat. In the event of his untimely death, Rumpi was under instruction to take the file to his rival,

Hari Kumar. Despite their differences, he and Hari had an understanding that they would not allow one another's murder to go unsolved.

The Most Usual Suspects file contained details of four individuals. A fifth name, that of a serial killer known as Lucky, had recently been removed after he had been 'awarded' the death sentence.

'Not so lucky after all,' chuckled Puri to himself as he looked over the other names. In no particular order, they were:

Jacques 'Hannibal' Boyé, the French serial killer, serving a life sentence in Tihar jail for murdering and eating seven Canadian backpackers.

Krishna Rai, the opposition MLA[1] from Bihar, whose son Puri had helped convict for murdering a bar girl.

Ratan Patel, the head of India Info Inc., serving six years for insider trading.

Swami Nag, the swindler, confidence man and murderer.

Without doubt, this last individual posed the greatest threat. There was a note on his page that read 'absconding, whereabouts unknown'. Before going into hiding, the Swami had sworn to kill Puri himself 'by any and all means'.

The detective decided to call his usual sources within the criminal underworld to find out about Swami Nag's whereabouts and whether any of the other three had put out a contract on his life recently. He would also ask Tubelight to make

---

[1] Member of legislative assembly.

some inquiries; no one else had better informants.

For now, that was as much as Puri could do.

There were hundreds of hit men for hire in Delhi; nearly all of them were ordinary, everyday people desperate to do anything to provide their families with their next meal. Their fingerprints were not on record; their weapons of choice were often 'country-made' pistols and rifles, which were impossible to trace. Puri closed the Most Usual Suspects file, put it on the couch next to him and opened another dossier containing details of the attempts that had been made on his life.

Today's incident brought the tally to twelve.

On six occasions, his enemies had tried shooting him; twice, they'd attempted poison (once using a *samosa* laced with arsenic); and during The Case of the Pundit with Twelve Toes, a hired thug had tried to force Puri's car over the edge of a hairpin bend on the road to Gulmarg.

The most ingenious attempt had been orchestrated by a cunning murderer (a naturalist by profession) working in Assam's Kaziranga Park, who had secretly sprayed Puri's clothes with a pheromone that attracted male one-horned rhinos.

The closest anyone had come (not including the three rhinos, who could move surprisingly quickly), had been a criminal hijra who had pushed a pile of bricks off the top of a building into an alley in Varanasi where Puri had been walking.

Hardly a day went by when Puri didn't relate

one of these stories to someone. Prospective clients, journalists, visiting children doing school projects and Scotland Yard detectives had all heard one or more.

'Danger is my ally,' he would tell eager listeners.

Fostering an image of fearlessness was vital to his reputation as a detective. But Puri was not lax about his own security. His Ambassador was a customised model fitted with bulletproof glass and a reinforced steel undercarriage. He kept two Labradors in the garden and employed an alert *chowkidar* armed with a shotgun. And he varied the route he took home.

Puri was also careful to appease the gods, visiting the temple at least once a week and observing all the major festivals.

If all that failed to protect him . . . well, the detective had not stared death in the face without being somewhat fatalistic. As he was fond of saying, 'We're all but one breath from this life to the next, isn't it?'

★ ★ ★

A couple of hours after the shooting, with the bump on his forehead no longer throbbing, Puri decided he was well enough to drive to Jaipur to begin work on the Kasliwal case.

Rumpi had other ideas.

'Chubby, you must rest,' she insisted in Punjabi, the language the two usually spoke with one another, returning from the kitchen with some tea for him. 'I'm making you some *khichri*

51

and later I'll rub mustard oil on to your head.'

Obediently, the detective sat on the couch again. He knew when it was prudent to do as he was told. Besides, spending the day at home would not be all bad. He could re-pot his chilli plants, watch some cricket and, in the evening, visit the temple.

Rumpi returned to the kitchen and Puri switched on the TV, surfing through the inordinate number of satellite channels until he found one showing the India vs. West Indies match in Hyderabad. It was the second test — the Indian batsmen having collapsed in the first — and the tourists were nearly eighty-two for one, with Lara two runs short of a half-century.

★   ★   ★

Half an hour later, as Puri was enjoying Rumpi's khichri with home-made curd and tart mango pickle, and reflecting on the perks of being shot at, a car honked its horn outside the front gate and the dogs began barking.

The detective listened as the gate was opened and a vehicle's tyres ground against the gravel. Two doors banged shut and footsteps approached the house. A few seconds later, Puri heard the sound of his mother's voice in the corridor.

'Namaste,' she said to Rumpi. 'I came directly, na. But traffic delay was there. So many cars you can't imagine. At Ring Road junction, the light was blinking, causing backup. Police were being negligent in their duty. Drivers were just honking

52

and shouting and such. But what a terrible thing has happened! Everyone is all right, though, na? Thank God. Where is Chubby? He is OK? That is the main thing.'

Puri heaved a drawn-out sigh and looked affectionately at the TV like a lover bidding his sweetheart a reluctant adieu. He switched it off and pushed himself off the couch. As his mother entered the room, he bent down and touched her feet.

'Thank God you are all right, my son,' she said, tears welling in her eyes as she raised him up by the shoulder. 'As soon as I came to hear, then directly I called your number. But the line was totally blocked. Must be there is commotion here and such. So I rushed right away. Of course, I felt certain everything would be all right. But Ritu Auntie was in agreement I should come. This shooting person must be found and I've little else to do.'

The fact that Ritu Auntie, an insatiable gossip, had encouraged Mummy to drive over came as no surprise to him. Nor did the fact that his mother had learned about the shooting so quickly. Although recently retired and living with the detective's eldest brother twelve miles away, Mummy-ji had a staggering number of mostly female friends and acquaintances who acted as her own intelligence network across the city (and often well beyond).

Puri was in little doubt that the leak had emanated from his servants. One of them had told the subzi-wallah about the shooting and he in turn had passed on the news to one of his other customers, more than likely one of the drivers working for a household a few doors down. This driver had told his mistress, who in turn had informed her *cousin-sister*, who in turn had called up the auntie living next door. In all likelihood, this auntie was a bridge player who had paired up with Mummy at a recent *kitty party* and they had swapped telephone numbers.

Puri had learned from hard experience that it was impossible to hide dramatic developments in his life from his mother. But he would not tolerate her nosing about in his investigations.

True, Mummy had a sixth sense and, from time to time, one of her premonitions proved prescient. But she was no detective. Detectives were not mummies. And detectives were certainly not women.

'Mummy-ji, there is no need to come all this way,' said Puri, who always sounded like a little boy when he addressed his mother. 'I am fine. Nothing to worry about. No tension.'

She made a disapproving tut. 'Tension is there most definitely,' she replied firmly. 'Quite a bad bump you've got, na.'

Mummy found the armchair nearest the door and perched on the edge of the seat, her back perfectly straight. Despite the abruptness of her departure from home and the race through Delhi's pollution and traffic, she was calm and composed. The former headmistress of Modern School, she wore her silver hair, which had only been cut once in her life, pulled back from her face into a sedate bun. Her cotton sari was a conservative green and matched her emerald earrings.

'For tension, bed rest is required. Two days minimum,' she continued.

'Mummy-ji, please. I don't need bed rest,' protested Puri, who was sitting back on the blue leather couch. 'Really, I am fine.'

A silence fell over the room. Puri noticed the Most Usual Suspects file still lying next to him and hoped that his mother wouldn't notice it.

'There are clues?' asked Mummy, suddenly.

Puri hesitated before answering. 'No clues,' he lied.

'Empty cartridges?'

'No, Mummy-ji.'

'You've made a thorough investigation of the scene?'

'Of course Mummy-ji,' he said, sounding as stern as he could when addressing his mother. 'Please don't get involved. I have told you about this before, no?'

Mummy replied impatiently: 'Peace of mind will only be there once this goonda is behind bars. He may be absconding, but he will revert. Meantime, there is one other matter I wish to discuss.' She hesitated before continuing. 'Please listen, na. Chubby, last night, I was having one dream . . . '

The detective let out a loud groan, but his mother ignored him.

'Just I see you walking through one big house,' she said. 'Lots of rooms there are and peacocks, also. I believe it is in Rajasthan, this place. You're entering one long passage. It is dark. One flashlight you are carrying, but it is broken. At the end, there is one young girl. Just she's lying

55

on the ground. She is dead. So much blood I tell you. Then from behind comes one goonda. Most ugly he is. And he's carrying a knife and . . . '

Mummy stopped talking and looked confused.

'And what, Mummy-ji?' prompted Puri.

'Well, see at that moment I was waking.'

'So you don't know the end?'

'No,' she admitted.

'OK Mummy-ji, thank you for telling me,' he said to appease her. 'Now let's have no more talk of knives or goondas or shootings. We'll take tea and then, you are right, I should take bed rest. Tension is most definitely building.'

The detective called out to Sweetu, who was in the kitchen. In double time, he appeared in the doorway, looking uncharacteristically alert.

'Bring *masala chai* and biscuits,' instructed the detective.

'Sir, what to do with Auntie's *tachee?*' he asked.

'Tachee?' repeated Puri.

'My trunkcase,' explained Mummy. 'I'll be staying for some days. It's my duty to remain, to make sure you are all right, na? I'm your Mummy after all. When you are safe, then I will revert. Meantime, don't go to Rajasthan, Chubby. I forbid it. There is grave danger and such awaiting you there.'

6

The following morning, Puri left the house at the usual time, saying goodbye to Mummy and Rumpi on the doorstep. He took with him his briefcase, stainless steel tiffin and a cardboard box holding files and papers.

The detective was not heading for the office, but he did not tell anyone his destination, not even Rumpi, for fear of having to listen to another of Mummy's lectures.

Handbrake only found out where they were headed once he had pulled away from the gate.

'We are going out-of-station,' said Puri, nursing the bump on his head, which was less sore than the night before but had turned a dark purple.

He addressed the driver in Hindi peppered with the odd English term and phrase.

'Where to, Boss?' asked a surprised Handbrake, regarding Puri curiously in the rearview mirror.

'Jaipur.'

'No bags, Boss?'

'I have packed my overnight things in that cardboard box. It was not possible to explain all this to you at home.' Puri reverted to English: 'Everyone is doing gossip.'

Handbrake decided not to pry further; he knew it was not his place to ask questions about his employer's business, nor to complain about the sudden departure and the fact that he had not been given the opportunity to bring along a change of clothes. Such was the lot of the Indian chauffeur. Still, he could not help wondering why Puri was being so secretive about his plans. Surely it must have something to do with the shooting yesterday?

Working for the detective was certainly proving exciting. Handbrake had started the job almost a month ago, a busy month in which he had found himself tailing errant spouses and working alongside undercover operatives. On one occasion, Boss had asked him to follow a client whom he suspected of keeping two wives. Last week, he had driven his employer to South Block for a meeting with the Defence Minister. Yesterday, someone had tried killing him. And now, it seemed, they were on the trail of a hit man.

Handbrake still couldn't quite believe his luck. For the past five years, he had worked at the Regal B Hinde Taxi Service behind the Regal Hotel. Home had been a dirty tarpaulin erected by the side of the road where he'd slept on a *charpai* shared on a shift basis with two other drivers. The hours had been gruelling and the owner, 'Randy' Singh, had been a miser who exacted a punishing percentage of all fares.

To add to Handbrake's woes, he had rarely been able to visit his wife and new baby girl, who remained in his father's house in the family's 'native place', a village in the hills of Himachal Pradesh, a ten-hour drive north of the capital.

But after visiting the Sai Baba temple off

Lodhi Road, Handbrake had seen his fortunes changed for the better.

That very afternoon, Puri's former driver had suddenly resigned due to ill health and Elizabeth Rani had had to call the Regal B Hinde Taxi Service and ask for a car. Handbrake had been first in line for a fare, and after picking up the detective from Khan Market he spent the day driving him all over the city.

That evening, Boss had complimented him on his knowledge and asked him four questions.

Did he have a family? Yes, Handbrake had replied, telling Puri about little Sushma, whom he missed so much it hurt.

Did he drink? Sometimes, he admitted, feeling ashamed because of the many times he'd got drunk on Tractor Whisky and blacked out.

Next the detective had asked him whether he knew what colour socks he was wearing.

'Yes, they are white,' Handbrake had replied, mystified by the question.

'And which newspaper have I been reading today?'

'*Indian Express.*'

Puri had offered him a full-time job with a monthly salary double his usual earnings on the spot, throwing in one thousand rupees to buy some new clothes and go for a haircut and shave. He'd even advanced him a further five hundred to rent a room in Gurgaon.

The job came with certain conditions.

Handbrake was not to discuss Puri's business with anyone, not even his wife. To do so was a sackable offence. So, too, was drinking on duty, turning up for work with a hangover, cheating on petrol, gambling and visiting prostitutes.

The driver was banned from sleeping on the back seat of the car during the day. And he was expected to shave every morning.

Handbrake had accepted all these conditions willingly. However, there was one proviso to which he had taken exception: his employer's insistence that he obey Indian traffic rules. Incredibly, Puri expected him to keep to his lane, indicate before he turned, and give way to women drivers. When he attempted going around roundabouts anticlockwise, cutting off autorickshaw drivers or backing the wrong way down one-way streets, he was severely reprimanded. Furthermore, when he exceeded the speed limit on the main roads, he was told to slow down. This meant that he often had to give way to traffic, which was humiliating.

Handbrake found the drive to Jaipur that morning particularly frustrating. The new tarmac-surfaced toll road, which was part of India's proliferating highway system, had two lanes running in each direction, and although it presented all manner of hazards, including the occasional herd of goats, a few overturned trucks and the odd gaping pothole, it held out an irresistible invitation to speed. Indeed, many of the other cars travelled as fast as 100 miles per hour.

Handbrake knew that he could keep up with the best of them. Ambassadors might look old-fashioned and slow, but the latest models had Japanese engines. Still, he soon learned to keep it under seventy. And time and again, as his competitors raced up behind him and made their impatience known by the use of their horns and flashing high beams, he grudgingly gave way, pulling into the slow lane amongst the trucks, tractors and bullock carts.

Soon, the lush mustard and sugarcane fields of Haryana gave way to the scrub and desert of Rajasthan. Four hours later, they reached the rocky hills surrounding the Pink City, passing in the shadow of the Amber Fort with its soaring ramparts and towering gatehouse. The road led past the Jal Mahal palace, beached on a sandy lake bed, into Jaipur's ancient quarter. It was almost noon and the bazaars along the city's crenellated walls were stirring into life. Beneath faded, dusty awnings, cobblers crouched sewing sequins and gold thread on to leather slippers with curled-up toes. Spice merchants sat surrounded by heaps of *lal mirch*, *haldi* and ground *jeera*, their colours as clean and sharp as new watercolour paints. Sweet-sellers lit the gas under blackened woks of oil and prepared sticky *jalebis*. *Lassi* vendors chipped away at great blocks of ice delivered by camel cart.

In front of a few of the shops, small boys, who by law should have been at school, swept the pavements, sprinkling them with water to keep down the dust. One dragged a doormat into the road where the wheels of passing vehicles ran over it, doing the job of carpet beaters.

Handbrake honked his way through the light traffic as they neared the Ajmeri Gate, watching the faces that passed by his window: skinny bicycle rickshaw drivers, straining against the weight of fat aunties; wild-eyed Rajasthani men with long handlebar moustaches and sun-baked faces almost as bright as their turbans; sinewy peasant women wearing gold nose rings and red glass bangles on their arms; a couple of pink-faced goras straining under their backpacks; a naked *sadhu*, his body half covered in ash like a caveman.

Handbrake turned into the old British Civil Lines where the roads were wide and straight and the houses and gardens were well set apart.

Ajay Kasliwal's residence was number 42 Patel Marg, a sprawling colonial bungalow purchased by his grandfather, the first Indian barrister to be called to the Rajasthani Bar. The house was named Raj Kasliwal Bhavan, and sat back from the road beyond two red sandstone pillars crowned by stone Rajasthani *chhatris*. A driveway led through a well-tended front garden where a mali stooped over the beds planting marigolds.

Handbrake pulled up in front of the grand, columned entrance and got out to open Puri's door. The detective was stiff after the long drive and grimaced as he stepped out of the car, his knees creaking under his weight.

'I'll be some time,' he told the driver, handing him thirty rupees. 'Take lunch and then come back. Also, don't call anyone in Delhi and tell them where you are.'

Puri mounted the three steps that led to a veranda with its cane furniture and rush blinds, and yanked the brass bell pull. There was a ringing somewhere deep inside the house and, before long, the door was pulled ajar by a young maidservant.

'*Ji?*' she said, her eyes darting over the top of her *chunni*, which obscured half her face.

'I am here to see Ajay Kasliwal,' explained Puri in Hindi.

The girl nodded and let him inside, her head bent shyly. She closed the door behind them and, without another word, led the detective down a hallway lit by an antique smoky-brown Manoir lamp. The inside of the bungalow was cool thanks to its thick, granite walls and stone floors. The sound of the maidservant's chappals scuffling over them was accompanied by the soft squeaking of the detective's shoes. When she came to the second door on the left, the girl indicated towards it as if something frightening lurked inside.

'Is Mr Kasliwal inside?' asked Puri.

She shook her head slowly. 'Madam,' she whispered with lowered eyes.

Puri opened the door and stepped into a large sitting room of diminished grandeur. It was furnished with dowdy couches and armchairs draped in crocheted throws. On the floor lay a twenty-foot Persian rug which was faded and, in places, threadbare. Overhead hung a sooty crystal chandelier, which gave a feeble light.

The decor did not detract from Mrs Kasliwal's regal bearing. She sat on a throne-like armchair next to the fireplace in a priceless silk sari. Although no great beauty, she benefited from strong bone structure, which suggested strength

63

of character. The gold and black *mangal sutra* necklace, large red *bindi* on her forehead and the *sindoor* in the parting of her hair also indicated a certain piety.

'Namashkar, Mr Puri,' she said, putting aside her knitting. Her tone was inviting but also slightly imperious. 'Such an honour, no? Not every day a famous detective visits. The Sherlock Holmes of India, isn't it?'

Puri did not like being compared to Sherlock Holmes, who had rather belatedly borrowed the techniques of deduction established by Chanakya in 300 BC and never paid tribute to them. But he hid his irritation well and sat down on the couch in front of the fireplace to the left of Mrs Kasliwal.

'Quite a bruise you've got there, Mr Puri. Some criminal type gave you a bash, is it?'

'Nothing so exciting as that,' replied the detective, quickly changing the subject. 'But what a fine house. Must be quite old.'

'They're not making them like this any more that is for sure,' beamed Mrs Kasliwal. 'It's been in the family for quite some time. Three generations, in fact. But where are my manners? Something to drink, Mr Puri? Chai?'

'I wouldn't say no, actually madam,' answered the detective.

Mrs Kasliwal rang a bell that sat on a side table along with a portrait of a young man in his graduation cap and gown.

'What a handsome fellow,' remarked Puri.

'So kind of you to say so,' she said, proudly. 'That's Bobby, taken earlier this year passing out

64

from St Stephen's. Such an intelligent boy, I tell you. And most considerate, also.'

'He is living with you now?'

'Living with us, of course, but currently studying in UK at School of Economics, London. In two years, he should be returning and joining Chippy's practice.'

Chippy was evidently Ajay Kasliwal's nick-name.

'So it's the legal profession for him, also, is it?' asked the detective.

'Bobby's always wanted to be a lawyer like his father, Mr Puri. He's got all kinds of idealistic visions. Wants to put the world to rights. But I keep telling him to get into corporate law. That is where the money is. You know these fellows are making crores and crores.'

A knock came at the door and the young maidservant reappeared carrying a glass of water on a tray. As she served the detective, Mrs Kasliwal watched her every movement with a deep frown.

'Will there be anything else, madam?' the girl asked timidly after Puri had taken the glass.

'Bring tea,' came the icy reply.

The maidservant nodded and withdrew in silence, closing the door behind her.

'Mr Puri, I should have told you that Chippy is running late,' Mrs Kasliwal said while the detective sipped his water. 'Some urgent business is there. You'll find him at the District and Sessions Court. But first you'll take lunch.'

'He's a busy fellow, is it?'

'Never stops, Mr Puri! One case after another. So many people seeking his advice. And he can never say no. He is far too accommodating, actually. That is his character. You will not find a more respected man in all of Rajasthan. And from such a well-to-do family. His grandfather was one of a kind and his father was a most distinguished person, also. Only problem is . . . ' Here Mrs Kasliwal faltered. 'Frankly speaking, I fear for his safety, Mr Puri. Such powerful people he is taking on. Even politicians and the like. I ask you, is it worth it? Sometimes it's best not to get involved, no?'

'Certainly one has to be careful,' said Puri, staying neutral despite his admiration for his client's strong convictions and courage.

'Exactly,' said Mrs Kasliwal. 'A man should put his family first and others after. Also, is it for lawyers to fix the whole country? Mr Puri, such terrible things they are saying about Chippy. But that is why you are here, is that not correct? You'll clear my husband's good name and the family name, also. People are getting all kinds of ideas, I tell you. Everywhere there is talk.'

'You can count on Most Private Investigators, madam,' he replied.

'But how will you find this girl, Mr Puri? She could be alighting anywhere, no? Who knows what has become of her? One day she is here, then absconding. Most probably she has made friendship with the wrong sort and paid the consequences.'

66

Puri nodded. 'Often shenanigans are taking place,' he agreed.

'I tell you, Mr Puri, I'm facing constant servant tension. I don't dare take my eyes off these people for one minute. Give them an inch and they take more than a mile. You provide good salary, clean quarters and all, but every time, someone is making mischief. I tell you, drivers are making hanky panky with maidservants. Cooks are stealing *ghee*. Malis are getting drunk and sleeping under trees. Then they are making demands, also! 'Madam give me advance. Madam give my daughter education. Madam give me two thousand *bucks* for Mother's heart operation.' Are we expected to take responsibility for every problem in India, I ask you? Don't we have our own stomachs to feed?'

Puri took out his notebook and asked Mrs Kasliwal how Mary had come to be in her employ.

'Just, she came knocking one day. I had need of one maidservant.'

'You have records? A photocopy of her ration card, a photograph?'

Mrs Kasliwal regarded Puri with amused pity.

'Why should I have a photograph of her?' she asked.

'What about her last name? You know it?'

'I never asked, Mr Puri. Why should I? She was just a maidservant after all.'

'Is there *anything* you can tell me about her, madam? She was a satisfactory worker?'

'Not at all! Always things were going missing,

67

Mr Puri. One day my comb; the next, two hundred rupees. When absconding she took one silver frame, also.'

'How do you know?'

'Because it was gone! How else?'

The detective wrote something in his note-book, ignoring Mrs Kasliwal's testiness.

'Mary vanished on what date exactly?' he asked.

'August 21st night. 22nd morning there was no sign of the girl. I found her room empty.'

'Was Mary having relations with other staff members?'

'You know these Christian types, Mr Puri. Always putting it about.'

'Anyone in particular?'

'She and Kamat, cook's assistant, were carrying on for sure. Twice or thrice, I saw him coming from her room.'

Puri made a note of this.

'You have been most co-operative, madam,' he said. 'But just a few more questions are there. Tell me when Mary left, her salary was owing, was it?'

Mrs Kasliwal seemed surprised by the question and took a moment to answer. 'Yes, it was due,' she said.

'You're certain, madam?'

'Quite certain.'

'Did you report her disappearance to the police?'

'And what should I tell them, Mr Puri? Some Bihari-type maidservant absconded? Police have better things to do with their time.'

'You are quite correct, madam,' he said. 'The police suffer from case overload these days. That is why substitute batsmen like myself are making good innings.'

Puri put away his notebook, but he wasn't quite finished with his questions.

'Madam, just you called Mary a 'Bihari-type',' he pointed out. 'But earlier you didn't say where she was from.'

'A slip of the tongue, Mr Puri,' said Mrs Kasliwal. 'So many servants these days are coming from Bihar and other such backward places. Naturally I assumed she was from there, also, being so dark.'

'She was very dark, is it?'

'Like *kohl*, Mr Puri,' she said with disdain. 'Like kohl.'

★ ★ ★

After an excellent lunch, Puri inspected the servant quarters.

The redbrick building stood in the back garden beyond a wide lawn and a screen of bushes.

There were five small rooms as well as a shared 'bathroom' equipped with a cold tap, an iron pail and a squat toilet.

Mary's room had remained empty since her disappearance. It was dingy and bare save for a cotton mattress that lay on the floor and posters of the Virgin Mary and the Bollywood hunk Hrithik Roshan on the wall. Puri knew that in winter, with no source of heating, it must have been brutally cold, and in summer, unbearably hot.

He spent more than five minutes in the room, scouring the place for clues. There were rat droppings scattered across the floor, and in one corner ash from a burnt mosquito coil. Lined up on the windowsill, Puri also discovered a dozen smooth little coloured stones. These he slipped into his pocket when Mrs Kasliwal wasn't looking.

'Regrettably, I found nothing,' said Puri as he emerged from the room, noting that the door was warped and it couldn't be closed or locked properly.

Together they made their way back across the lawn and down the side of the house to the driveway where Handbrake was waiting in the car.

'Madam, one more question is there, actually,' said Puri before he headed off to the court. 'What all were your whereabouts on August 21st night?'

'I was playing bridge with friends, Mr Puri.'

'I see. And you returned at what time exactly?'

'Quite late, Mr Puri. Some time after midnight if I'm remembering correctly. Before you ask, Mary's absence came to my attention the next morning only.'

'Must be there were other people around the house — servants and all?'

'Certainly, Mr Puri. But who knows what goes on when I'm not around. I shudder to think, really I do.'

'Can you list all of those who might have been

present at the time?'

'But of course, Mr Puri. Let me write the names down for you.'

She wrote:

Jaya, maidservant
Kamat, cook assistant
Munnalal, driver
Dalchan, mali

7

Outside Jaipur's District and Sessions Court, rows of male typists sat at small wooden desks bashing away at manual typewriters. The continuous tapping of tiny hammers on paper punctuated by the pings of carriage-bells was constant — the very sound of the great, self-perpetuating industry of Indian red tape.

Hovering behind each typist stood his clients: complainants, defendants, petitioners and advocates, all watching to ensure their affidavits, summons, wills, marriage applications, deeds, indentures, and countless other types of form were completed accurately. A rate of ten rupees per page was charged for this service, an unavoidable fee given the court's stipulation that all official documents should be typed (and one exploited to the full by the typing mafia who ensured that there was not a word processor in sight).

In front of the courthouse sat rows of advocates whose 'offices' were out in the open. Each had a desk with his name prominently displayed on a plaque, a few chairs, and a metal filing cabinet packed with bulging files tied with string.

Schools of hangers-on circled the lawyers, like symbiotic fish feeding off the parasites on sharks. Chai-wallahs moved between the rows of desks with trays of small glasses of sweet milky tea, calling 'Chaieee, Chaieee!' Grubby little urchins carrying wooden boxes with brushes, rags and tins of polish offered to shine shoes for four rupees. Hawkers sold roasted peanuts in newspaper cones.

Various businesses had also set up under a banyan tree. There was a barber's — a mirror attached to the gnarled trunk and a high chair — catering to anyone requiring a haircut or a shave before making their appearance in court. A table with a phone and a meter hooked up to a car battery also served as a 'telecon centre'.

Like any place in India where people gathered, the courts attracted beggars and a collection of wildlife as well. A man with no legs rolled around on a makeshift skateboard, holding his hand up in hopes of a handout. Rats and crows competed for discarded peanut shells. Pye-dogs lazed in the winter sun.

Puri passed through this throng with disdain writ large across his face. His aversion to India's courts had developed long before he became a private detective. In the mid-1970s, his father had been falsely accused of bribery and become embroiled in a court battle to clear his name, which had dragged on for nearly fifteen years and had sullied his reputation for ever. As a teenager, the young Puri had spent many a morning or afternoon waiting patiently outside the Rohini courts complex where he had seen for himself how corrupt and inefficient the system was. Often he would meet his cousin Amit there, trying to settle a property dispute that had started between his grandfather and great-uncle

73

some twenty years earlier and embroiled the next two generations in pointless quarrelling and exorbitant legal fees.

According to one newspaper article Puri had read recently, it would take half a century to clear the backlog of cases pending in India. And there were hundreds more being added every day.

The detective passed some of the system's victims in the corridors of the main building as he searched for the courtroom where Ajay Kasliwal was arguing a case. Many of them were poor and illiterate, unable to afford proper representation or the bribe money necessary to grease the countless palms of the many gatekeepers to justice. They crouched on their haunches, resigned and helpless in the face of endless adjournments, incomprehensible legal jargon and unchallenged violations of their fundamental rights.

A jostling crowd of advocates, defendants and their families blocked Puri's entrance to Court 19. He found a space on a bench outside, and waited for Kasliwal to emerge. Next to him sat an old man with the dry, cracked heels of a farmer who had spent long years ploughing parched fields.

Puri asked him what he was doing there and soon the farmer was telling him about his case. It had begun with a dispute over a water buffalo.

'My neighbour stole the animal at night,' he said. 'When I complained to the police, they beat me. The court said there was no evidence and I was ordered to pay my neighbour's legal fees.

Now I am in dispute with his lawyers because I cannot pay and my own lawyer is also charging to represent me. When I come here to appeal, either the lawyers do not appear or there is no time given to me in the court. Meanwhile the bills grow larger and still I cannot pay. In the end I will be bankrupt, they will take my land and I will have no choice but to take my own life.'

Puri asked him how much he owed. The amount was two thousand rupees.

'And how long have you been coming here?'

'Three years.'

It saddened him to think that in today's India, sixty years after the nation had won its independence, a man's future and that of his family hung in the balance over an amount equivalent to a restaurant bill. He felt inclined to take out his wallet and give the farmer the amount he required. But he knew cash handouts were not the answer; the money would just get swallowed up. What was needed was reform. Perhaps by defending Ajay Kasliwal, he could help achieve it.

⋆ ⋆ ⋆

'Case adjourned,' said Kasliwal, squeezing through the swell of people clambering to get inside Court 19. 'That's the third time this week.'

'On what grounds?' asked Puri.

'The key witness was supposed to be deposed before the judge, but it seems His Lordship has been bought by the opposition.'

75

The two men left the building and drove over to the Rajasthan High Court where Kasliwal had his office.

'The problem with the system is such that it is almost impossible to remain honest,' said the lawyer. 'So much temptation is there, I tell you. Everyone is involved. All these bastards are looking after one another's interests. If you get one good apple, then they're worried it will spoil the batch. They don't want honest fellows like me around who aren't ready to do match fixing.'

'It is a great conspiracy of interests,' he continued. 'I'm fighting the entire system, Puri-ji. My enemies are surrounding me on all fronts. But we must root out this evil. How can India expect to reach superpower status with all this corruption around? It is like a great hand around our throats. I, for one, am prepared to fight it with every bone in my body.'

Kasliwal's office was plainly furnished with just a desk, a few chairs and picture of Gandhi on the wall. In the bottom drawer of his desk, he kept a bottle of Royal Challenge.

'It's good for bad purposes,' he chuckled, pouring Puri a small glassful, then adding some soda.

The two men clinked glasses and sat down on either side of Kasliwal's desk, facing one another.

'Puri-ji, you are a good man,' said the lawyer. 'That is as clear as day. Come what may, we will be friends! That is for sure.'

The detective drank to his client's health, but looked troubled.

'Too much soda?'

'No, no, *badiya*!'

'Something is wrong?'

'Yes, there is something,' answered Puri. 'Before I proceed further, one thing should be understood. A detective must be thorough. He must leave no stone unturned. To reach the truth, he must go about where he's not wanted asking questions people don't want answering. He must pry into the darkest shadows. Sometimes he will discover skeletons hiding away in closets. Sometimes in trunks, also.'

'You've found something already, Puri-ji?'

'Nothing yet. But this is an old friend.' He touched the side of his bulbous Punjabi nose. 'It is as good as radar. Better, in fact! And it is telling me something terrible has happened. The circumstances surrounding Mary's disappearance are most peculiar. No way a maidservant leaves without taking her salary. However small an amount, such a female will want it.'

The detective stared into his whisky, deep in thought.

'If you want me to find out what happened, I must examine your affairs and those of your family. From top to bottom, inside out.'

'We have nothing to hide,' said Kasliwal.

Puri drained his glass and placed it on his client's desk. His countenance was grave. 'Let us suppose for a moment you were making mischief with this Mary,' he said.

Kasliwal sat up straight. 'What kind of question is that?'

'Sir, I need to know everything or no good will

77

come,' answered Puri, staring at him across the desk.

'Nothing happened between us, I swear it.'

'But you tried to make friendship with her?'

'Listen, I admit she was good for window shopping, but I never touched her. My father taught me never to do hanky panky with servants.'

'And with others?' probed Puri.

The lawyer stood up, looking agitated. He started to pace up and down.

'Sit. It is no good hiding the truth from Vish Puri,' prompted the detective.

'My private life is not open for discussion,' said Kasliwal firmly.

'Sir, I'm working on your behalf. What is said will remain between us.'

Kasliwal stopped by the window of his office looking out on the inner courtyard of the High Court. There was a long silence and then he turned his back on the window and said:

'I admit I'm not a man to always eat home-cooked food. Sometimes, I like something extra spicy.'

His words were met with a blank look.

'Come on Puri-ji, you know how it is. I'm only human. Married to the same woman for twenty-nine years. Arranged marriage and all. After so many innings, a man needs some extracurricular activity.'

'But not with servants?'

'Life is complicated enough, Puri-ji.'

The detective took out his notebook, referring to his notes from his conversation with Mrs Kasliwal.

'How about Kamat, cook's assistant? He and Mary got involved?'

Kasliwal shrugged. By now, he was standing with his hands on the back of his chair, leaning over it. 'I wouldn't know. With so much workload, I'm not around the house much.'

Puri flicked back to the notes taken during his first conversation with his client in the Gymkhana Club.

'The night Mary vanished, you were working, is it?' he asked.

The lawyer looked down and exhaled deeply. 'Not exactly,' he confessed. 'I was . . . '

'Making friendship?'

There was a pause. 'Something like that.'

'Anyone can verify?'

Kasliwal looked torn by the suggestion. 'Puri-ji, that could be awkward,' he said hesitantly.

The detective referred to the list compiled by Mrs Kasliwal of everyone who was supposed to have been in the house at the time of Mary's disappearance.

'What about your driver, Munnalal? He was with you?'

'He dropped me at the address, yes.'

'I'd like to talk with him.'

'I'm afraid one month back, he got drunk and abusive, so I fired him.'

'You know his address?'

'No, but he's round about. I pass him in one of those new Land Cruisers from time to time. Must be working for another family. I doubt it will be difficult to track him down.'

The detective checked his watch. It was already four o'clock.

'By God where does the time go? I'd better get a move on, actually,' he said.

Kasliwal saw him to the door.

As they shook hands Puri asked, 'Sir, is your wife aware?'

'Of what? Munnalal's address? Possibly I can ask her.'

'I was referring to your like of spicy food?'

Kasliwal raised a knowing eyebrow and replied: 'I never bring home takeaway.'

★　★　★

After he left the High Court, Puri asked Handbrake to take him to a hole-in-the-wall cash dispenser where he took out a wad of new one-hundred-rupee notes.

Their next stop was Jaipur's Central Records Office where the detective wanted to check if any unidentified bodies had been discovered around the time of Mary's disappearance.

The building matched the blueprint for most Indian government structures of the post-1947 socialist era: a big, uninspiring block of crumbling, low-quality concrete with rows of air conditioning units covered in pigeon excrement jutting from the windows.

At the entrance stood a walk-through metal detector that looked like a high school science project. Made out of chipboard and hooked up to an old car battery, it beeped every ten seconds irrespective of whether anyone passed through it.

The foyer beyond was dark with a half-dead potted plant on either side of the lift and several panels hanging precariously from the false ceiling. Two busybody male receptionists sat at a wooden desk cluttered with rotary dial telephones and visitors' logbooks. A sign on the wall behind them read:

FOLLOWING VVIPS ONLY MAY ENTER
WITHOUT SECURITY CHECK:
PRESIDENT OF REPUBLIC OF INDIA
PRIME MINISTER OF REPUBLIC OF INDIA
CHIEF MINISTERS MEMBERS OF LOK
SABHA MEMBERS OF RAJYA SABHA FOR-
EIGN HEAD OF STATE FORMER FOREIGN
HEAD OF STATE FOREIGN AMBASSADOR
(ORDINARY DIPLOMATS NOT EXEMPT
NOR AIDS) DALAI LAMA (RETINUE NOT
EXEMPT) DISTRICT COMMISSIONER
STRICTLY NO SPITTING

Puri did not have an appointment and, since he could not lay claim to being any of the above, had to part with a few minutes of his time and three of his new hundred-rupee notes.

Thus armed with the requisite entry chit, all properly signed and rubber-stamped, the detective made his way up the stairs (the lift was undergoing construction), passing walls streaked with red *paan* spit and fire buckets full of sand, cigarette and bidi butts.

On the fourth floor, little men with oiled hair wearing the semi-official uniform of the Indian bureaucratic peon — grey polyester pant suits

81

with permanent creases, and black shoes — made their way up and down the corridor. Coming face to face with the sheer size of the Indian bureaucracy never failed to amaze Puri. The system still employed hundreds of thousands of people and, despite the recent rise of the private sector, it remained the career of choice for the vast majority of the educated population.

Puri doubted this would change any time soon. India's love of red tape could be traced back centuries before the British. The Maurya Empire, India's first centralised power, which was founded around 2300 BC and stretched across most of the north of the subcontinent, had had a thriving bureaucracy. It had been a uniting force, implementing the rule of law and bringing stability. But now, the endemic corruption in India's administration was severely hampering the country's development.

Room 428 was near the far end of the corridor. As he strode purposefully inside, Puri took his fake Delhi police officer badge from his wallet, adopting the role of Special Commissioner Krishan Murti, Delhi Crime Branch. At the counter where all requests for records had to be made, he told the clerk that he wanted to see the file for unclaimed bodies found in Jaipur in August.

'Make it fast,' he said.

'Sir, request must be made. Procedure is there. Two days minimum,' replied the clerk.

At that moment, Puri's phone rang. He had pre-programmed the alarm to go off thirty seconds after he'd entered the office. He pretended to answer it.

'Murti this side,' he said, pausing as if to listen to a voice on the other end of the line. He allowed his eyes to widen. 'Bloody bastard!' he bellowed. 'What is this delay? Where are my results?'

The clerk behind the counter watched him with growing unease.

'Don't give me damn excuses, maaderchod! I want results and I want them yesterday! Top priority! I'm answering directly to the Home Minister himself. The man doesn't take no for an answer and neither do I! If I don't see action within one hour, you'll be doing traffic duty in Patna!'

Puri hung up the phone, muttered 'Bloody bastard', and turned on the clerk.

'What were you saying? Something about two days minimum, huh?'

'Yes, sir,' quivered the clerk.

'What bullshit! Get me the incharge. Right away. No delay!' bawled the detective, thoroughly enjoying himself. Oh how he loved watching bureaucratic types squirm!

Puri was ushered into a partitioned cubicle, the domain of C. P. Verma, whose seniority was denoted by the fact that he wore a jacket and tie.

'I want the record for unidentified bodies discovered in August,' Puri told the bureaucrat who had stood up. 'It's of national importance. Top priority.'

C. P. Verma, who had overheard the exchange between the desk clerk and Puri, hadn't risen through the ranks without learning how to respond to authority and recognising when to jump.

'Of course, sir! Right away, sir!' He called for his secretary, who swiftly presented himself in front of his boss's desk. C. P. Verma ordered the man to bring him the file, his tone no less abrupt than Puri's. '*Jaldi karo*! Do it fast!' he added for good measure, his face contorted with displeasure.

The secretary scampered off to dispense orders of his own to the subordinates ranked below him. The incharge's expression melted into an unctuous smile.

'Sir, you'll take tea?'

The detective brushed away his offer with a motion of his hand, busying himself with his phone.

'Just get me the file,' he said, flatly, pretending to make another phone call, this time to his assistant whom he accused of mismatching a set of fingerprints.

Less than five minutes later, the secretary returned with the file. Puri snatched it out of his hands and began searching through the pages. Nine unidentified bodies had been discovered in Jaipur in August alone. Of these, two were children, both suffocated and dumped in a ditch; four were hit-and-run victims found dead on the sides of various roads; one was an old man who fell down a manhole and drowned (he was not discovered for a month); another was a teenager whose headless torso turned up one morning on the railway tracks.

The ninth was a young woman.

Her naked body had been found on the side of

the Ajmer Road on August 22nd.

According to the coroner's report, she had been raped and brutally murdered and her hands had been hacked off.

A grainy, out-of-focus photograph showed extensive bruising around her face.

'Why only one photograph?' Puri asked C. P. Verma.

'Sir, budget restrictions.' It was evidently a phrase he was used to parroting.

'What happened to this woman's body?'

'Sir, it was held in Sawai Mansingh Hospital for requisite 24 hours and after no claim was made upon it, cremation was done.'

'Give me a photocopy of this report and the photo, also.'

'Sir, I'll need authorisation.' He ventured a smile.

'Authorisation is there!' shouted Puri, showing him his badge. 'Don't do obstruction!'

Within a matter of minutes, the photocopies were in Puri's hands.

C. P. Verma saw the detective to the door personally.

'Sir, anything else from me?' he asked.

'Nothing,' snapped Puri as he left.

'Thank you, sir. Most welcome, sir,' C. P. Verma found himself saying to the detective's back.

The incharge then returned to his cubicle, pleased with himself for having assisted such a highly ranked detective. He was even more senior than the other investigating officer Rajendra Singh Shekhawat, who had asked to see the same file the day before.

85

8

Ajay Kasliwal couldn't tell whether the girl in the coroner's photograph was Mary.

'So much of bruising is there,' said the lawyer, grimacing at the image when Puri showed it to him in the evening.

Mrs Kasliwal studied it for a few seconds and then said in a tone that might have been born of caution or confusion, 'These people look so much alike.'

'You can make out any distinguishing marks?' the detective pressed her.

'How should I know?' she answered brusquely.

Puri decided to show the photograph to the servants and asked that they be brought into the sitting room one by one.

Bablu, the cook, came first. A fat, greasy-faced Punjabi with bloated fingers, he gave the photocopy a cursory glance, said, yes, it could be Mary and then returned to his kitchen. Jaya, the shy girl who'd answered the front door for the detective in the morning, was next. She held the piece of paper with trembling hands, looked at the image, squealed and closed her eyes. Puri asked her if she recognised the girl, but she just stared back at him with wide, frightened eyes.

'Answer him,' Mrs Kasliwal instructed.

'Yes, madam . . . I . . . I . . . ,' Jaya said, her eyes darting between the Kasliwals and the detective.

'Don't be afraid,' urged Puri, gently. 'Just tell me what you think.'

'I don't . . . couldn't . . . say sir,' she said after further coaxing. 'It . . . well, it could be . . . Mary, but then . . . '

Puri took back the picture and Jaya was dismissed.

Kamat, cook's assistant, was equally nervous and no clearer on whether the woman in the photograph was his former co-worker. But he seemed remarkably unmoved by the shocking nature of the image and, with a shrug, handed it back to the detective.

That left the mali.

Mrs Kasliwal would not allow him to enter the house, so he had to be brought to the kitchen door, which opened into the back garden.

The gardener was evidently stoned and stood there with a silly grin and dopey eyes, swaying from side to side in time with a tune he was humming to himself.

Puri handed him the photograph and he stared at it for thirty seconds with his head moving back and forth like a rooster's.

'Do you recognise her?' he asked.

'Maybe, maybe not,' replied the mali. 'My eyesight is not what it used to be.'

All this went to confirm why Puri rarely bothered asking servants — or most people, for that matter — direct questions. Getting at the truth, unearthing all the little secrets that people buried deep down, required a subtler approach. And so later that evening, the detective made a few phone calls to Delhi, putting into motion the next stage of his investigation.

★ ★ ★

The detective spent the night in one of the guest rooms in his client's house, Raj Kasliwal Bhavan, and, after breakfast, announced his intention to return to Delhi.

Ajay Kasliwal looked taken aback by this news. 'But Puri-ji, you just got here,' he said.

'Don't have tension, sir,' the detective assured him. 'Vish Puri never fails.'

Soon, he and Handbrake were on the highway to Delhi, travelling at the legal and responsible speed that was not of the driver's choosing and certainly not to his liking.

By now, Handbrake was burning with curiosity about the detective's latest case. The servants at the house had been talking about little else and the driver had been privy to their theories. The subzi-wallah had told him that the lawyer Sahib had many lady friends and he had got Mary pregnant and had sent her away with a payoff. The cook had whispered that the mali, whom he hated, had raped the maidservant, killed her and buried the body under the spinach. And the Muslim who sold carrot *halva* on the pavement had been adamant that the girl had fallen in love with a fellow Muslim, converted to Islam and, consequently, been abducted by her family and murdered.

Puri smiled when Handbrake related all this to him.

88

'Did they ask about me?'

'All of them, Boss.'

'And what did you tell them?'

The driver looked suddenly unsure of himself. 'I told them that . . . you are . . . that you are an . . . idiot, Boss.'

Puri looked pleased. 'You told everyone?'

'Yes, just like you asked me to. I said that you forget everything from one day to the next because you are a drunkard and you spend all your mornings sleeping.'

'Excellent! Very good work!' said Puri.

Handbrake grinned, grateful for the compliment. But he was still confused by Puri's motive. It showed clearly in his expression.

'Vish Puri's third rule of detective work is to always make all suspects believe you are a fool,' explained the detective. 'That way they are caught unawares.'

'What is the second rule, Boss?'

'Pay no attention to gossip.'

'What is the first?'

'That I will tell you when you are ready.'

With that, Puri lay back against the seat and went to sleep. He did not wake until they reached the halfway point and Handbrake pulled in to the Doo Doo Rest Raunt and Rest Stop car park.

The detective went into the air-conditioned dining room where he sat at a clean table and enjoyed a cup of chai served in a china cup by a waiter.

Handbrake, meanwhile, went to the open-air *dhaba* where he sat amongst the flies and the truck and bus drivers, and the same tea was served in clay cups.

★ ★ ★

Puri had good reason for returning to Delhi: he had received a summons. Not the sort of summons issued by the courts (although he had been handed more than his fair share); this was from a potential client, a man whom the detective could not ignore or put off, a childhood hero no less.

Brigadier Bagga Kapoor, retired, was a decorated veteran of the 1965 Pakistan war. He had commanded a tank battalion during the legendary advance over the Ichhogil Canal, which marked the western border with India. In September of that year, he and his men destroyed eighteen enemy tanks, coming within range of Lahore International Airport. When his own tank was hit by enemy fire and two of his men were killed, Brigadier Kapoor pulled his unconscious gunner from the burning vehicle and carried him to safety. For this action, he was awarded the Ati Vishisht Seva Medal.

Puri had never had the pleasure of meeting the legendary Brigadier, although he'd heard him lecture at the Indian Military Academy in Dehradun in 1975. Naturally, he was thrilled at the opportunity of being of service to the great man. But when Brigadier Kapoor had telephoned Most Private Investigators the day before and spoken to Elizabeth Rani, he had not specified the nature of the case. He'd simply left instructions for Puri to meet him in Lodhi Gardens at four in the afternoon.

'I tried telling him that you are out-of-station, but he insisted,' Elizabeth Rani told Puri on the phone while he was still in Jaipur. 'He also asked that you must go alone.'

The detective stopped off at home in time for lunch to discover that Mummy had been trying to find witnesses to the shooting in the neighbourhood. According to Rumpi, she had spent all of yesterday and most of this morning knocking on doors.

'By God!' exclaimed Puri, angrily. 'I told her not to get involved! Why she always insists on doing such interference I ask you?'

'She's just trying to help,' said Rumpi as she and Malika prepared *rajma chawal* for lunch. 'Shouldn't you be out there doing the same — asking people what they saw?'

'My dear, I'm totally capable of running my investigations. Already I've got my own people doing the needful.'

This was true: Tubelight and one of his boys had been making discreet inquiries in the neighbourhood since yesterday; so far, though, they had come up with nothing.

'Mummy will only make a mess of things and put people on guard. It could be dangerous, also. Detective work is not child's play. Now please, when Mummy returns from doing her chitchat, tell her I want a word tonight. She's to stop this nonsense.'

★ ★ ★

After lunch Puri drove to his office, caught up with the latest developments in the other cases on his books, which included some run-of-the-mill matrimonial investigations, and then drove the short distance to Lodhi Gardens.

The car park at the Prithviraj Road entrance was full of Hindustan Ambassadors with official licence plates and red emergency lights on their roofs — just some of the thousands of courtesy cars assigned to India's senior babus, judges and politicians for conducting the business of the state. These days that included taking wives and their lapdogs for their afternoon walks, or so the ruling bureaucratic elite had come to believe.

Puri crossed the Athpula Bridge and followed the path through the gardens. He passed lawns where families sat enjoying picnics, groups of young men played cricket with tennis balls and toy sellers hawked balloons and kazoos. Cheeky chipmunks darted between the boughs of trees and long-tailed green parakeets with red beaks perched in branches overhead, shrieking noisily. The detective passed an old man practising his yoga exercises, breathing alarmingly heavily through his nostrils; and a bench half hidden between the bushes where two young sweethearts sat stealing furtive kisses.

Brigadier Kapoor was already waiting for Puri on the steps of the Sheesh Gumbad mausoleum, checking his watch impatiently and looking none too pleased that the detective was three minutes late. The war hero was a year short of eighty and his big military moustache, sideburns and correspondingly bushy eyebrows had turned white. Nonetheless, he was still remarkably fit. In American sneakers, socks drawn up to his knees, khaki shorts and a woolly ski hat, he was dressed for exercise.

'Puri, I've heard good things about you,' said Brigadier Kapoor, who had attended Dehradun and Sandhurst and spoke with an accent that reminded Puri of bygone days.

'It's a great honour, sir,' replied the detective with a salute, then a handshake.

'I do briskwalking for forty-five minutes every day at four o'clock without fail,' said Brigadier Kapoor, who carried a military baton with an ivory handle tucked between his chest and the upper part of his left arm. 'We'll talk along the way.'

Puri was hardly dressed for briskwalking; as usual, he was wearing a safari suit and Sandown cap. But without further ado, the older man set off along the jogging circuit at three times the pace of the detective's usual gait.

'I need you for something, Puri,' said Brigadier Kapoor, sounding as if he might ask him to parachute behind enemy lines. 'I don't have to tell you it's for your eyes only.'

'Understood, sir.'

'It's my granddaughter, Tisca.' They passed some copses of giant bamboo, which arched forty feet above them. 'She's to be married in two months. There's a big wedding planned here in Delhi. I was introduced to the boy two days ago. Mahinder Gupta's his name. He won't do. He won't do at all!'

The detective groaned inwardly. He had

hoped that Brigadier Kapoor was going to offer him more challenging work than another matrimonial. But he still managed to sound interested:

'I understand, sir.'

'I blame my son, Puri,' said Brigadier Kapoor as they approached the footbridge that led to Mohammed Shah's tomb. 'He's never been a good judge of character. His wife's even worse. Hopeless woman.'

By now, Puri had broken into a sweat and had to wipe his brow with his handkerchief.

'What sort of family the boy is from?' asked Puri.

'They do commerce, they're Guptas. *Bania* caste.'

'So this boy's occupied in the family business is it?'

'He's working at some place called BPO. You've heard of it?'

'BPO stands for Business Process Outsourcing. Such companies operate call centres and all.'

'I see,' said Brigadier Kapoor with a frown that suggested Puri's explanation did not make things any clearer to him.

'There's anything specific you have against this boy?' asked the detective.

'He's not a man, Puri. He hasn't served his country.'

The detective was developing a stitch in his left side. The direction of their conversation was also making him feel uncomfortable. Matrimonial investigations had become his bread and butter (he often dealt with several a week), but

94

usually his clients came to him seeking reassurance about a prospective bride or groom. Brigadier Kapoor, by contrast, had it in for the boy and wanted to scupper the wedding.

Unfortunately, turning the case away was out of the question. The detective could not say no to a man of such stature; to do so would damage his own reputation.

'What else can you tell me, sir?' panted Puri, growing ever shorter of breath.

'The boy has spent a good deal of time in Dubai. God knows what he could have got up to there. The place is a hotbed of Jihadists, Pak spies, dons, every kind of shady character.'

'He's here in Delhi these days, sir?'

'I believe so. Plays a lot of golf. Shoots four under par — or so they say.'

Much to Puri's relief, they got stuck behind three overweight society women in Chanel sunglasses, sun visors and unflattering leggings, and had to slow down.

Brigadier Kapoor soon lost patience and barked at the women to give way. With a collective tut, they moved to one side of the path and he marched past them muttering to himself.

'Sir, tell me,' said Puri, struggling to catch up again. 'Your granddaughter's what age exactly?'

'Thirty-four or thereabouts.' His tone betrayed not a hint of embarrassment, but she was ancient to be getting married.

'And the boy's age, sir?'

'Three years her junior.'

'Sir, it's the first time Tisca's getting engaged?'

'That's not the point, Puri,' said Brigadier

Kapoor, sharply. 'I want to know about this Gupta boy.'

The two men passed Sikander Lodhi's tomb and reached the car park, where Rumpi's rajma chawal was threatening to make another appearance.

'Sir, with your permission, I'll take my leaves,' said Puri somewhat sheepishly.

Brigadier Kapoor looked unimpressed. 'As you like, Puri,' he said. 'I'll have my file on Mahinder Gupta sent over to your office tomorrow morning. Report back to me within a week. Get me all the dirt on him. I'll take care of the rest.'

'Yes, sir.'

'And get yourself in shape, man,' chided Brigadier Kapoor, wagging his baton. 'At your age I used to run five miles every day before breakfast.'

'Yes, sir.'

Before the detective could mention his fee and explain his usual policy of a down payment for expenses, his new client marched off with his arms pumping like pistons, as if he was charging an enemy position.

Puri waited until he was out of sight and then sat down on a wall to catch his breath and wipe his brow.

'By God, thirty-four,' he said to himself shaking his head from side to side, disapprovingly. 'Well past her sell-by date. Off the shelf, in fact.'

★ ★ ★

At home that evening, Mummy was waiting for Puri in the sitting room.

'Chubby, I've something most important to tell you. One big development is there,' she said.

'Mummy-ji, if it's about the shooting, please save your breath,' he said, as he went through the motion of bending down to touch her feet but only reaching the halfway point.

'Chubby, you must listen, na. It's most important. One servant boy — '

'Sorry Mummy-ji but I won't listen,' interrupted the detective. 'I told you before, you're not to do investigation. It's not a Mummy's role, actually. You'll only make things more complicated. Now please, I respectfully request you not to go sticking your nose where it doesn't belong.'

'But Chubby, I — '

'No, Mummy-ji, that is final, no discussion. Now, I'm going to wash and take rest.'

Puri went upstairs leaving Mummy on her own in the sitting room to think things over.

Chubby had inherited his father's pride and stubbornness, she reflected. Om Chander Puri, too, had always been adamant that she should stay out of his investigations. Only on a few occasions, when he'd been completely stumped by a case, had he deigned to discuss the details with her. Although, each time, she'd helped him unravel the clues, he'd never been able to bring himself to openly acknowledge her assistance. Similarly, when Mummy had had one of her dreams, Om Chander Puri had rarely taken heed of it.

As a wife, Mummy had always felt compelled

to obey her husband. But as a mother, she did not feel constrained to ignore her natural instincts — especially now that her son was in grave danger.

Graver than he knew.

That morning, Mummy had met a young servant boy called Kishan, who worked in house number 23, a few doors down. When she'd asked him if he'd seen anything suspicious on the day of the shooting, he'd looked panicked and blurted out:

'I was nowhere near the back of the house!'

'What happened at the back of the house?'

'Nothing!'

'How do you know if you weren't there?'

Eventually, after being plied with a Big Feast ice-cream and having been assured of Mummy's trustworthiness, Kishan admitted that he had been behind the Puris' home at the time of the shooting.

'What were you doing there?' Mummy had asked.

'Um, well, Auntie, I . . . ' he'd replied, looking embarrassed.

'Let us say you went to the market to buy milk and took the long way back,' Mummy had suggested helpfully.

'Yes exactly. I'd forgotten.'

'What did you see?'

'I was behind a wall waiting for . . . um, well . . . '

'You had to do toilet?'

'Yes that's right and, well, I heard the shots. They sounded like firecrackers. Then two minutes later, I saw a man hurrying out of that building site.'

Kishan had caught only a fleeting glimpse of the man's face. But there had been something distinct about him.

'He was wearing red boots.'

Upon hearing this, Mummy had instructed Kishan not to mention what he'd seen to another soul. It was the kind of information that could get someone killed.

Chubby of all people would understand the significance of the red boots if only he would listen to her. But for now she would have to carry on with the investigation on her own.

'I'll show him mummies are not good for nothing,' she told herself.

9

Few men failed to notice the young peasant woman walking down Ramgarh Road three mornings after Puri left Jaipur. Her bright cotton sari might have been of the cheapest quality and tied jauntily in the style of a labourer, but it did justice to the firm, shapely body beneath. The demure manner in which she wore her *dupatta* over her head — the edge gripped between her teeth and one tantalising, kohl-rimmed eye staring out from her dark features — only added to her allure.

The more lecherous of the men she passed called out lustily.

'I will be the plough and you my field!' bawled a fat-gutted *tonga-wallah* from the front of his horse-drawn cart.

Further on, two labourers painting white lines on the concrete divider in the middle of the road stopped their work to stare and make lewd sucking noises. 'Come and be my saddle! You will find me a perfect fit!' cried one.

The Muslim cobbler who sat on the corner surrounded by heels and soles, gooey pots of gum and a collection of hammers and needles was more discreet. But he could not take his eyes off her ample bosom or the flash of alluring midriff beneath her blouse. Thoughts passed through his head that, as a married man blessed with three healthy sons, he knew he would have to ask Allah to forgive.

Despite her coy embarrassment, the young woman understood the licentious and perfidious nature of men only too well. She ignored their comments and stares, continuing along the uneven pavement with her small bag towards the entrance to Raj Kasliwal Bhavan. There, just beyond the gate, she spotted a mali crouched on the edge of one of the flowerbeds, a scythe lying idle by his side. His clothes were old and tatty and he went barefoot. But his pure white hair was a biblical affair. It began like the crest of a wave, sweeping back from his forehead and cascading down around his ears in a waterfall of licks and curls, before finally breaking into a wild, plunge pool of a beard.

The mali was staring into space with a dreamy, far-off expression, which at first the young woman assumed was a manifestation of old age. Drawing nearer and smelling distinctive sweet smoke trailing up from the hand-rolled cigarette, she realised that his placid state was self-induced.

'Namashkar *baba*,' she greeted him from a few feet away.

The old man stirred from his reverie and, as his drowsy eyes focused on the vision in front of him, his mouth broadened into a wide, contented grin.

'Ah, you have come, my child,' he said, drawing his beard through one hand. 'Good. I have been waiting.'

'We know each other, baba?' asked the woman with a bemused frown, her voice deeper than her youthful looks suggested.

'No, but I have seen you in my dreams!'

'I'm sure you have!' she mocked.

'Why not come and sit with me?' he suggested.

'Baba! If I wanted a corpse I would go to the graveyard!'

Her pluckiness caused the mali to laugh. 'Spend a little time with me, my child, and I will show you that I am no corpse!'

'I have no time baba. I must find work. Is there any available here?'

He patted his thighs. 'There is work for you here!'

'Enough, baba. I am no grave-robber! I was told *Memsahib* is hiring.'

'Memsahib is always hiring. She demands hard hours and pays little. No one stays for long.'

'But you are here.'

'Yes, I am content. I have a roof over my head and I can grow everything I need. What I don't smoke, I sell. But for you there is no charge. Make me feel young again and I will give you as much as you like for free.'

'Later, baba!' she said impatiently. 'I have mouths to feed.'

'What kind of work can you do?' he asked, sounding doubtful.

'Baba! Are you the sahib of the house? Are you the one to ask the questions? I'll have you know that I can do many things. I can clean, do laundry and cook. I even know ironing.'

The mali took another drag of his joint and gently exhaled, the smoke dribbling from his nose and trailing up his face.

'Yes, I can see that you have been many things,' he said.

His words caused the woman to chuckle, but the true reason was lost on the mali.

'A lady in the market told me Memsahib is looking for a maidservant,' she said.

'The last disappeared a few months ago.'

'What happened to her?'

'She was murdered.'

'How do you know?'

'I know.'

'Who did it?'

'It could have been one of many men.'

'She had lovers?'

The mali laughed again. 'That one was known as the 'Little Pony',' he continued. 'There can't have been a man in Rajasthan who hadn't ridden her! I took my turn! So did the driver, the subzi-wallah, Sahib — '

'Sahib?' interrupted the woman with alarm.

'You sound surprised?'

'I've heard it said he's a good man,' she added quickly.

'People are not all that they seem. Whenever Memsahib was away, Sahib would knock on the Little Pony's door. He made a feast of her on many nights! You could hear them from miles away. But it wasn't the sahib who killed her.'

'How do you know?'

'He was not here when she disappeared.'

'Then who is the murderer, Baba?'

The mali shrugged and drew the last from his joint, dropping the still-smoking end into the flowerbed. The woman turned away from him and looked up at the house.

'Where should I ask for work?' she asked.

'At the back. Go to the kitchen door.'

She started up the drive.

'Wait! You didn't tell me your name,' called the mali, admiring the way her silver anklets jangled around her slim, brown ankles.

'Seema!' she shouted over her shoulder without stopping.

'I will be dreaming of you, Seema!'

'I'm sure you will, Baba!'

Seema made her way up the sun-dappled driveway and along the right side of the whitewashed villa. A redbrick pathway led through flowerbeds planted with marigolds and verbena. Beyond, where the path led behind the house, finches gathered around a stale *roti*, chirping as if catching up on local news.

She reached the door of the kitchen and pulled out the letter of recommendation she had been carrying tucked into her waist. It was from a senior bureaucrat and his wife in Delhi, Mr and Mrs Kohli, and stated in English that Seema had worked for them for three years. They had found her 'to be an employee of the highest reliability, honesty, loyalty and integrity, also'. The letter bore Mrs Kohli's phone number. Prospective employers were welcome to call her and ask for further details.

Seema's knock was answered by the cook's assistant, Kamat, who, judging by the wisp of hair on his upper lip, was not a day over fifteen. He was carrying a knife with which he'd been chopping ginger. Kamat in turn called the cook,

Bablu, whose thick, wide nose flared when he frowned.

'Where are you from?' he asked, drying his hands on a cloth and eyeing her suspiciously.

Seema was careful to strike just the right tone when she answered — not too shy, but not overly confident either. She said: 'Sir, my village is in Himachal.'

Seema knew that everyone preferred servants from the hills; they were considered more reliable and trustworthy than those from the plains of the Hindi belt. Furthermore, hill people were not traditionally rag pickers so they were allowed to handle food.

'What can you do?' asked Bablu.

Seema listed her skills and some of her work experience.

'Wait there,' said the cook, snatching the letter out of her hand and shutting the door in her face.

Seema anticipated a long wait and it was nearly thirty minutes before the door opened again. This time it was Madam who appeared. Her hair was piled up on her head covered in a thick, green mud; she was having it dyed with henna.

'You are married?' Mrs Kasliwal asked Seema, looking her up and down.

'No, madam.'

'Why not?'

'My father doesn't have the dowry.'

'How old are you?'

'Twenty-six.'

Madam handed Seema's letter back to her.

'I made a call to Delhi,' said Mrs Kasliwal, without elaborating on her conversation with Mrs Kohli. 'I need one laundry-cum-cleaner maidservant. Can you start right away?'

Seema nodded.

'The pay is nine hundred per month with meals. You must be live-in.'

The amount was below the market rate, especially for a live-in position, which meant a seven-day week.

'Madam, that is low,' stated Seema, eyeing the woman's diamond wedding ring and her matching earrings, which were worth several *lakh* rupees. 'I want twelve hundred.'

Mrs Kasliwal tutted impatiently. 'Nine hundred is fair.'

'Eleven hundred and fifty?'

'Nine hundred and fifty. No advance.'

Seema considered the offer for a moment and then, with a reluctant wobble of her head, assented.

'Very good,' said Mrs Kasliwal. 'Sunday will be your day off and you can leave the house, but otherwise you must be here. I don't want any sneaking out, and no visitors. Is this understood?'

Seema nodded again.

'Bablu will give you your duties. Any stealing and I will not hesitate to call the police. If, in three days, I am not satisfied, then you must leave.'

Mrs Kasliwal led Seema into the kitchen where she instructed Bablu to put her to work immediately.

It was a long, hard day. First Seema helped out in the kitchen chopping onions, kneading *roti* dough, picking out the grit from the *moong daal*, and boiling milk to make *paneer*. Then she had to mop the hardwood floors in the corridors and the dining room. She was allowed thirty minutes for lunch, some *subzi*, which she ate on her own, crouched outside the kitchen. Afterwards, she was sent to a nearby market to pick up three heavy bags of pulses, as well as a packet of cornflakes for Sahib's breakfast. The rest of the early afternoon was spent doing laundry.

As she worked, Seema was left with little opportunity to interact with her co-workers, let alone get to know them. Bablu said little and when he did speak, it was to curse. Mostly this was on account of Kamat, who was clumsy and forgetful and overcooked the chawal and poured fat down the drain. The driver, Sidhu, who had been working in the house for only a month, spent the morning in the driveway chatting on his mobile phone while wiping, waxing and polishing Mrs Kasliwal's red Tata Indica, which he treated as if it was the *Koh-i-Noor*. Sahib's driver, Arjun, who had been hired to replace Munnalal, appeared at around twelve o'clock and, although there was no missing his reaction to the sight of Seema, he barely had enough time to eat his *khana* before returning to the office with his master's tiffin.

Seema found little opportunity to speak with any of the casual staff, either. The dishwasher girl who came for an hour to scrub all the pots and pans before continuing on to a number of other neighbouring households was evidently intimidated by Bablu and kept her head down at the sink. The beautician who came to give Madam threading and *maalish* had airs and didn't deign to say so much as a please or thank-you for a cup of tea. And as for the *dalit* toilet cleaner, who came from a rag pickers' colony on the edge of Jaipur, she was a mute.

The only person Seema managed to talk to properly was Jaya, the other young maidservant, who had been working in the house since early August.

In the late afternoon, when Madam went out visiting friends, the two of them worked together sweeping and mopping the veranda. Given that Jaya was intensely shy and evidently unhappy, Seema broke the ice by telling her about some of her adventures. She talked about her days with a travelling theatre troupe in Assam; the year she spent working as an ayah to a couple of Delhi socialites' children; and her experiences as a Bombay bar girl and how a crorepati businessman had fallen in love with her and proposed.

These stories were all true, even though many of the mitigating circumstances surrounding them were adapted for the audience.

Jaya liked listening to them and quickly took to her new friend. On a couple of occasions, she even had cause to smile.

★   ★   ★

That evening, when all the day's chores were done, Jaya led Seema to the servant quarters at the back of the compound.

There were five rooms in all. The mali occupied the first (starting from the left); the next belonged to Kamat; the third was empty; the fourth, which had posters of the Virgin Mary and Hrithik Roshan on the wall, was vacant as well; and the last room belonged to Jaya.

Jaya warned against staying in the fourth room because the door was warped and did not close properly. But Seema said she liked the idea of the two of them being neighbours. Besides, the door could be fixed.

Together they cleaned the room and took down the posters. Afterwards, Seema took her idols from her bag. Having arranged them on the narrow windowsill of the front window, she lit an incense stick and said a prayer.

The two maidservants spent the rest of the evening chatting and sharing a few dates. Seema related more stories about her adventurous past and, now and again, asked Jaya about the other servants.

Soon, she had learned that the mali was stoned all the time and always passed out in the evening. Bablu was gay, but pretended to be straight even though there wasn't a Salman Khan movie he hadn't seen. Kamat often drank and turned extremely aggressive; there was a rumour going round that he had raped a girl working in another house.

At ten o'clock the two decided to turn in and Seema went back to her room.

She heard Jaya close her door and turn the key in the lock and it was with some effort that she managed to do the same.

An hour later, Seema was woken by the sound of a whistle. And then someone tried opening her door.

She called out, 'Who's there?' But there was no reply and she heard footsteps running away.

Cautiously, Seema got out of bed, went to the door, opened it and looked outside. It was pitch dark and there was no one in sight.

In her right hand, she held the four-inch Nepali *Khukuri* knife that she always kept under her pillow at night.

10

There were fifteen phone lines running into the Khan Market offices of Most Private Investigators Ltd., only six of which were used, officially, by the company. The rest were for undercover operations.

Each of these nine lines had its own dedicated handset, answering machine and a voice-activated tape recorder arranged on a long table in the 'communications room' across the hallway from Puri's office. In front of each phone lay a clipboard with notes detailing how the line was being used and precisely how it should be answered.

These notes were for the benefit of Mrs Chadha, whose job it was to answer the nine phones in a variety of voices.

It was vital, but mostly uncomplicated work. Much of the time, all she had to do was pretend to be a receptionist or a phone operator and then connect the call to either Puri or one of his operatives.

Recently, for example, lines one to four had been assigned to 'Hindustan Pharmaceuticals' (as part of the investigation on behalf of the state of Bihar into the illicit sale of legally grown opium). Mrs Chadha had been required to pick up all calls to those numbers with the words, 'Hindustan Pharmaceuticals, your health is our business, how may I be of assistance?' before connecting them to Puri, a.k.a. Ranjan Roy, CEO.

But at other times, Mrs Chadha, who was a member of the South Extension Amateur Theatrical Society, a gifted impressionist and liked her job because she could spend most of the day knitting, had to play more complicated roles.

During one of the latest matrimonial investigations, line seven had been dedicated to the 'Hot and Lusty' escort service, and for that Mrs Chadha had had to adopt a husky voice and arrange bookings for a certain Miss Nina.

For the foreseeable future, line nine was allocated to a Chinese takeaway called 'Hasty Tasty' and for this Mrs Chadha sounded harried and impatient and asked questions like, 'How hot you want chilli chicken?'

To help make things sound authentic, the communications room was equipped with a multi-deck sound system. This had been set up by Flush and worked automatically. Whenever a call came though, the machine would start playing appropriate background noise.

For Hindustan Pharmaceuticals the ambience was nothing special, just general office sounds: typing, murmuring, the distant ringing of other phones. Calls to the Hot and Lusty line triggered a Muzak version of the theme to *Love Story*. And when anyone rang Hasty Tasty, Mrs Chadha found herself speaking over the clatter of pots and pans, gushes of steam and the cries of irate chefs.

Usually Puri was able to give Mrs Chadha a

rough timing for when a call was expected.

The same morning that Seema applied for work at Raj Kasliwal Bhavan in Jaipur, the detective told Mrs Chadha to expect line six to ring at around nine o'clock.

When the call came, it was closer to 9.30.

Putting aside the sweater she was knitting for her youngest grandson, Mrs Chadha answered the phone with a polite 'Ji?'

The woman on the other line asked for a certain Mrs Kohli.

'Yes, it is she,' she said in English, sticking to her own voice for once.

The conversation that ensued panned out just as Puri had predicted. The caller, a well-spoken lady called Mrs Kasliwal, divulged during a two-minute preamble that she had a large house in Jaipur, that her husband was a well-respected lawyer, and that her handsome son was studying in London.

Eventually she came to the point. Had a servant girl called Seema worked for the Kohlis?

'For three years or thereabouts,' answered Mrs Chadha. 'A most satisfactory worker she was.'

'Might I ask why she was terminated?' asked Mrs Kasliwal.

'Actually, my eldest son and his family returned from posting in Kathmandu and he brought back one ayah, so there is no need for the girl.'

'But you had no complaints?' asked Mrs Kasliwal, sounding as if she would need convincing.

'Not-at-all,' said Mrs Chadha. 'One can say

113

she's a cut above the riff-raff.'

The conversation drifted on to other matters, with Mrs Kasliwal dropping a few names and extending an invitation to tea the next time the Kohlis were in Jaipur.

After she hung up, Mrs Chadha logged the call on the appropriate clipboard and called Puri to tell him that the conversation had gone well. Then she got back to her knitting while she waited for the next scheduled call. A young, prospective groom was expected to call on line seven and ask for the services of Miss Nina.

★ ★ ★

Puri did not expect to hear from Facecream for at least 24 hours. She had not carried a mobile phone with her so she would have to go to an STD[1] booth out in the street to call him.

Getting away from the house could prove difficult, but after working with the Nepali beauty on several dozen operations, the detective was in little doubt that she would find a way.

At Puri's request, Tubelight had sent two of his boys to Jaipur as well. Zia and Shashi had arrived in the Pink City yesterday and been tasked with trying to locate Kasliwal's former driver, Munnalal.

Meanwhile, there was one other lead to follow: the stones Puri had found in Mary's room. He

---

[1] Subscriber Trunk Dialling allows a caller to call another telephone directly instead of via a manual exchange.

had arranged to have them sent to Professor Rajesh Kumar at the geology department of Delhi University.

'Perhaps Doctor-sahib can provide me with a clue to where they came from,' Puri told Elizabeth Rani who was waiting in front of Boss's desk as he placed the little stones, one by one, inside an envelope.

'We must leave no stone unturned, isn't it, Madam Rani?' said Puri, chuckling at his own pun. 'It's a long shot no doubt, but then no clue is ever insignificant, no?'

'Yes sir,' she answered efficiently before returning to her desk to make the arrangements for the envelope to be dispatched to Professor Kumar's office — Professor Kumar for whom, secretly, Elizabeth Rani had a soft spot.

Puri, who likened himself to a spider at the centre of a web with silky tendrils branching out all around him, eased back into his chair, confident that all the little secrets of the Kasliwal household would soon be his. There wasn't another detective in India, private or otherwise, who could have handled it better. And (as Puri acknowledged, begrudgingly) there was only one to equal him.

The young hotshots straight out of detective school (like that bloody Charlie, Harun what's-his-name, who always wore a silk suit and gelled his hair so every goonda could spot him coming a mile off) certainly offered little in the way of competition. The problem with such Johnny-come-lately types was that they watched too much American television, and imagined every case could be solved by turning up at a crime scene and using an ultraviolet light.

Not that forensics didn't have their place. As Puri had told a class of cadets at the Delhi headquarters of the Central Bureau of Investigation (the Indian equivalent of the FBI) during one of his recent lectures, Indians had been pioneers in the field.

'In the fifteenth century, one Delhi court investigator, Bayram Khan, solved the most brutal murder of the Great Mughal's courtesan by matching a hair he located floating in the baths where she was drowned by the eunuch, Mahbub Alee Khan,' the detective had read from a speech that had been typed — and the English grammar greatly improved — by Elizabeth Rani. 'Also let us not forget the Tamil alchemist, Bhogar, who led the way in substance testing. For example, he made extensive comparisons of tobacco ashes. This achievement came a full one century and half before British detective Sherlock Holmes wrote a monograph on the same subject without so much as acknowledging the earlier work.'

Puri had gone on to talk about the great Azizul Haque and Hem Chandra Bose, who developed the fingerprint classification system and opened the first Fingerprint Bureau in Calcutta in 1897 — although Sir Edward Richard Henry took the credit for their pioneering industry.

'So, as we can see, forensics certainly has its uses,' he'd added. 'But there is no substitute for good, old-fashioned intelligence gathering. The microscope cannot match the power of the human eye, we can say.'

Naturally in this field, India had also led the world.

'Some two thousand and three hundred years ago, Mr James Bond's ancestors were living in caves,' he'd said. 'In those dark, distant days, there was no Miss Moneypenny, no Mr Q, and the only gadgets were flints to strike together to make fire.'

This point had got a gratifying laugh from his audience.

'But in India at this time, we were having the great Maurya Empire,' the detective had continued. 'The founder of our greatest dynasty was, of course, the political genius, Chanakya. It was he who established what we can call the art of espionage. He was, in fact, the world's first spymaster, establishing a network of male and female secret agents. These *satris* as they were thus known operated throughout the empire and its neighbouring kingdoms.'

Puri had not needed to remind the cadets that it was Chanakya who had written the world's first great treatise on statecraft, the *Arthashastra*, an extraordinarily practical guide to running and nurturing a fair and progressive society — one that India's modern rulers, and indeed the world's, would have done well to study. But he had drawn their attention to the section on running a secret service and read an excerpt:

''Secret agents shall be recruited from orphans. They shall be trained in the following techniques: interpretation of signs and marks, palmistry and similar techniques of interpreting

117

body marks, magic and illusions, the duties of the *ashramas*, the stages of life, and the science of omens and augury. Alternatively, they can be trained in physiology and sociology, the art of men and society.''

Chanakya, Puri explained, had recommended numerous disguises to be adopted while conducting clandestine operations.

'Brothel keepers, storytellers, acrobats, cooks, shampooers, reciters of *puranas*, cowherds, monks, elephant handlers, thieves, snake catchers and even gods, to name just a few,' he said. 'For agents planning to infiltrate a city, Chanakya suggested adopting the cover of a trader; those working on the frontiers should pose as herdsmen. When a secret agent needed to infiltrate a private household, he urged the use of — and I quote — 'hunchbacks, dwarfs, eunuchs, women skilled in various arts, and dumb persons'.'

Nowadays of course, dwarfs were no longer easy to recruit since many of them had found work in Bollywood. The wealthy classes were no longer inclined to hire hunchbacks as servants. Disguising yourself as a nun was no longer a guaranteed way of gaining access to the home of a high official. And, ever since one-rupee shampoo sachets had become available at paan stalls, shampooing had ceased to be a viable profession.

But the *Arthashastra* remained the basis of Puri's *modus operandi*. The section on the recruitment, training and use of assassins aside, the treatise remained as instructive today as it had proven to the rulers of the great Maurya Empire.

In all that time, human character had changed little.

'Nowadays,' he'd concluded, 'a man can fly from one end of the planet to another in a few hours, only. Achievements in science are at a maximum. But still, there is more mischief going on than ever before, especially in overpopulated cities like Delhi.'

Puri believed this was because the world was still passing through Kali Yuga, the Age of Kali, a time of debauchery and moral breakdown.

'More and more people's moral compass is turning 180 degrees. So you must be vigilant. Remember what Krishna told Arjuna at the battle of Kurukshetra. 'The discharge of one's moral duty supersedes all other pursuits, whether spiritual or material.''

11

With Facecream now inside the Kasliwal household, Puri decided to turn to Brigadier Kapoor's case.

He spent a few hours on the phone checking into the prospective groom's background and soon learned that Mahinder Gupta was to be found at the Golden Greens Golf Course most evenings.

The club was in NOIDA, the North Okhla Industrial Development Area to the east of Delhi, which, despite its clumsy acronym, had become one of the most elegant addresses for Delhi's wealthy, image-conscious elite. To reach it, Handbrake took the road that passed the magnificent Humayun's Tomb and frenetic Bhogal Market with everything from toilets and bamboo ladders to cotton mattresses for sale on the pavements.

At around seven o'clock the Ambassador passed east on the toll bridge that spanned the Yamuna River.

Handbrake had overheard Puri bemoaning the fate of the holy river to someone recently. Apparently, he and his friends had swum in its waters when they were young. On summer weekends, they had crossed by ferry to buy watermelons from the farmers on the other bank. But now, as the terrible stink that filled the inside of the car attested, the Yamuna was a giant sewer — three billion litres of raw waste went into it each year.

On the other side, Handbrake found himself in unknown territory; he had never been to NOIDA before. He had hoped there might be 'signage' to point the way to the golf course, but none appeared. Risking a telling-off, he told Puri he didn't know the way.

'Sir, any directions for me?'

Such honesty did not come naturally to Handbrake. His instinct as a former Delhi taxi driver was never to admit ignorance of an address. Partly, this was an issue of pride. Behind the wheel was the one place in the world where he felt like a king. And what king likes to show weakness?

But mostly it was because his former boss, Randy Singh, owner of the Regal B Hinde Taxi Service, and Handbrake's mentor, had always insisted that if a passenger didn't know the way to their chosen destination, then it was a driver's God-given right to fleece them royally.

This philosophy had been instilled in Randy Singh by his father, old Baba Singh, who'd made his fortune rustling water buffalo. Thus the Singh family credo ran: 'They have it; why should we not take it?' Indeed, Randy Singh believed that it was the duty of every taxi driver to find ways and means of ripping off all his customers. In his office, he kept an up-to-date map of the current roadworks and diversions across Delhi. Every morning, he briefed his boys on the hot spots where they were sure to run into long delays. He also bribed the men from the

Department of Transport whose duty it was to install the government-issued fare meters, which were meant to protect passengers from fraud, to charge an extra three paisa for every mile. This extra profit he split with them seventy-thirty in his favour.

Not surprisingly, Regal B Hinde Taxi Service received a good many complaints from its customers. But Randy Singh never showed remorse. And he prepped his drivers on how to react to disgruntled passengers. Play the dumb villager newly arrived in the big city, he instructed. 'Sorry, sir! No education, sir! Getting confusion, sir!'

Handbrake's new employer saw things very differently. If you weren't completely honest and tried to bluff your way around; if you set off in any old direction hoping for the best and then stopped to ask the way from ignorant bystanders only to find yourself performing half a dozen U-turns, the detective was liable to get extremely hot under the collar.

'*Oolu ke pathay!* Son of an owl!' he'd shouted recently when Handbrake had pretended to know his way around Mustafabad and they'd ended up going round and round in circles in Bhajanpura instead.

Given the respect Handbrake was developing for Boss, such cutting insults hurt. But for all his great deductive powers, Puri was just as lost in many areas of New Delhi's newest suburbs. His map, which was the most up to date available in the market, had been printed two years earlier and did not include many of the roads and developments that had 'come up'.

It didn't help that, throughout Delhi, signages were rare. Nor that the many 'sectors' — which sounded like planetary systems in a Hollywood science fiction film — were just as mysterious as new galactic frontiers. A driver might reach Sector 15 expecting to find Sector 16 nearby, but to his frustration turn a corner and find himself in Sector 28 instead.

Recently, when Handbrake had been sent to Apartment 3P, Block C, Street D, Phase 14, Sector 17 in Gurgaon, it had taken him well over an hour to find it.

As for the Golden Greens Golf Course, Puri had never been there either. So when Handbrake came clean about not knowing the way, the detective told him to ask someone for directions. But not just anyone.

Migrant labourers were a no-no. According to Puri, they weren't used to giving directions because they came from villages where everyone knew everyone else and roads didn't have names.

'Ask them where anything is and they will tell you 'over there'.'

As for fellow drivers, they were not to be relied on, because half of them were probably lost themselves.

Puri sought out real estate brokers and bicycle-rickshaw-wallahs as good sources because they had to be familiar with the areas in which they worked. Pizza delivery boys could also be trusted.

Soon after turning off the NOIDA expressway, Handbrake spotted a Vespa moped with a Domino's box on the back and pulled up next to it at a red light.

'Brother, where is Galden Geens Galfing?' he shouted in Hindi to the delivery boy over the sound of a noisy, diesel-belching Bedford truck.

His question was met with an abrupt upward motion of the hand and a questioning squint of the eyes.

'Galden Geens Galfing, Galden Geens Galfing,' repeated Handbrake.

The delivery boy's puzzlement suddenly gave way to comprehension: 'Aaah! Golden Greens Galf Carse!'

'Ji!'

'Sectorrr forty-tooo!'

'Brother! Where is forty-tooo sectorrr?'

'Near Tulip High School!'

'Where is Tulip High School?'

'Near Om Garden!'

'Brother, where is Om Garden?'

The delivery boy scowled and shouted in an amalgam of English and Hindi: 'Past Eros Cinema, sectorrr nineteen! Turn right at traffic light to BPO Phase three! Enter farty-too through backside!'

Some time later, Handbrake delivered Boss to the front door of the clubhouse and drove to the parking lot. He expected a long wait. But for once, he wasn't bothered and sat back in his seat to enjoy the view.

It occurred to him to take a few photographs of the manicured landscape with the new mobile phone Puri had given him. How else would he be able to prove to the people in his village that such an empty, beautiful place existed?

*   *   *

Puri was not a member of the Golden Greens Golf Course, although he would have liked to be. Not for the sake of playing (secretly he couldn't stand the game — the ball was always ending up in those bloody ponds), but for making contacts amongst India's new money, the BPO (Business Process Outsourcing)-cum-MNC (Multi-National Corporation) crowd.

Such types — as well as many politicians, senior babus and Supreme Court judges — were often to be found on these new fairways to the south and east of the capital. In Delhi, all big deals were now being done on the putting greens. Playing golf had become as vital a skill for an Indian detective as picking a lock. In the past few years, Puri had had to invest in private lessons, a set of Titleist clubs and appropriate apparel, including Argyll socks.

But the fees for the clubs were beyond his means and he often had to rely on others to sign him in as a guest.

Rinku, his closest childhood friend, had recently joined the Golden Greens.

He was standing in reception wearing alligator cowboy boots, jeans and a white shirt embroidered with an American eagle.

'Good to see you, buddy! Looks like you've put on a few more pounds, *yaar!*'

'You're one to talk, you bugger,' said the detective as they embraced. '*Sab changa?*'

Rinku's family had been neighbours of the Puris in Punjabi Bagh and they had grown up playing in the street together. All through their teenage years they had been inseparable. But in their adult lives, they had drifted apart.

Puri's military career had exposed him to many new people, places and experiences, and he'd become less parochial in his outlook. By contrast, Rinku had married the nineteen-year-old girl next door, whose main aspiration in life had been to wear four hundred grams of gold jewellery at her wedding. He had followed his father into the building business and, during the boom of the past ten years, made a fortune putting up low-cost multi-storey apartment blocks in Gurgaon and Dwarka.

Few industries are as dirty as the Delhi construction business and Rinku had broken every rule and then some. There was hardly a politician in north India he had not done a shady deal with; not a District Collector or senior police-wallah to whom he hadn't passed a plastic bag full of cash.

At home in Punjabi Bagh where he still lived in his father's house with his mother, wife and four children, Rinku was the devoted father and larger than life character who gave generously to the community, intervened in disputes and held the biggest Diwali party in the neighbourhood. But he also owned a secret second home, bought in his son's name, a ten-acre 'farmhouse' in Mehrauli. It was here that he entertained politicians and bureaucrats with *gori* prostitutes.

It greatly saddened Puri to see how Rinku had become part of what he referred to as 'The Nexus', the syndicate of politicians, senior

126

bureaucrats, businessmen and crime dons (a good many of whom doubled as politicians), who more or less ran the country. Rinku stood for everything that Puri saw as wrong with India. The disease of corruption was slowly eating away at his friend. You could see it in his eyes. They were paranoid and steely.

And yet Puri could never bring himself to break the bond between them. Rumpi said it was because he had spent his childhood trying to keep Rinku out of trouble.

'So, *saale*, when did you get membership, huh?' asked Puri.

They had gone to the bar and sat down at a table that provided a panoramic view of the Greg-Norman-designed course.

'I'll let you in on a little secret, buddy,' answered Rinku. 'I'm a silent partner in this place.'

He put a finger to his lips, the chunky gold chains slipping down his wrist.

'Is it?' said Puri.

'Yah! And as a gift to you, I'm going to make you a member. No need to pay a farthing. No bloody joining fee. Nothing! You just come and go as you like.'

'Rinku, I — '

'No argument, Chubby! This is final! On the house!'

'It's very kind of you, Rinku. But really, I can't accept,' said Puri.

''Very kind of you, Rinku, I can't,'' echoed Rinku mockingly. 'What the hell's with all this formal bullshit, Chubby, huh? How long have we known each other? Can't a friend gift something to another friend any more, huh?'

'Look, Rinku, try to understand, I can't accept that kind of favour.'

'It's not a favour, yaar, it's a gift!'

Puri knew he could never make Rinku see sense; his friend couldn't accept that he did not live by his so-called 'code'. He would have to accept the offer and then, in a few weeks, after Rinku had forgotten about the whole thing, renounce his membership.

'You're right,' said the detective. 'I don't know what I was thinking. Thank you.'

'Bloody right, yaar. Sometimes I don't recognise you any more, Chubby. Have you forgotten where you're from or what?'

'Not at all,' replied the detective. 'I just forgot who I was talking to. It's been a long day. Now why don't you buy me a drink, you bugger, and tell me about this man I'm interested in.'

'Mahinder Gupta?'

Puri nodded.

'He's a Diet Coke,' said Rinku dismissively.

'A what?'

'Bloody BPO type, yaar. Got a big American dick up his ass, but thinks he's bloody master of the universe. Just like this lot.'

Rinku scowled at the young men in suits standing around the bar. With their degrees in Business Management and their BlackBerries, they were a different breed to Puri and Rinku.

'You know what's wrong with them, Chubby? None of them *drink*!'

The suits all turned and stared and then

looked away quickly, exchanging nervous comments.

Their reaction pleased Rinku.

'Look at them!' he laughed. 'They're like scared sheep because there's a wolf around! You know, Chubby, they go in for women's drinks: wine and that funny coloured shit in fancy bottles. I swear they wear bloody bangles, the lot of them. The worst are the bankers. They'll take every last penny from you and they'll do it with a smile.'

The waiter finally arrived at their table.

'Why the hell have you kept us waiting so long?' Rinku demanded.

'Sorry, sir.'

'Don't give me sorry! Give me a drink! For this gentleman one extra large Patiala peg with soda. For me the same. Bring a plate of seekh kebab and chicken tikka as well. Extra chutney. Got it? Make it fast!'

The waiter bowed and backed away from the table like a courtier at the throne of a Mughal conqueror.

'So what's this Diet Coke been up to, huh? Giving it to his best friend's sister or what?'

Puri tried to answer but he only got out a few words before Rinku interrupted.

'Chubby, tell me one thing,' he said. 'Why do you bother with these nothing people? After all these years you're still chasing housewives. What's your fee — a few thousand a day, maximum? I'm making that every minute. Round the clock. Even sitting here now my cash till is registering. Ching!'

129

'Don't worry about me. I'm doing what I'm meant to be doing. This is my dharma,' replied Puri.

'Dharma!' scoffed Rinku. 'Dharma's for sadhus and *sanyasis*! This is the modern world, Chubby. Don't give me that spiritual shit, OK?'

Puri felt a flash of anger and shot back: 'Not everyone is a . . .'

But he stopped himself speaking his mind, suddenly afraid that if he did, it would bring an end to their relationship once and for all.

'Not everyone is what? A bloody crook like me? Is that what you were going to say?'

They sat in silence for nearly a minute.

'Listen, I didn't come here to argue,' said Puri eventually. 'I'm not one to tell friends how to live or what to do. You've made your choices; I've made mine. Let's leave it at that.'

The Patiala pegs arrived, both tumblers filled to the brim.

Puri picked up his and held it above the small round table that separated them. After a moment's hesitation, his friend did the same and they clinked glasses together.

Rinku downed half his Scotch and let out a loud satisfied gasp, followed by a belch.

'That's a proper drink,' he said.

'On that, we agree,' smiled Puri.

★ ★ ★

'So this *Sardaar-ji* gets married and on his first night he has his way with his new wife. But the

130

next morning he gets divorced. Why? Because he notices a tag on her underwear that says: *Tested by Calvin Klein*!'

Puri roared with laughter at the punch line to Rinku's latest Sikh joke.

The two men were on their second drink.

'I heard another one the other day,' said the detective, when he had wiped the tears from his cheeks.

'Santa Singh asked Banta Singh, 'why dogs don't marry?''

'Why?' asked Rinku gamely.

'Because they're already leading a dog's life!'

Only a slick of grease and some green chutney remained on their snack plates by the time Puri broached the subject of Mahinder Gupta again.

'Your Diet Coke comes here most nights after work — around eight-thirty, usually,' Rinku told him. 'Sometimes his fiancée joins him. She's as bloody nuts about golf as he is. I played a round with him just one time. He wouldn't take my bet. Said gambling was against the club rules! I tell you, Puri these guys are as stiff as — '

'Anything else?' interrupted the detective.

Rinku drained his glass, eyeing his friend over the brim.

'He's got a place in a posh new block near here, Celestial Tower. All bought with white.[1] Can you believe it, Chubby? The guy's got a mortgage from the bank! What kind of bloody fool does that, I ask you? So you want to meet

---

[1] White money is declared income, not derived from the 'black' economy.

131

him — your Diet Coke?'

'Where is he?'

'In the corner.'

There were three men sitting at the table Rinku indicated. They had arrived a few minutes earlier.

'A thousand bucks says you can't guess which one,' said Rinku.

'Make it three thousand.'

'You're on.'

It took Puri less than thirty seconds to make his choice.

'He's the one in the middle.'

'Shit yaar! How did you know?' said Rinku, fishing out the money and slapping it down on the table.

'Simple yaar!' He pronounced it 'simm-pull'. 'The man on the right is wearing a wedding ring. So it shouldn't be him. His friend on the left is a Brahmin; I can see the thread through his vest. Guptas are banias, so it's not him. That leaves the gentleman in the middle.'

Puri looked more searchingly at Mahinder Gupta. He was of average height, well built and especially hairy. His arms looked as if they had been carpeted in a shaggy black rug, his afternoon shadow was as swarthy as the dark side of the moon, and the many sprigs poking out from the neck of his golfer's smock indicated that even the tops of his shoulders were heavily forested. But Gupta did not strike Puri, who always made a point of sizing up a prospective bride or groom for himself, as the macho type. If anything, he seemed shy. When he spoke on his

BlackBerry — he was using it most of the time — his voice was quiet. Gupta's reserved body language was also suggestive of someone who was guarded, who didn't want to let go for fear of showing some hidden part of his character.

Perhaps that was why he didn't drink.

'What did I tell you?' said Rinku. 'Guy doesn't touch a drop of alcohol! Saala idiot!'

'What time will he play?'

'Should be any time.'

A few minutes later, Gupta's golf partner arrived and the two of them headed off to the first tee.

'Chubby, you want to play a round?' asked Rinku.

'Not especially,' said the detective.

'Thank God! I hate this bloody game, yaar! Give me cricket any day! So you want to go to the farmhouse? I've got some friends coming later for a party. They're from Ukraine. They've got legs as long as eucalyptus trees!'

'Rumpi is expecting me,' said Puri, standing up.

'Oh, come on, Chubby, don't be so bloody boring, yaar! I'll make sure you don't get into trouble!'

'You've been getting me into trouble ever since we were four, you bugger!'

'Fine! Have it your way. But you don't know what you're missing!'

'I know exactly what I'm missing! That's why I'm going home.'

Puri playfully slapped Rinku on the shoulder before making his escape.

On his way home, the detective considered how best to proceed in the Brigadier Kapoor case.

Mahinder Gupta struck Puri as somewhat dull — one of a new breed of young Indian men who spent their childhoods with their heads buried in books and their adult lives working fourteen-hour days in front of computer terminals. Such types were generally squeaky clean. The Americans had a word for them: 'geeks'.

Being a geek was not a crime. But there was something amiss.

Why would a successful, obviously fit and active BPO executive agree to marry a female four years his senior?

To find out, Puri would have to dig deeper.

First thing tomorrow morning, he would get his team of forensic accountants looking into Gupta's financial affairs. At the same time, he'd assign Flush to find out what the prospective groom got up to outside office hours.

12

Puri did not reach home until ten o'clock, an hour later than usual.

The honk of the car's horn outside the main gate marked the start of his nightly domestic routine.

The family's two Labradors, Don and Junior, started barking, and, a moment later, the little metal hatch in the right-hand gate slid open. The grizzled face of the night-watchman, Bahadur, appeared, squinting in the bright glare of the headlights.

Bahadur was the most conscientious night-watchman Puri had ever come across — he actually stayed awake all night. But his arthritis was getting worse and it took him an age to open first the left gate, then the right, a process that Handbrake watched restively, grinding the gears in anticipation.

Finally, the driver pulled inside, stopped in front of the house and then jumped out quickly to open the back door. As Boss stepped on to the driveway, Handbrake handed him his tiffin.

The dogs strained on their ropes, wagged their tails and whined pathetically. Puri petted them, told Handbrake (who was renting a room nearby) to be ready at nine sharp and then greeted Bahadur.

The old man, who was wearing a monkeycap with earflaps and a rough wool shawl wrapped around his neck and shoulders, was standing to attention with his back to the closed gates. He held his arms rigid at his sides.

'*Ay bhai*, is your heater working?' asked Puri, who had recently installed an electric heater in the sentry box in anticipation of the cold, damp smog that would soon descend upon Delhi.

'*Haan-ji! Haan-ji!*' called out Bahadur, saluting Puri.

'You've seen anything suspicious?'

'Nothing!'

'Very good, very good!'

Puri entered the house, swapped his shoes for his monogrammed slippers and poked his head into the living room. Rumpi was curled up on the couch in a nightie with her long hair down around her shoulders. She was engrossed in watching *Kaun Banega Crorepati*, India's version of *Who Wants to Be a Millionaire?* but turned off the TV, greeted her husband and brought him up to date with what was going on in the house.

There were no visitors or guests, she told her husband. Radhika, their youngest daughter who was studying in Pune, had called earlier. Malika had gone home to her children, alcoholic husband and impossible mother-in-law. And Monica and Sweetu had gone to bed in their respective quarters.

'Where's Mummy?' asked Puri, perching on the arm of the armchair nearest the door.

'She went out a few hours ago. I haven't heard from her.'

'Did she say where she was going?'

'She mumbled something about visiting some auntie.'

'Mumbled? Mummy doesn't do mumbling. I asked you to keep an eye on her, isn't it?'

'Oh please, Chubby, I'm not one of your spies. I can't be expected to keep track of her all the time. She comes and goes as she pleases. What am I supposed to do? Lock her in the pantry?'

Puri frowned, hanging his head reflectively. His attention was drawn to the stain on the white carpet in the living room made by some prune juice Sweetu had carelessly spilled recently. It reminded him that he needed to have another word with that boy.

'I'm sorry my dear, you're right of course,' he conceded. 'Keeping up to date on Mummy is not your responsibility. I'll try calling her myself. First I'm going upstairs to wash my face.' This was code for: 'I'm hungry and I'd like to eat in ten minutes.'

After he'd freshened up and changed into a white *kurta pyjama* and a cloth Sandown cap, Puri went up on to the roof to check on his chillies. The plants that had been caught in the crossfire appeared to be making a full recovery.

The detective was little closer to finding out who had shot at him. His sources inside Tihar jail had heard nothing about a new contract on his life. Tubelight's boys had not been able to find any witnesses to the shooting, either.

All the evidence pointed to the shooter being an amateur, an everyday person, who would have passed unnoticed in the street.

There was only one lead and it was tentative at

best: Swami Nag had apparently returned to Delhi, but his whereabouts remained unknown.

Puri picked a chilli to have with his dinner and made his way downstairs. Rumpi was busy in the kitchen chopping onions and tomatoes for the *bhindi*. When the ingredients were ready, she added them to the already frying pods and stirred. Next, she started cooking the rotis on a round *tava*, expertly holding them over a naked flame so they puffed up with hot air like balloons and became nice and soft.

A plate had already been placed on the kitchen table and Puri sat down in front of it. Presently, Rumpi served him some *kadi chawal*, bhindi and a couple of rotis. He helped himself to the plate of sliced tomato, cucumber and red onion, over which a little *chat* masala had been sprinkled, and then cast around the table for some salt.

'No salt, Chubby, it's bad for your heart,' said Rumpi without turning around from the cooker.

Puri smiled to himself. Was he really that predictable?

'My dear,' he said, trying to sound charming rather than patronising but not proving entirely successful, 'a little salt never did anyone any harm. It is hardly poison, after all. Besides, you've already cut down on the amount you're using and we don't even have butter on our rotis any more.'

'Dr Mohan has ruled out butter and said you have to cut down on salt. This is your life we're talking about. You want to leave me a widow so I have to shave my head and live in a cell in Varanasi and chant mantras all day long?'

'Now my dear, I think you're being a little over-dramatic. You know full well that well-to-do middle-class widows don't have to sing mantras for a living. Besides, are we going to allow Doctor-ji to ruin every last little pleasure? Should we go through life living in fear?'

Rumpi ignored him and carried on preparing the rotis.

'All I require is a one small pinch to have with my chilli,' he continued. 'Is that really going to kill me?'

Rumpi sighed irritably and relented.

'You're impossible, Chubby,' she said, spooning out a little salt from one of the sections of her *dabba* and putting it on the side of his plate.

'Yes, I know,' he replied playfully. 'But more importantly, now I am also happy!'

He bit off the end of the chilli, dipped it in the salt and took another bite.

For most people this would have been equivalent to touching molten lead with the tip of their tongue. The Naga Morich chilli is one of the hottest in the world, two to three times as potent as the strongest jalapeno. But Puri had built up an immunity to them, so he needed hotter and hotter chillies to eat. The only way to ensure a ready supply was to propagate them himself. He had turned into a capsicum junkie and occasional dealer.

'So how is my Radhika?' asked the detective, who ate with his hands as did the rest of the family when at home. This was a convention he prided himself on; Indians were supposed to eat that way. Somehow a meal never seemed as

139

satisfying with cutlery. Feeling the food between your fingers was an altogether more intimate experience.

'Very fine,' answered Rumpi, who made sure her husband had everything he needed before taking her place next to him and serving herself a little kadi chawal. 'She found a good deal on one of those low-cost airlines so as to come home for Diwali. It's OK with you or she should take the train?'

More family news followed during the meal. Their second grandchild, four-month-old Rohit, the son of their eldest daughter, Lalita, had recovered from his cold. Jagdish-Uncle, one of Puri's father's four surviving brothers, had returned home from hospital after having his gall bladder removed. And Rumpi's parents were returning from their holiday 'cottage' in Manali.

Next, she brought Puri up to date on local Gurgaon news. There had been a six-hour power cut that morning (it had been blamed on fog). An angry mob of residents had stormed the offices of the electricity company, dragged the director out and given him 'a good thrashing'. Eventually, the police had intervened using *lathis* and roughed up a lot of people, including many women.

Finally, Rumpi broached the delicate subject of a holiday; she wanted to go to Goa.

'Dr Mohan said you need a break. You never stop working these days, Chubby,' she said.

'I'm quite all right, my dear. Fit as a fiddle, in fact.'

'You're not all right at all. All this stress is

taking its toll. You're looking very tired these days.'

'Really you're worrying over nothing. Now what about dessert? There's something nice?'

'Apple,' she replied curtly.

★ ★ ★

After Puri had finished eating, he washed the residue of kadi chawal from his hands in the sink, ladled out a glass of cool water from the clay pot that sat nearby and gulped it down.

Afterwards in the sitting room, he turned on his recording of *Yanni Live at the Acropolis*, relaxed into his favourite armchair and dialled Mummy's number.

She answered on the sixth ring, but there was a lot of static on the line.

'Mummy-ji where are you?' he asked her.

'Chubby? So much interference in there, na? You're in an auto or what?'

'I'm very much at home,' he said.

'You've not yet reached home! So late it is? You've had your khana outside, is it?'

'I'm at home, Mummy!' he bawled. 'Where are you?'

The static suddenly grew worse.

'Chubby, your mobile device is giving poor quality of connection. Listen, na, I'm at Minni Auntie's house. I'll be back late. Just I need rest. Some tiredness is there.'

She let out a loud yawn.

'This line is very bad, Mummy-ji! I'll call you back!'

'Hello, Chubby? My phone is getting low on battery and no charger is here. Take rest. I'll be back later, na — '

The line went dead.

Puri regarded the screen suspiciously.

'Who is Minni Auntie?' he shouted to Rumpi who was still in the kitchen.

'Who?'

'Minni Auntie. Mummy said she's at her house.'

'Might be one of her friends. She has so many I can't keep track.'

Rumpi came to the door of the sitting room, wiping her hands on a tea towel.

'Who are you calling now?' she asked Puri.

'Mummy's driver.'

He held the phone to his ear. It rang and rang, but there was no response and he hung up.

'She's out there looking into the shooting — I know it,' he said, wearily.

Rumpi made a face. 'Oh, Chubby, I'm sure she's just trying to help,' she said.

'It's not her place. She's a schoolteacher, not a detective. She should leave it to the professionals. I'm making my own inquiries about the shooting and will get to the bottom of it.'

'If you ask me, I think Mummy's a natural detective,' said Rumpi. 'If you weren't being so stubborn and proud, you might give her a chance. I'm sure she could be very helpful to you. It doesn't sound like you've got any clues of your own.'

Puri bristled at this last remark.

'My dear, if you want your child to learn his

six times table, you go to Mummy,' he said brusquely. 'If you want a mystery solved, you come to Vish Puri.'

★　★　★

As her son had rightfully surmised, Mummy was not at Minni Auntie's (although such a lady did exist; she was one of the better bridge players amongst the nice group of women who played in Vasant Kunj).

She was on a stakeout.

Her little Maruti Zen was parked across the street from the Sector 31 Gurgaon police station, five minutes from Puri's home.

With her was her driver, Majnu, and Kishan, the servant boy, whom she'd persuaded to come with her. She'd also brought along a thermos of tea, a Tupperware container packed with home-made vegetarian samosas and of course her handbag, which, amongst other things, contained her battery-operated face fan.

This had come in extremely useful when her son had called earlier. By holding it up to her phone she had created what sounded like interference on the line, which helped her avoid having to give away her location. This was an old trick she'd learned from her husband, who had occasionally used his electric razor to the same effect.

During forty-nine years of marriage, she'd picked up a number of other useful skills for a detective and a good deal of knowledge as well.

Take red boots, for example.

Mummy knew that they were part of a senior police officer's dress uniform and were supposed to be worn only during parades. Occasionally cops were known to wear them for their day-to-day work when their other boots went for repairs.

If the shooter was indeed an officer — who else would wear such footwear? — then the most logical place to start looking for him was the local 'cop shop'.

Of all the stations in Gurgaon, the one in Sector 31 had one of the worst reputations. Stories abounded about police-wallahs arresting residents of the *bastis* and forcing them to cook and clean for them; of beatings, rapes — even murders.

'We might be here for hours,' moaned Majnu, who was always whining. They had been outside the station for an hour already and he was annoyed at having to work late.

'We have no other choice,' Mummy told him. 'Everyone else is being negligent in this matter. Some action is required.'

★ ★ ★

At around 10.40, a man in plain clothes emerged from the station. Kishan recognised him as the person he'd seen leaving the scene of the shooting.

'Madam, please don't tell anyone it was me who told you! The cops will kill me!' he said when he realised that the shooter was a police-wallah.

'Your secret is safe,' Mummy reassured Kishan, giving him a couple of hundred rupees for his trouble. 'Now go home and we'll take it from here.'

The servant boy did not have to be told twice. He hurriedly exited the car and rushed off into the darkness.

On the other side of the road, Red Boots got into an unmarked car, started the ignition and pulled into the road, heading west.

Mummy and Majnu followed behind. But the driver kept getting too close and she had to scold him more than once.

'There's a brain in that skull or just thin air or what?'

Twenty minutes later, they found themselves pulling up outside a fancy five-star Gurgaon hotel.

Red Boots left his car with the valet and went inside.

'I'm going to follow him. You stay out here in the car park,' Mummy told Majnu.

'Yes, madam,' sighed the driver, who was by now in a sulk.

Puri's mother passed through the hotel doors — they were opened by a tall Sikh doorman with the kind of thick beard and moustache that appealed to tourists — into the plush lobby. Red Boots had turned left, past the bellboy's desk and the lifts. Mummy saw him disappear inside a Chinese restaurant, Drums of Heaven.

Outside the entrance, she stopped for a moment and looked down at what she was wearing in alarm; her ordinary *chikan kurta* and *churidaar pyjamas* were hardly appropriate for such a fancy place.

'But what to do?' she said to herself, continuing her pursuit.

Beyond a kitsch dragon and pagoda, Mummy was greeted by an elegant hostess, who looked Tibetan. Would Madam like a smoking or non-smoking table?

'Actually I'm meeting one friend, only,' replied Mummy. 'Almost certainly she's arrived. Just I'll take a look. So kind of you.'

The hostess escorted Mummy to the back of the restaurant where Red Boots was sitting with a fat-throated man in a white linen suit. They were both smoking cigarettes and drinking whisky.

Behind them there was a vacant table for two; Mummy made a beeline for it, sitting directly behind her mark.

'Must be my friend has yet to arrive,' she told the Tibetan lady. 'Her driver's always getting confusion.'

The hostess placed a menu on the table and went back to her podium.

Mummy pretended to peruse the dim sum section while trying to eavesdrop on Red Boots's conversation with Fat Throat, gradually inching her chair backwards as close as she dared.

The Muzak and the general murmur from the other tables drowned out most of their words. So Mummy asked the waiter to turn off the music — 'Such a headache is there' — and, after turning up her hearing aid to full volume, she was able to grasp a few clear sentences.

'You'd better not fail again. Get him out of the way or the deal won't go through,' Fat Throat was saying in Hindi.

'Don't worry, I'll take care of him,' replied Red Boots.

'That's what you said before and you missed.'

'I told you I'll get it done and I'll get — '

Just then Mummy felt a searing pain in her head.

The waiter had returned and asked to take her order. The effect was like having a screaming megaphone put up to her ear.

'Madam, are you all right?' asked the waiter.

Again his words boomed through her head and Mummy flinched in pain, managing to turn her hearing aid down to normal before he could ask anything else.

'Yes, yes, quite all right,' she said a little breathlessly. There was a loud ringing in her right ear and she felt dizzy. 'I think I'd better step outside. Some air is required.'

Gathering up her handbag, Mummy made her way out of the restaurant and the hotel.

She found Majnu lying back in his seat fast asleep.

'Wake up, you duffer!' screeched Mummy, banging on the window. 'What is this, huh? Dozing off on the job. Think I'm paying you to lie around? You're supposed to be keeping an eye out and such.'

'For what, madam?'

'Don't do talkback! Sit up!'

Mummy got into the back of the car and waited.

Forty minutes later, Red Boots and Fat Throat came out of the hotel, shook hands and parted ways. The latter got into a black BMW.

'You follow that car,' instructed Mummy. 'And pay attention, na!'

Soon they were heading through Sector 18. But Majnu had grown overly cautious and stayed too far back. When the BMW turned left at a light, he got stuck behind two trucks. By the time the light changed and the trucks had given way, Fat Throat's car was nowhere in sight.

'Such a simple thing I asked you to do, na! And look what happens! Ritu Auntie is doing better driving than you and she can't do reverse!' cried Mummy.

Having his driving compared to a woman's was the worst insult Majnu could imagine and he sulked in silence.

'Now, drive me back to my son's home,' she instructed. 'Tomorrow we'll pick up the trail. *Challo!*'

13

'Mr Puri, they've taken him!' shouted Mrs Kasliwal without so much as a hello when the detective answered his phone the next morning. She sounded more irate than panicked. 'Fifteen minutes back they came knocking without warning. There was such a scene. Media persons were running around hither and thither, invading our privacy and trampling my marigolds!'

'Please calm yourself, madam and tell me who it is who is taking who!' said Puri, never at his most patient or sympathetic when dealing with a hysterical or melodramatic woman (and even less so at 7.45 when he was in the middle of shaving).

'My husband, of course! The police arrested him! Never could I have imagined it could happen here! Some upstart police-wallah arresting Chippy like a . . . a common criminal for the whole world to see.'

'On what charge?' asked the detective. But she was still talking.

'Have these people no respect for privacy, Mr Puri? I've seen animals behaving with more dignity at the zoo!'

Mrs Kasliwal started berating someone in the room with her. One of the servants, evidently. Puri wondered if it could be Facecream. Then suddenly, she was back.

'How this can happen, Mr Puri? Is it legal?

149

Surely the police can't just go round arresting respectable people and casting clouds over family reputations whenever they fancy? There has to be some cause.'

It was true that before the age of 24-hour television news, the police would never have made a show of arresting a man of Kasliwal's status. But nowadays, high-profile arrests were public spectacles. This was the cops' idea of PR — to give the impression that they were doing something other than extorting bribes from drivers.

'Madam, please tell me with what is he charged?' asked Puri again. But Mrs Kasliwal still wasn't listening.

'I want to know what you're going to do about this, Mr Puri,' she continued, barely pausing for breath. 'Thus far, I must say the quality of your service is most unsatisfactory. I can't see you're getting anywhere. You came here for a few hours, asked some questions and then did a disappearing act. Have you made any progress at all?'

'Madam, will you *please* tell me with what your husband's charged?' said the detective.

Mrs Kasliwal let out an irritated tut. 'Pay attention, Mr Puri. I told you already. Chippy has been charged with murder. Police are now saying he killed that silly servant girl Mary. But it is all lies. They're trying to cook the case.'

'Have they a body?' asked Puri, calmly.

'They're saying she and the bashed-up girl in your photograph are one and the same. But it's not her. I know it.'

'Forgive me, madam, but you were not so

certain when I showed it to you before,' said Puri.

Mrs Kasliwal tutted again. 'Most certainly I was!' she said. 'I told you categorically it was not Mary. Your memory is faulty. Now, I'm going to ask K. P. Malhotra to represent Chippy. They are old friends and he's one of the best lawyers in India. He'll get him off for sure. The charges are all spurious. I'll talk to him about whether your services are still required. It could be he has his own detective.'

Puri kept the phone up to his ear, saying, 'Hello, Hello,' but realised she had hung up and that the dial pad of his mobile was now covered in shaving foam.

The detective hastily finished his ablutions and got dressed.

Had he let his client down, he wondered? Should he have seen this development coming?

Puri searched his conscience and found it clear. It was quite normal for people to lose confidence in his abilities in the middle of an investigation. To be fair, their lack of faith was understandable.

From the Kasliwals' perspective, Puri appeared to be doing nothing. They hadn't seen him down on his hands and knees scrutinising the floors with a magnifying glass. He hadn't threatened and cajoled the servants as most other private investigators and police detectives would have done. He hadn't even stuck around in Jaipur.

But Puri's methodology, suited as it was to the Indian social environment, had always proven infallible. And it could not be rushed. As he

151

often told his young protégés, 'You cannot boil an egg in three minutes, no?'

Nonetheless, the situation was urgent. If convicted, Kasliwal would face life imprisonment.

★ ★ ★

The detective considered an air-dash to Jaipur, but given his fear of flying and the fact that it would gain him at the most an hour, he opted instead for the highway.

By eight o'clock, he and Handbrake were on the road again.

Puri sat on the back seat calling his contacts to find out more on the charges brought against his client.

A source inside the Chief Prosecutor's Office (one of his uncle's daughter's husband's brothers) told him that the arresting police officer was called Rajendra Singh Shekhawat.

Shekhawat was a 'topper' — one of the most successful detectives in the state. He was said to be young, bright, ambitious and highly adept at keeping his superiors happy.

'So where did he find the body?' Puri asked his uncle's daughter's husband's brother.

'She was found on the Ajmer Road,' he said.

'Recently?'

'No, no! Long time back. August, I think.'

Puri hung up and called Elizabeth Rani, who had access to the World Wide Web on what she called 'whif-ee'. She soon located a transcript of the comments Inspector Shekhawat had made to

152

the press in front of Raj Kasliwal Bhavan minutes after the arrest. He'd claimed that the investigation into Mary's disappearance had been 'of the utmost professionality'. Furthermore, 'substantive evidence' had been 'unearthed by the use of modern detective methodology'. Ajay Kasliwal was, according to the inspector, 'a cold blooded killer' who had 'raped and strangled the maidservant girl until dead'.

When Inspector Shekhawat had been asked by a reporter about the motive for the murder, he'd replied:

'Clearly, the accused and the victim were having intercourse of one sort or another — who is to say? — and he was endeavouring to conceal his misdeed.'

Elizabeth Rani also told Puri that the story was running number two (after India's comeback against the West Indies) on the bulletins of the 24-hour news channels. Evidently all of them had been tipped off about the arrest and dispatched live uplink trucks.

'Sir, the scene was quite chaotic,' said Elizabeth Rani.

'Yes, I can well imagine,' said the detective before hanging up.

Puri had developed an intense disdain for India's news media. All that the burgeoning American-style news channels peddled was sensationalism. Standards in journalism had been thrown out the window; a new breed of editors would stop at nothing to attract 'eyeballs'.

'The three Cs now dominate the news agenda,' a senior commentator had written last month in a respectable news magazine. 'Crime, cricket and cinema.'

Recently, Puri had been watching one of the most popular channels in the middle of the afternoon and been shocked to see live pictures of a man committing suicide. He had jumped off the top of a building while journalists excitedly commentated below.

Last week, another so-called 'award-winning' news outfit had aired one of their 'stings'. They had placed hidden cameras in the office of a university professor and caught him canoodling one of his students.

But nothing caught the headlines in India like murder in a middle-class family.

Such cases — and the 'National Crime Region' supplied a goodly number nowadays — became orgies of speculation.

'Trial by media circus' was how the detective referred to it.

★ ★ ★

Halfway to Jaipur, Puri stopped at a dhaba and ordered sweet chai and a *gobi parantha*. The TV was tuned to Action News and, just as the detective had feared, their mid-morning bulletin was dominated by what a computer-generated graphic described as 'The Maidservant Murder'.

'BREAKING NEWS . . . PINK CITY SHOCKED BY BRUTAL MURDER OF HELP . . . HIGH COURT LAWYER CHARGED . . . POLICE SAY VICTIM WAS FIRST RAPED . . . MOUNTAIN OF EVIDENCE AGAINST ACCUSED' ran the ticker tape along the

154

bottom of the screen.

Simultaneously, the channel was running video of what an anchorman described as 'chaotic scenes' outside Raj Kasliwal Bhavan during the arrest.

It did indeed look like bedlam — but only because of the scrum of cameramen and reporters who mobbed the accused as he was led from his house. In the middle of the fray, Puri spotted his client being helped into the back of a Jeep. Cameramen surrounded the vehicle, trying to stick their lenses through the windows, but were repelled by the police. Then the Jeep sped away with some of the rabid pack chasing after it on foot.

The report then cut to a close-up of a pretty young lady reporter whose urgent demeanour suggested that the world might be about to end.

'The cops have intimated they've got a steel-tight case against High Court lawyer Ajay Kasliwal,' she said in an adolescent, nasal voice. 'Earlier today, he was taken from here under police escort to the local cop shop where he'll be held until chargesheeting. Arun.'

A suave, urbane young man sitting in a slickly lit studio appeared and in a voice that sounded like an Indian version of an American game-show host said:

'Extraordinary developments there in the Pink City, Savitri. Tell us what are the charges against Kasliwal exactly?'

'Well, Arun, the High Court lawyer stands accused of raping and murdering his maid-servant, Mary. Her body was discovered in a ditch on the Ajmer Road. I understand her face was very badly beaten so it took some time to identify her.'

'Now, sources inside the police department have told me' — for this read Inspector Shekhawat, Puri thought — 'that a number of witnesses saw Ajay Kasliwal dump the body in the middle of the night. I've also been told that the police have impounded his Tata Sumo and they'll be carrying out tests on it today. Arun.'

The anchor in the studio, who shared the screen with a little box which replayed the pictures of the arrest on a continuous loop said, 'I take it the police wouldn't have made such a high-profile arrest if they weren't pretty sure they'd got their man. What was Ajay Kasliwal's response to the charges?'

'Kasliwal refused to say *anything* at all when he was arrested this morning. Not one word left his mouth. I'm told he'll be held for twenty-four hours while the cops make further inquiries. They'll be focusing on his relationship with the maidservant, Mary. What exactly went on between them? We should have more answers later today. Back to you in the studio, Arun.'

'Thanks Savitri. Savitri Ramanand there reporting live from the scene of the arrest of Jaipur High Court lawyer Ajay Kasliwal. We'll be bringing you more on the Maidservant Murder throughout the day. In the meantime let us know what you think. Email us at the usual address on the screen. We want to hear from you.'

'Next, the latest on Team India's triumph in the second test. We'll be back after these

156

messages. Don't go away.'

Film star Shahrukh Khan then appeared on the screen, endorsing Fair and Handsome, one of the dozen or so different products he was currently advertising. Puri, who had unconsciously been grinding his molars for the past five minutes, told the waiter to switch off the TV.

Soon, the detective was enjoying his parantha and a fresh bowl of curd.

He was almost finished when his private phone rang. It was Professor Rajesh Kumar at Delhi University calling.

'Hello sir! Haan-ji, sir! Tell me!' bellowed the detective.

The pleasantries over, Professor Kumar informed Puri that he'd got the test results back on the stones from Mary's room.

'There's something most unusual about them,' he said. 'Where did they come from?'

'Jaipur, sir,' Puri told him.

'That's most peculiar,' said the professor. 'We found unusually high traces of uranium.'

'Did you say uranium?'

'Yes, Chubby, that is exactly what I said.'

14

The Jaipur police station where Ajay Kasliwal was being held was depressingly typical. The building was a concrete square, two floors high with steel supports jutting out of the roof in case a third floor was ever required.

Red geraniums spilled on to the well-swept pathway, but did little to soften its charmless architecture. Puri wondered how people elsewhere in the world could view police stations as sanctuaries. For Indians, they were lions' dens.

Seeing a well-fed man in a smart grey safari suit, polished leather shoes and a Sandown cap, the duty officer immediately stood up from his chair, looking as alert as if the Prime Minister himself was making an impromptu visit.

'How may I be of assistance?' he asked in Hindi with a convivial jiggle of the head.

Puri explained his credentials and his purpose for visiting the station: he wanted to see Ajay Kasliwal.

The duty officer took the detective's card and explained that he needed to refer the matter to his 'senior', who was in the next room.

A few minutes later the officer in question appeared.

'It will be our pleasure to help you in any way. Some cold drink? Some tea?' he asked.

For the sake of diplomacy, Puri sat with the police-wallah for ten minutes, dropping a few names into the conversation and leaving him in no doubt that he was someone with contacts at the pinnacle of power in Delhi. The detective also complimented the officer on the tidy appearance of the station.

'Our Indian police are most co-operative,' he said, in a deliberately loud voice with a grin.

Such flattery always went down well. 'Thank you, thank you, so kind of you, sir,' beamed the officer.

A stern-looking woman constable escorted Puri to the cells. They were at the back of the station, three in total, each twelve-feet square with a squat toilet positioned behind a low concrete wall that offered little privacy. There were no windows and no ventilation of any kind. The stench of sweat, piss and acrid bidi smoke hung heavily in the air. The bars and the doors were antiquated and the clunky locks required six-inch keys, which jingled from the constable's belt like reindeer bells.

The first cell contained seven prisoners who were racing captured cockroaches across the floor on a course delineated by empty cigarette boxes. Crouching over the contenders, the prisoners' voices alternated between cheers of encouragement, howls of disappointment, and whoops of victory.

At the back of the second cell, a half-naked sadhu with dreadlocks sat in apparent comfort on the hard concrete floor, while two old men with long white beards passed the time over a game of cards. Another man with a cadaverous appearance leaned up against the bars, staring

159

through them with a blank, melancholy expression.

Ajay Kasliwal had the last cell to himself. It was devoid of furniture and proper lighting. He was sitting in the semi-darkness against the back wall with his face buried in his hands.

When he looked up, Puri was shocked to see how exhausted he appeared. Deep creases had developed along his forehead. Bags the colour of storm clouds had gathered beneath his eyes.

'Thank God!' he exclaimed. Standing up, Kasliwal rushed to the front of the cell and clasped the detective's hands. 'Thank you for coming Puri-ji! I'm going out of my mind!'

For a moment, it seemed as if the lawyer would break down in tears, but he managed to regain his composure.

'I tell you, I never laid a finger on that poor girl,' he said, his grip still tight. 'You do believe me, don't you, Puri-ji? These charges are bogus. I'm a gentle giant, actually. Ask anyone and they'll tell you the same. Ajay Kasliwal could not and would not hurt a fly. I'm a *Jain*, for heaven's sake! We people don't like to kill anything, not even insects.'

The lady constable, who had been standing behind Puri, interrupted: 'Ten minutes only,' she said coldly and withdrew further down the corridor.

'Of course I believe you, sir,' said the detective. 'One way or other, we'll get you out of this pickle. You have Vish Puri's word on that.'

He let go of Kasliwal's hands and reached into his trouser pockets, taking out two packets of

160

Gold Flake cigarettes.

'These are for you,' he said, passing them through the bars.

Kasliwal thanked him, tore into one of the packets and, with trembling hands and fumbling fingers, put a cigarette to his lips. Puri lit a match and Kasliwal pushed the end of the cigarette into the flame. The detective surveyed his client's features in the flickering light, searching for clues to his mental state. He was concerned to see that he had developed a tic above his left eye. Such a spasm could be the first indicator of more serious problems to come. The detective had seen other men — confident, successful men like Kasliwal — reduced to blubbering wrecks after being put behind bars.

Ashok Sharma, the 'Bra Raja', who had hired Puri to investigate the bizarre set of events that had led to the death of his brother (The Case of the Laughing Peacock), had suffered a nervous breakdown after spending just one night in Delhi's notorious Tihar jail.

Of course, Kasliwal's cell was positively five-star compared to Tihar. But tomorrow morning, he had a date in front of a magistrate at the District and Sessions Court where he would be chargesheeted. And if bail was denied — and in the case of a 'heinous crime' it often was — he would be remanded into judicial custody and sent to the Central Jail. There, Kasliwal would be forced to share a dormitory with twenty convicted men. If he wished to remain unmolested, he would have to pay them protection money.

'The first thing I must know, sir, who is representing you?' asked Puri.

'My wife was here two hours back and says K. P. Malhotra has agreed to take the case. I haven't talked to him yet; my mobile ran out. He's meant to come this afternoon.'

'He's someone you trust?'

'Absolutely. We've known each other for twenty-odd years. He's a good attacker and adept at defending his wicket also.'

'Badiya — that's good to hear,' said Puri. 'But, sir, if I'm to continue, there can be no other private detective. It will make things too hot in the kitchen.'

Kasliwal stole a furtive glance at him; Puri guessed that the lawyer's wife had already sown the seeds of doubt about the detective's abilities.

'You're not satisfied with my work is it?' he prompted.

'Well, Puri-ji, frankly speaking, so far I've not seen much evidence of progress,' admitted Kasliwal. 'Now I'm behind bars charged with rape and murder. Can you blame me for shopping elsewhere? My life and reputation are at stake.'

'Sir, I assure you everything and anything is being done. But my methods are my business. It is for the client to place his trust in my hands. Not once I have failed in a case and I'm not about to start now. Equally, Rome wasn't built in the afternoon. These things can't be rushed.'

Kasliwal pursed his lips as he weighed his options over the last of the cigarette.

'I'll make sure you're the only one on the case,

162

Puri-ji,' he said eventually.

'Good,' said the detective. 'Now let us waste no more of time. Tell me exactly and precisely what occurred when you were brought in. Inspector Shekhawat read you the riot act is it?'

'He says he's got witnesses who saw me dump the body.'

'Police-wallahs can always find witnesses,' said Puri. 'A good lawyer will deal with them in court. What else?'

'He says a former servant is ready to testify that I raped her.'

'Who is she?'

'How should I know, Puri-ji? I kept quiet during the interview, refused to say a word, so naturally I didn't ask who this woman is.'

'Did Shekhawat mention any hard evidence?'

'No, but I'm sure he must be searching for something to spring tomorrow.'

Kasliwal took a last drag on his cigarette, let the stub fall on the floor and ground it under his heel.

'Tell me one thing, Puri-ji. In your opinion, the girl they found on the side of the road . . . she is Mary?'

'Seems that's what your Inspector Shekhawat is intimating.'

Kasliwal's chin sank on to his chest. 'So, someone murdered her after all,' he sighed. 'But who?'

'You have some idea?' asked the detective.

'No, Puri-ji, none.'

'What about Kamat? Your wife told me he's a drunkard and was having relations with the female. It's true?'

'I've no idea.'

'Tell me about your movements the night that body was discovered. August 22nd. Can you recall?'

'I was in court come the afternoon. In the evening, I freshened up at home and . . . ' Kasliwal flushed with embarrassment. Puri could guess what he had been up to.

'You had 'takeaway' is it?'

The lawyer nodded. 'My usual order.'

Howls of excitement came from the first cell. Evidently another cockroach race was reaching a thrilling climax. When the noise had died down, Puri asked about Kasliwal's hearing.

'It's set for tomorrow at eleven o'clock,' he told the detective. 'I'm trying to get it heard by one of the few honest judges. But seems no one's willing to lift a finger to help. My enemies have made sure of that.'

Kasliwal cast a look over his shoulder.

'Looks like I'll be spending a night in the penthouse suite, huh.' He laughed sardonically. 'Thank God there's a couple of cops in here I helped out some years back, so I shouldn't be facing harassment. But Puri-ji, a few hundred bucks wouldn't go amiss. That way at least I can get some outside food brought in.'

'You'll find five hundred stuffed inside the other cigarette packet, sir,' whispered Puri.

Kasliwal nodded gratefully as the woman constable called out, 'Time's getting over!'

The two men shook hands.

'I'll be in court tomorrow for sure,' said the detective. 'In meantime, don't do tension, sir.

Rest assured, everything is being done to secure your release. The responsibility is on my head. Already some very promising clues are there. Now take rest.'

★ ★ ★

As Puri was making his way out of the station, the duty officer informed him that Inspector Shekhawat wanted 'a word'.

'By all means,' said the detective, who was anxious to get the measure of his adversary.

Puri was led upstairs straight into his office.

Shekhawat was in his late thirties, stocky, well built, with a thick head of black hair, an equally thick moustache, and dark, deep-set eyes. He was the embodiment of the supremely confident Indian male who is taught self-assurance within the extended family from Day One. The *kundan* studs in his ears did not indicate a hip, arty or effeminate man; he was a Rajput of the *Kshatriya* or warrior caste.

'Sir, it's a great honour to meet you,' he said in Hindi in a deep, booming voice. Shekhawat offered Puri his hand with a big politician's grin. 'I've been an admirer of yours for quite some time. Thank you for taking the time to see me. I know that you are a busy and important man.'

Puri was not altogether immune to flattery, but he doubted Shekhawat's sincerity. Behind the smile and friendly handshake, he sensed a calculating individual who had invited him into his office with the sole purpose of ascertaining whether he posed a threat.

'I was hoping we would meet,' said Puri, replying in Hindi, his tone perfectly amicable. 'It seems we're working on the same case but from different ends. We might be able to help each other.'

Shekhawat seemed bemused by this suggestion. He smiled with slow deliberation as he resumed his place behind his desk and Puri sat down in a chair opposite him.

'It's my understanding that Ajay Kasliwal is your client, is that correct?' asked the inspector.

'That's right.'

'Then I'm not sure how we can help each other, sir. I want to see Kasliwal convicted; you on the other hand want to see him walk free. There is no middle ground.'

One of the phones on the inspector's tidy desk rang. He picked up the receiver. Hearing the voice on the other end prompted a subtle change in the man's bearing. He stiffened and his eyebrows slowly slid together until they were almost joined.

'Sir,' Shekhawat said. There was a pause as he listened. Then he said again, 'Sir'. He met Puri's gaze, held it for a second and then looked down. 'Sir,' he repeated.

While the detective waited, he looked up at the photographs and certificates that hung on the wall behind the desk. From these he was able to piece together much of Shekhawat's life. He'd gone to a government school in Jaipur where he'd been a hockey champion. He'd married extremely young; his wife could not have been a day over sixteen. They'd had four children together. He'd attended the Sardar Vallabhai Patel National Police Academy in Hyderabad and studied to be an officer. Three years ago, he'd been awarded a Police Medal for Meritorious Service.

'Must have been for a big case,' said Puri when Shekhawat hung up the phone after a final 'Sir'. 'The Meritorious Service award, I mean.'

'I caught the dacoit, Sheshnag,' he bragged. 'He'd eluded our forces for thirteen years but I personally tracked him down to his hideout and arrested him.'

'I read about it in the papers. So you were the one,' said Puri. 'Many congratulations, Inspector! It was a fine piece of detective work. Must have been very satisfying.'

'Yes it was. But frankly, sir, I take far greater satisfaction from arresting a man like Ajay Kasliwal. He is the worst kind of criminal. For too long, men like him have roamed free. Money and influence have kept them safe from prosecution. But thankfully times are changing. Now the Big Cats must face justice for their crimes like all the animals in the jungle. We are living in a new India.'

'I admire your principles,' said Puri. 'I'm all for even-handedness. But my client is a good man and he's innocent.'

'Sir, with respect, Kasliwal is as guilty as *Ravan*,' said Shekhawat with an arrogant smirk. 'I have all the evidence I need to put him away for ever. He raped and murdered that young woman.'

'You're certainly confident,' said Puri, hoping to coax the inspector into showing all of his hand.

167

'I've three witnesses who saw Mr Kasliwal dump the body by the roadside.'

'So I understand, but why was no charge brought against my client for two months?'

Shekhawat answered decisively. 'The witnesses took time to come forward because they were scared of intimidation from the client, who threatened them at the scene.'

Puri allowed himself a chuckle.

'I very much doubt that will hold up in court.'

'I have hard evidence as well.'

'How can there be more evidence when the accused is innocent?'

'For that, sir, you will have to wait until tomorrow. I am not at liberty to divulge anything more.'

The detective held up his hands in a gesture of defeat.

'Well, I can see I'm going to have my work cut out proving my client's innocence,' he said. 'Obviously you are determined to see this thing through, so I suppose I'd better get back to my work.'

Puri stood up but lingered for a moment in front of Shekhawat's desk, looking down absentmindedly as if he'd forgotten something.

'There's something else I can help you with?' asked Shekhawat in the patient tone reserved for children and the senile.

'There is one thing, actually,' said Puri, suddenly sounding unsure of himself.

He took out his notebook and flipped through the pages until he came to one in the middle crammed with illegible writing.

'Yes that's it,' he said, as if reading from it. 'From what I'm told, the girl's body was cremated after no one came to claim it. Is that correct?'

'That's true.'

'And the photograph taken by the coroner was out of focus and extremely grainy.'

Shekhawat eyed Puri suspiciously, no doubt wondering how he had come by this information.

'If you say so,' he said.

'Also,' continued the detective, 'her face was all bashed up, bloody and swollen. She'd obviously been given a severe beating.'

The inspector's nod was vague encouragement to go on.

'Given this, I'm curious to understand how you can be sure she is the maidservant Mary.'

'That's not in dispute. Two witnesses have identified her from the coroner's photographs.'

'Former or current employees of the Kasliwals, no doubt.'

'The defence will be informed at the appropriate time,' Shekhawat said officiously and then showed Puri to the door.

15

Facecream had discovered a gap in the perimeter wall behind the servant quarters just large enough for a person to squeeze through. She'd made use of it a couple of times in the past two days, sneaking out undetected to go to an STD phone booth a few streets away.

But Facecream was not the only person using this secret gateway: the earth there was well trodden.

This raised the alarming possibility that an outsider was entering the property unseen and unchallenged — perhaps the same person who had tried to open her door that first night.

Determined to find out who was coming and going through the wall, she had set a trip, stringing a tripwire — or rather a trip-thread — across the gap. Anyone passing through it would now inadvertently tug a bell hanging inside her room.

In the past two days, she'd had just one bite — a stray pye-dog. But the line remained taut. And now, as she set off for a midnight rendezvous with Puri, she was careful not to fall victim to her own ruse. Treading carefully over the thread, Facecream passed through the gap in the wall.

On the other side lay an abandoned property, an old bungalow with broken windows surrounded by a large garden overgrown with creepers and long grass. She stopped, surveying the shadowy terrain ahead for any sign of movement. Nothing stirred in the undergrowth save for grasshoppers. The only sounds were distant ones: the hum of an autorickshaw, the screech of an alley cat. Up above, bats darted through the air. In the moonlight, she caught glimpses of them swooping above the tree line where their black wings appeared momentarily, stretched against a hazy backdrop of stars.

Jaya feared the bats and the owl that lived in one of the *khejri* trees. She had warned her new friend Seema not to go into the garden at night.

The bungalow, she believed, was inhabited by malicious djinns. They had driven out the owners and guarded their territory jealously. At night, lying in her room, she claimed to be able to hear their terrible, mocking laughter and the cries and screams of those they had entrapped in the spirit world.

Djinns, Jaya told Seema, often possessed people. Just recently, one had attached itself to her aunt, forcing her to speak in strange tongues. It was only thanks to a travelling *hakim* that she had been cured. He'd taken her to the tomb of a Sufi saint and exorcised the malicious fiend.

But Facecream did not fear djinns. Parvati, the mountain goddess, whose magic talisman she wore around her neck, had always protected her against attacks from both ghoulish and human assailants. Living rough on the streets of Bombay when she'd first come to India had also given her a sixth sense for recognising danger. And just in case, her Khukuri knife was tucked into her waist.

171

Facecream set off across the garden and made her way down the side of the bungalow, nimbly avoiding the odd bits of rusting metal hidden under the tall grass and weeds, and stopping now and again like a deer testing the air.

When she reached the front of the property, she passed through the leaning iron gate that stood at the entrance to its neglected driveway, tugged her shawl over the back of her head so that it framed her face, and turned left into the quiet lane.

The security guards in the sentry boxes positioned outside the other neighbouring properties were all snoring loudly and she slipped past them unnoticed. The drivers at the bicycle rickshaw stand were all asleep as well, slumped on the seats of their vehicles with their legs stretched out over their handlebars.

Further on stood a large house surrounded by a high wall and a pair of gates mounted with bright lights. Soon after she had passed these lights, Facecream noticed a shadow creep along the ground in front of her. Then, gradually, it began to shrink.

She was being followed.

The distinctive sound of rubber chappals scuffing against the ground told her that her stalker was no djinn.

For a moment, Facecream considered turning around, drawing her Khukuri and charging. But then she remembered Puri's advice about controlling her reckless streak and decided to wait for better attack terrain.

She continued to the next junction, turned

right and broke into a sprint. Reaching the first parked car, she hid behind it, lying flat on the ground, and watched to see who came around the corner.

A few seconds later a pair of hairy male legs appeared. They stopped, shifted from left to right indecisively and then hurried on in her direction. Facecream could see from the man's skinny ankles that he was no match for her. She drew herself up on all fours like a cat and prepared to spring at him. But at the last moment, she held back and let out a loud 'boo!'

Tubelight staggered back in shock, looking as if he might keel over.

'What are you doing? Trying to give me a heart attack?' he cried.

'Ssssh! Keep your voice down! You'll wake the guards!' hissed Facecream. 'What are you doing here?'

'Boss is running late and asked me to let you know.'

'So why were you following me?'

'I knew you wouldn't want to be seen with me behind the house.'

'You weren't trying to sneak up on me?'

'Don't be ridiculous. If I'd wanted to do that, I could have easily taken you by surprise.'

Facecream laughed. 'You were making more noise than a buffalo in heat.'

'Listen, if I'd been on my guard you would never have been able to surprise me.'

'Whatever you say, *bhai*.'

★ ★ ★

Puri picked them up and drove to the Park View Hotel where he was staying. It was nowhere near a park (his room provided a view of a car park), though it was a modern affair with air conditioning, clean sheets, and western-style toilets.

The trio sat at a table in the otherwise empty restaurant. The night manager placed a bottle of Scotch, some bottles of soda, ice and glasses on the table before returning to the front desk.

Puri poured a peg each for himself and Tubelight and a plain soda for Facecream, who strongly disapproved of alcohol. (He'd once heard her describe it as 'a curse on women'.)

'So, Miss Seema,' he said. 'Your message said 'urgent'.'

In Puri's presence, Facecream was always serious, calm, respectful and, although it rarely showed, affectionate. She seemed totally removed from the party girl or cheeky village damsel she often played.

The detective surveyed her appraisingly. He found himself wondering who the real Facecream was. And whether she knew herself.

'Yes, sir, I have important information for you,' she said. Her soft, eloquent pronunciation was unrecognisable from Seema's coarse village burr.

'I've spent the past few days working side by side with Jaya. We've cleaned together and, in the evenings, cooked and shared all our meals. I've told her many stories about my — Seema's — past. She loves hearing them and a bond has formed between us.'

'Last night, Jaya started telling me about herself and the many difficulties she's faced. She was married off to her second cousin at fifteen. They had a son, but he died after two years. Cause unknown. It sounds to me like jaundice. Then two years ago, her husband was killed in a train accident. Her in-laws said she was cursed and threw her out of the house. When she tried to return to her parents' home, they refused to take her back.

'Jaya was taken in by her eldest sister here in Jaipur. This sister got her the job with the Kasliwals. Things started to go better for her. But one evening, when her sister was out working, her brother-in-law forced himself on her. Somehow the sister found out and blamed Jaya. After that, she had to come and live in the servant quarters.'

Puri nodded encouragement to go on.

'Jaya is extremely shy and nervous,' Facecream continued. 'She also gets very frightened at night and hates to sleep on her own. This evening, I discovered why.'

Tubelight lit a cigarette and squinted in the haze of smoke that swirled in front of his face.

'When the police arrived this morning and arrested Mr Kasliwal, Jaya became extremely distressed,' Facecream recounted. 'I found her making up the beds in tears. When I asked her what was wrong, she refused to answer. I sat with her for a while as she cried. And then she said: 'He didn't do it.''

'Who didn't do what?' I asked.'

'Sahib is a good man. He didn't kill Mary. It

175

was somebody else.'

'I couldn't get anything more out of her after that. For the rest of the day, she looked grief-stricken. At teatime, she dropped a cup. Mrs Kasliwal shouted at her and called her stupid. Jaya went to her room and in the evening she refused to eat.'

'After I had finished my duties, I took her some food and sat with her and combed her hair. Then she asked me if we were friends. I told her, 'Yes we are good friends.' She took both my hands in hers and asked me if I could keep a secret. She said it was a very big secret and that if I told anyone, we would both be in danger. I assured her that I would help her in any way I could. Then, Jaya told me in a whisper that she knew who had killed Mary. She said she'd seen the murderer disposing of the body.'

'Go on,' said Puri, shifting in his chair in anticipation.

'On the night Mary disappeared, Jaya was fast asleep. But at around eleven o'clock, she was woken by a commotion in Mary's room. She opened her door a crack and saw Munnalal, the driver, carrying away Mary's body in his arms. Jaya caught a glimpse of Mary's face. She says it was ghostly pale. Her eyes were wide open, but frozen.'

'Munnalal carried her to Sahib's Tata Sumo, laid her on a big piece of plastic in the back, shut the door quietly and then quickly drove away with his headlights off.'

'What did Jaya do next?' asked Puri, sipping his drink.

'She crept out of her room. On the ground, she says she noticed some drops of blood leading to the spot where the Sumo had been parked. She found the door to Mary's room half open and looked inside. The thin cotton mattress was soaked with blood. On the ground next to it lay one of the kitchen knives from the house, also covered in blood.'

'By God,' said Puri.

'Jaya ran back to her room and bolted the door behind her. She sat there for hours in the darkness, crying, terrified. Eventually, she fell asleep. In the morning, the trail of blood on the ground had vanished.'

'Did she look inside Mary's room again?'

'Yes. She says the door was wide open. All Mary's belongings, apart from the posters on the wall, had gone.'

'The mattress?'

'That too. The floor had also been washed.'

Puri thought for a moment, gently rubbing his moustache with an index finger.

'Munnalal must have come back and got rid of everything,' suggested Tubelight.

'Might be,' said Puri. 'Let's put ourselves in his chappals. In the dead of night, he returns to clean up his misdeed. He's got to get rid of her paraphernalia and all. So what next? Could be, he takes it all away. Gets rid of it elsewhere. Or he tosses it over the back wall.'

'That's the likeliest possibility,' Facecream ventured.

Puri shot her a look.

'You found something?' he asked eagerly.

She grinned and pulled up the leg of her baggy cotton trousers. Taped to her ankle was something wrapped in a plastic bag. She placed it on the table and opened it. Inside was a four-inch kitchen knife. The blade was rusted.

Tubelight let out a low whistle.

'I found it in the undergrowth,' she said.

'Absolutely mind-blowing!' exclaimed Puri with a big, fatherly smile.

'I've got other good news,' said Tubelight.

'Munnalal?'

'My boys found him today. He's living in the Hatroi district of Jaipur.'

'First class!' said the detective. 'Tell them to watch him round the clock and I'll pay him a visit tomorrow.'

'Any more instructions for me?' asked Facecream.

'Spend time with Kamat,' instructed Puri. 'Find out if Mrs Kasliwal was correct and he was doing hanky panky with the female.'

16

Mummy, like so many Indians, had a gift for remembering numbers. She didn't need a telephone directory; the Rolodex in her mind sufficed.

The late Om Chander Puri had often made use of her ability.

'What's R. K. Uncle's number?' he would call from his den in the back of their house in Punjabi Bagh as she made his dinner rotis in the kitchen. Seeing the digits floating in the air before her eyes she'd reply automatically: '4–6–4–2–8–6–7.'

Mummy had no difficulty remembering even the much longer numbers of 'portable devices'.

Jyoti Auntie, a senior at the RTO (Regional Transport Office), was on 011 1600 2340.

It was this lady, with whom Mummy had partnered at bridge on many a Saturday afternoon in East of Kailash, who she called now to ask about tracing Fat Throat's BMW numberplate.

'Just I need one address for purposes of insurance claim,' she told Jyoti Auntie when she called her the morning after Majnu had lost him in Gurgaon.

'Oh dear, what happened?' asked Jyoti Auntie.

'The owner was doing reckless driving, bashed up my car and absconded the scene,' she lied. 'Majnu gave chase but being a prime duffer, he

179

got caught in a traffic snarl.'

Jyoti Auntie sympathised. 'Same thing happened to me not long back,' she said. 'A scooter scratched my Indica and took off. Luckily I work at RTO so after locating the driver's address, Vinod paid the gentleman a visit and got him to reimburse me for damages done.'

'Very good,' said Mummy.

'You have a note of the numberplate?' asked Jyoti Auntie.

'No need, just it's up in my head. D-L-8-S-Y-3-4-2-5. One black colour B-M-W. It is Germany-made, na?'

Her friend tried to look up the numberplate in the system, but the computers were 'blinking', so Mummy had to call back after an hour.

'The vehicle belongs to one Mr Surinder Jagga, three number, A, Block Two, Chandigarh Apartments, Phase Four, Home Town, Sector 18, Gurgaon,' divulged Jyoti Auntie.

Mummy wrote down the details (she did not have a head for remembering addresses) and thanked her.

'You're playing bridge on Saturday, is it?' asked Jyoti Auntie.

'Certainly, if not totally,' said Mummy. 'Just my son, Chubby, is facing some difficulty and requires assistance.'

'Nothing serious, I hope.'

'Let us say it is nothing I cannot sort out,' said Mummy.

★ ★ ★

Less than two hours later, Mummy and Majnu pulled up outside Block Two, Chandigarh Apartments, Phase Four, Home Town, Sector 18, Gurgaon.

Fat Throat's black BMW was parked in front of the building.

'You wait here and don't do sleeping,' instructed Mummy. 'Just I'm going to check around. Should be I'll revert in ten minutes. But in case of emergency call home and inform my son's good wife. You're having the number, na?'

'Yes, madam,' sighed Majnu, who was only half listening and privately lamenting the fact that he had missed his lunch.

Mummy let herself out of the car and made her way to the entrance to Block Two.

Chandigarh Apartments was not one of the high-end super luxury developments. It housed call centre workers and IT grunts, most of whom hailed from small towns across the subcontinent and had flocked to Delhi to live the new Indian dream.

Like so much of Gurgaon's new housing, which had been sold for considerable sums amidst a blitz of slick marketing and — false — assurances of round-the-clock water and electricity supplies, Block Two was beginning to crumble. Less than two years after its 'completion', tiles had started falling off its façade; the monsoon rains had left enormous damp stains on the walls and ceilings; and the wooden window frames were warped.

The lift was out of order and Mummy had to climb the stairwell where the builders (who had

181

cobbled together the structure with substandard bricks) had failed to remove blobs of plaster from the bare, concrete stairs. Here and there, wires hung incongruously from the walls as if the very innards of the building were spilling out.

Mummy, bag in hand, soon reached the third-floor landing.

Flat 3A was on the immediate left.

A pair of men's black slip-on shoes lay in front of the door. On the wall to one side of it hung a plaque that read:

TRUSTWORTHY PROPERTY DEALERS LTD.
OWNER: SHRI SURINDER JAGGA

This was all the information Puri's mother required for the time being.

Now that she knew Fat Throat was a property broker, Mummy would ask around and find out more about him. With any luck, someone might be able to tell her what Jagga and his co-conspirator, Red Boots, were up to.

Mummy turned to head back downstairs. But just then, the door swung open.

Standing there in the doorway, eclipsing a good two-thirds of the frame, was Fat Throat, no longer dressed in his white linen suit but in a black cotton kurta pyjama. Behind him in the poorly lit interior she could make out another, smaller figure.

Surinder Jagga narrowed his eyes and stared at Mummy suspiciously, as if he recognised her, and said, in the same deep, chilling voice she remembered from the Drums of Heaven restaurant, 'Yes, madam? You're lost?'

Mummy, caught off guard and intimidated by the sheer size of the man and his thuggish bearing, stuttered, 'I . . . see . . . well . . . just I'm looking for, umm, Block Three.'

'This is Block Two,' answered Fat Throat, abruptly.

'Oh dear, silly me. Thank you, ji. So confusing it is, na?' she said and started down the stairs.

Mummy had taken only a few steps when Fat Throat called after her.

'Wait, Auntie!'

She stopped, feeling her heart beat a little faster. Without turning around, she reached inside her handbag and wrapped her fingers around her can of mace.

Could be, he spotted us following him home, Mummy said to herself. Curse that idiot driver of mine. It's all his fault, na.

'Which apartment you want?' Fat Throat asked.

'Um . . . a . . . apartment six number, A,' she ventured.

There was a pause.

'The Chawlas, is it?' he asked.

'That's right.'

'OK, auntie, it's across the way,' he said. 'You want I should send someone with you?'

'No, no, it's quite all right,' she said, breathing a sigh of relief.

Mummy continued on her way. As she made the first turn in the stairs, she heard another voice coming from the landing above her. Looking up, she saw a second man emerge from

Fat Throat's apartment.

He stooped to put on his black shoes and, in the shaft of light coming in through a window in the stairwell, Mummy got a good look at his face.

She recognised him instantly.

It was Mr Sinha, one of Chubby's elderly neighbours. And he was carrying two thick briefcases. One in each hand.

17

Pandemonium broke out when Ajay Kasliwal arrived at the Jaipur District and Sessions courthouse at eleven o'clock the following morning.

But it was carefully orchestrated.

Rather than being brought in through the building's back entrance, away from the eye of the media storm, he was escorted through the main gate in a police Jeep.

Twenty-five or so constables made a show of trying to hold back the baying pack of 'snappers' (which had grown significantly in number). But the determined press-wallahs quickly surrounded the vehicle. And as the accused stepped down from the back of the Jeep with the police around him, he was accosted by lenses and microphone-wielding reporters all screaming questions at once.

A couple of burly constables then took Kasliwal by his arms. With some of their colleagues acting like American football linebackers, they tunnelled a passage through the crowd, frog-marching him inside the courthouse.

Inspector Shekhawat — plenty of starch in his spotless white shirt; comb grooves etched in his wavy hair — stood to one side of the steps, watching the 'chaotic scenes' that he knew would play so well on TV.

After the media tidal wave crashed violently

185

against the entrance and was successfully repelled, he answered some of the reporters' questions.

'Is it true you've discovered some blood-stains?'

'Our forensics team put Ajay Kasliwal's Tata Sumo under the scanner and came up with dramatic results. Dried blood was found on the carpet at the back.'

'Anything else you can tell us?'

'We found a number of women's hairs. These we are analysing. Also, we found a woman's bloody fingerprint on the bottom of the back seat. So there's no doubt in my mind her body was placed there and driven to its final destination.'

'Can you confirm that Kasliwal refused to answer questions yesterday?'

'Yes, under interrogation he refused to answer any and all questions.'

'Why he chose to be silent?'

'It's his right, actually. But it's unusual. An innocent man has nothing to hide.'

Puri slipped past Shekhawat unnoticed and made his way inside. He found the corridor outside Court 6 crowded with defendants, plaintiffs, witnesses and a disproportionately large number of advocates in white shirts and black jackets. The court crier appeared, calling out the names of those to be summoned before the judge in the same affected, nasal voice which Indian street vendors use to advertise their wares. The presiding judge, Puri discovered, had an extremely busy day ahead of him. Kasliwal's arraignment, although the most high-profile case, was only one of twenty slated to be heard.

Some would require only a few minutes of His Honour's time: a deposition would be taken and then the case would have to be adjourned because a key piece of evidence had gone missing and the police needed time to track it down (a classic delaying tactic). Others might drag on for thirty or forty minutes while the lawyers wrangled over a precedent in law established in a landmark case dating back to Mughal times.

Puri chatted to an advocate he met while waiting in the corridor for Kasliwal's arraignment to begin. The young man was representing himself against a former client who had paid him with a bad cheque.

'How long has your case been going on?' asked Puri.

'Nearly two years,' replied the advocate. 'Every time I want to get a court date, I have to pay a bribe to the clerk. But then my client feathers the judge's nest and he adjourns the case, and so it goes on and on.'

'Judge Prasad has a sweet tooth, is it?' asked Puri.

The advocate smiled wryly, evidently surprised by the detective's apparent naïvety.

'His shop is always open for business,' answered the young man. 'You can pay at the bench as easily as you buy milk from Mother Dairy.'

It was another twenty minutes before the court crier stepped out into the corridor and summoned Ajay Kasliwal.

Soon, the accused was brought from the holding room where he'd spent the past thirty minutes consulting his lawyer.

Puri slipped into the courtroom ahead of him and, finding it packed to capacity, stood by the door. The gallery was cluttered with a hodge-podge of benches and old rickety cane chairs, some with holes in their seats. Before them, stretching across the breadth of the room, rose the bench, a solid wooden structure that looked like a dam designed to hold back flood waters. In the centre, wearing a black cape, thick glasses and a bomb-proof countenance, presided Judge Prasad. Two clerks and a typist sat on either side of him.

When Kasliwal was led inside, every head in the gallery strained to watch him escorted to the dock, a little platform surrounded by a waist-high grille. It might well have dated back to the sepoy trials following the Indian Mutiny against the British in 1857.

Puri's client had clearly not slept a wink on the hard concrete floor of his cell. The bags under his eyes had darkened to the hue of ink and the tic in his eyelid had grown more pronounced, causing him to wink with perturbing frequency.

The detective could only imagine how humiliated Kasliwal must feel. But he retained a dignified and defiant pose, standing erect with his arms behind him and chin held high. When he looked into the gallery and saw his immediate family sitting there, including his son, Bobby,

188

who had flown in from London the night before, his expression conveyed confidence and courage.

'State versus Ajay Kasliwal!' announced the court crier.

Silence fell over the gallery as the print and wire service journalists readied their pens and notebooks.

Judge Prasad was not one to stand on ceremony. His impatient manner suggested he would much rather be somewhere else (from what Puri had been told, his preferred location was the Jaipur golf course). This was hardly the Rajasthan High Court. There were no computers or microphones, no air conditioning, no coffee machines dispensing sweet, frothy cups of Nescafé.

This was a place of business.

The more hearings Judge Prasad could pack into a single day, the more he could enrich his growing property portfolio. Thus, he did not allow lawyers to stand at their desks and engage in tedious examinations and cross-examinations. That was another luxury only the High Court could indulge. Here in Court 6, trials were conducted with all those gathered directly in front of him. This way, monetary bargaining could be done and transactions made without anyone in the gallery overhearing.

'Approach!' he instructed Kasliwal's lawyer and the state prosecutor, Veer Badhwar.

Both men stepped forward and stood shoulder to shoulder in front of the bench.

The hearing, conducted in Hindi, took all of ten minutes.

First, Judge Prasad asked Mr Badhwar to

present the charges and he gladly did so. The prosecutor then called Inspector Shekhawat, who explained that bloodstains had been discovered in the back of Kasliwal's vehicle.

The accused was then read the charges of rape and murder and asked how he pleaded.

'Not guilty, Your Honour.'

His plea was entered into the record. Mr Malhotra then asked that his client be granted bail.

'Does the accused have an alibi for his location on the night of the murder?'

'Sir, I respectfully submit the police have not provided ample proof that the murdered girl is my client's former maidservant. The body was cremated 24 hours after it was discovered and was not properly identified at the time.'

'Answer the question,' said the judge impatiently as the typist hammered away at his keys, recording their verbal exchange.

'He was at a friend's house, Your Honour,' said Malhotra.

'Is this *friend* willing to come forward?'

'We have not been able to locate the friend at the present time, but we are confident we will do so within a few hours.'

'Does the police have any objection to the court granting bail?'

'We do, Your Honour,' answered Inspector Shekhawat. 'The crime is a heinous one. The accused is a danger to the public.'

Judge Prasad scribbled something on the file that lay in front of him, checked his watch and then said:

'Bail is denied. The accused is to be remanded into judicial custody. Constables, take him away.'

'Your Honour, I object. My client has no criminal record and is an upstanding member of the community.'

'Bail is denied. You are welcome to appeal the court's decision.'

The judge asked the clerk to search for a date for the trial to begin.

Files and papers were moved back and forth across the bench; ledgers were opened and closed. The clerk ran his index finger over pages and columns until it came to rest on a spare slot nearly five months away. 'April 9th at three forty-five,' he said.

Badhwar and Malhotra were dismissed and Kasliwal was led from the courtroom to be taken to the Central Jail. Within seconds, the gallery emptied as his family and the newspaper hacks went in pursuit of him.

By the time they'd left the courtroom, another group of file-toting advocates and their clients had gathered in front of the bench.

★　★　★

The detective caught up with Bobby Kasliwal on the steps of the courthouse where he was waiting for his mother and Malhotra, who had gone to bribe the appropriate clerk to set a date to appeal the bail verdict and bring forward the start of the trial.

Puri was struck by how much Bobby took after his father — nose, chin and height were

191

almost identical. He combed back his black hair in the same style. And he had adopted some of Ajay Kasliwal's mannerisms — the way in which he stood, for example, back straight and fingers laced together in a cradle.

But Bobby's youthful mien betrayed his lack of experience. His life was lived through books. This was evident to Puri from the small indentations on the sides of his nose, the ink stain on his middle index finger and his pullover's threadbare elbows, which he'd worn down during long hours leaning on his desk studying his textbooks. Fidgeting constantly, he appeared to be inwardly grappling with fear and some form of regret.

'Quite a journey you must have had,' said Puri after introducing himself.

'Yes sir, the flight was nearly ten hours and then three more hours on the road,' said Bobby, who was polite but made little eye contact. His right leg quivered nervously as if he was busting to go to the toilet.

'By God! Must have been exhausting, no?' said Puri.

'It was OK sir, thank you sir,' he said automatically.

'So tell me how is En-gland? Must be cold.'

'Very cold, sir. It rains too much.'

'But you're enjoying? London, that is?'

'Very much, sir. It's a wonderful opportunity.'

Bobby looked over Puri's shoulder, evidently searching for any sign of his mother.

'So your Mummy is doing all right, is it?' asked the detective.

'She's not been sleeping well, sir. She's getting migraines.'

Puri shook his head gravely.

'It is only right and correct that you have come home,' he said in a sympathetic, avuncular tone. 'Your Mummy and Papa need every last drop of support they can get.'

He took Bobby gently by the arm and, pulling him towards him, added:

'I can only imagine what anxiety you and your near-or-dear are experiencing. Must be something akin to hell. But rest assured everything is being done to clear your Papa's good name. By hook or crook we'll get these fraudulent charges reverted. I give you my word on that. Most Private Investigators never fails.'

He released Bobby's arm.

'Thank you, sir. I'm very grateful to you. There's no way my father could have done this thing. How they can even suggest it, I don't know. He never broke one law in his entire life.'

'I understand you're planning to work with him after your studies are complete?'

'Certainly, sir. It's always been my dream to work with Papa. There's so much I can learn from him. I want to make a difference the way he has.'

Puri fished out a copy of his business card and handed it to him.

'Call me if any assistance is required. I can be reached night or day. If there's anything you wish to discuss — anything at all — dial my number. Confidentiality is my watchword.'

'Right, sir,' said Bobby.

Puri turned to leave, but twisted round on his left foot and exclaimed:

'By God, so forgetful I'm getting these days! One question mark is there, actually.'

'Sir?' frowned Bobby.

'Your whereabouts on the night of August 21st of this year? You were where exactly?'

'In London, sir.'

'Accha! You already reached, is it?'

'I flew two weeks earlier.'

'That is fine. Just I'm ticking all the boxes.'

'No problem, sir.'

Puri lingered for a moment, looking down at the ground apparently lost in thought. Bobby put his hands in his pockets, took them out again and then folded them in front of his chest.

'Did you get to know her — Mary, that is?' asked the detective after a long pause.

'Know her, sir?'

'Must be you talked with her?'

'Not really, sir, she was, well, a servant. I mean, she made me tea and cleaned my clothes. That's about it. I was studying mostly.'

'Can you tell me her last name or where she came from?'

'No, sir, I wouldn't be able to tell you that. My mother should know.'

Puri reached inside his safari suit and took out a folded piece of paper, his copy of the photograph of the murder victim.

He handed it to Bobby without telling him what it was.

The young man unfolded it and grimaced at the gruesome image.

'Is that Mary?' asked the detective.

'I think so. It looks like her, sir,' said Bobby, still staring down at the image. And then he suddenly pushed the photocopy back into Puri's hands, ran to the side of the steps and vomited.

18

Brigadier Kapoor called while Puri was on the way to see Munnalal. It was his third attempt in as many hours, but the detective had been too busy to pick up earlier.

'Puri! I've been trying to reach you all day! What is your present location?'

'Sir, I'm out-of-station, working on a most crucial and important case — '

'More important than mine, is it?' scoffed Brigadier Kapoor indignantly.

'Sir, honestly speaking, my commitment and dedication to your case is one hundred and ten per cent. Just an emergency type situation was there and it became necessary for me to leave Delhi right away for a day or two.'

Puri sounded unreservedly conciliatory. He was, after all, in Brigadier Kapoor's employ, albeit temporarily, and it was expected that an employer would periodically berate his or her employees to keep them in line. If the detective had been in his client's shoes, he would have probably done the same. How had the Marathi poet, Govindraj, put it? 'Hindu society is made up of men who bow their heads to the kicks from above and who simultaneously give a kick below.'

'I don't want to hear excuses!' barked Brigadier Kapoor, sounding as if he was back on the parade ground. 'An entire week has passed without a word. I've not received one piece of intelligence! Now report!'

In fact, it had only been five days since Puri had agreed to take on the case and in that time the Most Private Investigators team had been anything but idle. As he explained, his top two researcher-cum-analysts had been doing the initial footwork: getting hold of Mahinder Gupta's financial statements and phone records and analysing all the data for anything suggestive or suspicious. At the same time, Puri's operative Flush had been ingratiating himself with the target's servants and neighbours.

He had also been going through the subject's garbage.

'Trash Analysis' was standard procedure in any matrimonial case, 'Waste not, know not!' being one of the detective's catchphrases. The stub of an airline boarding pass or a cigarette butt smeared with lipstick had, in the past, been enough to wreck the marriage plans of more than a few aspirants.

Fortunately, getting hold of people's garbage was a cinch. Indian detectives were much luckier than their counterparts in, say, America, who were forever rooting around in people's dustbins down dark, seedy alleyways. In India, one could simply purchase an individual's trash on the open market.

All you had to do was befriend the right rag picker. Tens of thousands of untouchables of all ages still worked as unofficial dustmen and women across the country. Every morning, they came pushing their barrows, calling, '*Kooray Wallah*!' and took away all the household rubbish. In the colony's open rubbish dump, surrounded by cows, goats, dogs and crows, they would sift through piles of stinking muck by hand, separating biodegradable waste from plastic wrappers, aluminium foil, tin cans and glass bottles.

Flush had had no difficulty whatsoever scoring Gupta's garbage, even though he lived on his own in a posh complex called Celestial Tower, which, according to a hoarding outside the front gate, provided a 'corporate environment' in which residents could 'Celebrate the New India!' But so far, Puri's promising young operative had discovered nothing incriminating.

'No condom, no booze, no taapshelf magazine,' he'd told Boss the day before on the phone.

Gupta subscribed to publications such as *The Economist* and *The Wall Street Journal Asia*. He was strictly veg and ate a lot of curd and papayas. His only tipple apart from Diet Coke was Muscle Milk, a sports drink. He also used a number of different hair and skin-care products.

Socially, he mixed in corporate circles and attended conferences with titles like 'BPO in the Financial Sector — Challenges & Opportunities'. He visited the temple once a week and kept a small puja shrine in his bedroom, complete with photographs of his parents who lived in Allahabad, and a number of effigies, including Ganesh, Hanuman and the goddess Bahuchar Mata.

Gupta employed a cook, who came for two hours in the afternoon; a sweeper, who, along with the floors, was charged with washing the three bathroom-cum-toilets every day; and a cleaner who was responsible for wiping everything the sweeper wasn't assigned to do.

The latter had told Flush that her employer was a private man who was meticulously tidy. Her only gripe was that he had recently purchased a '*dhobi* machine', which she resented because it had robbed her of the income she had been earning from washing his clothes.

The sweeper had grumbled about the low pay and the fact that Gupta shed a lot of hair, which blocked the shower drain in the master bathroom-cum-toilet. She'd also had plenty to say about the memsahib down the hallway who was apparently carrying on with another housewife in Flat 4/67.

Gupta's driver had not divulged any salacious secrets about his employer either. The two bottles of Old Monk rum with which Flush had plied him had elicited no stories of 'three-to-the-bed' orgies, nights of cocaine-fuelled debauchery or illicit visits to secret love children. Apparently, Gupta spent most evenings either playing golf or watching golf on ESPN.

'He's an oversmart kind-of-guy,' Flush had concluded.

Ordinarily at this stage in a matrimonial case, Puri would have advised his client against any further investigation. But he wasn't leaving anything to chance and had his team go to Phase Two.

Flush had been charged with tapping the subject's phone lines and tailing him. That very evening, assuming he could make it back to Delhi, Puri was also planning to gatecrash a pre-marriage party Gupta was having in his apartment, to plant a couple of bugs.

Puri explained the plan to Brigadier Kapoor, but he still sounded dissatisfied.

'What about his qualifications? Have you checked on them?' he asked.

'Gupta attended Delhi University as advertised. That much is confirmed.'

'Any girly friends?'

'We did interviews with two batchmates. Both told that Gupta kept himself to himself. A very studious fellow, it seems. Didn't so much as talk to females. No reports of hanky panky. Equally, he was strictly teetotal. Never touched so much as one drop of alcohol or *bhang*.'

'Other marriages?'

'We're getting on top of the registers, sir.'

'What about his time in Dubai? What was he doing there?'

'Working for a US bank. I've contacted my counterpart in West Asia. A highly proficient fellow. He's asking around.'

'Any affairs?'

'With females, sir?'

'Males, females — anything?'

'No indication, sir.'

Brigadier Kapoor let out an exasperated sigh.

'Listen, Puri, I want you on the case round the clock,' he reiterated. 'Time is running short. The marriage is only one month away. I'm more convinced than ever that something is not right with this man. He came for tea the other day to meet my dear wife and I could see it in his eyes. As plain as day. There's something missing.'

'Now,' Brigadier Kapoor carried on, after clearing his throat. 'I know a thing or two about men, Puri. When you've fought alongside them, sent them into battle, seen them felled by enemy fire and bleeding to death in front of your very eyes, you become a good judge of a man's character. This man is hiding something and I want to know what it is. I'll expect to hear from you day after.'

★   ★   ★

Munnalal lived at the far end of a long, dirty lane overhung with a rat's nest of exposed wires and crisscrossing cables. Caught within these tendrils, like bugs in a spider's web, forlorn paper kites and plastic bags floundered.

The lane and its narrower tributaries, which branched off into a seemingly endless warren, were lined with terraces of tall, narrow brick houses. Their diminutive front doors were overlaid with iron latticework and daubed with red swastikas to ward off the evil eye.

Puri had to abandon the Ambassador at the far end of the lane and proceed on foot.

He was acutely conscious of how conspicuous he appeared in such impoverished surroundings. Many of those he passed eyed him with apprehension, assuming, no doubt, that he was a plainclothes cop, government official or rich landlord.

A woman sitting on the front step of her home

picking lice from her daughters' hair dropped her gaze when she spotted Puri drawing near. Further on, three old men, crouched on their haunches against a wall, looked him up and down through narrowed eyes and then muttered surreptitious comments to one another.

Only the neighbourhood's squealing children, who ran back and forth playing with all manner of makeshift toys — metal rims of bicycle wheels, inflated condoms — were not intimidated by the detective's official bearing. Grinning from ear to ear, they cried with outstretched hands, 'Hello Mister! One pen!'

Fortunately, no one paid any attention to Tubelight, who led the way, walking ten steps ahead of the detective without giving any indication that they were together. Dressed in the simple garb of a labourer, he had spent the past few hours in one of the neighbourhood eateries, playing *teen patta* with a group of local men.

Gleaning information about Munnalal, who was not well liked in the neighbourhood, had proven easy. Word was that he had come into a good deal of money in the past few months and gone from driving the cars of rich sahibs to owning a Land Cruiser of his own. He hired out the vehicle in the local transport bazaar, mostly to 'domestic tourists' visiting Rajasthan from elsewhere in India.

'They say he's got a new plasma television, too,' Tubelight had told Puri when the two had rendezvoused on the edge of the Hatroi neighbourhood twenty minutes earlier and the operative had reported all he'd learned. 'Spends his days sitting and staring at it.'

Cricket was Munnalal's main staple, along with Teacher's Fine Blend.

'He's completely *tulli* most days,' Tubelight had added. 'A heavy punter as well. Into the bookies for twenty thousand.'

The local lassi-wallah had also proven a mine of information. Over a couple of glasses of his refreshing yoghurt drink, he'd told Tubelight that Munnalal was a wife beater. On a number of occasions the vendor had spotted bruises on his wife's face and around her neck.

The man sitting on the side of the lane, selling padlocks, combs, and wall posters of Hindu and Bollywood deities, had confirmed this. He'd also told Tubelight that Munnalal often fought with his neighbours. Recently there had been a dispute over a wall shared with the Gujjar family. It had resulted in a punch-up. Munnalal had put his neighbour in hospital with concussion and a broken arm.

'Sounds like quite a charmer, isn't it?' Puri had commented.

'Want me to keep an eye on him, Boss?' Tubelight had asked. 'See what he gets up to?'

'Such a fool will provide his own rope,' the detective had replied sagely. 'I'm going to shake his tree and see what falls to earth.'

'You're going to do a face-to-face?'

'Why not? I'm feeling sociable! Let us pay *Shri* Munnalal a visit. Lead the way.'

Puri soon reached the house and banged on the door. It was answered by a harried-looking woman with a bruise on her cheek, who looked him up and down suspiciously and demanded to know what he wanted.

'You're Munnalal's wife?' asked the detective in Hindi in a deep authoritative voice.

'What of it?'

'Go tell him he has a visitor.'

'He's busy.'

'Go tell him. Don't waste my time.'

The woman hesitated for a moment and then let the detective inside.

'Wait here,' she said as she went to fetch her husband.

By now Puri, who was wearing his aviator sunglasses, was standing on the edge of a small courtyard scattered with a few children's toys and bucket of wet laundry waiting to be hung on the washing line. In one corner, a charpai leaned against the dusty wall.

TV cricket commentary blared from an open door on the other side of the enclosure. A moment later, it suddenly stopped and Munnalal appeared to inspect his visitor.

One look at Puri caused him to stand a little straighter and to thrust the bottom of his vest into the top of his loose-fitting trousers. There was no hiding the fact, however, that he was a man loath to shift from his favourite mattress. Fat-faced, with a gut spilling over his waist, he had not shaved in days. Stubble had taken root on his bloated throat like black fungus, spreading over his chin and cheeks and threatening to engulf the rest of his features. His sunken eyes were bloodshot. And his vest, which failed to contain the great bunches of hair that protruded from his armpits, was dotted with spots of grease.

Still, what Munnalal lacked in looks and appearance, he evidently made up for in shrewdness. In Puri, he instantly recognised a threat. Rather than demanding to know his visitor's identity and purpose, he turned on the charm.

'Welcome to my home, sir,' he said in Hindi with a smarmy smile.

'You're Munnalal?' asked Puri with a perfunctory handshake, almost overcome by the stench of booze on the man's breath.

'Yes, sir.'

'I've come to offer you some help.'

'Help? Me, sir?' he said, surprised. 'How can I refuse?'

'You can't,' said Puri.

With a half-quizzical look, Munnalal offered the detective a plastic deck chair in the shade on the east side of the courtyard.

'Make yourself comfortable, sir,' he said before disappearing back into his room and calling his wife to bring the two of them refreshments.

When Munnalal re-emerged a few minutes later, he had put a comb through his greasy hair and changed into a clean, white salwar.

'So, sir, what can I do for you?' he asked Puri, drawing up a chair opposite his guest. He offered Puri a cigarette and then lit one of his own.

'I need some information,' replied the detective

'Ask me anything,' he said grandly with a

broad grin and a flourish of his hands.

'I understand you used to drive for Mr and Mrs Ajay Kasliwal.'

'That's right,' replied Munnalal. 'I was with Sir and Madam for a year or so.'

'So you knew the maidservant Mary?'

Munnalal's grin froze.

'Yes, sir. I knew her,' he said, cautiously. 'Is that what this is about?'

'You knew her well?'

'Not well — ' Munnalal broke off, clearing his throat nervously. 'Sir, why all these questions? Who are you — sir?'

Puri explained that he was a private detective from Delhi working for Ajay Kasliwal. Munnalal digested this information for a moment with a troubled frown, drawing on his cigarette a little harder each time.

'They're saying on the TV that Sahib murdered the girl,' said Munnalal, exhaling a cloud of smoke.

'Ajay Kasliwal is innocent. Someone set him up. I'd like to know what you know about it.'

Munnalal forced a laugh.

'Me? What could I know? I'm just a driver, sir.'

'You *were* a driver. But from what I hear you've gone up in the world. They say you're a rich man these days.'

'Who says that?' Munnalal asked sceptically.

'Your neighbours, mostly,' said Puri. 'They say you live like a maharaja. Munnalal-sahib they call you. Apparently, you drink Angrezi liquor. You bet big sums on cricket. Seems you've come into a lot of money recently.'

Munnalal shifted uneasily in his chair. 'It's my business how I live.'

'Where did the money come from?'

'An uncle died and left me his house,' he said defiantly.

'An uncle?'

'He was childless. I was his favourite.'

Puri surveyed Munnalal with steely eyes.

'What can you tell me about the night Mary disappeared, August 21st?'

'Nothing, sir.'

'Nothing at all?' Puri smiled. 'Come now, you must know something. Where were you that evening?'

'I took Sahib to a hotel and waited for him in the car park.'

'You didn't go back to the house?'

'Not until later when I dropped him home — that was around one in the morning.'

Munnalal stubbed out the end of his cigarette and quickly lit another one.

'That's strange,' said Puri, whose hands were folded neatly in his lap. 'I'm told you were at the house at around eleven o'clock and carried Mary's body from her room to the back of the vehicle.'

'Who told you that?' exploded Munnalal, his eyes filled with venom.

'That's not important,' answered the detective, coolly. 'What is important is that you tell me exactly what happened at Raj Kasliwal Bhavan on August 21st. Otherwise I might have to pass on what I already know to Inspector Rajendra Singh Shekhawat. Perhaps you know him? No.

207

Well, he's a very energetic young officer. I'm sure he's good at getting people to talk.'

Abruptly, Munnalal suddenly pushed back his chair and stood up. For a moment the detective thought he might lunge. But instead, he began to pace back and forth, regarding Puri like a caged tiger.

'You were there that evening, weren't you?' said the detective.

'I never left the hotel car park. The other drivers will back me up.'

Puri slipped his sunglasses down the bridge of his nose and stared at Munnalal over the top of them.

'I have a witness who saw you carry the body from Mary's room to Mr Kasliwal's Tata Sumo.'

'I never murdered anyone!' shouted Munnalal.

Puri held up a calming hand. 'There's no need to get angry. As long as you co-operate you've got nothing to worry about.'

Just then, Munnalal's wife emerged from the kitchen bearing two metal cups of water on a tray. She served Puri first and then her husband. Munnalal downed the contents in big gulps. Then he handed the empty cup to his wife, fished out a few rupees from his shirt pocket and sent her out to buy him another packet of cigarettes.

'What do you want?' asked Munnalal when they were alone again.

Puri placed the cup of water on the ground untouched.

'What any person wants? To be comfortable.'

Munnalal's lip twisted into a knowing sneer.

208

'How comfortable?'

'That depends. First I want to know what happened at Raj Kasliwal Bhavan that night.'

'What if I refuse to talk?'

'I don't need to tell you what the police will do to you to get a confession.'

Munnalal grunted knowingly and sat down again. A long silence ensued as he weighed up his options.

'Sir, I never killed that girl,' he said, sounding conciliatory. 'She tried to kill herself.'

His words were met with an expression of cold scepticism.

'That's the truth,' insisted Munnalal. 'I went to her room and found her lying on the floor. There was blood everywhere. She'd cut her wrists.'

'What business did you have going to her room?'

Munnalal faltered. 'I . . . she . . . she owed me money. I went to collect it.'

Puri sighed. 'Don't lie to me or it will be the worse for you. Now tell me: why did you go to her room?'

'I already told you, sir!' protested Munnalal. 'I went to her room to collect the five hundred rupees she'd borrowed from me. She was lying there covered in blood. She'd used a kitchen knife. But she was still alive. So I tied her wrists with cloth to stop the bleeding, carried her to the Sumo and drove to the clinic.'

'Then what?'

'The nurse took her in. That was the last I saw of Mary.'

'What was the name of the clinic?'

'Sunrise.'

Puri took out his notebook and wrote down the name.

'Then what did you do?' he asked.

'I returned to the hotel to pick up Sahib.'

There was a pause.

'You had blood on your clothes?'

'A little but I washed it off.'

'And the knife? How can you explain it ending up in the garden behind the house?'

Munnalal shrugged.

'Someone else must have thrown it there.'

'You never touched it?'

'When I first entered the room I picked it up. But I didn't return to the room after that.'

'Did you inform anyone the next morning?'

'No.'

'Why not?'

Munnalal looked cornered. He took another long, hard drag on his cigarette and said, unconvincingly; 'It could have meant trouble for me.'

Puri pushed his sunglasses back up the bridge of his nose.

'Let me tell you what I think *really* happened,' he said. 'You went to that room to have your way with Mary. Probably it wasn't the first time. She turned a knife on you. There was a scuffle and you stabbed her. Maybe she died then and there. Or, like you say, she was still alive. Either way, you carried her to the Sumo and drove away. Later, you came back to the house and cleaned up the blood, got rid of her things and threw

210

away her knife. Probably you also went into the house and took a silver frame to make it look like she'd stolen it and run away.'

'I told you, I didn't murder her and I never stole anything either,' objected Munnalal. 'Go to the Sunrise Clinic and they'll tell you she was brought in alive.'

Puri stood up.

'I'll do that,' he said. 'But there is still the matter of the knife and the witness who saw you remove the body.'

'Sir, I'm sure we can come to some arrangement,' Munnalal said. 'I'm a reasonable man.'

'When you're ready to tell me the whole truth then we'll find out how reasonable you can be,' said the detective. He handed Munnalal his card. 'You've got until tomorrow morning. If I don't hear from you before then, I'll tell Inspector Shekhawat everything I know.'

19

Puri and Tubelight sat together on the back seat of the Ambassador as Handbrake drove to Jaipur airport.

'How many of your boys have you got watching Munnalal?' asked the detective.

'Zia and Shashi are on the job, Boss.'

'They're experienced enough? I don't want anything going wrong.'

'They're good boys,' said Tubelight. 'Want me to check on this Sunrise Clinic?'

'Make it your top priority. I want to know if that bloody Charlie took Mary there. Ask the doctors and all. They must be knowing. Could be they'll tell us what became of her.'

'Think she tried suicide, Boss?'

'Munnalal is so used to telling lies he wouldn't be knowing the truth if it landed in his *channa*. But why he would concoct a cock and bull story about a clinic?'

'You think he killed her?'

Puri shrugged. 'We're still only having some of the facts. So many open-ended questions remain. There's been no satisfactory verification of the body. I'm certain the police are barking up a wrong tree. Let us be sure not to do any barking of our own.'

Puri's mobile rang and, after scrutinising the number on the screen, he answered it.

By the time he hung up, Tubelight had

formulated his own theory about what had happened at Raj Kasliwal Bhavan on the night of August 21st.

'Munnalal rapes the girl,' he said. 'Gets trashed and abuses her. She pulls a knife and there's a tussle. Mary gets stabbed and expires. Then he carries the body to the vehicle and dumps it on Ajmer Road.'

He looked triumphant, but Puri sighed.

'Baldev,' he said, using Tubelight's real name, 'why you're always insisting on doing speculation?' Puri's tone was not patronising. Tubelight was, after all, one of the best operatives he had ever worked with, even if he was prone to jumping to conclusions.

'A pen cannot work if it is not open,' continued the detective. 'Same with the human mind. Let us stick to what facts there are. According to police estimates, the body was dumped on 22nd night. So if Munnalal did the killing, seems odd he would hang on to the body for twenty-four hours.'

'He had to move it, Boss.'

'He's a fool, but not so much of a fool. Either Mary and the dead girl are *not* one and the same or something else transpired after Munnalal removed Mary from her room.'

Puri took off his sunglasses and rubbed his sore eyes.

'Ask yourself this: why a common driver should be opting to take the female to the private clinic who'll be charging a hell of a lot when the State Hospital is near to hand? Number two, what's he doing hanging around the house so late in the first instance? Not doing the dusting, that is for sure. Should be Jaya and other servants have the answers. Let us hope Facecream finds out. Three, if Munnalal didn't return to the scene, who cleaned away the blood and all?'

Tubelight nodded, impressed. 'I hadn't thought of that,' he said.

'Deduction is my speciality, actually. But deduction cannot be done with thin air. That is where you come in. After the Sunrise Clinic, find out where this bugger got so much of money. Must be he's doing blackmail. Question is, to whom he's giving the squeeze?'

Puri checked his watch as Handbrake pulled up outside the airport terminal. The last flight was due to depart for Delhi in thirty minutes. That was just enough time to buy a ticket and get through security.

'You're coming back tomorrow, Boss?' asked Tubelight as Puri got out.

'Handbrake's to proceed from here directly to Gurgaon. Tomorrow morning we'll revert at first light. Should be we'll reach by eleven, eleven-thirty.'

'You've got airsickness pills, Boss?'

Puri gave him a resigned look.

'Bloody lot of good they did me last time,' he said.

*　*　*

Puri didn't get airsick. It was a myth he perpetrated to disguise the real reason he avoided planes: being up in the air terrified him.

214

Over the years, he had tried all manner of treatments to cure his phobia, but so far nothing had worked. Not the Ayurvedic powders. Not the hypnosis. And certainly not the 'Conquer Your Worst Fears' workshop run by that charlatan 'Lifestyle Guru' Dr Brahmachari who'd taken him up in a hot-air balloon and only succeeded in giving him nightmares for weeks.

To make matters worse, Mummy was forever reminding him about the prophecy made at his birth.

According to the family astrologer (a complete bloody goonda if Puri had ever met one), the detective was destined to die in an air crash.

'Don't do flying,' Mummy had been telling him for as long as he could remember. 'Most definitely it will be your doom.'

Puri considered himself a spiritual man, but in keeping with his father's belief system, he was not superstitious. To his mind, astrology was so much mumbo-jumbo and had an adverse effect on people's thinking.

Rumpi did not altogether agree with him, of course. She couldn't help herself. But the detective had always told his three daughters that no good had ever come from soothsaying.

'Imagine some seer predicts you will marry a rich babu,' he'd told them one day when they were all teenagers. 'It will create a bias and get your thinking into an almighty jumble. You and your mother will pass over boys with greater qualities who are more compatible. Ultimately, you will not find contentment.'

'But I want to marry a prince, Papa!' Radhika,

215

the youngest, who'd been twelve at the time, had told him.

'Perhaps one day, *chowti* baby,' the detective had told her. 'But only the God knows. Trust to your fate and don't do second guessing.'

Of course, it is always easier to preach such credos than to live by them. Indeed, whenever Puri laid eyes on an aeroplane, he heard that voice in his head asking, 'What if?'

This was why, despite the three hundred deaths every day on India's roads, he still felt safer travelling by car. It was also why, given the option of a three-hour flight or a 36-hour journey on a Rajdhani train, he opted for Indian railways whenever he could.

But today Puri had no choice. The only way he was going to make it to Mahinder Gupta's party was by flying to Delhi.

And so it was an uncharacteristically nervous and skittish Vish Puri who made his way through security, having bought himself a business-class ticket (if he was going to meet his doom he might as well do it with extra leg room).

What his fellow passengers and the pretty young air hostess made of him can only be imagined.

Upon entering the cabin, Puri, who was by now feeling strangely disoriented, sat down in someone else's empty seat. When its rightful occupant arrived, the detective refused to budge and only did so when the air hostess intervened.

Next, Puri had to be asked to move his suitcase out of the aisle and place it in the overhead locker. When he complied, the case

216

sprang open and his Sexy Men aftershave and a pair of VIP Frenchie *chuddies* fell into the aisle.

By now, Puri's hands were trembling so much his seatbelt had to be buckled for him. During take-off, he sat as rigid as a condemned man in an electric chair. His hands gripped the armrests, his fingernails sank deep into the soft plastic, and he found himself muttering a mantra over and over.

'*Om bhur bhawa swaha tat savitur varay neeyam . . .*'

Once the plane was in the air, he began sweating profusely and built up a considerable amount of gas in his stomach. This he vented periodically — to the intense displeasure of the Australian lady tourist sitting on his right: 'Jesus! Do you mind?'

When Puri tried to calm his nerves with the remains of a quarter-bottle of Royal Challenge he'd brought on board, the air hostess informed him that it was illegal to consume alcohol on domestic flights and he had to put it away.

During the landing, Puri held his breath and closed his eyes.

The moment the aircraft left the runway, he unclipped his seatbelt and staggered to his feet. Once again, he found the air hostess by his side, this time ordering him to sit down until the plane had come to a complete halt and the overhead seatbelt light was switched off.

Puri complied. But the moment he saw the gangway through the window, he was again up out of his seat and, suitcase in hand, pushing his way to the exit.

'We look forward to seeing you again soon,' said the air hostess cheerily as he left the plane ahead of all the other passengers.

'Not if I can help it,' mumbled the detective.

★ ★ ★

Puri had hired a brand new S Class Mercedes to pick him up at the airport. The driver, who wore a white uniform buttoned up to his neck and a yacht captain's cap embellished with gold leaf emblems, was standing outside the arrivals gate holding up a whiteboard with the alias the detective had adopted for the evening written upon it: 'Monty Ahluwalia'.

Mr Somnath Chatterjee was also waiting for him in the car park.

Mr Chatterjee, of indeterminable age, had a severe hunch born of a lifetime bent over a sewing machine. His clothes were always too large for him — the sleeves of his shirts came down to his knuckles; his trouser legs were always rolled up around his skinny ankles, giving the impression that he had somehow shrunk inside them.

But anyone who had known him long enough, like Puri, could testify to the fact that Mr Chatterjee had always been extremely skinny. His inattention to the proportions of his own apparel was in no way a reflection upon his skills as a tailor. Indeed, he ran Delhi's most successful costume house.

Mr Chatterjee was, in fact, the scion of a noble line of Bengali tailors who had once fitted the

218

Nawabs of West Bengal. Under the rule of the British East India Company, the family had set up shop in Calcutta and adapted to its European tastes, providing uniforms for the (not-so) Honourable Company's troops, and supplying the British theatres with costumes. It was a source of much interest to Puri that Mr Chatterjee's great-grandfather had even provided disguises for Colonel Montgomery of the Survey of India — the real-life inspiration for Colonel Creighton in *Kim*, Rudyard Kipling's tale of intrigue and espionage during the Great Game with Russia.

Chatterjee & Sons had moved to Delhi in 1931, following in the footsteps of their British patrons. For the past twenty years, Mr Chatterjee had been providing Puri with his disguises.

Normally, the detective went for his fittings at Mr Chatterjee's premises, which were hidden down a long alleyway off Chandni Chowk in Shahjehanabad, or Old Delhi as it was now called.

The premises were filled to the rafters with hundreds of costumes and paraphernalia. Hindu deities were stored on the ground floor: Hanuman monkey suits, strap-on Durga arms, and Ganapati elephant trunks hung in rows. Uniforms from numerous epochs were to be found one flight up: the military regalia of Macedonian foot soldiers, Maratha warriors, Tamil Tigers, Vedic Kshatriyas, and Grenadier Guards. The third floor was home to traditional garb of hundreds of different Indian communities: from Assamese to Zoroastrian. There was a

219

special room set aside for headgear of all sorts, including the woven bamboo ceremonial hats worn by Naga tribesmen, the white *mande thunis* of the Coorg, and British pith helmets. And the fourth floor was the place to go to find all the props, including mendicant and beggar accoutrements: swallowable swords, snake charmers' baskets (complete with wind-up mechanical cobras), and attachable deformed limbs.

Crucially for Puri, Mr Chatterjee also provided a variety of Indian noses, wigs — his Indira Gandhi one was especially realistic — beards and moustaches. These he kept in the cool of the basement, where dozens of wooden boxes were itemised: 'Sikh Whisker', 'Rajasthani Handlebar', 'Bengali Babu'.

What Mr Chatterjee didn't have in stock he could have made. Twenty-seven tailors worked in a room on the top floor, sitting cross-legged in front of their sewing machines surrounded by swathes of silk, cotton and chiffon.

On a few occasions in the past, when Puri had come to Mr Chatterjee and requested something out of the ordinary at short notice, these men had worked late into the night to accommodate him — like the time he had needed an Iraqi *dishdasha* to attend a polo match.

Tonight, however, Puri required nothing as exotic. He had asked Mr Chatterjee to supply him with a standard Sikh disguise.

Puri clambered into the back of the tailor's clapped-out van where assistants with stage glue and a make-up kit gave him a quick makeover. Ten minutes later, he emerged wearing a large red turban, fake moustache and beard, a pair of slip-on black shoes and unflattering brown glasses with thick lenses. Puri slipped on several gold rings and put a ceremonial *kirpan* around his neck.

Mr Chatterjee inspected him from head to toe, craning his neck upwards like a tortoise peeping out of his shell, and made an approving gesture with his head.

'Most realistic, sir!' said the old man in Hindi, his voice wheezy and high-pitched. 'No one will ever recognise you! You would have made a great actor!'

Puri puffed his chest with pride.

'Thank you, Mr Chatterjee,' he replied. 'Actually as a young man, I was doing a good deal of amateur theatre. In the ninth grade I won the Actor of the Year award for my portrayal of Hamlet. Often, I considered joining the stage. But duty called.'

'What is the case this time?' whispered Mr Chatterjee, who always got a thrill from aiding the detective. 'Someone has been murdered?' he asked conspiratorially, his eyes lighting up with enthusiasm. 'Are you after that bank robber — the one in the paper who stole fifty crore?'

The detective did not have the heart to tell him that he was involved in a straightforward matrimonial investigation.

'I'm afraid it's top secret,' Puri whispered in English.

'Aaah, taap secret! Taap secret!' repeated the old man giving a delighted giggle as he accompanied the detective to his car.

'I trust my secret is safe with you, Chatterjee-sahib?' asked Puri, laying a fond hand on one of the old man's hunched shoulders.

'I would rather die than tell them anything, sir!' he cried with watering eyes. 'Let them pull out my fingernails! Let them blind me! Let them cut off my — '

Puri gave him a reassuring pat.

'I'm sure it won't come to that,' he interrupted. 'Now you'd better go. It's best if we're not seen together. I'll come to your office in a few days once the case is resolved and settle my account.'

'Yes, thank you sir, be careful sir,' said Mr Chatterjee, returning to his van.

Puri watched him climb inside and pull away, certain that on his way back to Chandni Chowk, the old tailor would check in his rearview mirror to make sure he wasn't being followed and, no doubt, call later in the evening to assure him that the coast had been clear.

★ ★ ★

Puri made a quick stop *en route* to Mahinder Gupta's apartment to pick up Mrs Duggal, his escort for the evening.

She was waiting for him in the reception of a five-star hotel. When she saw the Mercedes pull up, she came out to meet it. A moment later she was arranging herself on the comfortable leather seat next to the detective and admiring the swish interior.

'So I take it we'll be sticking to our usual routine?' she said to Puri after they had

222

exchanged pleasantries.

'You know the old saying: why fix what isn't broken?' answered Puri.

Mrs Duggal, a petite auntie who wore her sporty silver hair pulled back, smiled her innocent smile.

'I must say I do so enjoy our little forays, Mr Puri,' she said, in her quiet, lilting voice. 'Retirement is quite all right. It's wonderful seeing the grandkids growing up. Did I tell you Praveen won a silver medal in breaststroke on Friday? I can't tell you how proud we all are. I wouldn't have missed being there for the world. But sometimes I do find myself pining for the old days. I miss that sense of adventure.'

No one meeting Mrs Duggal or passing her in Panchsheel Park where she took her morning walk with her neighbour, Mrs Kanak, would have imagined that she had worked for RAW, India's secret service. During the 1980s and 90s, Mrs Duggal and her husband, a career diplomat, had been stationed in some of India's most high-profile foreign high commissions and embassies. Ostensibly, she had worked as a secretary, taking dictation, typing and answering the telephone. But secretly her mission had been to keep tabs on her compatriots — diplomats, bureaucrats, administrative staff and, most important, her fellow spies.

To this day, not even her husband or children knew of Mrs Duggal's double role and the fact that she was a decorated national heroine.

While based in Dubai, she had identified the traitor, Ashwini Patel, and prevented him from

223

betraying the identity of the highly placed Indian mole working inside Pakistan's secret service, ISI. During her four-year stint in Washington, Mrs Duggal had discovered that the Military Attaché was having an affair with a Chinese spy and seen to it that the hussy sent phoney naval plans to her superiors in Beijing. And in Moscow, she had collected evidence of the High Commissioner's involvement in the Iraq Oil for Food scandal.

For the past four years, though, Mrs Duggal had been enjoying her well-earned retirement back in Delhi. She passed her days playing bridge, spoiling her grandchildren with home-made *ladoos*, and spending long weekends with her husband, now also retired, by the Ganges in Haridwar.

Occasionally she also did freelance jobs for Puri. Her usual part was that of the detective's wife, for which Mrs Duggal needed no disguise. She was dressed in the understated style that had worked so well for her during her undercover days: a simple but fetching beige silk sari with gold *zari* design, a black blouse, a pair of sensible heels and a modest selection of kundan jewellery.

'You're very sober, Mrs Duggal,' commented the detective as the car pulled on to the main road to NOIDA.

'I'm glad you approve,' she replied. 'You know I'm not one for gaudy colours.'

Puri gave her a couple of Flush's ingenious sticky bugs, one of which looked like a wasp, the other a fly, and explained where he wanted them placed.

Mrs Duggal popped them into her handbag where she also kept her lock-picking tools: a couple of hair grips and a metal nail file.

'Should be child's play for two old professionals such as ourselves,' said Puri.

'Just as long as I'm home by eleven-thirty, Mr Puri. My husband will be expecting me. Any later, and he'll start thinking I've got a boyfriend.'

The two chuckled as the Mercedes sped along the new three-lane toll road.

Half an hour later, they were standing in the elevator heading up to the twenty-second floor of Celestial Tower.

A long, carpeted corridor with wood-panelled walls and air-conditioning vents purring overhead led to the executive penthouse.

Puri rang the bell and the door was promptly opened by a servant, who ushered them into a spacious, dazzling white apartment. He was relieved to find it crowded with members of the Gupta and Kapoor families and their closest friends. Amongst such a large gathering (the party was at least seventy strong), no one would notice a couple of old gatecrashers, let alone challenge them. Indeed, as the detective and his escort stepped through the door, looking for all the world like a respectable auntie and uncle, they were greeted warmly by Mahinder Gupta's parents. It did no harm that Mrs Duggal wobbled from side to side with 'arthritic' hips and grimaced each time she put her right foot forward.

'Monty Ahluwalia and my good wife,' Puri

said in halting English with a deep, provincial drawl as he shook Mr Gupta by the hand.

'Such a beautiful apartment,' commented Mrs Duggal to Mrs Gupta. 'You must be very proud.'

The four of them engaged in small talk for a few minutes. It wasn't long before the Guptas revealed the apartment's whopping price tag: five crore.

'Of course it's absolutely rocketed up since then,' said Mr Gupta. 'Our son spent fifteen lakhs on the bathroom alone.'

'Seventeen lakhs actually, darling,' cooed Mrs Gupta, going on to describe the Italian Jacuzzi bathtub. 'The toilet's also amazing. You know, it flushes automatically, has a heated seat, a sprinkler system and a bottom blow-dryer! You really *must* try it.'

As Mr and Mrs Monty Ahluwalia began circulating amongst the other guests (and trying the Japanese hors d'oeuvres, which the detective did not rate, grumbling to a fellow Punjabi that he was a 'butter chicken man through and through'), Puri began to understand why Brigadier Kapoor was so against his granddaughter's marriage.

The Kapoors belonged to the refined, elite classes of south Delhi: military officers, engineers, the odd surgeon, and one Supreme Court judge. Puri could picture them at cultural evenings at Stein Auditorium or the IIC, wine tastings at the Gymkhana Club and art exhibitions at the Habitat Centre.

Indeed, as the detective and Mrs Duggal mingled, they overheard some of them discussing a retrospective of the Indo-Hungarian artist Amrita Sher-Gil, which had been showing at the National Gallery of Modern Art. Elsewhere, an uncle in a blazer, striped cotton shirt with French cuffs and loafers was telling another uncle, who was dressed almost identically and had a matching greying moustache, about the cruise he and his wife had recently taken around the Great Lakes. And at the far end of the room, Brigadier Kapoor himself, dressed in a three-piece suit and standing with his silver-haired wife at his side, was telling another elderly auntie in a mauve sari about a charity dinner that he and Mrs Kapoor had attended at Rashtrapati Bhavan.

The Gupta clan, by contrast, was drawn from the Punjabi merchant castes. All the younger men seemed to have salaried positions with IT multinationals and worked twelve-hour, six-day weeks. They wore off-the-rack suits and gold watches, had gelled hair, and talked mostly about the markets, Bollywood and cricket. They smoked, drank and laughed raucously, occasionally giving one another matey slaps on the back. Their wives showed a fondness for chunky sequined heels, garish eye-shadow, and either sequined cocktail dresses, or Day-Glo saris worn with strapless, halter-style blouses. Four of them were clustered in the kitchen admiring the stainless steel extractor fan.

'Wow!' one exclaimed. 'So shiny, yaar.'

Puri and Mrs Duggal chatted for a while with Gupta's fiancée, Tisca Kapoor, who seemed like a sensible, articulate woman, if hugely overweight and clearly nervous about how the two families were getting along. As they talked, the detective dropped his napkin on the ground and attached a bug to the underside of one of the faux alligator-skin side tables.

He and his partner in crime then split up. The detective crossed the room to the gas fireplace where he attached another device to the back of one of the photo frames, and then went in search of a Scotch on the balcony.

Meanwhile Mrs Duggal hobbled over to the kitchen (where a few of the older Gupta aunties were discussing the attributes of the front-loading washing machine which, they all agreed, was worth the money) and attached the magnetic fly under the lip of the extractor fan.

She then made her way to Mahinder Gupta's bedroom. Having attached a wasp to the bottom of the metal bed frame, she stepped into the bathroom and locked the door behind her.

In one corner stood the Jacuzzi bathtub and in another the toilet.

Mrs Duggal washed her hands in the sink and, as she did so, noticed a metal medicine cabinet on the wall.

It was locked.

Curious, she took out a hair grip and metal nail file and, in a few seconds, popped the cabinet open.

On the shelves inside, she found an unmarked bottle filled with pale yellow liquid and two syringes. She took the bottle and put it into her glasses case in her handbag.

Just then she heard Mrs Gupta's voice in the bedroom. 'Come this way, it's through here.'

The handle on the door turned and there was a knock.

'One moment,' called out Mrs Duggal.

She locked the medicine cabinet, sat down on the toilet and quickly stood up again. Sure enough, it flushed automatically.

Mrs Duggal opened the door to find Mrs Gupta and three other women who had come to inspect the bathroom waiting on the other side.

'You're quite right, the toilet really is a wonder,' she gushed. 'So much easier on the hips.'

20

At about 10.30 that evening, just as Puri reached home after dropping off Mrs Duggal, the front door of Munnalal's house in Jaipur suddenly swung open with a thud.

A beggar with a horribly deformed hand who was crouching against a wall ten feet away watched as Munnalal stepped outside. In one hand he was carrying his mobile phone, his thumb working the keypad. From his pocket protruded the wooden butt of a revolver.

Munnalal's wife appeared in the open doorway with an anguished, searching expression.

'Your food is ready!' she screeched to his back as he set off down the lane. 'Where are you going? It's late!'

'None of your business, whore!' he bawled over his shoulder. 'Go back inside or I'll give you a thrashing!'

The beggar, seeing Munnalal striding towards him, made the mistake of holding out his deformed hand, which looked like a melted candle, and pleaded for alms — 'Sahib, roti khana hai.'

In return he received a hail of abuse.

'Bhaanchhod!' Munnalal called him as a passing shot, kicking his begging bowl and the few pitiful coins that it contained into the open drain.

The unfortunate man howled, scrambling on

all fours after the receptacle, which had landed upside down in fetid slime.

'*Hai!*' he moaned, after retrieving it and retaking his position against the wall where he had been sitting all evening.

A couple of passing locals, who had seen how cruelly Munnalal had behaved, took pity on the beggar and dropped a few rupees at his feet.

'May Shani Maharaj bless you!' he cried after them, picking up the coins and touching them to his forehead and lips.

The beggar watched his benefactors continue on their way, passing Munnalal's front door, which, by now, had been slammed shut. Then he stood up, collected his pitiful possessions and, when he was sure no one was watching, twisted off his deformed hand. He shoved it under his soiled *lungi*, and set off down the lane.

'Bastard Number One's on the move, heading in your direction,' said Tubelight's man, Zia, into the transmitter concealed in the top of his cleft walking stick.

'Roger that,' came back a voice in the clunky plastic receiver in his ear.

The voice belonged to Shashi, his partner, who had watched too many American cop shows and insisted on using the lingo.

'Who is this Roger?' hissed Zia into his communicator.

'Your papa, yaar,' quipped Shashi.

'Shut up, OK!'

'Ten-four,' replied his colleague.

Munnalal hurried down the lane, stopping briefly at the cigarette stand where he bought a sweet paan. Greedily he stuffed it into his mouth and tossed a grubby note on to the vendor's counter.

Soon, he reached the busy main road where he stepped beyond the broken, piss-stained pavement at the edge of the traffic. Amidst a haze of dust and diesel fumes, with horn-blaring Bedford trucks hurtling past, Munnalal went about trying to hail an autorickshaw.

Zia decided to watch him from the entrance to the lane, staying in the shadows and telling Shashi, who was parked nearby, to keep his Vespa's engine running.

Much to their shared — and in Munnalal's case obvious — frustration, all the autos that drove past were occupied. Some carried as many as eight people with six on the back seats and another couple clinging to the sides like windsurfers.

Five minutes passed. A blue Bajaj Avenger motorcycle driven by a man wearing a helmet with a tinted visor pulled up on the other side of the road.

At first, Zia paid the driver cursory attention. But after Munnalal succeeded in hailing an auto and drove away in the direction of the old city, the Avenger made a quick U-turn and set off after him.

Zia and Shashi were not far behind on the Vespa.

'Someone else is following Bastard Number One,' said Zia.

'Roger that. Did you get a pozit-iv eye dee?'

'Huh?'

'Po-zit-iv eye dee! Means did you recognise him?'

'How could I recognise him, you fool? He's got a helmet on and his numberplate is covered in mud.'

'Ten-four. Do you think he's a perp?'

'Speak Hindi, will you!'

'A perp means a goonda type.'

'I don't know!'

'Think we should get between them?'

'No, but don't fall behind.'

'Copy that.'

Munnalal's auto buzzed and spluttered its way down M.I. Road, past Minerva cinema. Occasionally, he spat great gobs of paan juice out the side of the vehicle, painting the road's surface with intermittent red streaks.

Ten minutes later, the auto turned down the lane which ran behind Raj Kasliwal Bhavan and came to a halt outside the deserted bungalow with the overgrown garden.

Munnalal got out and paid the driver, who promptly drove off in search of another fare. He looked up and down the street to make sure no one was following him and then slipped through the leaning iron gate. A second later he was lost amidst the long grass and shadows.

The motorcyclist, having dismounted and watched Munnalal's movements from a safe distance, took off his helmet and, leaving it on his bike, continued his pursuit on foot.

Zia and Shashi pulled up in time to see the motorcyclist pass through the gate and enter the garden.

'No way I'm going in there,' whispered Shashi as they crossed the lane. 'I heard an owl!'

'They're harmless, yaar. All they do is sit in trees and go hoo hoo.'

'OK hero, you go in there and I'll wait here and cover you.'

'What is this 'cover me' business? Bloody halfwit. Think you're Dirty Hari?'

'It's Dirty *Harry*,' corrected Shashi.

'Whatever, yaar. You stay here. Relax. Maybe take a nap.'

Cautiously, Zia headed into the garden. Shashi watched him go and, finding himself alone, had a change of heart.

'I thought I'd better watch your back,' he whispered when he caught up with his partner.

Together, the two of them crept forward through the long grass and weeds. The owl started hooting again, causing Shashi to grip Zia's arm. And then suddenly a figure ran straight into them, knocked them both to the ground and sprinted off in the direction of the lane. Zia and Shashi were dazed and it took them a few seconds to pick themselves off the ground.

'Go after him! I'll check ahead!' ordered Zia.

'Ten-four!'

Shashi gave chase, but he was too slow. As he reached the lane, the motorcycle kicked into start and, with a roar of the engine, made a 180-degree turn and sped away.

Shashi watched the Bajaj Avenger disappear from sight, knowing that his cousin's Vespa was no match for it, and went to find his partner.

They met outside the gate.

'He got away!' said Shashi in a loud voice.

'Keep your voice down, you fool!'

'Don't call me a fool!'

'OK, halfwit! What happened?'

'He took off. What about Bastard Number One?'

'He's dead.'

'What? Are you sure?'

'Yes, I'm sure!' snapped Zia. 'He's lying behind that abandoned house with a knife sticking out of his throat.'

Shashi's eyes widened.

'What happened?'

'Well, it wasn't suicide!'

Shashi held his hands over his face and kicked at the ground. A pall of dust rose around him.

'That's just our luck!' he cursed. 'Bloody fat bastard goes and gets himself terminated while we're on duty. Boss and Tubelight are going to *kill* us!'

'I know! It's all your fault. You should have rubbed the mud off the numberplate and written it down when you had a chance,' said Zia.

'What do you mean *I* should have? What about you?'

'It was your turn to do the thinking.'

Shashi paced back and forth a couple of times. Then a thought occurred to him.

'What about his mobile phone? Did you get it?'

'It wasn't there.'

'Sure?'

'I checked all his pockets!'

235

'Wallet?'

'Gone as well.'

There was a pause.

'What do we do now? Call the cops?'

'No, you idiot, we get out of here before someone sees us.'

'Right . . . I mean Roger that,' said Shashi.

★ ★ ★

'Bloody fools!' was Puri's reaction to news of Munnalal's murder and the events leading up to it.

It was Tubelight who broke it to him at two in the morning.

'Do the cops know?' asked the detective as he tried to shake off the deep, restful sleep he had been enjoying.

'Doubtful. The body is probably lying unnoticed, it being night time, Boss. Should I make an anonymous call? Tip off the cops?'

'Not yet. They'll trample the scene. I'll try to get there as fast as I can.'

Puri hung up the phone and switched on the light in the panel behind his bed. Rumpi stirred.

'What is it, Chubby?' she asked, sleepily.

'Trouble,' he answered.

'Pack my things, will you? I've got to return to Jaipur immediately. The case has taken a turn for the worse. Someone has been murdered.'

'Who?' she asked.

'The man who held all the answers.'

Puri changed and went into his study. Opening the safe, he took out his .32 IOF and slipped it into his trouser pocket.

By the time he went downstairs, his wife was standing by the front door with his packed overnight case, a few cold rotis wrapped in tin foil and a flask of hastily made 'dip tea'.

The detective smiled and gently took her cheek in his right hand. '*Meri achhi biwi,* my good wife,' he said.

She could feel the cold metal of Puri's pistol against her thigh as she gave him a fond hug.

'Take care,' she said.

The detective chuckled. 'Don't worry about me, my dear. When it comes to danger, I've got a sixth sense.'

'Danger doesn't worry me,' answered Rumpi. 'But those deadly pakoras and chicken frankies you like so much do.'

★ ★ ★

Puri managed to get a couple of hours' sleep and reached the Jaipur city limits at dawn. An apologetic and sleepy Tubelight was waiting for him at Ajmeri Gate. They headed straight to the murder scene. But the police had beaten them to it. Three Jeeps and the coroner's wagon, which looked like an armoured milk van, were parked outside the gate of the derelict house. Five gormless constables stood nearby, chatting amongst themselves.

Puri told Handbrake to stop the car across the road, from where he watched and waited. A few minutes later, a procession emerged from the garden. It was led by a couple of orderlies carrying a stretcher with a blanket draped over Munnalal's body. Two more constables with rifles slung over their shoulders followed. Bringing up the rear was Shekhawat, smoking a cigarette.

'Good morning, Inspector,' said Puri as he got out of the Ambassador.

'What are you doing here, sir?' he asked, surprised to see the detective.

'Just I was on my way to see my client's wife for an early morning conference,' he answered, cheerily.

'At this time?' The inspector looked at his watch. 'It's not even six.'

'What to say? I like an early start.'

Puri gave a nod in the direction of the stretcher, which was being slid into the back of the coroner's wagon.

'Who have you got there?' he asked.

'Male, mid-forties, found with this knife sticking out of his throat.'

Shekhawat held up the bloody murder weapon, which he'd put in a plastic bag.

'By God,' said Puri, feigning surprise. 'Any identification?'

'Nothing. So far he's a *Naamaalum*, unknown. He was carrying this.'

Shekhawat held up Munnalal's revolver, also now in a plastic bag.

'May I see the body?' asked Puri.

'Why all the interest, sir?'

'The murder occurred behind my client's house. Might be I know the victim, isn't it.'

Shekhawat led the detective over to the

238

coroner's wagon and told the orderlies to pull back the blanket.

Munnalal's face was frozen in an expression of sheer horror. The wound was on the left of the neck and the blood had soaked his shirt.

His lips and chin were also stained with paan juice.

'Do you recognise him, sir?' asked Shekhawat.

The detective made a face that suggested ignorance.

'Unfortunately not, Inspector.'

The orderlies replaced the blanket over Munnalal's face. Puri and Shekhawat turned and walked away.

'Any theories?' asked the detective.

'We got an anonymous tip-off in the middle of the night. Someone called and said he saw two men hurrying out of the garden and driving away on a Vespa. He gave us the numberplate. My guess is these two murdered him for his wallet and phone.'

'So a robbery then,' suggested the detective.

'Seems that way,' answered Shekhawat.

Puri was looking down at the dust on the street where a number of vehicles had left tracks, privately cursing the police for being such bunglers. If only he had reached the scene before them.

'Well, Inspector, I can see that you have everything well in hand,' he said. 'I'll wish you a good day.'

The detective got back into his car.

'Go straight to Raj Kasliwal Bhavan,' he told Handbrake tonelessly.

As the Ambassador pulled away, Puri watched the reflection of the inspector in the rearview mirror. Shekhawat in turn watched the back of Puri's vehicle. The curious expression on his face made the detective uneasy.

It was only a question of time before he found out that Munnalal once drove for Kasliwal and his murder was bound to reflect badly on his case. Puri could see tomorrow's newspaper headlines already:

HIGH COURT LAWYER'S FORMER DRIVER FOUND DEAD. COPS SUSPECT FOUL PLAY

'Can your boys' vehicle be traced back to them?' asked Puri, with some urgency.

'No way, Boss, but why?'

'Shekhawat has the numberplate.'

'How, Boss?' exclaimed Tubelight.

'Most probably the killer himself gave it to him. Your boys have been most careless. Tell them to go back to Delhi right away. I would want to talk to them once this thing is over.'

The Ambassador turned right at the end of the road, then right again and pulled into Raj Kasliwal Bhavan.

After it came to a stop in the driveway, Puri sat for a moment in a gloomy silence.

'What's wrong, Boss?' asked Tubelight.

'I've come to a theory about what all has been going on. If I'm right it would not end well for anyone.'

Tubelight knew not to ask Puri about his theories. There was no point. The detective

240

always kept his cards close to his chest until he was sure he had solved the case. This secrecy was derived partly from prudence and partly from his controlling nature.

'Any luck at the Sunrise Clinic?' he asked Tubelight.

'I chatted with the receptionist. Says no girl matching Mary's description was brought in. I think she's lying. I'm going back at seven to meet the security guard on duty the night Mary was murdered.'

'Allegedly murdered,' Puri reminded him.

'Right, Boss. What's your plan?'

'Just there's some checking up I need to do here. Take the car and send it back for me. I'll pick you up around eight o'clock.'

Puri got out of the vehicle, but turned and said through the open door:

'Be alert! Whatever miscreant did in Munnalal knew what he was doing.'

'A professional, Boss?'

'No doubt about it at all. A most proficient and coldblooded killer.'

21

Puri followed the brick pathway that led along the right-hand side of Raj Kasliwal Bhavan, rounded the corner of the house and paused outside the door to the kitchen. It was closed. All was quiet inside.

The detective surveyed the garden to see if anyone was around. Finding the coast clear, he walked over to the servant quarters and edged along the space between the back of the building and the property's perimeter wall.

Facecream's small window was easily identifiable from the thread that went up the wall and disappeared inside. Puri knocked on the glass three times and made his customary signal: the call of an Indian cuckoo.

A moment later, the window opened and Facecream appeared.

'Sir, you shouldn't have come!' she whispered in Hindi. 'It won't be long before everyone is up. Memsahib does her yoga at seven on the lawn!'

'Munnalal was murdered last night in the garden right behind this wall,' said Puri.

'Last night, sir? Just here? I didn't hear anything.' There was a wounded indignation in her tone.

'Could the killer have come from inside?' asked the detective.

'There's no way anyone can come in and out without my knowing, Boss,' said Facecream.

Puri brought her up to date with the events of the night before and told her how he had come to examine the knife wound for himself. When he was finished, Facecream said:

'Sir, was the motorcycle a blue Bajaj Avenger?'

Puri's eyes lit up with expectation. 'Tell me!' he said.

'Sir, Bobby Kasliwal has one. Last night he rode away on it at around eleven-fifteen.'

'By God! What time he returned?'

'Past midnight.'

Puri let out a long, resigned sigh. 'It's what I feared,' he said to himself.

'What is, sir?'

He didn't answer, but asked: 'Is the motorcycle kept in the garage?'

'Yes, sir.'

Puri nodded. 'I'll have a look. Anything else you can tell me?'

'Sir, I've been trying to find out what more the servants know about Munnalal. Nobody has a good word to say about him. Jaya claims he constantly harassed her. She says he groped her a number of times. Once, when he was drunk, he tried to force his way into her room.'

'Does she know if there was anything going on between Munnalal and Mary?'

'She's not sure, sir. She heard some sounds coming from Mary's room one night. This was soon after she started working here, in late July. But she couldn't say for sure whom Mary was with.'

Puri heard a rustling sound coming from the side of the servant quarters and signalled to

243

Facecream to close the window. Casually, he put his hands behind his back and pretended to be looking for something on the ground so that if anyone appeared asking him what he was doing there, he could claim to be searching for clues.

The rustling grew louder.

Presently, a large black crow hopped into view, turning over leaves with its beak.

'False alarm,' he gestured to Facecream who came back to the window and opened it.

'Can you tell me anything else?'

'Sir, I got the cook's assistant, Kamat, drunk. He liked Mary but I doubt there was anything going on between them.'

'Is he aggressive?'

'Yes but he's not that tough.'

'How do you know?'

'He tried it on and I slapped him. He ran off crying.'

It was Facecream's opinion that the mali, too, was no threat. 'He's smoking charas all day,' she said, 'and can no longer differentiate between reality and fantasy. He makes up stories about everyone. He seems to hate Kasliwal. Apparently he's been telling everyone that Sahib has been coming to my room at night!'

'By God,' murmured Puri. 'Anything more?'

'That's all,' she answered. 'But sir, have you considered that after you confronted Munnalal, he figured out that it was Jaya who saw him carrying away Mary's body and he was planning to intimidate her or silence her?'

'That would certainly explain why he was carrying a weapon,' said Puri. 'But there is one other possibility — '

His words were interrupted by the shrill sound of Mrs Kasliwal's voice. She was calling from the kitchen door.

'Seema? Seema! Chai *lao!* This instant!'

'Sir, I'd better go,' said Facecream reluctantly. 'I'm not in her good books. Yesterday I broke a plate and she's docking my salary forty rupees. That doesn't leave me much to take home!'

Puri laughed. 'Just a few more days and we'll have you out of here. Let's talk tonight at the usual time.'

The detective remained where he was while Facecream hurried off towards the kitchen.

'*Haanji ma'am. Theek hai ma'am*,' he heard her saying to Mrs Kasliwal.

The two women went inside, closing the door behind them, and Puri stole over to the garage, which was on the other side of the garden to the left of the house. He tried the side door, found it open, and stepped inside.

Bobby's Bajaj Avenger was parked at the back.

The numberplate was coated in red mud.

Upon further inspection, Puri found a spot of blood on the accelerator grip. There was another on the helmet.

★   ★   ★

'He's gone to visit his father in jail,' Mrs Kasliwal told Puri when he asked about Bobby's whereabouts.

She was on the front lawn in the *dandasana position*, squeezing shut one nostril with her

245

index finger and breathing out hard through the other.

'At what time, madam?'

Mrs Kasliwal snorted a couple more times and then laid her upturned hands on her knees. 'He left at six-thirty or thereabouts,' she said.

'You're certain, madam?'

'Of course I'm certain, Mr Puri!' she snapped.

Puri watched as she moved into the *Ardha Matsyendrasana*, or Half Lord of the Fishes, pose.

'He's carrying a mobile phone, madam?' asked Puri.

Mrs Kasliwal sat up straight again, exhaling as she did so.

'Certainly he's having one, Mr Puri. But why the sudden interest in my son?'

'Actually there's a certain matter I would like to discuss with him.'

'Tell me what exactly?'

'Actually I was hoping he might bring me one or two caps from London next time he's reverting to India. I'm particularly partial to Sandowns. By far the best quality is made by Bates Gentlemen's Hatter of Piccadilly. I hoped Bobby would bring me one or two. Naturally I would make sure he's not out of pocket.'

She looked at him with a baffled expression.

'Caps, Mr Puri? Caps are the priority, is it? What about the investigation? What progress is there?'

'Plenty, madam, I can assure you.'

'So you keep saying, Mr Puri! But I see no evidence of it. Thousands are being spent of our

246

money and for what? No progress at all! Frankly speaking, I don't know what it is you're doing all day.'

She lowered her chin to her chest and then added:

'Fortunately my lawyer, Mr Malhotra assures me the police case is shot full of holes. Only the flimsiest of evidence they have. Nothing concrete. He'll be getting Chippy off for sure.'

Puri fished out his notebook.

'What is Bobby's mobile number, madam?' he asked, pencil at the ready.

Mrs Kasliwal rattled off the digits too quickly for the detective, who had to ask her to repeat them three times before he had the number written down correctly.

'Very good, madam,' he said, putting away his notebook. 'I'll be on my way. One thing is there, though. Your former driver, Munnalal. Last night only, he was most brutally murdered.'

Mrs Kasliwal's body visibly tensed for a moment.

'It happened in the property directly abutting your own, madam, at eleven-thirty. You heard anything?'

'Nothing,' claimed Mrs Kasliwal. 'I was fast asleep I can assure you. Such a long tiring day it was. But how can you be sure he was murdered?'

'He was stabbed in the neck, madam.'

Mrs Kasliwal made a face as if she had smelt something unpleasant and shook her head from side to side.

'Such dangerous times we live in, I tell you,' she said. 'Most probably he got into an altercation with the wrong sort.'

'Anything is possible, madam,' said Puri. 'But seems odd to me he was murdered here — right behind your house.'

'Who knows what goes on, Mr Puri? These people live such different lives to us.'

'He wasn't coming to see you, madam?'

'Me, Mr Puri? What business would he have with me!' Mrs Kasliwal's words were liquid indignation.

'Could be he was in need of assistance?'

'What kind of *assistance* exactly?'

'I'm told he was facing financial difficulties.'

Mrs Kasliwal rolled her eyes. 'That is hardly news, Mr Puri! Munnalal was always asking for salary advance. These types are in and out of trouble. So much drinking and gambling is going on.'

'Did you ever give him anything extra?'

'Extra?' asked Mrs Kasliwal, regarding him with mild contempt.

'Like a bonus, say?'

'I gave him his salary. That is all. *Buss!* Now I've answered enough of your questions, Mr Puri. There's such a busy day ahead. Mr Malhotra will be arriving at nine-thirty to go over the defence. And I'm hosting the monthly meeting of the Blind Society.'

'No need to explain, madam,' said Puri. 'It's about time I pushed off. Till date, I'm without my breakfast.'

★　★　★

Puri picked up Tubelight ten minutes later from behind the Sunrise Clinic.

He could hardly control his excitement.

'Boss, the security guard remembers a girl being brought in on August 21st night!' he said, clambering into the car. 'Says she was covered in blood. But Boss! She was very much alive!'

'He's certain of it?' asked the detective.

'One hundred — no, three hundred and fifty per cent certain!'

'Why so certain?' Puri said, sceptically.

'She was dropped off by a man matching Munnalal's description in a Sumo and the very next night she left!'

'She left? How?'

'Taxi. Came and took her.'

'She was with someone?'

'The guard's got confusion on this point,' answered Tubelight. By this the operative meant that the guard had clammed up suddenly when asked.

'Could he tell you where the taxi went, at least?'

Tubelight grinned.

'No delay! Tell me!' insisted Puri.

'Train station.'

'He's certain?'

'Overheard the taxi-wallah being told where to go.'

'Very good!' exclaimed Puri. 'Tip top work!'

'Thanks, Boss,' said Tubelight with a grin.

The detective instructed Handbrake to head directly to the station.

'Boss, you don't want to interview the clinic

owner? He's Dr Sunil Chandran.'

'Naturally I would want to know why it was Mary was discharged and who all paid the bill,' he said. 'But I'll visit Dr Chandran later. For now, let us stick on the trail while it remains hot.'

★   ★   ★

On platform 2, where the Jat Express to Old Delhi was about to depart, hundreds of passengers with suitcases and bundles balanced on their heads were trying, all at once, to push through the narrow doorways of the already crowded second- and third-class carriages.

The weakest, including women with babies and the elderly and infirm, were ejected from the crush like chaff from a threshing machine, while the strongest and most determined battled it out, pushing, shoving and grabbing one another, their voices raised in a collective din.

Puri watched as an acrobatic young man clambered up the side of one carriage, scrambled along the roof and then attempted to swing himself inside over the heads of the competing passengers jammed into one of the doorways. But he was roughly pushed away and, like a rock fan at a concert, was passed backwards aloft a sea of hands and dumped unceremoniously on to the platform. Unperturbed, he scrambled to his feet and clambered up the side of the train to try again.

The detective continued along the platform where the calls of chai and *nimboo paani* wallahs competed with train tannoy announcements preceded by their characteristic organ chords. A knot of migrant workers, evidently waiting for a long-delayed train, lay sprawled over sheets of newspaper on the hard concrete platform, sleeping soundly.

Near the first-class retiring room, Puri found the men he was looking for: three elderly station coolies who were sitting on their wooden baggage barrows taking a break from the gruelling work of ferrying passengers' luggage on their heads.

Like the other coolies the detective had just interviewed at the main entrance to the station, they wore bright red tunics with their concave brass ID plates tied to their biceps. Their arms and legs were thin and sinewy.

Puri explained that he was looking for a missing girl called Mary who was said to have come to the station on the night of August 22nd. His description of her was derived from facts gleaned during his investigation — together with a certain amount of deductive reasoning.

'She is a tribal Christian from Jharkhand in her early twenties. She would have been extremely weak and probably had bandages wrapped around her wrists. I believe that if she boarded a train, its destination was probably Ranchi.'

The old men listened to the detective's description. One of them asked: 'What was the date again?' Puri repeated it. But none of them remembered the girl.

The detective made his way to the last platform. There he found a young coolie who

251

was carrying three heavy-looking bags on his head for a family travelling on the Aravali Express to Mumbai.

'Yes sir, I remember her well,' he said. 'She could hardly walk. She seemed sick. Yes, she had bandages around her wrists.'

'Did she board a train?'

'A man put her on board the — ' The coolie suddenly stopped talking. 'Sir, I'm a poor man. Help me and I will help you,' he said.

Puri took out his wallet and handed the man one hundred rupees. This was as much as the coolie made in a day, but his composed expression did not change as he tucked the note into his pocket.

'She boarded the Garib Niwas.'

'You saw her get on?'

'Yes sir, I helped her.'

'Did you speak to her?'

'I asked her if she needed a doctor, but she did not answer me. She looked like she was in shock, just staring blankly, not even blinking.'

'What happened to the man she was with?'

'He waited until the train departed. Then he left.'

'Describe him.'

Again the coolie pleaded poverty. Puri had to hand him another hundred rupees.

'Middle aged, salt-and-pepper hair, dark suit, white shirt, expensive shoes — well polished.'

Ever grateful for the observational powers of the common Indian man, the detective made a note of the coolie's name and went in search of the station manager's office.

Twenty minutes later, he was back at the car where Tubelight and Handbrake had been waiting for him.

'There is one 'Mary Murmu' listed on the manifest for the Garib Niwas train to Ranchi on August 22nd,' he said. 'Sounds like she was extremely weak.'

'What's our next move, Boss?' asked Tubelight.

'You and Facecream keep a close eye on Bobby Kasliwal. He is up to his neck in this. I want him watched every moment of the day and night.'

'Think he murdered Munnalal?'

'There's no doubt he was there on the scene.'

'And you, Boss?'

'I'm going to Jharkhand tonight to locate Mary.'

'Jharkhand. Could take for ever. Where will you look?'

'The uranium mines of Jadugoda.'

22

The passenger manifest showed that whoever purchased Mary Murmu's train ticket on August 22nd had opted for a seat in a non-air-conditioned three-tier carriage. The train from Jaipur to Ranchi had been a 'local' and had stopped at every station along its 740-mile, 30-hour journey east, across the subcontinent.

During his student days, Puri had always travelled in the cheapest trains and carriages out of financial necessity. He looked back on the experience with nostalgia. The hypnotic swaying of the train, the camaraderie between passengers, all of them poor, had been wonderful.

But he knew how unforgiving the conditions could be. And now, as he travelled in the comfort of a first-class carriage on a fast train (top speed 87 miles per hour) on the same route Mary had taken, he pictured her — weak, with nothing of her own to eat or drink, possibly fading in and out of consciousness — crammed into the corner of a bottom wooden bunk with the rough feet of the occupants on the bunk above dangling centimetres from her face.

Her carriage would have been heaving with labourers and rustics, who routinely clambered aboard slow-moving local trains between stations, occupying every inch of space. Mary would have been forced to share her bunk with up to six or seven other passengers. With no one to guard her place while she went to the toilet, she might well have found herself squeezed on to the floor.

When the train stopped during the day and the sun hammered down on the roof, it must have been like the inside of a tandoor oven. The circular metal fans bolted to the ceiling would have offered little respite. During the inordinate number of stops, there would have been no letup from the footfall of hawkers selling everything from biscuits and hot tea to safety pins and rat poison. Nor from the perpetual stench of 'night soil' which, on all Indian trains, went straight down the toilet chutes on to the tracks.

Had someone taken pity on Mary and helped her? Perhaps a sympathetic mother who had given the poor girl some water and a little something to eat from her family's tiffin.

Had she had made it to Ranchi alive?

The odds were not good. And without Mary, or at least irrefutable evidence that she had not ended up dead and mutilated on the side of Jaipur's Ajmer Road, Puri was going to have an extremely hard time proving what had happened on the night of August 22nd. A train booking with her name on the roster would not be enough to prove Ajay Kasliwal's innocence.

The detective watched the striking Rajasthani landscape slip past his window. The sun was setting over an intricate patchwork of small fields — the dry, baked earth rutted with grooves made by ox-drawn ploughs in expectation of the monsoon rains.

His eyes followed the progress of a herd of

black goats and a stick-wielding boy along a well-worn pathway that led to a clutch of simple homesteads. In front of one stood a big black water buffalo chewing slowly and deliberately. Nearby, on a charpoy, sat an old man with a brilliant white moustache and a bright red turban watching the train go by.

★ ★ ★

Puri reached Ranchi early the next morning. He had phoned ahead to arrange transportation and exited the station to find a driver who hailed from Jadugoda waiting for him.

Together they set off in a four-wheel-drive Toyota towards the mines.

'Sir, it's not a good idea to make this journey at night,' the driver told Puri once they had left behind the economically depressed city, which embodied little of the new India. 'Nowadays the roads are extremely dangerous.'

'Why's that?' asked Puri.

'Naxals,' replied the driver.

Much of Jharkhand, along with great swathes of eastern and central India — the 'Red Corridor' — were controlled by Naxals, short for Naxalites, or Maoist guerrillas. Their cause was ostensibly a just one: to fight against oppressive landlords and functionaries of the state, who had tricked or forced hundreds of thousands of people off their land. But like so many proxy rebel movements around the world, they had become the scourge of the people they claimed to represent. Naxal comrades levied taxes on

256

villagers, robbed them of their crops and indoctrinated their children.

They also killed hundreds of people each year.

'Just last week they murdered a truck driver who refused to pay their road tax,' explained the driver. 'They burnt him inside his cab. Last night they murdered an MLA in Ranchi. They put a mine under his car and BOOM!'

Puri had read about the murder in that morning's paper. The MLA was the third to die in so many months. Little wonder the Prime Minister had recently called the Naxalites the single biggest internal security threat faced by India.

Still, the detective asked the driver whether he thought the Maoist movement would continue to grow.

'Of course, sir,' he said.

'Why?'

'Because now the poor can see what the rich have — expensive cars, expensive houses. So they feel cheated.'

Yes, the genie has been let out of the bottle, Puri thought to himself. God help all of us.

★ ★ ★

Despite all the potholes, which caused his head to jerk up and down, and occasionally bounce off the window, Puri soon fell fast asleep.

He awoke when they were half an hour from Jadugoda town.

The landscape to his left was Martian: flat, rocky and arid. The only earthly features were the occasional thick, knotty trees — remnants of a great, primordial jungle, which had been cleared to grow monsoon-dependent rice. To the right rose hills with sharp escarpments. Here and there, the upholstery of patchy scrub was punctured by outcrops of rock and scarred by gullies made during heavy downpours.

The uranium mines lay deep beneath these hills. A barbed-wire fence encircled them. Large yellow Uranium Corporation of India signs warned trespassers to keep out.

Puri's vehicle was soon stuck behind a convoy of dump trucks. Each was carrying loads of ordinary-looking grey rock chips which, according to the driver, had been extracted from the mines and were being taken to the processing centre a few miles away. There, the rock would be crushed, and, after being put through a chemical process, the uranium extracted in the form of 'Yellowcake'.

'Sir, did you know our Yellowcake was used to make India's nuclear bomb?' said the driver, grinning with pride at his country's achievement and his native Jharkhand's contribution.

'Do you know anyone who works in the mines?' asked the detective.

'Sir, only tribal people do the manual labour underground,' he replied.

There was a subtext to his answer: the driver was a caste Hindu and although he had grown up in the area, he did not mix with the tribals, or *Adivasis*, the indigenous aboriginals who traditionally dwelled in the jungle.

'I had a cousin who used to drive these trucks.

He did the job for twelve years,' said the driver cheerily. 'But then he had to stop.'

'What happened to him?' asked Puri.

'Sir, he got sick. The company doctors diagnosed him with TB and gave him some medicine. But he did not improve and then he died.'

'What was his age?'

'Forty-two.'

The driver fell silent for a moment and then, with a confused frown, said:

'Sir, the anti-mining campaign-wallahs say the mines make people sick. They say people should not work there. But what else are people to do? There are no jobs. Driving a truck pays good money. If one or two people get sick, well . . . '

They were still stuck behind the dump trucks, unable to pass because of oncoming traffic.

A headwind had started blowing dust from the uranium rocks in their direction. Some of it settled on the windscreen. Although the windows were rolled up, Puri automatically buried his mouth and nose in the crook of his arm.

The driver laughed when he noticed the detective's reaction.

'Sir, don't worry, you can't get sick from a little dust! See?' He rolled down his window and took a deep breath. 'There's nothing wrong with me at all!'

⋆　⋆　⋆

Jadugoda was virtually indistinguishable from tens of thousands of other little roadside settlements to be found across the length and breadth of India, thought Puri as they stopped at the main intersection to ask for directions.

A collection of rickety wooden stalls stood along the sides of the road that led in and out of the town. There were several paan-bidi stands stocked with fresh lime leaves and foil pouches of tobacco, which hung like party streamers. There was a vegetable stand, a fruit stand with heaps of watermelons, and a butcher whose hunks of meat hung on hooks smothered by flies.

A fishmonger sat cross-legged on a plastic tarpaulin on the ground scaling a fresh river fish using a big knife that he held expertly between his toes. Next to him crouched an old woman selling *meswak* sticks for cleaning teeth.

The scene would not have been complete without a big neem tree by the intersection, which provided welcome shade for the local dogs and loafers who spent their days watching people and vehicles coming and going.

There was, however, one unusual feature about the place. In the middle of the intersection stood a statue of three Adivasis armed with bows and arrows — a memorial to local heroes who fought, albeit with primitive weapons, against the British.

In Chanakya's day, too, the tribals had offered fierce resistance to the Maurya Empire, staging raids on passing caravans from their jungle fastness. But since the formation of the Indian republic, these people had been exploited and disenfranchised, Puri reflected sadly. To their misfortune, their ancestral lands lay atop some of the largest mineral deposits in the world, and in the past fifty years most of these had been requisitioned for pitiful compensation. Hundreds of thousands of Adivasis had been made homeless and nowadays, all across India, scratched a living digging ditches, carrying bricks and cleaning toilets.

There was a good deal of prejudice against them.

'The tribal people are not so friendly,' complained the driver as they pulled away from the dusty intersection. 'They're dirty and backwards and they drink too much!'

A couple of minutes later they passed a small township built in the 1960s by the Uranium Corporation of India to house its full-time employees and their families, nearly all of whom hailed from elsewhere in India. Within its spruce perimeter there was a school, a hospital, blocks of flats and green playing fields.

Beyond the township, the driver took a left down a rocky lane and pulled up outside an ordinary, one-storey concrete building. Had it not been for the cross above the entrance, Puri would never have guessed it was the local church.

The detective got out of the Land Cruiser and knocked on the metal doors. They were soon opened by a middle-aged man who could easily have passed for an Australian Aboriginal. He was dressed in a shirt, jeans and a baseball cap, and around his neck hung a small, gold crucifix. His eyelids blinked in slow motion, giving the impression that he was half asleep, and his

261

mouth broadened into a wide, childlike grin.

'Good afternoon,' he said, welcomingly, as if it had been some time since he'd had any company. His English pronunciation mimicked the way it is spoken on 'Teach Yourself' audiocassettes.

'Good afternoon, just I'm looking for the priest,' said Puri.

'I'm Father Peter,' replied the old man. 'It's a pleasure to meet you.'

'Father, my name is Jonathan Abraham. I run a charity based in Delhi that offers assistance to Adivasi Christian families,' lied the detective.

The business card he handed the priest named him as 'Country Director' of the non-government organisation that he often used as a cover: 'South Asians In Need' — SAIN. The card listed two Delhi numbers — both of which, if dialled, would be answered by an extremely helpful lady by the name of Mrs Kaur, who would offer to send out an information pack about the charity.

The priest studied the card and his eyelids blinked in slow motion again.

'Ooh!' he said like an excited child. 'Are you from Delhi?'

'Yes, Father, my office is there.'

Father Peter grinned again. He had a dazzling set of white, perfectly straight teeth, which might have belonged to an American high school student. 'Then you are the answer to my prayers!' he said, inviting the detective inside.

★ ★ ★

262

Puri had reasoned that if he went around asking people in the local Christian Adivasi community about Mary's whereabouts, they would react with suspicion and he would be stonewalled. Furthermore, he didn't want Mary — assuming she was still alive — coming to know that an outsider was looking for her.

Ideally, he wanted to engineer a situation in which she would feel comfortable divulging the truth about what had happened to her in Jaipur. He would need to gain her trust.

Fortunately, the cover of a Christian was an easy one to pull off. Puri had attended a Delhi convent school as a young boy and the nuns had drummed the Lord's Prayer into him. The other sacraments of the Nazarene guru were also easily observed. (Pretending to be, say, a Muslim presented considerably more pitfalls. Mastering the Islamic prayers alone took hours and hours of practice.)

Christian priests, too, were easier to handle than the representatives of other faiths. They were generally nowhere near as greedy as Hindu pundits, who always had their hands out.

The only thing Father Peter really wanted was a new cross for his church. The existing one, which was made of wood, was being eaten by termites. 'Now it is 'holy' in more ways than one,' he joked as they drove back into town.

Over lunch — Puri took him to the dhaba on the main road, which was the only place to eat in Jadugoda — the detective promised to send him a new one from Delhi.

By the time they had finished their meal and

263

sat cleaning out the bits of mutton gristle from the gaps in their teeth with toothpicks, he had learned that there were only forty families in the Jadugoda area who had converted to Christianity (far greater numbers were to be found around Ranchi). The rest still clung to their animist religion.

Of those forty families, seven or eight bore the tribal name Murmu.

Puri told Father Peter that he wanted to visit their homes because the Government of India's Ministry of Development had identified the Murmus as the poorest and he wanted to assess their needs.

The priest accepted this explanation without question and offered to act as the detective's guide.

To reach the first house, they drove back to the main junction in the centre of the town and turned left along the narrow road. It passed through the hills, which were cordoned with high fences. More yellow 'No Trespassing' signs appeared and the driver explained that the uranium processing centre was off behind the line of trees on their left.

'See the pipe coming out of the jungle? That carries the waste from the plant — a sludge of toxic chemicals and crushed rock,' chimed in Father Peter.

Puri followed the path of the pipe with his eyes. It travelled under the road, crossed the narrow valley and climbed up the side of an enormous, 150-foot-high man-made dam that had been con-structed across the mouth of the adjacent valley.

'The waste is dumped there, is it?' he asked.

'Behind the dam lies what they call the 'tailing pond',' said Father Peter. 'No one is allowed there. But when I was a boy, we used to go up the hill and throw stones into the mud.' He grinned impishly at the memory of his childhood escapade. 'It's very thick. Sometimes when it is very hot the surface is hard and cows stray across it and get sucked down.'

Their destination was a hamlet that lay in the shadow of the dam.

By now, it was early afternoon and the sun was at its hottest. The little sandy lanes that ran between the mud and straw compounds were empty save for a few chickens.

Father Peter knocked on the first door and an Adivasi man with coal black skin, wearing a sarong and a baseball cap, answered. He was obviously delighted to see the priest and after a good deal more grinning and pleasantries, the detective was invited inside.

A large well-swept courtyard lay at the centre of the house. On one side rows of cowpats were drying in the sun; on the other grew a banana tree, holding up a direct-to-home satellite receiver dish.

Their host arranged a couple of chairs in the shade provided by the overhanging thatch roof and soon his daughter served them glasses of cold water and a packet of cream-filled biscuits.

The daughter was too young to be Mary and Puri quickly established that she had no sisters. But he went through the motions of taking out his notebook and enquiring about the family's financial circumstances.

The couple had had two other children, both boys. The elder was working down in the mines where he loaded rocks on to a conveyor belt all day without any protective gloves or breathing apparatus; the other son had been born physically and mentally handicapped and died at the age of seven.

'What problems do you face?' Puri asked them.

The father made a face as if he did not know where to begin. Usually, he said, his words translated for the detective by Father Peter, he worked alongside his son in the mines. But he had been feeling weak for the past few months and had not been able to work. Because of this the family's income had been halved. Like seven hundred million other Indians who were yet to see the benefits of the country's economic growth, they were surviving on less than two dollars a day. To make matters worse, the water in their well had been poisoned by the chemicals from the tailing pond.

'They can no longer drink it,' explained Father Peter, almost jovially. 'But they still use it for washing.'

'Have you thought about moving? It is dangerous to be here, no?' Puri asked them.

'This is the only land we have left,' said the father. 'The jungle is mostly gone and we have nowhere else to go.'

Puri made a show of writing down more details and, before heading off to meet the next family, gave the father a thousand rupees. He also tried to impress upon him that it was

266

hazardous to use the water from the well. But the man shrugged, resigned to his lot.

★ ★ ★

It was not until the following afternoon when the detective and Father Peter arrived at the eighth and final home on the list that Puri's search came to an end.

The house, which was much smaller than the others they had visited, stood next to a sal tree. In its shade a teenage girl and a young woman squatted playing a chequers-like game called *Bagha-Chall*, or Tigers and Goats. The board was a grid drawn in the sand; for pieces they were using twenty-four little pebbles. In shape and colour, they were indistinguishable from the ones Puri had found on the windowsill of the servant quarters in Raj Kasliwal Bhavan.

'Hello Mary, God bless you,' said Father Peter in Santhal, the local language, greeting them both with a big friendly smile.

'Hello, Father,' beamed Mary, who was wearing an unusually large number of bangles on her wrists.

She stood up, brushing away the hair from her eyes with her left hand, and a few of the bangles slid down her arm towards her elbow, revealing a scar on her wrist.

'Is your father at home?' asked Father Peter.

'He's inside, sleeping,' she said.

'Well go and wake him, child. This gentleman has come all the way from Delhi and would like to speak with him.'

267

Mary shot Puri a suspicious look.

'What does he want?' she asked.

'He's here to help us.'

'How?'

'Now don't ask so many questions, my child. Run along and bring your father,' said the priest.

Puri watched Mary walk over to the house. She was an attractive young woman, slim, with dark brown eyes and long black hair tied in a ponytail. Her features, dusky and distinctly Adivasi, were strikingly similar to those of the murder victim dumped on Jaipur's Ajmer Road.

'That poor girl has suffered a lot,' the priest told Puri when she was out of earshot.

'What happened to her?'

'I hate to think. She won't tell anyone, not even her mother. Like so many of our young women, she went to the city to find work. When she came back a few months later, she could hardly walk. It's taken her weeks to recover, God protect her.'

'How did she get here?'

'The Lord was watching over her. She collapsed at Ranchi station, but a member of our community took her to a hospital.'

Soon, Puri was sitting on a mat on the floor inside the house with Mary's father, Jacob, asking questions about the family's circumstances. Mary sat in the doorway listening to their conversation and sifting through a pot of lentils. All the while she watched Puri suspiciously.

Like most of the men Puri had interviewed in the past 24 hours, Jacob worked in the mines, which provided just enough money to feed the family. But he was getting old and complained that he had no son to help him. Last year, after the family's rice crop failed, he had sent his eldest daughter to the city to work. For a while, she sent money home.

'But she became sick and returned,' said Jacob. 'Now I'm afraid my health will give out and we will all starve.'

Puri made a note of this and then explained to Jacob that he ran a charity willing to provide the family with assistance. He made a show of taking out a calculator and punching in some figures and then announced that because they had no sons, they were eligible for an immediate payment of four thousand rupees. This was more than Jacob made in a month, and the sight of so much cash left him speechless. He took the wad from Puri with tears in his eyes and said to Father Peter: 'It is a miracle!'

★ ★ ★

Puri accepted the family's invitation to stay for dinner and, before the sun went down, managed to snap a surreptitious picture of Mary with his mobile phone.

After dark, by the light of a paraffin lantern, they sat eating a simple meal of fish, rice and daal. The food, which was prepared by Mary and her mother, was delicious. Throughout the meal, Puri complimented the cooking and ate seconds and thirds.

Afterwards, as he, Jacob, Father Peter and the

driver, who had joined them, shared the priest's pipe, the detective made his host an offer:

'I would very much like to give your daughter a job working in my house in Delhi,' he said. 'The salary would be three thousand rupees a month and she would stay in the servant quarters.'

Mary looked horrified by this suggestion. 'No, Father I won't go!' she protested immediately.

Puri ignored her protest, adding, 'Of course I can understand why you would be concerned about her safety. You are welcome to bring her there yourself. I will provide the train tickets and we can all travel together. Perhaps Father Peter would like to come as well and we can find him a new cross for his church?'

The detective knew it was too good an offer for Jacob to turn down. It was the answer to all his prayers.

Sure enough, despite Mary's misgivings, her father soon agreed to Puri's terms. They would leave for Delhi the next day.

23

Mummy's little Maruti Zen crept along the road in Mehrauli, south-west Delhi. The road was lined with imposing walls topped with shards of broken glass. Behind these lay 'farmhouses', some of the largest and most expensive properties anywhere in the capital, all of them built on land illegally appropriated by the wealthy and well-connected. Mummy had visited one a few years ago during Holi. It had been like a mini-Mughal palace — all marble archways and perfumed gardens.

'Twenty-two!' called Majnu, Mummy's driver, as they passed another set of ornate, wrought-iron gates and he read from the Italian marble plaque, which had been engraved with the owner's name: 'KAKAR'.

Mummy was looking for number nineteen.

She had been reliably informed by Neelam Auntie, one of her former neighbours in Punjabi Bagh, that it belonged to Rinku Kohli, Puri's childhood friend. Apparently, he spent most of his time in Mehrauli these days, often returning to Punjabi Bagh and his wife, children and elderly mother in the early hours of the morning.

Everyone knew what Rinku got up to in his farmhouse. It was an open secret. But his standing had not suffered in the community as a result. Punjabi Bagh's men admired him because he was rich, drove a Range Rover and liked to drink a lot of imported Scotch, watch cricket and tell dirty jokes. And the women were always ready to forgive a good Punjabi boy for his improprieties, just so long as he respected his elders, observed all the family rituals and raised strong, confident boys of his own.

'Must be making a packet,' Neelam Auntie had commented admiringly.

Mummy, though, had always understood Rinku's weaknesses. The fact that he had turned out rotten like his father had come as no surprise to her — nor that he and Chubby had chosen such different paths. But Rinku had practically grown up in her house and she had always been kind to him.

Which was why Mummy felt confident asking for his help now. A serial adulterer and crook he might be, but nice, grey-haired Punjabi Bagh aunties still commanded Rinku's respect.

'There it is! Stop!' she shouted.

Majnu, who was sulking again because he had been working long hours helping shadow Red Boots, pulled up to the gate. A uniformed security guard approached his window.

'Tell Rinku Kohli he's got a visitor,' Mummy called over the driver's shoulder.

'Madam, there's no one here by that name.'

'Just tell him Baby Auntie is here. I've brought his favourite *ras malais*.'

The guard hesitated.

'Listen, I know he's living here, na. So might as well get on with it!'

Reluctantly, the guard returned to his hut and picked up a phone. Mummy could see him through the glass talking to someone. Another minute passed before he emerged again and opened the gates.

Majnu started the engine again and pulled inside.

The 'farmhouse' was set in three acres of immaculate, emerald lawns trimmed with neat hedges and lush flowerbeds. The house defied elegance, however. A modern redbrick structure with oblong windows and yellow awnings, it looked like a House of Fun at a fairground. At the back, Mummy spied a swimming pool and two tanned goris in bikinis sunning themselves. A lean, attractive Indian man in shorts and sunglasses was standing nearby, talking on a mobile phone and smoking a cigar.

Majnu stopped in front of the house and, as Mummy got out clutching her Tupperware container, Rinku came bounding down the steps.

'Baby Auntie, what a surprise!' he said, bending down to touch her feet.

'Namaste beta. Just I was passing, na,' she said, patting him on the shoulder. 'No inconvenience caused, I hope?'

'Not-at-all! You're most welcome any time Auntie-ji, any time. Come, we'll have some tea.'

He was about to head back into the house and then thought better of it.

'Actually let's go on the lawn. It'll be quieter there.'

He led her to a spot where a garden table and chairs were arranged in the shade of a tree.

'Oi! Chai lao!' he called to a servant who had emerged from the front of the house.

Rinku and Mummy sat down and exchanged gossip about friends and family.

When the tea arrived, Rinku served her himself and then tucked into one of the ras malais, making suitably appreciative noises.

'*Wah!*'

Mummy saw her chance.

'Beta, you heard some goonda did shooting at Chubby, na?' she said.

Rinku's face darkened. He took off the sunglasses he'd been wearing and placed them on the table.

'I heard, Auntie-ji. I'm sorry.'

'So close it was. Just one inch or so and he'd have been through. Fortunately, his chilli plants saved the day.'

'Thank God,' intoned Rinku.

'Problem is, beta, Chubby's not doing proper security. When I help, he gets most upset. You of all people are knowing how stubborn he can be, na.'

'Only too well, Auntie-ji.'

'You know and understand. That is why I've come,' she continued. 'But beta you're not to tell Chubby we've talked. Equally, I won't go telling him you're helping in this matter.'

Rinku patted her fondly on the hand.

'Auntie-ji,' he said, 'Chubby has always been like a brother to me. And you've been like a mother. We are family. Just tell me what I can do.'

Mummy proceeded to tell Rinku about how she had tracked down Red Boots, a corrupt police inspector called Inderjit Singh; and how

274

he had met Surinder Jagga at the Drums of Heaven Restaurant, where, over spring rolls and whisky, they'd discussed a murder.

'Since then I've done checking. Turns out, this fatty-throated fellow has desire to build one office block on Chubby's home. Already he's bought up some nearby plots. Recently one elderly neighbour, Mr Sinha, sold out. Must be under pressure, but it has been hushed up.'

'Did Jagga come to Chubby with an offer?' asked Rinku.

'Rumpi says Jagga visited some weeks back and offered Chubby a large sum for the land, but he turned him down flat. Jagga didn't threaten him, so naturally my detective son is unaware he is behind the shooting.'

'Jagga and Singh must have decided the best course of action was to get rid of Chubby,' said Rinku. 'They probably thought someone else would get the blame and then Rumpi would take their offer and sell up.'

'Jagga and Inspector Singh are bad sorts, that is for sure,' added Mummy.

Rinku looked as if he couldn't make up his mind whether to congratulate Mummy on her brilliant detective work or scold her for taking so many risks.

'You've been keeping quite busy, isn't it, Auntie-ji.' Rinku smiled, quietly impressed.

'Well, what to do, beta? Someone's got to look out for Chubby, after all.'

'I know, Baby Auntie, we all worry about him. He's doesn't look after himself, actually. But at your age you shouldn't be running around getting involved in this kind of thing. These people can be dangerous. Property brokers are the worst kind.'

'Don't be silly, beta, I'm quite capable of looking after myself, na.'

Rinku laughed. 'I've never doubted that, Baby Auntie. But you've done more than enough. Leave this with me, OK? I'll take care of it.'

'You know this Jagga fellow, is it?'

'I know people who know him,' said Rinku, a little hesitantly. He paused. 'Auntie-ji, I promise I'll sort it out. Trust me.'

'Don't do rough stuff, beta, please.'

'Of course not, Auntie-ji!'

'And not a word to Chubby.'

'Not one word! Now I'll walk you to your car.'

★ ★ ★

Flush was also busy while Puri was in Jharkhand. Keeping tabs on Mahinder Gupta was proving to be deeply unsatisfying.

Never before had he trailed such a boring individual.

The man's routine was numbingly predictable.

On the day before Puri returned to Delhi with Mary, Gupta woke at a quarter to six, spent ten minutes on his automatic toilet (which sluiced and dried his bottom and told him to 'have a nice day'), changed out of his pyjamas into his tracksuit, and made his way to the kitchen.

There he gulped down a protein shake.

At 6.30, Bunty, his one-thousand-rupee-per-hour personal trainer arrived and, for the next thirty minutes, put Gupta through his paces in his personal gym.

Afterwards, the BPO executive had a shower and then changed into a smart business suit and tie.

At 7.30, he took the lift down to the underground car park to his BMW. Pavan, the *car-saaf-wallah*, had finished washing and waxing the blue paintwork to perfection, and for this he received payment of twenty rupees.

The car sparkled in the early morning sunshine as Gupta's driver pulled out of the gates and took the turning for the NOIDA expressway toll road. He did not have to fight too hard for space amid the frenetic traffic. Given the Beemer's Brahmanical status at the top of India's vehicular caste system (bicyclists being the dalits of the road), few cars dared to cut in front of it or venture too close lest they contaminate its uncorrupted, venerated bodywork.

Gupta, meanwhile, sat on the back seat with the automatic windows closed and the air conditioning on, blissfully isolated from the diesel fumes and wretched hawkers. He kept half an eye on his in-car LCD TV, which was tuned to a morning business programme, while reading his overnight emails from Hong Kong on his BlackBerry. He also put in calls to New York, Mumbai and Singapore.

At the main gate to Analytix Technologies, Gupta's employers, the guards stood to attention as the BMW left the dusty, bumpy feed road and glided over the pristine tarmac of the car park, pulling up at the entrance to the glass-panelled office block.

Briefcase in hand, Gupta took the elevator up to his office on the executive floor.

He stayed inside the building all day.

For lunch, he ate a *dosa* at his desk.

At precisely 8.15 in the evening, he left work, having already changed into his golf kit — green mock turtleneck, long Greg Norman plaid trousers and a Tiger Woods cap.

Gupta reached the Golden Greens Golf Course at 8.30 and teed off with a senior futures manager, Pramod Patel.

He scored an eagle on the fifth, a birdie on the eighth and finished seven under par.

Back in the clubhouse, he had a Diet Coke at the bar and, shortly after ten o'clock, returned home.

There he changed out of his golf clothes, took another shower and spent an hour talking on the phone, first with his parents and then his fiancée.

He fell asleep watching the second day of the Vallarta Golf Cup in Mexico.

'I bet all his dreams are about little white balls,' Flush muttered to himself as he sat in his white van, which was parked near Celestial Tower, listening to his mark snoring.

A week of surveillance had thrown up nothing incriminating. Gupta's bank and phone records were clean. He had not visited any porn sites. He was not in touch with illegal bookies. He had not made any big unaccounted-for cash withdrawals.

When he wasn't working, playing golf or sitting on his automatic toilet, Gupta went to the

Great Place Mall where he liked to watch sappy Bollywood love stories in the super-luxury Gold Class Lounge cinema and buy organic handmade lavender soap at Lush.

Flush was growing increasingly frustrated with his failure to dish up the dirt. Seeing middle-class Indians living such ostentatious lives while the vast majority of the population survived on next to nothing riled him. He wanted badly to put a dent in Mahinder Gupta's perfect life.

The only glimmer of hope was the unmarked bottle of yellow liquid Mrs Duggal had discovered in the medicine cabinet.

But what could it be? Was he HIV positive, perhaps?

One thing was for sure: he was not taking recreational drugs. Gupta had not had contact with any of the hundreds of dealers now operating in Delhi.

'He's not even had pizza delivered, Boss,' Flush had reported to Puri at the end of another fruitless day.

24

After returning from Jharkhand and leaving Mary and her father with Rumpi, Puri drove to his office.

Sitting behind his desk and feeling especially pleased with himself, he sent Door Stop, the office boy, to fetch him a couple of mutton *kathi rolls* with extra chutney. These he devoured in a matter of minutes, ever vigilant about getting incriminating grease spots on his safari suit, and then got back to work.

His first call was to Tubelight, whom he informed about his success in Jharkhand — 'A master stroke' was how he described his triumph. He also shared his plan, which did not involve breaking the good news to the Kasliwals just yet.

'I've something else in mind,' he said. 'What's Bobby been up to?'

'Doing timepass,' said Tubelight. 'He's hardly come out of his room. Facecream says he's depressed. Had a big argument with his mother.'

'What about?'

'She couldn't tell, but there was a good deal of shouting. That apart, he's gone to the Central Jail to visit his Papa every day.'

Next, Puri talked to Brigadier Kapoor to assure him that that the investigation was 'very much ongoing'. He promptly received a harangue on how he wasn't doing enough and should try harder.

Finally, the detective turned his attention to

the small matter of the attempt on his life and put in a few more calls to some of the informers and contacts to find out if they'd heard anything useful.

One, a senior officer at the CBI whom the detective had helped on a couple of cases in the past, ruled out Puri's top suspect, Swami Nag. There had been a confirmed sighting of the fraudster at a Dubai racetrack on the very day of the shooting, so he had not been in Delhi as previously thought.

'Unless of course His Holiness can bi-locate and be in two places at once,' joked the officer.

No one else had any leads.

Exhausted from the overnight train journey from Ranchi, Puri tilted back in his comfortable executive chair, put his feet up on the desk and closed his eyes.

In seconds, he was fast asleep and dreaming.

He found himself standing before the legendary walls of Patliputra, the ancient capital of the Maurya Empire, with its 64 gates and 570 towers. Nearby, under an ancient peepul tree sat a sagely figure with a shaven head, ponytail, and a stud in one ear. Across his forehead were drawn three parallel white lines denoting his detachment from the material world.

Puri recognised him as his guru, Chanakya, and went and knelt before him.

'Guru-ji,' he said, touching his feet. 'Such an honour it is. Please give me your blessings.'

'Who are you?' asked Chanakya, busy writing his great treatise.

'I'm Vish Puri, founder and managing director

281

of Most Private Investigators Ltd. and the best detective in India,' he answered, a little hurt that the sage had never heard of him.

'How do you know you are the best?' asked Chanakya.

'Guru-ji, I am the winner of the Super Sleuth World Federation of Detectives award for 1999. Also, I was on the cover of *India Today* magazine. It's a distinction no other Indian detective has achieved till date.'

'I see,' said Chanakya, with an enigmatic smile. 'So why have you come to me for help? What can I, a simple man, do for you?'

'Guru-ji, someone tried to kill me and I need help in finding whoever it was,' explained Puri.

Chanakya closed his eyes and gave the detective's request some thought. It seemed like an age before he opened them again and said:

'Do not fear, Vish Puri. You will receive the help you need. But you must accept you don't have power over all things. All of us require a helping hand from time to time.'

'Thank you, Guru-ji! Thank you! I'm most grateful to you. But please, tell me, how will I be helped?'

Before Chanakya could answer, Elizabeth Rani's voice broke in. She was calling him over the intercom. Puri woke with a start.

'Sir, I've the test back from the laboratory. Should I bring it?'

The detective looked at his watch; he'd been asleep for more than half an hour.

'Yes, by all means,' he said, drowsily, buzzing in his secretary.

The test Elizabeth Rani was referring to was the analysis of the mystery liquid Mrs Duggal had retrieved from Mahinder Gupta's bathroom.

After looking over the results, and drinking a cup of chai, Puri called Flush on his mobile phone to tell him the news.

'It's testosterone,' he said.

'Is that all, Boss?'

'You sound disappointed.'

'It's very common for guys to take that stuff these days, Boss,' Flush explained. 'Everyone who goes to gyms is taking it. They all want Salman Khan muscles, so they're pumping themselves full of dope. It's readily available on the black market. Most chemists will sell it to you.'

'I don't doubt Gupta wants big muscles,' said Puri. 'But from everything we've learned about this man and his habits, I have a feeling his motives are different.'

'HIV, Boss? Maybe that's why so much of his hair is falling out.'

'No, something else. Find out his doctor's name. Has he seen him lately?'

★ ★ ★

Puri had given Rumpi and the servants strict instructions to make Mary feel welcome and asked them to put away the Hindu idols for a few days (he had to keep up the pretence that he was Jonathan Abraham, after all). He'd also sent Sweetu to his cousin's house because he couldn't be trusted not to blurt out the wrong thing at the wrong time.

Mary's father stayed at the house for only a couple of hours and then headed back to the train station. His wife and younger daughter needed him at home, he explained to Rumpi.

A tearful Mary saw him off and then joined Monica and Malika in the kitchen, where she helped them prepare lunch.

When asked where she had worked before, she told them that this was her first job.

After lunch, Monica and Malika showed Mary the laundry room and taught her how to use the top-loading washing machine, which had to be filled with buckets of water because there was rarely any in the taps after eight o'clock in the morning.

Rumpi then took her shopping at a nearby market for new clothes. Mary picked out a few bright new kurtas, salwars and chunnis, some underwear and two pairs of chappals. Puri's wife also bought the new maidservant a hairbrush and various bathroom necessities.

The next stop was a small private health clinic run by Dr (Mrs) Chitrangada Suri, MD, who gave Mary an examination. The doctor found that she was suffering from dehydration, malnourishment, worms and lice, and immediately wrote out prescriptions for a couple of different medicines, vitamins, minerals and oral rehydration salts.

Talking in English so Mary would not understand, Dr Suri also told Rumpi that the girl had tried cutting her wrists within the past few months and although the blood loss had probably been significant, she was young and seemed to have bounced back.

That evening, after Malika returned home to her family, Mary and Monica made the evening meal, did the washing up, took down the laundry from the roof, ate their dinner and then went for a walk in the neighbourhood.

They passed many other servants working for other households out enjoying the cool evening. Monica stopped to chat and gossip and bought them both ice-creams from a vendor with money that Rumpi had given them specifically for the purpose.

At 8.30, they sat down with Madam in the sitting room to watch *Kahani Ghar Ghar Ki*, one of India's most popular soaps. Set in the home of a respectable industrialist family, the serial nonetheless featured shocking twists and turns with extramarital affairs, murders, conspiracies and kidnappings.

In the latest development, the main daughter-in-law had had a face-change operation and turned up as the wife of another man. But Monica said this was because the actress playing her had been fired after demanding a salary increase.

At nine o'clock, Rumpi said that Sahib was expected home and that it was time to sleep. A second mattress had been arranged on the floor in Monica's small room and lying on it was a new Bagha-Chall set. Mary's eyes lit up at the sight of the pitted wooden board and the bagful of pretty, polished stones and she eagerly accepted Monica's challenge to a game.

Mary proved a demon player, easily beating her opponent.

'I'm village champion!' she said. 'I could beat all the men if they would play me!'

The two of them then settled down for the night and Mary was soon fast asleep. Monica lay awake for a while, wondering why her new roommate was so sad and why she wore her bangles to bed. But eventually she fell asleep.

Around midnight, she awoke in a fright. Mary was sitting up, screaming.

Monica jumped up and turned on the light and then put her arms around her new roommate, telling her that it had only been a bad dream. Now awake, Mary fell back on her pillow and started crying.

'I lost him!' she sobbed. 'I lost him!'

'Lost who?' asked Monica.

But she didn't answer and cried herself back to sleep.

25

Flush called Puri the next morning to give him the name of Gupta's doctor.

'How did you find it so quickly?' he asked him.

'He went to see him before reaching office,' answered the operative.

'What's the doctor's name?'

'Dr Subhrojit Ghosh.'

'6-B Hauz Khas village,' said Puri.

'You know him, Boss?'

'Indeed I know him,' said the detective with a chuckle.

'Well Boss, it's definitely Dr Ghosh who prescribed Diet Coke testosterone. Afterwards he went and bought more supplies.'

'Good. Well done. Now pack up and get out of there.'

'The operation is finished, Boss?'

'I'll be taking over,' said Puri. 'If Gupta is seeing Dr Ghosh there is only one meaning.'

* * *

Puri drove to the leafy area of Hauz Khas in south Delhi, built amidst the ruins of the ancient Delhi Sultanate.

Dr Subhrojit Ghosh practised in the basement of the same two-storey house that his father had built and in which he had grown up.

287

It had been more than six months since Puri had been there, but he knew the place well. He and the doctor had met during one of his first cases. The erudite Dr Ghosh had been recommended to him as an expert on a medical matter. In the years since then, Puri had turned to him on many occasions for advice and the two had spent countless evenings sitting in the Gymkhana playing chess and talking politics.

Puri passed through the gate and made his way down the side of the building to the clinic entrance.

After letting him in, Dr Ghosh's assistant asked Puri to wait in reception. He sat down on the cane couch and picked up a copy of the Indian edition of *Hello!* The cover featured a leading Bollywood actress who had cropped up during one of Puri's more sensational matrimonial investigations a few years earlier — The Case of the Absconding Accountant. She had been an unknown then, and in the process of bedding half the producers, directors and leading men in Mumbai.

The spread pictured her sitting on a white couch with her parents and her pet poodles. 'Putting Family First' read the headline.

With a disdainful chortle, Puri tossed the magazine back on to the table just as the door to the doctor's office opened.

'Hello old pal, this is a surprise!' said Dr Ghosh with open arms. 'Long time no hear, eh, Chubby? How long has it been?'

'Too long, actually,' answered the detective, embracing his friend.

'Well, come in. You'll take some chai?'

'And some of those chocolate biscuits you keep hidden in your drawer.'

Puri stepped into the office and sat down in one of the two chairs in front of Dr Ghosh's desk.

'Extra sugar for my dear friend,' Dr Ghosh told his assistant before closing the door behind him and sitting down in the chair next to Puri.

'My God, it's good to see you, Chubby!' he said, giving him a friendly pat on the knee. 'How are you?'

'World class,' answered Puri. 'You?'

'All fine. But you've been neglecting me for too long.'

'I know, Shubho-*dada*.' Shubho was short for Subhrojit; dada meant older brother in Ghosh's native Bengali. 'But I'm non-stop these days. The city is going mental, I tell you. There's a crime wave like you wouldn't believe. Not a day goes by without some girl getting raped or a businessman getting kidnapped. You read about the shootings in CP?[1] Can you imagine? Goondas running around knocking off business-men in daylight hours! Someone even took a pop at me just the other day.'

'I heard. Rumpi called me. Said you're working too hard and your blood pressure's up. She asked me to have a word with you, Chubby. Frankly speaking, you *do* look tired.'

'Oh please, the woman is keeping me half starved. How am I meant to live on daal and rice?'

---

[1] Connaught Place, New Delhi.

'You're off the chicken frankies, I take it?' said Dr Ghosh, looking sceptical.

'Well, not entirely,' admitted Puri with a roguish grin.

'Hmm, I thought as much. And when's the last time you had a holiday?'

'You're doing an examination, is it, Doctor?'

'Tell me, Chubby. When was the last time you had even one day off?'

'I've no time for meter down, Shubho-dada,' he said. 'People look to me for help. Who else they can turn to? The cops? When the Director General, Central Reserve Force is getting his journalist lover stabbed and throttled to death? Do you know in NOIDA where gangsters are nightly holding up commuters with country-made weapons, the constabulary's phones are cut off through non-payment of bills? They're not even having petrol for their vehicles!'

'I know how bad it is, Chubby. Believe me. Only yesterday, Rajesh Uncle's house was broken into and they gagged and bound Sarita Auntie.'

'By God,' intoned Puri.

'Point is, it's not your responsibility. You're no caped crusader. This isn't Gotham City. It's Delhi. You can't clean it up single-handed.'

'Someone's got to bloody well do something,' said Puri, raising his voice. 'Papa worked every day of his life to build a better India. I owe it to him to — '

'Your Papa was a good man, we all know that,' interrupted Dr Ghosh. 'No one with a shred of decency could ever doubt it. Never mind the whispers. Let them be damned! But it's not your responsibility to make amends for what happened. You've got to think of your own health and well-being. Let's face it, you're not getting any younger. Or slimmer! Think of Rumpi? She needs you, too.'

The doctor's assistant brought in their tea on a tray and left it on the desk. Puri took his cup while Dr Ghosh went behind his desk, opened the drawer and took out an already open packet of milk chocolate McVities digestives imported from the UK.

'I shouldn't give you these, but you'll only accuse me of being tight,' he said, handing Puri the packet. 'There's only a few left anyway.'

'I'm sure you're having more stashed away there somewhere,' chided the detective.

'Could be,' said Dr Ghosh with a wink.

They both bit into their biscuits and sipped their tea. By now the doctor was sitting behind his desk. On the wall hung his medical degree from the All India Institute of Medical Sciences.

'So, Chubby, I take it this is one of your professional visits. What is it this time? You need to consult me on some poison? Or you've got another crushed skull to show me?'

'Actually it's about one of your patients,' said Puri.

'Oh?'

'Don't worry, Shubho-dada, I know all about your doctor confidentiality and all. No one's asking you to betray any secrets. Without naming names, I want to tell you what I know about a certain individual. If my theory is wrong just say the word.'

'Sounds fair enough, Chubby,' said Dr Ghosh.

'Your patient is male, thirty-one, a senior BPO-wallah. He's living in NOIDA in quite a fancy apartment. Has his own gym and talking toilet and all. Currently he is engaged and due to be married shortly. Quite the golfing fanatic. He is worryingly obsessed with golf, in fact.'

Dr Ghosh leaned forward on his desk, picked up a Parker pen and started doodling on his blotting paper.

Puri switched to Hindi:

'I've been studying his habits and they are extremely suggestive,' he said. 'At school he was a misfit, never had many friends and was prone to depression. Since then he has become extremely successful professionally, but he remains a private person in a way that very few Indians are. At the golf club, for example, he never uses the men's changing rooms, but comes home to shower. He never consumes alcohol, either, presumably because he needs to maintain control at all times.'

Puri paused for a moment to finish his tea and reached for another biscuit, the last in the packet.

'You've been prescribing him testosterone,' he continued. 'I'm guessing he's been taking it since his mid-teens. Given your specialisation, I would say that he has . . . well, let us call it a 'special problem' and it is something he has been keeping secret all his life.'

Puri chose his next words carefully.

'The irony is that he has nothing to hide, and that is precisely the problem,' he said.

The faintest of smiles played across Dr Ghosh's lips.

'Chubby, might I ask why you need to know?' he asked.

'I've been retained by his fiancée's family. Now that I have discovered this man's secret, I'm concerned for her future. If she's not aware of the truth, then she is being deceived and I'm obligated to tell her.'

The doctor nodded and, wetting the end of his finger, dipped it into the cluster of crumbs left in the packet and licked them off.

'It's certainly a *private* matter,' he said. 'All I can suggest is that you go and talk with the girl.'

'Fine. In that case I'll arrange an interview,' said the detective.

'Try to remember one thing, old pal,' said Dr Ghosh. 'Love can move in mysterious ways.'

The doctor stretched and looked at his watch.

'I've no more patients today. Shall we go to the Gym for a peg or two and a game of chess?'

'Think you can take me on, is it?' said Puri.

'As I recall, I won last time we played, Chubby.'

'You had me at a disadvantage.'

'How's that?'

'I was completely piss drunk.'

★ ★ ★

Later that evening, Mary and Monica returned from their evening walk to find that Sahib had come home early.

Much to their frustration, he had parked

293

himself in front of the TV; the prospect of being able to watch *Kahani Ghar Ghar Ki* now seemed remote. But Puri assured them he was only planning to watch the news headlines and that afterwards, the TV was all theirs.

Shyly, the two servant girls filed into the room and sat down on the floor at the foot of the couch, gazing up at the set in silence.

Five minutes later, the channel appeared to change (in fact Puri had pressed play on the VCR remote control) and a Hindi news report began about the Ajay Kasliwal case in Jaipur.

The pictures showed the High Court lawyer being led into court and Inspector Shekhawat telling the reporters that he could prove conclusively that the accused was guilty of killing his maidservant. The report, which was actually a number of reports Flush had edited together, cut to shots of the front of Raj Kasliwal Bhawan, then to a piece to camera by a reporter saying that the maidservant, Mary, had been taken away in Kasliwal's Sumo and dumped on the Ajmer Road. There followed more scenes from outside the court taken on the first day of the trial, including a few shots of Mrs Kasliwal. The report ended with a clip of Bobby addressing the cameras, insisting on his father's innocence.

Mary watched in wide-eyed disbelief, with her hand over her mouth as if she was suppressing a scream. When Bobby appeared, she pointed at the TV and let out a startled cry. Then her head flopped forward on to her chest and she fainted.

★ ★ ★

Mary came round to find herself lying on the blue leather couch with a cold hand towel on her forehead. Rumpi was sitting next to her; Mummy was nearby in an armchair doing some knitting.

'Are you all right, child?' asked Rumpi in a gentle, caring voice. 'Try to rest, you've had a fright.'

Mary stared up at her with dozy eyes and then took a sharp, frightened breath.

'Madam!' she exclaimed. 'I saw him!'

'You saw who?' asked Mummy.

'Him!' she said, turning away from her and burying her face in one of the purple silk cushions.

Rumpi put a gentle hand on her shoulder, saying, 'Please don't cry. Nothing is going to happen. Ask Mummy-ji, she will tell you.'

'Yes, nothing bad will happen to you now,' Puri's mother assured her, putting aside her knitting and joining Mary on the couch. 'We will look after you. Now stop your crying and sit up and have some tea. It is freshly made. Come. Sit up now.'

Mary did as she was told, rubbing her tear-stained face with the tissues that Mummy gave her.

'That's better, child,' said Rumpi, handing her a cup of tea. 'You are quite safe here. There's nothing to fear.'

After Mary had drunk half her tea, Mummy asked her again what it was that had caused her to faint.

'If you tell us then we can help you,' said Rumpi.

'Madam, I cannot say,' whispered Mary, looking frightened.

'Did it have something to do with what you were watching on television?' asked Mummy.

Mary bowed her head, staring down into her teacup. A few more tears fell into the brown milky liquid. Rumpi started stroking the back of the girl's head.

'Child, if you know anything about the case you saw on the TV, then you must tell us,' she said. 'It is very important. The man you saw, Shri Ajay Kasliwal, is accused of murdering a young maid who used to work in his house. She was called Mary — just like you. It is a serious charge. If he is convicted, Shri Kasliwal will spend the rest of his life in prison. There is even a possibility he will face the death penalty.'

Mary continued to stare down into her teacup.

'Dear me, child, this will not do,' said Mummy, firmly. 'Now you must finish your tea and tell us whether you worked for these people.'

Dutifully, Mary drained the cup and Rumpi took it from her.

'Now look at me, child,' said Mummy.

Mary's brimming eyes met those of the older lady.

'Tell me. Did you work for this family?'

The maidservant's lower lip started to tremble. 'Yes, I worked for them,' she admitted, and burst into another fit of sobbing.

When it had passed, Mummy said, 'If you are the same servant girl called Mary who worked for this family and you are alive, then Shri Kasliwal is innocent. You will have to go to Jaipur and help clear his name.'

The suggestion engendered a terrified reaction. 'No madam, I cannot go!'

Rumpi took Mary's hand in her own.

'Would you want Shri Kasliwal to go to prison for a murder he didn't commit? He is innocent.'

Mary hung her head again. 'Madam, I cannot go,' she repeated.

'You must,' said Mummy. 'It is your duty. You have no choice in the matter. The destiny of this man and his family is in your hands. But you will not have to face this alone. I will be with you.'

26

Before driving Mary and Mummy to Jaipur, Puri went to the Gymkhana Club to meet Brigadier Kapoor's grand-daughter, Tisca.

Their meeting was set for eleven o'clock in the morning, but the detective arrived a few minutes early to peruse the noticeboard in reception. The lunch menu promised 'Toad in a Hole' and 'Pinky Pudding'. Three more names had been added to the list of membership applicants. And there was a new notification signed by Col. P. V. S. Gill (Retd.), pointing out that hard shoes were to be worn in the building at all times.

RUBBER SOULS CAUSES SQUEEKING AND ANNOYANCE, it stated.

Wearing his non-squeaking shoes, which he'd changed into before entering the club, Puri made his way to the front lawn. There he ordered tea and cucumber sandwiches and sat down at the most secluded table he could find — a good twelve feet from a gaggle of aunties talking in loud voices about how much money they'd made on the stock market.

At the far end of the lawn, a mali was cutting the grass with a manual mower drawn by a buffalo.

'Uncle, I don't mean to be rude, but I don't have that much of time,' said Tisca Kapoor when she arrived, lowering herself into one of the cane chairs, which was barely wide enough to

298

accommodate her wide girth. 'Do you mind telling me what it's about?'

'Actually, my dear, I have come as a friend to discuss your proposed marriage,' said Puri.

Tisca Kapoor rolled her eyes. 'That's what I was afraid of,' she said. 'You've been asked by Brigadier dada-ji to talk some sense into me, no? Well you might as well save your breath, Uncle. Quite a number of aunties and uncles have tried before you. I love my grandpa very much and he's a national hero and all, but I've made my choice and I have my parents' blessing. That should be enough. Buss.'

'I'm asking for a few minutes of your time, only,' said the detective. 'You are quite correct. Your grandfather asked me to look into this matter and, during my investigation, I've come across certain information. This information is of a most highly delicate nature, to say the least. I'm in no doubt — no doubt at all, actually — that if your grandfather came to know what I'm now knowing, the wedding would be most certainly getting over in a jiffy. That is why I have come to you first. So, please do me the courtesy of answering a few questions. I have your best interests at heart, actually.'

'You're a private detective, is it — a kind of Indian Sherlock Holmes?' asked Tisca Kapoor.

'Sherlock Holmes was fiction, but I am very much real,' answered Puri. 'Yes, I am a private detective. The best in India actually, as many important personages will attest. They'll also tell you I am a man of great discretion.'

He poured them both some tea.

'Now, tell me how came you to know Mr Mahinder Gupta?'

Tisca Kapoor hesitated and then said with a sigh, 'We studied together — him and me.'

'At Delhi University, correct?'

'I see you've done your homework, Uncle.'

'You were sweethearts, is it?'

'Just friends, actually.'

'And then?'

'I stayed in Delhi; he went to Dubai. But we kept in touch. Last year he moved back to Delhi and we started spending time together. In August, we decided why not go the marriage way.'

'You've not considered marrying before?'

'There've not been a lot of takers — not with my weight and all,' she admitted.

'Why him all of a sudden?'

Tisca Kapoor smiled. 'We've always got along, actually.'

'So it's a love marriage, is it?'

'Certainly I love him, yes.'

'And he loves you, my dear?'

Tisca Kapoor hesitated again. 'I believe so,' she answered. 'Certainly he's very devoted and kind.'

Puri drank half a cup of tea, stuffed a cucumber sandwich into his mouth and chewed.

'So I take it you won't be wanting a family,' he said, his mouth half full.

'Why do you say that, Uncle?' she asked cautiously.

'You must be knowing about his problem.'

'Problem? What problem? I don't know of any problem.'

'It will do you little good to pretend, my dear,'

300

he said. 'My investigation has been most thorough. I know *everything*. My only concern is you are not being deceived. If Mahinder Gupta has been one hundred per cent honest, then that is your business. Certainly, I would keep his secret safe from your grandfather.'

She said nothing in response. Her expression betrayed both alarm and helplessness.

'It's my guess you've known what he is for many years. Perhaps he confided to you at university. Or you discovered it by chance,' prompted Puri.

There was a long silence and then Tisca Kapoor said in a quiet voice:

'It was at university. Everyone else teased me about my weight. None of the other boys gave me a second look. But Mahinder was always kind to me. We used to talk for hours and hours. About everything under the sun. I suppose I fell in love with him. One day I told him how I felt, but he ran from my room and after that he didn't talk to me for two weeks. Then, one day, he came to see me and told me that we could never be together. That was when he revealed his secret.' She lowered her voice. 'That was when he told me he was born a eunuch.'

Tisca Kapoor's throat had gone dry and so Puri poured her a glass of water.

'You mustn't be embarrassed, my dear,' he said. 'In my profession I'm often called upon to put aside the detective and become the psychologist. There is little I have not heard.'

Tisca Kapoor sipped the water gratefully and nodded.

'Understand, Uncle, this is something I've never told another living soul. Mahinder made me promise. He said his parents had hidden the truth from the world at his birth. Otherwise the hijras would have come and claimed him.'

'They were right to do so,' interjected Puri: 'They would most certainly have taken him.'

'That is why all through his childhood they kept it a secret. But also, had anyone at school ever found out, he would have been the laughing stock. That is why Mahinder has always been an extremely private person. He's kept himself to himself. But he's very sweet, I can assure you.'

'So now all these years later you're getting married. Is it only for convenience sake?' asked Puri.

'I've always loved Mahinder,' she said. 'But, yes, partly it is for convenience. There's so much pressure to marry, Uncle. My mother has been after me for so long! Now at least she'll be off my back!'

'She'll be after you for grandchildren next,' said Puri. 'What will you do?'

'We'll adopt,' she answered. 'One girl and one boy.'

'It's all decided, is it?' asked Puri

'We have it all planned out.'

The detective nodded knowingly. 'Well, it's as I suspected. Just I wanted to check you weren't being taken advantage of.'

'So you won't tell anyone?'

'My dear, you can trust me on that score. Confidentiality is my watchword, actually,' said Puri with not a little bravado.

Tisca Kapoor, soon to be Gupta, sighed with relief. 'You're too kind, Uncle. I can't thank you enough.'

The detective beamed with pride. 'No need for thank you, my dear. I'm only doing my duty.'

They walked back through reception and Puri saw her to her car. 'What will you tell my grandfather?' Tisca Kapoor asked before driving away.

'I'll tell him you're betrothed to a good man,' answered Puri, but it was not a conversation he was looking forward to.

27

Puri's Hindustan Ambassador reached the Jaipur courthouse at a quarter to five the following afternoon.

It was the first day of the Ajay Kasliwal 'Maidservant Murder' trial and the proceedings had been under way for a couple of hours.

Outside the main entrance, the media had gathered in full force. Six uplink trucks were parked on the pavement, their satellite dishes emblazoned with the logos of the nation's English and Hindi 24-hour news channels. Eager, earnest reporters posed in front of cameras mounted on tripods relaying live developments to tens of millions of potential viewers spread across the three million square kilometres that separated Kashmir from Kanyakumari. Photographers in sleeveless khaki jackets sat bent over their WiFi-enabled laptops transmitting the images they had captured an hour earlier of Kasliwal being led into court. Meanwhile a clutch of grizzled hacks milled around the chai stand, smoking laboriously, swapping disinformation and falling prey to their own self-deluding Chinese whispers.

Had any of them but known the identity of the shy, frightened young Jharkhandi woman who passed within a few feet of them, they would have surrounded her in much the same way Indian crows will ring and taunt a street cat if they spot it out in the open.

But the press-wallahs' scoop passed up the steps of the courthouse undetected.

Once inside, Puri led Mummy, who in turn was holding Mary by the hand, down the busy corridors until they reached the door of Court 6.

Already a crowd was waiting outside, all of them jostling for position and trying to cajole the peon on the door to let them in despite the sign that stated boldly, HOUSE FULL.

For once, Puri's powers of persuasion failed. The peon would not budge. 'Naat possi-bal,' he kept saying.

Mummy scolded her son for his failure.

'That's no way to go about things, Chubby,' she said after he had been rebuffed for the third time. 'How a son of mine ended up with cotton wool in his brain, I ask you? Evidently, a woman's touch is required, na. I will take care of it.'

Puri bristled. He had had grave misgivings about bringing along Mummy. But he had been left with no choice. Mary needed a chaperon and Rumpi needed to be at home to oversee the preparations for Diwali.

'Mummy-ji, please. I told you, don't do interference. I will sort it out,' Puri insisted.

'Chubby when you'll accept you don't have power over everything, na? A helping hand is required from time to time.'

Mummy's words echoed those spoken to Puri by Chanakya in the dream he'd had in his office two days earlier; for once, he was dumbfounded.

'What did you say, Mummy-ji?' he asked her.

She tutted impatiently. 'It's time to put away your pride, Chubby. I'm your Mummy after all. I've your best intentions at heart. Right now, a woman's touch is required. Now, you two go and sit. *Jao!*'

For once, Puri did as he was told and took a seat with Mary on a bench a few feet down the corridor.

With all the noise created by so many people coming and going from the courtrooms, Puri was unable to make out what Mummy said to the peon on the door. But gradually the man's demeanour softened and then tears welled up in his eyes.

Finally he signalled to the detective that he could enter the court after all.

'What all you said to him?' asked Puri.

'No time for explanations, na,' she answered. 'Let us say mummies have their uses after all. Now go quickly. Might be he's changing his mind. So corrupt these people are. We'll wait right here.'

Inside the courtroom, the gallery was packed with spectators, all of them sitting in silent, rapt attention to the cross-examination of Inspector Shekhawat by the defence counsel, Mr K. P. Malhotra, who was living up to his reputation as a fearsome advocate.

'Inspector, you say you found bloodstains in the accused's Tata Sumo,' he was saying. 'But I put it to you that this blood could have come from anyone. Another passenger with a bleeding nose, perhaps.'

'There is no doubt in my mind that the blood

306

belonged to the victim,' answered Shekhawat.

'Surely it is the responsibility of the police to offer proofs, is it not? Two and two should always equal four. Is that not correct, Inspector Shekhawat?'

'I can provide three witnesses who saw Ajay Kasliwal pull up in his Sumo and dump the servant girl's body on the Ajmer Road,' he answered.

'We will come to that in a moment,' said Malhotra. 'But let us first consider these bloodstains. I put it to you . . . '

Malhotra lost his train of thought as he read the note Puri had managed to pass to him.

'Mr Malhotra?' prompted the judge. 'Are you with us?'

'My apologies, Your Honour,' answered the lawyer, looking up from the note with a bewildered expression. 'I have just been informed of what could well be an extremely dramatic breakthrough in my client's defence. Might I take a moment of the court's time to confer with one of my associates?'

'This is highly irregular, Mr Malhotra, but I will grant you sixty seconds.'

'Thank you, Your Honour.'

Lawyer and detective exchanged a few quiet words and then Malhotra continued with his cross-examination, taking it in a new direction.

'Inspector Shekhawat, how can you be so sure that the Kasliwal family's maidservant, Mary, and the body found on the Ajmer Road are one and the same?' he asked.

'Two of her co-workers identified the victim

from a photograph taken by the mortuary photographer. Three part-time employees at the house did the same.'

'And if Mary was alive today — let us imagine she walked in here right now, for example — those same witnesses you mentioned would be able to identify her?'

Inspector Shekhawat replied confidently with an arrogant smirk. 'Without doubt.'

'I have no further questions for this witness,' said Malhotra. 'But I reserve the right to recall him.'

Shekhawat was excused.

'Your Honour, I would like to call a new witness who, I feel confident, could save a great deal of the court's time,' said Malhotra as the inspector resumed his seat in the gallery to watch the rest of the proceedings.

'It is tea time,' grumbled the judge.

'Your Honour, if you will allow me five minutes I believe we can clear up this whole matter.'

The judge gave his consent.

'The defence calls Mary Murmu,' announced Malhotra loudly.

'Who is Mary Murmu exactly?' asked the judge.

'Mary Murmu is the alleged victim, sir, the Kasliwal family's former maidservant,' replied the lawyer nonchalantly.

Malhotra's answer elicited a collective gasp. Every head in the court turned to look at the main door.

In the dock, Ajay Kasliwal stood on his toes

and craned his neck to see above the sea of heads.

The door opened again and Mary stepped through it, her head covered by her *pallu* and eyes cast down, with Mummy by her side. Together they walked slowly through the gallery until they reached the bench and the former maidservant was escorted to the witness stand.

'State your name for the record,' she was told by Judge Madan in Hindi as Mummy took a seat nearby.

Mary mumbled a response.

'Speak up, girl, and show your face!' he ordered.

She stated her name again and pulled back her pallu.

'My name is Mary Murmu,' she said clearly for all the court to hear.

'Liar!' screeched a woman's voice in the gallery.

Mrs Kasliwal was standing, pointing an accusing finger at the witness.

'That's not her!' she screamed. And then she fainted and fell to the floor.

The courtroom descended into bedlam.

28

Facecream was crouched behind a shrub in the back garden of Raj Kasliwal Bhawan. It was nearly eight o'clock and pitch dark. She had been there for over an hour keeping watch at the rear of the house in accordance with Puri's orders — delivered by Tubelight when the Kasliwals were still in court.

'Boss will arrive around eight,' he'd explained. 'Munnalal's murderer is still at large. He might try to take out Boss. So, be on your guard.'

Facecream's position to the right of the servant quarters provided a commanding view of the garden and the interior of the sitting room. The curtains had not been drawn, which was unusual. But then, today was proving to be anything but routine.

At breakfast, Madam had been in an uncommonly pleasant and buoyant mood, talking confidently on the phone about how Mr Malhotra was going to make short work of Shekhawat's case.

'It will soon be over,' Facecream had overheard her tell someone.

But at around 6.30 in the evening, when her freed husband had brought her back from the courts, Mrs Kasliwal had been completely hysterical.

'Vish Puri will ruin us all!' she'd screamed. 'Don't let him into the house!'

Shortly afterwards, the family doctor had arrived and given Madam a sedative that had put her to sleep. His patient was not to be disturbed, he'd insisted. The arrest and trial had exhausted her.

In accordance with the doctor's instructions, Ajay Kasliwal had excused all the servants from their duties for the evening — apart from Jaya who'd been told to make sure there was a ready supply of cold hand towels to cool Madam's forehead and ice for Sahib's whisky.

Facecream could see Jaya through the kitchen window now; she was taking something out of the fridge.

The other servants were all accounted for. Bablu had gone home. Kamat was in town watching a film. And the mali was stoned in his room, tendrils of sweet smoke drifting out of his open window.

Boss should be arriving any minute now, Facecream told herself.

If Munnalal's killer did make a play for him, he was likely to approach through the back way. But she was ready. Before taking up her position, she had checked her trip thread and it was still taut.

No one else had passed through the gap in the wall since Facecream had laid her trap and she was beginning to wonder if she would ever know the identity of the person who had tried her door that first night.

'Backside clear, over,' she whispered into the mini transmitter Tubelight had smuggled into the grounds earlier along with the earpiece receiver.

'Frontside clear, also — over,' responded Tubelight, who was loitering on the main road in front of the entrance to Raj Kasliwal Bhavan.

* * *

Puri's Ambassador pulled into the driveway at 8.10. Tyres crunched on gravel as the vehicle came to a halt.

'Boss has made penetration, over,' reported Tubelight.

The detective stepped up to the front door and paused to take a deep breath.

Rarely had he found himself in such an unenviable position.

True, he had accomplished what he had been hired to do: against all the odds, he had managed to track down the missing servant and ensure that the spurious, half-baked charges against Ajay Kasliwal had been dropped. By any standard, it had been a brilliant piece of detective work — one that would rank in Puri's self-congratulating oratory in the years ahead.

But a great injustice had been done — not to mention a gruesome, premeditated murder — and Puri could not see it go unpunished no matter how devastating the truth might prove for his client.

The detective patted the outside pocket of his jacket, reassured by the feeling of his trusty .32 IOF pistol, and pulled the bell chain.

Footsteps clipped and echoed down the corridor inside the house. A lock was unlatched. The door opened and Ajay Kasliwal's face appeared in the gap.

'Puri-ji! Thank God you're here!' said the lawyer.

'How is she?' asked Puri.

'Sedated. The doctor's with her now. He says she's suffered some kind of mental breakdown. He's recommending she be kept here overnight and taken to his clinic in the morning for testing. She's been saying the craziest things, Puri-ji. Like you're out to ruin the family.'

'I'm sorry it's come to this, sir,' said the detective. 'But I had to produce Mary in court. It was the only way.'

'I don't understand. Why did my wife insist it wasn't her?'

'I'll need to explain a few things,' answered Puri. 'But first thing is first. Something more urgent is there. Bobby has — '

'Yes, where is Bobby?' demanded Kasliwal, interjecting. 'He was at the courthouse, but disappeared. I couldn't find him anywhere and had to bring home his mother on my own. The media nearly ate us alive!'

'Sir, Bobby tried to — '

The detective's words were swallowed up by the sound of a vehicle tearing into the driveway and braking hard behind the Ambassador. It was a police Jeep. Inspector Shekhawat stepped out of it and opened one of the back doors. Bobby emerged into the light cast from the veranda.

'What's this?' exclaimed Kasliwal as the inspector led his handcuffed son to the door. 'Bobby, are you all right? What's happened? Puri-ji, for God's sake explain!'

'He was caught trying to enter Mary's room at the hotel where Mr Puri and Mary are staying,' butted in Shekhawat, officiously. 'I was going to take him down to the station for questioning. But given Mr Puri's co-operation in the past few hours, I agreed to do as the detective asked and bring him here first.'

'Those handcuffs aren't necessary,' said Puri. 'He's not going to abscond.'

The police-wallah appraised the prisoner like a fisherman trying to decide whether or not to put his young catch back into the river.

'I suppose you're right,' he said, although he didn't sound convinced. 'But I'm only willing to play along a little longer, Mr Puri. I want to know what's been going on here. If I don't get some answers soon, then we'll do things my way.'

Shekhawat unlocked the cuffs and Ajay Kasliwal ushered the party down the corridor.

Entering the sitting room, they found Mrs Kasliwal lying deeply sedated on the couch wrapped in a blanket. Her doctor, a man in his fifties with salt and pepper hair, was sitting at her side monitoring her pulse. At the sight of them, he made an irritated gesture.

'What's this, Ajay-ji?' he hissed, standing up. 'I said no visitors. She's not to be disturbed.'

Walking around the couch, he addressed Puri and Shekhawat directly.

'You must leave immediately! She's extremely sick. Ajay-ji, I don't know who these gentlemen are . . . '

'I'm Inspector Rajendra Singh Shekhawat,' said the inspector, flashing his badge. 'And this is

Vish Puri, a private detective. Who are you exactly?'

'I'm Dr Chandran, Mrs Kasliwal's personal physician,' he answered, haughtily.

'Dr Sunil Chandran, is it?' asked Puri.

'Yes, that's right.'

'I understand you are Madam Kasliwal's *rakhi-brother*. Is that so?'

'Yes, we grew up together. We're like brother and sister. Now what's all this about?'

'There's been a murder and we're here to find out who did it,' Shekhawat answered.

'Well, now's not the time. She's had a mental breakdown. You'll have to come back another time.'

'I'm afraid it won't wait,' said Puri. 'Why don't you pour yourself a drink, Doctor-sahib, and sit down? I'm glad to see you, actually. You've saved us time in coming here.'

'But I'm finished for the time being.'

'You're *finished*, that is for sure, Doctor-ji,' said Puri, sternly. 'Now sit down.'

'I'll do nothing of the sort!' shouted the doctor. 'Ajay-ji, I'm leaving. Take Savitri's temperature every hour and let me know of any change. You'll be able to reach me on my mobile.'

Dr Chandran gathered up his stethoscope and bag and made for the door. But he found his exit blocked by Shekhawat who had one hand on the revolver peeking out of his shoulder holster.

'Do as Mr Puri says, Doctor-sahib,' said the inspector, his muscular jaw rigid with determination.

315

Puri positioned himself by the fireplace. Bobby knelt next to his mother, a mixture of anger and anxiety clouding his young face. His father stood expectantly, looking at the detective for answers. The doctor was sitting involuntarily in one of the armchairs with his arms crossed in defiance. The inspector guarded the door.

'The case has been a complicated one and required all my skills as a detective, but fortunately I was up to the task,' began Puri.

Shekhawat rolled his eyes and looked at his watch.

'Mr Puri, please, I don't have all night,' he interrupted impatiently. 'Who killed Munnalal?'

The detective bristled at the younger man's impertinence. If there was one thing he couldn't stand, it was having people butt in while he was trying to conclude a case. This was his moment and he would not be rushed.

'During my many years of service and duty I have learned not to share information about ongoing cases with my clients,' he went on. 'Often it is important they remain in the dark. This gives the impression that I am sitting idle. In reality, nothing could be further from the truth. Vish Puri does not do meter down. Thus on the very day Munnalal met his fate, I went to his residence.'

Puri paused to clear his throat.

'An extremely unpleasant and most slippery fellow he was all round,' continued the detective. 'There and then, I confronted him with certain evidence. Namely, I told him I knew it was he who carried Mary's body from her room and placed it in the back of Kasliwal-ji's Sumo on August 21st night.'

'Mr Puri, please,' said Bobby, suddenly snapping out of his reverie. 'What's this about Mary's body?'

'Allow me to explain. The maidservant, Jaya, saw Munnalal carrying Mary from her room to your father's vehicle and placing her inside. At the time, she assumed he had murdered her. Terrified, she told no one.'

'But what happened to Mary?' asked Bobby.

'This same question I put to Munnalal. He did not deny taking her away. But he denied totally murdering the girl. He said she attempted the suicide, only. Afterwards he drove her to the Sunrise Clinic.'

At the mention of the clinic's name, Bobby and his father both turned and stared hard at Dr Chandran: 'That's your place, Doctor-sahib,' said the elder Kasliwal.

'I'm well aware of that,' replied the doctor. 'But I don't remember any girl. Clearly, this Munnalal was lying. The detective himself called him a 'slippery fellow'.'

'Munnalal was a first-class Charlie, that is for sure,' said Puri. 'But for once, he was not lying. Your night security guard remembers Mary most clearly, Doctor-sahib. He says after her admittance, you returned to the clinic. Must have been around midnight. Thus it seems you cared for her yourself.'

'I've no idea what you're talking about,' said

the doctor dismissively.

'Then why is it, the following night, you took Mary by taxi to the train station?' asked Puri. 'Knowing full well she was too weak to make the journey and might easily die along the way, you bought her a ticket on a local train to Ranchi. A coolie identified you at the scene.'

By now Bobby was glaring at Dr Chandran contemptuously. 'Uncle, is . . . is this true?' he asked him.

'Not one word of it, beta. Don't listen to him. He's trying to blacken the family name, divide and conquer like the British.'

'He's doing nothing of the sort,' snapped Kasliwal. 'But what I don't understand is how a maidservant tried killing herself in my own home and I knew nothing about it?'

'Sir, you are never around. Your work keeps you at the office, and at night you are out a good deal. You're a very *sociable* individual, we can say. Running of the house, with servants and all, is Madam's responsibility. Thus the facts were kept secret from you.'

'But to continue,' added Puri, urgently, before anyone else could get a word in, 'after dropping Mary at Sunrise Clinic, Munnalal returned here to Raj Kasliwal Bhavan. In the wee hours, Mary's blood was washed away and her possessions taken. The kitchen knife she used Munnalal threw over the back wall from where it was recovered and is now in my possession. Only things left behind were two wall posters and a few stones.'

Puri modestly revealed his foresight in having

318

Mary's stones analysed and how they had led him to Jadugoda. But his client was not interested in the deductive process, only the results.

'What about Munnalal? Why was he murdered?' he asked.

'Just I was coming to that, sir. You see he was an instrument only. Some other person did direction of his actions. When he found Mary bleeding to death in her room, he called that person to ask what to do. Thus he was ordered to rush the girl to hospital. But along the way Munnalal got thinking. For him, Mary's suicide attempt was a golden egg. Such a man knows many secrets. He stores gossip for rainy days. Thus he understood why Mary tried the suicide and why it had to be hushed up. Next day, he demanded compensation to the tune of many lakhs.'

'But that can only mean . . . ' said Kasliwal.

Bobby finished his sentence in a flat monotone: 'Ma. It had to be Ma.'

There was a long silence. Every pair of eyes in the room save Mrs Kasliwal's were now riveted on the detective.

'The boy is correct: it was your wife, sir,' said Puri. 'She told Munnalal to take Mary to the Sunrise Clinic and asked her rakhi-brother, Dr Chandran, to patch her up and send her on her way.'

'Puri-ji, I've been married to this woman for twenty-nine years and I can't believe she'd do that.' Turning to Dr Chandran, he implored him: 'Doctor-sahib, tell me this isn't true!'

'I tell you Ajay-ji every word is a filthy lie,' sneered the doctor. 'We should call Mr Malhotra and ask him to come here immediat — '

'Dr Chandran, your mobile phone records show you made four calls to Mrs Kasliwal on the night Munnalal was murdered,' interrupted Puri. 'One was twenty-five minutes after he was killed.'

'We've always talked a lot. She was having trouble sleeping and — '

'Oh, shut up!' broke in Ajay Kasliwal. 'I want to hear the rest. Carry on, Puri-ji; tell us what happened.'

The detective went on to explain that, minutes after his meeting with Munnalal, the former driver had called Mrs Kasliwal. He'd asked for more money to buy Puri's silence. She in turn had asked him to come to the house after dark. That evening, he'd set off by auto. Following behind on his motorcycle was Bobby, who wanted to ask Munnalal if he knew of Mary's whereabouts.

'Bobby followed him all the way into the empty property behind the house only moments after Munnalal was murdered,' said Puri. 'Stumbling upon the body in the dark, he got blood on him and ran from the scene. Shocked and totally confused, Bobby passed the time since mostly in his room. Must be he was asking himself many unanswered questions about what all happened to Mary and why someone killed Munnalal. Also he was scared he'd get accused of doing the murder. But he was never Vish Puri's suspect.'

'Well if it wasn't Bobby who murdered Munnalal, who was it?' demanded Shekhawat.

'From the wound I could make out it was a professional. He surprised Munnalal from behind. One hand drove the knife into the neck, the other was placed over the mouth — hence there was so much of betel juice on Munnalal's lips and chin. Must be you came to the same conclusion, Inspector?'

'Yes, of course,' lied Shekhawat, shifting uneasily. 'It was obvious. But you assured me earlier today you knew the identity of the killer!'

'Most certainly I know, Inspector,' said Puri. 'He is one hit man called Babua.'

Bobby piped up: 'But Mr Puri, are you saying Ma . . . she had . . . she had Munnalal . . . *murdered* . . . ?'

'It is hard to believe she could not have known. But there's no conclusive evidence connecting her to Babua. Dr Chandran took out the contract. He made a number of calls to the killer in the hours before the murder.'

'How do you know that?' asked Shekhawat.

Puri hesitated before answering. 'We all have our ways and means, Inspector.'

'But for God's sake, why?' broke in Kasliwal. He was gripping the back of the couch where his wife lay. 'Why, Puri-ji? None of this makes any sense!'

'Unfortunately, it makes perfect sense, sir,' answered the detective calmly. 'An Indian mother will do almost anything to protect her son and his reputation.'

There was another long silence. And then

321

Bobby broke into deep, shameful sobs.

'Papa I . . . I should have told you,' he said. 'But I . . . I didn't know what had happened. I . . . I never meant . . . for *any* of this . . . '

'*What* happened, Bobby? I want to hear it from you. Tell me once and for all,' said Kasliwal, now standing over his son.

'Papa I . . . '

'Out with it!'

The boy swallowed hard.

'It was this summer, before . . . before I went to London. Most days I . . . I was here alone in the house studying . . . and Mary . . . well, you see, Papa, sometimes we'd, um, talk. She was . . . so . . . so *nice*, Papa. And *smart*. We used to sit together . . . in my room. I . . . I was teaching her to read and write and we used to play Bagha-Chall. She always beat me.' Bobby's lower lip was trembling. 'Well, one day . . . you see . . . I loved her, Papa . . . '

Ajay Kasliwal held up a hand to silence his son.

'I understand,' he said. He turned and addressed the detective. 'I take it my wife found out, Puri-ji.'

'About a month after Bobby left for London, Mary discovered she was pregnant,' said Puri.

'Pregnant?' exclaimed Bobby.

'Desperate, she went to Madam. But the idea of a servant — a dirty tribal — being with her son disgusted her. She abused Mary verbally, threatened her and ordered her to leave the house immediately.'

' . . . And so that poor girl took a knife from

322

the kitchen, went to her room and cut her wrists,' murmured Ajay Kasliwal.

★ ★ ★

Facecream watched the evening's events unfold through the French windows of the sitting room.

First Boss appeared with Inspector Shekhawat and Bobby. Then, Boss gave one of those long-winded soliloquies he so enjoyed. And finally, Ajay Kasliwal broke down in tears and attacked the doctor, punching him in the face.

Bobby, Shekhawat and Boss tried to restrain him and in the confusion, the latter was knocked over.

Now, Facecream watched as the inspector clapped a pair of handcuffs on the doctor and led him away.

Puri came and stood silhouetted by the French windows, nursing his bruised cheek, while Bobby sat with his distraught father.

Facecream decided to stay put. Munnalal's murderer was still at large, after all.

Another five minutes passed. Jaya appeared again in the kitchen, standing at the sink, her face framed in the window. Suddenly in the quiet night, Facecream heard the sound of the bell tinkle inside her room.

Someone had come through the gap in the wall.

A twig snapped underfoot. And then a man of average height appeared round the corner of the servant quarters carrying something long and narrow in one hand. He stopped, looked furtively from left to right, and then set off across the garden, sticking to the shadows on the left side of the lawn.

Facecream sprang forward and raced after him, her bare feet moving nimbly and silently over the grass.

She covered the distance that separated the two of them in just a few seconds and tackled the man from behind. He went down flat on his face and, in a flash, she pinned him to the ground, pulling back one of his arms.

The intruder let out a cry of agony and begged to be let go. His pleas brought Jaya running from the kitchen.

'Seema, what are you doing?' she cried. 'Have you gone mad? Let him go!'

'No, Jaya, stand back!' insisted Facecream. 'This man is dangerous! He killed Munnalal!'

'Dangerous? That's Dubey! He's a rickshaw-wallah! He's my — friend.'

'You're sure?'

'Of course I'm sure! He wants to marry me.'

Facecream released Dubey and the poor, shaken man stood up. He was still clutching a red rose that he'd brought for Jaya, but it had been badly crushed.

'I'm so sorry. I thought you were . . .' said Facecream.

But the rickshaw-wallah had taken to his heels with Jaya hurrying after him.

★ ★ ★

Ten minutes later, Puri stood with Shekhawat next to his Jeep in the driveway. On the back

324

seat, in handcuffs, sat Dr Chandran. He was glaring with venomous eyes at his captors through the window.

'You think he'll give her up?' asked the inspector.

'I doubt it,' said Puri. 'To do so would be to admit his guilt. He'll claim he's been framed, try to buy off or intimidate the witnesses. His trial will go on for years. It takes time to put away a man with his kind of connections.'

'And her? She goes unpunished?'

'Oh no, Inspector. It is all over for her. She might have escaped prison, but no human being ever escapes punishment. One way or another, justice is always served. All of us must answer to the God eventually.'

Puri rubbed his stomach and grimaced.

'Personally I'm now answering for the *kachoris* I ate at lunch,' he added with a smile.

Shekhawat remained stony-faced and aloof. His pride was badly wounded. And he was not about to admit his mistakes — not here and now, and certainly not in his official report.

'Well, I'll be going,' he said. 'There's the killer Babua to track down and I've got a good idea where to find him.'

'Oh there's no need, Inspector,' said Puri, airily. 'Didn't I tell you, I've got him locked in the boot of my Ambassador?'

For once, Shekhawat was visibly dumbstruck.

'There?' he asked, pointing to the car, his eyebrows knitted together.

'That's right, Inspector. One advantage with Ambassadors is they have large secure boots.'

'But . . . ?'

'I picked him up this afternoon after tracing his mobile phone. Let me show you.'

They walked over to the car and Handbrake opened the back. Inside lay a burly man, bound and gagged, his eyes defiant and angry.

'Allow me to present one Om Prakash, alias Babua,' said Puri, triumphantly. 'A right bloody goonda if ever there was one.'

29

At the end of every big case, Puri dictated all the details of his investigation to his personal secretary, Elizabeth Rani, who could do fast typing.

He did so for two reasons.

Firstly, it was not uncommon for trials to drag on for years, sometimes decades. So it was imperative to keep a detailed record of events, which the detective could refer to when he was called upon to give evidence.

And secondly, Puri was planning to leave all his files to the National Archive because he was certain future generations of detectives would want to study his methods and achievements.

The detective also liked to entertain the idea that some day a writer would come along who would want to pen his biography. He had thought of the perfect title: CONFIDENTIALITY IS MY WATCHWORD. And what a spectacular Bollywood film it would make. Puri's favourite actor, Anupam Kher, would play the lead and Rekha would be perfect for the part of Rumpi. Her screen persona would be that of a good, homely woman who also happened to be a talented and alluring exotic dancer.

'Sir, one thing I don't understand,' said Elizabeth Rani after Puri had finished relating the twists and turns in The Case of the Missing Servant. 'Who was the dead girl found on the Ajmer Road?'

Puri's secretary always asked such elementary questions. But he didn't mind spelling it out for her. Not everyone could have a mind as sharp as his, he reasoned.

'She's just one of dozens upon dozens of personages who go missing across India every year,' he explained. 'No doubt we'll never know her name. So many girls are leaving the villages and travelling to cities these days. And so many are never returning. Just they're turning up dead on railway tracks, in canals, and getting raped and dumped from vehicles. With their near and dear so far away, no one is there to identify the bodies. I tell you, frankly speaking Madam Rani, it is an epidemic of growing proportions.'

Elizabeth Rani moved her head from side to side mournfully.

'Such a sad state of affairs, sir,' she said. 'Thank the God there are gentlemen such as yourself to protect us.'

'Most kind of you, Madam Rani!' beamed Puri.

The two of them were sitting in the detective's office: he behind his desk; she in front of it with a laptop computer. Elizabeth Rani saved the document in which she had typed his dictation and closed the screen.

'Sir, one other thing,' she said as she stood from her chair to leave.

'Yes, Madam Rani,' said Puri, who had been expecting more questions.

'You said Mary got pregnant, sir. But what happened to the baby?'

'Sadly she lost it on the train to Ranchi.'

'That poor girl,' commiserated Elizabeth Rani. 'How she has suffered. Is there any hope for her and Bobby?'

'Sadly, there is no Bollywood ending. Mary refused to see him. Most likely, it is for the best. Too much hurt is there, actually. The poor girl has gone through hell. This morning we brought her to Delhi, Rumpi and I. We've made arrangements for her to start work with Vikas Chauhan's family. Ajay Kasliwal has also promised to pay for her dowry so she might one day go the marriage way. He's being most generous and appreciative, I must say.'

'And Bobby, sir?'

The detective rubbed the end of his moustache between his fingers in a contemplative fashion before answering.

'Seems like he and his mother will never speak again, Madam Rani,' said Puri sadly. 'He's sworn he'll not so much as be in the same room with the woman.'

His secretary sucked in her breath and said, '*Hai, hai*.'

'Mrs Kasliwal's actions were certainly deplorable. Which one of us could forgive her in our hearts?' continued Puri. 'But Bobby's actions, although innocent, were hardly decent. Such a well brought up and educated young man should have known better, actually. There is a right and proper place for physical relations and it is between husband and wife only. When young people go straying outside those boundaries, there can only be hurt and misfortune.'

'Quite right, sir,' said Elizabeth Rani.

Puri tucked a pen he'd been using into the outside pocket of his safari suit next to the three others.

'India is modernising, Madam Rani, but we must keep our family values, isn't it? Without them, where would we be?'

'I hate to think, sir,' she said.

'Well, Madam Rani, that will do for now. Place the file in the 'conclusively solved' cabinet. Another successful outcome for Most Private Investigators, no?'

'Right away, sir. And what about this other file?' She held up the binder to show him. 'The most recent attempt on your life? The shooting?'

Puri thought for a moment. He had no leads; none of his contacts or informants had anything new to go on. But the words of his guru came back to him: 'Do not fear, Vish Puri. You will receive the help you need.'

'Mark it as 'ongoing',' he answered. 'One day I'm sure I'll come to know the truth. Like everything else, it will surely come out in the wash.'

Elizabeth Rani returned to her desk, closing the door to his office behind her.

Puri leaned back in his chair and looked up at the portraits of Chanakya and his father on the wall, both of them wreathed in garlands of fresh marigolds. Putting the palms of his hands and fingers together, he respectfully acknowledged them both with a namaste.

★ ★ ★

With Diwali, the festival of lights, the biggest holiday in the Hindu calendar, due to begin the next day, Puri gave his staff the afternoon off and asked Handbrake to drive him to the airport to pick up his youngest daughter, Radhika.

He could hardly contain his excitement as he waited outside the arrivals hall. It had been three months since he'd seen his chowti baby, the longest they'd ever been separated. He'd missed her sorely.

As the other passengers emerged from the building pushing trolleys piled high with baggage, and taxi-wallahs vied for their custom, the detective stood up on his toes, trying to peer over the heads of the crowd gathered around the exit.

When he finally spotted Radhika, her young, eager face searching for his amongst the banks of strangers, he felt a lump form in his throat and cried out his nickname for her:

'Bulbul! Bulbul!'

'Hi, Papa!'

Grinning from ear to ear, she skipped forward, flung her arms around him and gave him a kiss and a big hug.

'By God, let me look at you,' he said, holding her by the shoulders and giving her a fond, appraising look. 'So thin you've become, huh! They're not feeding you at that college or what? Come! Mama's making all your favourites and she can't wait to see you. Mummy-ji's at home, also. Both your sisters are arriving tomorrow.'

He took hold of her trolley and they headed into the car park to find Handbrake and the Ambassador.

'So, all OK?' he asked.

And from that moment until they reached the house, Radhika regaled him with everything that had happened to her in the past few months.

'Papa, you know we've been learning . . . '

'Papa, you'll never guess what my roommate Shikha said . . . '

'Papa, something amazing happened . . . '

'Papa, did you know that . . . '

Puri sat basking in her youthful enthusiasm and innocence, succumbing to her infectious laughter. Occasionally, he reacted to her anecdotes by saying things like: 'Is it?' and 'Don't tell me!' and 'Wonderful!' But for the most part, he just sat and listened.

By the time they pulled up in front of the gates and Handbrake honked the horn, he felt the weight he'd been carrying on his shoulders — the weight he'd become so used to — had vanished.

⋆　⋆　⋆

Like millions of other Hindu, Sikh and Jain households across India, every inch of Puri's house had been cleaned ahead of Diwali. In the kitchen, all the cupboards had been emptied and the shelves wiped down. The marble floors had been scrubbed and scrubbed again. Dusters had swished away cobwebs. Special lemon and vinegar soap had left all the taps, sinks and mirrors gleaming. And all the wood in the house had been lovingly polished.

The exterior wall that surrounded the

compound had been whitewashed and a cracked tile on the porch replaced.

Rumpi had also been busy making preparations for entertaining all the family members and friends who were expected to visit over the next few days.

Gift boxes of dried fruit, almonds, cashews and *burfi* had been packed and wrapped, and then stacked in one corner of the kitchen. Monica and Malika had been preparing huge pots of *chhole* and carrot halva, and deep frying batches of onion and paneer pakoras. And Sweetu had been sent to the market to buy bagfuls of 'perfect ice', savoury *matthis* and oil for the *diyas*.

Puri's remit (he knew it only too well but Rumpi reminded him more than once) was to buy all the liquor, firecrackers and puja offerings — in the form of coconuts, bananas and incense — that would be made to Lakshmi, the goddess of wealth.

It was also his responsibility to pick up new decks of playing cards and some poker chips. No Punjabi Diwali could be complete without a bit of friendly gambling. And if this holiday was anything like last year, they were in for at least one all-night session of teen patta.

After dropping Radhika at home, Puri went to the nearest market. He found it packed with people rushing around buying last-minute items. The shops were decked with coloured lights and tinselly decorations. Devotional music blared from the temples. Every few seconds, bottle rockets whizzed and exploded overhead.

He returned after dark to find Rinku's Range

Rover — licence plate 1CY — parked in the driveway.

Before entering the house, Puri gave Hand-brake his Diwali bonus and enough money to get an auto to Old Delhi railway station. By mid-morning the following day, he would be home with his wife and baby daughter in their village in the hills of Himachal.

'Thank you, sir,' said the driver, beaming with happiness. 'But sir, one thing you promised me. The first rule of detection. What is it?'

Puri smiled. 'Ah yes, the first rule,' replied the detective. 'It is quite simple, actually. Always make sure you have a good *aloo parantha* for breakfast. Thinking requires a full stomach. Now you'd better be off.'

Puri saw Handbrake to the gate and made his way inside the house.

'So we've got our first visitor, is it?' he shouted as he stepped into the hallway.

He found Rumpi, Mummy and Radhika sitting with Rinku having tea and sharing platefuls of pakoras.

'Happy Diwali, Chubby!' Rinku said, greeting Puri with a hug and the usual matey slap on the back.

'You too, you bugger. Let me fix you something stronger.'

'No, no, I've got to be off,' said Rinku. 'The traffic to Punjabi Bagh will be murder.'

'Just one peg! Come on!' insisted Puri.

'OK, just one,' replied Rinku who never needed much convincing when alcohol was on offer. 'But you're going to get me into trouble.'

'Then we'll be even!'

The detective poured both Rinku and himself generous glasses of Scotch, and soon they were telling *Sardaar-ji jokes* and splitting their sides with laughter.

Forty minutes and several more pegs later, Rinku stood to leave.

'Baby Auntie, have you seen my car?' he asked Mummy, his eyes twinkling.

'No, I must see what everyone is talking about,' she answered, gamely. 'Just I'll fetch my shawl. Such cold weather we're having, na?'

Rinku said goodbye to the rest of the family at the door and he and Mummy stepped outside.

'I've taken care of Chubby's little problem,' he said in a hushed voice as they walked over to his Range Rover. 'Those two gentlemen won't be troubling him again.'

'I heard Inspector Inderjit Singh is suspended pending an inquiry into illegal activities,' said Mummy.

'And it seems his friend has dropped plans for building a new office block,' added Rinku.

'Just they're saying the market is doing slowdown, so it is best, na,' said Mummy.

Rinku stooped down to touch her feet and wished her a happy Diwali.

'You too,' she said. 'And, thank you, beta. I'm very much appreciative.'

She waved him off and returned to the house.

'What were you two talking about, Mummy-ji?' asked Puri who had been watching them closely from the doorway. 'It can't be such a long chat about a car?'

'Just I've been discussing one investment proposition.'

'With Rinku?' laughed the detective. 'What's he trying to sell you? The President's Palace?'

'Don't do sarcasm, Chubby. Rinku has given me one hot tip. Just some land is coming up and we're in discussion.'

'You watch your back, Mummy-ji. He's a slippery fellow,' said the detective, closing the door behind them.

'Oh Chubby, when will you learn, na? Just I can take care of myself. Now, come. Let's play cards. Tonight I'm feeling very much lucky!'

Glossary

AACHAR	pickle. Most commonly made of carrot, lime, garlic, cauliflower, chilli or unripe mango cooked in mustard oil and spices.
'ACCHA'	Hindi for 'ok', 'good' or 'got it'.
ADIVASI	literally 'original inhabitants'. These Indian tribals comprise a substantial indigenous minority of the population of India.
AGRAWAL	a community in India, traditionally traders.
ALOO PARANTHA	flat Indian wheat bread stuffed with a potato and spice mixture, pan-fried and served with yoghurt and pickle. Often eaten for breakfast.
ANGREZ	Hindi for 'English' or 'British'. Also means 'Englishman' or 'Britisher'. Angrez noun, Angrezi adjective.
ASHRAMAS	the four phases of a Hindu's life.
AUTO	short for autorickshaw, a three-wheeler taxi that runs on a two-stroke engine.

337

AYAH	a domestic servant role that combines the functions of maid and nanny.
'AY BHAI'	Hindi for 'hey brother'.
BABA	father.
BABU	a bureaucrat or other government official.
'BADIYA'	Urdu word for 'wonderful', 'great'.
BAGHA-CHALL	a strategic, two-player board game that originates in Nepal. The game is asymmetric in that one player controls four tigers and the other player controls up to twenty goats. The tigers 'hunt' the goats while the goats attempt to block the tigers' movements.
BAHU	daughter-in-law.
BAKSHISH	a term used to describe tipping, charitable giving and bribery.
BALTI	a bucket.
BANIA	a trader or merchant belonging to the Indian business class.
BARSAATI	from *barsaat* meaning rain. A barsaati is a room at the top of the house used for storage

or servants' quarters that bears the brunt of the falling rain. Today, barsaatis in posh Delhi neighbourhoods rent for hundreds of dollars per month.

BASTIS colonies of makeshift houses for the poor.

BATCHMATES students who attended the same school, college, or military or administrative academy.

BETA 'son', or 'child', used in endearment.

'BHAANCHHOD' Punjabi expletive meaning, 'sister fucker'.

BHAI brother.

BHANG a drink popular in many parts of India made by mixing cannabis with a concoction of almonds, spices, milk and sugar.

BHAVAN home or building.

BHINDI okra.

BIDI Indian cigarette made of strong tobacco hand-rolled in a leaf from the ebony tree.

BINDI from the Sanskrit *bindu*, 'a drop, small particle, dot'. Traditionally a dot of red colour applied in the centre of the forehead close to the eyebrows worn by married Hindu women, or by any girl or woman as a decoration, often coloured to match the clothes they are wearing.

BUCKS   as in America, but used to mean rupees instead of dollars.

BURFI OR BARFI   a sweet made from condensed milk and cooked with sugar until it solidifies. Burfi is often flavoured with cashews, mango, pistachio and spices and is sometimes served coated with a thin layer of edible silver leaf.

'BUSS'   Hindi for 'stop' or 'enough'.

CAR-SAAF-WALLAH   wallah is a generic term in Hindi meaning 'the one' or 'he who does'. Car-saaf-wallah is typical Hinglish, a mixture of Hindi and English, in this case meaning 'he who washes the car'.

CHAI   tea.

'CHALLO'   Hindi for 'let's go'.

CHANNA   spicy masala chickpeas, also known as *chhole*.

CHANNA BHATURA   Indian fried bread, very oily, chewy (and delicious!), served with curried chickpeas.

CHAPPALS	Indian sandals usually made of leather or rubber.
CHAPPATIS	see *roti*.
CHARAS	handmade hashish, very potent.
CHARPAI	literally 'four feet'. A charpai is a woven string cot used throughout northern India and Pakistan.
CHAT	a savoury, spicy, tangy street food common to northern and western India. Chat is comprised of crispy fried *papris* or savoury biscuits, topped with yoghurt, spices, sliced onions, mango powder, and tamarind and green chilli chutneys.
CHAWAL	rice.
CHHATRI	literally 'umbrella' or 'canopy', a dome-shaped pavilion commonly used as an element of Indian architecture.
CHHOLE	see *channa*.
CHIKAN KURTA	Kurta is a long shirt worn by men and women in Pakistan and northern India. Chikan refers to a unique embroidery style from Lucknow, believed to have been introduced by the emperor Jehangir's wife, Nur Jehan. Traditionally, it

341

uses white thread on white muslin cloth.

CHOWKIDAR	watchman.
CHOWTI BABY	in Hindi chowti means little.
CHUDDIES	Punjabi for underpants.
CHUNNI	long scarf worn with drawstring trousers and a knee-length *kameez* or *kurta*.
CHURIDAAR PYJAMA	a style of leg-hugging drawstring pyjama with folds that fall around the ankles like a stack of churis, or bracelets.
COUSIN-SISTER	a colloquialism emphasising that in India a first cousin is like a sibling.
CRORE	a unit in the Indian numbering system equal to ten million.
CROREPATI	an extremely rich person, a multimillionaire.
DAAL	spiced lentils.
DABBA	a lunch box, usually round and made of stainless steel with several compartments.
DALITS	untouchables, low caste; means 'suppressed' or 'crushed'.
DANDASANA POSITION	in yoga the simplest form of the sitting position.

DHABA	roadside eatery, popular with truck drivers in northern India, which serves spicy Punjabi food.
DHARMA	a Sanskrit term that refers to a person's righteous duty or any virtuous path.
DHOBI	a person who washes clothes.
DISHDASHA	an ankle-length garment similar to a robe worn in the Arab world, most commonly in the Gulf states.
DIYA	a lamp usually made of clay with a cotton wick dipped in vegetable oil.
DOSA	a South Indian crêpe made from rice and lentils.
DOUBLE-ROLE	one actor playing two opposing roles (good brother/bad brother) in Indian films.
DOUBLE-ROTI	sliced white bread.
DUPATTA	in women's dress, a scarf usually worn over the head and shoulders, made of cotton, georgette, silk, chiffon, etc.
GHEE	clarified butter.
GOBI	cauliflower.
GOONDAS	thugs or miscreants.

GORA/GORI	a light-skinned person; the term is often used in reference to Westerners.
'HAAN-JI'	Hindi for 'yes sir/madam'.
'HAI!'	an exclamation indicating surprise or shock.
HAKIM	a Muslim physician.
HALDI	turmeric, deep orange-yellow spice made from the rhizomes of the turmeric plant.
HALVA	a dessert made from wheat flour, semolina, lentils or grated carrots mixed with sugar and ghee and topped with almonds. Often served in Hindu and Sikh temples as blessed food for worshippers to eat following prayers.
HIJRA	a member of 'the third sex', neither man nor woman. Most are physically male or intersex (formerly known as hermaphrodites). Some are female. Hijras usually refer to themselves as female and dress as women. Although they are often referred to in English as 'eunuchs', relatively few have any genital modifications. A third gender has existed in the subcontinent from the earliest records,

and was clearly acknowledged in Vedic culture, throughout the history of Hinduism, as well as in the royal courts of Islamic rulers.

HINDUSTAN
AMBASSADOR
until recently India's national car. The design, which has changed little since production started in 1957, is similar to the British Morris Oxford.

INCHARGE
noun meaning 'boss'.

JAINS
a small but influential and generally wealthy religious minority with at least ten million followers.

'JALDI KARO'
Hindi for 'hurry up'.

JALEBI
pretzel-shaped, bright orange sweet made of fried batter soaked in sugar syrup.

'JAO!'
'Go!'

JEERA
cumin seeds.

-JI
honorific attached to the end of nouns.

'JI'
'yes'.

KACHORIS
a snack eaten in north India and Pakistan. The Rajasthani variety is a round flattened ball made of fine flour filled with a baked stuffing of yellow

daal, beans, gram flour, red chilli powder and other spices.

KADI CHAWAL   kadi is made from gram flour fried in butter and mixed with buttermilk or yoghurt to produce a spicy, sour curry. Served with chawal, rice.

KATHI ROLL   a type of street food similar to a sandwich-like wrap, usually stuffed with chicken tikka or lamb, onion and green chutney.

KHANA   Hindi for food.

KHICHRI   a cupful of rice cooked with yellow lentils and spiced with cumin, salt and coriander. Generally eaten when one is sick or in need of comfort food.

KHUKURI   a carved Nepalese knife used as a tool and weapon.

KIRPAN   a ceremonial sword or dagger that all baptised Sikhs are supposed to wear.

KITTY PARTY   women in India organize kitty parties to socialise, but also as an interest-free way of loaning each other money. The kitty is a collective fund. The carefully chosen guests bring their next instalment of cash to each party. One name is drawn from a hat, with that woman receiving twelve instalments all at once to use as she pleases.

KOH-I-NOOR the 'Mountain of Light', a 105 (21.6g) carat diamond that belonged to various Mughal and Persian rulers and is now part of the British crown jewels.

KOHL a mixture of soot and other ingredients used predominantly by Middle Eastern, North African, sub-Saharan African and South Asian women (and to a lesser extent men) to darken the eyelids and as mascara for the eyelashes.

KOORAY WALLAH one who collects the rubbish. See *car-saaf-wallah*.

KSHATRIYA the military and ruling order of the traditional Vedic-Hindu social system as outlined by the Vedas; the warrior caste.

KUNDAN a style of jewellery dating back to Mughal times in which precious and semi-precious stones are set in pure gold, often with coloured enamel at the back.

KURTA PYJAMA long shirt and drawstring trousers.

LADOOS	a sweet that that is often prepared to celebrate festivals or household events such as weddings. Essentially, ladoos are flour balls cooked in sugar syrup.
LAKH	a unit in the Indian numbering system equal to 100,000.
LAL MIRCH	ground red cayenne pepper.
'LAO'	Hindi for 'bring'.
LASSI	drink made from buttermilk, can be plain, sweet or salty, or made with fruit such as banana or mango.
LATHI	length of bamboo or cane carried by police or schoolmasters.
LOAD SHEDDING	a phrase referring to the period when Indian power companies cut off the electricity when they cannot meet demand.
LUNGI	a garment that covers the lower half of the body, tied around the waist.
'MAADERCHOD'	literally 'motherfucker' in Punjabi.
MAALISH	oil massage.
MALI	gardener.

MANDE THUNIS	a turban worn by the Coorg men of southern Karnataka.
MANGAL SUTRA	a symbol of Hindu marriage, consisting of a gold ornament strung from a yellow thread, a string of black beads or a gold chain. It is comparable to a Western wedding ring and is worn by a married woman until her husband's death.
MANGLIK	astrological term referring to a person born under the negative influence of Mars. It is believed that a non-Manglik marrying a Manglik will die. Two Mangliks marrying each other cancel out the negative effects. Mangliks can also perform a ceremony in which they 'marry' a tree or a golden idol to transfer their bad luck.
MASALA CHAI	spiced tea.
MATTHIS	fried savoury biscuits, often served with tea.
MEMSAHIB	formerly a term of respect for white European women in colonial India, but now used for well-to-do Indian women.
MESWAK	a natural toothbrush made from the twigs of the *Salvadora Persica*

tree, also known as the Arak or Peelu tree.

MOONG DAAL   a split bean with a green husk and yellow inside.

NAAMAALUM   like a John or Jane Doe, a corpse or hospital patient whose identity is unknown.

NAMASHKAR/ NAMASTE   traditional Hindu greeting said with hands pressed together.

NIMBOO PAANI   lemonade, usually with salt.

'OOLU KE PATHAY'   Punjabi curse, literally translates as 'son of an owl'.

PAAGAL   Hindi for crazy.

PAAN   betel leaf, stuffed with betel nut, lime and other condiments, used as a stimulant.

PAKORA   a deep-fried snack. They can be made from pretty much anything dipped in a gram flour batter.

PALLU   the loose end of a sari.

PANEER   un-aged cheese made by curdling heated milk with lemon juice.

PARANTHA   a flatbread made with wholewheat flour, pan fried in oil or clarified butter and usually stuffed with vegetables like potatoes and cauliflower.

PEG	a unit of measurement for alcoholic spirits. Peg measures can hold anywhere from 1 to 2 fluid ounces (30–60 ml).
PRESS-WALLAH	a journalist.
PUJA	prayer.
PUKKA	Hindi word meaning solid, well made. Also means 'definitely'.
PURANAS	a group of Hindu, Jain or Buddhist religious texts.
RAJMA	red kidney beans cooked with onion, garlic, ginger, tomatoes and spices. A much-loved Punjabi dish eaten with *chawal*, rice.
RAKHI-BROTHER	the Hindu festival of *Raksha Bandhan* celebrates the bonds between brothers and sisters. The sister ties a *rakhi* or holy thread on her brother's wrist in exchange for a vow of protection. Any male can be adopted as a brother by tying the thread.
RAS MALAIS	dumplings from cottage or ricotta cheese soaked in sweetened, thickened milk delicately flavored with cardamom.
RAVAN	the demon king of the Hindu epic, the Ramayana, who kidnaps the wife of Lord Ram.

ROTI OR CHAPATTI	Indian wheat flatbread cooked on a hot griddle.
'SAALA, MAADERCHOD'	'bastard, mother fucker'.
'SAALE'	'bastard'.
'SAB CHANGA'	Punjabi for 'all well'.
SADHU	a holy man who has renounced the material world to devote himself to spiritual practice.
SAHIB	an Urdu honorific now used across South Asia as a term of respect, equivalent to the English 'sir'.
SALWAR	baggy trousers worn by men and women common to Afghanistan, Pakistan and northern India.
SAMOSA	a triangular fried savoury snack stuffed with potatoes, peas and spices.
SANYASI	a Hindu who has renounced the material world.
SARDAAR	a male follower of the Sikh religion.
SARDAAR-JI JOKES	Sikhs are traditionally the butt of jokes in northern India.
SARI	India's national dress for women. Usually six yards of

material wrapped and pleated over a blouse and petticoat.

SHRI a Sanskrit title of veneration. An honorific, whose equivalent is Mr in English.

SINDOOR a red powder used by married Hindu women and some Sikh women. During the marriage ceremony, the groom applies some to the parting of the bride's hair to show that she is now a married woman. Subsequently, sindoor is applied by the wife as part of her dressing routine.

SONF plain or sugared fennel seeds eaten to aid digestion and to freshen the mouth after a meal.

SUBZI a vegetable.

SUBZI-WALLAH vegetable seller.

TACHEE Indian English for suitcase, derived from 'attaché case'.

TAVA a large, flat or slightly concave disc-shaped griddle made from cast iron, steel or aluminium used to prepare several kinds of flatbreads.

TEEN PATTA an Indian card game, also known as Flush. Usually played at Diwali, the Indian new year, it is a betting game in which the player with the best hand (three aces, or three consecutive cards of the same suit) wins the pot.

TIFFIN	steel lunchbox usually with three round, stackable compartments.
TIMEPASS	Hindi/English word meaning any pointless activity to pass the time.
TONGA	a horse-pulled cart.
TULLI	Punjabi slang for 'drunk'.
'YAAR'	equivalent to pal, mate or dude.
ZARI	a type of thread made of fine gold or silver wire woven into silk to create intricate patterns, Mughal in origin.

NOTE

The rupee exchange rate at the time of writing is
£1 = 75 Rps
$1 = 44 Rps

We do hope that you have enjoyed reading this large print book.

Did you know that all of our titles are available for purchase?

We publish a wide range of high quality large print books including:
Romances, Mysteries, Classics
General Fiction
Non Fiction and Westerns

Special interest titles available in large print are:
The Little Oxford Dictionary
Music Book
Song Book
Hymn Book
Service Book

Also available from us courtesy of Oxford University Press:
Young Readers' Dictionary
(large print edition)
Young Readers' Thesaurus
(large print edition)

For further information or a free brochure, please contact us at:
Ulverscroft Large Print Books Ltd.,
The Green, Bradgate Road, Anstey,
Leicester, LE7 7FU, England.
Tel: (00 44) 0116 236 4325
Fax: (00 44) 0116 234 0205

A CURE FOR ALL DISEASES

Reginald Hill

Superintendent 'Fat' Andy Dalziel may have been in a coma, but he's not down for good. In the meantime a few weeks bedrest in Sandytown, a pleasant seaside resort devoted to healing, seems just the ticket. And when a fellow newcomer appears in the shapely form of psychologist Charlotte Heywood, Dalziel develops an unexpected passion for alternative therapy. But Sandytown's principal landowners are at war over grandiose plans for the resort. One of them has to go and when one of them does, in spectacularly gruesome fashion, DCI Peter Pascoe is called in to investigate — with Dalziel and Charlotte providing unwelcome support. Pascoe soon finds dark forces at work in a place where holistic remedies are no match for the oldest cure of all . . .

INHUMAN REMAINS

Quintin Jardine

Oz Blackstone, screen hero and sleuth, has died of a ruptured aorta. His wife, Primavera Blackstone, is in Spain with their son Tom. Prim's mind is still occupied with thoughts of Oz when her aunt, Adrienne McGowan, arrives. It seems that Auntie Ade's roguish son Frank has disappeared. Prim flies to Seville to track him down, only to become a fugitive with her life under threat, as her aunt goes missing, and Tom is forced to flee to safety. As she and her companion in danger cross Spain to free Adrienne, Prim is at the centre of a maelstrom of mystery, until the final solution springs from the unlikeliest of sources. The Blackstone legacy is in good hands, but will they, and it, survive?

THE WATCHER

Brian Freeman

One murder has haunted Lieutenant Jonathan Stride for thirty years. In 1977 his girlfriend's sister was savagely beaten to death. Stride came face to face with the suspect — and let the man escape. And when writer Tish Verdure begins a book about the murder, he's reluctant to re-open the case. But Tish has new evidence that raises questions about the actions of the police . . . and even Stride's own wife. Then Tish receives threats, and a teenage girl is hounded to her death. Stride investigates a voyeur who may hold the key to two brutal crimes. Then as he finds himself in a devastating confrontation high above the deadly waters of Lake Superior, he and Tish must face their worst fears — and the truth about the past.

OXFORD MENACE

Veronica Stallwood

Kate Ivory should be writing her latest novel, but her partner, John Kenrick, wants her to concentrate on their relationship. The last thing Kate needs is a cry for help from her friend, Sam Dolby. Blake Parker, director of an Oxford research unit, has financial worries. He and his team must produce useful results soon, or lose their funding. The last thing Blake needs is an attack on his lab by an animal rights group. Kate agrees to keep an eye on Sam's girlfriend Kerri, while he's away in China. Unfortunately, Kerri is working in Blake's lab, and the animal rights activists aren't alone in making life uncomfortable for the scientists. Kate finds herself entangled in a mystery where all is not what it seems . . .

OSCAR SEASON

Mary McNamara

The Pinnacle is *the* place to stay during the Oscars, and this year the pre-Awards crises have reached fever pitch: a very recognizable body is found in the hotel pool; Hollywood's most famous leading man is secretly holed up in the Presidential Suite; and the larger-than-life producer of the Oscars will stop at nothing for higher ratings. A consummate professional, the hotel's PR manager Juliette Greyson must do a careful dance to rescue the Pinnacle's reputation while somehow sparing herself and her famous clientele in the process. But first Juliette must figure out what is real and what is staged. Who is lying and who is acting? And when does murder stop being murder — and start becoming damn good publicity?

This Large Print Book for the partially sighted, who cannot read normal print, is published under the auspices of

THE ULVERSCROFT FOUNDATION

FORGET-ME-NOT-CHILD

FORGET-ME-NOT-CHILD

by

Anne Bennett

Magna Large Print Books
Long Preston, North Yorkshire,
BD23 4ND, England.

British Library Cataloguing in Publication Data.

A catalogue record of this book is
available from the British Library

ISBN   978-0-7505-4435-1

First published in Great Britain 2017 by Harper,
an imprint of HarperCollins*Publishers*

Copyright © Anne Bennett 2017

Cover illustration © Gordon Crabb by arrangement with
Alison Eldred

Anne Bennett asserts the moral right to be identified as the author of
this work

Published in Large Print 2017 by arrangement with
HarperCollins Publishers Ltd.

Magna Large Print is an imprint of Library Magna Books Ltd.

Printed and bound in Great Britain by
T.J. (International) Ltd., Cornwall, PL28 8RW

I dedicate this, my 20th book, to my family for their love and encouragement over the years. I love and appreciate you all greatly.

ONE

Angela could remember little of her earlier life when the McClusky family lived in Donegal in Northern Ireland. As she grew she had understood that her name was not McClusky but was Kennedy, and she was the youngest daughter of Connie and Padraig Kennedy, and that Mary and Matt McClusky were not her real parents at all, though she called them Mammy and Daddy. She also learned that she had once had four older siblings all at school and so when Minnie the eldest contracted TB and Angela's mother realized it was rife in the school, she asked Mary McClusky, who was a great friend of hers, to care for Angela, then just eighteen months old, in an effort to keep her safe. Mary had not hesitated and Angela lived in the McClusky home, petted and feted by the five McClusky boys who had never had a girl in the family before.

However, before Angela was two years old she was an orphan; for her parents succumbed to TB too as they watched their children die one by one. Mary was distraught at the loss of her dear friend and all those poor young children. And Padraig too, for he was a fine strapping man and well able, anyone would have thought, to fight off any illness.

'Ah, but maybe he hadn't the will to fight,' Matt said. 'He'd watched his children all die and then his wife had gone as well before he developed it.

11

What was left for him if he had recovered? I imagine he didn't bother fighting it.'

Whatever the way of it, there was a spate of funerals and though Angela attended none of them she was aware of a sadness in the McClusky family without understanding it.

Eventually Mary had to rouse herself for she had a family to see to, including little motherless Angela, and Matt had a farm to run. Mary did wonder if there was some long-lost relative who would look after Angela, but after the last funeral it was apparent there wasn't and Mary decided that she would stay with them. She knew there would be no opposition from Matt who had by then grown extremely fond of her, as they all had, and he just nodded when Mary said it was the very least she could do for her friend. Matt too had been badly shaken by the deaths of the entire Kennedy family and was well aware that a similar tragedy could have happened to his family just as easily. This time they had got through unscathed and he readily agreed that Angela should continue to live with them and grow up as their daughter.

'Angela will be your new little sister,' Mary told her sons. Not one of them made any objection but the happiest of them all was her youngest, Barry. At five years old, he was three years older than Angela and she was petite for her age with white-blonde curls and big blue eyes that reminded him of a little doll. She was better than any doll though for she seemed to have happiness running through her, her ready smile lit up her whole face and her laugh was so infectious all the McClusky boys would nearly jump through hoops to amuse

12

her. 'I will be the best brother I know how to be,' Barry said earnestly. 'I was already fed up of being the youngest.'

Mary laughed and tousled Barry's hair. 'I'm sure you will, son,' she said, 'and she will love you dearly.'

And Angela did. Between her and Barry there was a special closeness though she loved all the boys she thought of as brothers and all were kind and gentle with her.

However the farm didn't thrive. A blight damaged most of the potato crop, and heavy and sustained storms left them with barely half of the hay they would need for the winter, meaning they would have to buy the hay needed from elsewhere, while many cabbages, turnips and swedes were lost to the torrential and ferocious rains that eventually flooded the hen house, resulting in many hens also being lost. That first bad winter they just about managed although empty bellies were often the order of the day and later Barry told Angela she was lucky not to remember those times.

Everyone looked forward to the spring after the second bad winter. Matt and his sons knew that if the spring was going to be a fine one nothing would go awry and with tightened belts they might survive. Matt had a constant frown between his eyes because the weather wasn't good. 'Surely this year will be better than last,' Mary said.

Matt's lips tightened. 'We'll see,' he said grimly. 'For if it's not a great deal better we will sink.'

In the early spring of that year a cow died giving birth and the female calf died, a fox got into the

hen house and killed most of the hens, and one of the lambs scattered on the hillside was savaged by a dog and had to be put out of his misery. As their finances were on a keen knife edge these things were major blows. Matt knew he would have to leave the farm where he had lived all his life and his father before and his father. That thought was more than upsetting, it was devastating, but he had to face facts. One evening in late March after Angela and Barry had gone to bed and the dinner pots and plates had been put away, Matt and Mary faced their four eldest sons across the table and told them they didn't think they could survive another year.

There was a gasp from Sean and Gerry, but Finbarr and Colm, who helped their father on the farm, were not totally surprised. They knew as well as anyone how badly the farm had been hit, but they still thought their father might have a plan of some sort and it was Finbarr who asked, 'What's to do?'

'We must leave here, that's all,' Matt said.

'Leave the farm?' Sean asked.

'Yes,' Matt affirmed. 'And Ireland too. We must leave Ireland and try our hands elsewhere.'

That shocked all the boys for not even Finbarr thought any plan would involve them all leaving their native land, though Mary, heartsore as she was, knew that was what they had to do.

Finbarr glanced at his brothers' faces and knew he was speaking for all of them when he said, 'We none of us would like that, Daddy. Is there no other way?'

'Aye, the poorhouse if you'd prefer it,' said Matt

and he spoke with a snap because leaving was the thing he didn't want to do either. 'They have one in the town.'

At Finbarr's look of distaste, he cried out, 'Do you think this is easy for me? This is where I was born and where I thought I would die. It's my homeland but we can't live on fresh air.' Then he added with an ironic smile, 'Though we have made a good stab at it this year.'

Finbarr knew that well enough and didn't bother commenting, but instead asked, 'But where would we go?'

'Where Norah Docherty has been urging me to go this past year,' Mary said. 'And that's Birmingham, England. She's in a place called Edgbaston and she says it's not far from the city centre and she can put us up until we get straight with our own place and she says she can probably even help you all with jobs.'

Finbarr nodded for they all knew the Dochertys had left Ireland's shore four years before when they were in danger of having to throw themselves on the mercy of the poorhouse to save the children from starving to death. Then an uncle living in Birmingham had offered them all a home with him in exchange for looking after him because he was afraid of being put in the poorhouse too. It was a lifeline for the Docherty family and they had all grasped it with two hands and were packed up and gone lock stock and barrel in no time at all.

Mary knew Norah found the life hard at first for Norah had written and told her that the house was terribly cramped. Her uncle couldn't make the stairs and his bed had to be downstairs. But a man

15

who lived just two doors down called Tim Bishop was the gaffer at a foundry in a place called Aston and he had put a word in for Norah's husband Mick. He had jumped at the job they offered him and Mary said he'd been tired coming home especially at first, for the work was heavy, but then a job was a job and with Birmingham in the middle of a massive slump, to get one at all was great. She said you really needed someone to speak on your behalf to have a chance at all and Norah's uncle had once worked at the same place as Tim Bishop and been well thought of and Tim Bishop approved of the family coming over to see to him in his declining years, for they all knew well the old man's fear of ending up in the poorhouse or the workhouse, as it was commonly known.

'This Tim Bishop Norah speaks of seems to be a grand fellow altogether,' Mary said. 'He had Mick set up in a job before he had been there five minutes. Please God that he may do the same for us.'

'Yeah, but what sort of job?' Colm grumbled. 'Don't know that I would be any good in Birmingham or anywhere else either,' he said. 'The only job I know how to do is farming.'

'Well you can learn to do something else can't you?' Matt barked. 'Same as I'll have to do.'

'We'll all have to learn to do things we're not used to,' Mary said. 'Life is going to be very different to the life we have here but that's how it is and we must all accept it.'

Mary had a way of speaking that brooked no argument, as the boys knew to their cost, and anyway Finbarr knew she made sense and he sighed and said, 'So what happens now?'

'Well travel costs money,' Mary said. 'And that's something we haven't got a lot of, so we sell everything we don't need. Your father has sold all the cattle and even got something for the carcasses of the cow and young calf but it isn't enough. We'll sell everything on the farm because we can hardly take anything but essentials with us anyway.'

Sad days followed as the children watched the only home they had ever known disappearing before their eyes. The neighbours rallied, one took the cart and horse and another took the hens the fox hadn't killed and rounded up the sheep and yet another said he would have the plough and even the tools were sold. It was hard to get rid of the dogs and though Angela could only remember flashes of that time she remembered crying when Matt said the dogs had to go. All were upset. 'They are going to good homes,' Matt promised her and she remembered his husky voice and the way his eyes looked all glittery.

Barry hadn't liked to see the dogs go either but knew he had to be brave for Angela and so he said, 'We can't take dogs to this place Mammy said we're going to, Angela, so they have got to stop here.'

'They'd hardly like it in Birmingham anyway,' Mary said. 'Their place is here.'

'I thought mine was,' Gerry said.

'Gerry, you're too old to moan about something that can't be changed,' Mary said sharply. 'What can't be cured must be endured – you know that.'

'Who's having the table?' Barry asked.

'The person who has bought the cottage,' Mary said. 'That's Peter Murphy and he asked me to

leave the table and chairs, my pots and all, the easy chairs, stools and settle, the butter churn and the press and all the beds. I was happy to do it and he gave me a good, fair price for them too.'

'Funny to think of someone living here when we've gone,' Gerry said.

'I suppose,' Mary said. 'But I'd rather someone was getting the good out of it than it just falling to wrack and ruin.'

They all agreed with that but when they assembled the following Saturday very very early that late April morning Mary looked at their belongings packed in two battered cases and two large bass bags and her heart felt as heavy as lead. She wasn't the only one. As they left the farmhouse for the last time they all felt strange not to see the clucking hens dipping their heads to eat the grit between the cobbles outside the cottage door, nor to hear the barking of the dogs. As they made their way to the head of the lane where the neighbour who bought the horse and cart would be waiting for them to take them down to the rail bus station in the town, they missed seeing the horse and cows sharing the field to one side, and to the other side of the lane the tilled and furrowed fields, now bare with nothing planted in them. They missed seeing the sheep on the hillside pulling relentlessly on the grass.

Sad though they were to leave, the children were also slightly excited, but Mary's excitement was threaded through with trepidation for she had never gone far from home before, none of them had, and she looked at the youngsters' eager though slightly nervous faces and hoped to God

they were doing the right thing.

All knew where the McCluskys were bound and even at that early hour some neighbours had come to see them off and wish them God speed and their good wishes almost reduced Mary to tears as she hugged the women and shook hands with the men and led the way on to the rail bus where she and Matt got them all settled in.

They were soon off, the little rail bus was eating up the miles, but it was only the start of the long journey to Birmingham. They would leave the rail bus at a place called Strabane and from there get a train to the docks at Belfast. Then a boat would take them across the sea to Liverpool where another train would take them from there to Birmingham. The rail journey to Strabane had begun to pall but they all perked up a bit when it was time to board the boat.

Mary was very nervous of going up the gangplank and once on deck the way the boat seemed to list from one side to another was very unnerving, but what worried her most was the safety of the children. Not the older boys, they should be all right, but it was Barry and little Angela she was concerned about. What if one of them was to fall overboard? Oh God, that didn't bear thinking about!

She didn't express her fears, she knew the boys would only laugh at her, but she said to Finbarr and Colm, 'You make sure you look after Barry and Angela. Make sure you keep them safe,' knowing they would more than likely want to explore the ship. Her gallivanting days were over and she was finding it hard enough to keep her balance

now and they hadn't even set off yet.

'I don't need anyone to look after me,' Barry declared. 'I can look after myself.'

'You'll do as you are told,' Mary said sharply to Barry. 'And you mind what Finbarr and Colm say.'

Barry made a face behind his mother's back and Finbarr clipped his ear for his disrespect. 'Ow,' he said holding his ear and glaring at Finbarr.

'Never mind "ow",' Finbarr said. 'You behave or we'll not take you anywhere. We'll just take Angela because she always does as she is told.'

'Yes,' Colm said, 'you'd like to see around the ship wouldn't you, Angela?'

Angela wasn't sure, it looked a big and scary place to her, but she knew by the way the question was asked what Colm wanted her to say so she nodded her head slowly and said, 'I think so.'

Barry said nothing more because he definitely did want to see over the ship and Finbarr could be quite stern sometimes and he knew his Mammy would never let him go on his own. Anyway he hadn't time to worry about it because the call came for those not travelling on the boat to disembark and exhilaration filled him for he knew they would soon be on their way. Finbarr put Angela up on his shoulder because she couldn't see over the rail and from there she watched those wishing to disembark scurry down the gangplank to stand on the quayside and wave as the sailors raised the gangplank and hauled in the thick ropes that had attached the ship to round things on the quayside that Finbarr told her were bollards. Then the ship's hooter gave such a screech Angela nearly

jumped off Finbarr's shoulder. The ship's engines began to throb and Finbarr lifted her down and Angela felt the whole deck vibrate through her feet as the ship moved slowly out to sea.

Matt and Mary joined the children at the rail as they watched the shores of Ireland slip away and Mary suddenly felt quite emotional, for she had never had any inclination to leave her native land. The sigh she gave was almost imperceptible, but Matt heard it and he put his gnarled, work-worn hand over Mary's on the deck rail. 'We'll make it work,' he said to her. 'We've made a right decision, the only decision, and we will have a good living there, you just see if we don't.'

Mary was unable to speak, but she turned her hand over and squeezed Matt's. It was hard for him too for farming was all he knew, but he was a hard worker and had always been a good provider, and she had a good pair of hands on her too. She swallowed the lump in her throat and said, 'I know we will, Matt, I'm not worried about that.'

And while the children went off to explore they stood together side by side and watched the shore of Ireland fade into the distance.

Mary was to find that she wasn't a very good sailor though the children seemed unaffected and wolfed down the bread and butter Mary had brought. It had been a long time since that very early breakfast, but Mary could eat nothing and Matt ate only sparingly. Mary thought that he had probably done that so that the children could eat their fill rather than any queasiness on his part.

Mary was very glad to leave the boat and be on dry land again, but she was bone weary and it

would be another couple of hours before they would reach Birmingham. All the children were tired and before the train journey was half-way through Angela climbed on to Mary's lap and fell fast asleep. She slept deeply as the train sped through the dusky evening and did not even stir when it pulled up at New Street Station. Oh how glad Mary was to see a familiar face as she stepped awkwardly from the train, for Mick Docherty was waiting with a smile of welcome on his lips. He was unable to shake Mary's hand for she had Angela in her arms. But he shook hands with Matt and the children one by one, even Barry, much to his delight.

He led the way to the exit and Mary was glad of that for she had never seen so many people gathered together. The noise was incredible, so many people talking, laughing, the tramp of many feet, thundering trains hurtling into the station to stop with a squeal of brakes and a hiss of steam, steam that rose in the air and swirled all around them smelling of soot. There was a voice over her head trying to announce something and someone shouting, she presumed selling the papers he had on the stall beside him, but she couldn't understand him. Porters with trolleys piled high with luggage weaved between the crowds urging people to, 'Mind your backs please.'

'We'll take a tram,' Mick said as he led the way to the exit. 'We could walk, and though it's only a step away, I should say you're weary from travelling. Yon young one is anyway,' he went on, indiating Angela slumbering in Mary's arms.

'Aye. And little wonder at it,' Matt said. 'We've

been on the go since early morning and I'm fair jiggered myself.'

'Aye, I remember I was the same,' Mick said. 'Well you can seek your bed as soon as you like, we keep no late hours here, but Norah has a big pan of stew on the fire and another of potatoes in case you are hungry after your journey.'

The boys were very pleased to hear that. They had hoped that somewhere there might be food in the equation, but now they were out of the station on the street and no one said anything, only stood and stared for they had never seen so much traffic in the whole of their lives. Mary was staggered. She'd thought a Fair Day in Donegal Town had been busy, but it was nothing like this with all these vehicles packed onto the road together. Hackney cabs ringed the station and beyond them there were horse-drawn vans and carts mixed with a few of the petrol-driven vehicles she had heard about but never seen and bicycles weaved in and out among the traffic. A sour acrid smell hit the back of her throat and there was a constant drone, the rumble of the carts, the clip clopping of the horses' hooves sparking on the cobbles of the streets mixed with the shouts and chatter of the very many people thronging the pavements.

And then they all saw the tram and stopped dead. They could never have imagined anything like it, a clattering, swaying monster with steam puffing from its funnel in front and they saw it ran on shiny rails set into the road. Getting closer it sounded its hooter to warn people to get off the rails and out of the way and Mary found herself

23

both fascinated and repelled by it. 'That's good,' Mick said as he led them to a tram stop just a little way from the hackney cabs, 'we've had no wait at all.'

'Yes,' Mary said, 'but is it safe?'

Mick laughed. 'It's safe enough,' he said. 'Though I had my doubts when I came over first.'

Mary mounted gingerly, helped by the boys because she still had the child in her arms. She was glad to sit for even a short journey though she slid from side to side on the wooden seat for Angela was a dead weight in her arms. It seemed no time at all before Mick was saying, 'This is ours, Bristol Street.' And once they had all alighted from the tram he pointed up the road as he went on, 'We go up this alleyway called Bristol Passage and nearly opposite us is Grant Street.'

Mary saw a street of houses such as she never knew existed, not as homes for people – small, mean houses packed tight against their neighbours and Mary felt her spirit fall to her boots for she never envisaged herself living in anything so squalid. The cottage she had left was whitewashed every winter, the thatch replaced as and when necessary and the cottage door and the one for the byre and the windowsills painted every other year, and she scrubbed her white stone step daily.

She could not say anything of course nor even show any sign of distaste. One of these was the house of her friend, besides which she didn't know how things worked here. Maybe in this teeming city of so many people houses were in short supply.

She hadn't time to ponder much about this as

24

Norah had obviously been watching out and had come dinning down the road to throw her arms around Mary, careful not to disturb Angela, but her smile included them all as she ushered them back to the house. 'I have food for you all,' she said, but added to Mary, 'What will you do with the wee one?'

'I think she is dead to the world,' Mary said. 'I see little point in waking her. She'd probably be a bit like a weasel if I tried. She hates being woken up from a deep sleep.'

'Oh don't we all?'

'Yes,' Mary agreed. 'I suppose I'd hate it just as much. So if you show me where she is to sleep, I'll take her straight up.'

'That will be the attic,' Norah said. 'And you, Mick, get those boys sat around the table with a bowl of stew before they pass out on us.' The boys sighed with relief and busied themselves sorting chairs around the table as Norah opened up the door against the wall and led the way up the two flights of stairs to the attic. There was a bed to one side, a chest and set of drawers, and a mattress laid on the floor. 'That will do you two and Angela,' Norah said. 'The boys I'm afraid will have to sleep elsewhere for now.'

Mary was completely nonplussed at this though she knew Norah had made a valid point for she had four children of her own and the walls were not made of elastic. 'Where will they sleep then?'

'In Tim Bishop's place,' Norah said. 'You know I told you he got the job for Mick?'

'Oh yes,' Mary said as she laid Angela down on the mattress and began removing her shoes.

'Where does he live?'

'Just two doors down,' Norah said.

'I suppose it's him we shall have to talk to anyway about a job for Matt.'

'Of course, I never told you Tim died last year.'

That took the wind right out of Mary's sails because she had sort of relied on this Tim Norah had spoken so highly of to do something for them too and it might be more difficult for them than it had been for Mick Docherty. But a more pressing problem was where her sons were going to lay their heads that night. 'So whose house is it now?'

'His son Stan has it,' Mary said. 'Tim died a year ago and before he died he gave permission for Stan to marry a lovely girl called Catherine Gaskell. They had been courting, but they were only young, but unless they were married or almost married when his father died, Stan as a single man wouldn't have had a claim on the house. Anyway they married and sheer willpower I think kept Tim alive to see that wedding for he died just three days later and now Stan and Kate have an unused attic and the boys can sleep there.'

'I couldn't ask that of perfect strangers.'

'They're not perfect strangers, not to me,' Norah said. 'They're neighbours and I didn't ask them, they offered when I said you were coming over and I couldn't imagine where the boys were going to sleep. Stan said he's even got a double mattress from somewhere. Anyway I can't see any great alternative. Can you?'

Mary shook her head. 'No and I am grateful for all you have done for us, but I'd rather not have Barry there. He is only seven and for now can

share the mattress with us and let's hope Matt gets a job and we get our own place sooner rather than later.'

'I'll say,' Norah said. 'And you can ask Stan about the job situation because he's the Gaffer now. Apparently Mr Baxter who is the overall Boss said there was no need to advertise for someone else when Stan had been helping his dad out for years. So if anyone can help you out it's him.'

That cheered Mary up a bit. And she did find Stan a very nice and helpful young man when she saw him later that evening. He had sandy hair and eyes and an honest open face, a full generous mouth and a very pleasant nature all told, but Mary did wonder because he was so young whether he would have as much influence as his father had had.

Still she supposed if he agreed to put in a word for Matt and the boys, for only Barry and Gerry were school age, the others could work and if he could help them all it would be wonderful, but only time would tell.

TWO

Every morning for the whole of her short life Angela had woken early to the cock crow. She would pad across to the window and listen to the dogs barking as they welcomed the day and the lowing of the cows as they were driven back to the fields from the milking shed. When she dressed

and went into the kitchen the kettle would be singing on the fire beside the porridge bubbling away in the pot and the kitchen would be filled with noise, for her father and brothers would be in from the milking after they had sluiced their hands under the pump in the yard and thick creamy porridge would be poured into the bowls with more milk and sugar to add to the porridge if wanted. It was warm and familiar.

The first morning in Birmingham she woke and was surprised to see Danny beside her for she couldn't remember that ever happening before and she slipped out of bed, but the window was too high for her to see out of. She wondered if anyone else was awake because she was very hungry. She wandered back to bed and was delighted to see Barry's deep-brown eyes open and looking at her. 'Hello.'

'Ssh,' Barry cautioned. 'Everyone but us is asleep.'

Angela thought Barry meant just their Mammy and Daddy and then she saw the children lying on the other mattress. She couldn't remember the Dochertys from when they lived in Donegal but she remembered Mammy telling her they had four children now. And so she lowered her voice and said, 'I'm ever so hungry, Barry.'

Barry didn't doubt it because Angela had had none of the delicious supper him and the others had eaten the previous evening and he was hungry enough again, so he reckoned Angela must be starving. 'Get your clothes on,' he whispered. 'Not your shoes. Carry them in your hand and we'll go downstairs.'

'What if no one's up?'

'They will be soon,' Barry said confidently. 'It's Sunday and everyone will be going to Mass.'

'Is it? It doesn't feel like a Sunday.'

'That's because everything's different here,' Barry said. 'Hurry up and get ready.'

They crept down the stairs quietly holding their shoes, but there was no kettle boiling on the range, nor any sign of activity, and no wonder for the time on the clock said just six o'clock. On the farm the milking would have all been done by that time, but in a city it seemed six o'clock on a Sunday is the time for laying in bed. And then he remembered there might be no breakfast at all because they were likely taking communion and no one could eat or drink before that. It wouldn't affect Angela, nor he imagined the two youngest Dochertys, Sammy and Siobhan, whom he'd met the night before. They were only five and six, but the other two, Frankie and Philomena, were older. He had no need to fast either for he hadn't made his First Holy Communion yet. Had he stayed in Ireland he would have made it in June, but here he wasn't sure if it would be the same. It did mean though he could eat that morning and he searched the kitchen, which wasn't hard to do since it was so tiny and, finding bread in the bin, he cut two chunks from one of the loaves, spread it with the butter he'd found on the slab and handed one to Angela.

But Angela just looked at him with her big blue eyes widened. 'Here, take it,' he said.

'It must be wrong,' she cried. 'We'll get into trouble.'

29

'I might get into trouble but you won't,' Barry assured Angela. 'But you must eat something because you have had nothing since the bread and butter in the boat dinner time yesterday. We had stew last night but you were too sleepy and Mammy put you to bed, so you must eat something and that's what I'll say if anyone is cross. You won't be blamed so take it.'

He held the bread out again and this time Angela took it and when she crammed it in her mouth instead of eating it normally Barry realized just how hungry she had been and he poured her a glass of milk from the jug he had found with the butter on the slab to go with it. 'Now you've got a milk moustache,' he said with a smile.

Angela scrubbed at her mouth with her sleeve and then said to Barry, 'Now what shall we do?'

'Well, it doesn't seem as if anyone is getting up,' Barry said, for it was as quiet as the grave upstairs when he had a listen at the door. 'So how about going and having a look round the place we are going to be living in?'

'Oh yes, I'd like that.'

'Get your shoes on then and we'll go,' Barry said.

A little later when Barry opened the front door Angela stood on the step and stared. For all she could see were houses. Houses all down the hill as far as she could see. She stepped into the street and saw her side of the street was the same. And she couldn't see any grass anywhere. There had been other houses in Ireland dotted here and there on the hillside, but the only thing attached to their cottage was the byre and the barn beyond that. There wasn't another house in sight and you

would have to go to the head of the lane to see any other houses at all. To see so many all stacked up tight together was very strange.

'Where do you go to the toilet here?' Angela asked, suddenly feeling the urge to go.

'Down the yard,' Barry said. 'I'll show you. Mr Docherty took me down the yard last night, we need a key.'

He nipped back into the house to get it before taking Angela's hand and together they went down to the entry of the yard. As Barry had seen in the dark, now she also saw that six houses opened on the grey cobbled yard and crisscrossing washing lines were pushed high into the sooty air by tall props.

Barry said, 'Norah told us last night some women wash for other people. Posh people, you know, because it's a way of making money and they have washing out every day of the week except Sunday. And this is the Brewhouse where Mick says all the washing gets done,' he added as they went past a brick building with a corrugated tin roof.

The weather-beaten wooden door was ajar and leaning drunkenly because it was missing its top hinges. Angela peeped inside and wrinkled her nose. 'It smells of soap.'

'Well it would be odd if it smelled of anything else,' Barry said, 'and these two bins we're passing have to be shared by the Dochertys and two other families. One is for ashes, called a miskin, and the black one is for other rubbish.'

'Don't you think it's an odd way of going on?' Angela asked.

31

Barry nodded. 'I do,' he said in agreement. 'And you haven't seen the toilets yet, they're right at the bottom of the yard and two other families have to share them as well. They have a key to go in and you must lock it up afterwards. The key is always kept on a hook by the door.'

Angela found it was just as Barry said and as she sat on the bare wooden seat and used the toilet she reflected that Mammy had been right, they had an awful lot of things to get used to.

Stopping only to put the key back on its hook, the two started to walk down the slope towards Bristol Street and Barry wondered what Angela was thinking. He'd had a glimpse of the area as he had walked up Grant Street with everyone else the previous evening. He didn't think they looked very nice houses, all built of blue-grey brick, three storeys high with slate roofs and they stood on grey streets and behind them were grey yards. He didn't think his mother had been impressed either, but she had covered the look of dismay Barry had glimpsed before anyone else had seen it.

So he wasn't surprised at Angela's amazement as she looked from one side to the other. 'There's lots of houses aren't there Barry?' she said as they started to go down Bristol Passage.

'Yeah, but this is a city and lots of people live in a city and they all have to have houses.'

'Yes, I suppose,' Angela said.

'D'you think you'll like living here?' he said as they strode along Bristol Street. Despite it being still quite early on a Sunday morning there were already some horse-drawn carts and petrol lorries on the road and a clattering tram passed them,

weaving along its shiny rails. There were plenty of shops too, all shut up and padlocked. Angela said, 'I don't know.'

'It's all strange here isn't it? Not a bit like home.'

'No, no it isn't.'

'Tell you what though,' Barry said. 'This is probably going to be our home now, not Mr and Mrs Docherty's house, but this area. So I'm going to make sure I like it. Don't do no good being miserable if you've got to live here anyway.'

That made sense to Angela but Barry always seemed to be able to explain things to her so she understood them better. 'And me,' she said.

'Good girl,' Barry said with a beam of approval and he reached for her hand as he said, 'We best go back now because we'll probably be going to an early Mass and we daren't be too late.'

Everyone was up at the Dochertys' and Mary asked where they had both been and would have gone for Barry when he attempted to explain, but Norah forestalled her. 'It was obvious Angela would wake early,' she said to Mary, 'because she had her sleep out and it was good of Barry to take her downstairs and let us have a bit of a lie in.'

'But to take food without asking!'

'Well he couldn't ask me without waking me up first and that wouldn't have pleased me at all,' Norah pointed out and added with a little laugh, 'It was just a bit of bread and it's understandable that Angela would be hungry. Don't be giving out to them their first morning here.'

'I was starving,' Angela said with feeling.

'Course you were,' Norah said. 'You hadn't eaten for hours.'

Barry let out a little sigh of relief, very grateful to Mrs Docherty for saving him from the roasting he was pretty sure he had been going to get from his mother, and when she said, 'Anyway come up to the table now for I have porridge made for you two and Sammy and Siobhan,' the day looked even better.

St Catherine's Catholic Church was just along Bristol Street, no distance at all, and Norah pointed out Bow Street off Bristol Street where the entrance to the school was. 'I will be away to see about it tomorrow,' Mary said. 'I hope they have room for Barry and Gerry for I don't like them missing time. Wish I could get Angela in too because she's more than ready for school.'

'I thought that with Siobhan and was glad to get her in in September,' Norah said. 'I think when they have older ones they bring the young ones on a bit.'

'You could be right,' Norah said. 'I know our Angela is like a little old woman sometimes, the things she comes out with.'

'Oh I know exactly what you mean,' Mary said with feeling. 'Mind I wouldn't be without them and I did miss the boys last night. Be glad to see them at Mass this morning.'

The boys were waiting for them in the porch and they gave their anxious mother a good account of Stan Bishop and his wife Kate, who they said couldn't have been kinder to them. That eased Mary's mind for her children had never slept apart from her in a different house altogether and she thought it a funny way to go on, but the only

solution in the circumstances.

After Mass, Norah introduced them to the priest, Father Brannigan, and he was as Irish as they were. Mary's stomach was growling embarrassingly with hunger and she hoped he couldn't hear it. She also hoped meeting him wouldn't take long so she could go home and eat something, but she knew it was important to be friendly with the priest, especially if you wanted a school place for your children. Matt understood that as well as she did and they answered all the questions the priest asked as patiently as possible.

It might have done some good though, because when he heard the two families were living in a cramped back-to-back house with the older boys farmed out somewhere else, he said he'd keep his ear to the ground for them.

'Well telling the priest your circumstances can't do any harm anyway,' Norah said. 'Priests often get to know things before others.'

'No harm at all,' Mary agreed. 'Glad he didn't go on too long though or I might have started on the chair leg. Just at the moment my stomach thinks my throat's been cut.'

It was amazing how life slipped into a pattern, so that living with the Dochertys and eating in shifts became the norm. Gerry and Barry were accepted into St Catherine's School and went there every day with all the Docherty children and Angela was on the waiting list for the following year when she would be five. Better still, Stan Bishop said he could get Sean into the apprentice scheme to be a toolmaker and Gerry could join him in two years'

time, and he could find a labouring job for Matt the same as Mick, so that by the beginning of June the two men and the boy Sean were soon setting off to work together.

Sadly, Stan could find nothing for the two older boys who were too old for the apprentice scheme, which had to be started at fourteen, and there was no job for them in the foundry. They were disappointed but not worried. It wasn't like living in rural Donegal. Industrial Birmingham was dubbed the city of one thousand trades and just one job in any trade under the sun would suit Finbarr and Colm down to the ground.

So they did the round of the factories as Stan advised, beginning in Deritend because it was nearest to the city centre and moving out to Aston where the foundry was. They started with such high hopes that surely they would be taken on somewhere soon. 'The trick,' Stan said, 'is to have plenty of strings to your bow. Don't go to the same factory every day because they'll just get fed up with you but don't leave it so long that they've forgotten who you are if they have given you any work before. And if you're doing no good at the factories go down to the railway station and offer to carry luggage. It's nearly summer and posh folk go away and might be glad of a hand and porters are few and far between. Or,' he added, 'go to the canal and ask if they want any help operating the locks or legging the boats through the tunnels.'

'What's that mean, "legging through the tunnel"?'

'You'll find out soon enough if they ask you to do it,' Stan said with a smile. 'Just keep going and

something will turn up I'm sure.'

They kept going, there was nothing else to do, but sometimes they brought so little home. Everything they made they gave to their mother but sometimes it was very little and sometimes nothing at all. They felt bad about it, but Mary never said a word, as she knew they were trying their best, and while they were living with the Dochertys money went further, for they shared the rent and the money for food and coal. But she knew it might be a different story if ever they were to move into their own place.

However, that seemed as far away as jobs for her sons, but life went on regardless. Barry did make his First Holy Communion with the others in his class, and not long after it was the school holidays and they had a brilliant summer playing in the streets with the other children. Mary wasn't really happy with it, but there was nowhere else for them to play. Anyway all the other mothers seemed not to mind their children playing in the streets, but she was anxious something might happen to Angela. 'You see to her, Barry,' she said.

'I will,' Barry said. 'But she can't stay on her own in the house. It isn't fair. Let her play with the others and I'll see nothing happens to her.'

'Don't know what you're so worried about,' Norah said. 'That lad of yours will hardly let the wind blow on Angela.'

'I know,' Mary said. 'He's been like that since Angela first came into the house, as if he thought it was his responsibility to look after her. He's a good lad is Barry and Angela adores him.'

'He's going to make a good father when the

time comes I'd say,' Norah said.

'Aye. Please God,' Mary said.

Angela thought it was great to be surrounded by friends as soon as she stepped into the street. She had been a bit isolated at the farm. Funny that she never realized that before, but having plenty of friends was another thing she decided she liked about living in. Birmingham.

Christmas celebrated by two families in the confines of one cramped back-to-back house meant there was no room at all, but plenty of fun and laughter. There was food enough, for the women had pooled resources and bought what they could, but there was little in the way of presents for there was no spare money. Many of the boots, already cobbled as they were, had to be soled and heeled and Mary took up knitting again and taught Norah. The wool they got from buying old cheap woollen garments at the Rag Market to unravel and knit up again so that the families could have warmer clothes for winter.

January proved bitterly cold. Day after day snow fell from a leaden grey sky and froze overnight, so in the morning there was frost formed on the inside of windows in those draughty houses. Icicles hung from the sills, ice scrunched underfoot and ungloved fingers throbbed with cold.

Life was harder still for Finbarr and Colm toiling around the city in those harsh conditions to try and find a job of any sort to earn a few pennies to take home. So many factory doors were closed in their faces and when the cold eventually drove them home they would huddle over the fire to still

their shivering bones and feel like abject failures. No one could help and neither of them knew what they were going to do to help ease the situation for the family.

Slowly the days began to get slightly warmer as Easter approached. Angela would be going to school in the new term and she was so excited. She was just turned five when she walked alongside Mary for her first full day at school on April 15th. She was so full of beans it was like they were jumping around inside her. At the school she was surrounded by other boys and girls all starting together and they regarded each other shyly. When their mothers had gone their teacher, Miss Conway, took them into the classroom, which she said would be their classroom, and told them where to sit.

Angela was almost speechless with delight when she realized she had a desk and chair all to herself. After living with the Dochertys for months, she was used to sharing everything. She looked around and noticed what a lot of desks there were in the room, which was large with brown wooden walls and very high windows with small panes. There were some pictures, one with numbers on it, one with letters, and a map above the blackboard that stood in front of the high teacher's desk.

Another little girl was assigned the desk next to Angela and she turned to look at her, envying the pinafore she wore covering her dress. In fact most of the girls wore pinafores but her Mammy said funds didn't run to pinafores and she knew

better than to make a fuss over something like that. The girl had straight black hair that fell to her shoulders and dark brown eyes, but her lips looked a bit wobbly as if she might be about to cry and her face looked as if she was worried about something, so Angela smiled at her and the little girl gasped. What the little girl thought was that she'd never seen anyone so beautiful with the golden curls and the deep blue eyes and pretty little mouth and nose. Spring sunshine shafted through the tiny windows at that moment and it was like a halo around Angela's head. 'Oh,' said the little girl with awe. 'You look like an angel.'

Angela laughed, bringing the teacher's eyes upon her. She thought maybe laughing wasn't allowed at school and she was to find that it wasn't much approved of.

Nor was talking, for when she tried whispering to the other girl, 'I'm not an angel, I just look like my mother,' the teacher rapped the top of her desk with a ruler, making most children in the room jump. 'No talking,' she rapped out and Angela hissed out of the corner of her mouth, 'Tell you after.'

And later, in the playground, she told the whole story of how she ended up living with the McCluskys, according to what Mary had told her. 'Funny you thought I looked like an angel,' she said. 'Because my real mammy thought so too and she insisted I was called Angela. All the others looked like my father.'

'And they all died,' the girl said. 'And your mammy and daddy as well?'

Angela gave a brief nod and the other girl said,

'I think that's really sad.'

Angela shook her head. 'It isn't really, because I can't remember them at all. Mammy, I mean Mary, has a photograph of them on their wedding day. It was stood on the dresser at home and I suppose it will come out again when we have our own house, but I have stared at it for ages and just don't remember them. And Mary and Matt McClusky have loved me as much as if I had been one of their own children and the boys are like brothers to me.'

'Huh,' said the other girl, 'I have no time for brothers. I have two, both younger than me, and a proper nuisance they are.'

Angela laughed and said, 'What's your name?'

'Maggie. Maggie Maguire and my brothers are called Eddie and Patrick. But I think Mammy is having another one and that will probably be a boy as well. I'd love a sister.'

'So would I,' Angela admitted. 'Shall we just be good friends instead?'

'Yes, let's.' And so a bond was formed between Angela Kennedy and Maggie Maguire from that first day.

THREE

Just after Angela began school, the priest heard of a house that would shortly be vacant due to the death of the tenant and Mary went straight down to see the landlord. She took her marriage

lines with her and the birth certificates of the children and to prove her honesty she carried a recommendation from the priest and she secured the house, which was in Bell Barn Road and only yards from Maggie's house in Grant Street.

Mary was delighted to get a place of her own though she did wonder how she would furnish it, but when she said this to Matt he had a surprise for her. 'With the sale of the farm and land I had money over when I bought the tickets to get here,' he told her. 'Not knowing when I would get a job when we arrived, I put it in the Post Office and it's still there, so we'll go off to the Bull Ring Saturday afternoon and see what we can pick up to make the place more homely at a reasonable price.'

Mary was really pleased that Matt had kept the money safe and that he had kept knowledge of it to himself as well, or she might have been tempted to dip into it from time to time, and where would they be now if she had done that? They'd have a house but not a stick of furniture to go into it.

In fact it wouldn't have been that bad because the previous tenant had died and his family didn't want much of his furniture, so the house already had two armchairs, a small settee and a sideboard downstairs, and a bed and wardrobes were left in the bedroom upstairs. Norah went to inspect the house and agreed with Mary it needed a thoroughly good clean before anything else and they undertook that together. In the Bull Ring Mary and Matt bought oilcloth for the floor, a big iron-framed bed for the boys in the attic and two chests for their clothes. For Angela there was a truckle bed that was to be set up in the bedroom because

Mary declared it wasn't seemly for her to share the attic with so many boys when she was not even officially related to them.

The purchases severely depleted Matt's savings and money from day to day was tighter than ever and Norah was finding it hard to make the money stretch. If some days they seemed to eat a lot of porridge it was because a pair of boots needed repair or there was a delivery of coal to pay for. Mary worried about the meals often. 'Men need more than porridge,' she said to Norah. 'If Finbarr and Colm do get a job they'll hardly be able for it and Matt works hard now and needs good food or he might take sick.'

Sometimes she would take Angela with her when she went to the Bull Ring on a Saturday afternoon and she would hide away and send Angela into the butcher's and ask for a bone for the dog. The butcher knew there was little likelihood of there being any sort of dog; most people had trouble enough feeding themselves. But he would be charmed by the look of Angela, her winning smile and good manners, and she usually came out with a bone with lots of meat still on it. Often the butcher would slip her something else, like a few pieces of liver, or a small joint because he would have to throw them away anyway at the end of the day.

And Mary would boil up the bones and strip them of meat for a stew along with vegetables and dumplings to fill hungry men. She would do the same with pigs' trotters if she had the pennies to buy them. She could make a couple of loaves of soda bread almost without thinking about it

43

and if there was no money for butter, mashed swede would do as well. Cabbage soup was also on the menu a lot so though no one starved, the monotony of the diet got to everyone, but no one complained for there was little point.

Finbarr and Colm were filled with shame that they couldn't do more to help and knowing this, Gerry felt almost embarrassed to join Sean on the apprenticeship scheme in 1902 when he turned fourteen and left school. 'Don't feel bad about it,' Finbarr said. 'You go for it. I would do the same given half a chance.'

Both apprentice boys were full of praise for Stan Bishop and thought he was a first-rate boss, always patient with them if they made mistakes in the early days. 'He's a decent man,' Mary said. 'I always thought it.'

'He's a happy bloke, I know that,' Sean said. 'He's always humming a tune under his breath and he sings at home.'

'He does that,' Colm said. 'He's good, or it sounds all right to me anyway, and Kate has a lovely voice.'

'Well she's in the choir,' Mary pointed out. 'That's why they always go to eleven o'clock Mass. She sometimes sings when she is in the house on her own because I have heard her a time or two when I have been up visiting Norah. She has got a lovely voice, but then she seems a lovely person. She always seems to have a smile on her face.'

She had. It was evident to everyone how happily married they were and there was speculation why there had been no sign of a child yet, though

Mary had confided to Norah that she thought Kate looked rather frail. 'I don't think it would do her good to have a houseful of children,' she said. 'It would pull the body out of her.'

'We none of us can do anything about that though,' Norah said. 'It's God's will. The priests will tell you that you must be grateful for whatever God sends, be it one or two or a round dozen.'

'I know,' Mary said and added, 'They're quick enough to give advice. But no one helps provide for those children, especially with jobs the way they are.'

'I know,' Norah said. 'And then wages are not so great either. I mean, my man's in work and I am hard pressed to make ends meet sometimes. At least Sean and Gerry are learning a trade, that's lucky.'

'Aye, if there is a job at the end of it.'

'There's the rub,' Norah said, because many firms would take on apprentices on low pay and get rid of them when they were qualified and could command far better wages, and take on another lot to train as it was cheaper for them.

'I'm not looking that far ahead,' Mary said. 'I'll worry about it if it happens. As for Kate Bishop, she seems not to be able to conceive one so easy, so I doubt they'll ever be that many eventually.'

'Don't be too sure,' Norah said. 'I've seen it before. They have trouble catching for one and then as if the body knows what to do, they pop another out every year or so.'

'Proper Job's comforter you are,' Mary said and added with a smile, 'Are you going to put the kettle on or what? A body could die of thirst in

this place.'

There was no change in the McClusky household over the next couple of years. Sean, now
halfway through his apprenticeship, got a rise,
but it was nothing much, and Matt too was earning more so the purse strings eased, but only
slightly. Towards the end of that year, Norah told
Mary she was sure Kate Bishop was pregnant.
There was a definite little bump that hadn't been
there before. By the turn of the year Stan was
nearly shouting it from the rooftops and though
he was like a dog with two tails, Kate was having
a difficult pregnancy and was sick a lot and not
just for the first three months, like the morning
sickness many women suffered from.

Many women gave her advice of things they had
tried themselves, or some old wives' tale they had
heard about, for all the women agreed with Mary
that Kate Bishop couldn't afford to lose weight for
she had none to lose. She was due at Easter and
she hardly looked pregnant as the time grew near.
'God!' Mary said to Norah. 'I was like a stranded
whale with all of mine. I do hope that girl is all
right. I saw her the other day and couldn't believe
it, her wrists and arms are very skinny and her skin
looks sort of thin.'

'She's still singing every Sunday morning
though,' Norah said. 'And she practises through
the day, does her scales and everything.'

'I suppose it helps keep her mind off things.'

'Maybe. Can't be long now though.'

On the fifteenth of April Kate Bishop's pains
began in the early hours and though Stan had

engaged a nurse, it was soon apparent that the services of a doctor were needed and he booked an ambulance, and while he was waiting for it to come Kate had a massive haemorrhage and died.

Stan was distraught at losing his beloved wife and he couldn't cope with his new-born son. Both Mary and Norah were often in the house with Stan, mainly caring for the baby and making meals for Stan he had no appetite to eat. Sometimes he seemed almost unaware of their presence and both Mary and Norah felt quite helpless that they could do nothing to ease Stan's pain and were glad when Kate's older sister Betty arrived.

She was married to Roger Swanage and though they lived in a nice house that Roger had inherited from his widowed mother, still they had no children though Betty had been trying for years to conceive. She took charge of Stan's son and Roger took it upon himself to organize the funeral for Kate because Stan seemed incapable, though he did insist on choosing the hymns because Kate had favourites and he chose those.

Betty seemed surprised at the numbers who turned out for the funeral but Kate had been popular and very young to lose her life in that tragic way, so the church was packed, including many men, as the foundry was closed that day as a mark of respect. Even those not going to the Mass stood at their doorways in silence as the cart carrying the coffin passed, some making the sign of the cross, and any men on the road removed their hats and stood with bowed heads.

The Requiem Mass seemed interminable and Mary heard many sniffs in the congregation as

Father Brannigan spoke of the grievous loss of the young woman leaving a child to grow up without a mother's love, and the loss would be felt through the whole community, but particularly by her grieving husband and her family, and the choir where she had been a stalwart member. Eventually it was over and the congregation moved off to Key Hill Cemetery in Hockley, as St Catherine's didn't have its own cemetery.

The wind had increased during the Mass and it buffeted them from side to side, billowing all around them, and when they stood by the open grave the wind-driven rain attacked them, stabbing at their faces like little needles – a truly dismal day. As the priest intoned further prayers for the dear departed and they began lowering the coffin with ropes, Stan gasped and staggered and would have fallen, but Matt reached out and put a hand upon his shoulder. 'Steady man. Nearly over.' The clods of earth fell with dull thuds on to the lid and they all turned thankfully away and walked back through the gusty, rain-sodden day to the back room of The Swan where a sumptuous feast was laid out, made by the landlord's wife and her two daughters.

Everyone seemed to think that it was right and proper that Kate's childless sister should rear the motherless child. Even Father Brannigan saw it as an ideal solution when he called to see them a week after the funeral to discuss the child's future and baptism.

'And you are fully prepared to take on the care of the child?' he asked Betty, though his gaze took in Roger too.

It was Betty who answered, 'Oh yes, Father,' she said. 'Kate was my own younger sister and I'm sure she would wish me to do this, and how can I not love her child as if he were my own?'

'And have you children of your own?'

'Sadly no,' Betty said. 'The Lord hasn't seen fit to grant me any and we have a fine house waiting for a child to fill it.'

'Well I think that eminently suitable,' the priest said.

'What of you, Stan? Are you in agreement with this?'

Stan turned vacant eyes on the priest. He wondered how he could explain to the priest, without shocking him to the core, that he cared little for the tiny mite held in Betty's arms so tenderly, the mite his wife had died giving birth to. And he contented himself giving a shrug of his shoulders.

Father Brannigan saw the intense sorrow in his deep eyes and knew for Stan the pain of his loss was too raw to discuss things to do with the child, and so he thought it a good thing his sister-in-law was there. He turned again to Betty. 'And have you chosen names?'

'Yes,' Betty said decidedly. 'I want him called Daniel.'

Stan's head shot up at that and the priest was pretty certain he hadn't known of Betty's plan. And he hadn't, and though he and Kate had discussed names, Daniel hadn't been mentioned, yet Betty said Kate would approve of Daniel. 'It was the name of our late father,' she said to Stan.

Stan hadn't the energy to protest and felt anyway he had no right. Betty was going to raise

the child, therefore she should have the right to name that child too. And Betty could be quite right – since it was the name of Kate's father she might have called him Daniel in the end. 'I don't mind what the child is called,' he said, 'but I want Matt and Mary McClusky as godparents.'

Mary was delighted to be asked but she noted the jealous way Betty held on to the child. While she was willing for Mary to take him from her and hold his head over the font so that the priest could dribble water over it, she took him back afterwards and would let no one else, not even his own father, hold him and Mary felt the first stirrings of unease. Stan on the other hand was pleased initially to leave everything to Betty and for Daniel to be taken back to their fine house in Sutton Coldfield after the christening.

'Where is Sutton Coldfield?' Mary asked Matt a few weeks later.

'I'm not sure myself,' Matt said. 'I know it's a fair distance and a posh place, so Stan was telling me. He said Betty and Roger live in a big house built of red brick with a blue slate roof. And although it's not on the doorstep it's easy enough to get to because a little steam train runs from New Street Station and then the station in Sutton is just yards from their house.'

'He's going to see him soon isn't he?'

Matt nodded. 'This Saturday afternoon,' he said. 'He'll have been with them nearly three weeks then and he wants to see how he has settled down and everything.'

Later Stan talked to Matt about how it had gone. 'Tell you, Matt, when I saw him, I had the urge to

grab him and bring him home where he belongs. But how could I care for him and work? Betty, on the other hand, already has the nursery fitted out for him, which is far more salubrious than any attic bedroom I could provide. There's also a garden back and front and I could see much better surroundings unfolding for Daniel if I left him there with his aunt and uncle, though I know he will probably call them mammy and daddy and will grow up thinking of them as his parents.'

'Like Angela did?'

'Ah but, the difference was she was told from the start who her real parents were and that they had both died, which was the truth, but Daniel has a father, though he will hardly be aware of that.'

'Why not?'

'Because Betty said it would confuse the boy if I kept popping up every now and then, and it wasn't as if I could offer him anything. She told me that if I cared for the boy I should stay out of his life and let them bring him up. The point is I know I can offer the child nothing, but I still wanted to see him, take him out weekends, you know, get to know him a bit, but Betty said if I intended doing that I would have to make alternative arrangements. She would only look after Daniel as long as I stayed away.'

Mary sighed when Matt told her that night what had transpired when Stan had gone to see his son. She wasn't totally surprised. She had thought Betty was the type of person who wouldn't want to share her dead sister's child. In a way in her mind she was probably trying to forget he had parents and make believe that he was her own

child she had given birth to.

In Mary's opinion secrets like this were not healthy and they had a way of wriggling to the fore eventually, spreading unhappiness and distrust. 'That's very harsh,' she said. 'I mean at the moment it's hard on Stan, but the longer Betty and her husband leave telling Daniel of his father, the greater the shock for the child. Stan might not be able to care for him and work, but that doesn't mean he can't be part of his life. I think he's a lovely man and I'm sure the child as he grows would benefit from knowing him.'

'I couldn't agree more,' Matt said. 'He said Betty was adamant. I think I might call her bluff in time. If she loves Daniel like he says she'd not want to give him up so easy, but Stan probably won't want to risk it.'

'Does he miss him?'

'I asked him that myself,' Matt said. 'I suppose that what you never had you can't miss but Stan said he always feels like something is missing and he copes because he knows Daniel will be happy and well loved, for Betty dotes on him and her husband does too, only slightly less anxiously. He said he would never have to worry that they would ever be unkind to him and he will want for nothing – no going barefoot with an empty belly for him. As long as the boy is happy that's all that matters to Stan.'

'That's what most parents want,' Mary said. 'Their children's happiness, and he is a decent man for putting the needs of his son before his own.'

Angela was unaware of what had happened to

Stan's baby. She knew about the death of his wife giving birth to the child, that couldn't be hidden from the children, but the baby had just seemed to disappear. Even Maggie living only doors away from Stan Bishop knew no more. It was no good asking questions because things like that were not discussed in front of children so the girls concluded the baby must have died too. 'Shame though, isn't it, for Stan to lose his wife and baby.'

'Mm,' Maggie said. 'Though I don't think men are that good at looking after babies.'

'No, maybe not,' Angela agreed. 'I just feel sorry for him being left with nothing. Doesn't seem fair somehow.'

'My mammy says none of life is fair and those that think it is are going to be disappointed over and over,' Maggie said and Angela thought that a very grim way of looking at things.

FOUR

Stan seemed to get over the loss of his wife in the end as everyone must, but for ages a pall of sadness hung over him. Barry started on the apprenticeship scheme in 1907, the same year his brother Sean finished, and Stan's sadness wasn't helped by the news he had to impart to Mary. 'He was heartbroken when he came to tell me that the boys would have no job at the end of their apprenticeships,' Mary told Norah. 'Sean is out of work now like his older brothers and I

suppose Gerry will be the same in two years' time. Stan said he could do nothing about it because it was the company's policy. It was a bit of a blow but not a total shock because that sort of thing is happening everywhere.'

'I know but it isn't as if they can get a job somewhere else using the skills they have learnt because there are no jobs.'

'Aye that's the rub,' Mary said. 'And now there'll be another mouth to feed on the pittance they will be able to earn. I mean you can only tighten a belt so far. And when Gerry is finished too in two years' time God knows what we are going to do.'

'I'm the same,' Norah said, 'and this has decided me.'

'What?'

'My eldest Frankie is just eighteen so half-way through his apprenticeship and my brother Aiden was after writing to me, offering to find him a job in the place he works. They're taking a lot of young lads on.'

'But Aiden is in the States?'

'I know, New York.'

'But... But surely to God you don't want your son going so far away?'

'Course I don't,' Nora said. 'What I want is for him to get a job somewhere local and meet a nice Catholic girl to marry and give me grandchildren to take joy from. But it's not going to happen, not here. I know when we bid farewell that will be it and I'll never see my son again but I can't deny him this chance of a future. I see your lads day after day worn down by the fact they can get no job. Unemployment is like a living death and how

54

can I put Frankie through that when Aiden is holding out the hand of opportunity to him?'

She couldn't, Mary recognized that, but she knew Norah's heart would break when her eldest son went away from her. And though her own heart ached for her sons she couldn't help feeling glad that they had no sponsor in America.

Unbeknownst to her, though, Finbarr and Colm were very interested in Frankie Docherty's uncle's proposal. 'He seems very certain he will have a job for you,' Finbarr said.

'Yes he is.'

'What line of work is it?'

'Making motor cars.'

Finbarr stared at him. There were a few petrol-driven lorries and vans and commercial vehicles but personal motor cars were only for the very wealthy, they had taken the place of carriages, and Finbarr didn't think even in a country the size of America they would need that many. Frankie's career might be short lived when he got to the States.

Frankie caught sight of Finbarr's sceptical face and he said, 'My Uncle Aiden says that America is not like here and that everyone who is someone wants a motor car. They can't keep up with the demand. And they want to train mechanics too so that they can fix the cars when they go wrong.'

'Right,' Finbarr said. 'You excited?'

Frankie nodded eagerly. 'You bet I am,' he said, and added, 'I have to hide it from Mammy though.'

'I can imagine,' Finbarr said with a smile. 'Well I wish you all the very best and I only wish Colm

and I were going along with you.'

'Wouldn't you mind going so far away?'

'Won't you?'

'Of course,' Frankie said. 'I expect to miss my family but that's the choice you have to make, isn't it. And you've got to deal with homesickness otherwise you will waste the chance you've been given.'

'That's pretty sound reasoning, Frankie,' Colm said. 'I imagine I would feel much the same.'

'And me,' said Finbarr.

'Maybe I can get my uncle to speak for you too,' Frankie said. 'He'll know your family for they were neighbours in Donegal and then Mammy helped when you first came over and my mother and yours are as thick as thieves now.'

'We would appreciate it,' Finbarr said. 'See how the land lies when you get over there.'

'Yes,' Frankie said. 'I won't forget. It will be nice for me to see a familiar face anyway. I'll write.'

So Frankie left a few days later. His mother cried copious tears and his siblings sniffled audibly. Even Mick's voice was husky and even Frankie was struggling with his emotions, and he hugged his family and shook hands with all the well-wishers gathered to wish him God speed.

'It will break my heart if Mammy is as upset as Norah was when we go,' Colm said.

'She will be,' Finbarr said. 'Worse maybe for there are two of us. But however sad she is, remember we are not just thinking about this for ourselves alone but also for Mammy and the others. All she has coming in now is what Daddy brings in and a pittance from Gerry and Barry's

apprenticeship money, and Gerry will be out on his ear before long too.'

'Yeah I suppose.'

'We need to leave, Colm, and go as far as America if things are as good as Frankie's uncle says. The life we have now is no life at all, and even worse, we have no future to look forward to.'

It was sometime later Frankie wrote the promised letter and told them things were just fine and dandy for him in America and he was looking forward to them joining him. The even better news was that knowing the family personally from when they all lived in Donegal, their uncle was not only willing to sponsor them but loan them the £10 each needed for the assisted passage tickets, which would be easy to pay back from the good wages they'd be earning over there. Finbarr let his breath out in a sigh of utter relief, for he hadn't known how they were going to raise the money for the fare, and this generous man was coming to their aid. All they had to do now was tell their parents and he thought that was better done sooner rather than later and give them time, particularly their mother, to come to terms with it.

If Finbarr and Colm thought Norah Docherty was upset when Frankie left, that was before they had seen their mother's distress, for she was almost hysterical with grief. Never in her wildest dreams had she thought her sons would do what Frankie Docherty did and leave everything behind and travel to another continent entirely. She thought if nothing else, financial constraints would prevent them, for they would never raise the £10 needed to avail themselves of the assisted passage

scheme. Aiden had paid for his nephew and it appeared he was prepared to loan her two sons the money needed and sponsor them too.

'We have no life here, Mammy,' Finbarr cried. 'There is no future for us, our lives are dribbling away.'

Mary continued to cry, but Matt had listened to his sons. Finbarr had a point, he realized, for he was twenty-four now and Colm twenty-three. They should be working at a job of some sort and have money in their pockets for a pint or two now and then, go to the match if they had a mind, court a girl perhaps, and all they could see in front of them were years of the same struggle. There was no light at the end of the tunnel because they were unable to procure some meaningful employment, so Matt's wage added together with a minute portion from his two sons still at the foundry had to keep them all. It was only Mary's ability to make a sixpence do the work of a shilling that stopped them from starving altogether.

The situation couldn't go on however, especially when there was every likelihood of the situation worsening when Gerry finished his apprenticeship in a year or two and subsequently Barry. His sons had the means of alleviating things for them and securing a future for themselves. It was bad that this involved them leaving home to move so far away but he didn't see any alternative. Though he knew he would be heart-sore to lose them, for the good of them all it had to be.

Finbarr and Colm had their arms around their mother saying they were sorry and urging her not to upset herself, and her tears had changed to

gulping sobs, and Matt waited till he was totally calm and then told Mary quietly the thoughts that had been tumbling around his head. As a pang of anguish swept over Mary's face Colm moved away so Matt could hold Mary's arm. Neither Finbarr nor Colm had been aware of Matt's thoughts and the fact that he had listened to them and understood their concerns meant a great deal since the one person their mother listened to and took heed of was Matt.

'But America, Matt,' Mary wailed. 'It's so far away. We'll never see them again.'

Matt gave a slight shake of his head. 'We might not and there will be a part of my heart that will go with them, but we can be content, thinking that we have given them the potential for a full and happy life.'

Mary was still silent so Matt went on. 'We left our native shores for a better life, remember.'

'We only crossed a small stretch of water though.'

'Never mind how long or short the journey was. We came for a better life,' Matt said. 'And for a time achieved it, but the system failed our boys and they are on the scrapheap. They want better than this and who can blame them? And if they have to go to America to achieve it, so be it.'

Mary gave a brief nod. Though tears shone in her eyes and she was unable to speak, she knew she had no right to deny a better life to her sons.

The rest of the family were astounded when they heard and more than a little upset, though they all could see why the boys had to go. Father Brannigan disapproved, but then he disapproved

59

of so much, you wouldn't know what you had to do to please him.

'You will lose your faith if you go there.'

'Don't see why you say that, Father,' said Finbarr. 'They have priests and churches and plenty of Catholics already there.'

'It's a dangerous, lawless place.'

'Oh, have you been over there, Father?'

'No I haven't been,' the priest snapped. 'I wouldn't go to such a place if you paid me, but I can read the papers.'

'Even if it's as bad as you say,' Colm said, 'Fin and I wouldn't get involved in anything like that. We just want to do a job of work and get paid a wage that will enable us to enjoy life a little.'

'Frankie Docherty has been there some months now and he writes to us but never mentions any trouble of any kind,' Finbarr said and the priest was silent, because he had tried to talk Frankie out of going and he hadn't been dissuaded either.

The boys would not be going until the spring of 1908 as it was too close to the end of the year to cross the Atlantic, so Christmas that year had poignancy to it as they knew they might never ever be all together like that again. Stan came to wish them all Happy Christmas. He had grown fond of the boys and he felt a measure of guilt that he had been unable to help them in finding employment. Neither of the boys bore him any ill will however, and though they'd undoubtedly miss their family, Frankie described New York in such glowing terms, they couldn't wait to see it for themselves.

Mary had got a battered case from someone, not that her sons had much to put in it – sparse sets of

ragged underwear, everyday clothes holed and patched and the two jumpers Mary had knitted them both for Christmas, for she said from what she'd heard New York winters were severe. They would be travelling in the suits they wore for Sunday, though they were thin and quite flimsy now and the trousers shiny and shapeless, and the only boots they possessed they had on. They had no top coats or any money to buy them which was another reason for crossing the Atlantic in the spring.

The day arrived and the family assembled to say goodbye for there was no money for the fare to accompany them to the docks. Mary had thought of this day often and had shed tears each time she had thought of it, and now she held her sons tight, for it was a hug that would have to last a lifetime, and tears were also raining down Finbarr and Colm's face when Mary released them. Matt also hugged his two sons and wished them God speed. They bade farewell to Sean and Gerry and Barry and as he hugged Angela Finbarr said, 'You better behave yourself now I'm not around to look after you.'

'Huh, as if I ever took any notice of you anyway,' Angela said with a ghost of a smile.

Finbarr gave a watery smile back, glad of her lightening the atmosphere, even slightly, for the whole family had seemed steeped in misery, and it was hard to leave them like that, but they had a boat to catch. Mary stood on the pavement and waved till they turned down Bristol Street and so were out of sight. Then she came in, gave a sigh, plopped in a chair and burst into tears, wiping her eyes with her apron.

Finbarr and Colm's departure had left a gaping hole in the family and they maybe were aware of that but they certainly knew how their mother would worry and so they wrote a letter while on the ship just saying that they were well and quite excited and on course for America. They hadn't expected to be able to do that but it was a practice on some ships to encourage it, even providing the paper, envelopes and pens, since it was known it helped homesickness for many of the passengers, at least in steerage or third class, who were often not there through choice but forced through poverty and unemployment to make for the Brave New World.

The next letter came after they had met up with Frankie and his uncle and were taken to share a bedroom in Aiden's quite sizeable home. Finbarr wrote:

Before we came to America we had to go to a place called Ellis Island to see if we were free from disease. We were prodded and poked and examined and in the end the doctor said I was fit enough but needed more flesh on my bones. Colm was told the same and we were mighty glad because if you fail that medical you're sent back. We were asked questions, general knowledge sort of thing, and an account of why we have come to America and we found the Christian Brothers had beat enough knowledge into us for us to be able to give a good enough account of ourselves.

Colm wrote:

From Ellis Island you can see the New York skyline

62

and all the skyscrapers some of the fellows on the ship had told us about. What a sight it was. And dominating the waterfront was the huge Statue of Liberty. Liberty that burns in the heart of every Irish man. This is truly the land of the Free and neither of us can wait to experience that.

'They seem happy enough anyway,' Matt said. 'So far at least.'

And they continued to be fine as they described the long straight streets of New York that had numbers instead of names and the shops and the buildings that towered above them till you could almost feel they were actually scraping the sky. They described the tramcars and the trains that run underground that the Americans called the subway and they talked of the job they did building motor cars.

Mary wished they wouldn't write in such glowing terms of the great life they were leading for she saw the same restlessness in her two younger sons, which intensified when Gerry finished his apprenticeship in 1909 and was immediately laid off. Angela knew that Mary was worried they would want to follow their brothers to America, but she also knew how tight the financial budget was. Maybe if she got a job and could contribute a bit and things were a little easier they would stay.

In 1910 Angela would be fourteen and could leave school but as her birthday was in early April it was after Easter before she could leave school and only then if she had a job to go to, otherwise she had to stay until July. From the experience her brothers had had she knew any job might be

difficult to find.

'I don't like the thought of you in a factory anyway,' Mary said in early March.

'Mammy, I don't think I can be that fussy,' Angela said. 'Think of the way Finbarr and Colm searched for employment and they were willing to do anything and in the end they had to go to America to get a good job. Maybe,' she added with a grin at Mary, 'I should try that too?'

'Don't even joke about that,' Mary said. 'We'll keep looking. There must be something and we have got time yet.'

It was Norah who told her about the vacancy at George Maitland's grocery shop. It was a little out of the way for them, but she had gone visiting an old neighbour who had moved there and seen the card in the window.

'People around said he had a boy helping him but he caught rheumatic fever. They did think at one time the boy wasn't going to make it but when it was obvious he was going to recover George Maitland didn't advertise his position in case he wanted to come back to work, so my friend said. She said, "He's a decent sort that way, George." He even had his crabbed wife to help him a time or two but she insulted more than she served, my friend said, and if she was more in the shop in general and not just when he was short handed people would go elsewhere for their groceries.'

Angela wrinkled her nose. 'She doesn't sound very nice. But if the boy is recovering, I don't see why he's advertising now for someone new.'

'That's it,' Norah said. 'Apparently he is as well as he ever will be, but he's left with a weak heart

and the doctor said the work in the shop is too strenuous for him, so as he can't go back there's a vacancy. Do you know the shop I'm talking about?'

Angela nodded, 'I'll go up tomorrow.'

'What about school?' Mary asked.

'I think this is more important,' Angela said. 'Jobs are snapped up these days and it's nearly holidays anyway and if I secure this job my school days are numbered and I'll be earning money almost straight away.'

Mary couldn't argue with that. 'I think you do right. We'll sort out the school later and I hope you get it.'

So early the next morning George Maitland turned as the bell tinkled and saw one of the most beautiful girls he had ever seen standing in his shop. She had white-blonde hair and the most vivid blue eyes and when she smiled at him it was as if someone had turned a light on inside her.

Angela in her turn saw an oldish man in his late fifties, if she had to hazard a guess. He had a pleasant face rather than a handsome one for he had a large nose and a wide and generous mouth set in slightly sallow skin. He had plenty of hair but it was a bit like pepper and salt in colour and matched his big, bushy eyebrows. Beneath those eyebrows were the softest kindest eyes she had seen in a long time and he said, 'Can I help you?'

'Yes, please,' Angela said. 'I've come about the ad.'

'The ad?'

'Yes it's in the window,' Angela said. 'About a

shop assistant.'

'You want to work in the shop?' George said. He had never thought about employing a girl before but there was no rule against it and he realized he would like to see that pleasant and attractive face every day.

'It's five and a half days a week,' he said. 'All day Saturday and half day Wednesday, that all right?'

'That's fine, sir,' Angela said, hardly daring to believe that this man was going to employ her. She could go home and put a smile on Mary's face, because it was nearly the holidays so she could start work straight away. 'Thank you, sir,' she added and wondered if it was bad form to ask about wages. She needed to know, but wouldn't like to scupper her chances.

George wondered if she knew how expressive her face was. He was surprised she hadn't asked straight away what she was to be paid when he told her the hours she would be working, but knew from her face she was working up to do it now.

And so he forestalled her. 'And the wages are ten and six a week,' he said, knowing if he had employed a boy he would have started him on twelve and six.

However, Angela didn't know that and ten shillings and sixpence sounded fine, to her, especially when George added, 'And a basket of groceries every Saturday.'

George readily agreed to write a note for the school so that Angela could be released from school early and she began in the shop at the start of the Easter holidays. She was a hit with most of the customers and soon he didn't know what he

had ever done without her. She loved serving in the shop and it showed. She greeted every customer, even the awkward ones, with a bright smile and if someone had a sick child they were worried about or a doddery mother or chesty husband she would remember and enquire about them. Added to that, she was quick and efficient and could reckon up faster and more accurately than any boy he had ever employed.

He felt quite paternal towards Angela. She could easily have been his daughter and how he wished she was. He had thought by the age he was now he would have sons to help him in the store and carry on after his day, as he had done with his father, and maybe a daughter or two to gladden his heart.

But it was not to be, for Matilda didn't like that side of married life. That hadn't worried him at first for girls of her class were not supposed to like sex and as they were heavily chaperoned during their courtship he was unable to ask or reassure her about it. In fact they had both been so constrained and had such little time totally alone that he knew no more of Matilda when he married her than when the courtship had begun.

She was completely innocent of sexual matters or what you did to procreate a child. In that she wasn't unusual of her station; very often it was expected that the husband would teach a girl what was what on their wedding night. So George imagined that he would talk to her about sexual matters and any problems could be sorted out.

However, she didn't even like discussing such things. She said it was 'dirty talk' and was completely disgusted when he explained how they

might conceive a child together. She threw him from her with such force that he almost fell out of bed while she screamed at him that she was surprised at such dirty words spilling from his mouth and she never wanted to hear a word about it again. So nothing was sorted out at all.

Matilda agreed to share a bed and often lay beside him as stiff as a board, but that was all. She wouldn't allow George to touch her in any way. He had initially thought she might come round in the end, but as time went on her attitude became more and more entrenched. He begged and pleaded, cajoled, but Matilda wouldn't budge an inch. 'But don't you want a child, my love?' he'd asked in desperation and frustration one night.

'A child!' Matilda had shrieked, as if she had never heard of such a thing. 'No I don't want a child. I have no desire to find myself lumbered with some smelly, bawling brat.'

George felt a stab in his heart as he realized he had fallen for a beautiful face, for in her youth Matilda had been a stunning beauty and he had been overawed that she had agreed to walk out with him. Her parents made no objection to their courtship for though George was 'Trade' he was known as a steady, sober and easygoing sort of chap who would inherit the shop after his father died.

What George got was a shell instead of a real flesh-and-blood woman. One who looked good on the top but with nothing underneath. He was heartbroken that his dreams of a family to fill the rooms above the shop would only ever be dreams and never become reality. However, he believed

marriage was for life and if you made a bad choice you had to live with it, and as he wasn't the sort of man to force himself on a woman he settled for a loveless and a sexless marriage.

He felt ashamed that his wife spurned him so totally and he threw himself into the shop, knowing there he was in charge and a success, but it was a sterile success for he was working only for a woman who had no interest in it and was only interested in the profit made.

And now Angela had brought brightness to his days he was almost content.

Angela could have told him he had brought contentment to Mary with the groceries she took home each Saturday. In fact it was more than contentment. In fact that first Saturday, as she unpacked the bag and laid all the articles on the table, Mary burst into tears and wiped her eyes on her apron as she felt the worry of making nourishing meals for them all slide from her shoulders.

And so when Angela gave her her wage packet unopened she extracted sixpence from it and gave it back to Angela. 'I don't want it, Mammy,' Angela said. 'The money is just for you.'

Mary shook her head. 'It's right you keep something, for the men hold back their ciggy money, so you should have something.'

'But I don't smoke.'

'I should think you don't,' Mary said. 'But there might be something else you want. Save it if you can think of nothing just now, but you can rely on sixpence coming your way every week.'

'Thank you Mammy.'

'Yes, and talking about smoking, I wish your

father didn't do so much of it,' Mary said. 'He has that hacking cough and smoking can't help. Smoking less might help his stomach too.'

'What's wrong with his stomach?'

'Oh I don't know,' Mary said. 'Indigestion most likely. It only seemed to start when you started bringing the food from Maitland's. His stomach's not used to good food, too rich for him.' And then she added as she saw Angela's brow creased in concern, 'But don't worry yourself, Angela. If that is what's upsetting him he'll get used to it in the end.'

FIVE

Mary thought life had finally reached a more or less even keel. She had no idea what the future held, but just for the moment things were going along nicely. True, like their elder brothers, Sean and Gerry could find no permanent jobs, but that wasn't so important now that Angela was bringing in ten shillings a week and a big bag of groceries. Barry, now two thirds of his way through his apprenticeship, had had a raise and he was able to also tip up ten shillings a week and Matt earned three pounds and kept little back for himself. It meant if Sean and Gerry had earned anything it was a bonus and if they hadn't managed that, it didn't matter.

Barry knew that wasn't how his brothers viewed things because he had discussed it with

them. They felt failures and they viewed the lives of their brothers in America with unbridled envy. 'I don't think I'm asking a lot,' Sean said. 'I want a job of work that pays enough for me to live independently, pay rent and bills with enough over to buy some much-needed clothes, or have my leaky boots mended, or go out for an evening and have a few beers. Now I call that living a life.'

'Well you can't do that here,' Gerry said. 'Just at the moment a person needs to go to America to live at all.'

'Well why don't you go then?' Barry asked.

'Basically because of you, mate,' Gerry said.

'Why me?'

'Because we're dropping you in the mire.'

'How?'

'Well we can't all swan off and leave Mammy and Daddy on their own.'

'They won't be on their own,' Barry said. 'I have no yen to go to America and how will you not going to America help any of us?'

Both boys had to admit it would make little difference, but Gerry still felt bad about leaving Barry to shoulder all the responsibility of their ageing parents on his own, but Sean said, 'At least Angela loves our mammy as much as we do, so there will be no problem when you wed.'

'What d'you mean when we wed?'

'Well you will wed won't you?' Gerry said. 'Everyone knows that you are crazy about her. Plain as the nose on your face.'

'Yes but Angela is little more than a child. She's not even sixteen until the spring and I don't know if she feels the same about me.'

71

Sean laughed. 'Course she does. The love-light's shining in her eyes every time she looks at you. Think Mammy's aware of it and I reckon nothing would please her more because she loves Angela like the daughter she never had.'

What Sean said was true. Angela had no memory of her earlier life with her birth parents but the memories that were rock solid for her were of Mary cuddling her tight and tucking her into bed at night with a kiss. Angela knew she was truly loved by the whole family and especially Mary and Matt, and she loved them in return. Barry knew she loved him too and always had, but she was so young. It might be a childish love she had for him and not yet the love of a woman for a man, a love that would last a lifetime and stand strong and true against all that life might throw at them. He couldn't ask such a young person to make a commitment like that, it wouldn't be fair. He decided to stick to his original plan and wait until she was eighteen and he was through his apprenticeship before admitting how he felt about her and hoping she felt the same. So Barry never spoke to Angela but the boys wrote to Finbarr and Colm and said they wanted to try their hand in America.

The elder boys were delighted their younger brothers wanted to join them and they recommended that they travel in ships on the White Star line for there was more comfort for the third-class or steerage passengers.

Finbarr wrote further:

If I were you I'd take the train to Southampton and sail on the Titanic. *I've been reading up about it and it's*

the largest passenger ship in the world. It's been made in Belfast and it has its maiden voyage on 12th April, a grand time to cross the Atlantic. There are electric lights, you sleep four to a room, three meals a day is all included and served in one of two dining saloons and there is running water in the shared bathrooms. And best of all it's unsinkable. Just say the word and I'll book you two places now if I can because lots might want a place for her maiden voyage. Our journey across was comfortable enough but it didn't have the facilities like the Titanic. *I wish Colm and I had been able to travel on it, but we'll be here to meet you on the dockside.*

Sean and Gerry were terribly excited to be given the chance to travel on such a magnificent ship and they read up all they could about it. Mary was absolutely astounded that her two other sons wanted to go to America too. 'You'll be next I suppose,' she snapped at Barry.

Barry knew she wasn't cross but frightened and he said gently but firmly, 'Not me, Mammy. I've no yen to go travelling.'

'What if they lay you off when you finish your apprenticeship?'

'Shall we cross that bridge when we come to it?' Barry said. 'But even then I promise I am going nowhere.'

Mary let out a sigh of relief, but she didn't want Sean or Gerry to go either, but what could they do? The slump seemed deeper than ever in Britain. There was a slump in America too but Finbarr and Colm seemed immune to it and they had guaranteed they could get their brothers jobs

as soon as they came over. Matt could see the lads' point of view though he too would miss the two of them sorely. Mary could see it, though wished she didn't have to, and Angela felt a deep sadness that two more brothers were going to live an ocean away from her.

The boys did their best to reassure their mother. They showed her a picture of the ship and told her about all it had on board and everything, but as Mary said to them, there was always the chance they might fall ill or something. A few years ago the people in Ireland were leaving in droves for America and so many perished in the ships they began calling them coffin ships.

'I know,' Barry said. 'Things are much improved now. I mean Fin and Colm gave a good account of their journey and the *Titanic* is supposed to be the best of its kind.'

They were travelling down to Southampton on Tuesday 9th April, which was Angela's sixteenth birthday. Fin and Colm had paid for their train fare to Southampton and booked them into a lodging house near the docks and they would board the *Titanic* from there the following morning. 'Get a good night's sleep,' Finn advised, but Sean and Gerry were far too excited to sleep. This was the start of the greatest adventure of their lives and they didn't want to waste the whole night sleeping, and spent most of the night talking of the journey which they were looking forward to and of arriving in America where their lives would really begin.

On Monday 15th April a very excited woman

arrived in the shop with news that the unsinkable *Titanic* had gone down in the Atlantic Ocean, sunk when it hit an iceberg. Apparently the news had appeared on an American newsreel and her aunt in America had sent a telegram to her as her son had been due to sail on the *Titanic*. But he had been taken ill and had to cancel.

The blood had drained from Angela's face and eventually the woman noticed. 'God, Angela, you've gone ever such a funny colour.' Then she clapped her hands over her mouth and said, 'Oh me and my big mouth, blurting it out like that. Your brothers were on it weren't they? I remember talking about it when my Tom was due to go too.'

George had heard every word too and he said consolingly to Angela, 'There will be lifeboats to get the people off, don't worry. A big new boat like that will have enough to cope with any eventuality. And the ship might not even be fully sunk, people might still be on it.' Then he turned to the woman and said, 'Did it say anything else about those rescued, the survivors?'

The woman shook her head. 'Don't know if there's any more to tell yet, not that you can get it chapter and verse in a telegram.'

'No, course not,' George said and he turned to Angela and said, 'You should go home. What this woman has heard others can hear. You should be with your mother and send for Barry and his father. You need to be together.'

Angela went round for Barry before going home, for if Mary had heard any inkling she might need their support. When she told Stan what she had heard that morning he was upset himself and fully

agreed Barry and Matt needed to be at home and when they were sent for she told them both what she had heard that morning. Matt gave a sharp intake of breath and his face drained of colour, but he said only, 'This will hit your mother hard, Barry.'

It would hit Barry hard if anything bad had happened to them. They were his big brothers and he loved them. And yet he said to his father, 'We know nothing concrete yet, Daddy. We must hold on to that.'

'You're right, Barry,' Stan said as they left. 'Sometimes these snippets of news are anything but helpful. Come and tell me as soon as you know anything definite. I was very fond of those young men.'

They walked home almost in silence, each busy with their own thoughts, but all were relieved to find Mary knew nothing, and they were able to tell her gently and hold her as she wept.

A telegram arrived the followed day from Finbarr. He didn't know if the news of the sinking of the *Titanic* after hitting a massive iceberg had reached British shores so he explained that first and explained another ship called *Carpathian* had picked up survivors and was estimated to be arriving in New York on 18th April. The news gave everyone renewed hope. The men returned to tell Stan, who relayed the news to the workforce. Angela went to tell George, and neighbours hearing of the sinking of that gigantic vessel with two of the McClusky sons on it came to say how sorry they were, and they too went home cheered that survivors had been picked up by another ship.

76

They existed in a kind of limbo for a couple of days. Norah Docherty, knowing the same fate could have happened to her son, was great company for Mary in keeping her spirits up and Mick took Matt to The Swan for a pint. In fact, Matt, the very moderate drinker, had far more than one pint since many of the men wanted to buy him one – their way of showing sympathy – and it ended up with Mary and Angela helping the very drunk Matt up the stairs to bed. As they lowered him on to the bed, Angela said, 'Are you going to undress him?'

'I am not,' Mary said emphatically. 'I'm not even trying to move his hulk around to get him more comfortable. I'll just remove his shoes, that's all, and I'll tell you, I'd not have his head in the morning for a pension, and yet I can envy him because for the last few hours he has been able to stop worrying about those lads.'

'They'll be all right,' Angela said. 'They probably had a fright and might have got a bit wet, but they are big strapping lads and know how to look after themselves.'

'Of course they do and you are right,' Mary said and Angela so hoped she was right as she followed Mary down the stairs.

On 18th April just before eight in the evening, Finbarr and Colm had stood just outside the harbour in New York and watched the *Carpathian* sail in. And once the *Carpathian* had docked, the two young men surged through with the rest to check the list of survivors to see if their younger brothers had been among the lucky ones. A sailor from the rescue ship, seeing their anxious scrutiny

of the lists pinned up, asked who they were searching for, and when they told him he said that few men had got off. 'I heard as how there weren't even enough lifeboats for everyone.'

'Not enough lifeboats?' Finbarr repeated almost in disbelief.

'Well wasn't it supposed to be unsinkable?'

Finbarr nodded. 'That's what they claimed wasn't it, Colm?'

'Yes,' said Colm in agreement. 'I mean, that was one reason we encouraged them to travel on the *Titanic*.'

'Well it hit a gigantic iceberg, see. Most of an iceberg is below the water, you only see a bit of it, and whatever way it happened, it hit the iceberg and started to sink. I heard this from the sailors we pulled onto our ship,' the *Carpathian* sailor said. 'One of them said when the iceberg was spotted there wasn't time to turn such a large ship to avoid it. He said if they hadn't tried to avoid it and had hit it head on it probably would have been all right but, as it was, it crashed into the side and the iceberg ripped straight through it and it started to fill with water.'

'What were you doing picking up sailors when more passengers could have been in the lifeboats?' Finn asked.

'They were the sailors chosen to row the lifeboats,' the *Carpathian* sailor said. 'If they hadn't rowed away from the ship as quick as possible when it sank it would have pulled the lifeboats down with it. Then we'd have had no survivors at all to rescue. There were a few other men as well. Travelling first class, some were let on the boats

78

straight away, but then the crew found out how dire the situation was and after that it was women and children only that were loaded into the lifeboats.'

'And the rest of the men?' Finbarr asked, though he knew the answer.

'They went down with the ship,' the sailor said bluntly. And then, looking at the clothes Finbarr and Colm had on, which marked them as working men, the sailor went on, 'Would your brothers be travelling steerage?'

'They were,' Finbarr said. 'What of it?'

'Nothing,' the sailor said. 'That is, nothing good. It's just that these sailors told us that few steerage passengers, carried in the bowels of the ship, made it to the lifeboats anyway, not even the women and children. One told me some hadn't even got to the deck when the ship sank without trace.'

'People wouldn't have been picked up by other ships, would they?' Colm cried, desperate to find some glimmer of hope. 'Like if they were clinging to some wreckage or something like that to keep afloat?'

The sailor shook his head. 'Sorry, mate. First off, there were no other ships in the area. Ours was the only one who answered the distress call, so probably any other ships were too far away to be of any use. And secondly, even if someone had managed to hang on to wreckage, how long do you think they'd last in water cold enough to have huge icebergs floating in it? One minute? Maybe two, but no more than that before they froze to death.'

Colm staggered at the news. They bought papers on their way home and read the reports of the

collision that sank a ship claimed to be unsinkable on her maiden voyage. It was news that shocked the world, and their brothers had died, and the way they died was horrendous, and Finbarr in particular felt as guilty as Hell for urging Sean and Gerry to follow them.

When they returned to their lodgings they decided to say nothing to their mother and father about the things the sailor from the rescue ship told them. 'It would serve no purpose and only upset them further,' Finn said. 'Anyway, it's not the thing to put in a telegram, and that's what we must send first thing tomorrow and we can write them a fuller letter later.'

Colm agreed, 'Aye and it will be hard enough to cope with the loss of two sons and enough to be going on with.'

And so the bare telegram just said that neither Sean nor Gerry were among the survivors on the *Carpathian*. They had been waiting for the telegram and yet Angela's fingers shook as she took it from the telegraph boy. 'Any message?' the boy asked.

Angela shook her head. 'No message.'

She shut the door and turned and gave the telegram to Barry, for she couldn't bring herself to open it. Barry took it from, her and read the few bald words out to them all as his own voice was breaking with emotion, and tears sprang from his eyes as he felt the aching loss of his brothers. Angela did too, but she pushed aside her heartache to deal with Matt and Mary who were in pieces.

She knew that until the arrival of the telegram Matt and Mary would have hoped it wasn't as

bad as they feared. They had encouraged this. They had all hoped themselves because it's what people did. But now all hope was snuffed out, Sean and Gerry were gone and she would never see them again, and if she felt the pain of that loss so keenly, she could only imagine what it was doing to Matt and Mary, and the anguish etched in both their faces tore at her heart.

Even after the telegram Barry and Angela couldn't understand the scale of this tragedy and in the papers Barry had brought in they had both read about the proverbial unsinkable liner, on its maiden voyage, that had indeed sunk and sunk so quickly when it struck an iceberg that though 705 had managed to get into lifeboats and so were saved, 1,517 perished. Most of the fatalities, the papers claimed, were steerage or third-class passengers and any that were rescued were women and children. The lack of enough lifeboats for all the passengers was also discussed, and the fact that a lot of the lifeboats were not full when they pulled away from the ship, for the *Titanic* sank quicker than anyone thought it would.

The newspapers made grim reading and Angela hid the papers away in the cellar with the kindling for the fire, intending to burn them when she got the chance, for she and Barry both thought dealing with the death of their sons was quite enough to be going on with, without constantly reading about such a disaster. But that was hard to do without Matt or Mary catching sight of the headlines and so on, because they seldom left the sitting room.

Coming into the room the evening following

the arrival of the telegram, Mary had sobbed afresh as Angela helped get her ready for bed. Angela said, 'I understand Mammy's distress really because I suppose the telegram snuffed out the last glimmer of hope that she kept burning in her heart. I know it did for me, for I loved them just as if they had been my true brothers.'

'Yes,' said Barry with a sigh. 'I know you did and they knew, it too. And I know the casualty figures are shocking, but knowing that two of those left to die are your own flesh and blood is hard to take. But that is what happened, and they are dead and gone, so that neither of us will see them again. But that's how it is and we must deal with it.'

Everyone felt sorry for the McCluskys and many understood the spiral of depression Matt and Mary had sunk into when the telegram arrived, cutting off all hope that either of their sons might have survived. So they continued to pop in and out as they had when the news first broke and didn't usually come empty-handed. Unable to do anything to ease the situation, they brought a bit of stew they had left over and cakes they'd made, and Angela marvelled that these people, some of whom had little enough for themselves, were willing to share with them. Norah also visited, and Stan were always popping in and out.

The priest, Father Brannigan, came too, purporting to show support and sympathy in their loss, but managed to turn it round to slight condemnation against Matt and Mary for letting the boys go in the first place. While he drank two cups of tea he ladled three sugars into them and

ate all the scones that one of their neighbours had brought round for them earlier that day.

Eventually, annoyed at the implied criticism Angela knew Mary and Matt were unable to cope with, she said, 'Sean and Gerry had no permanent work, Father. They had to go each day to the factories to pick up a few hours' work if they could. Often they arrived home empty-handed.'

'Many work that way.'

'But maybe they haven't an alternative,' Angela said. 'But Sean and Gerry had two brothers already in America who could find them good jobs and have them lodging in the same house as themselves. It was a wrench for them to go for all of us, but I know they felt bad when they could contribute nothing at home. They saw themselves as a drain on the family and could see no future for themselves. No-one did anything wrong and yet Mammy and Daddy have lost two sons and maybe prayers, rather than censure, would be more helpful at this point.'

Had Mary and Matt been thinking straight they probably would have been surprised at Angela talking to the priest that way, but it all went over their heads and even Father Brannigan didn't come back with a sharp retort as he would normally, for he was unused to any form of criticism from his parishioners. However, Angela's words had hit home and he had seen the sadness lurking behind her eyes that glittered with unshed tears, and so they all knelt and said the rosary together and before the priest left he promised to say a Mass for the repose of the boys' souls.

That comforted Angela a great deal but it

didn't seem to sink in to Mary and Matt. As the loss turned into a manageable ache, Barry had to go back to work, for they had to eat, and Matt made no effort to return. Mary seemed incapable of caring for the house or cooking anything and so Angela tried to give up the good job she had at Maitland's grocer shop to look after them both.

However, Mr Maitland wasn't happy losing his assistant who worked so hard and was a favourite with the customers because she was always so cheerful, and he said it had been a terrible tragedy and it was unreasonable to expect the parents to get over the loss of two sons straight away, and he gave her another week before he advertised for someone else. Barry was glad about that because he was the only one working and he hoped Angela could return to work before too long because money was so short.

However, the extra week was drawing to a close as one day slid into another with no change, and that night as Barry made his way home from work he'd made a decision, but first he had to talk to Angela. He had a bit of a wait but he was a patient man. Angela had cooked liver and onions and Barry tucked in with relish, glad that Angela was such a good cook and an economical one. His parents, he noted, had eaten little and he knew if they were to recover from this, he had to give them something to look forward to.

Eventually, with Mary and Matt helped to bed, Angela sat down on the settee before the hearth opposite Barry with a sigh. 'Tired?' Barry asked.

Angela nodded. 'A little but it's the emotional part of it that wearies me most.'

Barry shook his head. 'I don't know how you put up with it day by day.'

'Well I owe your parents my life and love them dearly anyway. But I could cope much better if I could see some light at the end of the tunnel and for their sake more than mine.'

Barry suddenly moved to sit beside Angela and caught up her hand, something he hadn't done since she'd been small and she wasn't sure how to react. But she had no time to think because Barry looked deep into her eyes as he said, 'What do you think of me, Angela?'

Angela looked at the dear and familiar face and his intense dark eyes and felt her stomach turn over like she had butterflies fluttering inside and her mouth was dry enough to make her voice husky when she said, 'Wh... What d'you mean?'

'You know what I mean,' Barry said almost impatiently. 'But if you are shy of saying so I will tell you what I think of you. That all right?'

Angela gave a brief nod and Barry went on, 'I love you, every bit of you. I think I've loved you from the moment I first saw you with your blonde curls, your lovely blue eyes. But those eyes in the early days were sad and confused, and I wanted to help you and so I was determined then to be the best big brother I could be.'

'And you were,' Angela assured Barry. 'But you were more than that. You were my protector, my knight in shining armour. I wouldn't have got on half as well without you and I loved you too.'

'As a brother?'

Angela swallowed deeply and said, 'Yes, as a brother.'

'You were a child and I was a child,' Barry said. 'But my love for you has changed and deepened and now I love you as a man loves a woman and I need to know if you feel the same.'

Angela didn't answer straight away but then what she did say was, 'I think it's wrong for me to feel towards you any other way than as a brother.'

'Why?'

'Well we were brought up as brother and sister.'

'Yes but we are not brother and sister. There is no blood between us and that's what counts,' Barry said earnestly. 'Look, I had no intention of speaking of this, not because I was unsure of my own feelings but because I know you are only just sixteen and I am only nineteen. I intended leaving it two years till my apprenticeship is over and I'm earning decent money.'

'You might be in an even worse state financially then, if you are laid off when you turn twenty-one as your brothers were,' Angela said.

'Yes and I'm afraid it may well be,' Barry said and it did worry him that he would end up the same, but there was nothing he could do about that. He shrugged. 'It's a chance I must take,' he said. 'But whatever happens I'll want you by my side, loving me as a woman with a love strong enough to withstand anything life throws at us.'

He hoped she felt the same, for he would not force her, and so he said almost tentatively, 'Angela, could you love me even a little bit?'

Angela had been having strange yearnings flowing through her body when she was near Barry, or sometimes even when she just thought of him for months. She wasn't sure what they were and she

had tried to ignore them, pushing them down into her subconscious, certain the Church would say they were sinful. Most enjoyable things were.

But Barry's words and passionate eyes boring into hers had unlocked her feelings and so she answered, 'No.' She saw his face fall and she added with a smile, 'There's no way I can love you a little bit, I can love you an enormous big bit.'

Barry felt as if his heart had stopped in his breast and he looked at Angela incredulously. 'You mean that?'

'I most certainly do. I can't say when I stopped loving you just as a brother; I just know that I tried to push the feelings down, but the thought of not having you in my life fills me with fear. But now we have admitted our feelings for each other I think we will have to keep them secret from Mammy.'

'Well my brothers seemed to think she knows already.'

'Oh, she's maybe guessed a bit but she won't know for definite,' Angela said. 'I think we must hide our happiness for a wee while.'

'Why?'

'Well, out of respect, I suppose.'

'You knew Sean and Gerry as well as I did,' Barry said. 'And if it is as the priests say and they are in a better place and can look down on us, knowing them well, do you think they'd be happier in Paradise if we lamented long and hard and went round with faces that would turn the milk sour?'

'Yes but...'

'Angela, don't think me heartless,' Barry begged, 'for I'm really not and there's not a day goes by

when I don't miss my brothers, but they would want me to get on and live life. Besides, I'm not just thinking of me in this but of Mammy too, particularly Mammy, for if we wed soon she will have to take a grip on herself because there would be a wedding to plan and the thought of grandchildren to gladden her heart. It will give her something to look forward to, something to live for.'

Angela wasn't at all sure that Barry was right in his assumptions, but now they had admitted their feelings for each other she doubted they could continue to be discreet, and anyway, she didn't want some hole-in-a-corner affair. Barry had at least convinced her that they were doing nothing to be ashamed of, so she didn't want to go skulking around her own home and perhaps lying to Mary and Matt, for that wouldn't be showing either of them any respect at all. No, it had to be out in the open. 'You're right Barry, it's only right that they be told as soon as possible.'

'Yes,' said Barry. 'I'll speak to them tomorrow after dinner.'

SIX

The following evening Angela had made an excellent stew from a selection of vegetables and a scrag end of mutton she had queued for hours in the Bull Ring to get. She wanted to make something a bit special for she knew Barry was intending to speak to his parents that night and in their

present lethargy and sadness she wasn't at all sure how they would react to it.

As they sat at the table Angela thought Mary looked just a shade better. There was a spark in her eyes that she hadn't seen in a long while and she was pleased to see that Mary at least had got her appetite back, for she attacked her dinner with relish. Small signs of recovery, surely, and she couldn't help feeling that what Barry was going to say might knock her right back again. When everyone had finished, Angela cleared away and made a cup of tea.

Normally they would take the tea to drink before the fire, but Barry asked them to sit at the table and drink it because he had something he wanted to say to them. Angela saw Mary gazing at Barry fearfully. Angela's mouth went suddenly very dry and she watched Mary's face with apprehension as Barry explained that the brotherly love he had always had for Angela had changed to real love and just the previous day Angela had admitted she felt the same way. 'So now we know we truly love one another, we want to get married,' Barry said.

Mary smiled wryly and she wondered if her young son thought he was telling her news because she'd seen how it was for the young people some time before. They had betrayed themselves in just the way they gazed at one another in odd moments. His brothers had been aware of it too, for she had overheard them discussing it and she couldn't have been happier, for she had prayed for just such an outcome in her nightly prayers for years.

Before she was able to say this however, Matt

spoke and as he hadn't spoken since the arrival of the telegram, Angela was pleased that their discussion seemed to have got through to him, even though his words were ones of censure. 'Talking of marriage when your brothers are barely cold?' he said to Barry and his voice was almost a growl and the words seemed wrung out of him. 'At best it's unseemly and disrespectful. I'm ashamed of you, Barry.'

'And not getting married will bring the boys back, will it?' Mary demanded, before Barry had a chance to speak.

Angela looked at Mary in astonishment. Mary caught the look and with a sigh admitted, 'I've been thinking for a while that maybe I have been selfish, wallowing in self-pity.'

'Ah no, Mammy,' Angela contradicted. 'You haven't a selfish bone in your body.'

Mary shook her head with a sad smile and said, 'I am no saint, my dear, and you have done your best to shield me from what happened on that tragic boat. But today when you were in the market, your father was feeling a bit chilly and so I went down to the cellar to get the makings to lay the fire and there I saw the old papers you kept from me and I read that entire families were lost on that ship and...' Mary's voice faltered and stopped as she recalled her shock and horror reading the words Barry and Angela had sought to protect her from. The anguish in her heart had forced a cry from her and tears stood out in her eyes for her own lost sons. And yet she knew they weren't the only sons lost, there were also husbands, fathers and brothers lost. All no doubt

beloved members of families who would always miss them, because even the relatively few passengers from steerage that had been rescued were women and children, the lucky ones.

Remembering this now she said to Barry, 'Were there no men at all from steerage saved?'

'Well it was women and children first,' Barry said. 'In the papers I read it said that at first, when the sailors began loading the lifeboats, it was first-class passengers first and there were men too. When they realized how bad the situation was, the men were refused and they only took women and children.'

'Well I read in one paper that there weren't enough lifeboats for all on board anyway,' Mary said. 'I think that a scandalous state of affairs.'

'It was supposed to be unsinkable,' Barry pointed out. 'I imagine Finn and Colm feel bad because they encouraged Sean and Gerry to go on that ship.'

'Because it was supposed to be the safest way to cross the Atlantic,' Mary said. 'And yet nothing changes, for aside from the men, most of those who were left to die in the icy sea were steerage passengers. Women and children, even wee babies.'

'It was a dreadful thing to happen,' Angela said. 'I was beginning to think you would never recover from such tragedy.'

'I was beginning to feel that way myself,' Mary said. 'But even before I found the papers in the cellar I had told myself that I must get over it. I mean I don't think there will be a day goes by when I'll not miss those boys and wish with all my

heart they hadn't died and certainly not in that awful way, but had they not died I was hardly likely to see them again, for few people ever return from America, and so it's as if they are dead in a way.

'Oh, they could have written as Finn and Colm do and I am pleased they have such good jobs and, please God, one day they will write and tell me of the girls they intend to marry and later the birth of children I will never see. It is hard rearing children who are unable to find any sort of future in the country where they were raised so that they have to go so far across the foam, but the reality is four sons have already been lost to me.'

Angela's heart bled for the abject sorrow on Mary's face because every word she spoke was the truth. And then Mary gave a sigh and went on, 'However, some in that fated ship lost all belonging to them, while I still have one son left and I have Angela, who is as close as any daughter. For the two of you to wed is what I have longed for and though both of you are young, life is uncertain and I think we should go ahead and plan the wedding.'

'I see you are determined upon it,' Matt said. 'Going on as if our sons had not existed.'

'If they lived they would applaud us,' Mary said. 'And I doubt they'd feel any different dead. They knew the way the wind blew between Barry and Angela probably before they realized it themselves. I know you are hurting, for I am myself, but we can't undo this terrible tragedy. Sean and Gerry died a painful death and that will stay with me always. But this is a new start for us all and if you can't see that then you're a numbskull.'

'Oh, it's a numbskull I am now, is it?' Matt said, affronted.

'Yes you are,' Mary said unabashed. 'If you can't see that this is the way forward, the only way, something in life to look forward to and in time rejoice in.'

Matt was quiet and Angela could tell he was thinking over Mary's words as she knew he often did. She was astounded at the rapid turnabout Mary had made and wondered if they'd been right to try to shield her. She was a lot stronger than either of them had given her credit for and this truth was compounded when she turned to Angela and said, 'Now weddings cost money and I know there is precious little to spare so how about trotting off to Maitland's Grocery tomorrow morning and seeing if you can have your old job back. Didn't you say he was keeping it open for you?'

Angela nodded. 'Till this Monday.'

'Well tomorrow is Saturday, so if he has kept his word your job will still be there for you.'

'Shall you be all right?'

Mary nodded. 'I might be better if I have less time to think.'

'Shall you mind going back?' Barry asked.

'No,' Angela said with a laugh. 'Why should I mind? I loved my job and I know the money is needed. I can't wait to start if you want the truth.'

'Good,' Mary said. 'That's settled then.'

The next morning Angela set off for Maitland's Grocery Store early, fairly certain that George Maitland would be there getting ready for the first

customers, and when she tapped on the door he opened it with a beam. 'Am I pleased to see you,' he cried, throwing the door wide. 'Come in, come in and give me the news.'

'Well the first thing is I would like my job back, please,' Angela said.

George sighed in relief as Angela explained that she now felt able to leave Mary and Matt to fend for themselves and return to work. 'They are much improved,' she told George when he enquired after them. 'At least,' she added more honestly, 'Mammy has improved. I think Daddy will never really get over it and I think he sort of blames Fin and Colm for encouraging the two younger ones to go. Mammy doesn't and she says that tomorrow she is going to write and tell them so because you know they write regularly and we expected a letter from them after the telegram but we have heard nothing. Barry thinks they might be a little scared to write and he could be right, but anyway if that's the case Mammy intends to remedy it.'

George nodded. 'She's a great woman, Mary.'

Angela nodded. 'She is indeed and I know that more than most.'

'But Matt hasn't got much better you say?'

Angela shook her head and added, 'You would hardly know what he thinks, because he seldom says anything at all and none of it good since the arrival of the telegram.'

'No sign of him getting back to work?' George asked. 'That might help him get a grip on himself.'

Angela shook her head vehemently. 'He's not fit,' she said. 'Not physically I don't mean, though

he's thinner and frailer than he was because he eats so little and has started having pains in his stomach again, but he's had those pains for ages. Mammy thinks it's indigestion. But I'd be more worried about his emotional state. Barry thinks he might never work again.'

'It must be hard for you financially with Barry not out of his apprenticeship yet.'

Angela shrugged. 'It has been hard but we have managed just about. Needs must and all that.'

'Well I'm delighted you're back. The customers have been asking for you. Mrs Maitland has had to come and help me at busy times.'

Angela wrinkled her nose, for Matilda Maitland had scarcely set foot in the shop since she had been working there. 'Bet that didn't go down too well.'

George didn't speak, but shook his head with a smile before going on to say, 'Well this has decided me. I have thought about it time and enough. I am putting your wages up two shillings to twelve and six.'

Angela gave a gasp. 'Oh Mr Maitland. Are you sure?'

'Quite sure, my dear,' George said. 'And I will pack you up a big bag of groceries to take home with you today and every Saturday night after we close.'

Tears were standing out in Angela's eyes and she brushed them away impatiently and determinedly swallowed the lump in her throat as she said, 'Thank you so much, Mr Maitland. You are very kind.'

George Maitland's voice was gruff as he an-

swered the girl he had grown so fond of in the two years she had been working at the shop and he said with a twinkle in his eye, 'Not at all, my dear. I'm looking after myself, that's all. It's just a ploy to get more hours' work out of you, for people can work harder if they are not hungry.'

Angela knew it wasn't that at all but she didn't bother arguing, but instead began removing her coat. 'Shall we make a start then?'

'Now? You mean start right now?' George asked.

'Why not now?' Angela said. 'I have to start sometime and it might as well be today as Saturdays were always busy and usually needed two of us.'

Angela spoke the truth as George knew well. He'd actually thought that morning that he'd probably have to ask his wife to lend a hand before the day was out. He hated asking her, because she detested serving in the shop and made that abundantly clear and was so short and abrupt when she served people that she upset some of his best customers. And now here was Angela offering him a solution. 'Well if you're sure?'

'Course I am,' Angela said. 'Looks like I'm needed too because there's already a queue forming outside waiting for you to open up.'

There was and George hurried to open the door. The people poured in, most only too delighted to see Angela behind the counter again.

The day passed swiftly as busy days often do. Though she assumed the family would know why she hadn't returned home after seeing George Maitland, she found a small boy in the street who agreed to go and tell them for two ounces of

monkey nuts. She had no dinner with her, but Mary realized that and sent a sandwich back with the child. Angela was very grateful and ate it in the store room as she always did.

When George returned to the shop he appeared pensive. 'What are you thinking about so intently?' she asked with a smile.

'I'm thinking that it's madness for me to go upstairs for my dinner every day while you sit in the store room eating a sandwich.'

'Why is it?' Angela asked. 'I don't mind. I've done that since I started here.'

'I know, for that's how Matilda wanted it,' George said grimly. 'But you will feel more able to do a full afternoon's work with a good dinner inside you and Matilda is a good cook, I will give her that.'

Angela was quite happy with a sandwich and knew that however good the food, she wouldn't take full enjoyment of it in the stilted atmosphere there would be, because she'd only be there on sufferance. But then she knew it would save money for them all if she was to be given her dinner at the shop. She would only need a light tea and a meal only had to be cooked for Barry when he came in from work. She knew Mary would as usual see to herself and Matt at dinner time and then they could have tea with her. That surely was more important than Matilda Maitland's bad humour. And yet she said, 'Mrs Maitland might not like it.'

'You leave Matilda to me,' George said. 'From now on you will eat dinner with us. Agreed?'

'If you say so, Mr Maitland,' Angela said with

an impish grin. 'You're the boss.'

'Glad you realize that at least,' said George, but he had a smile on his face as he turned the sign to OPEN and unlocked the door.

Mary cried when she unpacked the two shopping bags George had filled with groceries for them all. There were three loaves of bread that George said would only go stale if they stayed in the shop, a block of lard, and another of butter and a chunk of cheese. There was the ham and corned beef that had been left at the end of the day and a side of bacon left on the bacon slicer and a dozen eggs, and then he had added a jar of jam and a packet of biscuits. Mary could see the makings of many meals with the food George Maitland had given them and when Angela told her about the raise and the new arrangement Mary felt the nagging worry slide from her shoulders that they wouldn't have enough to eat, heat the house and pay the rent.

'You must take a little more for yourselves,' she said to Angela.

Angela shook her head. 'I don't want anything.'

'Listen to me,' Mary said. 'You think you know all there is to know about Barry, but you know him as a brother. You need to get to know him as the man you will spend the rest of your life with and, please God, as the father of any children you may be blessed with and for that you two need to get out more on your own.'

'We haven't the money for that sort of thing.'

'With your increased wages and Barry's money we have enough,' Mary insisted, 'especially if you

are guaranteed a hot dinner every day and George sends home groceries every week. Anyway you don't have to spend a lot. Now and again you could maybe go to the cinema, or the Music Hall, or if money was tight you could just go for a walk, or go down the Bull Ring on a Saturday evening where there is great entertainment to be had I've been told.

'And another thing,' Mary went on before Angela had time to form any sort of reply, 'tell everyone about your impending marriage so the two of you can openly go down the street hand in hand, for you are doing nothing wrong.'

'I know that,' Angela said. 'I wasn't sure about it myself at first, you know, with Barry nearly a brother to me, but he convinced me that it was all above board to feel as we do.'

'Hmph, and he might have to do some more convincing before he is much older.'

'What d'you mean?'

'Why did you think it might be wrong?'

'Well I suppose because we had been brought up so closely,' Angela said. 'I knew Barry loved me. He said that when I arrived at your house first, though, he couldn't understand much of it, but he felt sorry for me because he said I looked so sad and he was determined to be the best big brother he could be. And he was and I always loved him. I loved you all of course but there was always a special place in my heart for Barry, my big brother, so when those feelings changed I thought they must be sinful, so sinful I nearly told it in confession.'

'But you didn't,' said Mary with a smile.

99

'No I didn't because to give voice to it would make it more real,' Angela said. 'At the time I was trying to convince myself that I was imagining things. And I suppose I was sort of ashamed.'

'Well all I'm saying is that others may feel as you did at first,' Mary said. 'In fact some around the doors think you are brother and sister. We came here as a complete family and I thought of you as my daughter by then, and you were a wee sister to all the boys, and so many will think these feelings you have for each other very wrong indeed. And so I don't want you to hide away as if you were guilty of some crime. Hold your heads up high.'

SEVEN

How wise Mary was, Angela often thought in the weeks that followed that little chat, for there was open condemnation from neighbours. George Maitland had been slightly alarmed when she told him as well as being surprised, though he knew they were unrelated because Angela had told him when she first came to work in the shop how it had transpired that she was living with the McCluskys. But he knew what people were like and many he knew would take a dim view of this state of affairs, and the customers in the shop were shocked at first and it didn't entirely stop when Angela told them she wasn't Barry's sister, for some still considered it bordered on an incestuous relationship.

Added to that was what they saw as a lack of

respect shown to their two boys drowned in the Atlantic Ocean. 'There was no decent period of mourning at all,' women muttered among themselves around the doors.

'And that cock-and-bull story of her not being related to the McCluskys at all doesn't ring, true to me.'

'Yes they're all the same family as far as I'm concerned,' another agreed. 'I'm surprised Mary doesn't put a stop to it.'

'Wait till Father Brannigan gets to hear. He'll roast the pair of them alive.'

Some women showed their displeasure initially by refusing to be served by her. Angela found the animosity hard to take for she had never encountered it before; she'd always thought she was well liked.

Mary told her to take no notice, that their news would be a seven-day wonder, that was all, and then it would be someone else they turned their attentions upon. Angela knew that that was probably true, but meanwhile she found it hard to approach a group of chattering women, who fell silent as she grew near and ignored any tentative greeting she offered, and she felt their eyes boring into her back as she walked away. 'Miss hoity toity,' someone called after her as she passed. 'Marrying her brother with no respect for the dead.'

Barry seemed not to notice, or at least not to care. 'Why worry?' he asked Angela one Saturday night as they made their way to the cinema. 'While they're pulling us to pieces they're leaving some other poor devil alone.'

But it was almost a fortnight since the news that Angela intended to marry Barry McClusky became public, and just that morning a woman had refused to be served by Angela. She dreaded the day when George Maitland would ask her to leave and although the money she earned as well as the groceries given ensured their survival, she would still be glad not to face the bevy of scornful, judgemental women day after day. She turned to Barry now and said, 'Don't you care what they are thinking about us and what some are even saying?'

Barry gave a little laugh as he shook his head. 'Slides off me like water off a duck's back,' he said. 'It would matter only if it were true, but it isn't. You and I are doing nothing wrong and you must really believe that, or it will taint the time we have together.'

Angela knew Barry was right and cuddling up tight against him as they walked, she felt safe and secure and it was easy to tell that she cared not a jot for the opinion of the neighbours.

After a while the animosity calmed down a little when George eventually took his customers in hand and assured them Angela was no blood relation to the McCluskys and far from showing lack of respect to the two boys that drowned, they decided to marry early to give Mary some reason to go on, to give her something to look forward to, for she was in danger of falling into depression.

Most customers accepted that. Many of George's customers were Catholics and went to St Catherine's and knew the McCluskys to be a respectable family, and no wonder Mary was so very desolate, losing two sons like she had. Giving

her a reason to go on would seem to be a good idea. However, over three weeks later another customer, one Edith Cottrell, known for her caustic tongue, still refused to let Angela serve her.

Angela turned away with a sigh and George Maitland saw the tears in her eyes and it angered him. He knew there were plenty of shops on Bristol Street that people could go to if they decided to boycott his shop. And yet he felt that he could no longer stand by and allow Angela to be treated so badly by some of his customers and so he faced the woman and said, 'Angela must serve you, because I'm busy.'

The woman was affronted. 'I'm a respectable person I'll have you know,' she said. 'And I am particular and I will not have that hussy serving me.'

Angela's head shot up and her eyes were no longer full of tears. Instead they flashed fire and her face was flushed as she demanded angrily, 'Who are you to call me a hussy? Let me tell you my foster mother Mary McClusky would likely wash my mouth out with carbolic if she heard me using that word about another person, especially if it was totally unfounded as yours is. I called Mary McClusky my foster mother because that's who she is and the fact that people think she is my mother speaks only of her generosity of spirit that allowed her to take into her home the orphaned child of her dear friend, my mother. She cared for me and gave me as much love as she did her own sons. My name is Angela Kennedy, but soon, when I marry Barry, I will be called McClusky and will be proud of that.'

'Hmph,' Edith Cottrell snapped irritably as she added, 'And does Barry McClusky know what a she-devil you are and one with an evil temper?' She swung round from glaring at Angela to face George Maitland and said, 'You should take care who you employ, or you'll find decent people won't come in here. I'll go elsewhere and I'll spread the news, never fear.'

Angela knew by giving way to that outburst, however justified she might have thought it was, she had alienated one of George Maitland's customers and she knew the knock-on effect that could happen from that. She bitterly regretted risking making life more difficult for such a kind man who had helped her, and therefore the family, a great deal. So she gave a small sigh before saying to Edith Cottrell, 'You needn't bother going anywhere because it's me that's leaving.' And she removed her apron as she spoke.

'What you doing?' George cried. 'Put that apron back on!' And he leaned across the counter and said, 'Angela will not be leaving, Mrs Cottrell, but you will, for I don't want your sort in here abusing my staff for no reason and, if any of your friends are of like mind, they can stay away too. Good day to you.'

Edith Cottrell looked from Angela biting her bottom lip in anxiety and still clutching her apron in her hands to the resolute George and she said, 'I hope you know what you are doing.'

'I do absolutely,' George said. 'And as I said before, good day to you.'

Edith Cottrell had no option but to leave and as she flounced through the door and shut it behind

her with a slam Angela looked at George and said, 'Oh Mr Maitland. What have you done?'

'Something I should have done a while ago. Never could stand the woman anyway.'

'But won't she destroy your business?'

'She may try,' George conceded. 'But the woman isn't liked whereas you are, by many people, and so I think the majority will have more sense than to heed her. Mind,' he added with a little chuckle, 'they may have a peep into the shop to see this she-devil I have working for me.'

'But, George, they should know me,' Angela protested. 'I've been working here ages now and, to be honest, I was surprised anyone had any sort of negative reaction when I told them about me and Barry.'

'It was shock, that's all,' George said. 'And some who moved here after you probably did think that Barry was your brother, for you were all brought up like one big family. Most now, knowing the truth of it, are fine, but you always get the odd ones, like Edith Cottrell, who see sin when none exists. Take no heed of her.'

Angela tried to do just that and it was easy enough to do as Edith never went near the shop. Others did though, for George was right. Whatever it was Edith told them, a stream of women entered the shop over the next few days to buy sundry items, but really to see if Angela had overnight turned into the screaming she-devil virago Edith Cottrell probably described.

They found her unchanged and thought it wrong of Edith to bad-mouth her so, for the girl was doing no harm at all. In a way Edith did

Angela a favour because after that everyone behaved as they always had towards her and many even offered their congratulations.

Some expressed concern that she was very young to marry but then others put in that it wasn't as if they didn't know one another. And it wasn't as if Barry and Angela would be totally alone starting married life for they would live with Mary. Barry had made that abundantly clear and Angela didn't seem to mind that either. Truly, if Barry had suggested leaving she would have done her best to dissuade him, for she couldn't bear Mary to be left alone with Matt, who was so still and silent it was as if the lifeblood had been sucked from him.

There was just about enough money to buy everything needed in the house, but little slack and Barry suggested to his mother that she should see if Matt was entitled to anything as he was unable to work.

Mary shook her head. 'There's nothing for the likes of us Barry,' she said. 'If you don't work you starve.'

'No,' Barry cried. 'There's something called the National Insurance Scheme that looks after you when you're sick. Dad has been paying in for a year or so. I don't know much about it because it doesn't apply to apprentices, but the Gaffer – you know Stan Bishop – said to tell you and for you to have a word with him, like. He's been on about it since that last time he called to see Dad.'

Mary knew Stan was an honest man who would put her right about things and she went see him expecting nothing, only to find Matt, like all

workers, was in a scheme where he paid four pence a week, the employer three pence and the government two pence, which entitled him to seven shillings for fifteen weeks, but he had to be deemed unfit to work in the first place by a doctor. It might have ended right there because Mary hadn't money to spend on a doctor who might say there was nothing wrong with Matt at all, and then they would get nothing and still have a doctor's bill to find, and this was what she said to Stan.

'Oh, you don't have to pay for this doctor, Mary,' Stan assured her. 'He's on the panel. That means part of the scheme and paid out of the contributions.'

'And what if they find nothing wrong?' Mary asked for in her heart of hearts she thought Matt was suffering from extreme sadness, because she was suffering from that too, only she had forced herself to get on with life for the sake of the two left to her and the sadness receded slightly to a constant but bearable ache. She had tried talking to Matt who would look at her with rheumy, anguished eyes and just mumble, 'I can't, Mary. I just can't.'

'I think he'll find Matt is too sick to work,' Stan said. 'It hasn't got to be anything physical, but there again he's not a well man, Mary. When I called to see him last time I was shocked at his appearance. He was skin and bone.'

Mary shook her head. 'I know, he won't eat.'

'Well, there is something radically wrong when a fit man shrinks away to nothing,' Stan said. 'Let's get the doctor to have a look at him shall we?'

Matt didn't want to see any doctor and it took the combined efforts of them all to convince him to agree to it, but when the doctor called Mary was on her own, because Barry and Angela were both at work. The doctor was as aloof as most of them were, but he wasn't there to be a friend but to find out if there was something wrong with Matt, or just the loss of his sons that had caused this malaise and weight-loss. She had to admit that the doctor seemed to know his stuff and he checked Matt all over and asked him loads of questions and then he faced him and said directly, 'How long have you known?'

'Known what?' Mary demanded. 'What you on about?'

Matt ignored Mary and it was the doctor he addressed as he said, 'Not long all told.'

Mary looked from one to the other and said, 'Will someone please tell me what's going on?' And then all of a sudden the men's faces were so grave she didn't know whether she wanted to hear what they were going to say. But even as she mentally backed away she told herself it was yet one more thing to be faced. She swallowed the nervous lump that had formed in her throat, faced the doctor and said, 'Go on.'

'Your husband, Mrs McClusky, has a tumour in his stomach,' the doctor said gravely.

Mary wasn't totally sure what a tumour was, but it didn't sound a great thing to have and so she said, 'So can you take it out?'

'I'm afraid not.'

'So what happens now?'

'Nothing happens,' the doctor said, and went on to say to Matt, 'I can give you something for the pain.'

'You never said you were in pain,' Mary said to Matt almost accusingly.

'I was, but I was in such agony at losing the boys anyway,' Matt said. 'That hurt so much, any other pain didn't seem to matter. And then you were suffering too, so how could I load it on you?'

'And were you in a lot of pain?'

Matt shrugged, but the doctor said, 'A great deal of pain, I would have said, judging by the size of the tumour now.'

'Aye,' Matt said. 'The pain was bad enough at times but still nothing to the loss of two sons drowned in the Atlantic Ocean.'

The doctor raised quizzical eyes to Mary and she said, 'Our two sons were lost at sea, making for America to join their older brothers. They travelled on the *Titanic*.'

Everyone knew about the loss of life on the *Titanic* and Mary saw the doctor's eyes widen in sympathy and he quite knew why the man before him had ignored the pain he must have had for some time. Not that it would have made any difference to the outcome, but maybe he could have made him more comfortable.

'Is that really all you can do,' Mary said, 'just give him painkillers?'

'The man can't work miracles, Mary,' Matt said. 'I've come to the end of the road and that's all there is to it.'

Mary had not realized the doctor would be able to do nothing. Doctors were important and

109

powerful and to seek their advice usually cost more money than she ever had, and what was the point if they could offer no cure? Matt on the other hand seemed to accept his fate and he just asked the doctor, 'How long have I got?'

'It's impossible to be absolutely accurate, Mr McClusky,' the doctor said. 'However, the tumour has grown very large and seemingly quite quickly, so I would say months rather than years.'

Mary gave a gasp of shock as she realized that soon she would lose her man, who had been by her side for many years. They had shared in good times and lean ones and she knew she would miss him a great deal.

Matt looked across at her and gave a wan smile as he said, 'Best tell our Barry and Angela to get a move on planning that wedding if they want me at it.' And only Mary saw the tears glittering behind his eyes.

Angela and Barry were devastated to hear what the doctor had said when Mary told them as soon as they arrived home from work. Angela felt tears spring to her eyes because she loved Matt and she would miss him very much. She remembered when she was small and he was fit and strong he would lift her up onto his broad shoulders and carry her around the room. He had a special smile just for her and called her his wee little lassie. However, she didn't let the tears fall because she knew it would be worse for Mary and felt she had to be strong for her, but Mary had had time to come to terms with the doctor's prognosis. Her tears were spent, helped in part

by Matt who had urged her not to take on so. He said everyone has to die some time and he'd had a fairly good innings.

And because Matt accepted his imminent death so well, everyone in the family took their cue from him. The Gaffer could hardly believe the report the doctor left with him and he came to see Matt and was sad to see that he had deteriorated further since he'd last seen him. Matt though had accepted his fate and so they chatted together about old times and the years they had worked together.

When the Gaffer left Matt he sought out Barry in the factory. 'Sorry to hear about your father.'

Barry was touched by the Gaffer's such obvious concern and he said, 'Thank you. It was bad news, you know. We thought he was just still grieving over my brothers. Mammy said she feels bad she didn't see how ill Daddy was, but she was distracted by the loss of the lads as well. Neither of them were thinking straight at the time.'

'Of course not,' the Gaffer said. 'That's quite understandable and Mary is not to blame herself in any way. Now this is something else I don't want to load onto her either. With the doctor's diagnosis she is entitled to money but there are forms to fill in and I called at the Post Office on my way back here and got them. But they are so detailed I think they might flummox your mother.'

'I'd say so Gaff,' Barry said. 'Mammy can barely read, let alone fill in forms. Angela and I will see to them.'

'Yes,' Stan said. 'You'll soon be head of the house, young Barry. You must look after your mother.'

111

'You haven't really to remind me of that, Gaffer, I would do that anyway,' Barry said a trifle stiffly.

'Of course,' Stan said. 'No offence intended.'

'None taken either.'

'Good,' Stan said. 'Good. Now if you pop into the office before you leave here tonight I will give you the forms.'

EIGHT

News of Matt McClusky's illness was sweeping the factory and many patted Barry on the back and said they were sorry to hear it and asked him to pass on their best wishes to his father. When he came home and said this Mary shook her head as she said, 'I know there are no secrets in the back-to-backs, but how they have heard of this so quickly beats me. I mean, two women asked me if it was true that Matt was very sick when I was at the grocer's.'

'I had a customer quiz me too,' Angela said. 'And Maitland's is a step from here.'

'Ah well, you know the three quickest ways to spread news?' Matt said.

'Yes, we know,' said the other three, for they'd heard it often. And they chorused together, 'Telephone, telegraph and tell a woman.'

They laughed gently for it was Matt's stock phrase and Mary marvelled, but was pleased to see Matt taking part in family things again and realized it was probably pain that had paralysed

and exhausted him. Now with the strong pain-killers prescribed by the doctor, the life that he had left was more bearable and her conscience smote her afresh for not realizing how sick Matt was.

Mary didn't say this, but what she did say was, 'Well this woman has said nothing about your illness and yet I know it will be common know-ledge across the county by the morning, and the one who probably doesn't know yet is the priest, and if he gets the news from other people's tittle tattle, when he does come I will be given a lecture. We need to see him anyway to bring the wedding forward.'

No one asked why. They had decided on a six-month mourning period before marriage out of respect for the two drowned boys and so as they had declared their feelings for one another in May their wedding was set for mid-October. Now there was a real chance that Matt might be dead by then.

And so the following day Mary went along to see the priest and told him about Matt and saw by his face he hadn't known, and he said how sorry he was to hear it, and Mary wished that she could be-lieve one word coming out of his mealy mouth.

When she said they had decided to bring the wedding forward she saw his eyes narrowed in suspicion and he said, 'Is there another reason for this untimely haste? Barry and Angela are very young as I said initially.'

Mary bridled and though usually she was respectful to the priest she was angry enough to forget that as she snapped, 'If you're implying what I think you are, then all I can say is you've

got a mucky mind. My Barry and Angela love one another, but they know right from wrong. I have just told you that my man is dying, the man is father to both of them and they love him dearly and they want him at their special day, and it is Matt's dearest wish that he walks his daughter up the aisle and that, and only that, is the reason for bringing the wedding forward.'

The priest was outraged. 'Mrs McClusky!' he almost roared. 'That is no way to speak to a priest.'

Mary was completely unabashed. She shrugged and said, 'Maybe it isn't, but it can't be right implying that our young people have been up to something they shouldn't.'

'I was merely asking...'

'No you wasn't,' Mary contradicted. 'You was judging and there isn't anything to judge.'

Suddenly she lost patience with the man and said, 'Now I haven't time for this. Are you going, to marry Barry and Angela or aren't you, because if it offends your sensibilities then I'll pop along to St Chad's and ask them to do it?'

She didn't mention this altercation with the priest at home nor did she say that she had rendered the priest almost purple in the face with rage. And he was angry with her for he knew if she did go to St Chad's and said he refused to marry two of his own parishioners it would reflect badly on him.

Mary watched his face working and guessed many of the thoughts running round his head and knew she had him over a barrel. No need for anyone to know that and she said only that the wedding was rescheduled for mid-August and that

114

didn't leave them much time to organize anything and it was a good job they wanted nothing lavish.

Mary was right, the news spread like wildfire. There was a constant stream of visitors to the house for Matt had been a very popular man, and with the wedding of his youngest son Barry to add to all that had happened to him, there was a lot of feeling in these visits. Father Brannigan was less welcome than most and he was stiff with Mary initially, but when he saw Matt, he knew he should have come to see him sooner or at the very least enquired after him when he hadn't been seen at Mass and excused Mary for her outburst, thinking she had a lot on her plate. As for Mary, she was surprised how little it mattered to her that the priest was friendly with her or not.

However, she knew they would soon need the services of a priest so she tried not to antagonize him further and so the visit passed well enough and he promised to call again and possibly hear Mart's confession if he'd like that.

Matt gave a wheezy laugh, 'If you want, Father,' he said. 'And I know it's your job and all, but sitting here day after day has been the most sinless time in my life. I think my soul must be only the slightest bit grey at the moment.'

Mary was smiling as she opened the door for the priest and even he had a grin on his face and she was glad she had kept details of their disagreement from the others so that Matt was able to behave quite normally towards him.

Angela thought it was very hard for her to get totally excited about her wedding. As spring gave way

115

to summer, which was proving to be a warm one and mostly dry, she was aware that as each passing day was one day nearer the day she longed for, when she became Barry's wife, it was also nearer the day when Matt would breathe his last and she would say goodbye to the only father she had ever known.

Barry too was affected by the imminent death of his father and he was also terribly worried about finance. He didn't earn that much as an apprentice, but it was better than nothing and he was concerned that when he qualified he might be laid off as his brothers had been, and if that happened he didn't know how they would survive. At the moment they were all right with Angela working at Maitland's shop and bringing home a pile of groceries every week as well as her wages. And the extra seven shillings a week they had been awarded due to Matt's illness was a godsend, though Mary saved most of it, knowing it was money she could not rely on, but it did mean she could afford to get the medicine to make Matt's life a little easier and dull the pain that he said was like a wild beast tearing his insides out.

Angela knew that Barry was worried about money and so when they went for a walk one sunny evening in late July, she assured him her job at Maitland's would be safe even after she married because George had told her so. 'He said he can see no problem at least till the babies come.'

'Huh, not too many babies I hope,' Barry said. 'God, Father Brannigan would scald me alive if he heard me, but I have no desire to see the body pulled out of you with a baby every year.'

'Barry, I long to hold your child in my arms,' Angela cried.

'I know,' Barry said, slipping his arm around her. 'And when you do I will be the proudest man in the universe. And I want to be the best father in the world and see that the child wants for nothing, and how can I guarantee that if we have too many mouths to feed?'

'But doesn't the Church say that we must be grateful for what God sends?' Angela said, quoting the Church's mantra. Planning your family if you were a Catholic was expressly forbidden.

'I know what the Church says but the Church hasn't to provide for them,' Barry said. 'And you haven't seen the ragged-arsed urchins running the streets. I mean, when I was growing up I was always adequately fed, but some of these children look as if they have never had a square meal in their lives. Their arms and legs are like sticks and they beg for any leftover food at the factory gates when we leave at night. Some get their wives to put up extra and share what they have left but it's so little and there's so many of them. It breaks your heart to see them.'

'Ah, it must do,' Angela said. 'Poor wee children.'

'Yes and I never want my child to suffer like that,' Barry said almost fiercely. 'You've no idea Angela. One chap was telling me he lives near the coal yard and every day at the crack of dawn a gang of them are there with their buckets because when the lorries come out laden with coal, some falls off when they go over the cobbles and they scrabble around and fight each other for these scrappy bits of coal. I never want our son or

117

daughter to be forced to do that either.'

'But how will you stop babies?' Angela asked. 'If we love each other and show that love, don't babies just come from that?'

'Yes, but there are ways of preventing that without spoiling the fun altogether,' Barry said with a coy smile.

'What ways?'

'Don't you be worrying your pretty head about that.'

'I bet it's something the priests wouldn't approve of.'

'Almost certainly,' Barry said. 'And if you knew more you would just worry over it.'

'And you won't?'

'I won't give a tinker's cuss,' Barry said. 'Look, you'll be my wife and we will decide when we'd like to add to our family, not some unmarried priest. Agreed?'

'Yes Sir!' Angela said with a mock salute and a cheeky grin, and Barry caught her up around the waist and spun her round and Angela felt she might burst with happiness.

The days folded one into the next and the kindness of people came to the fore, like the women down the yard who pooled resources to make a cake. A girl she barely knew from Grant Street, who'd got married the previous year, was willing to loan Angela her dress. And Mary took some of the money hoarded from the seven extra shillings a week she was getting from the Insurance and took Angela down to the Rag Market in the Bull Ring on the Saturday before her wedding, set for 17th August. George had given Angela the day

off as the Rag Market sold fish through the week and it was only Saturday when it sold clothes, but it was definitely where the bargains were to be found, and Mary bought the softest, loveliest underwear, a silk nightgown and stockings and the prettiest white shoes.

Angela had never owned such lovely things, and thanked Mary as they walked home. 'You don't get married every day of the week,' Mary said. 'And because we went to the Rag Market it wasn't a big cost all together. You are getting married on a shoe-string, my girl, and it wasn't what I wanted for neither of you, nor Matt either. We wanted more of a big splash.'

'Oh I'm not interested in all that sort of razzmatazz,' Angela maintained. 'The important thing is that I am marrying someone I love and that's Barry.'

'It does my heart good to hear you say that because you truly are made for each other.'

'I'm just glad that Daddy has come round about it now,' Angela said. 'It would have put a blight on the day if I was aware of his disapproval.'

'I know,' Mary said. 'I think much of his testiness then was due to the pain he was in, he has admitted as much to me. But I didn't know that and really went for him about the way he was when you announced how you felt about one another, which was no surprise to me and shouldn't have been to Matt if he had eyes in his head. Mind, he did say it's hard to think that just four months after two of our sons' bodies are lying in the Atlantic Ocean we are going to be celebrating a wedding, almost as if their deaths were of no

119

account. And yet his greatest wish in the world is to walk you up the aisle which will be the last act he will do for you.'

Matt seldom walked far now, for the tumour had grown so big it made walking difficult and the way it was positioned made breathing difficult too. 'D'you think he'll manage it?' Angela asked.

Mary shrugged. 'Who knows,' she said. 'I have the offer of the loan of a wheelchair and if he will agree to get into it to be pushed to the church, he has a chance but...' and she spread her hands helplessly and added, 'I think we'll just have to wait and see how he is on the day.'

'Yes,' Angela said. 'That's all we can do.'

Angela was such a beautiful bride it brought a lump to Mary's throat. The two had gone up into the bedroom the morning of the wedding so Mary could help her dress. They had given themselves plenty of time because there was something special Mary had to give to Angela. But first there was the dress and no matter that it was loaned, she looked a treat and Mary told her so as she stood before the mirror, now hardly able to believe her reflection.

Mary smiled at the look on her face as she said, 'Now, you must have something old, something new, something borrowed and something blue.'

'Well something new are all my fine under-clothes and my shoes are new too,' Angela said. 'And I borrowed the dress and veil and I have the blue lace handkerchief George presented me with, but for something old...'

'I have that,' Mary said. 'Something old and

very beautiful and it belonged to your mother.'

Angela gasped. 'What is it?'

'It's this,' Mary said and she peeled off the tissue paper from the article in her hand and there in her palm lay a beautiful silver locket. 'When your mother gave you into my care she said that if anything happened to her, then I must give you this on your wedding day, because she received it on hers, as it was a present from your father.'

'It's beautiful,' Angela said, slightly awed to be holding something that had once belonged to her mother. 'Is there anything in it?'

'Why don't you look?' Mary suggested, holding it out to her. 'It belongs to you now.'

Angela took it from Mary and pressed the catch and the locket opened. In one side was a miniature of the picture that stood on Mary's sideboard that she said was a picture of Angela's parents on their wedding day. She remembered as a child spending hours staring at the picture trying to remember something, anything about her real parents, but there wasn't even a glimmer of memory there. But now she would carry them near her heart always for she vowed then and there she would never take it off.

'That's your hair,' Mary said and in the other half of the locket there were three tiny, but absolutely perfect ringlets tied up with a red silk thread. Angela lifted them out gingerly. 'Was my hair really like that?'

'It was,' Mary said. 'Like a little doll you were. Connie always intended to have a photograph of all of you and a miniature from that for the other side of the locket, but that sort of thing is expens-

ive and when you have a fine houseful of children there is always plenty to spend any spare money on.'

Angela could well understand that but wished it had happened for she had no idea what her siblings had looked like. All she knew was that they were nothing like her because they had all taken after their dark-haired, brown-eyed father, so Matt told her, and she alone took after her golden-haired, blue-eyed mother.

Angela thought of all the times when money must have been tight and she thought of the grinding poverty that had driven them to England in the first place. Though she couldn't remember those austere times herself, Barry had told her how it had been for them and she was amazed that, due to a promise made to a friend, Mary had never felt tempted to try and sell the locket, or at the very least pawn it.

So her gratitude was heartfelt. 'Thank you, Mammy,' Angela said. 'Thank you for keeping it so safe, I will treasure it always.'

The lump in Mary's throat was back and to prevent the tears lurking behind her eyes trickling down her cheeks she said briskly, 'Come, we must be away, for though it's fashionable for a bride to be late, you can't be so late that Barry thinks you're not coming at all.'

Angela gave a gurgle of laughter as she said confidently, 'Barry would never think that.' She hurried nevertheless and when they entered the room Matt was rendered speechless for a moment and then he said with awe, 'Oh, my darling girl, you're beautiful, so you are.' He was immensely

122

glad he had agreed to be pushed to the church in the wheelchair because it meant he might be able to walk the length of the church to the altar, to walk Angela down the aisle. This was terribly important to him for he couldn't have loved her more if she had been his own and as her father he had to do this one last thing for her. He remembered how tickled pink he had been to have a wee girl in the family, when in the aftermath of the tragedy of losing an entire family he had known and liked so well he had realized Angela was theirs for keeps. She was so different to the boys and would love to climb onto his knee, wind her arms around his neck and kiss his leathery cheek. The boys had seldom done such a thing and it always gladdened his heart when Angela did it.

It was only a short walk to St Catherine's Church and a pleasant one that warm, sunny summer's morning. It was far enough for Matt though, and Mary was well aware of that, and she padded the chair with cushions to make it more comfortable for him. As the wheels rumbled over the cobbles neighbours not going to the Nuptial Mass stood in the doorways and cheered them on their way.

The priest was waiting for them in the porch and told them Barry and his best man Stan Bishop were already there. Angela had known Barry had spent the night with Stan so he wouldn't catch sight of the dress, and Stan had assured Angela he would get the groom to the church well ahead of her, and he was a man of his word.

In the porch Matt was eased out of his wheelchair and, biting his lip against the pain, he stood

123

with his arm through Angela's as the Wedding March began. Angela was aware that every step was agonizing for Matt and so their pace was slow down the aisle of that packed church. Barry slipped from the pew and stood before the altar with Stan and by the time Angela and Matt reached them, there wasn't a dry eye in the place.

Matt sank thankfully into the wheelchair Mary had brought for him. Angela stood beside her husband-to-be and threw back her veil. Barry looked at her and saw the radiance in her face and felt his heart miss a beat, and Angela felt her mouth was suddenly very dry and her own heart was hammering in her breast and she knew she loved Barry McClusky more than life itself, and she reached for his hand and squeezed it tight, for soon they would be as one, man and wife.

The wedding. had taken a great deal out of Matt but there was no opportunity to rest once they reached home, for in their absence the neighbours had been busy and the house was decorated and the table was groaning with food, adding to the things Mary and Angela had prepared. The two-tiered cake was in the centre and Angela marvelled that people who had so little themselves would go to such lengths to make their day a special one.

And it was so special. Even the weather was kind to them, which was a bonus for the previous few days had been unsettled. 'Ah well,' said Barry when she commented on this, 'The sun shines on the righteous.'

'Oh you, Barry McClusky,' said Angela, giving him a push.

'D'you see that, ma?' Barry said in an appeal to

his mother, though he had a great grin plastered to his face. 'Not five minutes married and she's abusing me already.'

'Oh I saw it and I'd say she had reason,' Mary said. 'Sun shines on the righteous indeed.'

The weather did make a difference though because they were able to spill onto the street from the cramped little back-to-back which couldn't hold one quarter of all those who wanted to share in Angela and Barry's special day.

Later when everyone had gone home as it got dark, Mary said she was dropping with tiredness and so Barry helped his father to bed, and Mary followed suit, and Barry and Angela were alone for the first time, and Barry led Angela to the settee and sat beside her and said, 'Hello Mrs McClusky.'

'Hello Mr McClusky,' Angela replied in like vein.

Barry smiled and put his arm around her and kissed her lips and though the kiss was a chaste one, he felt the blood coursing round his body and heard his heart thumping against his ribs, and he knew he wanted to pick Angela up in his arms, carry her upstairs and ravish her, but he knew he would have to proceed a lot more slowly.

He didn't even know if Angela had any idea what went on in the marriage bed and he asked her gently. Immediately she felt a crimson flush flood her cheeks as she said almost in a whisper, 'I know a little bit Mammy told me. I know about coming together to make a baby. She said it may hurt.'

Barry nodded. 'The first time it may hurt a little, but I'll try to hurt you as little as possible. We'll go

up now and I may do things you might think are wrong, but they're not, not now we're married.'

Angela was looking at Barry with large, apprehensive eyes and he laughed gently. 'Don't look at me like that. You trust me don't you?'

'Of course I do, Barry.'

'Come on then,' Barry said, getting to his feet and pulling Angela up next to him and hand in hand they climbed the stairs. They elected to sleep in the attic as they both agreed the bedroom would be more comfortable for Matt and Mary at the moment.

It was a novel experience for Angela because she had never slept in the attic and she had slept in the corner of the bedroom with Mary and Matt, which Mary had curtained off as she grew, for privacy.

Barry was no stranger to the attic and he led his young wife across the oilcloth laid on the floor to the double bed Mary had insisted on buying for them, and he laid her down and began to slowly undress her until she lay naked, shivering and slightly embarrassed. She reached for the silken nightgown she'd laid ready, but Barry took it from her. 'You have no need of this, my love,' he said, as he threw off his own clothes, snuffed out the lamp and got in beside her, 'I will warm you. Lie back now and let me love you properly.'

And Angela did just that and was glad Barry had warned her, because his hands were all over her body stroking and caressing her most intimate parts. Even worse was the fact that she was enjoying it too. She wanted him to go on and on and when a little moan burst from her it was too

dark for her to see the small smile of satisfaction that flitted across Barry's face, for he knew he was awakening her sexuality. Angela had an ache inside that she didn't fully understand and when she pleaded, 'Barry, please...' she didn't really know what she was asking for.

And then Barry entered her and there was one short, sharp pain but that was followed by waves and waves of exquisite joy that flowed all through her. And when it was over and she lay spent, she thought, so that's sex. The one thing you must stay away from until you are married and no one ever even hinted that it could be so enjoyable. 'Are you all right?' Barry asked, a little concerned by the silence. 'Did I hurt you?'

'Oh no, my darling you didn't hurt me at all,' Angela said. 'You loved me properly, that was all, and it was the greatest thing I have ever experienced and oh, Barry McClusky, I love you more than life itself.'

'And I love you too my darling girl and let's hope we have years ahead of us when I can show you just how much.'

NINE

The following morning, the glowing look on Angela's face told Mary that whatever happened in the marriage bed the previous night had pleased her and she was relieved. She hadn't been able to discuss such things with Barry, for it would have

just embarrassed the pair of them, but she had hoped he would go slowly as Angela was so young and quite naive about sexual matters. Maybe he had worked that out for himself though! He seemed delighted as he walked to Mass that morning holding his wife's hand, a wide grin plastered to his face.

They were congratulated by many both before and after Mass that morning, especially by Angela's friend Maggie that she didn't see so much of now they were both working except for meeting after Mass. Maggie threw her arms around her friend and then Barry and wished them many many congratulations. Others were lining up to shake Barry by the hand and hug Angela and some even kissing her on the cheek, causing the familiar crimson flush to flow over her face.

The wedding had taken it out of Matt and anxiety about him was draining Mary and yet she urged Barry and Angela to enjoy the lovely summer's day. 'Soon you will both be back at work,' she said. 'So make use of the time you have together. Looks like the sun is still continuing to shine on the righteous, as Barry maintains.'

Despite her words though, Angela saw the lines of strain pulling Mary's mouth down and she said firmly, 'We will take a walk out this afternoon after I have eaten the dinner I will help prepare and I am quite determined on that.' Mary didn't argue as she well might have and protest she was all right and would manage fine, and Angela knew she would be glad of her help though she'd probably never admit it, so the women worked amicably together as they had done many times before and

Barry sat beside his father and read snippets out of the paper to him.

So it was much later as Angela and Barry walked through Cannon Hill Park that Angela said, 'Do you think we should have let your father go to the wedding?'

'Doubt we could have stopped him,' Barry said. 'He wanted to go so much he agreed to be pushed in a wheelchair, that's how important it was, the prerogative of all fathers to walk their daughters down the aisle and to all intents and purposes he is your father. He'd have probably felt a complete failure if he hadn't been able to do that.'

'But he's ill,' Angela cried. 'I mean he has gone downhill so fast, overnight, for he was a different man yesterday.'

'He was putting on an act yesterday,' Barry said. 'It was our wedding day and he wanted nothing to spoil it.'

'I suppose,' Angela said, and added, 'Your mother has seen the deterioration in him and she's worried. She told me that though he says nothing she knows the pain's worse and she's going to get the doctor tomorrow.'

'Mammy does right calling in the doctor,' Barry said, 'for he said he'd keep Daddy pain free as long as possible and it is all they can do for him now. And that's really the point,' he said to Angela. 'We have to face the fact that my father and your foster father is dying. He has a few months at best and we cannot change that in any way. Now if I was the one dying...'

'Oh don't...'

Barry smiled at Angela's horror-struck face and

said, 'Just imagine if I was, I'd rather be let do things I wanted to do even if it shortened that life, because if you lay in bed and did nothing you would still die anyway.'

They began to make their way back and Angela was assimilating Barry's words when he put in, 'You know if you were to ask Daddy now, I bet even though he feels rough today, he won't regret what he did yesterday. And it wasn't just walking you up the aisle, though that was a big thing for him to do, but added to that was the party that followed the wedding that meant he didn't get any rest at all.'

'He seemed to enjoy that,' Angela said. 'Everyone was so pleased to see him.'

'Yes, they were and he did,' Barry said. 'So if he pays for it now then he does. But the doctor should be able to make his life a little more comfortable.'

The doctor did come the following day and upped Matt's morphine and it eased the pain, but made him drowsier. But Mary wouldn't let Barry and Angela waste their holiday sitting with him now when he slept so much of the time.

Barry still hesitated and Mary gave him a little push. 'Go on,' she urged. 'I will be fine, honestly... You just go on and enjoy yourselves while you have the chance.'

They hadn't any money but the weather was kind to them and Angela didn't care where they went as long as they were together, for she was loving Barry more with every passing hour. They could only go where they could walk to and thinking it was no good going to the town looking

at things they couldn't afford to buy, they went the other way. Calthorpe Park was a favourite of hers anyway and they walked beneath the avenue of trees still in full leaf though there were a few leaves already littering the ground. She said, 'On a warm day like this it's had to think of these trees stripped bare in the winter.'

'It's hard to think of winter at all,' Barry said. 'I don't know who does like the dark and the cold and the leaden skies, so let's not think about things to come but enjoy this glorious day, which is ours to share and I am here with the most beautiful woman in the world, my wife.' The words and the way he looked at her as he said them caused Angela's stomach to give a lurch and her heart to begin hammering in her breast, and so when Barry drew her into the shadow of some nearby trees and kissed her, she melted into his arms and responded eagerly. They could have easily gone further for they both wanted to, but they controlled themselves with difficulty and Barry knew he had got himself a treasure, a woman he loved who enjoyed sex as much as he did.

And long may it continue, he thought and it had a chance if Angela wasn't having a child every year. Bringing babies into the world, she might struggle to cope and finding enough for them to eat would be a constant headache... What woman in that situation would enjoy sex when at the end there might be yet another mouth to feed?

'Penny for them,' Angela said.

'Oh they're not worth a penny,' Barry said dismissively. 'I was just thinking how much I want to ravish my lady wife but will have to contain myself

till tonight.' Angela laughed and Barry grabbed her around the waist and whispered huskily in her ear, 'But it will be all the sweeter for the wait.'

'Barry!' Angela protested. 'Stop it, you are getting me all of a fluster. Hold my hand while we go round the flower beds and try and control yourself.'

With a broad grin on his face, Barry did as Angela asked but she wasn't really cross, rather she felt wanted and desired by the person she loved most in the entire world.

The next day Barry took Angela to the canal. He was no stranger to the canal for he had learnt to swim in there like his brothers before him. Most boys learnt to swim in the 'cut' as it was called, but it was skinny dipping so nice girls didn't go near. Angela had been one of the nice girls, Mary had seen to that, and she'd looked at the dirty, torpid oil-slicked water that smelled quite rank and thought she hadn't missed much not being allowed near the canal. And she also knew that whatever inducement had been offered, she wouldn't have gone into that water for a pension and she was glad she was a girl and would never have been expected to.

However, it was very pleasant walking along the towpath and periodically stepping out of the way of the shaggy enormous-hooved horses that pulled the highly decorated barges through the water. 'Why are they decorated with elephants and roses?' Angela asked.

Barry shrugged. 'Don't know,' he said. 'Always have been so maybe no one remembers the reason why now. Dad told us lads that what the boat

132

people really don't like is being called river gypsies.'

'Why?'

'Cos they aren't I suppose,' Barry said. 'Dad said they were farmers and thrown off the land when the railways came in. I suppose this was the only way of earning a living and giving them somewhere to live as well.'

'I suppose,' Angela agreed. 'Really that's what life is all about isn't it, making enough money to live on?'

She felt sorry for the boaties, as Daddy said they were known, and she had heard many talk of them in a disparaging way. They wore a uniform of sorts, thick boots, cord trousers, cotton shirt, a waistcoat and always a cap. The women wore dark dresses nearly to the floor though often, their boots could be seen peeping out beneath them. Their shawls though were more colourful and their bonnets were trimmed with lace. Their children in comparison were very scantily clad in a variety of items and usually barefoot and skipped nimbly from boat to towpath and back again with ease, helping their parents operate the locks.

She had found the whole thing fascinating and she had enjoyed their couple of days off. They couldn't afford any more time off work however and so the next day Angela was back in the shop and customers found that though she'd always been a happy person before, now it was like she had a sort of glow about her, for though she was still young she had become a woman like them. Something else gave her more self-assurance than before and

that wasn't totally due to being loved up so effectively by Barry – it was to do with her feeling of belonging.

The McCluskys had welcomed her freely into their home and treated her as one of the family and though she loved them all and she couldn't have loved Mary and Matt more if she had been born to them, as she grew up it had bothered her that her name was Kennedy for Matt and Mary had not adopted her in the normal way, but just took her to live with them. She had not been lacking in love and it shouldn't have mattered what her name was. It did, however, and she wasn't sure why it did, and she could never have told Matt or Mary, for they would never have understood and would undoubtedly have been upset. However, now legally she was a McClusky and Barry's parents were hers too and that made her very happy and contented.

Life continued as it always had. Some days Matt was quite bright and other times very ill. Barry reminded her that each day was a bonus and on days when Matt was well, Barry often spent most of the evening reading snippets out of the paper for him and they'd fall to discussing the articles. Mary liked to see Barry showing so much concern for his father and giving him some time, for Mary said he looked forward to Barry coming home because time hung heavy on him.

None spoke of how long Matt had, though they all knew it couldn't be long and privately Angela wondered if he would see Christmas.

When December arrived, however, Matt was still with them, though he slept most of the day and it

was Angela who was feeling under the weather and when she was sick in the chamber pot a few mornings running Barry was beside himself with worry. 'You're doing too much in that bloody shop,' he railed. 'Caught a chill, most likely as well, going out at the crack of dawn. You'll have to tell him it's too much for you.'

Angela knew that Barry was more anxious than angry and she hid her smile because she was fairly certain she knew what ailed her. She hadn't had her monthlies either and she knew they stopped when you were expecting a baby, Mary had told her that, and part of her wanted to catch up Barry's hands and tell him he was going to be a father and dance him around the room at the delight of it all. But she hesitated to say anything because Barry had gone on about the body being pulled out of her if they had a lot of children too close together. He might think this pregnancy too soon, though he must have known there was a good chance of her becoming that way with the sex they enjoyed nearly every night.

Mary couldn't understand her. She had noticed the absence of rags steeping in a bucket of disinfected water every month and heard Angela being sick in the morning and wondered why there had been no announcement. She knew Angela was excited and yet it was a muted excitement and Barry seemed to be totally unaware, at all, and so it was about halfway through December when she said to Angela as she came in from work one evening, 'Isn't there something you need to share with Barry?'

Angela stared at her. 'You know!'

'Course I know,' Mary said. 'I've got eyes and ears and a brain in my head, but apart from all that there's a sort of look about you, oh I don't know how to describe it, just something different, but men don't see these things. Barry doesn't know does he?'

Angela shook her head.

'But why haven't you told him?' Mary asked.

Then Angela told her about Barry wanting to space any family they might have so that she wasn't worn down with it.

'Well,' Mary said, 'I don't know how he intends to do that. I think you just must be grateful for whatever God sends.'

'I thought he might feel it was too soon.'

'Now, listen to me,' Mary said. 'All that planning your family rubbish is for the future surely. This is your first child and I'll tell you if I know my son, he will be tickled pink at the news and I should not delay telling him. Oh,' she added, 'and when you do don't let on that you've mentioned it to me first. It's important that the husband is the first to know.'

Mary was right, Barry was so delighted he didn't know what to do with himself and he picked Angela up, spun her round, declared she was a clever girl and kissed her passionately and the next thing he said was, 'Who else knows?'

'No one.'

'No one?' Barry repeated. 'Not even Mammy?'

'No one,' Angela assured him, 'Though maybe your mother guesses something's up. We'll tell her together tonight.'

Barry suddenly clasped his hands to his head

and cried, 'God, I can scarcely believe I'm going to be a father.'

'You'd better because it's going to happen,' Angela said.

'My darling you've made me the happiest man in the world,' Barry said, holding Angela tight.

Angela laughed lightly and said, 'Especially when I deliver a son for you.'

'Son or daughter makes no odds to me.'

'I thought all men wanted a son?'

'I am not all men,' Barry said. 'And how could I not love a baby you and I have made with love?'

'Ah, Barry,' Angela said and she melted into his arms.

Barry was so concerned about Angela's pregnancy that he began to irritate everyone. He would barely let Angela lift a finger and said that she definitely had to give up her job. In the end, Angela told him to stop fussing. She wasn't ill and now that she was over the sickness she felt as fit as a fiddle. 'And as for giving up my job, don't you think I will be giving that up soon enough and then won't we miss my money and the bags of groceries I bring home every week?'

Barry knew Angela spoke the truth and seeing the sense of her words said grudgingly, 'All right, keep your job if it means so much to you but I don't want you climbing steps or on chairs to reach things.'

'George wouldn't let me do anything like that,' Angela said reassuringly. 'He's almost as bad as you.'

And he was, Angela was being honest, but he wasn't that happy about Angela's pregnancy be-

cause he knew that he was soon to lose her and would have to get someone else in to help him. He had thought and hoped, being so young, it might be some time before they began a family.

Angela liked George and they got on well together but she often sensed an inner sadness in him that seemed to make him a more caring person and he was extra solicitous towards Angela once he knew of her pregnancy and she told this to Barry to set his mind at rest. Barry was relieved but as he held Angela close he told her what he really wanted was to earn a decent wage so that he could provide for them all.

TEN

Even before Angela announced her pregnancy Barry knew he would have to get Angela's old bed downstairs for his father, because now he was too ill to make the bedroom on his own and the stairs were so narrow, it was difficult for Barry to carry him. It was even more cramped in the small living room with the bed in place but no one bothered complaining, there was nothing else to be done. Now someone would have to sit with him all night too, dozing as well as they could in the chair. 'That will be my job of course,' Barry said.

'Why you of course?' Angela said.

'Because it's not a job for you,' Barry said. 'Not for women, particularly you and my mother. It will be too much for her.'

138

'Isn't that for me to say?' Mary asked her son. 'And let me tell you, I have more experience of spending the night in a chair and taking what rest I can, for when three of your brothers got the whooping cough I stayed up night after night so Matt could get his rest, for he had a job to do. And so if you think you are doing this by yourself you are mistaken, for you will not be fit to do your job if you were to do that. And remember, Matt is my husband, so my responsibility.'

Barry shook his head. 'Not totally, Mammy,' he said. 'He is my father and if he was of right mind what d'you think he'd say to me letting you sit up with him night after night and me seeking my bed as if he was nothing to me?'

'Why don't we take it in turns then?' Angela said. 'And before anyone says a word, Matt is my father too and this way we will only have to do it every third day and we still won't be leaving him alone.'

And so it was established and when she told Barry of her pregnancy he did balk a bit at her missing sleep and spending her nights in an uncomfortable chair, but he was overruled by Angela and Mary. In this way they limped through Christmas as Matt took a downward turn. He was slipping in and out of consciousness and everyone knew one time he wouldn't wake up again. The neighbours came to see if they could help but there was little they could do, and when the priest saw the state of him he said he should have been told how ill he was and he needed to administer the Last Rites, and it didn't matter a jot that he was unconscious. Mary was greatly comforted

when the Last Rites had been given to Matt who, she knew, would soon meet his Maker. The doctor also popped in periodically and when he came just after Christmas, he told Mary Matt was holding on by a hair's breadth and he could go any time.

That was not news to any of them and yet Mary was very glad that she was the one with Matt when the end came in the early hours of Tuesday 8th January 1913. Matt had been restless that night and so Mary had been unable to settle and was sitting beside his bed wishing she could do something, anything to ease his passing, when he suddenly opened his eyes. Mary was startled because she hadn't seen his eyes wide open like that for a while and they weren't rheumy and pain-riddled, but seemed quite clear and she was even more amazed when he fastened those eyes on her and said, 'We were a good team, Mary,' for Matt had said nothing except the odd unintelligible mumble for some time. However she replied in like manner, 'We were, Matt, a very good team indeed.' They weren't a couple to show affection for one another. It wasn't their way, but uncharacteristically Mary leant forward and kissed Matt's dry paper-thin cheek. She saw his lips turn upwards in a slight smile before his eyelids slid shut again. Mary sat back down in the chair and held Matt's hand firmly and eventually his rasping gasps for breath slowed and she knew he was nearing the end even before she heard the death rattle in his throat.

The room was suddenly very still and Mary knew Matt was gone. With a sigh Mary got to her feet and pulled the sheet over her husband's face

before going upstairs to wake Barry.

Barry had thought that because he knew his father was dying, had known for a while, that when he eventually did it would be easier to bear, but he found that wasn't the case at all. 'I suppose it's because death is so final,' he said to Angela.

'I suppose so,' she replied brokenly. 'Oh God, Barry, I will miss him so very much.'

Both Angela and his mother seemed awash with tears and Barry envied them those tears because what he wanted to do was throw himself on the floor and howl his eyes out. But he knew that was a luxury he couldn't allow himself for everyone was relying on him. He was a bit at sea himself and very grateful to Stan Bishop who had told him when his father was diagnosed with terminal illness he would help him with the arrangements for the funeral and so forth if he wanted him to. Barry did indeed need his advice. He had to see him anyway to take a few days off and Stan proved to be a tower of strength.

As was the custom, the neighbours had a whip-round for flowers and though Mary accepted the flowers with good grace, she told Angela she wouldn't be surprised if Matt was turning in his grave. 'Couldn't abide flowers on a grave that would just wither and die in no time at all,' she said. 'He always said if the one who died is the man of the house and maybe the sole bread-winner any money collected should be given to the widow to buy food or to help with the rent. No one can eat flowers.'

Maybe not, but a good send-off was considered

of great importance so on the day of the funeral the wreath from the neighbours was laid on the coffin before the altar at St Catherine's alongside the family flowers. It was also fairly littered with Mass Cards, which were sent by Catholic relatives and good friends, including Matt and Mary's two sons in America. They both sent loving letters of condolence and each had folded a ten-dollar bill inside the envelope which they said was to 'help' with things. It was more money than Mary had ever seen in her life and Barry advised her to put it straight into the Post Office where they would change it to sterling.

The day was a keen one and it was cold enough in the lofty church during the long and mournful Requiem Mass, despite the fact that it was packed. Angela dreaded the walk to Key Hill Cemetery in Hockley in such cold and as they stepped out of the church their breath escaped in wispy trails from their mouths and they were assailed by a biting wind sending flurries of ice-laden snow that fell from a leaden sky.

The coffin was pushed before them on a cart as they walked in a procession, led by Father Brannigan. Barry came after him, with his arm around his mother and Stan Bishop took care of Angela. Everyone else followed behind and stood dithering at the graveside while Father Brannigan intoned prayers for the dear departed.

Eventually it was over, the prayers said, the coffin lowered, the clods of earth thrown on top and the crowds turned thankfully to make their way to the back room of The Swan public house on Bell Barn Road where Mary and Angela had

made enough food to feed the masses, helped greatly by George Maitland who had donated a great deal of the food and willingly gave Angela time off to be with Mary and help her through this dreadful time. Mary shed tears at George's generosity and only wished she could thank him in person but it was Saturday, and that was his busiest day in the shop and though he would have liked to close to attend the funeral he knew he would let a lot of people down if he did that.

Many people marvelled at the spread the two women had managed to conjure up in those austere days. They certainly appreciated it and Angela watched the food they had taken days to prepare disappear faster than the speed of light. She couldn't begrudge them, though, for by coming to the funeral they were showing respect for Mary, and Angela knew if Mary thought she had the support of the neighbours it would help her cope better.

And the neighbours did gather around Mary after the funeral which meant Angela could stop worrying about her and mourn Matt herself. But life must go on and she returned to work the day after the funeral and accepted condolences from George and many customers, knowing that the pain at the loss of Matt would eventually settle to a bearable ache and she would be able to look forward to the birth of her baby who she thought would help them all.

However before the birth Barry came home one day in March with good news. He was just a fortnight away from his twentieth birthday and Stan had called him into the office because he had

a proposal to put to him. Although Barry couldn't officially finish his apprenticeship for another year, Stan had seen the chap in charge of the apprentices and he said that there was really no more he could teach Barry and that he was a good and conscientious worker and so Stan decided to finish his apprenticeship a year early. It needed the approval of the management, but the death of Matt who had worked for the firm meant that Barry was now the sole breadwinner and had glowing praise from his superiors, so they decided to stretch a point. And so from his birthday his wage would rise to £3 a week which had been what his father earned. The women were very pleased, particularly Angela who had been concerned at how they would manage financially when she had to give her job up at Maitland's shop.

George was pleased at her news though he had to admit to himself that part of him had hoped that finances would ensure Angela stayed working for him, leaving Mary to care for the child. Now he knew that wasn't going to happen. Not only was Angela a good worker, she was also like a ray of sunshine and he knew he would miss her greatly. But he didn't betray his inner thoughts in any way and congratulated Angela and said to pass on his good wishes to Barry before going on to say, 'You surprise me, though, for most employers I know of are not generally concerned with the welfare of workers unless it affects their ability to work hard and make them plenty of profit.'

'I think that it's Stan that made a difference,' Angela said. 'He was very fond of Matt and suffered alongside him when the boys were drowned, and

144

when he saw how ill Matt was he was shocked and came to see him many times and sorted out the sick pay and everything. He felt guilty about Barry's two brothers who were laid off as soon as they were through their apprenticeship.'

'That's what I mean,' George said. 'That's common practice.'

Angela nodded. 'I know,' she said. 'But then those boys decided to try their hand in America and perished in the sea. It made me wonder if they would have been so keen to go if they were regularly employed. And if I thought that, I bet it crossed Stan's mind too. He told Barry that his hands had been tied over that, but he would ensure it never happened to him, and now this news.'

'I know. It's almost unbelievable.'

'Stan thinks it's likely there's going to be a war.'

'A war?' George repeated. 'What gives him that idea?'

'I asked Barry that and he said it's because of all the unrest in Europe.'

'There's always upset in Europe,' George said dismissively. 'If we bothered about everyone we'd never be away from the place. Very volatile, the Europeans are, generally. Anyway, what happens over there doesn't affect us.'

'No I suppose not,' Angela said. 'Stan asked Barry if there was a war, would he go, enlist you know? Barry said, not likely, not unless he was forced to, that is. He said he had to look after his mother and me and our baby and that was enough to be going on with. Stan said he was glad Barry was so sensible and he wished all young fellows felt the same.'

'I'd agree with him there,' George said. 'Some young fellows are hot-heads altogether. So let's hope England doesn't allow herself to be pulled into a war that is really no concern of ours and we keep our young fellows at home, where they belong, until they mature a bit.'

'Ah, yes indeed,' Angela agreed.

According to Iris Metcalf, who was the woman most neighbours called on when their babies were due because few used the services of a doctor un-less in an emergency, Angela's baby was due towards the end of May, maybe 24th or there-abouts, and so when March drew to a close Barry told Angela she should think about giving in her notice. However, Angela felt incredibly well and with Mary doing the lion's share of the housework and cooking, she didn't see the necessity.

However, someone else was concerned about Angela continuing at the shop, or maybe incensed might be a better name for it. Matilda thought, even assumed that Angela would give in her notice as soon as she became pregnant. It was after all what any decent woman would do, but George said the family needed her wages to survive. And so she continued to come and flaunt herself. Matilda had told George it wasn't seemly to have Angela at the front of the shop serving people and he reminded her that he made the rules in the shop, not her.

In all other ways in the home and even the marriage Matilda held sway and got everything she wanted, but from the first George had made it clear that the shop was his domain, as it had been

146

his father's and before him his grandfather's, and he made the decisions. This suited Matilda mainly because it gave them a good living and she had no desire to enter the smelly shop let alone work there. She had once hankered after a terrace house in some grander area far away from the cramped houses in the mean little streets, but George always said it was more practical to live in the flat above the shop. 'It's plenty big enough for us two,' he'd said the first time she had asked him and he had stuck to it like a mantra and in the past would often go on, 'I mean it isn't as if we have a house full of children.' He had stopped using this as another stick to beat her with because she couldn't help not liking children. And she really thought what women had to endure to conceive was too disgusting for words and she was having no truck with that. But George's paternal feelings had been turned on when Angela McClusky came to work in the shop. He was more than just fond of her and that was like a thorn in Matilda's side and she begrudged every mouthful of the dinner she took as her right because George said so. But she knew Angela couldn't go on much longer. So when she was still there the first week in April she said to George as they sat eating their evening meal, 'I just hope you have honed up your midwifery skills, that's all I can say.'

'What?'

'I think you heard,' Matilda said testily. 'I hope you know just what to do when Angela McClusky goes into labour in the shop in front of all the customers.'

George blanched at the thought, but said firmly

enough, 'That won't happen.'

'And how are you going to ensure that, pray?' Matilda said. 'According to what I hear, babies have an annoying habit of coming unannounced whenever they please and the more inconvenient the time the better. Tell you what,' she added, 'I am surprised that young husband of hers has not been up to see you before now, because you are putting Angela at risk, not to mention their un-born child if she carries on like this. And you can't even use the excuse that they need the money any more because from what I hear he is on good money now.'

Matilda's words hit home for George knew a lot of what she said was right and he thought himself selfish and insensitive not to encourage Angela to leave, just because he was dreading not seeing her again. But he may have put her at risk. Pregnant women should rest, he had heard, and though Angela had never said she wanted to leave, he knew he should have insisted and before he could talk himself out of it, then and there he went down to the shop, packed a bag of groceries, and went down to see Angela with two weeks' wages in his pocket to tell her that for her own sake she mustn't come to the shop any more.

Both Barry and Mary were relieved that Angela was released from the shop and she could rest more, and though Angela missed the shop and had never complained, the ponderous weight she was now carrying around did wear her out, so she knew it was probably for the best.

Now that money was easier Barry gave Angela money to buy some things for the baby and she

went to the Bull Ring with Mary. They wandered around the stalls comparing prices and chose what to buy with care. Eventually they bought some soft sheeting to cut into squares to make nappies and they also bought rubber pants. 'A marvellous invention,' Mary called them. 'There were none of these sorts of things in rural Ireland when mine were growing up,' she said. They added long night-dresses, little vests, a couple of crocheted matinee jackets, a bonnet, bootees, a couple of warm wool blankets and a shawl. 'Now,' Mary said, as they set off for home, 'we're all ready. All we're waiting on is the baby.'

'Oh yes,' Angela said. 'I hope it's soon. Nine months is such a long time.'

'It's no time at all to grow a new life,' Mary said. 'Don't fret, your baby will come when he or she is ready and that's how it should be.'

ELEVEN

Angela's pains began in the early hours of 24th May. It was Saturday and Barry worked half a day and so Angela said nothing to him. Although she longed to meet the baby she had carried for so long, she was nervous of the birth and Mary understood this and so gave her some idea of what to expect. 'A first baby usually takes its time,' she said. 'After that it's as if the body knows what to do. But the labour with a first is usually longer and when your pains start they are little more than a

149

grumbling, not unlike the pain you sometimes get with your monthlies.'

And lying in the bed that morning, Angela thought Mary had been right, for the pains were like the drawing pains she'd had each month before she became pregnant, when she would search out the cotton pads she always had ready in the cupboard. 'Best thing in the early stages is to keep moving,' Mary had advised and Angela knew that she was probably right about that too, but she could hardly leave her bed so early and walk the floor.

All that would do would be to wake Barry and then once he realized what was happening he would probably not want to go to work but stay at home fussing all around her and worrying himself into an early grave. No, it was better Barry was kept in ignorance for a wee while yet and she closed her eyes and tried to rest, drawing her legs up to ease the pains slightly.

Next to her in the bed, Barry was awake though he kept his eyes shut. Since Angela's time drew nearer he had tended to sleep more lightly and so he had been aware of her slight movement when the pain woke her first and was aware of her beside him now with her knees pulled up and sometimes giving small gasps that she tried to smother. Angela was right that he was anxious, for as his darling wife had grown bigger and ungainly he realized what he had done and what Angela would have to go through to give birth to the child.

He loved Angela more than life itself, but she was young, surely too young to start having babies when she had scarcely finished maturing. He had

said as much to his mother out of Angela's hearing and she had said, 'Tell you the truth, Barry, I have thought the same myself. But see, son, what's done is done. Angela might be small and young, but she's strong enough and I have sounded out Iris Metcalf and you know she's helped the birth of nearly every child in this street, so she knows her stuff. We just have to put our trust in God, that's all.'

It wasn't that reassuring and Barry hadn't the same belief in prayer as his mother and he felt totally helpless. But he reasoned there was no need for him to lie there when Angela was obviously in pain and trying to cover it up, so he whispered, 'Angela.'

'Oh I'm sorry,' Angela whispered back. 'Did I wake you?'

'I was awake anyway,' Barry said. 'Are you all right?'

'Right as rain,' Angela said and then gave a gasp as another pain gripped her.

'Doesn't sound it to me,' Barry said. 'Shall I fetch Mammy?'

'No,' Angela said firmly and added, 'Look Barry, it is the baby coming but your mother assures me that first babies take ages.'

'Even so, I won't go in today,' Barry said. 'They'll understand I have to stay with you.'

'To do what exactly?'

'What d'you mean?'

'I mean what is the point of you staying away from work?' Angela said. 'I told you your mother said it takes ages and she meant hours, not minutes, and you can do nothing during that time.

151

You might not even be let in the room. I know your mother thinks it's no place for a man when a woman is giving birth and it's more than likely the midwife will feel the same way. You'd just be kicking your heels and worrying more than ever.'

'I feel so useless.'

Angela gave a wry smile. 'I imagine most men do,' she said. 'Your work is over until the baby's born and then you can prove that you are the best father in Christendom.'

'I will be that all right,' Barry said fervently. 'But can I do anything for you now? How about me making you a nice hot cup of tea?'

Angela knew there was going to be no further sleep or rest for either of them that night and said, as she attempted to get out of bed, 'Your mother said it was best to move around.'

Barry pushed her gently back onto the pillows and said, 'Don't care what my mother said. I am going downstairs now to make a cup of tea for my lady wife because it is all I can do for the woman who is soon going to make me the proudest man on earth.'

Angela's eyes filled with tears at Barry's lovely words and she knew it was important that he made that tea. 'Are you sure?' she asked.

'Course I'm sure,' Barry said, slipping his trousers on as he spoke. 'If only to prove to you that I'm not bloody helpless.'

He pushed his feet into his boots, gave Angela a kiss and left the attic. And Angela heard the clatter of his boots on the stairs in the still night and knew it was unlikely Mary would sleep through it and would probably work out why Barry was going

downstairs so early.

Angela was right and a few minutes later she heard Mary's laboured breath as she ascended the stairs. She was wearing an old robe wrapped over her nightdress but Angela was pleased that she had the warm slippers on her feet that she had bought her for Christmas. 'Is it time?' she asked Angela, but she was in the throes of another contraction that answered her question.

'And where's his Lordship off to?' Mary asked. 'It was like a herd of elephants going down the stairs.'

Angela smiled. 'I know,' she said and despite the fact she felt bad about waking Mary it was very reassuring to have her there. 'He's making me a cup of tea,' she told Mary. 'He insisted. He said he feels useless.'

'Well he will,' Mary said. 'Most men are useless when it comes to the birth. But making a cup of tea won't hurt him and drinking it won't hurt you. After he is packed off to work I want you to move down to the bedroom where you will be more comfortable and that will be your room from now on and I will relocate to the attic.'

'Are you sure?'

'Course I am,' Mary said. 'It's right now for me to move to the attic. But I must try and protect the mattress by covering it with some rubber sheeting I got hold of.'

'Barry did threaten not to go in today,' Angela said to Mary. 'He wanted to stay with me.'

'Stuff and nonsense!' Mary said impatiently. 'Men are neither use nor ornament when a woman is giving birth and I wouldn't have him, or

153

any other man cluttering up the bedroom, so going to work is the only sensible thing to do and I shall tell him that when he gets here with the tea.' And Mary did tell Barry and in a tone that brooked no argument though he did try.

Mary went down to see to the bed and when Angela had finished the tea Mary and Barry helped her down to the bedroom, and Mary told her to rest between contractions while she followed Barry downstairs and cooked him breakfast. It was too early for him to go to work so Mary asked him to top up the coal scuttle with coal from the cellar and also fill the kettle and the large pan with water from the tap in the yard, and Mary hung those over the fire so there would be plenty of warm water when it was needed.

As soon as Barry left Mary cooked porridge for Angela to give her strength for the ordeal ahead. She took it up to her to find her in quite a lot more pain. She didn't really want the porridge, but ate it to please Mary, but she was grateful for the second cup of tea she brought.

Despite Mary saying it was better to move around in the early stages Angela found it hard to stand and with each contraction she had the desire to crouch. When she told Mary this she said, 'You might surprise us all and give birth quicker than I imagined. Will you be all right if I pop along to tell Iris you've started?'

'No I'll be fine and I'd really like to see her,' Angela said for she liked the doughty little woman. She felt safe in her hands; she knew what she was doing and she was clean.

When she said this to Mary she agreed. 'Some

dirty ones about. Most around here have Iris now, but before she moved here about ten years ago women would get who they could to help if they had no handy relatives, and the tales they have told me about some of these old hags, gin sodden many of them and completely useless! I've heard some right horror stories. There's none of that sort of carry-on with Irs. Anyway I won't be a tick.'

Mary was much longer than a tick. But then she brought Iris back with her and Angela was relieved to see her because the space between the contractions had shortened considerably and the pains were much stronger. 'Let's have a little look, ducks,' she said throwing back the bedclothes. She gave a grunt of satisfaction as she stood up again and said with a smile to Angela, 'You're almost ready. Not be that long till you're holding your wee baby in your arms.'

Angela felt a thrill of excitement run through her even though Iris went on to say, 'Still a wee bit of work to do yet, I need to see everything is going well inside, but I need to scrub my hands well before I do that.'

'I have warm water ready,' Mary said and led the way downstairs. Iris was very gentle in her examination and declared everything was as it should be and they just had to wait. And that's what they did while Angela's pains grew in intensity. Mary made tea for them all and when Angela began to writhe in the bed, trying to escape the wild beast tearing her insides out, Iris tied a towel to the bedhead for her to pull on when the pains got bad. 'They are bad already,' Angela wanted to say but she wasn't able to say much as a massive contraction disabled

155

her and then there was a sudden rush of water from her body. 'That's your waters gone,' Iris said. 'Won't be long now.'

Mary positioned herself at Angela's head and suffered with her though every pain as she bathed her face, which was shiny with sweat, and she offered her sips of water and encouraged her gently. 'Come on, my bonny lassie,' she said, using the endearment Matt always used. 'You can do this. Ride the pain, lassie.'

Sometime in this maelstrom of pain and discomfort Barry came home from work. Mary would not let him see Angela who she said wasn't fit to be seen and also said she had work in the room above and if he wanted anything to eat he had to make it himself. Such a thing had never happened before to Barry, and yet this was a special day and, please God, at the end of it he was going to be a father.

That exhilarating thought coursed through his body and he had no intention of sullying the day with any trace of ill humour and so he said, 'I'll knock up a sandwich for myself, never fear. Go back to Angela. I'd say her need is greater than mine.' Mary scurried back upstairs and took her place again at the head of the bed and she hadn't been there that long when Angela said she wanted to push.

This last stage of the birth was what had worried Mary the most, thinking Angela might tear herself badly, or even haemorrhage if the strain on her slim young body was too great. Iris knew what Mary was concerned about because she told her that morning as they walked to the house and so

she examined Angela swiftly. 'She's wide enough,' she said reassuringly to Mary and to Angela she said, 'Push away, ducks. This baby is anxious to be born.'

Now Angela understood the reason for the towel which she pulled on so hard she threatened to pull the bedhead down on top of her because she had never experienced such pain. She felt as if she was on fire and was trying to give birth to a red-hot cannon ball and her low moans had turned to shrieks. And Mary and Iris were encouraging her to give one more push and yet one more. She wanted to tell them to shut up but hadn't breath left to do it.

Just when she really thought she could do no more Iris called out 'I can see the head! Come on, Angela, give it all you've got.'

Angela gathered all her strength and pushed with all her might. 'Good girl,' Iris said approvingly. 'Give another like that.'

Angela did but then she lay back on the bed and said, 'I can't do any more.'

'Every woman feels like that,' Iris said airily. 'Have a breather and when the urge to push comes again then go with it and push with all your might. One more decent push might do it.'

The urge to push couldn't be ignored and when it came Angela's whole face was contorted as she pushed with all the strength she had left. There was a sudden extreme pain and her breath left her body in a scream and then she felt something slither between her legs and newborn wails filled the room.

'Oh Angela, you clever girl,' Mary said and her

voice was husky with unshed tears as she went on, 'You have a beautiful little daughter.'

'Oh let me see her,' Angela said, struggling to sit up.

Iris wrapped her in the shawl Mary had ready and placed her in Angela's outstretched arms. She gazed into her beautiful face and the milky-blue eyes flickered shut as Angela rocked her gently. She felt such a powerful tug of love for the child that she gave a gasp. 'I didn't think it was possible to love a child as much as this,' she said in awe. 'I love Barry but this is...'

'Mother love, that's what that is,' Iris said. 'I think it's the most powerful emotion in the world.'

'I agree with you,' Mary said. 'Matt always said it was nature's way of ensuring that mothers would protect their young.'

'Yes, fortunately human beings don't have to do much of that,' Iris said. 'Now where's that young husband of yours, for I'm sure he would like to get acquainted with his new baby daughter?'

'Don't know where he is,' Mary admitted. 'Thought he'd be wearing the floorboards out in the room below to be honest. I best seek him out.'

In the end there was no need to do that. Barry had been pacing the room like a caged tiger but each time he opened the door to the stairs he heard his young wife's moans and it tore at his heart-strings. He wanted to run up and see what was happening to her but he knew his mother and the midwife wouldn't let him in.

So, as he could do nothing to help her, he had to be somewhere where he couldn't hear her suffering and the only place was outside and so

he went out. He needed to keep moving, to walk, but he didn't intend to go far from the house and so he was walking aimlessly along Bell Barn Road, down Bristol Passage to Bristol Street and back again.

He was approaching the house when a neighbour sitting on her doorstep taking the air said as he passed, 'Hope everything's all right, Barry. Your Angela gave out such a scream a few minutes ago.'

The blood ran like ice in Barry's veins and he tore down the street to the house, wrenched open the door of the stairs, leapt up them two at a time, yanked open the bedroom door and just stood and stared at the woman he loved so dearly holding a baby, their baby, in her arms as if she had done it every day of her life. He had eyes for no one else and his eyes were so full of love and amazement it was beautiful to see.

Iris whispered to Mary, 'Let's go and have a cup of tea. I'll have to clean the baby up later and check she's all right, but it can wait. I think those two need some time to bond with their baby.'

Neither Angela nor Barry were really aware of Mary and Iris leaving the room and Barry continued to gaze at his child as if he couldn't believe his eyes. 'It's a girl, Barry,' Angela said gently. 'Are you disappointed that I haven't given you a son?'

'Disappointed?' Barry repeated as if he couldn't quite believe his ears. 'My darling girl, what are you thinking of? Between us we've created this perfect child and she'll grow to be as beautiful as her mother, inside and out, and gladden our hearts with every passing year, and you ask if I am

159

disappointed? I am not, not in the slightest and I don't care if I never have a son.'

Angela sighed with relief. 'The next one will be a son,' she said.

'Son or daughter will make no odds when the time comes,' Barry said. 'But I meant what I said before this one was born. I want you fully recovered from the birth and to have a few years enjoying our daughter before we give her a playmate. Have you a name for her? You would never discuss it before the birth and as you did all the work it should be your decision.'

Angela smiled. She had never discussed names with anyone, thinking it unlucky, but she had decided almost from the time she realized she was pregnant what to call a girl and she said, 'I would like her called after my mother and yours, Constance Mary. D'you like it?'

'I love it,' Barry said. 'And it's right that you should honour your mother in that way and my mother will be over the moon.' Barry leant forward and kissed the baby's soft, soft skin gently and said, 'Hello, Constance Mary McClusky, welcome to our family.'

And Angela thought she just might burst with happiness.

Neighbours had streamed into the house those first few days after Connie's birth all carrying a gift of some sort, a rattle or teething ring, a small cardigan or pretty nightgown, and they all admired the child who they said was the image of her mother. Even George came and Angela was delighted to see him and he brought a complete

pram suit for the baby to wear as she got older when the winter set in. Barry's brothers sent a couple of beautiful dresses trimmed with lace and bedecked with ribbons that they said were all the rage in the States.

'And they might well be too,' Mary said. 'But they're not very practical. When you are out of your lying in we'll take a dander up to the Rag Market for more everyday clothes for Madam here.'

However, before they could do this Mary opened the door to see Maggie outside with a pram full of baby clothes. 'What's all this?'

'Hello, Mrs McClusky,' she said, 'I've come to see Angela and the baby and these are from me mother. She had a clear-out and thought you might like these old baby things and the pram because she doesn't need that either.'

'How kind of her,' Mary said. 'Is she sure?'

'She is,' Maggie said with an emphatic nod of her head and added with a grin, 'She said she is giving up all that sort of nonsense now and said my father must tie a knot in it. I think Mammy is glad to get rid of the stuff for wee Maurice is six now. And it's too cramped in the attic to keep clothes she has no use for. She said take them and welcome.'

Angela was very grateful for the bag of clothes, which were lovely and she lifted one after the other with a cry of delight. 'There's a christening gown at the bottom,' Maggie said. 'It's well-worn for we have all been christened in it.'

It didn't look at all well worn, Angela thought as she peeled back the tissue paper it had been

wrapped in and sat gently stroking the silken fabric. 'It's so soft and so white,' she said. 'It looks brand new.'

'Oh that's Mammy,' Maggie said. 'She has this thing that the gown shouldn't ever look second-hand and so every time it's worn she washes it in that soft Lux soap and whitens it with Becket's Blue in the final rinse water and when it's dry she wraps it in tissue paper and stores it in a drawer in her room because the bedroom is not as damp as the attic.'

'Well it worked, will you tell her, and I am very grateful,' Angela said.

'I will,' Maggie promised and added, 'She's sent over her old pram as well, that she was glad to be shot of I think.'

'Oh I will be so glad to have that,' Angela said fervently, her face a big beam of happiness because she hadn't known how they were going to afford a pram and though the baby would be fine in a shawl for now, when the winter came she would like her tucked up warm and cosy.

'Hey,' Maggie said suddenly, 'can I have a wee cuddle?' Angela smiled as she lifted the sleeping baby from the cradle at her side of the bed and placed her into Maggie's outstretched arms. The baby just wriggled a little, protesting at being disturbed, and then she settled and her breathing became steady as she slumbered on. Over the child's head, Maggie's smiling eyes met those of Angela and she hugged the baby a little tighter and said, 'Oh isn't she just lovely? You are so lucky, marrying the boy of your dreams and having this beautiful baby and still just seventeen.

Everyone is envious of you.'

'Oh I hope you're wrong about that,' Angela said. 'Being envious is not a good thing to be.'

'It's not said in a horrible way,' Maggie assured Angela and went on, 'People are pleased for you. I suppose it's because you had such a bad start and people are just glad it has turned out so well for you.'

'I never felt I had a bad start really,' Angela admitted. 'I mean, I know I lost my entire family and that might be thought of as sad, but I was too young to remember them and I was lucky enough to be given a whole new family, the McCluskys. I never lacked love or care and that's really what matters to a child. And as for Barry, though I love him dearly I never think of him as the boy of my dreams, he was just always there and I always felt safe when he was around.'

'But you don't think of him as a sort of brother, do you?'

'Not now I don't,' Angela said. 'Anyway, what about you and Mike Malone?'

Maggie gave a shrug. 'Oh he's just a neighbour, a friend that's all.'

'No great passion then?'

'No,' Maggie said, but a smile played around her mouth and Angela could make a good guess that Maggie would have liked Mike to be more than a friend. She liked him too because he was a really nice lad and as he was the same age as Barry, they had been firm friends when they had been at school together.

So Angela said, 'You don't know that your feelings won't change. They often do as you grow.

163

I mean, look at me and Barry, I only thought of him in a brotherly way for years. But then I began to realize that I loved him in a different way and now our love has deepened and become stronger.'

'There's still hope for me then,' Maggie said.

'I'd say.'

'And you do truly love Barry now, I mean properly like a husband?'

Angela smiled as she said, 'Yes, well it isn't as though I've had a plethora of other husbands to practise on, but for example we didn't get young Connie there from holding hands.'

Maggie's peal of laughter caused the baby to jump slightly before settling again to sleep as Maggie said, 'I never thought for one moment you did. But didn't you miss your mother more when you had a child of your own?'

'How could I miss what I never had?' Angela said. 'This is all I have of my parents.' And she opened the locket she always wore around her neck for Maggie to see. 'This was given to me on my wedding day. It was my father's present to my mother when they married and it will be Connie's on her wedding day. I look at that picture sometimes and try to remember, but it's still all a blank to me. I have named the baby Constance after my mother, though, and Mary as well after Barry's mother.'

'Constance Mary,' Maggie said. 'They're good names.'

'Glad you like them,' Angela said, 'because I'd like you to be Connie's godmother.'

Maggie was astounded because it was the last thing she'd expected, but she was obviously

pleased. She grabbed at Angela's arm and cried, 'Oh my God, do you mean it? I would be so thrilled... Oh I never expected that. Oh Angela I am so thrilled.'

Angela was quietly amused by Maggie's reaction because she had thought of Maggie straight away and Stan Bishop was to be godfather.

'I take it you'll accept?' she said.

'You bet I accept,' Maggie said. 'You couldn't have said anything that would please me more.'

And so, a few days afterwards Constance Mary McClusky was baptized at St Catherine's Church. Even Father Brannigan seemed a little more human. At Mass he announced the baptism that would take place that afternoon and a great many people congratulated Angela and Barry outside the church. When she saw Maggie Angela said quietly, 'Did you see Father Brannigan? He almost had smile on his face.'

'No,' Maggie said. 'I thought so too at first, but I think it was just a touch of wind he had.'

Angela bit her lip to stop a giggle escaping for she could see Father Brannigan making his way towards them and she remembered Maggie had whispered things like that to her before at school, causing her to laugh at inappropriate times and get into trouble, and she could hardly laugh in the priest's face. 'All ready for this afternoon?' he asked Angela.

'I think so, Father.'

'I do think the names you have chosen eminently suitable,' the priest said. 'It's right that you honour the woman who gave birth to you and the woman who reared you.'

Angela nodded. 'I thought that, Father, and Mary was so pleased to be included and she deserved to be for she was a wonderful mother to me. Now she is so much looking forward to having a baby in the house again.'

'And you having Maggie here to look after her spiritual welfare.'

Maggie gave a grin and said impishly, 'I'll do my best, Father. And I will have Stan Bishop to help me so, between the two of us, we'll endeavour to ensure that Connie McClusky turns out a good little Catholic.'

Father Brannigan frowned slightly, not sure that Maggie wasn't making fun of him. It wasn't the words she said, but her manner, yet her face looked innocent enough and he decided he might have imagined it and he turned back to Angela. 'So I look forward to seeing you all this afternoon at four-thirty sharp.'

Angela thought how different a church is with so few people in it. Voices seemed to carry further and had an echoing sound and even shoes sounded loud on the marble floor and despite the fact that it was now early June, it was chilly in that stone edifice with its vaulted ceilings.

Connie bawled her head off when she was roused from her slumber by some strange person pouring cold water on her head. Mary said it was good to yell, it was getting the devil out of her. Angela looked across at the baby in Maggie's arms and thought she was innocent and pure and had no devil inside her, but now was not the time to argue about it. Everyone, including Father

Brannigan, was going back to the house for a bite to eat for it was a special day and she had helped Mary make a fair few fancies as well as lots of sandwiches. Connie behaved angelically once the water-pouring was over and in the house she was passed from one to another with barely a murmur. 'Isn't she a little star?' Barry said that night as they undressed for bed with the baby slumbering in the cradle beside them.

'She is,' Angela said and added with a grin, 'Takes after her mother there.'

'Ho! And one who thinks a lot of herself as well,' Barry said and gave Angela a playful tap on the bottom and then he turned her around and kissed her.

Angela felt frissons of desire run through her body and when Barry said huskily, 'My darling girl, you have made me the happiest man in the world,' she answered, 'If you come to bed, I know a way to make you happier still.' And Barry lost no time in getting beneath the covers and cuddling up to Angela and she sighed in contentment.

TWELVE

Angela never forgot the wonderful summer of 1913. The whole family doted on the child. Just to look at her made Angela's heart melt and she wasn't the only one, for she helped to mend Mary's heart, which Angela thought had been broken when she lost her sons and badly bruised

167

too at the death of Matt.

In fact, Connie's birth helped everyone because she was a sunny, happy child and Angela took her out every day, pushing the pram proudly. She went to see George when Connie was just over a fortnight old and he had tears in his eyes as he gazed at her.

The lack of any child of his own to follow after him hit him afresh. A grocery shop was cold comfort next to a living, breathing child to hold in his arms. So though he was pleased for Angela, he was also envious of the love shared between her and Barry, which was obvious from her radiant smile and the softening of her voice when she spoke of him And most of all George envied her the child that she was so clearly besotted with and he knew she would hardly relish leaving her and returning to work in the shop again.

He had tried two assistants since she had left and both had proved useless and he was limping along on his own. He did tentatively mention coming back to Angela, but she was vehement in her refusal. 'I don't think Barry would like it,' she said. 'He earns well enough now and we can manage and though Mary isn't old, she's too old to start looking after babies. She's done enough of that and anyway I would miss my wee girl if I didn't see her all day, every day. Unless there is no alternative I don't see the point of having children and giving them to someone else to rear.'

'I do quite understand my dear,' George said. 'It was just a thought.'

'And kindly meant I'm sure,' Angela said. 'You were always very good to me, all of us really and

if I had to have some form of employment I would be back here like a shot.'

But that wasn't likely to happen and George knew he had to accept it and move on as Angela had. She bade goodbye to George as customers appeared, but it wasn't so easy to leave because they all wanted a peep of the baby and they oohed and aahed over her and said she was a darling wee dote.

Angela didn't mind because she was immensely proud of her baby, but later as she was making her way home she was a little anxious about George. It was common knowledge that his wife wasn't an easy woman. She was a fine-looking woman still and must have been a stunner in her youth, but Angela doubted she had a kind or loving bone in her body.

'It's often the way with very beautiful women,' Mary said when Angela mentioned her concerns about George when she got home. 'The men have their heads turned and Matilda Maitland would have made a play for George because of the shop.'

'But she doesn't like the shop.'

'Doesn't like demeaning herself to serve in it, but I bet she likes the living it brings in,' Mary said and added, 'Women like that seldom have children. I wouldn't be a bit surprised if George is lacking in that area as well, and you know what I'm talking about.'

Angela did but she was still young enough to blush discussing even mildly intimate things. But she thought Mary was probably right and it might explain how emotional George had become when he saw Connie. She felt sorry for him, for he was

a kind and generous man and she was sure he would pay Matilda back a thousand-fold for the merest scrap of affection.

'It wouldn't happen in the Catholic Church for the man would have the priest out to give the wife a talking to, but he's Church of England and likely they don't do that kind of thing.'

'No I suppose not.'

'And I know what you think of George and I am fond of him myself,' Mary said, seeing Angela's woebegone face. 'But there is nothing you can do and there is a saying that he has made his bed so he must lie on it, so if I were you I would try to put George's problems out of your head and get ready to feed Miss Connie for she's stirring in her pram and will be hollering in a minute.'

Mary was right, she thought as she lifted Connie from the pram, really what ailed George was none of her business and she could do nothing to help him and she sighed as she sat down and began unbuttoning her blouse.

Connie was almost five weeks when she smiled for the first time and Angela thought for a moment her heart had stopped beating and she lifted her up in her arms and held her tight and called to Mary to come and see. And she did see because now that Connie knew how to smile, she seemed to do a lot of it.

'Wait till her Daddy sees that,' Mary said. 'He'll be turning cartwheels, so he will.'

Angela laughed. 'He might well,' she said. 'For he's one proud father. I think as she grows she will wrap him around her little finger.'

'I believe it's the way with fathers and daugh-

ters,' Mary said. 'And sure, didn't you have Matt where you wanted him? He never cuddled the boys as he did you.'

Angela knew Mary spoke the truth and she smiled wistfully. 'I would have loved him to see Connie,' Angela said with a sigh.

'Then he would have wanted to live long enough to see her grow up,' Mary said. 'Anyway, if we believe the priests that there is something after this life, he might well be looking down on us just this minute.'

'Do you doubt there's an afterlife then?'

'No,' Mary said. 'Not really. I can't afford not to believe for then I would never see my boys again, or Matt of course. As it is I can hope that all those I've loved and lost will be waiting for me at the other side.'

'And my parents and siblings,' Angela said. 'Comforting thought that, isn't it.'

'It is,' Mary said with an emphatic nod. 'And so I will believe it until I'm proved wrong.'

'And so will I,' Angela said and she removed the baby from her breast and sat her up, rubbing her back to get her wind up. Connie sat groggily, almost replete and then she gave an enormous burp. 'I hope that's not an opinion, young lady,' Mary said in mock severity and both women burst out laughing.

Angela relished every day and took delight in every milestone Connie passed like the first time she rolled over, or a tiny tooth peeping through the swollen red gums, often after many fractious and fretful nights. Then there was the first time she held a rattle in her hand without dropping it,

and a few days later she could pass it from one hand to the other. Barry was absolutely delighted when she shouted 'Dada' one day as he came through the door and she learned to clap her hands and sit up unaided without a pile of cushions around her in case she fell over.

'She'll be walking soon and then she will be one body's work,' Mary remarked one day. 'So you best get ready to run after her, because my running days are over.'

Angela knew that only too well. She could never linger at Mass nattering to Maggie now because as Connie became more mobile, she went to the early Mass at nine with Barry while Mary minded the baby and she had to hurry home so Mary could go to the one at eleven and Angela did the dinner for them all. So the girls agreed to meet on Saturday mornings as they did their shopping and Connie loved her Auntie Maggie very much. 'To-morrow's Barry's favourite day in the week,' Angela said as they were wandering around looking for something cheap but tasty for Sunday dinner.

'Why, because he gets a lie in?'

'No he doesn't have one of those, he wakes the same time, which is just as well, as Connie thinks six, or sometimes before six is a grand time to get up. No, he looks after Connie while I get on with the dinner. He says it's the only time he has her all to himself and they do have some fun together.'

'He's good to do that,' Maggie maintained.

'I suppose,' Angela said. 'He always said she's his baby too.'

'Well that is true, but some men think looking

172

after a baby is beneath them, women's work. He doesn't go for a drink then on Sunday morning?'

Angela shook her head. 'Nor at any other time in the general way of things. He earns enough to pay the rent, the gas, put good food on the table, have a cellar full of coal in the winter and buy clothes for Connie as she grows and for us all to have good boots on our feet. Many aren't as comfortable as we are but there is little slack. If there is any money left he tends to put it in the Post Office, so there is always something put by for that proverbial rainy day.'

'So he doesn't go to the football either?'

Angela shook her head and Maggie said, 'Angela you have got a good man there.'

'You don't have to tell me that,' said Angela.

It was coming up to Christmas, which hadn't been fully celebrated the year before because of Matt's terminal illness, but Barry said they must do the works with a child in the house, although she was far too young to know anything about it.

Mary had made the cake some time ago with Angela's help and they had all had a stir of the pudding. Now with just a fortnight to go Barry and Angela got the tree, streamers and decorations down from the attic where they were stored while Mary made mountains of mince pies. 'Mammy, you're not feeding an army,' Barry complained good-naturedly.

'Well Stan's coming too isn't he?'

This was true. Barry had asked the Gaffer when he found out he would be spending Christmas on his own, again. He had spent every Christmas alone since his wife had died, but unless they had

173

been related Barry couldn't have asked him while he was an apprentice. People might have thought he was sucking up. 'Stan is only one more person, Mammy,' Barry said.

'I know,' Mary said. 'But I want to make plenty so he can take some home with him and I know you when you get started on mince pies.'

'It isn't my fault,' Barry said. 'You shouldn't make them so tasty.'

'Hmm, the term "greedy guts" springs to mind.'

'Oh come on, Mammy,' Barry protested. 'Christmas is one day in the whole blessed year when you can indulge yourself.'

'You're right and so that's why I'm making so many mince pies.'

Angela listened to Barry sparring with his mother with a smile on her face because it was all play acting. Mary would cook them a wonderful Christmas dinner and not stint on anything so that they would be hardly able to move after it. The mince pies would be for the tea along with chicken sandwiches, sausage rolls and pickles and slices of Christmas cake. And then Stan Bishop would go back to his lonely house.

'It is a shame Stan Bishop would be by himself if you hadn't asked him to our house for Christmas,' Angela said to Barry as they scurried home from Mass the Sunday before Christmas. The day was icy so wisps of vapour surrounded her mouth as she spoke and her feet crunched on the frosty ground and she cuddled closer to Barry as she went on, 'He is such a lovely, considerate man, I'm surprised he's still single. I mean his wife has been

174

dead some years now. I couldn't remember all of it because I was just a child, but Mammy told me all about that and I could sort of remember the funeral. It was ever so sad and then to lose the baby as well.'

'He didn't lose the baby,' Barry said. 'Not in the way you mean. He's been brought up by his wife's sister.'

'So why isn't he spending Christmas Day with him?'

Barry shrugged. 'I don't know,' he said. 'He never mentions him.'

'Never mentions his own son? That doesn't sound like the Stan I know.'

'Well he's pretty good about keeping things close to his chest is Stan,' Barry said. 'Maybe you should ask him.'

'Oh I don't know that I'd like to do that,' Angela said. 'There might be a good reason for him not mentioning him. I am intrigued, though, because I always thought he would make a good father, a bit of a doting parent, you know?'

'Yeah, I would have thought that too.'

What Barry had told Angela about Stan made her feel differently about the man. She felt incredibly sad for him, but the subject wasn't broached again until they were sitting round the table eating their Sunday dinner, Connie on her father's knee. Angela said Barry had told her about Stan's son that she thought had died and that he never mentioned.

'He's not let see him,' Mary said. 'So I suppose there's nothing to say.'

'Not let see him?'

175

'No,' Mary said. 'You have to see the situation as it was then. First of all, I have never seen a happier couple than Stan and Kate, and they had a bit of a wait for Daniel because he wasn't born till 1905. And then tragedy. I wasn't surprised Stan was so distracted, they were so kind and loving the pair of them. Awful it was and when Kate's sister Betty came with her husband Roger, I really think Stan saw her as a Godsend, at first. Anyway, even when she took the baby to live with her, because he was all at sixes and sevens and wasn't in any fit state to look after a baby, and he knew he couldn't look after him and work.'

'Yes,' Angela said. 'But if he had kept in contact with Daniel and got to know him a bit, he might have come back to live here with him in the end when he was older.'

'I doubt that,' Mary said. 'If he was brought up in the lap of luxury as he is, according to Stan.'

'No he'd never settle to life here,' Barry agreed. 'And why should he? His home, his life, his friends, his school and his doting parents are there. Why would he want to leave all that?'

'Anyway, that wouldn't be at all the way Betty would want it. I met her at the funeral and didn't take to her at all. She wasn't a bit like her sister Kate. She was quite a lot older and she has never been able to have children.

'Now I am not saying she wasn't sorry her sister died and she did mourn her, but the consolation for her would have been the newborn child. She was certainly one of the first ones to hold him, she could almost have given birth to him. She was possessive about him and only begrudgingly

handed him over when I was at the font and took him back straight afterwards. I think she wants to pretend the child is hers and Roger's and doesn't want Stan in his life. She wants all the child's love directed towards her.'

'I don't think that's a healthy way of looking at things,' Angela remarked.

'It isn't and the losers are Stan and his son.'

'He's still a decent bloke though,' Barry said. 'And a good boss. I know he was upset when my brothers were sacked when they finished their apprenticeships, but look how he fought to keep me on.'

'Yes, I often wondered about that,' said Angela.

'It was a bit because of my brothers,' Barry said. 'Apparently, Stan told them that it was unlikely the boys would have gone to America if they had been kept on in regular work at the factory and they ended up being drowned at sea. And then with Dad taking sick and dying, he said they had to bear some responsibility.'

'Even though all Stan said was true,' Mary said, 'I'm surprised they took any notice. Places like that are not generally noted for their charitable gestures.'

'You're right, they're not,' Barry said. 'But just at the moment they needed experienced workers like Stan and to a lesser extent even me.'

'Why?'

'Well it's a bit hush hush,' Barry said, remembering too late that Stan advised him not to say anything just yet. 'Don't tell anyone, will you?'

'What sort of anyone?' Mary commented dryly. 'I don't know many Russian spies and the people

I do know will not, in the main, be the slightest bit interested and I think Angela would say the same. Your secrets are safe with us.'

'Well it's just that we are starting up new lines. It means employment for some, and that's the good news, and it means all the qualified men have to learn how to work the new machines so we can train the new ones.'

'Is that all?' Mary said. 'That's what all that cloak and dagger stuff was about?'

Barry nodded as Angela, watching his face, said, 'So what are the new lines?'

'We have a whole new section starting up and the people working there will be making bullets. There will be about fifty jobs going.'

'Bullets!' Mary echoed. 'What would we want with so many bullets?'

Barry didn't answer, he just said, 'And that's not all, because two of the forges are having new dies fitted in the new year to make long narrow tubes, and they will be the barrels for rifles, and batches will be sent along to the gun quarter to be assembled.'

'But what's it all about, son?' Mary asked. 'It isn't as if we are at war or anything.'

Barry was suddenly very still and Mary said, 'You think there's going to be a war don't you?'

'I don't know,' Barry admitted. 'But Stan thinks we might be dragged into that business in Europe.'

'How could we be?' Angela asked. 'It's miles away.'

'I know,' Barry conceded. 'But the company must know or suspect something, or they wouldn't go to all this trouble and expense, and if we do go

to war then I'd like to think that we were semi-prepared. We can't wait till the bullets are flying to make our own.'

Just at that moment Connie started shouting and wriggling and Angela had to take her from Barry so he could eat the rest of his dinner in peace. She put her arms out to Connie who rewarded her with a smile that nearly split her face in two and Angela's heart constricted with the love beyond measure she felt for this child. As she took her in her arms she knew without a shadow of a doubt, however hard life might be, she would never give her child away for someone else to bring up.

THIRTEEN

That Christmas was a magical one for Angela and she was woken by Barry kissing her lips very gently. 'What is it?' she asked him drowsily.

'Nothing,' Barry said. 'I mean, that is, nothing bad. I just couldn't wait one more minute to give you my Christmas present.'

She fully understood Barry's impatience when she sat up in bed and opened the large box he handed her, for he had bought her a good, warm coat in navy with a fur trim and matching hat. 'Oh, Barry, it's wonderful,' she cried as she lifted it out of the box.

She knew few women had a coat of any description and none would have one of this quality and

she did wonder how Barry had managed to afford it, but she couldn't spoil the moment by asking him. It was much later when she found out he'd seen it in the Rag Market and Stan had bought it for him and he had paid him so much a week, cutting down his cigarettes to do so. She had been further moved when she heard that, but on Christmas morning she was looking forward to wearing it to Mass.

Oh how proud Angela felt as she stepped out for Mass that crisp, cold Christmas morning. She barely felt the icy chill of the day, wrapped in her warm coat and hat. Even her hands were covered with thick, black, woollen gloves which had been Barry's present to her the previous Christmas.

She had her hands on the handle of the pram because Connie had to go along with them that morning as they were all going to nine o'clock Mass. Angela made sure though that Connie was wrapped warmly, from her flannelette vest and petticoat beneath her winter-weight dress and cardigan to the pram suit covering all that, one of the two from her two brothers in the States. They said in the letter sent with them that they were all the rage in America, made to protect babies from a harsh New York winter. One was a sort of royal blue and one dark red and Angela had chosen the red one for that morning.

Although there were pram suits in Britain they were woolly, knitted ones but the American coat, leggings and bonnet and even mittens and bootees were made of some sort of fleecy material. The bonnet was trimmed with lace and Barry thought Connie looked enchanting with the lace framing

her pretty little face, tendrils of blonde curls escaping at the sides and over her forehead. More important than how she looked though was how warm she would be and with the fleece suit on and tucked into the commodious pram with a couple of woollen blankets she would be as snug as a bug in a rug and with a bit of luck might sleep all the way through Mass.

Just before they left for Mass Barry had gone upstairs for his overcoat and as he was coming down again he saw Angela holding Connie in her arms and he felt such love and pride for them that his heart stopped beating for a moment and he wanted to wrap his arms around them and never let harm come to them.

He remembered that when Connie had been born, her hair was so blonde it looked as if she had no hair at all if a person didn't notice the down on her head. But now she was seven and a half months old she was developing the curls Angela had as a child. Mary always said she was the image of her mother at the same age and Barry could plainly see why Angela's mother named her so because angelic was the word that sprang to mind whenever he looked at his daughter.

He loved them both with an intensity that almost frightened him, for times were precarious for the working classes, because diseases were rife and people were fragile and sickness spread like wildfire in the cramped, insanitary hovels they lived in, and women like Stan's poor wife could also die in childbirth and he knew he really wouldn't want to go on if he lost them. 'Barry,' Angela called and Barry realized he was still standing on the stairs

caught up in reverie. 'Are you all right?'

'Fine. Just thinking.'

Angela laughed. 'You don't want to do much of that on Christmas Day,' she said. 'Leave that for every other day of the year.'

'I will,' Barry promised. 'I will close my mind from this moment on and not think of another thing for the rest of the day.'

'You are a fool,' Angela said, but fondly. 'If you get your coat on we're ready.'

Angela loved going to Mass on Christmas morning. She liked the church all ready to celebrate the birth of Jesus, the white and gold altar cloths, the flickering candles lighting up the whole altar, the figure of Baby Jesus put into the manger at last completing the nativity. And when the priest came to begin Mass she knew his vestments would be white and gold too and he would carry a candle set in a golden candlestick that would gleam and glisten and behind him would be four altar boys in red cassocks and white surplices keeping pace with the priest.

She also enjoyed meeting friends and neighbours and wishing them Happy Christmas, but as they neared the church Angela noticed a lot of the poorer women looking at her coat with envy and she felt so sorry for them, because a good few had only a threadbare dress, a thin shawl and down-at-heel boots to keep out the cold of the day, and for a moment the joy went from her.

Maggie voiced what many of the women who passed Angela in the porch might have wanted to say. She grabbed Angela by her two wrists and spun her round. She cried, 'Well will you look at

the set of you. Tell me, is this all from Santa?'

'It is,' Angela said with a broad grin in answer to Maggie's pleasure.

'Well then, my girl, I'd have said you have been thoroughly spoilt,' Maggie declared.

Angela agreed with her, but she wasn't the only one spoilt that Christmas, for Santa had left Connie a truck full of coloured bricks and a number of board books courtesy of Maggie's mother. 'Wouldn't take a penny piece for them,' Mary said. 'Was a bit offended I had offered. She said she was glad to see the back of them, but it has certainly made Christmas for Madam here.'

And her Christmas got better for that morning Maggie had given her a monkey on a stick and when Stan arrived just before lunch, he had a large bag with him and from it he pulled out a big soft brown teddy bear almost as big as Connie. 'He's lovely,' Angela said, taking it from Stan and stroking his soft fur. 'But you needn't have bothered, you only had to bring yourself.'

'Not at Christmas,' Stan said. 'And it gave me great pleasure to buy a present for a child.'

Angela could say nothing to that but, 'Well thank you, it was very kind of you.'

'You and Mary have not been forgotten either,' Stan said. 'I thought most women like perfume, but there is so much of it I hadn't a clue what to buy. But the girl advised me.' And he took from the bag two small packets. 'I got them different so you could share,' he explained. 'The girl told me the younger women go for this one,' he said, handing one to Angela. 'April Violet,' she said, opening it up and revealing a little bottle, then dabbing

183

some on her wrists. Even the bottle was beautiful and the perfume inside looked deep purple.

'Mary this is yours,' Stan said and handed Mary a yellow packet. 'Tiara Bouquet,' Mary read. 'Oh I can't wear this unless I have my tiara on.'

'Won't get much wear then,' Angela said with a laugh. 'Come on, stretch a point because it's Christmas and dab some on your wrists and we can compare. Thank you, Stan, for such lovely gifts.'

'Oh yes, thank you, Stan. That was such a thoughtful thing to do and we never expected it.'

And neither woman said that they had never had proper perfume in the whole of their lives. Even at Christmas and birthdays, it was too expensive to contemplate and now Angela had got perfume she didn't know when she'd use it for the only place she went was church for Mass. But surely even the Church couldn't object to a dab of it. It would seem criminal not to use something Stan had spent so much money on.

Stan hadn't finished however and out of the bag came a bottle of whisky and cigars for Barry that caused his eyes to open wide with delight. 'Oh you couldn't have done better mate, I love a drop of whisky.'

'Do you?' Angela said. 'I didn't know that.'

'That's because I don't allow myself to indulge in it,' Barry said. 'As for cigars I don't think I've ever tasted one, but my Dad used to speak of them with reverence. Not that he ever had many, just like this, a few bought at Christmas.'

'Well you seem to have pleased everyone in the room,' Mary said. 'Makes my presents to you

seem a bit mundane and ordinary.'

'I didn't expect a present from you at all,' Stan said in surprise. 'You'll be giving me a fine dinner and the chance to celebrate Christmas with your family and that is present enough for me. My gifts were just to say thank you.'

'I only bought you socks,' Mary said. 'In my experience men are very bad at shopping for themselves and no one can have too many socks.'

Stan laughed. 'Well,' he said, 'they may seem like mundane presents to you, but I am immensely grateful because you are right, I am bad at buying things for myself and I don't think I own a pair of socks that haven't holes in them somewhere, so new ones will come in very handy.'

'Mammy,' Barry said suddenly, 'the smell of that dinner cooking is making me feel light-headed, for I hadn't much breakfast after Mass, to make room for it.'

'Get away with you,' Mary said. 'And you know the best thing you can bring to a dinner table is a good appetite. But we have the soup first anyway and that's just to be heated up so it will be ready in a jiffy.'

'Right, I'll sort out the table,' Barry said.

'And I'll cut the bread,' Angela said, sitting Connie on the mat in front of the guarded fire, her truck full of bricks beside her.

'What shall I do?' Stan asked.

'Nothing, you're a guest.'

'Oh please, that makes me feel uncomfortable and I'd rather be doing something.'

'All right then, I have a very important job for you,' Barry said and he jerked his thumb towards

Connie as he spoke, 'and that is to entertain Madam there.' Stan felt panic rise in him. He would rather do any job but that one, for he wasn't any good with kids. He turned his gaze almost with dread towards the baby who was regarding him with large blue eyes. And then Connie smiled and the smile was so wide and radiant Stan felt his heart give a flip and the next he knew he was on his knees beside her on the rug and building a tower with the bricks. Connie crashed it down with a cry of delight and chuckled at the very dismayed look on Stan's face.

Her laugh was so infectious Stan built another tower which had the same reaction, and another, and was almost sorry to be called to the table despite his hunger. Angela had caught sight of his face as he got to his feet after playing with Connie and thought Betty hard and unfeeling to keep him apart from his son.

Maybe he couldn't be a father in the normal way, but he certainly should have been given the chance to build some sort of relationship with him. The fact that Betty and Roger were not Daniel's real parents would eventually come to light as these things inevitably do, and Angela wondered if the boy would resent the pair of them for separating him so totally from his natural father.

Still, she told herself, it really was none of her business and anyway, it was Christmas Day and no sad thoughts allowed. There could be few sad thoughts around the table with Connie there. She could understand little but seemed to delight in everything and her infectious chuckle and her

evident pleasure that caused her to clap her hands with glee amused everyone and chased any mournful thoughts away. So it was a cheerful meal and Angela thought Stan such good company she thought he might easily become a regular guest at Christmas.

The meal was fabulous and after it the women washed up while the men sat before the fire and smoked a cigar and kept an eye on Connie. And when it was all done and put away, Angela remarked, 'Not the weather for a walk today,' for icy sleet was falling from a sky the colour of gun metal.

'No,' Stan agreed. 'Not the day at all.' And then he added, 'I suppose we could always have a sing-song. I used to sing a lot at one time.'

'Did you?' Angela said because it was the last thing she had expected Stan to say, but his word tugged a memory for Mary who said, 'Oh my goodness, that struck a chord. You used to sing with your wife, Kate. She had a lovely voice.'

'Did you do it professionally?' Angela asked.

'Good Lord, no,' Stan said. 'We'd just do it for our own selves though Kate used to sing in the choir at Mass, so we'd sing any new hymns she had to learn at home and it would help her remember the words and then we might do others we both knew well just for fun.'

'I'd hear you,' Mary said. 'Anyone passing would hear you and Kate used to sing even if you weren't there.'

Stan nodded. 'She used to sing to the child she was carrying, who turned out to be Daniel,' Stan said. 'Some people thought she was crazy. She

187

used to sing him lullabies because she said he could hear and he would know the songs when he was born, and when she would sing them to him he would remember and know how much she loved him. I have never sung a word since the day of Daniel's birth. Even at her funeral I chose her favourite hymns and found I couldn't open my mouth.'

There was a sudden silence as Stan stopped speaking because they had all been hanging on every painful word. There were tears in Angela's eyes and in Mary's and Barry had an unaccountable lump in his throat. Even Connie sitting on the rug watching them all was silent, feeling the solemn atmosphere.

Suddenly, Stan got a grip on himself and said, 'I don't know what came over me. I'm sorry. Here I am, a guest, and this is how I repay your hospitality, doing my best to put a damper on Christmas.' He gave a sudden sigh and almost immediately launched into 'O Little Town of Bethlehem'.

It was too much for Angela. She had been moved by what Stan had said and now his rendering of the carol and the look on his face, showing what it had cost him to sing again after all this time, caused the lurking tears to start to trickle down her cheeks. To cover herself she lifted the baby onto her knee and began to sway in the chair in time to the music. There was a spontaneous burst of applause when Stan had finished, with Connie joining in enthusiastically, much to everyone's amusement.

'You have a fine voice,' Barry said and the

women agreed.

Stan went very red in the face, he was not used to being praised, and he held up his hands.

'Oh, stop please,' he cried. 'And it's not that I am ungrateful, far from it, and I found it very hard and very emotional to sing that, for it was Kate's favourite carol and I never sang it on my own, we always sang it together. You know, it would help me if you all join in.'

And they did and sang all the carols they could remember. Some time into the singing, Angela realized Connie had fallen asleep and she laid her in the pram in the room knowing the bedroom would be icy.

'She's a lovely child you have,' Stan said. 'I'm usually useless with kids.'

'I'm sure that isn't true,' Angela said.

'Oh I assure you it is,' Stan said. 'You all know I have a son?' They nodded and Stan continued his story. 'Kate's sister Betty is bringing him up and she doesn't want me around. When I got to think about it when I thought I was more or less over Kate's death, well maybe not over it, but coping better at least, I wanted to get to know my son and I booked the weekend off work and I went to Betty and said I wanted to have Daniel for the weekend and get to know him a bit.'

'How old was he then?' Angela asked.

'Not very old,' Stan said. 'He was just over two and of course didn't know me from Adam and he didn't like my house and wanted to go home. I took him to the park and spent hours pushing him on the swings and roundabouts and kicked about with a ball I'd bought, and we had fish and

chips for dinner but the child still wanted to go home, wanted his "Mammy and Daddy". I tried to soothe him, but he wouldn't be soothed, so I picked him up and he started to scream as if he was being murdered and then he was screaming that he hated me. He squirmed, kicked and punched me so I had to put him down and he curled himself in a tight ball and wouldn't uncurl himself, or speak one word to me, and I was worried to death.'

'I bet you were,' Angela said. 'But Daniel was only a very little boy and he was probably confused and frightened. So what did you do then?'

'I tried to think what Kate would want me to do and I knew she would want me to do what was best for the child, so I repacked the little case he had brought with him and the child uncurled himself quick enough when I told him I was taking him home.

'As we approached I saw Betty was looking out of the window and I thought she was probably bewildered and maybe a bit anxious because I was supposed to have Daniel for the whole weekend and here we were, back already. Betty hadn't been keen on the idea of my taking him for the whole weekend anyway because she said that was a long time for a small child to stay with someone he didn't know that well and she was dead right. She knew Daniel far better than I did.

'Anyway she came out to meet us to find out why I was bringing Daniel back so soon. Daniel gave a cry as he saw his mother approach and he pulled his hand from mine and ran down the road towards her and into her waiting arms.

When she lifted him up he wrapped his arms tight about her, buried his head in her neck and burst into sobs.'

'Ah poor wee boy,' said Mary.

'Aye,' Stan agreed. 'I saw that after. But at the time, I couldn't speak and if I'd tried I would have bawled my eyes out too. So though I saw Betty looking at me quizzically I could only shrug my shoulders and spread my arms wide.

'And then Daniel sat away from his mother's embrace, scrubbed at his eyes with his sleeve and pointing at me he said, "Don't make me go with that nasty man again, Mammy. He is horrid." 'Course, Betty accused me of doing something to the boy and I could only shake my head and then I just handed Betty the case, turned on my heel and left. I have seen neither of them since that day and it was five years ago.

'Betty and her husband applied to adopt Daniel about a year after that. By then I was feeling like a real rubbish father.' He looked at them all listening to him and he said, 'The hardest thing in the world after the death of my wife was to hear my son screaming out over and over that he hated me. I really thought Daniel would be better off not knowing anything about me and I signed the papers, so Betty and her husband are Daniel's parents legally. His name is Daniel Swanage and I have no part in his life.'

'I think that is one of the saddest things I have ever heard,' Angela said. 'If his adoptive parents really love him, Daniel will survive this. I am testimony to that, but it's you that will be hurting and you that have lost the most.'

191

'And don't think a little boy meant those words,' Mary said. 'If you had got to know him first, defied Betty and gone to see him every weekend and took him out and gave him a fun time, the outcome of that weekend might have been different.'

'I know, I have thought that myself,' Stan said. 'And the beggar of it is, it's too late.'

'Aye,' said Mary. 'That's the rub.' She got to her feet and said, 'Throats need lubricating after all that singing,' and she got up to make tea, but Barry waved away her offer of tea for him and Stan. 'We've got something more interesting,' he claimed and got up and brought bottles of beer he had got in for the festive season and the bottle of whisky Stan had brought him and put them all on the table as Stan got a deck of cards from his pocket.

He showed them some card tricks-first and they were amazed at his skill. 'D'you know any card games?' Barry asked. 'I never had a pack of cards because Daddy didn't approve of gambling.'

'I don't approve of gambling either,' Stan said. 'My money is too hard-earned to lose it all on a game of chance. I do it just for fun and it's great entertainment for a winter's evening.'

Mary still looked doubtful. 'Do you think it right though to play cards on Christmas Day?'

'I can't see that we are doing anything wrong,' Stan said. 'Honestly I can't. As long as no money changes hands it's just a game. Let me teach you all to play whist and you will see how harmless it is.'

'All right,' Mary said and Angela was glad because she too wanted to learn a few card games.

In fact the McCluskys picked up the rules of whist very quickly and thoroughly enjoyed themselves.

They had played four games when Connie woke. 'I best get tea,' Mary said and everyone groaned for no one was hungry, but Mary insisted. 'Well I'll put it out and cover it with tea towels and you can please yourselves. Connie will probably be ready for something anyway.'

'Shouldn't bank on it,' Angela said, holding the baby in her arms. 'She's had a good plate of her own mashed-up dinner and then a fair few forkfuls of Barry's because he had her on his knee and he of course gives her anything she wants.'

'You can't be giving out to the child,' Barry said. 'It's Christmas Day for goodness' sake.'

'Who's giving out to the child?' Angela said to Barry. 'It's you I'm giving out to. You'll have her spoilt, if you're not careful.'

'Fathers always spoil daughters,' Barry said. 'It's their prerogative. Anyway my own Daddy used to say better that way than the other way.'

Angela well remembered hearing Matt say that and she smiled at the memory. And it was true and she was glad that Barry loved Connie so deeply and was not afraid to show it. 'Hand her over,' Barry said to Angela. 'Me and Stan will keep her amused while you're busy.'

'I need to change her first,' Angela said. 'Unless you would like to do that too?'

'No,' Barry said, giving Angela a cheeky grin. 'Women are much better at that type of thing. I'm more than ready to admit that.'

'Oh I bet you are,' Angela said, but she laughed

as she took Connie upstairs to make her more comfortable, for she had to agree with him, men didn't change nappies. And if any did, and it was found out, they would be a laughing stock. In fact most of the day-to-day care was down to the women, but Angela considered that right and proper.

When she returned to the room though and handed Connie to her father she said, 'Don't throw her around much, you may drop her.'

Barry stared at Angela as if he didn't believe his ears and then asked incredulously, 'Why would I drop her? I have never even come close to dropping her before.'

Angela knew that but she also knew how many beer bottles had been emptied and vast inroads had been made in the whisky too and she was a bit concerned because Barry was unused to alcohol and she doubted Stan was a big drinker either generally.

However, her words fell on deaf ears and Barry and to a lesser extent Stan were soon tossing Connie in the air and spinning her round the room till she was breathless. There was no doubt that she enjoyed these games for she was screaming with laughter and shouting for more although Angela's heart was often in her mouth.

It meant though that Connie was far too wound up to eat much tea yet, despite this, Angela put a veto to any more rough-and-tumble games with Connie after tea lest she lose the bit she had eaten.

Undeterred, the men carried her over to the rug for more tower building. As the women washed up they could hear Connie's squeals of excitement as

she sent the towers crashing and Mary remarked to Angela, 'You'll never get her to bed tonight.'

'Well not till Stan goes home,' Angela agreed. 'Her father is as bad, but I can manage him. But I think Stan has had a good day, don't you?'

'He would be a hard man to please if he hasn't,' Mary said with a smile. 'And I don't think for one minute that he's an unreasonable man.'

Stan had had a wonderful Christmas with the McCluskys and though he was usually quite a sober man, he had imbibed a little too freely and Mary thought him too unsteady to go home on his own, clutching the parcel of goodies Mary had packed in his bag along with his socks. 'Go along with him, Barry,' Mary urged. 'See he gets home safe.'

Barry was almost as drunk as Stan was and had no desire to go out into the cold and the wet, and Grant Street was no distance away. But then he surveyed Stan standing swaying slightly as he bid them goodnight and knew when the cold night air hit him he could easily overbalance. What if he did that and hit his head or something? He said to Angela, 'All right if I go up with him?'

'More than all right,' Angela said and she hitched Connie further up her hip as she said, 'Little Miss here will settle easy if you two are out of the way.'

Barry grinned at her for he knew she had a point and he said, 'Wait on Stan. I'll come along with you. I'll just get my coat.' And Angela gave a sigh of relief when the door closed after the men.

FOURTEEN

'Happy New Year,' Stan cried, bursting through the McCluskys' door holding aloft the bottle of whisky. He also had with him a lump of coal and half a crown, because he was first footing. The first foot of the New Year had to be a man with the darkest hair and so that had to be Stan rather than Barry, as that ensures good luck for the family. The whisky is to signify the fact that they would never go thirsty, the coal that they would never be cold and the money so that they might have enough to last them all year. It was a custom the McCluskys brought with them from Ireland and though Stan had never done it before, he played his part beautifully, sneaking out just before twelve o'clock and as the hour was struck and some factory hooters sounded and people banged dustbin lids together he went back in to wish a Happy New Year to one and all.

Everyone had such high hopes for the New Year. For some time there had been unrest and clashes in Europe, though none had affected Britain and no one seemed to think Britain should get involved in countries so far away. They should deal with their own affairs.

Nearer to home though there was unrest among workers striving for better working conditions and living wages, and some workers had gone on strike. These strikes usually achieved very little

and didn't last long as the people couldn't exist for long without their wages, however meagre they were. Barry had great sympathy for them for he knew that but for the grace of God and the goodness of Stan Bishop he could have been one of them, and he understood the desperation of Gerry and Sean to sail to America where Colm and Finbarr were making such a good living. He sincerely hoped that some of those problems could be solved in 1914.

Then there was the Home Rule for Ireland supposed to be brought into being this year. He knew it would be marvellous if it ever came to pass because freedom from the yoke of England beat in the heart of every Irish Catholic who thought Ireland, being a separate island, should have a separate government and not be under British Rule. He knew too the Ulster Unionists would oppose the Bill, but if it became law there would be nothing they could do about it, surely.

'Oh I think they'll likely have something up their sleeves,' Mary said when Barry said this to her. 'They'll not give in without a fight. We just must wait and see.'

They hadn't long to wait before England began to unravel. In the early spring of 1914 some bricklayers began agitating for reform and the unrest began to spread to other towns and cities. And then the management's response in London was to lock the bricklayers out of their place of work.

'That will cause severe hardship and sooner rather than later I'd say,' Barry said one evening as he threw down the paper down in disgust and

added, 'The Boss said they're probably taking a hard line in London to dampen down the protests in other places.'

Angela nodded. 'He could be right, but you'd think they would at least listen to the workers' concerns, possibly compromise a bit.'

'I don't know why you're so surprised,' Mary said. 'Since when have these top-notch people given a tinker's cuss for the rest of us?'

'It is a bit short sighted though isn't it?' Angela said. 'I mean, factories and so on need workers. I'm sure if they treated them right, even if they couldn't meet all they demand straight away, they would work harder.'

'Maybe,' Mary said. 'But the bosses can behave how they want really, because there are so many on the dole queues now, they can easily replace whoever proves troublesome enough.'

However, after three weeks there was no sign of any softening on either side, but Angela knew the strikers would have to give in in the end because they were starving and so were their wives, and worse, their children.

Angela hated reading the paper for she imagined the despair of the bricklayers striving for a living wage and watching their children cry with hunger. God, she thought it would tear a man to bits, yet she felt she had to read it and when she said this to Barry, he admitted he felt the same way.

'That's what I'm on about, I suppose,' Barry said. 'There are people working here in Birmingham at various places full-time and yet not being paid enough to feed their families. Now we're

seeing even more stick-thin, barefoot kids in the streets. I always leave something from the dinner you put up now, for somehow it's even worse than it was before. Lots of us do it now, because it's hard to see such abject desperation on a child's face and not be moved by it. But you can only help one or two and some days there's so many of them.'

'From now on I will make you extra,' Angela promised, 'and if all wives with husbands in work did the same at least we could help more of them.'

'Yes we could,' Barry said. 'What makes me mad is if these blokes who have no job just give a mate a hand, say by helping out on a stall down the Bull Ring a time or two and the dole office get to hear of it, they stop the money altogether.'

'It's the wives that come to the rescue,' Mary said. 'I've seen them taking in washing, sometimes two loads as well as their own, and they beg for old orange boxes and the like, and chop them into sticks in the cellars to make up bundles of kindling they sell around the doors of the posh houses. It's them that ask for tick in the shops and they are seldom away from the pawn shop.'

What Mary said was true and it depressed Angela and she thought it was small wonder that there was such unrest in the country. 'And that Lloyd George seems to think more of foreigners than us,' Angela said, jabbing at the paper. 'All this happening in his England and he's more worried about the "build-up of weaponry in Europe". He calls it "organized insanity", but who really cares?'

Barry thought they might be made to care a great deal before too long because no one built up

199

weaponry for the sake of it and yet, on the other hand, there were always skirmishes and England had always kept well clear of any involvement, so this was probably the same. Anyway they could do nothing about anything other than making extra sandwiches to stop the children starving to death and thanking God that their daughter wasn't suffering the same fate. For he knew it must tear the heart from a man when he couldn't provide for his family.

Meanwhile he took such joy in his own child for she seemed to learn something new each day. She had 'Mammy' and 'Daddy' off pat and Mary she dubbed 'Ganny', and she was making a stab at Stan and Maggie but was not quite there yet. But then she would surprise them by suddenly saying 'door' or 'bed' and shouted 'more' and 'again' if she wanted another game, or more food. And then one day at the beginning of February Connie, who had been getting on her hands and knees for a week or two, crawled across the floor for the first time and pulled herself up by the guard surrounding the fire and hearth. The three adults looked at each other knowing that Connie would no longer stay where she was put. 'We'll have to make sure the door to the stairs is kept closed at all times,' Mary said.

'Yes,' Barry agreed, 'and I'll get some wood on Saturday to make a gate for the cellar steps, because I definitely don't want her falling down there.' The gate was in place and secure by Saturday evening and a good job too, for now Connie had mastered the art of crawling she could go across the floor in seconds, and what fascinated

her were the places she hadn't been allowed before, and one of those was the cellar. 'Oh wouldn't she just love to be down there playing with the coal?' Mary said with a chuckle as she removed her from the gate yet again and brought her into the room. 'Told you it's one body's work when they're at this stage.'

And no doubt about it now, they were at that stage. Connie wasn't prepared to sit in the pram while Angela did the washing, and she had to take her with her and make sure the door was shut when she did the bedrooms, and ironing had to be done when she was in bed and safely out of the way. And yet Angela wouldn't change a thing, for her love for the child was immeasurable and she felt privileged to watch her developing into a real little person.

'And won't it be lovely when the spring comes?' Angela said to Mary one day in late February as she stood at the window and watched the rain lashing the grey pavements. 'I will be able to take Connie to the park and let her crawl all over the grass!'

'I think we could all do with some warmth in our bones,' Mary agreed. 'And it's a pity we can do nothing to hurry it along.'

But the spring hadn't really taken hold when the Home Rule for Ireland Bill was passed in Parliament. But there was a clause for those opposed to the break-up of the union. The Conservative opposition leader Bonar Law issued pledges to all the Ulster Unionists who opposed Home Rule for Ireland. In the end Antrim, Armagh, Derry and Down had the majority of pledges necessary to use

the clause the government had put in place to opt out of Home Rule for six years. 'Six years, sixty years,' Mary said disparagingly. 'They are already watering down what they promised us. We will never have a united Ireland now, mark my words.'

'Maybe it was a way of avoiding civil war,' said Angela. 'I think the Unionists are ready for it because in the paper it said that the Ulster Volunteer Force is over 100,000 strong and they did that military exercise last month in Tyrone. That surely was to show the government what it could do if it wished. It's a bit like bullying really.'

'It's a lot like bullying,' Barry said. 'But the damage is done now.'

'Yes and I think the Government have their hands full with them suffragettes,' Mary said and she glanced at Angela and added, 'Good job you haven't taken up with all that nonsense.'

'No, it's not all nonsense,' said Angela. 'The point is I agree with much of what they say, because if men have the vote, we should have it too.'

'Why?' Barry said. 'Surely you would vote the same way I did?'

'No,' Angela said. 'Not necessarily. If you have the vote it is your right to choose and I wouldn't vote the same as you if I didn't believe in that party. That's what it's all about. Someday I think we will be very grateful to the Pankhurst women and all the other suffragettes who have gone through a great deal and I even understand their frustration too. It's just another example of governments not listening, but I can't agree with their methods.' And Angela had a point because the suffragettes had begun to set fire to empty

houses, railway stations, sport stadiums and had vandalized golf courses.

'Good job,' Barry said with a forced little laugh. 'What would Connie do if you were sent to prison?'

Really Barry was quite shocked. He'd always thought Angela would follow his lead, as head of the house, if women ever did get the vote and that idea had been turned right on its head. After a few moments though his thought patterns changed and he was proud of Angela and it showed she was a woman of integrity, saying what she did. Even the way she spoke showed she had a thinking brain and had thought things through. Surely he wasn't thinking of her not using that brain? He realized that though he loved Angela, he had thought of her as his wife and Connie's mother, not as a person in her own right as she so obviously was.

'D'you think it will ever happen that women will get the vote?' he asked. Angela shook her head. 'Couldn't tell you, but some women have died or been made very ill for the cause, usually because of the harsh treatment they have received in jail and I would hate to think their sacrifices were for nothing.'

The protests went on and more sacrifices were made but Europe and Ireland were in such turmoil all over that the British government weren't as shocked as they would normally have been when the following month in London, a suffragette named Mary Richardson took a meat cleaver to a Velazquez painting in the National Gallery. No one knew how or when the violence was going to end and suffragettes were viewed as

just another headache for the government. Barry said he couldn't see why the government couldn't just give women the vote and be done with it.

Angela agreed with him, but she was not that bothered about politics. Her concern was keeping Connie as healthy as possible and she took advantage of the warm spring weather to push Connie to the park every fine afternoon. Barry fully approved of Angela taking the child out of the unhealthy streets and on Sundays he would join them on their jaunts.

Mary was invited, but she always refused. Barry was concerned about this, especially if they were going further afield, but Mary encouraged them to go, waved them off cheerfully enough and always had a meal waiting when they returned. 'She will never come with me either,' Angela said. 'Sometimes I think the walk might do her good and it isn't as if anyone can gallop along pushing a pram. I have told her this but she always says her gallivanting days are over.'

'She doesn't seem to mind,' Barry said.

'I really don't think she does,' Angela said. 'Between you and me I think she gets tired. She wouldn't admit it in a thousand years, but I think she finds Connie a bit of a handful. She loves her to bits, no doubt of that, but children are very wearing at this age. With us out of the way she can put her feet up and have a wee nap.'

Barry nodded his head. 'Yes I think you're right.'

'So while there's no harm in asking her along, and you never know, she might surprise us one day, but if she says no then we have to accept that she prefers being left behind,' Angela said. 'And

knowing Mammy as I do, the last thing she would want would be us wasting the day worrying and fretting over her, so let's set out to enjoy ourselves. And she's always keen to know what we've done and where we've been isn't she?'

And enjoy themselves they did. Sometimes they went to nearby Calthorpe Park, or Cannon Hill a little further away, or they visited the Botanical Gardens or walked down to the canal to see the brightly painted barges pass, or they'd go for a dander down the Bull Ring, always a colourful place with lots going on while the constant banter between the barrow boys and potential customers and between the barrow boys themselves always made Angela smile.

Returning from an outing to Calthorpe Park one day Angela said, 'D'you think Connie would appreciate a tea party for her birthday next week?'

'I think she'd love it, but who would you invite?' Barry asked.

'Well as she's only a year old she hasn't a wide circle of friends just yet,' Angela commented drily. 'But there will be us, and I'm sure Maggie and Stan would like to be asked, and it falls on Sunday so it couldn't be better. And there will be a cake and a candle, though one of us will have to blow that out this year at least, and lots of little cakes and fancies and presents. What else does a twelve-month-old child want or need?'

So the party was planned for the following Sunday and during that week Angela bought a pram second-hand for the rag doll she knew Maggie was buying and Mary made a mattress and little blankets for the pram. However the best

present of all was brought up from the cellar by Barry. He had been working every night that week and he had made a rocking horse, which he had painted white and red. It was an incredibly beautiful horse and Connie's eyes opened wide in surprise and delight. She had stood up holding on to the guard and she suddenly loosed hold of it and set off walking, on her own, across the room towards the rocking horse. She only managed half-way before collapsing and made the rest of the way on her hands and knees, but Angela knew her baby girl was on her way and though she knew she would have to develop eyes in the back of her head, her heart rejoiced.

Less than a week later Stan called Barry into the office. 'I wanted to sound you out,' he said. 'Just so you know, if the balloon goes up I'm enlisting.'

'Balloon goes up, what you talking about?'

'If war is declared.'

'You said this before and nothing happened,' Barry said. 'You sure you're not just scaremongering? I mean, I agree that those Europeans seem a fiery lot and they have spats all the time and get over them. We rightly don't get involved in what is really their own business, so why should we get involved now?'

'I think we will be dragged into it this time, that's all,' Stan said. 'The government can't see what's staring them in the face. All their energies seem directed on stopping the Irish killing one another.'

'Look Stan, I can't leave Angela, my mother and baby daughter to fend for themselves and

join in a war I have no interest in.'

'You don't have to,' Stan said. 'I will and you can take my place in the factory. I have put in good reports about your work over the years and I will recommend you. They take more notice of my opinion now. So if the call-up comes, you can claim exemption because you will be in a reserved occupation. The factory is taking on war-related work now.'

'But why should you do that?'

'Why not?' Stan said. 'Think about it. I have neither chick nor child belonging to me.'

'What about your son?'

'Huh, he doesn't even know I exist,' Stan said bitterly. 'And if he did ever find out, what would he think of me, sitting pretty here while others risk their lives?'

Barry shrugged. 'So what of my child?'

'That's totally different,' Stan said firmly. 'As she grows, Connie will understand that you had her to care for and her mother and grandmother. She would never blame you, but I'm not bringing my son up and in fact have no rights with regard to him because I signed them away. So no one will mourn me if I don't make it.'

'Well that's not true,' Barry said. 'Haven't you ever heard the saying that you are stuck with your relatives and thank God you can choose your friends?'

'Yeah I've heard it.'

'Well then you've got friends who'd miss you. Mammy thinks the world of you, you know she does. She's never forgotten what you did, letting my four older brothers lodge with you when we

207

first came here, and she never will, and Angela also thinks the world of you. As for Connie, you are her favourite uncle and a damn sight more use than her real uncles who she'll probably never see. And you might be a right silly sod at times but I am quite fond of you myself.'

Stan was forced to laugh. 'All right then,' he said. 'So you'd miss me if I wasn't here?'

'Like Hell I would,' Barry said. 'So let's hope this latest skirmish comes to nothing and blows over like it has other times and you won't have to go anywhere.'

Stan said nothing for he saw that was how Barry wanted to deal with what he'd said. There was little point in arguing about it because it wasn't as if he knew anything definite, just a feeling in his bones that Europe was building up to something big, like a big melting pot of unrest with old rivalries and resentments bubbling to the surface and he felt certain it would soon overflow.

There was another reason for him wanting to keep Barry safe that he never let himself think about in the day, but there were thoughts that disturbed his sleep at night, and that was the fact that he loved Angela. He knew however Angela viewed him only as a friend, a good friend, but that is all he would ever be, a good friend of Angela McClusky because the love of her life was Barry. They were soul mates and he wanted Angela's happiness above all else and so if any of these skirmishes turned to a war England was dragged into, he wanted to keep Barry safe for Angela's sake.

FIFTEEN

Barry said nothing to either Angela or Mary about the conversation he had with Stan for he saw no reason to alarm them, but he started bringing in two papers on his way home from work. The *Birmingham Mail* dealt with mainly local news, but the *Daily Mail* he scrutinized from cover to cover and he saw that Europe was not a comfortable place to be in at that time. He was glad that he was in Great Britain although even there it was hardly comfortable with half the country on strike for better pay and conditions.

And then on Sunday 28th June, the heir apparent to the dual monarchy of Hungary-Austria, Archduke Franz Ferdinand, was assassinated in the Bosnian capital Sarajevo by a Serbian nationalist called Gavrilo Princip. The Archduke Ferdinand's wife Sophie, Duchess of Hohenberg, who tried to protect her husband, was shot in the stomach and she also died. Barry knew with a sinking heart that something big would come from this. It was splashed all over Monday's papers and he knew he couldn't protect his mother or Angela from news like this so he read the article out to them as they sat having a drink before bed.

They were both understandably shocked and then Barry added, 'Apparently, they weren't very popular, particularly in Budapest and Vienna.'

'They weren't very popular,' Mary repeated and

added, 'I would have said that was a barbaric sentence to pass on someone whose only crime appears to be one of unpopularity. Besides which, if you did away with all the people you didn't like the look of, or the way they went about things, the world would be near empty.'

'Yes it would,' Angela agreed. 'And however unpopular they were, no country can stand by and let the heir of their emperor be killed in that way. What's likely to happen now?'

Barry shook his head. 'I'm not sure,' he admitted. 'I suppose this Hungary-Austria alliance could attack Serbia.'

'Well that won't affect us,' Mary said complacently.

Barry opened his mouth but closed it again without speaking. He had said enough for the time being. He would say more when he knew more.

Barry didn't know much more for nearly a month, except for finding out that Princip was an Austrian subject. Stan was right, the British Government had their eyes completely off the ball and so were unaware that the Emperor Franz Joseph wanted to attack Serbia in retaliation as the assassination had taken place on Serbian soil and he had asked the Kaiser for help. Russia came in on the side of Serbia and mobilized 1,000,000 troops and when they wouldn't withdraw Germany declared war on Russia on the 1st of August and two days later declared war on France. Italy decided to keep out of it and Belgium's neutrality was assured by a treaty signed in 1839 by Britain, France and Germany. When German troops went into Belgium on 4th August, breaking that treaty,

Britain was plunged into war the following day.

In a way it was so quick and unexpected because Britain had been unaware of it until it was too late to even try to prevent it. Mary and Angela were extremely worried by the news. 'Shall you be called up?'

'I don't know if there will be a call-up but anyway I am safe,' Barry said and told them of Stan's proposal. Angela couldn't help but be pleased that Barry would be safe, but worried about Stan. 'Suit me if we could keep them both out of it,' Angela said. 'What do they know of war?'

'What does any ordinary person know?' Mary said. 'And I bet young lads will enlist in droves, like it's some big adventure they're going to.'

Mary was right and the very next Sunday just as they were finishing dinner they heard the military band going along Bristol Street 'I wonder where they're making for,' Angela said.

'Let's go and find out,' Barry suggested.

'Oh I can't,' Angela said. 'There's the dishes to see to.'

'I'll see to the dishes,' Mary said. 'You go and see what it's all about.'

'Are you sure?' Angela asked.

'Course I'm sure,' Mary said firmly. 'And I bet young Connie here would like to see the soldiers marching behind the band, wouldn't you, pet?'

Connie nodded her head emphatically for she had heard the band and loved music. 'Let's away then,' Barry said, scooping Connie from her chair and on to his shoulders in one movement.

'Wait,' Angela cried. 'She needs her coat.'

'Not on a day like this she doesn't, woman,'

Barry said. 'Hurry up or it'll be over before we get there.'

They weren't the only ones setting out for when they stepped out of the door they saw many doing the same thing and all making their way to Bristol Passage, which led down to Bristol Street. And what they saw when they reached the main street stopped many in their tracks.

A man in full regalia led the band. He had a cap with a shiny peak pulled down so low, Angela doubted his eyes were visible, but what was visible was his dark, curling moustache above his resolute mouth. He was wearing white gloves and in one hand he carried a twirling ornamental stick. He looked neither right nor left but straight ahead and his boots rang with each precise step on the cobbles and set the beat for the musicians to follow, reinforced by the big drums at the back.

The band were followed by the regular soldiers, khaki bags slung across their bodies, rifles over their left shoulders and all perfectly in time. A cheer rose in the air and rippled through the watching crowd and small boys ran whooping and cavorting along the pavement, caught up in the excitement of it all.

Behind the soldiers were civilians, many mere boys, younger than Barry, and he could well understand the lure. For the band and the spectacle were a promise of a more exciting life than one played out on those mean streets where they mightn't even have employment. Even from the people standing with them, one or two broke away and joined the motley crew following the army.

'Shall we follow them and listen to what they have to say?' Barry asked.

'You... You won't be tempted to join them?'

'Are you joking?' Barry said. 'I'm not a boy to be swayed by a few marching soldiers. I'm a married man with responsibilities and in the job I do, I'm helping the war effort, so I'm doing my bit that way.'

Relieved and reassured, Angela let out the breath she hadn't been aware she was holding and said, 'We may as well then.'

As Barry and Angela had guessed, the army marched into Calthorpe Park and a man with a bristling moustache and a shiny peaked cap, like the one the band master wore, leapt up onto the steps of the stadium. The band played on and the man made no effort to speak while the people were still streaming in through the entrance.

Eventually, a large crowd had assembled in front of the stadium, the band had stopped playing and laid their instruments down, and the man began to speak. He spoke first of what a privilege he'd always thought it was to serve his country, as he had done for many years in the British Army, and the finest way to serve any nation was to fight for them if that's what had to be done, especially in a war situation.

'So now our country is at war again, but it is an honourable war to bring freedom and justice to oppressed nations. The British Army's aim is to rid the world of brutal aggressors, for they are our enemy and we must crush them so that innocent men and women can live in peace. Many have already answered the call and come forward

to help in this task. But we need more to ensure we win this righteous war. Which of you young men have the courage to join us? Who amongst you will be able to wear the British Army uniform with pride knowing they have been part of making the world a safer place?'

It was stirring stuff, Barry had to admit, and despite his words to Angela his feet seemed to want to move of their own volition. He planted them firmly on the ground and he knew fighting in a war would be bloody and dirty and probably quite frightening at times and he might be injured or killed. And then where would that leave his mother and Angela and his baby daughter? He might not see her grow up so he was glad that wasn't in his life plan anyway, and yet he couldn't help wishing desperately that he could be part of this honourable war.

He wasn't a bit surprised though when young men and boys began peeling themselves away from the crowd to join the ranks of those who had followed the army. At first it was one or two that went, but that became a trickle and then a flood until a great many young men were there to sign on the dotted line and be part of the great British Army.

'Shall we go now?' Angela said for she had seen the zeal in her husband's face and, for all his assurances, it had disturbed her. 'Unless you want to see if Stan is here. I did look but didn't spot him.'

'Oh he won't be here,' Barry said. 'He has already been to see them at Thorp Street Barracks. He's already in.'

'Oh,' Angela said and then she exclaimed, 'Look, there's one that isn't in yet, but looks as if he's about to remedy that.' For a little way ahead of them in the crowd was Maggie and she had her arm linked with Michael Malone and as they watched he stepped away from her and joined the other boys and young men waiting to join up. 'It's Michael,' she said. 'Thought he would have more sense.'

'Maybe sense has less to do with it than lack of money,' Barry said. 'He was laid off six months ago and hasn't really earned a penny since then. In fact that may be why a lot of boys are joining up.'

'Dangerous path to tread.'

'Needs must,' said Barry.

The weeks that followed were strange ones. All the young fellows at the foundry gave notice as they said they were joining up and the only people applying for the jobs were women. The factory was noisy, greasy and grimy and a lot of the work was heavy and Barry didn't think it was a place for women to work and took the problem to Mr Baxter who was the manager of the whole factory. 'I think you must get over that prejudice against women, young Barry,' he said when he'd heard him out.

'It's not prejudice, sir,' Barry protested. 'Or at least not in a nasty way. I'm thinking of them, sir, for the work is really not suited to women.'

'So what's to be done?' Mr Baxter said. 'Those orders have to go out for they are for the war effort. How are we to expect our soldiers to face the enemy with no weapons or rifles?'

'Well no.'

'Look, Barry,' Mr Baxter said, 'ours will not be the only factory to be nearly empty of all its young man. You need a great deal of men to fight a war and have a chance of winning. You also need a great deal of ammunition too, so if there's no men to make it there's only the women left. Give the jobs to the women, Barry, and believe me they'll tell you if the work is too much for them.'

Barry was very surprised as the weeks passed. The women came in overalls with scarves wrapped turban-style around their heads. They were a cheerful lot, full of laughter and fun, and they changed the atmosphere of the factory floor, though the noise of the machines prevented them from talking a great deal when they were working, but they made up for it in the canteen when they were at their dinner or tea break when the noise level was sometimes very high indeed. But Barry put up with that because in all other ways they were no trouble. They arrived promptly and worked hard and never complained about the job as the young lads were wont to do and Barry had to revise his opinion of the work a woman can or should do.

He was further astounded when he saw women as conductresses on the omnibuses and trams, but completely flabbergasted when he saw women driving them, and they were driving horse-drawn wagons too and petrol-driven ones. He heard they were working in factories all over the country, leaving their homes and families some of them and taking lodging in the bigger houses. Cramped back-to-back houses usually had no space to

accommodate these intrepid souls who took work where they could, in drop forges, or steel works or Dunlops making tyres for military vehicles. Then there were many types of weaponry made in special-munitions workshops and it was women now who assembled and tested guns in the gun quarter.

All these used to be men's jobs, but there were few fit men about and Barry often felt he stood out like a sore thumb, for those he did see were all in uniform. Angela could have told him of the askance looks she had from some neighbours when she explained that Barry wouldn't be enlisting because he had exemption as he was in a reserved occupation. Some of the women went further and made snide remarks about him sitting pretty while others fought his battles, and others snubbed her completely. Although it hurt her because she would have said that she was well liked, Angela understood some of their reactions for they all had loved ones, husbands, brothers, sweethearts who had enlisted without a thought.

She said nothing about it to Barry, for it wasn't as if he could do anything about it and it would only worry him. She knew Mary had taken a bit of stick too because she mentioned it one day when she came in from shopping. 'What did they say?' Angela asked.

'Oh what I might have expected,' Mary replied, 'jibes about keeping my little lambikin safe, and similar stuff.'

'Oh, Mammy I'm so sorry,' Angela said.

'Don't know what you're sorry about,' Mary said. 'T'isn't your fault. Anyway don't you worry

217

about me. Their abuse rolls off me like water off a duck's back.'

'I suppose it will all be sorted out when the men are back home again and the war's over,' Angela said. 'It can't last for ever anyway. Some people at the shops were saying it might be all over by Christmas.'

'Nice if it was,' Mary said. 'But I doubt it. There are too many countries involved for it all to be wrapped up so quickly.'

'So we just live with the insults?'

'That's about the shape of it,' Mary said. 'Count to ten or bite your lip or whatever. Don't say anything you might regret because when the world is back to normal you will have to live alongside these people.'

Angela didn't argue with Mary. She was very wise and Angela hated confrontation anyway, but she avoided her neighbours as much as possible.

A very welcome letter came from Stan in late October. He had a spot of leave and there were no people he would rather spend it with. He said he would be staying in his old house because the neighbours had been keeping an eye on it for him and he was keeping the rent up to date so far.

Mary wrote and welcomed him warmly, only sorry that she couldn't offer him a bed too. 'I bet it's in a bit of a state as well,' she said to Angela. 'Looking after a place is all well and good but it's sure to be damp not being lived in, especially now the cold weather is setting in. His bed could easily be damp too.'

'Well he can't sleep in a damp bed,' Angela said. 'He'll go down with pneumonia.'

'What say you and I go and look at the place and maybe light the fires to warm it up before he gets here?' Mary suggested. 'He left me one of the keys for safe keeping.'

They went up together leaving Connie at Norah's to mind but when they surveyed Stan's house however they knew they would have to do more than light a fire and check the sheets for dampness. The house had an unloved look about it and a sour smell lingered in the air. Dust was thick on every surface and cobwebs festooned the corners of the room, the fender was dull and the grate badly needed black-leading.

Because Stan had plenty of coal in the cellar they first dealt with the hearths and the one in the bedroom too and when that was clean and tidy Mary lit fires in the living room and the bedroom before tackling the rest of the house. It took some time and they were very glad of the cups of tea Norah brought round when they had been hard at it for a couple of hours. 'This is just the job,' Mary said as she accepted a cup gratefully. 'My throat's that dry.'

'And mine,' Angela said. 'It's the dust. What have you done with Connie?'

'The wee angel went to sleep on my knee and so I put her in the pram,' Norah said and she looked around the room. 'You two have done wonders. I'd love to see the look on his face. When does he arrive?'

'About half ten Saturday,' Angela said. 'Barry's taking the morning off to welcome him.'

Stan arrived at the McCluskys' first but he wouldn't stay because he had all his kit with him

and he said that it would be better to dump it all in his house first. So Angela left Connie with Barry and went up with him and Mary followed her because they wanted to see his reaction to what they had done to the house. And when he opened the door he stood on the threshold and just stared. He had never seen the house so clean and tidy, gleaming with polish and a cheerful fire burned in the black-leaded grate behind a shiny brass fender with extra coal in the scuttle on the hearth.

'I got you a few bits,' Mary said. 'Not a lot because you'll be eating most meals with us, a small loaf and butter, tea, sugar and oatmeal to make porridge for your breakfast if you want to. I didn't leave any milk because it would only go sour but you can bring some from our house, I have a can you can use.'

'You are so very kind,' Stan said, his voice husky with emotion at their thoughtfulness. He tried, to get a grip on himself as he valiantly tried to swallow the lump in his throat and stop the tears trickling down his cheeks and thoroughly embarrassing everybody.

'It was nothing, really,' Mary said and then as she turned to go she suddenly said, 'Oh and don't worry about the sheets being damp, Angela here has had them warmed up with hot water bottles.'

'Like I said, I'm overwhelmed.'

'It's been no trouble honestly,' Angela said. 'We've lit the fire in the bedroom too so that the place will be cosy and warm for you.'

'I don't know what to say,' Stan said. 'Thank

you seems so inadequate.'

A catch in Stan's voice caused Angela to look up and she spotted a tell-tale tear seeping from Stan's left eye and knew he would hate them to see him crying and she said 'There's nothing to say. It's obvious you appreciate all that we've done for you and that's all that matters. We'll leave you to get sorted and come down when you're ready.'

Stan just nodded.

'D'you know,' Mary remarked as they walked down Grant Street, 'Stan Bishop is one of the nicest and most generous people I know and yet I don't think he has ever had much kindness shown to him. Look how he reacted over what we had done.'

Angela agreed, 'You could be right, so let's make sure he has a good leave and we'll be as kind to him as we know how.'

'Aye,' said Mary and the two women were smiling as they went in the house.

Stan hadn't seen Connie when he had just called before going to his own house and when he arrived about lunchtime he was astounded at the change in her in just a few months. But one thing hadn't changed and that was her love for her 'Uncle Stan' which she attempted to say, and Stan hugged her tight and said to Angela later as they sat to eat the delicious meal that Mary had cooked, 'I thought she would have forgotten all about me.'

'What,' said Angela in mock horror, 'forget the finest tower builder in the universe? I'd say not.'

'Yeah,' Barry agreed. 'Ideally children need more than their parents in their lives and Connie's a bit

short on real relatives and she picked you as her pseudo uncle.'

'Suits me,' Stan said. 'Shame I'm not going to be around much in the near future for this is embarkation leave. God knows when I'll get leave again.'

Barry nodded. 'I guessed it was embarkation leave,' he said. 'I might not know much about the army, but I know that much.'

'And how are you finding training?' Mary asked.

'Oh I have no trouble with the training,' Stan said. 'It is after all what I joined up for.'

'Are you ready to go?'

'Is any man ever ready for war?' Stan said. 'Although I have sometimes been as angry and frustrated as any other man, I have never wished to inflict harm on another human being. And yet most of our training was about that, learning all the different ways one man could kill another.' He paused slightly and then continued, 'We were told about these "Pals Regiments" they've set up so people from small towns and villages will all be together. The cities will be split into areas so, for example, there are a number of Birmingham Pals Regiments and I shall be in one of these.'

'Isn't that a good thing?' Angela asked. 'Isn't it better to have someone you know and trust at your back in battle?'

'There is that of course,' Stan said, 'and probably that was the idea behind it, but it means that the men will know one another, might be related even. We are told that even if their brother falls before them, they must step over him and go on.'

Angela gave a slight gasp, for she was quite

shocked at Stan's words, though she thought she had no right to be for she wasn't a fool, but when she had used the terms 'going to war' or 'in conflict' she didn't immediately think of the human cost of it. But in actual fact, in brutal terms that's what war boiled down to, killing more men than your opponent so as to be declared the winner, and Stan, watching her face, said, 'I'm sorry. Have I upset you?'

Angela shook her head. 'No, not really. It's just I've never thought of it that way before and now I have, I don't think I could ever kill anyone.'

'I could kill anyone who threatened my family,' Barry said, vehemently.

'Well all right,' Angela conceded. 'But the Germans aren't threatening us.'

'No, but they have invaded Belgium,' Stan said. 'And Belgium signed a treaty some time ago that they could claim neutrality.'

'Why?' Angela asked. 'I mean why just Belgium?'

'I don't know,' Stan admitted. 'Maybe because they're only a small country and have little in the way of defences in the event of being attacked by other countries round about and Germany ignored that treaty.'

'But why did they do that?' Angela cried. 'Did anyone think of asking them why before beginning a war that will undoubtedly kill many people?'

'D'you know Angela?' Stan said. 'I don't think anyone thought of that. I saw this coming for some time though because Europe was so volatile, our government seemed to be taken on the hop. I suppose many of the countries in Europe had had various skirmishes and squabbles amongst them-

223

selves so many times and got over them without our involvement and they must have thought or hoped this would be the same. I had a sort of premonition that this might be different. Mind you, I didn't envisage all the other countries joining in too. I thought it might be some major skirmish we might be pulled into and maybe it would have been like that if it hadn't been for the Archduke being killed, giving the Emperor a reason to attack Serbia and asking for the Kaiser's help.'

'According to the paper, Germans are committing gross atrocities in Belgium as well,' Barry said.

'We might almost expect behaviour like that,' Stan said. 'I would have said many invading armies intent on taking over a country don't treat the people so well.'

'Yes I think the same,' Barry said. 'It's a way of establishing control from the start. Anyway, whatever could have been done to avert all-out war wasn't done and now it's too late.'

'And I'm fed up of war talk,' Mary said. 'And such things shouldn't be discussed in front of Connie, for most of it goes over her head. Doesn't it pet?' she said, tousling Connie's curls.

Mary was rewarded with a beautiful smile, for though Connie didn't understand all the words said, she picked up on the atmosphere and knew all about serious faces and solemn ones, and she was glad when her Daddy smiled at her and it appeared to be over. To Mary he said, 'Sorry, Mammy, you're right of course.' He looked across at Angela and said, 'We could take Connie to the park if you like. That's if Stan wants,' he finished,

glancing across at his friend.

'I can't think of anything I'd like better,' Stan said.

'That's settled then,' Barry said. 'Shall we take the pram?'

'No,' Angela said. 'She'll be tired on the way back and if she's in the pram she'll sleep and then I'll never get her to bed tonight.'

'Righto,' Barry said and he fastened Connie into her coat before going out the door holding her hand.

'That won't last long, her walking on her own,' Angela said. 'A few yards along the road and she'll have her hands up to be lifted onto Barry's shoulders.'

'And he'll oblige of course?'

'That doesn't even need saying,' Angela said. 'He would have her totally ruined if I didn't watch him.'

'Ah well,' Mary said, 'better than taking no notice of her at all.'

Angela didn't argue for she knew she was lucky that she had a husband in a million and one who loved spending time with his child. She knew some men had no time for the babies once they were born but when she said to Barry how much she appreciated the help he gave her, he said Connie belonged to both of them and he missed enough of her growing up away at work all day. 'Not all fathers feel that way,' Angela said.

'I know it,' Barry said. 'And they are the losers because they don't know what they're missing.'

The sad thing was, Angela thought as she washed up the pots from dinner, Stan was one in

the same mould as Barry and his son was as lost to him as if he had died.

There was no point in saying anything though because it wasn't as if talking would make a ha'p'orth of difference. She gave a small sigh and standing on tiptoe gave her husband a kiss on the cheek. He was pleased, but surprised and with a smile on his face he said, 'I'm not complaining or anything, but what was that for?'

'Does there have to be a reason to give my husband a kiss?' Angela asked 'Let's just say it's because I know how lucky I am.'

SIXTEEN

The next day as Stan joined the family for Sunday dinner he said, 'They are recommending that all men who haven't already done so should make a will before they are sent overseas.'

Angela gave a shiver and Stan said, 'Just because I have been asked to make a will doesn't mean that anything is going to happen to me. It's a precaution to help your loved ones if anything did happen.'

'Well no good me making a will,' Mary said. 'For I would have nothing to leave.'

'Ah but I have a son,' Stan said. 'A son that I have had no hand in rearing. Meanwhile I have been given a good salary over the years and only me to spend it on and I am not a great drinker, do not gamble, only have the one packet of fags

a day and for years now any money left over from my wages has been put in the Post Office for Daniel. I want to make sure he will get it if anything happens to me though I will put in a codicil that the money be kept in trust for Daniel until he is twenty-one. My commanding officer helped me when I admitted I didn't know the least thing about making a will. He told me the firm to go to in the city centre too. Apparently they do a lot of military wills.'

'But do you really need a will when Daniel is with family?' Mary said. 'Surely Betty would make sure the boy got the money?'

'How would Betty explain it?' Stan asked. 'I signed all rights to my son to Betty and her husband and have no contact at all really because she said it would just confuse him.'

'Don't see how it could,' Mary said. 'Betty was wrong to ask you to do that. You were still mourning your wife.'

Stan nodded. 'My head was all over the place in the beginning and I couldn't have coped with Daniel. I was glad of Betty then.'

'I know you were,' Mary said, for she remembered it well.

'Didn't give her the right to steal your son,' Barry said. 'You couldn't have been in your right mind when you signed those papers because I could never sign my child away.'

'Aye, Barry,' said Angela. 'But we have had Connie eighteen months, think if you were faced with a newborn baby and a dead wife?'

'Yes,' Mary said. 'Stan was very vulnerable then and Betty took advantage.'

227

'And the plus side of all this is that Betty and Roger love Daniel,' Stan said. 'I know that they will love and care for him as if he was their own son and that's what Betty wants him to be. How then will she explain the money? I don't think for one moment that she will steal the money from him but she could very easily say it was a gift from them, her and Roger. I want a solicitor to deal with it and so I intend writing Daniel a letter explaining everything to him.'

'And what will that do to the lad?' Mary asked quite sharply.

'What d'you mean?'

'Well if Betty has her way, Daniel won't know you even exist,' Mary said. 'And then out of the blue when he's twenty-one he gets money from a stranger and a letter, and in that letter the stranger claims to be his father. If he thought Betty and Roger were his parents he is bound to be upset they've lied to him, upset that he never got to know you when you were alive. Whatever way he takes it, he is bound to be disturbed in some way.'

'You think I should say nothing?'

'No,' Mary said. 'I think there has already been too much secrecy in this whole business. If Daniel had been told Betty and Roger had adopted him as soon as he could understand and especially if you were a fixture in his life, then he would be able to take this in his stride long before he reaches twenty-one. If you didn't survive the war he would be upset and would mourn, but because he loved you and knew you loved him, the strength of that love would enable him to go on with his life and he probably would be grateful to Betty and Roger for

caring for him so well. But this way...'

'Someone is bound to get hurt,' Stan said. 'And I'm afraid it's going to be Daniel, the person I would cut off my right arm for.'

Angela felt so sorry for Stan and yet she knew every word Mary spoke was the truth. She couldn't see how anyone could make things any better. But then Mary said, 'There is only one thing to be done, you must write to Betty.'

Stan shook his head, 'No communication, that was the deal.'

'War changes everything,' Mary said. 'Tell her you have enlisted and what arrangements you have made for Daniel when he reaches twenty-one, if you do not survive the war. Don't look like that,' she went on, seeing the look of protest on Stan's face. 'Betty won't be able to touch that money or the letter if you wrap it up legally. That way if you don't survive the war she would be a fool if she didn't tell Daniel the truth about his parentage. It will still be a blow but better than receiving that bombshell with no warning on his twenty-first birthday.'

'Mammy's right,' Barry said. 'It is the only thing to do. Put the ball in Betty's court. They must be the ones to tell David the truth since they were the ones that didn't tell him the truth in the first place and cut you out of the boy's life into the bargain.'

'I agree with Mammy and Barry too,' Angela said. 'And being as you can't see the solicitor till tomorrow I'd get the letter to Betty written straight away.'

'And the one for Daniel to leave with the solici-

tor,' Stan said. 'I'll see to them both this evening. Something else I have decided and that's to give up the tenancy on the house. I don't know when I'll have leave again and while I know the house is not much cop, it's better than nothing and a family could have the use of it. It's selfish to keep it on.'

'And if all else fails,' Barry said, 'you can always have the use of our settee.'

'Or floor,' Stan said. 'I'll be a seasoned soldier by then and able to sleep anywhere.'

So all was done by the time Mary and Angela, with Connie between them, assembled at New Street to see Stan off, as he was joining his company on the South Coast, and they all knew without much doubt that he would be off to France soon. Angela's insides trembled, and she held Connie's hand so tight the child complained.

Angela knew anyone watching them would think them a family and though Angela had grown to love Stan, she didn't love him as she loved Barry – that love was special. However, that morning she did embrace him and kiss his cheek and Mary followed suit for it just felt right. 'Look after yourself,' Mary said and then remarked ruefully, 'What a daft thing to say to a man off to war.'

Stan smiled. 'I promise I'll keep my head down,' he said as he lifted Connie into his arms. 'Will that do?'

'I suppose it will have to,' Mary said gruffly. 'Connie, give Uncle Stan a kiss. He has to be on the train shortly.'

Connie wound her podgy little arms around Stan's neck and kissed his cheek soundly. 'Bye

Unky Tan.'

'Bye-bye my darling girl and I will be back to see you as soon as I can,' Stan said and he handed Connie into Angela's arms. 'You will write to me?' he said as he stepped into the train.

'Of course,' Angela said. 'Promise I will.'

The train doors were slammed, the whistle blew and billows of smoke filled the air as the train began to chug its way out of the station, leaving behind the acrid smell of coal dust. And Angela's eyes blurred with tears as she wondered if she would ever see Stan again.

Life continued as before as rumours of battles in strange places with foreign names filled the papers and now that Stan was probably embroiled in it, Angela read the papers as avidly as Barry, though previously she had only skimmed the headlines.

Stan wrote to them, but could tell them nothing of his location or any other war-related news, for the censor would cut it out if he tried. Instead they got little missives that gave them snapshots of army life, like the dugout assigned to the men when they had time to relax:

In the middle of a war our appearance still matters a great deal and I really can't see the point of being so particular…

In early December Stan sent a clue that he was in France when he wrote:

Sometimes I really can't stomach the food in the Naafi and it would be nice to be able to go into town

231

*for a home-made pie and some of the pastries they are
so famous for.*

'Got that through the censor,' Angela said.

'It doesn't say anything.'

'It says enough. "The pastries they are so famous
for" – that's France surely?'

'I'd say you're right, Angela,' Mary said. 'Anyway this has decided me. I will make him a small
Christmas cake of his own and mince pies too
and put them in the box I am making up.' She had
already bought him gloves and a scarf and Angela
added ten packets of cigarettes, a set of men's
handkerchiefs and a big bag of the bullseyes he
was partial to.

'Good English food,' Mary said in approval.
'No need to eat the French stuff unless he wants
to. And I'm sure pastries are all very well, but
they would hardly fill a man. You need things that
stick to your ribs a bit in cold weather like this.'

Angela thought Mary not far wrong because the
days leading up to Christmas were raw ones. It
didn't help that as December took hold there was
little in the shops to buy and often the grocery
shops' shelves were half empty. Everyone was
talking about it. It was said that the wealthy were
parking their cars or carriages in side streets and
sending the drivers in with long lists of things. This
left the poor, who couldn't afford to stockpile, to
manage the best way they could, although it was
hard to feed families without even basic com-
modities.

'I've never actually seen this myself,' Angela
said, 'though a lot of things I used to buy from

the grocer aren't there any more and in the paper they said there's a lot of it going on and it must be true because the food I used to buy has got to go somewhere. Surely it's wrong.'

'Of course it's wrong,' Mary said. 'How can you manage without bread and milk and tea? And some of the butchers' slabs are near empty as well and the greengrocer's hadn't a potato in the shop the other day. Shopping takes all day because you go from shop to shop along Bristol Street to get a bit here and a bit there and still come back with your bag half empty. And,' she added, 'at least we have the money to do that. What of the poor devils who are tied to the one shop because they'll let them run up tick till pay day? What are they living on if there's nothing on the shelves?'

Angela thought about the number of people George Maitland gave tick to and knew Mary had made a valid point. 'It's a disgrace,' she said. 'The government should do something to stop it.'

'They won't care about the likes of us,' Mary said. 'They have a war to win. As long as the soldiers are adequately fed I would say, as far as the government are concerned, the rest of us can sink or swim. But I'll tell you what, the war can't go on for ever and people have long memories and they won't forget those shops who let down their loyal customers. They'll go somewhere else when the war's over.'

'We all have to live till then,' Angela said. 'Barry is working the long hours he has to just now and needs good solid food inside him, and Connie too, for she has a lot of growing to do.'

'Well if it comes to that we all need proper

233

food,' Mary said. 'What would happen if you or I were to go down sick because we were so malnourished?'

'You're right,' Angela said. 'So let's start our boycott now. I'm going to start getting the groceries at Maitland's. It's a bit of a trek, but at least I will be able to get all I need.'

'How do you know he isn't into this selling to the toffs as well?' Mary asked.

'Because I know him,' Angela said, with assurance. 'He is an honest man with integrity and he would see this as wrong and have no part in it. And added to that he is no great lover of toffs. As for the greengrocery and the meat, we can buy all that from the Bull Ring because any toff or toff's lackey would get short shrift there.'

'Aye,' said Mary with a chuckle.

'And not a word to Barry,' Angela warned. 'He has enough on his plate just now.'

Angela was in fact quite worried about her young husband whose eyes often looked quite haunted and his face had a definite greyish tinge to it. The hours he put in at the factory were punishing, for the Government was pressing for greater production. Even more lines were set up and the employees had to work longer hours and much faster than before to make the products that were needed. Not many grumbled, for most had loved ones at the Front and wanted to do their bit too.

Barry always told Angela he was 'fine' when she asked him if he was all right, for he could never tell her what was really tormenting him, which were the pictures he had seen in the papers of the in-

jured soldiers returning to Britain. He didn't want to be among them, of course he didn't, he just felt bad about the whole thing. And worse were the others, who had made the ultimate sacrifice and whose bodies littered a foreign field somewhere.

So Barry never knew of the women's journey to buy decent food in sufficient quantity to put on the table. George Maitland, when he heard why they were changing grocers, said he'd had toffs' drivers target him too, but he had sent them packing.

'This man I'd never seen before gave me this big order, like a roll of wallpaper it was,' George said. 'And I said that as I hadn't seen him before he must be a stranger to the area and if so, didn't he have a local grocer to deal with such a large order.

'He said that he didn't, so I asked him why he needed so much food and if he was buying it on someone else's behalf. 'Course he coloured up then and so I said, "If I fill your order it will nearly empty my shelves, so then what do the customers do who've been coming to me for years if I have nothing left for them to buy to feed their families?"

'"Can't you restock?" said the cocky young chap.

'"'Course I could," I told him,' George said to Angela and Mary. 'But then I said to him, "I couldn't do that immediately. It might be three or four days before stock was back in the shop. So you sling your hook and don't come back and tell your Mistress she'll have to tighten her belt like the rest of us are having to do.'

Angela shot Mary a smile of triumph for she'd known just how George would behave. And then

George said, 'It might have been more difficult to do if Dorothy had been in the shop, though I would still have done it because I make the decisions, but Dorothy would tell Matilda and she would moan at me and Dorothy would put her oar in as well.'

'Oh dear,' Angela said. 'Is Dorothy your new assistant's name?'

George shook his head, 'No, worse luck. My assistant left to work in the munitions where the money is better and she didn't have to cope with Matilda. Dorothy is Matilda's sister. She's recently been widowed and Matilda wanted her here till she gets over it. Upshot is she's moved in lock, stock and barrel and Matilda suggested she works in the shop at busy times. I seem to spend a lot of time in the shop at the moment.' Both Mary and Angela could understand why and Mary said, 'You should take yourself to the pub a time or two and leave them to it.'

George smiled. 'That's never been my way.'

'Well maybe it should become your way,' Mary said. 'Make some friends of your own. All work and no play, you know?'

'I'll be all right,' George said, reaching into the lollipop jar to give one to Connie as he went on, 'And it will be lovely seeing you on a regular basis. I did so miss Angela when she left, but I bet you have your hands full now.'

'Oh yes,' Angela said. 'Connie takes some watching all right, but she is really the light of our lives.'

'Was he asking you to go back?' Mary asked as she pushed the pram back home.

Angela nodded. 'I think he was sounding me out.'

'Would you be tempted?'

Angela shook her head vehemently. 'I wouldn't want to leave Connie unless I had to and I definitely think Barry would be against it.'

'And he's bringing home plenty of money now too,' Mary said.

'That's all the overtime,' Angela said. 'And it can't go on at that rate for the hours are quite mad at the moment. I'll be glad when it's Christmas and he can have some time off, because he looks a little strained to me.'

'I've noticed he's quieter than usual,' Mary said. 'Let's hope you're right. Thank God Christmas is no distance away.'

The McCluskys woke on Christmas morning to find it had snowed in the night and was still snowing, the snow turning to shimmering pools of gold beneath the lamps which gleamed in the night sky, for it would be a few hours yet till daylight. Connie had never seen snow and she was enchanted and straight away wanted to get dressed and go out in it despite the cold and the darkness.

Downstairs however, Santa had paid a visit and left Connie a jack-in-the-box that amused her immensely. And that wasn't all. She also had a new fleece-lined winter coat from her American Uncle Finbarr. It was royal blue and there was a matching bonnet and mittens. She looked as pretty as a picture in it. But more importantly Angela knew she would be as warm as toast in that coat and she

237

intended to write and thank Finbarr heartily for he also sent ten dollars for them to treat themselves.

She wanted to congratulate Finbarr too for he wrote that he was getting married to a girl called Orla McCann who he had met at Mass. Mary gave a sigh of relief when Angela read that out because if he had met this Orla at Mass then she must be a Catholic. But it was even better than that for not only was she of Irish descent, but her family came from Donegal as the McCluskys did. She couldn't be more suitable and Mary was relieved that Finbarr's future at least looked set.

Colm hadn't any news like that himself but there was another ten dollars inside his letter and he said that Mammy need have no worries because Orla was a great girl altogether and he was to continue to live with them after they married until he was ready to settle down himself. He hadn't forgotten his little niece either and for her there was a beautiful large book and Angela gave a gasp as she lifted it out because she had never owned anything so fine. It was called *The Treasury of Nursery Rhymes* and every nursery rhyme anyone could think of was written on the wonderfully illustrated pages. Angela stroked the book almost reverently and looked forward to hours of enjoyment for her and Connie as they shared the book together.

There was another parcel too that year and it was from Stan who explained in the letter that he had found himself billeted near a small French town as Christmas approached and so was able to buy them some authentic French presents, so both women had silk stockings and they were truly magnificent and felt delicious against the

skin, but neither woman could think of an occasion when they would wear them for they were too ostentatious for Mass and they seldom went anywhere else. Barry on the other hand was very appreciative of the French Cognac.

'I think it's really lovely for Stan to remember us at all,' Angela said with a small sigh. 'And it seems horrible to seem ungrateful, but he seems not to have a clue what women like us would find useful.'

'Well how would he know?' Mary said. 'I think women are a great mystery for men, for Matt never had a clue what I might want or need either. There was no money ever for fripperies, but now and then I would have been grateful for a pair of stout boots, or warm slippers, but unless I gave out huge hints I usually went without.'

'Well we'll write and thank him anyway,' Angela said. 'And at least we won't have to pretend when we say Connie was delighted with her present, for she loved the kaleidoscope he sent when she had been shown how to twist it round.' And so Christmas went by and Barry tried to lift his despondent mood because it was Christmas after all. Angela wasn't fooled and she listened to her husband's restlessness in bed at night and worried about it, but she never shared her concerns even with Mary.

SEVENTEEN

The New Year was quiet and January was cold enough to numb fingers and feet, to form icicles on window ledges, to freeze the tap in the yard rock solid and for snow to fall from leaden skies, driven into drifts by the bone-chilling biting wind.

Getting about was hazardous, but groceries had to be fetched because there was little left to eat. Angela refused to let Mary come with her to Maitland's. 'It's too far for you. You might fall and break a leg.'

'So might you.'

'Yes, I might,' Angela conceded. 'So I'll be extra careful and if I should break something, I'll likely heal quicker than you. Look, it would be really helpful if you mind Connie for me and I'll take the pram. I can bring more back that way.'

Mary crossed to the window and gazed out. 'You'll never push the pram in this,' she declared. 'And it's still coming down thick and fast.'

'I'll be fine,' Angela said. 'Someone has to go and I've got that lovely warm coat from last year so I'll not freeze and if I can't push the pram I'll pull it. I did it a time or two before.'

However, despite her spirited words to Mary, Angela found the trek to Maitland's was challenging for the roads were thick with snow on top of impacted ice, the icy wind buffeted her from all sides and the pram she pulled behind seemed

to get heavier and heavier, and that was when it was empty, so she didn't relish the journey home. She intended getting a full week's worth of food to keep them going longer so she wouldn't have to make this journey again in a hurry.

George, though glad to see her, expressed concern that she had ventured out on such a day.

'Needs must,' Angela said. 'The cupboards were nearly bare. I was waiting for a better day myself, but each one is worse than the one before and if we were going to eat I had to get supplies. I've left Connie with Mammy though, the day is not fit for either of them to go out.'

'Oh no it isn't,' George agreed. 'You did the right thing there. Now let's have that order and I'll fill it out for you as fast as I can, so you can be home warm and safe and dry as quickly as possible.'

And George lost no time in filling the order and as Angela was packing it all away in the pram, she marvelled that she could buy a full week's food. She knew many of her neighbours couldn't, even if their husbands were in full-time work, for wages were so low, many lived from hand to mouth.

The wages the men brought home were usually enough for the wives to pay the rent and any tick they had owing in the shops, get their husband's suit out of the pawn shop, buy food for the weekend and if there was any left at all, maybe buy a hundredweight of coal. On Monday morning they would pawn the husband's suit and use the money for foodstuffs and if there was more week left than money, they would run up tick at the grocery shop.

That had been the lot of many women. There was very little slack and anything could tip the balance, boots needing heeling, a harsh long winter meaning an extra hundredweight of coal, a sick child needing the services of a doctor, any of these could send them into rent arrears.

She had remarked on this just that morning to Mary. 'I can't help feeling a bit guilty,' she admitted. 'I served many women like that in the shop while we are sitting pretty because Barry is an indentured toolmaker, and a supervisor to boot, so he gets good money and even if there is a call-up he will not have to go and fight anyone, but these women's lives will just get worse.'

'Maybe not,' Mary said. 'Those women married to heavy drinkers or gamblers might fare better. I don't know what a soldier is paid but I imagine there is some system in place to pay something out to their wives and more especially if they have children. T'isn't as if they'll have a boozer on every corner of a French field, or a cosy betting shop set up in the trenches they say they're fighting in. Now if, as well as the Army pay, they were to get themselves a little job, which seems as easy as blinking these days, they might have more money than they have ever had in their lives without a husband tipping it down his throat, or putting it all on a horse. Tell you, Angela, while I can never agree with war and there will be a great many men killed and terrible hardship, this war will be the making of some women.'

Angela had agreed with Mary and as she trudged home that day, lugging the overloaded pram after her, she thought of the women she'd

242

served who'd had even less to spend than their neighbours because of their husbands' excesses. They were the fathers of the children hanging around the pub doors on a Friday night, each trying to get some money from their father before he blew it all. They were the fathers who gave their wives so little she could only afford to feed one person anything decent and that had to go to the husband because he was the breadwinner. The woman and children would usually live on bread and scrape and not much of that and the children were usually dressed in ragged clothes and were barefoot.

It always saddened Angela to see them so skinny, with their gaunt pasty faces. Oh yes, if the women married to such men could now get enough to feed themselves and the children properly and have boots on their feet and coats on their backs, it had to be a good thing. And as she reached home with an immense sigh of relief, she thanked God that she was married to such a good, kind and considerate man.

The big freeze went on through January, but soon people had more to worry about than the weather because on the night of 9th January two Zeppelins dropped bombs on King's Lynn and Great Yarmouth killing four, injuring many more and causing £7,000 worth of damage. The whole country was stunned and scared. They knew England was at war, but that was about soldiers and sailors and battles. The thought that innocent and unarmed civilians could be killed by bombs from the air was beyond their understanding. It

243

was pulling everyone into the front line.

Barry felt sick to the pit of his stomach as he looked at the grainy photographs in the paper a couple of days later and saw the scale of the destruction and bemused people standing in the ruins of what had once been their houses and he wondered how Britain could hope to fight this airborne enemy.

Just days after this, Barry picked up the letter from the mat that had been pushed through the letter box and when he opened the envelope three white feathers fell out and he suddenly felt very cold and ashamed. Angela, coming into the room at that moment with Connie in her arms, saw his white face and the opened envelope beside him and fearing further bad news cried, 'What is it?'

Barry moved his arm so she could see the feathers as he said, 'Nothing much. Just what they send to all the cowards dodging war.'

'You're no coward.'

'Am I not?' Barry said sarcastically. 'Didn't I grasp Stan's get-out clause a little too eagerly?'

'It made sense, that's why,' Angela said. 'You have a wife and child.'

'D'you know, Angela, there are thousands of men at the Front,' Barry said. 'Don't you think some of them might be husbands and fathers too?'

Angela wasn't ready to face this yet, so instead of answering she said, 'I can't understand who would do this and upset us all so.'

'Oh you would be spoilt for choice as to who has done this,' Barry said. 'I can't meet the eyes of some I see at Mass knowing their sons will never come home again. And we're being snubbed by

families we have known for years. I've noticed so I'm sure you have.'

Angela couldn't disagree with him and she nodded her head mutely.

'And that's another thing,' Barry said. 'One of the reasons Stan went to war was for Daniel. He said if he doesn't make it Daniel will get to read the letter he has left for him when he is twenty-one when he will also find out about the money. Knowing Stan as I do, when Daniel reads that letter he'll know straight away what a fine man his father was and be proud that he died doing something worthwhile.

'Stan said it would be totally different for Connie and how readily I believed him. He said she would understand that I couldn't go to war and leave everyone, but will she understand that when she's a little older and the other children are recounting what their dads did in the war? What will she say then? And there will be plenty about to tell her what a coward I was because they would overhear adults talking. I might never know who sent those feathers but whoever it was, they were only expressing what everyone else is thinking.'

Angela would have liked to refute what Barry said but she couldn't for she knew it was too true. She had been snubbed and had snide remarks directed at her, and she knew children were very cruel when they wanted to be. She had experienced bullying herself, but not for long because she had Barry and his four big brothers to protect her, but Connie might have no one and any of the children who had lost a father, a favourite brother

or an uncle might think taunting and mocking Connie might be a suitable distraction to help them cope with the pain of loss. And Connie would be considered fair game because her father was named as a coward.

Angela tried not very successfully to stem the flow of tears as she said, 'So you've decided to enlist?'

Barry nodded. 'I think it's time I did,' he said and his arms encircled his wife and the child she was still holding as he went on, 'What finally decided me were the bombs. They could be dropped from the sky to land anywhere and Britain has got nothing to counteract them and so we have to go over there and stop them now, for I don't think that attack will be the last by any means and I think the Army needs every man jack of us. No one should sit on the fence on this one because our loved ones here are in danger. I always said I would fight if my family were threatened and bombs dropping from the sky mean just that and I must try and protect you.'

He lifted his hand, suddenly releasing Angela as he said, 'Ssh, I hear Mammy stirring in the attic. Not a word to her now, I want to tell her when I have got time to explain it all, for it will be hard for her because she has already lost two sons, but I'll have to leave now really.'

'You've had no breakfast,' Angela said. 'Not even a sup of tea.'

'No matter,' Barry said. 'I can probably pick something up in the canteen.'

Angela heard Mary's ponderous tread on the lower steps and she quickly scrubbed the tears

from her eyes and scooped the envelope and feathers into her cardigan pocket as Mary came into the room. But she had eyes only for her son. 'Are you still here?' she said for he was late leaving.

'I'm just away, Mammy,' he said, taking his coat from the hook at the back of the door as he spoke and with a kiss for Angela and Connie he was gone.

Barry told Mr Baxter of his decision immediately and could see how pleased he was and he got from behind his desk and shook him by the hand. 'I'm sure you're doing the right thing,' he said decidedly and Barry was glad of Mr Baxter's enthusiasm for it buoyed up his own, which had evaporated somewhat on the journey to work.

'Now,' Mr Baxter said. 'Have you anyone earmarked to take your place?'

'No, not really,' said Barry. 'Though I have been mulling through the idea of enlisting for some time, I only made the final decision when those bombs were dropped in Norfolk.'

'Yes, shocking wasn't it?'

'Yes and bombs from the air mean our loved ones aren't safe,' Barry said. 'Britain hasn't got anything like those Zeppelins, I don't think. So I thought the only thing to do was get over there as quick as possible and stop whoever is sending them. And I thought they would need every man they could get and what was I doing in a cushy number like the factory when I could be helping?'

'As for who will take my place?' Barry went on. 'Sir, those women have shaped up better than I could ever have imagined and I could name half a dozen that could do the job quite as well as I

247

can, but Pearl Mason will have a little bit of authority among the younger girls and she's well liked and also has a head on her shoulders.'

'Good, those are the qualities needed,' Mr Baxter said approvingly. 'Now I suggest you make your announcement to the girls on the shop floor immediately before the machines are started up, then you can make your way to Thorp Street Barracks. Send this young Pearl Mason to me.'

'You want me to go to Thorp Street Barracks today?' Barry cried incredulously.

'One thing I do know about war is that there is no place for shilly-shallying,' Mr Baxter said. 'You already said that you've thought about it for some time. Well waste no more of it thinking.'

'I haven't even told my mother yet, sir.'

'And is there anything your mother can do to turn you from this decision?' Mr Baxter asked.

'No, sir,' Barry said decisively.

'Well if I were you, I would get it all signed and sealed anyway,' Mr Baxter suggested. 'For in my experience a mother's tears can be very persuasive, but if it is all signed and sealed, whatever she says the die is cast.'

Barry could see the sense of that because he did find it hard to stand against his mother's tears and was well aware of his place in the family as her only son. First though, he had to tell the girls on the shop floor his intentions for he couldn't just disappear.

He could see the workforce were intrigued when they were asked to assemble by the steps that led up to the offices and when Barry appeared at the top of those steps and told them he was enlisting,

248

there was a little ripple of applause.

But some were perplexed for Barry had often been the topic of speculation and many had assumed, since he wasn't in uniform like most young men his age were, he must have failed the medical. Now it appeared he hadn't even had a medical. Barry heard the murmurings and explained that as the factory was turning out a great deal for the war effort he was in a reserved occupation, but he thought now he would be more use in the army. He got a cheer of approval for this and those who were the loudest were those who already wore the widow's bonnet and the black armband on their overalls.

The recruitment room at Thorp Street Barracks was a long one. The wooden floor gleamed with polish and the tramp of Barry's work boots sounded very loud as he walked the length of it to stand before the desk at the back of the room, with his heart banging in his breast and his mouth unaccountably dry.

There was a little queue of people at the barracks facing two men in uniform behind a desk. The line of men shuffled forward slowly but at last it was Barry's turn and he saw that one of the men seemed much older than the other. The older one had a florid face and grey hair, not that Barry could see much of his face, for it was partially obscured by his large handlebar moustache. His eyes were not obscured though and they were steely blue, and he introduced himself as Colonel Sanders.

Barry was surprised at such a high-ranking

officer dealing with recruitment, till he remembered Stan said they had taken a lot of the military men out of retirement to do the routine desk jobs. The other man was younger and his face was more open. He was Corporal Withers and his eyes and hair were the same soft brown.

Barry had thought his mouth too dry for him to speak normally and if he made any sort of sound at all it would come out as a squeak. However, he was able to give all the details the two men asked for and explain himself when they expressed surprise at his age for most recruits were younger.

Barry explained about the factory where he had worked since he'd left school and the vast amount of war-related things the factory was churning out. 'I was in a reserved occupation,' he said. 'You see most of the workforce, who were men and boys, enlisted when war was declared, even the previous Gaffer, and someone had to teach the girls and women what to do, as none of them had done any sort of work like that before. But now the women in the workforce are up to speed as it were.' Barry went on, 'One of them is now quite able to take my place while I play a more active part in the war.'

'Good man,' Colonel Sanders said admiringly, so that even his large moustache seemed to bristle with approbation. 'A man choosing to join in this just war, is worth ten conscripts who have to be nearly dragged in to do their duty.'

'I didn't know you had started the call-up, sir.'

'We haven't yet,' Corporal Withers said. 'We are getting enough volunteers at present, but that might change before the war is won, so then we will have conscription and we'll have to try and

turn reluctant young men into a fierce fighting force. But the next step for you now is for us to find out how healthy you are.'

Neither of the men were worried about Barry's fitness for he looked a fine, strapping chap, but he was sent to the male white-coated doctor who had a stethoscope hanging around his neck. The doctor had done this many many times and took Barry's temperature and checked his pulse rate before he weighed and measured him and sounded his chest and back. He asked him if he had any aches and pains and though Barry said he hadn't, he was still prodded and poked. The doctor looked into Barry's ears and his throat and examined his eyes and then, having told Barry to strip to his vest and pants, paid great attention to his legs and feet and finally he stood before the doctor who held his testicles in his hand and asked him to cough.

Barry had never been so embarrassed in his life, but for the doctor it was all in a day's work and part of the procedure and he asked Barry to dress and said he was A1 and well able to travel overseas after training.

Barry was joining the Royal Warwickshires and he asked how much he would be paid. It was Colonel Sanders who answered, 'You've heard of the King's shilling I suppose?'

Barry gave a brief nod.

'Well that's what you get, a shilling a day, seven shillings a week.'

It wasn't a lot but then Barry reasoned he didn't need a lot, as there wouldn't be that much to spend it on. 'I have a wife and a child,' he said.

'Yes, sixpence will be deducted from your allow-

251

ance for your wife and a penny for your child. The government will pay a weekly sum of one shilling and one penny a day to your wife together with the contributions from you and tuppence extra for your child from the government.' He made a swift calculation on a notepad and said, 'Altogether it comes to eight and fourpence a week.'

Eight and fourpence re-echoed in Barry's brain. It was not enough, not nearly enough. By signing on the dotted line he had reduced his family to penury. Almighty Christ, what had he done? How in God's name could they live on so little? But it was too late to think of that. His fate was sealed. 'Can I give my wife something from my pay?' Barry asked.

Corporal Withers nodded. 'You can indeed. Many men do that. To claim it your wife must take your marriage lines and the child's birth certificate and the child to the Town Hall. She must go herself, no one can go in her stead and as it may take some time to process it, she must do this without delay as soon as you start training. Have you to give notice to your present employer?'

'He said a week, that's all,' Barry said.

'Right, that will be a week today, Colonel Sanders. The 29th January, so how about you coming to the Barracks the following Monday, 1st February? Seven a.m. sharp. Don't be late. There's a truck leaving at a quarter past and I want you on it.' Barry knew he wouldn't be late, he was an early riser. That was the least of his problems and, unable to face Angela and his mother, he went back to work although Mr Baxter said he could go home after he was finished at Thorp Street. He

had no desire to go home and tell them what he had done for he had made their lives even harder.

Everyone seemed to think he had done the right thing and yet the thought of them all going hungry and Connie dressed in rags and running around barefoot would be his worst nightmare come true. He groaned aloud, glad he had the office to himself, for Mr Baxter had taken himself home and advised Barry to do the same.

EIGHTEEN

Afterwards, Barry was not sure how far he walked that night, but eventually he realized he couldn't walk all night and, even if he could, it would change nothing and he turned for home. He was mightily relieved that only Angela was in the room. She started when she saw him and her eyes he saw were full of concern and trepidation. He felt slight guilt that he had worried them so as he whispered, 'Where's Mammy?'

'Putting Connie to bed,' Angela said. 'And having a time of it because I kept her up to see you, only she got too tired to wait any longer, though she of course she didn't agree. Where on earth have you been till this time of night?'

Barry didn't answer that, but what he did say was, 'Shall I go up now?'

'What on earth for?' Angela asked. 'No, you may make matters worse. Connie's been quiet this long time so maybe Mammy's got her off at

253

last. I've kept your dinner hot, though you scarce deserve it, scaring us so. Where did you go?'

Barry said nothing until his dinner was in front of him and though he was hungry, for he had eaten nothing for hours, he felt slightly sick and he looked at Angela and said, 'I enlisted today.'

Angela gave a small gasp and yet she asked herself why she was so surprised because she knew that that was Barry's way. Once he'd made a decision he acted upon it. 'Is that what kept you?'

Barry shook his head. 'No, Mr Baxter gave me the time off for that. I thought I would enlist and be sent for the other formalities later, but they did it there and then. I think the mad dash for joining up has eased a bit though there were a fair few in front of me and as I left I saw a crowd of young fellows going in. As it was, I had my medical and everything.'

'When do you start?'

'I have to report on 1st February.'

'So soon?'

'For training just.'

'Even so,' Angela said, 'where will you train?'

Barry shrugged. 'Your guess is as good as mine,' he said. 'A couple of women on the shop floor said their chaps trained at a place called Cannock Chase. I don't know where that is and I don't much care, because it doesn't really matter where you train in the end as long as the training is done properly.'

'Oh, Barry, I am so going to miss you.'

'I won't be a million miles away,' Barry said. 'Not at first at any rate.'

'D'you realize we have never been apart?' Angela

said. 'Not for one single day and night since I was just over eighteen months old. You have always been there for me and I thought you always would be.'

Barry knew Angela was very near to tears and he pushed his empty plate away and gathered her up in his arms, saying as he did so, 'Angela, I love you more than life itself, my absolute love for Connie often overwhelms me and I love Mammy too and feel responsible for her too. You are the three most important women in my life and I can't stay with you, because I must fight for you and try and make the world a safer place.'

Angela would have much rather Barry was staying here at home and keeping her safe where his strong hands would encircle her if ever she was afraid and she would feel protected and cherished. But what was the point in saying any of this now the decision had been made and so her sigh was imperceptible as she said, 'Is that why you didn't come home, because you haven't told Mammy what you've done?'

'Partly,' Barry admitted and then added, 'I didn't want to face you either because you don't know everything, but I suppose it's better to tell you together?'

'Here's your chance,' Angela said. 'I hear Mammy on the stairs. I was about to send out a search party for she's been upstairs ages. I'll make her a cup of tea, it's just a pity we haven't got a drop of something stronger. I have a feeling she might need it.'

Mary came into the room wiping her sleepy eyes with her apron. 'What d'you think?' she said. 'I

255

have just woken up. I lay on your bed beside the cot to please Connie and I don't know whether I dropped off first or she did.' And then she looked at Barry and said, 'So you decided to come home in the end?'

'Yes, Mammy, as you see.'

'You been in some pub?'

'No, just walking, Mammy, trying to collect my thoughts.'

'Must have been some thoughts that took you so long.'

'They were, Mammy, and now I want to share them with you.' Angela gently pushed Mary down on the settee, and placed a cup of tea in her hands. 'You may have need of this,' she said and sat down beside her as Barry began to tell his mother what he had done and try to explain why he had done it. The tea was forgotten as Mary listened to the words spilling from her son's mouth. She couldn't believe she was hearing right. Stan had said he was safe and he needn't go to war for he could claim he was in a reserved occupation even if conscription was introduced, and he had done it anyway.

Oh dear Christ, her mind was screaming, how would they manage without Barry? How could she bear to see the only son she had left march off to a war he might not come back from? When shock caused her to shake, Angela took the tea from her and put it on the table and wrapped her arms around Mary and felt the abject despair and sorrow flowing through her that caused Angela to cry too, and the two women tightly embraced as their tears mingled together. And Barry, not able to bear to see the sadness he had inflicted on these

two women that he loved dearly, fell on to his knees before the settee and held them both tight, and he too shed tears of guilt and shame.

A long time later when the crying eventually eased and they were all feeling a bit light-headed, Mary pulled herself from Barry's arms and sat up straighter in the chair and said as bravely as she could, though her voice wavered slightly, 'Well, Barry that was a shock for me all right, but crying never did any good at all. If you have enlisted then you have and there's nothing to be done. Angela, Connie and I will have to get along without you the best way we can, like so many more are doing.'

Barry, amazed at his mother's stoicism, took a deep breath and deciding he'd better tell the whole of it, went on to say, 'I haven't told either of you one of the worst aspects of my decision to join the army.'

Angela groaned, 'Oh God,' she said. 'Does it get worse?'

''Fraid so,' Barry said. 'I didn't know any of this from talking to Stan. 'Course he hadn't anyone else to consider. I know he cares about Daniel, but he hasn't got to provide for him. I really thought though that if you were prepared to put your life on the line your family would be looked after.'

Angela knew what Barry was getting at and she said sharply, 'Just tell me how much you will be getting,' and when he said how much it was, her mouth dropped open in disbelief. 'Eight and fourpence?' she repeated incredulously. 'What am I to do with eight and fourpence when the rent is three and six?'

257

'I will send you more,' Barry promised. 'I can't say how much because I don't know what expenses I might have, but it will be as much as I can afford.' And he went on to tell her how to claim the money and to do it the minute he left for training. 'By the time they process it, I will know how much I can send you and will get it set up straight away.'

'Barry,' Angela said, 'you'll have less than six and six with the money already taken out to give to me and Connie and you must keep some money for yourself, but even if you were able to give me the whole untouched seven shillings, it's not going to be enough.'

Barry nodded his head miserably.

'Well, I think it's a shabby way for a country to treat its army,' Mary said.

'I agree with you, Mammy.'

'And I'm a drain on you,' Mary said. 'Have been for years. I mean what am I but a useless old woman?'

'You're not that old,' Angela protested. 'And you better not be useless for I'm going to rely on you.'

'What d'you mean?'

'We don't know how long this war is going to go on for,' Angela said. 'If we're going to survive it at all, one of us needs to get a job and that's down to me and I can't do that without you. But,' she added with a twinkle in her eye, 'if you're too old and useless we'll have to tighten our belts and hope for the best.'

Barry marvelled at Angela's resilience She had been overcome with sadness and shed tears, but once she knew how bad the situation was she had

a plan of action and one that involved Mary too for she said to Angela, 'You know I didn't mean that. Looking after Connie is a pleasure not a chore.'

'I think you're right about getting a job,' Barry said. 'What sort of work are you thinking of looking for?'

'Anything well paid,' Angela said.

'Not munitions,' Barry cautioned. 'They pay well because they are dangerous places. I don't want you working somewhere like that.'

Angela stared at him. 'I didn't particularly want you rushing into war,' she said. 'But you're going anyway, but you don't want me in any sort of danger.'

'Is that so wrong?'

'Well it's only that I don't want you in danger either. I mean when you're in France it's not to go to a vicar's tea party is it?'

Barry got Angela's point, he was leaving them in the lurch and they had to do the best they could. And so he said, 'All right. I'm sure you'd get something suitable and I really have no right to say anything about it.' And then he added, 'I could probably get you set on at our place. The work is heavy, but not dangerous.'

'I'd rather get something off my own bat,' Angela said and suddenly gave an enormous yawn. 'Let's go to bed,' she pleaded. 'I'm too tired to think straight and I want to wake early tomorrow and make the most of the short time we'll have together.'

Angela did fall into an exhausted sleep only to wake in the early hours, the time when everyday

problems magnify, and found she was unable to sleep again as sorrow at what Barry had done that day overwhelmed her. She fought tears, as Mary had said they did not help and anyway they could disturb Barry and Connie too, but sorrow filled her brain and lodged in her heart and drove all thoughts of sleep from her.

She was almost pleased when she heard Connie begin to stir in the cot and she heaved herself out of bed and picked her up, though her eyes were gritty from lack of sleep and her whole body felt like a bit of chewed string.

However, mindful of her words the previous night, she fought her fatigue to spend most of the afternoon at Calthorpe Park though the weather was squally and cold. And that night, much to Connie's surprise and delight it was her daddy who bathed her in the tin bath hanging from a hook on the back of the cellar door, which he filled with kettle upon kettle of water. And after he had bathed her and washed her hair, he carried her upstairs to where her Mammy had her pyjamas warming by the fire. Later it was Barry who carried her up the stairs to the cot Angela had warmed with firebricks wrapped in flannel and he tucked her up snug and warm and even read her a story before he left her to sleep. His heart ached as he descended the stairs. He had so wanted to see his child grow up and yet he knew that once his training was over and he set off for France he might not see her again for years and there was always the chance he wouldn't return from the war he had volunteered for and that thought made him feel very sad. But he could not

load this on Angela for the situation was of his own making.

At Mass the next morning, the news filtered through the congregation that Barry McClusky had enlisted, for it was hard to keep things private in the cramped houses with paper-thin walls and anyway this was hardly a private matter. They would all know anyway when he disappeared for training.

Angela, looking around for a fairly vacant pew, spotted the three spinster women who always came to Mass together and then sat towards the front of the church behind the children. The three spinsters were regarding the whole family disapprovingly. They had snubbed the McCluskys when they heard that Barry was in a reserved occupation and Angela thought they were just the type of people to send white feathers out. She was more certain of this when a woman behind them leant forward and whispered something to one of them. A lot of whispering and nudging went on and then the three women swung round and the look on all their faces could only be described as a satisfied smirk.

Angela glanced at Barry, but he was dealing with Connie and had seen nothing untoward and neither had Mary. She was glad and knew there was no point in making them aware of it and so she contented herself with a baleful look at all three of them and then took her place beside Barry as people began shuffling to their feet for the first hymn.

Afterwards so many people wanted to shake Barry's hand and wish him 'all the best' that

261

Angela, who'd had nothing to eat or drink because of taking communion, was beginning to think her throat had been cut. The priest hadn't been aware of what Barry had done until one of the altar boys mentioned it as they were changing in the sacristy after Mass and he too hurried out as soon as he could. 'God speed my boy,' he said. 'I will remember you in my prayers. Right is with you and will always prevail in the end.'

Barry wasn't so sure of that, but he wasn't going to argue with the priest at this juncture. Anyway now he had a hot line to God and he thought it good to have him on his side when he would be risking his life on a daily basis. As they walked home a little later he reflected that life was a funny thing. People who had snubbed him openly, even crossing the street to avoid meeting him, were breaking their neck to shake him by the hand that morning because he had done what they considered right and he wished he was so absolutely sure.

Many times that week, Angela wished she could stop time just there but never more poignantly than that last day. The following morning he would report to Thorp Street Barracks and life would never be the same again. So though it wasn't really the weather for it, after Mass they took the little steam train to Sutton Park from New Street Station. They left the pram behind and Barry lifted his small daughter onto his shoulders. She squealed with excitement swinging her little legs and beating Barry about the head with her podgy little hands as they walked into the town.

At New Street, Connie was fascinated by the noisy, bustling station where there was a sour smell and steam mixed with the coal dust wafting in the air. Sat atop her daddy's shoulders she wasn't afraid of the roaring monsters that seemed to hurl themselves into the station to stop with a clatter of wheels and hiss of steam. She didn't mind the man feeding the firebox at the front of the train with the orange and yellow flames licking around the coal he was shovelling. Sweat ran down the man's shining face, while smoke billowed out of the funnel above him into the already grey and sooty air.

A sudden shriek from another waiting train did make Connie jump, but before she could give voice to protest about it, Barry lifted her from his shoulders and put her in the train and got in beside her and so did her Mammy. Connie was so excited her tears were stopped before they'd properly begun. A train journey was a novel experience for Angela too, so she could perfectly understand why Connie was fizzing with the thrill of it all.

Industry, factories, houses and shops soon gave way to fields as they left the town behind. And this stirred a distant memory of a train journey undertaken through a similar landscape when Angela had travelled from Ireland to England years before.

There were fields of cows, some looking over five-barred gates to see the train pass with no sign of alarm and all chewing as if their lives depended upon it. Barry told the wide-eyed Connie that the creatures were called cows and

the milk that she liked to drink came from a cow. Connie said nothing but she looked at her father rather oddly, not able to understand what those peculiar animals had in common with the man who ladled their milk into the milk pan they took out to him.

Angela laughed at the expression on her young daughter's face because she knew what she was thinking. 'You'll know what these are in the next field,' she said confidently.

'Hoss.'

'Horse, that's right,' Angela said.

She knew Connie would recognise horses, which were a common sight in Birmingham for many wagons were horse-drawn and not all omnibuses were petrol-driven either. Their own coalman used a horse to pull his cart and in the Bull Ring there were many horses carrying all sorts of things and the ones pulling the barrels of beer were usually the smartest and some had their manes and tails plaited and their coats were always shiny and smooth.

Some of the fields were cultivated and Angela remembered the little tufts of green that had been on top of many furrows when she had travelled from Ireland, but now the only thing on the top of these furrows was a dusting of frost. Angela pointed to another field further off, full of sheep relentlessly tugging at the grass.

'See their woolly coats, Connie,' she said. 'They're called fleeces and that's what many of your warm jumpers are made from.'

Connie looked suitably impressed by that and the train began slowing down to pull to a halt at

a small station and Barry suddenly said, 'We've arrived.'

They stepped out onto the wooden platform and Barry said, 'This is it, the Royal Town of Sutton Coldfield.'

'Royal Town?'

'Yes, Henry the Eighth I think had something to do with the royal bit,' Barry said. 'He used to hunt here, it was all natural then, and he sort of bequeathed the park to the town, or that's what Stan said. He also said the people of Sutton are very proud of the royal title and the park and unless you live in Sutton Coldfield you have to pay to go in it.'

Angela shook her head, 'Surely not, Barry,' she said. 'Anyway how would you know such a thing because you told me you've never been here before?'

'Stan told me all about it,' Barry said as he put Connie back on his shoulders and led the way out of the small country station. 'He said he knew every inch of it because Kate's family lived in Erdington and he did all his courting in Sutton Park. They had to have Betty along as chaperone. She was quite a lot older than Kate and cross that her young sister had a boyfriend before she had and so she wasn't up to taking herself a little way off so they could have some privacy, or turning the other way so they could steal a kiss.'

'Be fair,' Angela said with a little laugh. 'If Betty was the eldest her parents would expect her to look after her sister. They didn't want their daughter ravished by some lusty young man if Betty took her eyes off her for a moment. Anyway,

Betty has her own man now and Stan didn't have his beloved very long all told.'

'No, he didn't,' Barry agreed. 'And I think I can safely say that with Betty in charge there was precious little ravishing went on either.'

'Barry McClusky, you say that as if it's a bad thing,' Angela said. 'And you don't even know Betty.'

'I know of her,' Barry said as they left the station and set off down the slight incline and Angela realized that Barry must have taken great notice of what Stan told him because he seemed to know just where he was going.

'You mean you know this woman that you've never met because of what Stan told you?' Angela said.

'No, not really,' Barry said. 'You know Stan's not one for bad-mouthing people. Plenty of other people said things though. I was a kid, but I overheard a lot and she seemed to want to control everything. I bet that Roger's hen-pecked.'

'Oh how can you say that without a shred of evidence?'

'I just know that's all,' Barry said. 'People say she went after Roger for the house. He was one of the bosses in a place she worked at as a lowly filing clerk. Roger's father had died a few years before and he had looked after his mother ever since. The old lady had become very infirm and I don't know how it all transpired but Betty ended up caring for her and she moved in completely in no time at all.'

'What's wrong with that?'

'Nothing,' Barry admitted. 'Only that Roger's

parents probably had someone earmarked for him to marry, someone from his social circle which certainly would not have included Betty, or people like her in the general scheme of things. They were middle class, and Roger was their only child, went to university and all.'

'Well circumstances dictated differently that's all,' Angela said. 'Look at me and how differently my life turned out. Happens all the time and people make the best of it. Strikes me this Roger was very grateful to Betty for being kind to his mother. He might have seen a different side to her that no one else was that aware of.'

Barry shrugged. 'You could be right. Anyway, they were married and when the mother died a few years later they inherited the house and I admit it must have been a hard cross to bear not to be able to have their own child. In a way I can understand them spiriting Daniel away.'

'So can I,' Angela said. 'What I can't understand is their apparent desire to cut Stan out of his life altogether and for Stan to comply, thinking it's better for the boy. I'm sure this is all going to come out some day.'

'I agree with you,' Barry said. 'But Stan won't rock the boat unless he has to. Anyway,' he said as he came to a wooden gate, 'we're here now, so what d'you think of Sutton Park? Apparently, according to Stan, we have to come in the summer to see it in its glory.'

'Well what we can't change is the seasons,' Angela said. 'But as I haven't seen it before it looks quite impressive enough to me in the winter.'

They were in front of a hut and the man inside

it took the money Barry offered and issued tickets and Angela was a bit surprised. 'Told you,' Barry said, holding up the tickets as they went through the gate.

'Well I've never heard of that before.'

'Nor me,' Barry admitted. 'But Stan said this is bigger than anything he had seen before. It has something like five lakes for a start. Anyway now we have paid hard-earned money to get in, let's at least have a look at the place.'

Angela had no problem with that and she looked out at the frost-filled meadow in front of them with a playground set to one side of it, which caused a cry of delight from Connie. The slide was too wet and crusty with frost but the swings were all right and the roundabout and Barry was quite happy to push Connie as high and fast as she wanted to go.

In the end he called a halt though because he said Stan had told him about something and he wanted to see it for himself. 'What is it?' Angela asked.

'Something called the Crystal Palace,' Barry said. 'He said to follow the stream round and we'll come to it and if I'm not mistaken the stream runs by the edge of the meadow by that bank of trees.'

The stream was where Barry thought it was and they walked by the edge of it and Connie tripped over so many protruding tree roots that Barry lifted her on to his shoulders again. It was worth it though when they saw the palace for the first time, for it was truly magnificent. It was built on the edge of a lake and three floors high and on

each floor were rows and rows of big tall windows looking down on to the large lawn in front of it. And stretching out to one side was a wondrous structure made completely of glass with a glass dome at the end. 'The conservatory,' Barry said.

Angela nodded. 'That must be the crystal bit,' she said. 'Love to see inside it.'

'Have to come back in the summer for that I'd say,' Barry said and added, 'It's built as sort of a replica of the Crystal Palace in London.'

'And is it a good likeness?'

'How would I know?' Barry said. 'I've never been to London. It was Stan told me that, but he hasn't been to London either.'

'So it might look nothing like the one in London and you'd not know the difference?'

'No,' Barry said. 'Nor care that much if you want the truth, but I'd like to come back when everything is open, play croquet on the lawn maybe and take a boat out on the lake.'

'That sounds nice,' Angela said. 'And what's that mass of stuff all covered over with something?' she asked, pointing to quite a massive pile of things at the edge of the gigantic lawn.

'That must be the fair Stan told me about,' Barry said. 'They've probably broken it down for the winter and I should say that's some sort of tarpaulin sheeting covering it to protect it from the winter weather.'

'A fair?' Angela repeated in surprise. 'A proper fair?'

'Oh yes, with all the rides and a little train that runs round the edge of it,' Barry said and grabbed Angela's hand suddenly as he said eagerly, 'We

must come here one summer's day when this damned war is over. I want to see Connie enjoy the rides and hold her hand and let her paddle the stream or fish for tiddlers. I want her to be free and happy and ultimately that's what we're fighting for.'

A sudden shudder ran through Angela and dread gripped her heart. A premonition of things to come? Surely not. Not able to share these thoughts, she said instead, 'I think this would be a good place to stop and eat the sandwiches. There's a shelter I spotted at the other side of the grass and it would be good to get out of the icy air while we eat.'

It was too cold for sitting long though and so they finished their sandwiches quickly. Even Connie didn't linger. No snow had fallen, but frost lay thick on the grass sparkling in the weak winter sun and crunching beneath their feet as they made their way to the woods.

The trees were bare, the branches stretching skywards like huge, glacial skeletons and they walked hand in hand kicking at the piles of frost-rimmed leaves, much to Connie's delight, and atop her father's shoulders she clapped her hands with glee. Then he delighted her still further when he put her down where she stood almost knee-deep in snow while he gently lifted a gilded spider's web from between two branches and even Angela, not a great lover of spiders in the general way of things, was slightly awed by the silver beauty of it.

However, the cold drew them back home in the end where Mary had soup heating over the fire. Angela was glad of it, but the cold stayed within

270

her and she knew it was the kind of cold no soup could ease because from tomorrow Barry would start his training to be a soldier, to learn to use weapons he had only heard of, to learn to kill, a world she could not share where he would have to kill or be killed. She would lose part of Barry to the British Army and she must bear it as bravely as she could.

So when she said goodbye to Barry early the next morning, she did not cry though her eyes were very bright. She remembered their love-making of the previous night that had an energy and urgency to it though even then, Barry had been careful for he said he couldn't leave her with another mouth to feed, especially now.

Barry saw the smile playing around Angela's mouth and, knowing her well, guessed her thoughts and kissed her tenderly, proud of her control. He saw the tears brimming behind her eyelashes, but she didn't let them fall and even managed a watery smile for him.

His mother, on the other hand, sobbed copiously and Barry, even knowing her level of distress, was slightly impatient with her for crying wouldn't change the situation and he said, 'Give over, Mammy, for Christ's sake. You're upsetting Connie.'

It was true. Connie was in Angela's arms and her bottom lip had begun to tremble as she saw her Granny so upset. Mary made a valiant effort to control herself and Barry lifted Connie into his arms and kissed her. 'Don't cry, darling,' he said. 'There's nothing to cry for. I'll be back before you know it when I am a proper soldier.'

It was doubtful that Connie understood every-thing Barry said but she always felt safe held in her father's arms and so she sagged against his shoulder with a sigh. Barry's heart melted and his eyes met Angela's over the child's head and she knew what it was costing him to leave them. But it was something he had to do and so she lifted Connie from her father's arms gently and said, 'Daddy must go now, pet, and you must stay at home and look after Mammy and Granny. D'you think you can do that?'

Connie nodded her head sagely and Barry kissed his mother, wife and child on their cheeks, picked up his case and stepped into the street. They watched him stride away from the doorway, a shadowy figure illuminated now and again when he walked under a street lamp. The he turned down Bristol Passage and was lost to view entirely. Angela closed the door with a sigh and saw Mary was poking the fire with vigour and she smiled at Connie and said, 'Soon have some porridge made for you and I could do with a sup of tea. Puts new heart in a body that.'

The words were spoken in such a plaintive voice that Angela looked up and said to Mary, 'Are you all right?'

'Angela, I won't be all right till this war is over and done with and Barry is home where he be-longs,' said Mary. 'But I'm not the only mother feels like this and I must bear it the same as them.'

'We will bear it together,' Angela said, reaching out and catching hold of Mary's hand. 'I feel exactly the same.'

272

'Oh Angela, you are such a lovely girl,' Mary said. 'I bless the day I took you in for you have never given me a day's worry and now we can be a comfort to one another.'

Just after breakfast, mindful of Barry's words about haste being needed in applying for a portion of his wages to be paid to her, Angela got together her marriage lines, Connie's birth certificate and her rent book for good measure and put them all at the bottom of the pram. 'Pity you got to take the wee one out in this,' Mary said. 'It's bitterly cold outside.'

'Mammy, the wind will hardly blow on Connie,' Angela said. 'I'm putting her in the coat Finbarr sent her for Christmas with the matching bonnet and mittens and she has fleecy leggings and the stout shoes Barry bought her. She'll have blankets over that will be tucked so well I don't think the cold weather will touch her. Anyway,' she added, 'there's no way around it, for if I want the money this is how it must be.'

'I suppose so,' Mary said. 'Stickler for rules, the army.'

'Have to be I should think,' Angela said. 'Oh and I might call in and see George on the way back. I've made a list of a few bits we could do with.'

'Are you going to sound him out about a job?' Mary asked.

'Not with him,' Angela said. 'He has Matilda's sister, Dorothy installed in there now, but he might know some shop that is losing their male assistant to the war or something like that. Any-

273

way,' she added, 'Maitland's is the last place on earth I would work now. And if I ever allowed myself to be persuaded to, it wouldn't be long before I was arrested for assault.'

Mary laughed. 'That isn't like you, Angela,' she said. 'Who would you attack, Matilda?'

'Oh yes, her too for good measure,' Angela said grimly. 'But the biggest clout would be reserved for her sister Dorothy. She's supposed to "help" George at busy times, though I think she must do more to turn customers away than anything else. I made the mistake of going in once at a busy time and was served by her. She is a hard-faced, foul-mouthed harridan. She has a fat red face and two piggy eyes set into it like currants in a lump of dough, only they are bluey grey and as cold as steel, and added to that she has a bulbous nose and slack mouth.'

'Oh you took to her then,' commented Mary ironically. 'All right so she was at the back of the queue when the looks were given out, but it isn't like you to turn against someone because of the way they look.'

'Oh Mammy, if it were only that,' Angela said. 'Though if she cracked those features into a smile it might make her look better. She made it obvious she had no time for me, but then she seemed to have no time for any of the customers, goes on as if they were an intrusion. She was rude to each and every one of them one way or another. I got the full treatment and George couldn't really help because the shop was so busy.

If it wasn't for George I would never go near the place, but because I worked there I know

274

when the shop is busy and I avoid those times.'

'And are you sure that it will be a quiet time today?'

'By the time I get there it will be,' Angela said. 'There is a rush first thing but by the time we have walked to the Town Hall and back the rush will have gone.'

She sighed suddenly and said, 'When I worked there I would often wish he had married a softer and kinder woman... And now he has Dorothy too, and she's much worse than Matilda.'

'Oh,' Mary with a wry smile, 'Devil incarnate then?'

Angela answered in like manner. 'Good contender for it anyway. And you know I don't think George is coping with it at all well. Sometimes he reminds me of a whipped dog. Still,' she said, as she bounced the pram down the front step, 'there's nothing I can do about it and I best be on my way.'

But even as she made her way to town she thought of the life she imagined George had with the two women constantly badgering him about anything and nothing. She looked forward to seeing him though because she seemed able to cheer him up a bit.

Connie fell asleep on the way to the town and she was still slumbering nicely when they reached the Town Hall. The woman behind the desk dealing with the forms said they just had to see the child and there was no need to disturb her and Angela was grateful because Connie could be right grouchy if she was woken from a deep sleep.

All in all it hadn't taken very long in the Town

Hall and the woman promised to process the claim as soon as possible and with a sprightly step, Angela set off for Maitland's shop.

NINETEEN

Angela turned the corner and stopped in shock for the shop was closed and shutters covered the windows. 'What happened to the shop?' she asked a boy playing in the street.

'It shut,' he said. 'After the man fell over.'

'What man?'

'The man what owned it,' the child said and added, 'Heard our Mom say as he'd had a heart attack and died.'

Normally such matters were not discussed in front of children, but this child seemed to be in the know and so Angela said, 'Are you talking about George?'

'Yeah that were his name, George.'

'And you're sure he had a heart attack?'

''Course I am,' the boy said. 'Our Mom was telling Beattie next door and I heard her and that's what she said.'

Angela felt suddenly sick as a wave of sadness almost overwhelmed her and she leant against the wall as her legs felt decidedly wobbly. She closed her eyes against the pain of the thought that she would never see George again.

'His posh wife's still here,' the boy said and Angela opened her eyes to see him still standing

276

there looking at her in a concerned way.

'What?'

'That George's posh wife and the other one are in the flat 'cos I seen them through the window.'

Angela knew he could easily have done that for one of the windows did overlook the street. The flat could be accessed by going through to the back of the shop, but there was an entrance from the street, though Angela had never used it. She thanked the child, turned the corner and approached the front door with some trepidation, but she felt bound to at least say how sorry she was, for though the marriage was not what anyone could call happy, death is so final.

Anyway she would like details of the funeral and she pressed the bell and heard it jangle in the flat. And then there were footsteps on the stairs, the door opened and Matilda stood in the threshold and glared at Angela as she demanded, 'What are you doing here?'

'I ... I've just heard about George and...'

'I hope you're not going to say that you'd like to express your condolences,' Matilda said. 'Not needed for I am far from sad. In fact it's what I wanted to happen for years.'

Angela gasped and was glad of the pram handles she held on to so tight for she could hardly believe what Matilda had just said.

'Shocked you have I?' Matilda said with a sneer.

'Yes, you've shocked me if that was your intention,' Angela said through gritted teeth. 'It's also the cruellest thing I have ever heard anyone say. I won't trouble you further if you would just give

me the details of George's funeral...'

'Oh that's been and gone,' Matilda said, smiling at the evident disappointment in Angela's face. 'Died on Monday and was buried on Saturday. No point in hanging about. As for the shop I am selling it lock, stock and barrel and intend to buy a bigger and better house as far from here as possible so there's nothing here for you.' And with that she slammed the door in Angela's face.

Angela stared at it for a moment fighting the insane desire to beat on the door and tell Matilda and her sister what she really thought of them but she knew it would achieve nothing and she turned for home, glad that Connie had wakened. She propped her up so that she could see more and chatted to her all the way home and it kept her mind off the unpleasant scene she'd had with Matilda Maitland.

Mary had broth waiting for them both and as they sat and ate it Angela told her what had happened when she went to the shop. She was sorry at George's passing and just as shocked as Angela had been at the things Matilda had said. 'And I'm sorry that you knew nothing of the funeral as well,' she said. 'But you know you couldn't have gone to it anyway.'

'Why not?' Angela said. 'I mean I know the rules that Catholics can't go to services in other churches, but I thought funerals would be a bit different.'

Mary shook her head. 'Not in the eyes of the church I don't think,' she said. 'Mind you with the war raging people of all religions are being killed so that rule might have to be more relaxed.'

'Yes,' Angela said for the casualty figures made frightening reading and she thought of Barry soon to enter the fray and Stan already in it and no end in sight, and felt totally dispirited and her sigh was heartfelt.

Another nagging worry was that she had no job. She knew George would have helped her if he could and now that avenue was closed. She knew she had to find something though for if she didn't they'd never manage. The worry of that was etched on her face and Mary felt for Angela and the body-blow she had received that day.

'Tell you what,' she said suddenly. 'Let's have a Mass said for George. I know he's not a Catholic, but the good Lord won't mind and I don't think Father Brannigan will object either and it will settle your mind maybe.'

Angela thought it a very good idea. It seemed alien to her to be laid in the ground with no sort of ceremony at all and no people even asked if they would like to pay their respects.

'You don't know people weren't asked,' Mary pointed out.

'Oh I sort of do, Mammy, because this boy knew everything,' Angela said. 'You know the sort who does a lot of earwigging and very useful in this instance and if he'd known about the funeral he would have said so. Because he'd probably think it a bit unusual, you know, with no one asked and that.' She sighed and went on, 'You know I bet the only ones at George's funeral were Matilda and Dorothy. It's as if they couldn't wait to get rid of him, as if his life was of no account.'

'A Commemorative Mass will make all the

difference, you'll see,' Mary said, giving Angela's hand a squeeze.

And strangely it did. The Mass was arranged for the following Monday and the priest announced it on Sunday so the church was fairly full of George's old customers on Monday. They greeted Angela like an old friend and afterwards they stood outside the church chatting.

The general consensus was that poor George had been nagged to death.

'Miserable cows, the pair of them, his wife and her sister.'

'Language,' admonished another. 'And you just outside the church.'

'Only word to describe them,' the first woman said. 'See, she came round collecting all the tick owed.'

'Matilda did?'

'No the other one, Dorothy or whatever they call her. It were the same day George died. God, he'd be barely cold. Anyroad my Bert has only had three days' work the last few weeks so I'd run up a bit of tick. He'd had a full week that week though and I intended paying some of the arrears, but she demanded it all. Well I didn't have it and told her straight and she said she'd send for a constable. Well I couldn't have that so I had to pawn all the blankets in the house, and till I can get them out again Bert, me and the kids have to go to bed in our clothes with every coat we possess on top of us.'

'I was the same,' another put in. 'My old man's suit is so old and thin now that I don't get much for it. One of these days it will fall off his back and

Christ knows what I'll do then if I can't pawn it. Anyroad there she was at the door, that Dorothy, all threatening like and saying she'd fetch the law out. I pawned my mother's old grandmother clock that she'd had as a wedding present years before. God she thought the world of that clock and it was beautiful and worth a bit you know, the only valuable thing I own and I just hope I can get it out of pawn before too long.'

And so it went on, a list of people hocking essential items because they were intimidated by Dorothy's threats of calling in the police. No one wanted to get mixed up with them. Some of the younger women had men in the forces, friendlier with Angela now her husband would soon be facing the same dangers as their own, and Angela noted with slight horror that two of the group wore the black bonnets of widowhood. They had five children between them and she wondered at their fortitude.

'Oh they're tough all right,' Mary said when Angela commented on this as they made their way home. 'And we must be tough too. I am ashamed of myself crying and carrying on so when Barry was only going for training.'

'Ah but...'

'Don't make excuses for me, Angela,' Mary said. 'I spoke to a lady back there with a black arm-band on. Her and her husband were married years with no sign of a child. In fact the woman said to me she thought she was past the age of childbearing and when her periods stopped she thought she was in the change. But she wasn't and she gave birth to a son. They knew there

281

could be no more and so this son was very precious to them both. He was the light of their lives, their reason for living and yet though they were proud of him as he marched off to war, they worried about him too. They began to say the rosary every night, like making a pact with God to keep him safe, but maybe God wasn't listening for whatever way it was, he was killed in late November.'

Angela had tears in her eyes as she said, 'How do they go on after such devastating news?'

'I asked her that,' Mary said. 'And she said that they go on because it's what their son would want them to do. I hope we are never asked to make that sacrifice, but if we are we must be strong, as Barry would want us to be, and between us we have a child to rear and that child is special because she is part of Barry.'

Angela thought this wasn't the time to tell Mary she didn't just want part of Barry, she wanted all of him, hale and hearty to wrap his arms around her and hold her tight. And when the madness in Europe ended they could bring up their special child together.

Angela was to find anything could be borne if you have the right mind-set. She did miss Barry but his frequent letters sustained her. He couldn't tell her where he was, but he gave out enough hints for her to have a good idea that he was in Sutton Park. She remembered that last day often and it pleased her to think that she had seen the place where he would spend the weeks of training.

He could tell her little of what they were doing either, but she remembered what Stan had said

about his training. Stan astoundingly was proving himself a first-rate soldier. She imagined it would be a surprise to him too. He could tell her little about it, but leading a company of men safely through enemy lines after their officer was killed earned him three stripes on his jacket.

Barry seemed to be enjoying the training, getting on fine with the other soldiers and as there was much he couldn't say his letters were full of fun instead as he described his fellow soldiers and the camaraderie between them all.

Angela wrote to him about the death of George but most of her letters were more cheerful, things Connie said or a skill she'd mastered, or places Angela had taken her. She said nothing about the money problems she had. His contribution, which was going to be five shillings a week, had not come through yet. Even Mary, used to letting one shilling do the work of two, was finding it hard to stretch the money and also pay the rent.

Part of that was because the shopkeepers on Bristol Street where she now had to take her custom had upped their prices since before the war. 'I think it grossly unfair,' Angela railed one day, surprised how little there was in her shopping bag considering the amount of money spent. 'And you know another thing, you can't ask for tick in many of the shops. There are notices to tell you not to bother asking because "refusal often offends".'

'Really,' said Mary. 'Oh that's bad. That's the only way some people have to manage the pittance they get.'

'Don't I know it,' Angela said. 'Anyway that

means us as well. Though I have never had to ask for tick yet, I might be reduced to it now unless I do what I've been threatening to do and get a job. I've dithered because I don't want to work full-time, I would miss Connie so much and I think it's a lot for you too.'

'Don't you worry about me, Angela,' Mary said. 'I'm as strong as an ox and me and Connie can look after each other, can't we, pet?'

Connie didn't really know what they were on about, but she smiled anyway and said, 'Yeth' and Angela picked her up and hugged her. 'I'll have a word with Maggie when I see her tomorrow,' she said. 'She only gets eight shillings for a ten-hour shift five days a week packing meat pies and sausages and stuff and I know she's fed up.'

And Maggie was fed up. 'I've had enough,' she said almost as soon as they met the following morning. 'D'you know what the boss said yesterday morning?'

'No. What?'

'He said that we're doing important war work cos all the stuff we pack is for the troops. Anyway I said it was a shame it wasn't better paid then, when most war-related work was. All right so we're not making shell cases or bullets, but food is important to the troops too. After all they say an army marches on their stomachs.'

'Do they?'

'Yes. Haven't you ever heard that expression?'

'No.'

'It means... Oh it's obvious what it means,' Maggie said. 'Anyway this has decided me. I'm off to the munitions.'

'And I might be going with you.'

'You? I thought you said Barry didn't want you working there?'

'Maggie, given the choice I wouldn't work in those sort of places,' Angela said. 'But needs must. We really can't manage on the money. Even when Barry's extra five shillings filters through it will be little better.'

'Won't you miss this little one?' Maggie said indicating Connie. 'People tell me the hours are long.'

Maggie had brought Connie a game that one of her brothers had had that consisted of putting stiffened thickish cord through large wooden beads and Connie was concentrating so hard her little pink tongue was sticking out. Angela felt a rush of love for her and she answered fervently, 'I will miss her like mad, but the war can't last for ever.'

''Course it can't,' Maggie said assuredly. 'And we've got to deal with the here and now. Another reason I'm going is because of our Mom. See I'll be twenty soon and our Syd is just two years behind me and I reckon he will get called up sometime this year and our Mom will miss his money, so it will help if I am earning a bit more. Mind you,' she added fiercely, 'we wouldn't be sailing so close to the wind all the time if my father hadn't got such a thirst on him.'

Angela said nothing for it was well known Maggie's father liked his hooch and he was a regular down The Swan and they sometimes heard him sing his way home on Friday and Saturday nights.

'Anyway,' Maggie added, 'I will help while I am

at home while I wait for my knight in shining armour astride a white horse to ride off with me into the sunset.'

'Oh yeah,' Angela said. 'Is this likely to happen sometime soon and is his name going to be Michael?'

'That would be telling,' Maggie said.

'Well he asked you to write to him.'

'Yeah and that's what I do, write to him,' Maggie said. 'And so far he hasn't said the magic words and proposed, but it's always best to be prepared.'

'You are a fool,' Angela said fondly.

'Takes one to know one,' retorted Maggie and their eyes met and they both burst into laughter. Connie looked up, in astonishment and for Maggie and Angela it was as if the years had rolled away and they were girls again at St Catherine's School. And Angela knew working in the munitions with Maggie would be much better than working without her, so when she said, 'Shall I make some enquiries then?' Maggie nodded her head. 'Do,' she said. 'It's no good putting it off.'

Mary was reluctantly relieved at Angela's decision for they couldn't survive on what they had coming in, but she was worried from a safety angle. 'It can't be that bad,' Angela said. 'There's plenty of people at it. Anyway no one seems to be really safe in this war. Look at those bombs that fell in London last week. They killed people and injured more and they were only going about their lives like everyone else when they were blown to bits.'

'Oh yes,' Mary said. 'That was really dreadful. I

am really scared they might drop one of those horrible bombs in Birmingham.'

'I know,' Angela said. 'And I'm doing my bit to stop them because the soldiers can't fight if they have nothing to fight with. I will only be making munitions as long as the war lasts and it can't last for ever. And think of the money we can save during that time. So if Barry has a time finding a job after the war it won't be a disaster but if he goes straight back to his old job that money can be used for something else.'

'Like what?'

'Connie's education,' Angela said. 'If she is bright enough Barry wants her to matriculate and go on further than that if she can.'

'And what happens when you have a houseful of children?' Mary asked. 'Surely you're not intending bringing her up as an only child?'

Barry had said his mother must never know his views on limiting their family. It was against the Church's teaching and she would never understand and so Angela just said, 'We'll cross that bridge when we come to it. But more importantly for the moment, Mammy, is that you understand why I have to go for this job?'

'I do see that we've all got to do the best for our families and that's what you are trying to do. But I shouldn't tell Barry till you are actually working at the place. He didn't tell us about him enlisting till the deed was done so you can do the same.'

'And what of Stan or Barry's brothers who write regularly?'

Mary shook her head. 'They need to know nothing either,' she said. 'The time has come when

women have to make their own minds up about their lives and not to look to their men's approval because most of them won't be around to give it or not. No, Angela, you take your job and we'll keep it to ourselves as long as we can.'

TWENTY

The Boss of the munitions factory, Mr Potter, had been clear about the rules when Angela was interviewed for the job. 'Everyone clocks in as soon as they arrive,' he'd said. 'And lateness is not tolerated. If a person is up to fifteen minutes late, they lose half a day's pay. The gates are closed at 6.15 and anyone arriving after that time will not get in and will not be paid for that day at all.' Then he fixed Angela with a beady eye and went on, 'In this industry we carry no passengers and can have no slackers or late-comers for it affects the output of the whole team. Now what you will do here is important work, for our troops cannot fight effectively without the means to do so. We expect our workers to realize the importance of what they do, arrive on time and work hard but carefully, for mistakes can mean accidents. Now are you up to that Mrs... Mrs...?'

'McClusky,' Angela finished for him. 'And yes I'm ready for it or I wouldn't be here.'

'I see you have a young child,' he said, scrutinizing the form she had filled in. 'Have you adequate care arranged?'

'Oh yes,' Angela assured him. 'I live with my mother-in-law. We have discussed it and she is quite willing to mind the child. My husband is training for the army and she knows as well as I how desperately the money is needed.'

'Well that seems all in order,' Mr Potter said. 'We'll see you bright and early on Monday morning.'

Angela never forgot her first day at the factory. She was always an early riser, but five o'clock was earlier than she usually rose, so Mary gave her the alarm clock that usually stood by her bed. When it shrilled out in the dark morning, she shut it off immediately, worried that it might have wakened Connie, but the child just murmured in her sleep, turned over with a sigh and slumbered on.

She had left her clothes ready on the chair beside the bed. She reached for them in the dark and carrying them and her boots in her arms she crept downstairs to dress. She also made a cup of tea and spread bread with marge and a smear of jam for she didn't know when she might eat again. Anyway it surely was not at all sensible to go to work hungry for she imagined you needed to keep your wits about you and a steady hand dealing with explosives.

As arranged, Maggie was waiting for Angela at the bottom of Grant Street and they greeted each other as they scurried down Bristol Passage to catch the half-five tram at the stop just around the corner on Bristol Street to take them to town. The ride was only a short one and usually they would walk such a distance easily, but once the tram reached the city centre they had to make their way

to the Bull Ring and cross over it to Deritend where the factory was and they couldn't risk being late.

It was strange walking around the dark and almost silent town, the gas lamps throwing pools of light now and again and the only people they met were groups or pairs of women obviously, at that time in the morning, walking to a job of work the same as they were.

Strangest of all was to look down on the Bull Ring, usually a centre of bustle and busyness and often tumultuous noise. Then Angela realized it wasn't completely silent for though the shops were shut, the barrow boys were running up the cobbled hill. The rumble of the carts they pushed and their boots were the only sounds in the early morning as they parked their carts according to the dockets in their hands. Many of the costers shouted over to the two girls or gave them a cheery wave as they carried on down the hill. 'A barrow boy was telling me once a pitch by the Market Hall opposite Woolworth's is the best place,' Maggie said.

Angela nodded for she had heard the same. The Market Hall was an impressive building. A set of wide stone steps was in front of it with gothic pillars at the top of the steps and beautifully decorated arched windows all around and as they passed it Angela remarked, 'It seems strange to see those steps without a scattering of people on them.'

'Ah, yes,' Maggie said because often men injured by this still-raging war would sell bootlaces and razor blades and the like from trays hung

around their necks and sometimes groups of them fair littered the steps. 'Speaking of which,' Maggie said, 'I always feel sorry for them, poor souls.'

'You'd have to be real hard-hearted not to feel sorry for them,' Angela said. 'But one thing I do miss is having the flower girls around Nelson's Column.'

'And they used to have some round St Martins too,' Maggie said pointing to the attractive church built of honey-coloured bricks at the bottom of the hill. It was a lovely church, all the windows were of stained glass, but the frames themselves were ornate too and the main window had an elaborate pattern of weaved stonework across the top of it. Added to that the main church had a series of small towers surrounding it and a magnificent steeple in the middle. Then in front of the church a line of trees and a fence where the flower sellers used to stand if the area around Nelson's Column was full as it often was.

'Precious few of them about now,' Maggie said with a sigh. 'I asked my dad why not and his answer was that we can't eat flowers.'

'Well he had a point,' Angela said. 'Things are bound to be different when we are at war.'

They were through the Bull Ring now and out the other end hurrying along narrow dark streets as Maggie said, 'Oh I'll say. Would we be going out at the crack of dawn to make weapons if we weren't at war?'

'I'd say not,' Angela said. 'If I ever thought of my future I would never have envisaged that one day I would be working in a factory making

291

things for our chaps to kill others.'

'You nervous?'

'A bit,' Angela said, 'but more than nervous I'm sad.'

'Why?'

'Well because when you said the hours were long you were right. I mean six till six is bad enough, but Saturday morning was supposed to be voluntary, but then I read in the paper that there is a crisis, a shortage of shells, and that's what we will be making, artillery shells, so I think Saturday morning will be semi-compulsory, like they'll make life difficult for you if you don't do it.'

Maggie nodded. 'You may well be right and not just to be awkward, but because they really are worried about this lack of shells. Mr Potter intimated as much to me when he interviewed me and said that most girls don't moan about it because they see it as a sort of duty to help their loved ones at the Front.'

'I do see that,' Angela said. 'Of course I do, only I feel sad for the hours I will be away from Connie. Mr Potter asked me about the care I have organized for her and that isn't an issue. What is an issue though is that I'd like to see something of her too.'

'Poor Angela,' Maggie said. 'I do see what you're saying and just at the moment I can see no way round it.'

'Nor me,' Angela said. 'But these long hours are going to be a strain on Mary too. I mean I know Connie is lovely, but they are a handful at this age. The point is though even when it's all over

292

no one knows how hard life is going to be and if there will be enough jobs for all those returning soldiers, and that's why I thought it best to get a well-paying job and build a little nest egg for that rainy day that Barry was always so concerned about.'

'If it helps at all,' Maggie said, 'I think you are doing absolutely the right thing and Connie I'm sure will understand that when she is older.' There was no chance to say any more for they had reached the factory and as they went in through the gates, Maggie said, 'Remember we have to get that card and clock in straight away. I'm sure the other girls will put us right in what to do.'

And the girls might well have done, but their supervisor, who introduced herself as Mrs Paget, was waiting for them, and Angela looked at her slightly pinched features and her, sharp eyes and knew that she would miss nothing and also stand no nonsense. She was welcoming enough to Angela and Maggie though and showed them how to get their card from the rack on the wall, which was in alphabetical order, and put it in the slot beneath the large clock and pull the handle, and the time recorded was seven minutes to six.

Then Mrs Paget took them to the changing rooms where they changed into boiler suits, rubber shoes and hats. Neither girl had ever worn any form of trousers in their lives for it would have been considered fast and Angela thought it felt very odd to have her legs enclosed but she was to find that they were the most practical and comfortable article of clothing she had ever worn.

The other girls, all togged up, had left now and Mrs Paget said to Angela and Maggie, 'Every bit of metal has to be removed and put in that steel box on the table.'

'Everything?' Angela questioned. 'Even my wedding ring?'

'Even that,' Mrs Paget said and went on in explanation, 'We can't risk anything generating a spark.'

Angela saw the sense of Mrs Paget's words but she still hated taking off the wedding ring that had never been off her finger since Barry had put it there and taking the locket from round her neck and even the take-out kirby grips that helped keep her bun in place. With a barely perceptible sigh she dropped the items in the metal box with all the others followed by a number of grips from Maggie which she used to try and tame her curly locks. 'Good girls,' Mrs Paget said, but she'd been watching their faces and added to Angela, 'I know that was hard for you, but we have to insist because we can't take any chances with explosives.'

'I do understand,' Angela said. 'It's just that those things... Well you know they're special to me. What happens to them now?'

'Don't worry,' Mrs Paget said. 'They will be quite safe. This box will be locked away in the safe till the end of the shift. Now,' she said to both of them, 'will you be all right for tomorrow? I mean you know what to do and everything?'

Both girls nodded and Mrs Paget said again, 'Good. Now all you need are masks and gloves which must be fitted before you go onto the shop floor.'

Angela thought the gloves weren't bad but it seemed very strange to have a mask around her face, but she told herself they probably know what they are doing and everyone would presumably be dressed the same. Even Mrs Paget had her mask and gloves on as she led the way out of the room and along a metal meshed floor to a padded door. Despite the padding they could hear the thump of machinery before Mrs Paget opened it.

But oh, when she did open it, the noise was such that it caused Angela to recoil from it. She had never heard noise like it for it was all-consuming, the roars and clanks and screeches and thumps filled her brain and hurt her ears, but a nudge from Maggie caused her to take a step forward. There was no way she wanted to go into that factory, but her feet seemed to move of their own volition until she stood beside Mrs Paget at the top of the steps looking down on the workforce.

As she descended the stairs behind Mrs Paget, she marvelled that the women didn't appear bothered by the noise, nor the acrid, sour smell that had lodged in Angela's nose, nor the yellowy-grey swirling dust that was everywhere.

Her eyes felt gritty and dribbles of water started running from them down her cheeks. Then it was as if something caught in her throat and she began to cough and cough and cough till it was difficult for her to draw breath. She couldn't work in that place she decided. She'd never even been inside a factory before and she didn't particularly want to do so now either. She would get some other form of war work. Maggie would under-

stand and, catching sight of her panicky eyes above her mask, Angela thought there was a good chance she was feeling the same way, and if she did it would be even better and they could go together to some other place.

And then, she thought of Barry choosing to enlist as she chose to work in a munitions factory. How would it be for him if war wasn't quite what he expected so, when the order came to go over the top, he would ignore it and set off for home to choose something more suitable? The Army would take a very dim view of that and shoot him as a traitor.

Now she could walk away and do something else, but it was shells and more shells that were needed and someone had to make them, or the soldiers would be left unprotected. Was she the sort of person to do something else that suited her better although she knew what she was doing was not as vitally needed as making shells? The answer was obvious, of course she could not just walk away. She was no fragile flower and for better or worse she was sticking to making shells for the duration.

That evening Angela was so tired it was hard to put one foot in front of the other as they left the factory and crossed the almost empty Bull Ring, and Maggie admitted she was just as done in. 'I can't understand it,' Angela said. 'I used to work long hours in George's shop standing on my feet all day and I was often up and down the steps to fetch things down from the upper shelves so it's not that I'm unused to work.'

'Yes,' Maggie said. 'But Maitland's was a pleasant place to work, I'd say, and not a noisy one?'

'Well, no,' Angela said. 'But what's noise to do with it?'

'I think constant noise like that is hard to cope with,' Maggie said. 'It sort of drains you of energy. I mean did you still hear it through your dinner hour even though we were in the canteen?'

Angela nodded, but added, 'You might have a point and I think the heat doesn't help the tiredness either.'

She'd never felt heat like it when she had occasion to go near the furnaces. Not that you could go too close because they were heated white hot to soften the carbon sheets so that they could be made into a basic shell shape. They sizzled like mad when they were then placed in vast sinks of cold water and billows of steam rose in the air. And when the rudimentary shapes cooled they had be made smooth on the grinding machine before being filled with explosives and the detonators. But the heat from those furnaces permeated the whole factory, so by mid-morning, Angela could feel sweat running down her back.

'I suppose we'll get used to it,' Maggie said.

'Well all the others seem to,' Angela said.

'Yeah,' Maggie said. 'One of the women who's worked here since the beginning of the war asked me how I was doing in the dinner queue today. She said it's a culture shock to everyone at first because few women had worked in any sort of heavy industry before the war began. She assured me that we would get used to it and that we have to stick at it because our lads couldn't fight a war

with no shells. Mind you, she said when she saw this place first she nearly turned tail and ran.'

Angela smiled ruefully. 'I nearly did just that,' she admitted. 'I couldn't believe I was going down those steps into my idea of Hell.'

'I thought there was something wrong,' Maggie said. 'I was pretty unnerved myself to tell you the truth, but you were like a coiled spring. What stopped you taking off?'

'What the lads are going through, to be honest,' Angela said. 'I got to thinking that however bad it is in France, Barry will have to deal with it. Anyway, I didn't know how you felt about any of it and I could hardly ask you anything over the noise of the factory and in front of Mrs Paget. Anyway, come on, our tram's in and will I be glad to get the weight off my feet, even for the relatively short journey home.'

Angela thought it hard being away from Connie all day and she told herself she would make it up to her when she got home in the evening, but she found she was weary enough to be thankful that Mary had a meal ready, and she only had to sit up to the table and eat it, and that Mary had washed Connie and she was all ready for bed in her pyjamas, and firebricks wrapped in flannel were warming the cot. All she had to do after they had eaten was carry Connie up to bed and read her a fairy tale from the book her Uncle Colm had sent from America before tucking her in.

Downstairs Mary was anxious to know how her first day at the factory had gone, for Angela had said nothing in front of Connie and even to Mary

she played it down a little, though she mentioned the noise.

'Well that's no surprise for all factories are noisy places,' Mary said.

Angela nodded, 'I know, I just wasn't ready for the level of it. But almost as bad as the noise is the acrid stench. One of the women said when we stopped for lunch that the really awful smell was from the sulphur. She said it smells like rotten eggs and she was not wrong either and the yellow dust swirls in the air and gets everywhere. You should have seen my boiler suit before I changed to come home, it was covered and even stained my underclothes.'

'You wear boiler suits?' Mary said in amazement.

'It's the most practical thing,' Angela said with a slight shrug. 'And we have rubber boots and hats that all our hair has to be covered with.'

'Goodness!'

'And that's not all,' Angela said. 'Every bit of metal has to be taken off, so from tomorrow I'm going to be leaving my wedding ring and locket at home.'

'Surely to God they don't expect you to take off your wedding ring?'

Angela nodded, 'Everything, even grips in your hair.'

'But why?'

'It's safer that way, Mammy,' Angela said. 'Remember we're working with explosives and anything metal could potentially raise a spark. They can't take the risk. Today I had to leave them in a metal box they put in the safe until we're ready

for home so tomorrow and every day I'm at work I may as well leave them here.'

'I suppose so,' Mary said. 'I'll take good care of them, never you fear.'

'We have to wear a mask too,' Angela said. 'It's supposed to protect our mouths and noses, but the dust particles still get in and there's nothing to protect our eyes. Mine were streaming most of the day and the dust made me cough. Something else no doubt I will get used to. Oh and we wear gloves. I am glad of those because some of the carbon is quite rough when we get it first and also covering our hands means that we have fairly clean ones to eat our dinner.'

'Angela, it doesn't sound a safe or even healthy place to work,' Mary said. 'Could you not find something else? I'm sure that if you were to ask at Barry's works they would find a place for you. Maggie too most likely. I know the money won't be as good but...'

'It isn't the money alone, Mammy,' Angela said, 'though I admit it was the money attracted me first, but there is a shell shortage. Our soldiers are running out of shells. Making them isn't pleasant and I can't pretend it is, but fighting a war I shouldn't think is any picnic either. This way I feel I am really doing my bit for Barry and Stan and all the other chaps. It is important and essential work and we can't run away from it.'

'Do the other girls all feel the same way?'

'I would say the majority at least feel that way,' Angela said. 'I doubt the money alone would keep them there if they didn't feel they were making a difference.'

However it was tiring work because it was relentless and they were constantly under pressure to make more and more shells. Because of this she didn't keep late hours and Mary was never long after her seeking her bed either for she said Connie was the best early morning call in the world.

Angela had been at the munitions factory for five weeks when a letter arrived from Barry that chased all thoughts of tiredness and lethargy away, for he was coming home. The news was tinged with a little sadness for Angela knew it would be embarkation leave and yet she longed to see her beloved husband and hold him tight and feel his strong arms envelop her.

Barry was due to arrive on Thursday morning 25th March and he was returning the following Monday morning early and so as soon as Angela arrived at work that day she sought out Mrs Paget and asked for time off. She thought there would be no problem and so was stunned when Mrs Paget said she was very sorry but there was no time off allowed. Angela stared at her as if she couldn't believe her ears. 'It's my husband's embarkation leave,' she said.

'I understand that,' Mrs Paget said and added, 'I'm sorry.'

'It changes nothing that you are sorry,' Angela said angrily. 'This is about the husband I love, the father of my child that we haven't seen for weeks and when he returns to his regiment and they sail for France I might never see him again and you know that as well as I.'

'Of course I know,' Mrs Paget said. 'And you're

not the only person who has asked this and the answer has been the same. It's company policy recommended by the government. None of the women working here has had a holiday of any sort. If the crisis about the lack of shells eases, some time in the future, then we may be able to be more flexible, but at the moment they are the rules I'm afraid.'

Well it might be company policy but Angela didn't think much of it and she said, 'I'd like to see Mr Potter please.'

She could see Mrs Paget was annoyed for Angela heard her sharp intake of breath and her nostrils pinched together as she said tight lipped, 'Mr Potter is a very busy man, but I'm sure he will agree to see you if you need further clarification. You will find however that he will say the same as me and you must go in the lunch hour as we have wasted enough time on this already this morning.'

Angela had no option but to follow Mrs Paget to the factory floor. Maggie looked up when she spotted her on the steps. She'd been as excited as Angela who had showed her Barry's letter on the way to work that morning. She had known too that she was going to ask for the time off. The noise prevented speech but above the mask her eyes lifted in a query and she was surprised at Angela's unhappy eyes and the shake of the head.

Standing in the dinner queue she was able to tell Maggie only the bare bones of what had happened between her and Mrs Paget so she hadn't really discussed it with anyone when she was summoned to the office to see Mr Potter and she

went with a growling stomach and hoped they hadn't stopped serving by the time she returned.

And it did no good, for just as Mrs Paget had said, Mr Potter reiterated exactly what she had said and Angela used the same arguments to no avail. 'Look how many women we have in the workforce at any one time. What if many people wanted to spend time with loved ones bound for overseas? How would we go on if we allowed that and not fall badly down in the quota of shells we have to produce each week? We would be in trouble then, but that wouldn't worry me as much as the Army being short. You say your husband will probably be setting sail for France soon. Well it will be a short visit and an abortive one if he has no shells, because he cannot fight the enemy if he has nothing to fight with.'

Angela was still silent and so Mr Potter went on, 'Think of this from the other way round. Say you had a few days free and wrote and told him at the training camp, would you expect him to be able to go up to his Commanding Officer and be given time off to spend with you?'

'No of course not,' Angela said. 'But he's in the Army.'

'And so are you in a way,' Mr Potter said. 'The job you are doing is a very important one and one that carries responsibilities. Remember, the people who make the ammunition are just as important as the people who use it and they rely on us to produce the goods. Shortly your husband may rely on us and we cannot let our boys down. You do see that?'

Dumbly Angela nodded her head and Mr

303

Potter said, 'Good girl. And I'll tell you what I'll do, I'll give you Saturday morning off so you can have two full days together.'

It wasn't enough, not nearly enough, but Angela knew it was all she was going to get and so she thanked him and went back to the canteen to find Maggie had saved her a beef pie. It was cold but Angela was too hungry to care and as she ate she told Maggie what Mr Potter had said.

Both Mary and Maggie were astounded by the factory's lack of understanding. Angela had not told Barry she was making shells, just said she was doing war-related work and was deliberately vague. In this letter she admitted the truth and then he could quite see why the factory had taken the stance it had because they had been warned about the lack of shells. In fact they had had a pep talk the same day that Angela's letter arrived. The Commanding Officer, knowing the men were heading off to start their embarkation leave the following day, had them all assembled in the drill hall and explained he wanted to talk about the womenfolk they had left behind back home.

'Many of you have been brought up to respect and protect women and in particular mothers, wives, sisters, girlfriends, but all that has been turned on its head with this war. You are no longer around to protect them and they have not only coped with that, but many are out at work and are running the country in our absence, doing jobs only men have done in the past. They are also making virtually all the weaponry we use. Make no mistake, without them we would be lucky to win this war. So when

you go home, do not forbid them to work in these industries, tell them to take all reasonable precautions of course, but that's all. Support their efforts and tell them how valuable their work is and how proud you are of them, and you should be proud, for the women of this land have proved to be truly remarkable.'

With words like that ringing in his ears Barry thought he could do no other than be supportive of what his wife had chosen to do, just as he had chosen to fight, though the thought of his lovely Angela in a noisy, dirty, smelly factory secretly filled him with a horror that he knew he couldn't show for he had no right to do so.

The following morning Angela went to work reluctantly and then had to fight to keep her mind on the job for she kept thinking of Barry and wondering what he was doing. But she forced herself to focus for shoddy work could cause accidents and accidents in an explosives factory had to be avoided at all costs.

Barry in fact spent ages getting to know his daughter again who had changed so much in the weeks he had been away. Now going on for two, she was a little girl rather than a baby and knew a raft of words and sentences and used them constantly and was a regular little chatterbox and an amusing one. Her smile seemed to light up the whole room and sometimes she would sing the nursery rhymes or lullabies she had learnt from her mother or grandmother. Barry loved her so much he ached at the thought of saying goodbye

to her on Monday morning.

He took her with him when he went to meet Angela from work that night, and as the two stood in the road the lamplighter came round because the dusk was beginning to tinge the day, and Connie was very excited for she was seldom out in the dark and she danced from one foot to the other. Despite the gloom they had been spotted by one of the first women surging towards the gate. One woman shouted back over her shoulder, 'Handsome soldier waiting for some lucky lady.'

The cry was taken up by the women following. 'I bet it's Angela's husband,' called another. 'She said he was coming home on leave today.'

There was a collective sigh of sympathy for every woman there knew what that leave signified.

But Angela had heard them and was battling her way through and they parted to let her go and when she saw Barry she gave a cry of unadulterated joy and dashed across to him and as his arms went around her, just as she imagined they would, she put her arms around his neck and burst into tears.

She wasn't the only one for the naked love between the young couple was emotional for the others as well and especially Maggie, and they all knew that soon they would be parted again and no one knew what the future held for any of them.

It was Connie broke the spell. Fed up with being ignored, she let out a cry and Barry's response was to lift her into his arms and plant a kiss on her cheek. Then he lifted her onto his shoulders and extending a hand to Angela said, 'Shall we go home?'

'Oh yes,' Angela agreed. 'But I usually go home with Maggie,' she added as Maggie came towards them to shake Barry by the hand. She had heard Angela's words though and she said, 'But these are not usual times are they? Your time together is limited and I'd say you need to make the most of every minute, so tonight I will go for the tram on my own.'

'Oh, but...'

'But nothing,' Maggie said. 'I'm off and I will see you in the morning.'

'Let her go,' Barry said, putting a restraining hand on Angela's hand when she would have called Maggie back. 'Maggie is a very wise girl and she knows that I need time with my wife and child before I share them even with Mammy. I had thought to walk, unless you are too tired?'

The shroud of weariness fell from Angela and the aches in her feet and legs ceased to matter because to walk would give them more time together and what was a little discomfort measured against that?

As they walked Barry told Angela a little of what his life had been like since he had left. He talked of the scratchy uniforms and the route marches in boots that gave him blister on top of blister till an old hand told him to wee in the boots to soften them.

'Ugh and did you?' Angela asked, the look of disgust plain on her face.

Barry laughed as he caught sight of her face as they passed under a street lamp. 'You wouldn't look like that if you had seen the state of my feet, believe me I would have tried anything, so I did as

this old lag said and it worked a treat and the boots are more supple altogether and I wasn't the only one to take his advice either. Do you wear boots?'

Angela nodded. 'Um we do, but they're rubber ones,' and she went on to describe the care taken to ensure they were wearing nothing metal that might generate a spark. Barry was glad of the precautions for the girls' safety. 'I would say it's necessary,' he said. 'Shame about your wedding ring though.'

'It just seemed more sensible to leave it at home.'

'Oh yes I can see that. I'd love to see you in those boiler suits though.'

'What about your uniform?' Angela said. 'It's too dark to see it properly.'

'Oh wait till you see the shiny buckles and buttons that I have to polish every day. I don't see what point there is to it. T'isn't as if we are going to worry about such things in the heat of battle. The Sergeant said he wanted to see his face in our boots. For what purpose? They say the trenches are filled with mud and completely waterlogged a lot of the time, so it is a useless exercise unless we are going to have a quick polish of everything polishable before we go over the top.'

A mental image flashed through Angela's brain of Barry climbing out of the relative safety of the trench to meet a hail of bullets from the other side. She shut her eyes against the scene and felt tears stinging them as she said, 'Don't.'

'What?'

'Talk about going over the top.'

'Angela that's what will happen. It's what I'm

308

training for.'

'I know that,' Angela said. 'And don't you think I'll have time enough to think of that when you are gone? Do we have to spoil the few days' leave you have discussing it now?'

Barry could see the level of Angela's distress and he said, 'You are right, no more war talk.'

Barry saw Angela's shoulders sag in relief and he was glad he hadn't told her how they were shown how to fix a bayonet to the barrel of a rifle and then charge at a straw-filled dummy bellowing and roaring like some sort of wild beast. 'And when you have the bayonet right in, give it a twist before you pull it out and you will have gutted him good and proper,' the Sergeant said.

It had made Barry feel quite sick and he said later back in the barracks, 'I don't think I could do that to another human being.'

'Haven't you learnt anything, McClusky?' a fellow soldier said. 'They are not human beings they're the enemy.'

'Yes, but...'

'There ain't a but, not in this,' said another soldier. 'Tell you straight, if it was him or me, I'd make sure it was him and if he touched my family, like they'd done in Belgium, I'd pull his guts clean out and lose no sleep over it.'

'Penny for them,' Angela said and jerked Barry out of his reverie.

'Sorry,' he said. 'And they're not worth a penny. Good job we're nearly home for Connie seems to be dropping off on my shoulders.'

Barry's words caused the drowsy Connie to jump and she said mulishly, 'Not tired.'

Barry's twinkling eyes met those of Angela and he said, 'Are you not, young Connie? Well in that case I think you can walk the last few yards home.'

When he let her down on the street though, she stumbled and would have fallen had Angela not caught up her hand. Barry caught up the other one and they swung her home and arrived through the door full of laughter and Angela stored such memories in her heart.

It was the first time that Angela had a real good look at Barry. In the light from the gas lamps she felt a thrill of pride run through her because he was so incredibly smart in his uniform. There was something about his manner too, he held himself straighter so he appeared taller. Even his walk was different, all those route marches Angela supposed, and if anything she loved him more than ever.

But if she thought Barry had changed Barry thought Angela had turned into a woman he hardly recognized. He had left behind a young girl and came back to a woman, and what's more a more self-assured and confident woman, and where once she would have always deferred to him, he could guess that she would no longer do that for now she had to make decisions for herself. He was immensely glad the Commanding Officer had taken time to warn all those going home how life had changed for the families and particularly the women left behind, for in his heart of hearts he wasn't sure he liked the new Angela. He knew he could never say this to her, but he was used to being the master in his own

house and he appeared to be that no longer.

On the other hand, he was immensely proud of Angela for the way she had coped and taken up the reins of the house and worked long and arduous hours to put food on the table and pay the rent, and though the job was dirty and exhausting she was glad to do it because it was essential to the war effort, and he knew whatever personal misgivings he might have, he would say nothing about them and only tell Angela how proud he was of her.

Angela was not used to being overly praised by her husband and was a little embarrassed, but even allowing for the fact she had changed considerably Barry was unprepared for what she said later as they sat before the fire with their last cup of tea before bed. Barry had asked her what she did in the factory and she had told him and then added, 'I can't ever say that I think war could possibly ever be a good thing and I know so many have died and we at home have tasted tragedy and suffered loss already and still it goes on. And yet this job, that I would never have done had the country not been at war, has opened up new horizons for me.'

'In what way?'

'Well I suppose like learning to drive the petrol-driven trucks.'

Barry stared at her with his mouth open. And then repeated, 'You're learning to drive petrol-driven trucks?'

Angela nodded. 'Not on the road yet,' she said. 'I started off in the warehouse just learning how all the controls on the truck work and how they

control the engine.'

'Control the engine,' Barry repeated again. 'God I'm beginning to sound like Little Sir Echo, but this is mind-boggling. Do I take it that you actually know how a petrol engine works?'

'Basically yes,' Angela said. 'Sometimes mechanics are hard to find and if you are stuck miles from anywhere and your truck breaks down, you need to be able to get it going again as quickly as possible, especially if it's stacked with shells that are needed somewhere.'

'Oh I agree with that,' Barry said. 'But you don't ride on the roads you say?'

'No, I've had to practise in the yard till they were confident I'd got the hang of it,' Angela said. 'But they said last week that I'll be all right to go out soon, this week probably.'

'Well I think you're a marvel,' Barry said in admiration. 'What d'you think, Ma?'

'I'll tell you straight I wasn't for it at first,' Mary said. 'I thought it was too dangerous hauling those shells about the place, but Angela said that it was no more dangerous than what she was doing every day; shaping them and filling them with explosives and this way at least she gets out of that smelly, dirty factory.'

'I see what Mammy's saying,' Barry said. 'But you will take care won't you?'

'Of course I will,' Angela said. 'I have no wish to blow myself to Kingdom come. But just now I must seek my bed for the morning is not that far away.'

TWENTY-ONE

The next morning Angela just bit back a groan as the alarm went off. It had roused Barry too and he stretched out his hand and murmured, 'Morning, Mrs McClusky.'

'Hush,' whispered Angela. 'You'll wake Connie and she wakes up early enough without an alarm believe me.' And so saying she gave Barry a kiss on the cheek, slipped out of bed and gathering her clothes in her arms and went downstairs to dress as she did every morning.

She was just making a cup of tea when Barry entered the room and Angela turned in surprise, 'What are you doing up?'

'I wanted to say a proper goodbye to my wife, what's wrong with that?'

'Nothing,' Angela said. 'It's just so early.'

'Angela I'm a soldier,' Barry said. 'We can be up at any time and sleep on a clothes line, near enough. Come on and wet that tea and come and give me what I left my bed for.'

Angela melted into Barry's arms with a sigh of contentment. 'I really wish they had given me the day off,' she said. 'I really don't want to go in today.'

'I know,' Barry said. 'I have the feeling it will be the hardest thing in the world to leave you on Monday. I must though or they would shoot me as a traitor and a coward.'

Angela sighed as she said, 'Mr. Potter said our job making the shells was just as important as the soldier firing them.'

'He's right too,' Barry said. 'Now you give me that kiss I have been waiting for, and be on your way, and I will be at the factory gates when you finish.'

The kiss could have been their undoing, but for the thought that Maggie would be waiting on the road and Angela knew she had absolutely no right to risk her being late. Barry quite understood that but when he released her he was breathless and Angela moaned and her whole body yearned for more. 'Hold on to it until tonight,' he advised.

And Angela had a broad smile on her face as she lifted her coat from the peg for they had made love the previous night, although Barry had been hesitant, knowing how tired Angela was. Angela wouldn't hear of it, knowing they had to squeeze every last second from their brief time together.

'You all right?' Maggie said as the two girls met.

'Fine. Why?'

'You're just going round with a dirty great grin on your face that's all,' Maggie said as they hurried down Bristol Passage. 'I was expecting you to have a face on you that would sour cream, having to go in today.'

'No point being like that is there?' Angela said. 'I mean I said it to Barry and he sort of said that lots of people have to do things they don't like when your country is at war. However hard it is for him to leave on Monday, if he didn't he'd be shot as a traitor, but a real rollicking is all we'd

get. So having made the decision to come in, it's not fair to make everyone else's life a misery because of it.'

'Mighty glad to hear that,' Maggie said. 'Good, here's the tram. This March wind is a bit bleak at this hour of the morning.'

Maggie was right and Angela tucked her scarf well around her neck when they left the tram to walk across the town to the factory. She was glad to reach the shelter of it because as she'd walked across the Bull Ring she'd felt as if she had been blown to bits.

She wished the day to speed by, but never had she known a day to pass so slowly and many a time she felt her mind wandering, imagining what Barry was doing and yearning to be with him and she constantly forced herself to concentrate.

Eventually though the endless day drew to a close and at the gate Barry was waiting for her, but alone this time. 'Where's Connie?'

'At home,' Barry said. 'Mammy was getting her ready for bed when I left, though she said she will keep her up till we get in. She was exhausted, but then I've had her out most of the day.'

'Oh it's lovely to be spending so much time with her,' Angela said as she waved Maggie off towards the Bull Ring and took hold of Barry's arm.

'Well I have to make the most of every minute don't I,' Barry said. 'Anyway it's no hardship to spend time with Connie for the child is a joy to be with. But it suits me to have you to myself like this for I need to talk to you.'

'That sounds ominous.'

'No, it's nothing like that,' Barry said. 'It's just that I can't see a way round it. You know what they say about two heads being better than one?'

'What is it?'

'Well without putting too fine a point on it, Connie is getting too much for Mammy.'

'Has she said so?'

''Course not,' Barry said. 'Can you see Mammy admitting to that, especially when she knows how important it is?'

'Then I don't see what I am to do.'

'There aren't any part-time positions?'

Angela shook her head. 'No,' she said. 'All munitions jobs I have heard of are full-time. Some work shifts, I've heard. Any other than war work isn't so well paid and while the war lasts we do need the money. When the war is over and you are home again everything will be as it was before, but this is how it must be for now.'

No more was said about it though Angela did worry because she knew Mary was no spring chicken and as Connie grew she became more and more active and hard for Mary to keep an eye on.

When Angela arrived home she could see the lines of strain on Mary's face which was grey with fatigue and Angela's conscience smote her for not even noticing that until it was pointed out to her. Mary though was her usual self and greeted them warmly and bade them sit up to the table for she had a delicious meal ready for them.

Angela slept badly that night. She was tired and they had spent a lovely evening together after both Barry and Angela put Connie to bed. And when they went to bed themselves a little while

later, though Barry had loved her so tenderly, sleep still evaded her. She had been bothered at what Barry had said about his mother and annoyed that she hadn't spotted it herself and yet, if she had noticed, what could she have done? What could she do now?

However, she knew the sleeplessness was also caused by the thought that on Monday morning her husband would march off to war and she might never see him again. She couldn't stand it! It was too much to ask! The thought of losing Barry tore at her heart, and yet she knew she would have to stand it. He wouldn't be the only beloved husband and father at the Front and she knew she would have to cope as every other woman had to. But when he went away she knew one part of her heart would die.

Tired though Angela was, she was up early the following morning, not wishing to waste one minute of the short time they had left. After breakfast she made up a picnic for Barry and Connie and herself, and said Mary should have a day on her own to rest, and Barry said that they would bring in fish and chips for dinner and so she had nothing to worry herself about. His mother protested and said it was nonsense spending their money that way. But they both expected her to react like that so they paid no heed.

The morning was mild though a slight breeze was riffling through the trees as they made for Cannon Hill Park with Connie in the pram for it was a long trek for little legs. The day was a magical one and though poignantly sad for the

317

adults, Connie felt no constraint and when she was tired out from running around the grass with her daddy he took her to the playground. Barry helped his small daughter climb the steps of the high slide and come down in a whoosh, or pushed her as high as high on the swings or spun her so fast on the roundabout she was dizzy when she came off.

They had their picnic on a grassy incline overlooking the lake; Angela spread the blanket while Barry got out the sandwiches and as Angela sat she thought everywhere looked fresh and clean, the grass verdant green and the daffodils bright yellow in the borders. The sky was Wedgwood blue and the wind sent white fluffy clouds scudding across it and rippled the water, the low sun glinting on the waves. It was so beautiful, so peaceful and it was hard to believe that just across another small stretch of water, men were holed up in trenches shooting at one another. Barry was thinking the same thing and he said, 'Hard to believe we're at war isn't it?'

Angela nodded and said, 'It is indeed.'

'This is what we're fighting for really, so that we keep England like this, a green and pleasant land.'

'I know.'

'Some things are worth fighting for.'

Angela swallowed hard before saying, 'I know that too. I just wish that it wasn't you doing the fighting. But as it is, I wish we could stop time now here, just for a wee while.'

'I wish that too,' Barry said urgently. 'But as that won't happen at least I will take another

318

memory to sustain me when I am away.'

Angela sighed and lay back on the grass and closed her eyes.

'Connie and I are going to feed the crusts to the ducks,' Barry said. His words jerked Angela from her little doze and she said, 'Hold on to her then.'

She sat up and watched the two walk down to the water hand in hand, with their bag of crusts, and her heart constricted with love for them both.

Ducks fed, Connie seemed sleepy and so Angela lay her down in the pram and as they walked around the park, she dozed and Angela gave a sigh. It could have been contentment, but Monday morning was looming ever closer. 'Where are we going tomorrow?' she asked Barry and went on, 'Sutton Park might be nice now the weather is a wee bit warmer.'

Barry shook his head. 'Not any more,' he said. 'Not with the Army commandeering so much of it. I heard tell they were building a prisoner-of-war camp there too. Anyway I did most of my training there, so I saw plenty of it. The next time I want to go there is in peacetime, when I am home again for good.'

'Fair enough,' Angela said.

'There's something else as well,' Barry said. 'I know we have been trying to take the burden off Mammy by taking Connie out and about, not that that has been in any way a chore, but she might feel a bit neglected if we take off for the whole day on my last day home.'

Angela could see that, for trying to spend most of his precious leave with his wife and daughter

319

meant that he hadn't spent a great deal of time with his mother. 'We haven't worked up any sort of solution to Connie's care while I work,' Angela said.

'No,' Barry agreed. 'I suppose we'll have to leave things as they are for the time being.

'Well let's not spend any more time worrying about a problem we can see no way of fixing,' Barry said. 'I'm looking forward to feeding the inner man at the moment, so shall we head home via the chip shop?'

'Oh I should say so,' Angela said with a smile as she turned the pram around.

Next morning before Mass Angela saw Maggie in the porch. 'No point asking how you are,' Maggie said to Angela. 'You're like a cat that's got the cream.'

'Ooh it's been lovely,' Angela said. 'But it's Barry's last day and tomorrow he will be gone and I will be back at work and worrying about Mary.'

'What about Mary?'

'Barry thought she looked tired. I felt bad I hadn't noticed it myself because when I really studied her myself, he was right. It's no good asking her because she always claims she's fine, but really she's not. Barry thinks she might be finding Connie a bit of a handful.'

'Well she is a bundle of energy that child,' Maggie said with a chuckle. 'My own mother said just the other day that Mary was getting very tired looking. Why don't you put Connie in the nursery?'

'What nursery?' Angela asked.

'The one set up for mothers engaged in war work,' Maggie explained. 'Think there's one on Bristol Street.'

Angela would have asked more but the strains of the organ were heard and she had to join her husband and child for Mass was about to start, so it was after Mass she learned more. The nursery was free to mothers who were engaged in war work and they took babies from six months. 'How d'you know so much about it?' she said.

'From Sonia,' Maggie said. 'I was working with her when you were learning to drive in the yard.'

'Isn't she a widow?'

'Yeah and left with two nippers, three and just eighteen months,' Maggie said. 'She told me straight she couldn't feed and clothe them adequately if she didn't have the nursery and the kids love it. Sonia said they have three meals a day too.'

Barry joined them then with Connie in his arms and Angela and Maggie filled him in about the nursery and he was impressed. 'Sounds just the job,' he said and turning to his daughter he asked, 'Would you like to go to nursery, Connie?'

Connie didn't answer her Daddy but her eyes were perplexed for she didn't know the word.

'Nursery is a place where you will have lots of toys and children to play with.'

Connie's face was a beam of happiness. 'Yes,' she said. 'Me go.'

'Well she's easily persuaded,' Barry said.

'Barry, she is not yet two years old,' Angela said. 'Your mother will be a different kettle of fish altogether.'

And Mary wasn't at all keen on the idea. They didn't attempt to tell her anything until she had eaten a good Sunday roast dinner when she might be feeling a little more compliant. Angela put Connie to bed for a rest so that Mary could have their undivided attention but the strategy didn't work all that well for they had barely begun to explain when Mary snapped, 'I am not in my dotage totally you know.'

'We know you're not,' Angela said soothingly, 'and no one is suggesting you are, and it isn't as if you are not doing a good job, because you are. But I don't want you to make yourself ill with exhaustion.'

'Well I won't, will I, looking after one small granddaughter?'

'Mammy they're very tiring at this age,' Barry put in.

'D'you think I don't know this when I've had a fine big family of my own?'

'Mammy things were different then,' Barry said.

'All I ask is that you let her try it?' Angela said. 'If she is unhappy she needn't stay.'

'And what will I do all day when she is away at this nursery place?' Mary demanded.

'You could always rest more, take it easy you know?' Barry said.

'I'll have rest enough in my box,' Mary growled and then looked at Angela accusingly. 'You said you needed me, that you couldn't do this job without me.'

'Mammy I swear to you I had never heard of this nursery until today,' Angela said. 'But I will probably still need you because it's unlikely they

will open to cover the hours I work or Saturday mornings. I will have to find that out, but I think I will still need you to take her there in the morning and fetch her home in the evening.'

'And how will you be able to find anything out about this nursery when you are working all day every day?'

'I'll take the day off.'

Barry gasped. 'I thought you couldn't have days off just like that?'

'You can't,' Angela said. 'And I'll likely get into trouble for it, but I don't care. What's the alternative anyway?'

Barry had so wanted Angela to come and see him off at the station, but knowing the situation he hadn't asked. And now, because she had to check out the nursery, she would be able to see him off properly first.

But then Angela said, 'Even before this business with the nursery, I had a mind to defy Mr Potter. I think it is unreasonable to expect us to just carry on as if something momentous isn't happening in our own lives. And I can think of nothing that will change my life more than when my husband steps on that train on his way to fight in a war. I will try hard to hold the tears back, but I will be upset and sometimes that makes me all jittery inside, and for the job I do you need a steady hand, and I doubt my mind will be on the job either and it would be easy make a mistake, and a mistake in a munitions factory can be fatal. I think it will be far better and safer for me to stay away from the place the day you leave.'

'I think you do right,' Mary said. 'It shows a

lack of compassion in your employers to not understand that.'

Barry said nothing, too choked by Angela's words, but when his arms went around her and his lips met hers words weren't necessary.

Connie was shouting and Barry went to fetch her and as he came down, he said to Angela, 'Let's see if we can find this nursery and not have you searching for it tomorrow and take Connie down to the canal later to see the barges.'

Angela was agreeable to this and they set off with Connie in her preferred place on her father's shoulders.

The nursery, called The Acorns, was the other side of Bristol Street over Pershore Road which was where Angela always turned down the other way on her way to Calthorpe Park, which was why she hadn't noticed it, especially as Maggie intimated that it was fairly new. It was a long low building and it had quite a large playground at the front and the windows Angela could see were decorated in some way. 'This is your nursery, Connie,' Barry said. 'What do you think?'

Connie gazed at it and then looked at her father who had told her about the children and toys at the nursery, but her tongue couldn't quite master the word children. 'Toys,' she said.

Angela knew what her daughter was getting at and she said with a smile, 'All the toys are inside.'

'That's because it's closed,' said Barry. 'Locked see,' he went on, lifting Connie and showing her the lock fastening the large metal gates together. 'When Mammy brings you tomorrow, it will be open and you can see it for yourself. Now we're

off to look at the canal.'

Connie was quite interested in the water though it was slightly brown and oil-slicked and had a pungent smell, but she was fascinated by the boats that her Daddy called barges. They were pretty and painted on the sides and moored to the rings on the towpath.

'Elephants and castles,' Barry said when Connie pointed out the painted barges. 'They always paint elephants and castles and don't ask me why because no one seems to know.'

'They are pretty though,' Angela said. 'Imagine having our house painted like that, Connie, because those barges are like people's floating houses where they live.'

'Tell you what,' Barry said. 'A few elephants and castles or any other damned design might cheer our back-to-backs a treat.'

Angela laughed. 'Barry, I don't think there is anything anyone could do to make those houses a bit cheerier. That would be a lost cause altogether.'

They walked along the towpath with Angela holding tight to Connie's hand and all was quiet and still. 'Because it's Sunday,' Barry said in a low voice. 'They're all resting up. I was hoping to see a barge going through the locks, but we're out of luck today. Shall we make our way home and give Connie a turn in the playground in Calthorpe Park on the way.'

Angela nodded. 'Well we are nearly at the entrance to it.'

However when they left the park there was a hurdy-gurdy man at the entrance with his barrel organ and monkey. He had a weather-beaten face

with two twinkling black eyes and he had on a well-worn dark-red jacket and black corduroy trousers tucked into well-cobbled boots. Angela was delighted to see the monkey was dressed too and more flamboyantly in black and white striped trousers, a red shirt and a black waistcoat with a felt hat on his head.

Connie's eyes opened wider still when she spied the monkey, and then the barrel organ started to play and the monkey danced up and down on top of it as Connie clapped her hands in excitement. The music brought a fair crowd. Other children playing in the street left their games and others came out of their houses and some adults too, all clustered around the hurdy-gurdy man listening, tapping their feet to the music, some humming along and some clapping the beat and everyone laughed at the antics of the lively monkey.

The music drew to a close and there was a ripple of applause and then further laughter as the monkey took off his hat and proffered it to collect donations. Many then turned regretfully away, but Barry dropped three pennies into the hat before they too left the hurdy-gurdy man and turned for home.

Seeing the hurdy-gurdy man was the high spot in Connie's life and when they arrived home, she tried with her limited vocabulary to explain to her grandmother, her obvious delight keeping them all entertained especially when she tried to copy the dances the monkey did.

Much later and with Connie in bed, closely followed by Mary, Angela was putting the last few bits in Barry's kitbag when she said, 'D'you

think you'll see much of Stan when you're over there?'

She had so hoped this was the case because Stan was a Sergeant now and so might be more protected than the ordinary privates, and with Stan a friend of the whole family and with him not wanting Barry to go in the first place, maybe he could see a way of keeping him safer.

However, Barry dashed those hopes straight away. 'The Western Front goes for miles and miles,' he said. 'Involving thousands of soldiers. Unless we had joined together into the same Pals Regiment I think the chance of finding an individual soldier a very slim one.'

'But he's a Sergeant now.'

'And so are countless others,' Barry said. 'And my time is not my own don't forget. I doubt I can wander around on my own asking questions, which is not a very safe thing to do in wartime anyway, and it would be frowned on for a private to be too friendly with a superior. Whatever you were in civvy street has to be left in civvy street. My fellow soldiers would probably see it as toadying up in the hope of getting special privileges. And it wouldn't do Stan any good either, the others might easily think he was the other way, you know?' Barry finished with a wink and a jerk of his head.

'No I don't know,' Angela said, completely perplexed. 'What are you on about? Other way from what?'

Barry sighed, 'If an older soldier took too much interest in a young private, they might think he was the sort of man who likes men the same way

that most men like women.'

Angela was totally shocked for she hadn't known there were any men like that and at the thought of it she felt the heat flood her face and knew her cheeks would be crimson with embarrassment as she said, 'Oh surely not?'

'Oh it's a distinct possibility,' Barry said. 'And proof isn't needed. Just a hint of scandal like that and Stan's life would be ruined. So you see it's better that we don't meet at all.'

'I do indeed,' Angela said.

'And now we have talked enough,' Barry said. 'I want a special memory to take with me when I march out tomorrow.' He took Angela by the hand as he spoke, but she made no protest as he led her to the stairs and they went up hand in hand.

TWENTY-TWO

The smoky steam-filled station was full even at that hour and Angela saw she wasn't the only one saying goodbye to her husband or sweetheart. Some had brought children, as she had brought Connie because Barry had wanted her there. And all the men were in uniform and some of the women were crying. Angela didn't blame them for she felt like doing the same, but iron resolve prevented the tears from trickling down her cheeks, lest they upset Connie.

Barry felt, as if his heart was breaking for he

was leaving behind the two people he loved best in all the world, and yet he couldn't in all honesty say he regretted his decision because it was not right for him to sit pretty at home while others risked their lives daily. 'This is it then,' he said as they walked towards the waiting train.

'Yes,' Angela said, her husky voice barely above a whisper.

Barry knew Angela was perilously near to tears and so to help her compose herself he picked Connie up into his arms. 'Now Connie,' he said, 'I want you to be a big brave girl for Daddy. Can you do that?'

Connie nodded her head and Barry went on, 'I must go away and I want you to be a big brave girl and look after Mammy.' Connie's eyes opened wide for she had never seen her father so serious before, but when he went on, 'Will you do that?' she nodded her head again and he placed her in Angela's arms and put his arms around them both and said, 'And Mammy will look after you too, until I come home again.'

Angela thought her heart was breaking into pieces as Barry said, 'That is the picture I want to take to France and the one I want to see when I come back, though you might not be in your Mammy's arms then, Connie, for you are a big girl now and it takes time to win a war.'

Angela gave Barry a watery smile but she did not speak for if she'd tried she'd have burst into floods of tears as many women were doing all around them. Barry knew there was no point in prolonging the parting any longer for it didn't help. And so with a sigh, he kissed his wife and

young daughter and boarded the train. He closed the door, for the guard was slamming the others, but slid the window down.

'I will say the rosary every night,' Angela promised, and God will protect you.'

'Aye,' Barry said with a wry smile, 'the bullets will bounce off me, or I may catch them in my teeth and spit them back.'

It was too much and Angela could no longer hold her tears in her brimming eyes and Barry leaned forward and kissed them as they trickled silently down her cheeks.

'All aboard.'

The last few stragglers got onto the train, the guard slammed the last few doors shut, there was an ear-splitting shriek and the engines began to throb. The guard then blew his whistle and stepped onto the footplate as the train began to chug its way out of the station and Connie and Angela waved until they could see Barry no more.

As she turned to leave the station Angela felt a sadness so deep it was as if she had lead weights attached to what was left of her heart. Connie noticed her tears and touched them gently with her finger. 'Cry?' she asked.

Angela swallowed the lump in her throat and said, 'No, it was just the smoke in the station making my eyes water. Now shall we go and see about this nursery for you?'

'Ooh yes,' Connie said, and Angela was glad she was distracted so easily and was too young to feel the loss of her father, for she imagined Mary's sorrow would be enough for her to cope with.

However that would be later because she had

told Mary she would go straight to the nursery after seeing Barry off. 'I only have this one day and I want to see around the place and talk to them and possibly put Connie's name down for they might not have a place right now.'

'Would they be open so early?'

'They're sure to be,' Angela said. 'They're for mothers doing war work.'

Angela was in fact pleased to have something to do after seeing her husband set off to join his regiment and presumably sail over to France in the very near future. She knew she couldn't break down, but must be strong for Mary and Connie as well as herself for she knew they must bear it the same as everyone else.

So she turned her energies to checking out the place where she hoped her daughter would be spending many hours of the day. She was delighted with the light airy rooms, and the staff who seemed to really care about the children, and the array of toys sent Connie into raptures.

The nursery was open from 7.30 to 6.30 so Angela would not be able to bring her or pick her up, but Mary wouldn't mind that so it wasn't a problem. Because many children came early and stayed till late they had breakfast at eight o'clock, a full dinner and pudding at twelve o'clock and a tea at four thirty, Mrs Cassidy the superintendent of the nursery said, 'And children of Constance's age will be put down for a nap after dinner.'

'That sounds wonderful, and the charges?'

'For women engaged in war work it's free, paid for by the government. You are doing valuable work and we are looking after your child so you

can continue to do that. I don't think I could ever work in a factory, but I am doing my bit this way.'

'And just as valuable work as mine I'd say,' Angela said. 'When could she start?'

'Well,' Mrs Cassidy said. 'The question is, is your daughter used to being left?'

'I don't know,' Angela admitted. 'I have only ever left her with my mother-in-law and that was all right until she got more active. My husband was on leave and he said it was getting too much for his mother.'

'Did she agree?' Mrs Cassidy asked with a smile.

'Not straight away no,' Angela said. 'My husband persuaded her and she listens to him. She will be the one bringing Connie and taking her back at the end of the day, because I work from 6.30 to 6.30, and when she sees this place I'm sure all doubts will leave her.'

'It's nice of you to say that,' Mrs Cassidy said. 'I was going to suggest that your mother-in-law brings her next Monday, just for the morning and stays with her. And then on Tuesday leave her to go shopping or whatever for a few hours, and gradually extend it so that she is ready to start full-time the following week. Not all mothers can do this but for those who can, we find the children settle quicker.'

'I don't think Mammy will have any problems with that,' Angela said.

And Mary didn't of course and was looking forward to seeing the place herself. But that was for the future; when Angela rose from bed on Tuesday morning she knew she was in for a telling off at the very least. 'And I have my answer

ready too,' she said when Maggie asked if she was nervous. 'Because for a start Mr Potter shouldn't be able to run our lives and tell us what to do.'

'He has the power to sack you.'

'Yes,' Angela said. 'And if he does how long do you think I would be out of work as an experienced munitions worker who can also drive?'

'I'd hate you to leave.'

'I've no intention of it,' Angela said. 'But I won't be treated as if I am Connie's age.'

So Angela wasn't surprised when Mrs Paget asked her to see Mr Potter before she began work and moments later she was standing facing him across the desk. 'I am very disappointed with you, Mrs McClusky,' he said.

'Oh,' said Angela. 'Why is that exactly?'

'I think you know why,' Mr Potter said testily. 'I explained how important the work we do is and that was the reason you could have no time off even though your husband was on leave, and you defied me.'

'Yes,' Angela said. 'I did.'

Mr Potter was a little taken aback by Angela's directness. 'And why is that?' he asked.

'Mr Potter,' Angela said, 'I am not claiming to be a special case, for many here love their husbands, but I have known mine since I was eighteen months old, as his parents took me in and brought me up when my parents and siblings died. I loved Barry as a brother before I loved him as a husband. He has been a big part of my life always and it was an inhumane request for me not to go to the station and kiss my man goodbye, knowing that I might never see him again. In fact if I had come in

333

I would have felt a failure as a wife, and just as importantly a hazard to myself and my fellow workers because I would be upset and my mind definitely not on the job in hand, and lacking in concentration can lead to accidents. I would say your directive is dangerous.'

Mr Potter was affronted. 'You, Mrs McClusky, are being presumptuous.'

'No. I'm not,' Angela retorted. 'I am talking sense. But I was off for another reason. When I began here my mother-in-law took on looking after my daughter, but she's not a young woman and it was getting too much for her and I had to find a nursery place for my daughter, or I would be standing before you now giving notice because my child-care arrangements had fallen through. Would you have preferred that?'

Mr Potter could find nothing to say to Angela because what she said made eminent sense, but the way she spoke to him was not exactly respectful. So he contented himself with saying curtly, 'You will of course lose a day's pay.'

'I expected no less,' Angela said. And then because Mr Potter's pompous attitude annoyed her she added, 'You're all heart.'

Mr Potter glared at her and Angela knew he would have liked to have given her the sack there and then, but he couldn't because she was needed. 'Will that be all?' she asked and he growled, 'Yes get back to work. You've wasted enough time already.'

'You've made an enemy there I'd say,' Maggie said when Angela told her what had transpired as they made their way home.

'Well that won't give me sleepless nights,' Angela said. 'It's the constant worry about Barry that's going to do that.'

Mr Potter had assumed that when confronted and accused of defiance Angela McClusky would have been apologetic, cowed even, and her assertive attitude had stunned him. After she had gone though, he had to concede that much of what she said made sense with regard to saying goodbye to loved ones and he vowed to be a bit more understanding in the future.

Angela was unaware of this and as far as she was concerned nothing had changed but she was far too busy to let it concern her unduly. On the home front there were no problems. Mary had been very impressed with the nursery at the first session when she had stayed with Connie. 'Not that she cared whether I was there or not,' she said to Angela that evening.

Mary was right and Connie who'd never before had so many friends to play with nor so many toys and she was in her element and settled to nursery as if she had been going to it every day of her life.

Angela wrote and told Barry all about it because he said he wanted to know all the news from home, however trivial, and everything concerning Connie. In his reply he included a copy of the photograph the army had taken for their records. Angela had already received a similar photograph from Stan who asked her to give it to Daniel if he didn't survive. Angela promised she would and put it away in the box where she kept the letters.

However, when Barry's came she took it to a

photographer in the town the first Saturday after-noon and had it enlarged, and bought a silver frame to put it in and it had pride of place in the bedroom. She was so glad to have it, not only for her own sake but also to show Connie the fine man her father was, lest as time passed, she might forget him. Every night Connie asked God to bless her Daddy and kissed his picture before settling down to sleep. And Angela had his picture before her each night as she knelt to say the rosary for she had made a bargain with God, a decade of the rosary every day in exchange for Barry's safety.

Mary too was glad to get a photo of her son for Angela had given her the original. And she too be-gan praying for his survival and safe return. Time hung heavy on her hands to begin with and she missed Connie sorely though she owned caring for her full-time had been a strain and yet without her she didn't know what to do with herself.

Angela encouraged her to rest, but Mary said resting had never been a major part of her life and anyway a person can have too much of a good thing and she was done resting now. However, few people need to be idle in wartime and she was soon engaged in knitting for the troops. It was a social event, arranged by the church and all the wool was donated and they knitted gloves, socks and a strange thing called a balaclava. Another day she rolled bandages for the military hospitals and on another she helped out at the canteen at the Barracks. That together with the shopping, cooking, cleaning and taking Connie to nursery and bringing her home again kept her happily

busy and made her feel she was doing something useful.

So life settled down to as even a keel as it could in wartime. Worry about Barry was always there like a nagging toothache and Angela was concerned for Stan too. Barry had written that he had seen no sign of Stan and as he had said it was highly unlikely they would meet up, Angela wasn't surprised. But she lived for Barry's letters for they at least showed he was alive.

Angela didn't know where he was, but by that time there was talk of a campaign at a place called Gallipoli and some other place called the Dardanelles and she supposed he could be involved there. But in the *Evening Mail* one night was a map showing the whole of the Western Front and she studied it for a long time trying to take in the vastness of it and could quite see why it was highly unlikely that Stan and Barry would ever catch sight of one another.

Connie continued to love her nursery and would have gone Saturdays and Sundays if it had been open and in just a few short weeks she was more independent and her speech had improved tremendously, so when her second birthday loomed, 24th May, Angela decided to have a little tea party for her birthday and invite some of her special friends from the nursery too. Her birthday was on Monday that year so Angela decided to have the party the day before. Mary threw herself into cooking for this special party and the centrepiece was a beautiful chocolate sponge cake. 'I don't know where you got all the stuff,' Angela said, surveying the table, for around the cake there were

iced biscuits, fairy cakes, ginger loaf, sausage rolls and scones, small sandwiches cut into quarters and a jug of homemade lemonade.

'It wasn't easy,' Mary said. 'It wasn't like before the war when you could just go to any shop and get everything you would need, now you have to pop from one shop to another and buy up what they have on the shelves.'

'Oh don't you miss George at times like this?'

'Yes I do,' Mary said. 'I would have probably got everything in Maitland's shop because, like you always said, he was a man of integrity and didn't sell to the nobs and leave his regular customers in the lurch like so many are doing.'

'I do miss him still,' Angela said. 'He was always so good to us and I wish he hadn't had to die like that.'

Mary nodded. 'Me too. Nagged to death, poor soul. Still they got their come-uppance. What goes around comes around they say.'

'Mammy what are you on about?' Angela said, perplexed.

'Oh I forgot to tell you,' Mary said. 'Some woman at the Knitting Club was telling me that Matilda and that sister of hers Dorothy bought a house in Pershore Road, near to this woman, and she said that Dorothy had a stroke not long after they moved in and she is completely helpless and Matilda has to do everything for her.'

'No!' Angela exclaimed, a bit ashamed of the smile on her face.

Mary nodded. 'It's true enough,' she said. 'See, Matilda wanted to get Dorothy taken to the hospital, but they told her straight they hadn't the

space, or beds, or doctors. She was telling this woman all about it. Doesn't do to be sick now because most common wards are earmarked for casualties from the war and many doctors have joined the Medical Corps and are serving overseas and nurses the same.'

'You know I never thought of that.'

'Apparently they have these women called VADs in some places, it's the Voluntary Aided Detachment and these are girls and women over the age of twenty-three from posh homes who don't need to be paid and they're there to help the nurses. But I heard lots of those have gone to the Western Front as well.'

Angela nodded. 'I read about that in the paper. A lot of these posh folk were in the suffragette movement before the war and they stopped all campaigning once war was declared to help in the war effort.'

'Well since war was declared women have done so much they are virtually running the country, which I would say has done more to advance their cause than all the protests and demonstrations they made before it.'

'You could be right,' Angela said. 'And they're game enough. The nurses say they couldn't run the hospitals without them and it's pretty stalwart of them to travel to France to work in the field hospitals. They must see some horrific sights and it's not exactly safe and yet I can't help wondering if they see it as a bit of an adventure too.'

'D'you think so?'

'Yes I do,' Angela said. 'I think I'd feel that way for these girls were very constrained before, they

had to be chaperoned everywhere and there were so many things they weren't allowed to do. Even now they can't be paid.'

'Oh that's because if they were paid, it would bring shame on their fathers because people would say their fathers couldn't afford to keep them.'

'That's exactly what I mean,' Angela said. 'But really whatever reasons they have for doing it matter less than the good job they are doing as general nursing aides freeing the trained medical staff to attend where the injuries are more severe. I mean, I'd like the best doctors and nurses out there treating Barry if he was injured, and Stan as well.'

'I agree,' Mary said. 'And it means that Matilda has to care for her own sister.'

'And with anyone else I would feel sorry for them having to do that,' Angela said. 'But with those two horrible people I can't help feeling it serves them right.'

'Don't blame you, girl,' Mary said. 'Cos I felt a bit the same. Anyway without Maitland's I did get all the stuff I needed for the party in the end and Connie's delight made it all worthwhile.'

And Connie was in a fever of excitement and so were the four little girls she had invited from the Nursery. Two of the mothers worked making shells at the same place as Angela and Maggie, and Maggie popped in too and so it was a merry little party. And when Angela watched the children sing Happy Birthday to Connie she felt a surge of happiness and stored it all in her head and her heart to tell Barry in her next letter.

TWENTY-THREE

Both the spring and summer of 1915 were in the main warm and sunny and it was even warmer in the factory and although Angela like all the rest stripped down to her underwear under her boiler suit, after just a short time in the factory her face would be red and glistening and she would feel beads of sweat running down her back and by the time she had finished her shift her clothes were usually sticking to her.

She knew she was luckier than many, because sometimes she had the opportunity to get out of the factory and drive the lorries which was a lot more pleasant. But she was always grateful for the bowl of warm water Mary had ready for her at home as well so she could wash herself all over before, she ate. She knew she owed Mary a lot for though she worked long hours, life would be much harder for her if she had to cook a meal when she got in every evening and somehow manage to shop and clean as well.

The nice weather did mean though that almost every Sunday and sometimes Saturday afternoon too she could go somewhere nice with Connie. She valued the time spent with her a great deal as she saw so little of her generally.

But the summer passed and by the time Christmas was approaching the summer was just a

memory. She was driving more now which she thought far more interesting than making shells ad infinitum. She had tried, to get Maggie to take a driving course but she said she was too scared and she tried to encourage her again one day as they travelled into work in mid December. 'I'd crash into something,' Maggie said.

''Course you wouldn't,' Angela said. 'Why would you do that? You steer with the wheel and there is a brake if you feel you are too close and you can go as slow as you like to start with.'

Maggie shook her head. 'It's never been something I've ever wanted to do.'

Angela laughed. 'Well I bet making shells wasn't on your list of things to do either.'

'Well no, 'course it wasn't, but the money's good.'

'But this is an opportunity that we wouldn't have any other time,' Angela said. 'This is a dreadful war, the casualty figures are scary and I wish Barry and Stan were not involved at all and I wish the country had not emptied itself of men, but it has and we couldn't stop it. And because that has happened women have had the opportunity to do things we have never done before and driving to me was just one more thing. I never in my wildest dreams thought I would get behind the wheel of a truck and drive it to factories and distribution depots all over the place. I couldn't pass up the chance and I'm glad I didn't because I love it.'

'I know you do,' Maggie said. 'But it really isn't for me so stop bullying me about it.'

Angela grinned. 'All right,' she said. 'You have

got a point. I have been badgering you and it isn't fair. If you really don't want to learn to drive that should be your choice.'

Maggie sighed with relief and to change the subject a little asked Angela if she'd finished the Christmas Boxes for Barry and Stan. 'More or less,' Angela said. 'Still it will be a funny old Christmas with just Mammy and myself. If it wasn't for Connie I wouldn't be bothered putting up decorations or anything.'

'Well it doesn't give a person much heart when they just have the one day off.'

'I know. Stingy lot,' Angela said. 'Mammy couldn't believe we just had Christmas Day.'

'Mmm,' Maggie said. 'I suppose what you have got to tell yourself is that fighting men don't even get that and me and our Mom will be filling our own Christmas Box next year.'

'Syd?' Angela said for that was the name of Maggie's eldest brother.

Maggie nodded her head. 'Only turned eighteen a few weeks ago. Mom's cut up about it but there's nothing to be done. He must go like the rest.'

'Does he mind?'

'I'll say not. He can't wait, silly fool,' Maggie said. 'He thinks it's like some Boy Scouts' Jamboree. He's trying to hide it from Mom but I know our Syd.'

'I suppose it's better that he's keen rather than the other way round when he has to go anyway,' Angela said.

'Maybe you're right,' Maggie said. 'They don't hang about. Provided he passes his medical, he

will be in before Christmas.'

'That's not that far away now,' Angela said. 'And then the turn of the year. I wonder what 1916 will bring, the end of the war perhaps?'

'Not a chance,' Maggie said. 'I stopped believing in fairy tales years ago.'

In the Eastertide of 1916 there was an insurrection in Dublin when rebel forces known at the time as The Brotherhood took over the General Post Office and various other strategic places in Dublin. 'I suppose they imagined with England fighting Germany the government had their hands too full to worry about them,' Mary said.

'Can't see it myself. Can you?' Angela asked.

Mary shook her head. 'No,' she said. 'And I dread to think of England's response to this. I don't think it will achieve anything. I mean I'm angry like we all are, England promised us independence if we helped them in the war but since then they have done nothing about it. All those young men, 125,000 of them, joined up in all good faith and many have been badly injured or have not returned at all and England is still silent about the promise it made. Well to be honest I expected nothing else, in my heart of hearts, but violence is not the way to protest and it is affecting their own. It tells you in the paper about the ordinary Dubliners unable to walk the streets for fear of being shot at. In fact it says many shops have put up their shutters and ceased trading to try and prevent looting.'

'Well soon there'll be nothing to put in the shops,' Angela said, 'for they have hold of the

344

railway station and they are letting nothing out.'

'I know,' Mary said. 'And the poor people have had their cars and carts and all else purloined to form the barricade in a place called St Stephen's Green. It's supposed to be a beautiful place and they have dug trenches all through it.'

'It can't be let go on,' Angela said. 'Germany or no Germany, England won't stand for this much longer.'

And it didn't for the next day a field gun was placed on the roof of the Sherbourne Hotel, which stood facing one corner of St Stephen's Green, and began shelling and shooting the rebels and they fled to the Royal College of Surgeons. There was another rebel contingent set to guard Mountford Bridge, which was the bridge leading from the Kingstown Docks where British ships off-loaded 10,000 extra soldiers. Another field gun was installed in a place called Merrion Square and it routed those guarding the bridge, and on Wednesday of that week the gunship *Helga* sailed up the Liffey pounding those occupying Liberty Hall.

Surrender was a foregone conclusion and it came on Saturday 29th April. The rebellion had lasted six days and left 450 dead and 2,000 injured. 'It will take a sight longer than six days for Dublin and the Dubliners to get over this,' Mary said grimly. 'Dublin has been burnt, battered and bruised, there is little food to be had, people's businesses have been looted and other lives destroyed with the loss of those cars and carts, and I feel sorry for the families of those men who have lost their means of making a

living, not to mention the maimed and the dead.'

'Will they all be shot d'you think?'

'I can't see what other outcome there could be for whatever they choose to call themselves, the English will only have one word for them and that is traitors and they shoot traitors.'

Mary was right. Three hundred people were arrested and one hundred and eighty of those were sent to England and held without trial, including a man called Roger Casement and another called Eamon de Valera who had his execution changed to a life sentence because he had an American passport. Over the next fortnight ninety people were condemned to death. Later it became known that fourteen leaders had been killed in the stone breaker's yard in Kilmainham Jail, just days after the uprising.

Upsetting though this news was, war news took precedence and also worry about their loved ones fighting a bloody war somewhere in France. Angela was delighted when she heard that the private soldier's wages were raised from a shilling a day to two shillings. Barry said he was sending the extra seven shillings to her together with the five shillings he was already sending. Angela said she didn't need it with her wages but he insisted.

I know you to be no spendthrift, he wrote. *Any money left put in the savings account.*

He had no need to write that really for Mary looked for bargains to make her good nutritious meals with, and with Connie having her dinner at the nursery and Angela having hers at the subsidized canteen, money went further anyway and any surplus went straight into the Post Office.

346

Throughout the spring there had been talk of a new Front opening in France which might shorten the war. No one really knew a great deal but rumours were rife. The Front was going to stretch for fifteen miles to the north of the river Somme, and soon the river would give its name to the bloodiest battle in the war so far, the Battle of the Somme. The earth was chalk and so the trenches criss-crossing the area were white and crumbly.

Some of the men assembled that early summer's day were new recruits held back for this campaign to fight next to seasoned soldiers now battle hardened, all part of Kitchener's New Army. As usual the British had been bombarding the enemy. It had been going on for a week and so the men were told opposition would be minimal.

Unbeknownst to the British, the Germans, used to this pre-battle bombardment, had moved their lines back, digging deep down into the crumbly chalk to make shell-proof bunkers, so when the British bombardment was over and the British began to advance, expecting little opposition, the Germans crawled out of the bunkers ready to face the enemy. Certain of victory, the British Army invited the newsreels in for the first time.

And so there were banks of reporters and cameramen everywhere and the newsreels rolled and captured the men leaving the trenches in waves, some not making it over the top as a bullet found its mark, and the soldier would jerk and fall back into the trench he had just left. Others were hit as

347

they ran towards the coils of barbed wire. The cameras could not go further into No Man's Land but the press could hear all right, the barking of the guns and the whine of shells, mixed with the screams and cries of men that went on and on.

Towards evening, with the Germans eventually in retreat, quietness descended. One or two intrepid cameramen took their cameras from their tripods and, carrying them, slithered under the wire as they had seen the soldiers do, though some hadn't made it and were impaled on the wire, and then they were through and stood and surveyed No Man's Land, shocked to the core. So the cameras recorded the ground littered with bodies and parts and pieces of bodies and the men with half a skull or limbs missing often lying in a pool of their lifeblood which was soaking into the chalky soil. Some were still alive, twitching or lying still with bleak deadened eyes in too much pain to even cry.

The orderlies were using the cover of the gathering dusk to move the bodies and the cameramen helped them with tears in their own eyes. And later when they found out it was estimated that 2,000 men died in the first hour of the conflict they weren't surprised. On that first day alone there were 60,000 casualties. They knew that many in England would scarcely believe that things were as bad as they had seen for themselves because the soldiers' letters were censored and the reporters and cameramen all thought it was about time the general public knew the truth, because what they had witnessed was more

348

like a massacre than a battle.

And so no punches were pulled when the newsreel was published and it was shown at cinemas. Angela never visited the cinema, but many of her workmates had been and so had seen the newsreel and shared the full horror of it with the rest of them the next day. The girls listened in horrified silence as they spoke about the absolute slaughter of British soldiers that day and the words they spoke caused the blood to run like ice in Angela's veins. She could scarcely believe what they were hearing and Maggie too was shocked to the core and before they caught the tram home that night, they bought a selection of papers each and Angela noted that the fiasco of the Somme was on the front page of every one.

Later, with Connie safely tucked up in bed, she studied them with Mary that night. There was no guarantee that Barry or Stan were anywhere near the Somme that day and yet she felt in her bones that they had been. 60,000 casualties in 24 hours, the numbers reverberated in her head and the harrowing pictures showing the scenes captured on the cameras hours after the virtual bloodbath she knew would haunt her forever.

Before that day while everyone at home knew war wasn't a great experience and men were maimed and killed and that was awful and dreadful, it was the newsreels and the newspaper articles that brought what had happened in the Battle of the Somme into their own living rooms.

'My God,' Angela said. 'The death toll's colossal.'

Mary sighed. 'I know, they must have just been

mown down. Some never even got out of the trenches and others were impaled on the barbed wire as they reached No Man's Land.'

'And how the injured suffered,' Angela said with feeling. 'They had lost limbs ... oh many had perfectly dreadful injuries and the battle was so fierce they had to wait all day in the hot sun to be tended.'

She was affected even by the grainy pictures from the newspaper, they were quite graphic enough, capturing the savagery of it so well. She was glad that they were just black and white and didn't think she could bear to see the film. 'And Barry could be part of this,' Angela said. 'And Stan could.'

'We would have heard if anything had happened to them,' Mary said. 'They would send a telegram.'

Angela knew that that was how many learned the bad news of their loved ones, but thought it might take some time to work out just who was killed, or badly injured and send the relevant telegrams, especially as the Battle of the Somme was still going on, and the loss of life was still high though it was not as high as on that first day.

However Angela saw no purpose in telling Mary her inner thoughts, time enough for her to worry when there was something to worry about and so she contented herself by saying, 'The point is, Mammy, every man killed was someone's father or son, husband, sweetheart or brother and they will all be missed and I'm thinking there will be many grieving people throughout the land just now.'

Mary sighed. 'I know and I know too I'm being selfish, but it isn't totally wrong to be glad that your lad is still living even though another person's might be dead, is it?'

Angela gave Mary's shoulder a squeeze as she said, 'No of course it isn't and you haven't a selfish bone in your body.' And then she added, 'This was supposed to shorten the war, according to the Government. Huh! If it means carnage on this scale I would say it's too high a price to pay.'

Angela waited daily for the buff telegram to be delivered to their door. It affected her nerves and disturbed her sleep but she could do nothing about it. The only good thing was that after such a tremendous loss of life, at a stroke many areas in cities, as well as small towns and villages, had lost all their young men. The Pals Regiment idea was dropped.

Barry used to write once a week, but when he had been in the army a while sometimes a fortnight would pass and then two or three letters would arrive together. But when it had been over three weeks since a letter from Barry came through the door, Angela was coming to terms with the fact that Barry was not ever coming home again. So when a letter was waiting for her as she came home from work one evening in early August and it was in a hand she didn't recognize, she assumed it was from some Department of the War Office to formally announce Barry's death and with a heavy heart she opened the envelope and withdrew the letter and then cried out with joy.

Mary had had her head down, trying to prepare

herself for the bad news she was sure the letter contained and now her head shot up and she noted the light shining in Angela's face, and the tears glistening in her eyes and she cried, 'What is it?'

'Barry.'

'Barry,' repeated Mary incredulously. 'He isn't dead?'

Angela knew that despite Mary saying they would hear officially if anything happened to Barry, she had begun to lose heart that she would ever see her son again.

Angela threw down the letter and caught Mary's hands up in her own and said, 'No, he's not dead, but very much alive. He has been injured though and still can't write because his arms are in plaster and so a VAD is writing this on his behalf.'

Barry had found that he was unable to express himself as he normally would when telling a third party rather than committing the words to paper himself, which meant he was unable to say many things due to embarrassment. He also had no intention of telling Angela of the fever that nearly killed him, nor of the very real fear that he might lose his arm, peppered as it was with shrapnel. Angela didn't have to know, but it meant that he had very little he could tell her as he was not allowed to mention that hell-hole at the Somme either.

But Angela didn't care how brief the stiff little missive was because it told her all that she needed to know and that her Barry was alive and as well as could be expected when fighting a war. 'He did

catch sight of Stan too,' Angela said to Mary scanning the letter again. 'He calls him just S but that's who he means, but he said he was too far away to speak or anything and he doesn't know what happened to him afterwards. Who would be informed if anything happened to Stan?' Angela asked.

'Betty I suppose.'

'Doubt she'd welcome telegrams or whatever arriving if she hasn't told Daniel the truth about his father.'

'She might have no say in it.'

'Well I hope she'll tell us if she does hear bad news,' Angela said. 'Or anything could happen to him and we'd know nothing. It could have already happened because we usually hear from him every fortnight or so and it has been a month now. I mean he might not have made it.'

'Write to her, why don't you?' Mary said. 'Ask her straight.'

'I will,' Angela said. 'But I will write a reply to Barry first. Have to get my priorities right.'

TWENTY-FOUR

Before Angela had a chance to write to Betty she received a letter from Stan explaining that he had been unable to write before because he had been injured. He didn't explain his injuries, seeing no purpose in telling her that he had been in a coma for a week, or that when he came round he had

been raving. The savage butchery he'd witnessed, and contributed to, was too much for his brain to cope with.

No need telling Angela any of that but he did want news of Barry and was immensely relieved to hear that he had survived too. So was Angela, knowing that in hospital they were safe. The Military Hospital was on the South Coast and with the job she had, she knew she wouldn't be given time off to visit either of them, but she was able to write.

'I suppose we must just be grateful that they have been shipped to Britain,' Angela said. 'In his letter Barry said many were being treated in Field Hospitals. I mean a proper hospital is bound to have better facilities.'

'I should hope so,' Mary said. 'So probably the severity of illness or injury determines who will be sent back to Britain.'

'D'you think they will have leave after, you know when they've recovered a bit?'

Mary shook her head. 'I would like to say yes,' she said. 'But I doubt it. That battle that started with that terrible loss of life on the first day is still raging.'

And it was, day after day with no side gaining much ground, for Angela avidly read the news in the papers. 'I would say that losing so many soldiers would mean that they want these patched up and back on the battlefield in short order.'

Angela thought Mary was right. Everywhere she went now she saw more and more widows' bonnets, more people with black arm-bands which signified how bad the losses were on a daily basis

and she knew if they were to have any chance of winning this brutal, savage war they couldn't really do without all those trained soldiers. So many had died, those who could recover would be needed again.

The long summer was a good one and most days the sun shone from a sky of cornflower blue and Angela was glad to be out of the hot stuffy factory, for most of her time now was spent delivering the shells. Mr Potter was pleased with Angela, despite their disagreement about her taking time off to say goodbye to her husband. In fact it had made him rethink his rigid stance and relax it a little and so it was common now for any woman in a similar position to be given time off. Mr Potter knew Angela was no shirker and a natural driver and she had been sent to areas of that teeming city she didn't know existed and she loved the freedom of the roads.

In late August Barry wrote the weekly letter on his own and said his arms were nearly as good as new, he just needed a bit of physio. He was then going back to the fray and Stan too wrote that he was improving daily. Angela was relieved they were both getting better but she knew when they left the safety of their hospital beds the dread would settle in her heart again.

Part of her thought that because they had both survived that ferocious first day of the Battle of the Somme, and so had Maggie's Michael, when so many hadn't, it could be seen as a sort of talisman for them both surviving the war. It wasn't as if they had got away unscathed.

In her heart of hearts though, she knew the fight

was far from over. Those who had said the Somme would be the deciding battle in the war were proved wrong and, as for shortening the war, it had done the opposite and had been an abject failure and she had to face the fact that they might lose the war altogether, or they might win after all but the cost would be the body of her darling husband and the father of her child left in a French field, and that would destroy her totally. She wanted nothing bad to happen to Stan either for he was very dear to them all and when they returned to the melee in France, worry could have overwhelmed her if she'd let it. During the day though, especially if she was driving, she had to push these worries to the back of her mind and concentrate on the road.

There was torrential rain in October putting an end to the lovely summer, but while no one enjoyed it much it was much worse for the troops trying to advance across battlegrounds turned into muddy quagmires. Because the war had been brought into homes via the newspapers illustrating the first day of the Battle of the Somme, Angela and Mary knew how much the soldiers must be suffering.

They knew more about this battle now, though it wasn't one battle but comprised many battles and they didn't seem to be going forward very quickly. As Mary said, it was like them taking one step forward and two back, and it did seem a bit like that and it was hard to remain hopeful.

Halfway through November though the battles on the Somme were over. In one of the bloodiest battles in history the British had suffered 420,000

casualties, the French nearly as many, and they had gained just 8 kilometres, about 5 miles of enemy ground.

The figures were staggering. It was hard even to imagine so many people. It was as if the world had gone mad. There would be no young men left, because those casualty figures were only for the battles fought around the river Somme. Soldiers had been killed before 1916 and were still being killed in battles being fought elsewhere.

Angela's eyes were full of pain when she lifted them from the paper and met Mary's, and she imagined all the families getting the telegrams to tell them their father, son, husband, brother or uncle was never coming home again. He was littering a foreign field in France with comrades who were killed alongside him. 'This is not a war,' Angela said to Mary. 'This is carnage on a massive scale.'

Neither woman had much heart for Christmas, but Connie was only a child so for her sake Angela got down the tree and the decorations from the attic and put them all around the room and Santa visited with books to read, colouring books and a paintbox, and a whip and top. So for her it was a good Christmas.

Connie had stopped asking about her father and though she kissed his picture at night he was really a stranger to her and that bothered Angela. She was not the only one, many other children's daddies were soldiers as well and most of them hadn't a clue what daddies did. 'Why worry about it?' Mary said. 'Barry can't fix that till he's

home again.'

'I know,' Angela said. 'It's just sad that's all. Not just for Connie. I mean for all the children.'

'War is sad,' Mary said. 'There is no better word for it.'

The year turned 1917 and peace seemed as far away as ever. The winter was bleak and snowy, gusty winds driving the snow into drifts. It was hard for people to get around, Angela had to take great care driving the trucks on the wet, slippery roads, and even basic things were in short supply in the shops, which was also blamed on the weather.

March was drier, but blustery. 'Well it is supposed to come in like a lion and go out like a lamb,' Angela remarked to Maggie, both holding on to their hats for grim death as they crossed the Bull Ring after leaving the tram.

'We're a third of the way through the month,' Maggie complained. 'Anyway I wish that wretched lion didn't have such a roar. These winds could take a person off their feet.'

'You're right,' Angela said. 'Hold your hat with one hand and link arms with the other and we might get to work in one-piece.'

They did, though even linked they were blown from side to side and everyone was talking about it as they clocked in.

'I never thought I would be so pleased to see the factory as I was today,' said one girl and there was a ripple of laughter at that.

'I know what you mean,' said another. 'It's blooming hard going and it takes your breath away.'

'Hope it dies down a bit before home time,' Maggie said. 'Pity you, driving in this, Angela.'

'Maybe I'll not have to do much today,' Angela said. But barely had the words left her mouth than Mrs Paget entered the room as they were changing into their overalls and said that Mr Potter wanted to see her.

Immediately one of the girls said teasingly, 'Oh what you done, Ange?'

'Been a naughty girl I reckon,' said another.

'That will do girls,' Mrs Paget said. 'On to the shop floor if you're changed and stop wasting time teasing Angela.'

Grumbling good-naturedly they made their way down to the factory and, slightly intrigued, Angela went down to Mr Potter's office and was astounded by what he asked her to do. 'The coast, Mr Potter? I've never driven anywhere near a distance like that.'

'I know but really you're the only one I can send,' Mr Potter said. 'You are the best driver and one who can read maps.'

'Yes, but...'

'Angela there is a container ship leaving on the afternoon tide and there is room on it for more shells and you know how important those shells are. We have them made but they are doing no good here. They are lading the big truck as we speak.'

'I've never taken the big truck out,' Angela protested. 'Bert always drove that. He'd not like anyone touching his truck, you know that.'

'He hasn't got to like it,' Mr Potter said. 'The fact is, Bert came out of retirement when the war

359

began and he had a heart attack last night. He's not dead, but the doctor has said he is no longer fit for work.'

'Sorry to hear that,' Angela said. 'He was a nice old fellow.'

'He was,' Mr Potter said. 'Still is, but it is too much for him. He often looked strained. His wife is pleased because she's been worried about him for ages. I've been a bit concerned myself just lately. Even if he had been at work today I would have hesitated to send him on such a journey.'

'Oh that would really have set the cat among the pigeons,' Angela said. 'You know how possessive he always was about that truck.'

'I do indeed,' Mr Potter said. 'But it's time now for Bert to take life a little easier and as it is, at the moment there is only you.'

'I think I'd be nervous driving that.'

'It's not that much different to driving the smaller one,' Mr Potter said. 'And a sight safer in the wind today. Now, after you're done, get something to eat in the town before heading back,' Mr Potter went on giving her a ten-shilling note along with the paperwork needed to give access to the docks. 'You might be later back than usual, is that a problem?'

Angela shook her head. 'No. Maggie will call in and tell Mammy if I'm late back.'

'Good,' Mr Potter said. 'And I will be still here whatever time you arrive. I want to see that you are in one piece and make the truck secure for the weekend.'

'Righto.'

'You're all set then,' Mr Potter said. 'The truck

should be ready for you now.'

The truck was ready, filled with as many shells as it could carry with tarpaulin sheeting roped on top of it and it looked very big, enormous in fact. 'Are you ready?' Mr Potter asked.

'As ready as I ever will be I suppose,' Angela said as she climbed into the cab. She seemed very high up and that gave her good visibility. The engine growled into life and Angela found it was surprisingly easy to manoeuvre and though she edged her way a little cautiously out of the yard, once on the open road she felt more confident. The sky was just beginning to lighten and she set off at a steady lick for Plymouth was some distance away and if the ship was sailing on the afternoon tide she had to be there in time to have the shells unloaded to catch that tide.

Mr Potter had drawn Angela a very detailed map and she followed it meticulously and found the docks easily. All her paperwork seemed to be in order and she was waved through. She was in a queue of trucks on the same errand and she saw only two of the drivers were men. The queue was moving slowly as they were offloading the shells straight from the trucks to the cargo holds of the ship and Angela was very glad she had made good time, there being many trucks trailing along the road behind her. She was suddenly aware of how stiff she was and as the trucks before her were stationary she got out to stretch her legs. The girl from the truck behind her got out too. 'God,' she said to Angela, 'I'm as stiff as a board.'

'Me too.'

'Come far?'

'Birmingham. What about you?'

'Exeter. You've come a fair distance.'

Angela shrugged. 'They need the shells don't they?'

'Oh I'll say they do,' the girl said. 'After the battle of the Somme I'm surprised they had any left. Did you see the newsreel?'

Angela shook her head. 'Couldn't bring myself to watch it.'

'You got a chap in the forces?'

Angela nodded. 'A husband. He was injured at the Somme, but it wasn't life-threatening. He was one of the lucky ones.'

'He was certainly.'

'How about you?'

The girl shook her head vehemently. 'Not getting involved with anyone till this little lot's over. I have two sisters, my eldest sister's husband was killed and our middle sister's fiancé too. It's not worth the heartache, but I sometimes wonder if there will be anyone left for us when it grinds to a halt. Seems to me the whole world is being stripped of young men. Oh looks like we're moving again.'

The girl was right and Angela climbed back in the truck, but as she moved forward the girl's words reverberated in her head, 'a world stripped of young men'. A whole generation lost. It was a sobering thought.

Angela's truck was unloaded shortly after this and she set off for the town for something to eat. It was a rare occurrence for Angela to eat out, but she avoided anywhere that looked any way posh,

for she was in her work clothes, eventually settling for a small cafe where she had fish and chips with two slices of bread and butter and two mugs of very strong tea and felt in great shape for the journey back.

It was slower going home though, because she encountered more traffic as she neared the cities and then had to negotiate her way through them. The dusk deepened as she approached Birmingham and that meant that she had to cut her speed because the lamps were not very effective.

She gave a sigh of relief as the factory loomed before her. Mr Potter must have heard her coming because he had the gates open and she was able to drive straight into the yard, where she stopped, turned the engine off and jumped down with a sigh of relief. 'All right?' Mr Potter asked anxiously.

'Fine, just a bit stiff sitting in one position so long,' Angela said. 'I'm more tired than I imagined I'd be as well.'

'All that concentrating would tire anyone,' Mr Potter said. 'And it has been a long day for you. It's half past seven now.'

'Yes, I'll just take my boiler suit off and get my coat and be on my way,' Angela said. 'I'll be glad to reach home tonight.'

As she got out of her boiler suit though she heard the jingle of coins in her pocket and so before she left she sought out Mr Potter who had returned to his office. 'These are yours,' she said, placing the coins on the desk. 'The meal was only two shillings.'

'Keep it,' Mr Potter said. 'You earned double

that by what you have done today.'

Angela was quite surprised. Mr, Potter was not known for gestures like that, though he was usually fair and she hadn't expected extra cash for doing what she had today. It was all part of doing her bit. 'Thank you Mr Potter,' she said. 'It's very generous of you.'

'Not at all my dear, not at all,' Mr Potter said. 'Least I could do. Now do you want me to call a taxi for you?'

Angela had never been in a taxi and she imagined the hoo-hah in the street if she arrived home in one and so she said, 'There's no need, Mr Potter, I only live a step away.'

'If you're sure?'

'Positive,' Angela said. 'I'm just glad the wind has died down. Maggie and I were nearly blown here this morning and I hadn't a great desire to be blown back home again this evening.'

'See you tomorrow then.'

'Yes see you tomorrow,' Angela said and reflected as she walked across the Bull Ring that she would rather Mr Potter had given her the morning off than let her keep the eight shillings change. But he hadn't and that was that and she was sure when she had eaten the meal Mary would have kept warm for her and had a good sleep she would feel as right as rain.

She alighted from the tram and went up Bristol Passage, only yards from home now, when she suddenly found her way blocked by three soldiers. Even in the dimness of the passage it was apparent that all three were very drunk and she gave a sigh of impatience as she said, 'Can you let

me pass please?'

'Oh hoity toity,' said one of the men. 'What if we don't want to?'

Another said, 'What are you doing abroad this time of night anyway?'

'Oh let me pass,' said Angela. 'I'm just coming from work.'

'And what manner of work is it that you do at near eight o'clock at night?' the first man asked.

'You're a street woman aint ya?' the second man said accusingly.

'Don't be ridiculous,' Angela snapped. 'I am a respectable married woman.'

The man nearest to her lifted up her left hand. 'No ring,' he said. 'Who you trying to kid?'

He threw her hand down and it brushed against her coat pocket where she had put the coins Mr Potter told her she could keep and they jingled together. The soldier heard it too and his hand dived into her pocket though she tried to stop him and withdrew the coins with a cry of triumph. 'And these are her earnings for this night's work.'

All of a sudden Angela was blisteringly angry. 'How dare you harass and assault me this way. That money was earned honestly so please return it to me and move out of my way and let me pass. What if I was to scream?'

'I wouldn't suggest you do that, lady,' said the first man. 'See we're professional soldiers and we know how to silence people.'

'Are you threatening me?' Angela asked as a sense of unease flowed through her.

'Take it how you like, but you be nice to us and no one gets hurt,' the first one said. 'All we want

is only what you've been doing all night anyway for mugs what pay. We're taking it for free, that's all, cos we don't pay for sex.'

'You've got it all wrong,' Angela protested, but got no further. One of them pulled a dirty hanky out of his pocket and tied it so tight around her mouth it cut into the sides and as she protested, he growled, 'Too much talking, lady. We want action.'

Another tied her hands behind her back with a bit of string and she was dragged struggling into a nearby entry, hearing buttons pop off her coat and the tear of her dress as she fought like a tiger, throwing her head from side to side, kicking out and suddenly the string tying her wrists loosened and she began wriggling one hand free.

The man who had spoken to her initially was the one to take his turn with her first and she felt nausea rise in her, for apart from the shame and degradation, the man stank and his putrid breath smelled of stale beer and cigarettes and possibly rotting teeth and even in the dimness she could see the vivid red scar that ran the length of his creased cheek. And then one hand was free and she attacked him with her nails, scoring deep scratch lines down his face.

With a howl of rage he turned her round and pushed her face against the bricks and re-tied her hands so tight the string cut into her skin and she moaned with the pain of it. 'Shut up, you stupid bitch,' the man said. 'I haven't started yet. I warned you, I said to be nice to us and what you did was not nice at all.'

Angela began to tremble as the man grasped her

by the shoulders and swung her round, throwing her against the wall, her head hitting it with such force she almost lost consciousness. And before she had time to recover from that he aimed a punch at her face and she felt her nose spurt with blood and the second punch closed one eye completely. She wasn't aware of much after that. Her coat was open because it had lost so many buttons and the man took hold of her dress and ripped it straight down the middle and the petticoat the same and then pulled at her knickers till they fell to the floor. 'Now spread your legs, bitch,' he snarled but Angela seemed incapable of even understanding what he was saying so he kicked them open. 'Oh I'm going to enjoy this,' he cried.

Angela only felt the pain of it though she was drifting in and out of consciousness as one after the other had their way with her. When the last one finished she sank to the ground. She was in agony, her body was on fire and the first man aimed a kick and when his army boot powered into her abdomen she curled into a ball groaning with pain so intense she wanted to die.

She wasn't sure how long she lay there in too much pain and too frightened to move, but she knew she had to move or Mary would be worried enough to send out a search party. Getting up was a major undertaking but after several attempts, eventually, she was on her feet, bent over because of the kick and staggering despite balancing herself on the wall.

Her home was only yards away, but it took a long, long time to get there and she stumbled

367

and nearly lost her footing often. She almost fell through the door and Mary who was tending the fire looked up. Her mouth dropped open. 'Almighty Christ!' she cried, throwing down the poker and darting to Angela who was sagging on the doorstep. 'What in God's name happened to you?' she asked again as she helped her to the settee.

Angela told the astounded Mary what had happened to her when she had nearly reached home and safety and Mary was shocked to the core and said it was a dreadful thing to have happened, absolutely dreadful and she wanted to inform the police, immediately. 'No men should get away with this,' she declared.

'I agree,' Angela said speaking with difficulty because of her smashed nose and a split lip. 'Yet they will, because I don't want to tell the police. It would be all round the neighbourhood in no time at all and what if someone thought Barry should know? Can you imagine how he would feel to hear about me violated like that and him not here to protect me? Don't you think he has enough to deal with without this worry on his mind?'

And the devil of it was that Angela was absolutely right and her abusers would walk the streets to do it again to some other young woman. Mary got a bowl of warm water and began to tend Angela's face. 'We must put it behind us,' she said. 'For if we cannot do that they will have won.'

'Huh, haven't they done that already?'

'No I don't think so,' Mary said. 'They abused your body. Don't let them have your mind as well.'

Angela sighed and said, 'I do see what you're saying and I will do my best, but I can't promise not to be nervous walking home on my own in the dark now, though that has never bothered me before. The best of it is Mr Potter offered me a taxi home and I refused it. I think I'll say a resounding "yes" next time.'

When Mary had done what she could for Angela's face she left her eating a bowl of stew she had warmed up for her and went to tell Maggie that she wouldn't be at work. 'What excuse shall I give?'

'If you can get Maggie on her own, you can tell her the truth,' Angela said.

Mary did get Maggie on her own and she came back to the house with her. She was as appalled as Mary had been when Angela told her the whole tale and quite understood why she didn't want the authorities alerted. 'The point is they have made quite a mess of your face and you will need a few days off till your face is more or less back to normal. You can't come to work like that.'

'What will you say is wrong with me?'

'That you've had a bad fall down the cellar steps,' Maggie said. There was a pause and then Maggie added quietly, 'Angela have you had any thoughts on what you will do if there are consequences?'

'Dear God, don't wish that on me,' Angela cried. 'Dealing with the memory of the whole thing is enough for me just now.'

'Sorry, Angela,' Maggie said. 'You are right. And should the worst happen we will cross that bridge when we come to it.'

369

TWENTY-FIVE

The following morning when Angela opened her eyes she groaned for her whole face throbbed, and between her legs, which she was to find out had bled, and her stomach felt as if she had been kicked by a mule. When she struggled from her bed she found it difficult to stand up straight. As she stood holding on to the wall for support, waiting for the room to stop spinning, she heard Mary and Connie go past her door on their way downstairs. Connie had moved into the attic to share a bed with her grandmother because Angela had to get up so early, but not today.

Gingerly and very slowly she followed them after a minute or two. When, she opened the door into the room it was to see Connie with her warm dressing gown and slippers on sitting up to the table eating a bowl of porridge. Connie hadn't been aware her mother was home because normally she wasn't on Saturday morning so she was pleased to see her but could see there was something wrong. 'Your face,' she said.

'Yes I fell down the cellar steps yesterday,' Angela said.

Connie nodded gravely. She knew all about falls, they happened to her all the time. 'Poor Mammy.'

'Yes indeed poor Mammy,' Mary said. 'And one that should still be in her bed. Here,' she said

370

holding out a bowl of porridge, 'get that down you and I'll make us both a cup of tea and then you get back to bed. And don't even bother protesting,' she said as Angela opened her mouth.

Mary sat down with her own porridge and said, 'When we've finished this me and Connie will get dressed and go shopping like we do every Saturday morning and you sleep if you can, for it's just turned half past seven.'

It was two full hours after Angela's usual time of rising and yet she felt more tired than she'd ever felt in her life and as Mary seemed to have everything in hand she decided to do as she was told for once and returned to bed. It was such a relief to lie down and ease her aching body and she closed her throbbing eyes and when Mary looked in later just before she went shopping Angela was in a deep sleep.

She woke with a shriek and a yell two hours later and this became the pattern over the next few days. Angela was constantly tired, but wary of closing her eyes because memories of the abuse would crowd into her mind. She knew she would be better off back at work with less time to think, but Mary was worried about her emotional health as well as physical and thought a good rest was needed because she wasn't the same girl she'd known and loved all these years.

Angela knew she wasn't the same person and couldn't seem to do anything about lifting her spirits. Anyway her face took time to heal and in the end Angela had the entire week off work. She was glad to return and Mr Potter was very glad to see her and she was busier than ever now Bert

was in full retirement.

But as the days passed, from when she opened her eyes in the morning till she closed them at night she was filled with the dreadful thought and fear that one of those monsters who had raped her might have made her pregnant. Mary knew and shared that fear and when eight weeks after the attack there had been no sign of any of the cotton pads soaking in the bucket she mentioned it to Angela one night after she had eaten and Angela said she had had no sign of her monthlies. 'It could be just the shock of it all,' Mary said. 'You know shock can do that sometimes.'

'And what if it isn't shock?' Angela said. 'What if the unthinkable has happened and I am carrying a child, then what the Hell am I going to do?'

Mary shook her head helplessly and then she said resignedly, 'Bring it up I suppose.'

'Bring it up!' Angela repeated 'Are you mad? I must get rid of it.'

'Ah no!'

'What's the alternative?' Angela said. 'You know the life we'd live here if they knew I was pregnant by someone else, with my husband away fighting. I would be shunned and castigated in public and by association so would you and can you imagine the life the child would have? He or she would be vilified, he or she would be taunted and bullied and guess what, Mammy, and this will shock you, but I shan't care what happens to this child. It will have no love from me because I don't want it and never shall.'

'You may feel differently when it's born.'

'How would I, Mammy?' Angela asked. 'The

father of this child is not my beloved Barry, the father of the child I might be carrying is a cruel, beer-sodden rapist. I don't know which one of those three drunken soldiers is responsible for putting me in this position, but it doesn't really matter for one was as bad as the other. Yet you want me to love this child, and Barry to return from war and bring up another's bastard? You ask too much, Mammy.'

Mary was in tears as she answered, 'I do my darling girl, but there isn't any other solution.'

Angela decided she needed to see Maggie, she might have some other ideas. However, getting rid of an unwanted pregnancy was not something she could talk about when anyone might over-hear because it was illegal to abort a pregnancy. And so on the tram that morning she asked Maggie if she would call round that evening as she had something she needed to ask her.

And Maggie, looking at Angela's face and her anxious eyes, had a good idea what it would be about, but also knew she couldn't speak about it in public, she had to wait until they were alone. And so that evening Maggie sat opposite Angela and Mary and said to Angela quite bluntly, 'I'm telling you straight there is no easy way of stopping a pregnancy once it has begun because it means aborting the baby.'

'Is there anything?'

Maggie nodded and added, 'There are a few back-street abortionists but they are hard to find 'cos asking around is risky and they keep changing addresses to keep ahead of the police. But these places cost and sometimes it doesn't always work

and that can mean that the baby is damaged in some way, but I can try and find out if you like.'

'Yes. Yes please.'

'No,' Mary said. 'Thank you, Maggie, but the answer is no.'

Angela shot round annoyed at Mary's interference and Mary said, 'Hear me out, Angela. I don't know where these people are and neither does Maggie and the minute she begins asking questions others would wonder why, because you don't enquire about the whereabouts of a backstreet abortionist to take afternoon tea together.

'Then there's the safety element because these people are not qualified. Some know bugger all, others are dirty devils that leave a woman with an infection that means she can never conceive again. I said I know no abortionists and that's true, but over the years I have seen their handiwork enough times and it's not pretty, like the young lass who bled to death, too scared of going to prison to summon an ambulance. You can't put your life at risk in the hands of these butchers for you have Connie to think about.'

'I agree really,' said Maggie.

'Right,' Angela said testily, 'both of you are busy telling me what not to do, so I'm sure you must have a great plan of what I must do instead.'

'Have the baby and put it up for adoption,' Mary suggested.

'And have someone write and tell Barry that I was carrying on with another man and had given birth to his child.'

'Barry would never believe you had found someone else.'

'No, not if he was home he wouldn't, where he saw me every day, but being over there it's different and they have been away a long time, and some women do play away. Barry's mate received a Dear John letter from his sweetheart a few days ago. Barry might well believe malicious gossip and that would destroy me.'

'You could write and tell him first,' Maggie said.

'We thought of that,' Angela said. 'But it would mean telling him about the attack and... Well we're told not to worry them unduly.'

'You can see why,' Maggie said.

'Absolutely,' Angela said. 'But it means we're right out of options, not that we had a great bundle of them to start with.'

There was silence for a moment and then Maggie said, 'Can I tell Mammy about you?'

'Why?' Angela said. 'The fewer people that know the better just at the moment.'

'I know, I'll pick my time don't worry. No one else will hear the news, but I have a special reason for Mammy to know about this attack, but I must have your absolute promise you won't tell anyone else what I'm going to tell you.'

'You have it,' Angela said.

'Aye I promise,' Mary said, wondering what secret Maggie was about to reveal.

'This happened to my mother,' Maggie said. 'No one knows, not even my father but she told me I suppose to try and keep me a bit aware. She was in service and raped by the son of the house. He put the blame on to her, said she was gagging for it and ... well you know the sort of thing?'

Both women nodded and Maggie went on, 'He was believed of course and she was dismissed without a reference and when she went home her mother wouldn't let her in.'

'Didn't she believe her either?' Angela asked, slightly incredulously for she could never envisage a time when Mary would turn her back on her.

'I don't know if she did or she didn't,' Maggie said. 'Maybe she thought it was probably true but couldn't take the stigma, you know?'

Again Mary and Angela nodded. 'What happened?' Angela asked because for poor destitute women there was only the workhouse.

'Auntie Phyllis happened,' Maggie said, 'and she was the sister of Mammy's mother. So Mammy wrote to her Aunt Phyllis telling her what had happened, and Phyllis went to the workhouse and got Mammy out. She looked after her until the baby, a boy, was born and took it to the Sisters of Mercy at the Catholic Orphanage and told the tale of a young, single Catholic girl who had lost her life giving birth. They took the child and Mammy recovered and she went on with her life and no one is any the wiser. Point is, Phyllis is older now and I don't know if she would be up for doing this again, but if she is you could bide with her, moving in just before you begin to show, have the child and put it up for adoption.'

'I think that is the best plan all around,' Mary said.

'So do I if Phyllis is willing to do it, but what about work?'

'You leave that to me,' Mary said. 'Don't give

notice or anything and I will tell them you have been called over to Ireland for a family crisis.'

'They know I haven't parents or siblings.'

'But they don't know that you haven't grandparents, or aunts, uncles or cousins,' Mary said. 'Don't worry. I will be deliberately vague, but stress it was unavoidable.'

'I will talk to Mammy tonight,' Maggie promised. 'She will believe what I will tell her, shocked by it I imagine, for she knows you to be a respectable girl from a good family and she'll tell Phyllis that too.'

'Thank you,' Angela said. 'I suppose it's as well to have a plan in place sooner rather than later.'

Phyllis Crabtree (Auntie Phyllis) lived in a fine brick house in Albert Road, Aston, and a fortnight after the talk with Maggie, Phyllis had asked to meet Angela on her own on Sunday afternoon so she could see for herself the type of girl she was.

Angela had felt rather nervous meeting this stranger who could change the course of her life or not, and when she saw the house she was more nervous still, for it had large bay windows overlooking a small garden behind an ornate fence, and a cobbled path and a white scrubbed step led to a good solid wooden door with a half moon of stained glass set in the top of it. Angela nearly turned tail and headed back home but she reminded herself what was at stake and rang the bell.

Phyllis was very friendly though. She was a tall woman, Angela noted, and her brown hair, which

was liberally streaked with grey, was caught up in a round bun on top of her, head, making her look even taller. She was very smartly dressed in a navy skirt that reached almost to the floor, just showing soft leather shoes from underneath, and a pink long-sleeved silk blouse fastened at the neck with a cameo brooch.

'Come in do,' she said as she opened the door, 'you're very welcome,' and as she led Angela down the black-and-white-tiled hall she pointed out the parlour and the sitting room before they came to the cloakroom where Phyllis said Angela could leave her coat. As she hung it up Angela thought how wonderful it would be to have a room just to hang coats in. And that wasn't all, for there was another room Phyllis referred to as a breakfast room plus a kitchen Mary would die for.

On the stove in the kitchen a kettle bubbled away and beside it was a tray laid for tea with two cups and saucers, milk and sugar and a plate of delicious-looking cakes. Phyllis poured the boiling water into the teapot and said to Angela, 'Can you bring the tray?'

Nervously Angela lifted it and followed Phyllis as she made for the very finely furnished parlour. 'Put the tray on the small table,' Phyllis said. 'And please take a seat.'

Angela did as she was bid and sat a little tentatively on the cream brocade settee as Phyllis poured tea for the two, of them. Angela studied the woman she might spend some time living with. She had quite a long face, with high cheekbones and quite a large mouth, but her eyes were

kindly and full of concern. And now those eyes were turned on Angela as Phyllis handed her a cup of tea and said, 'Now tell me about yourself.'

So Angela told Phyllis about growing up in the McClusky household after her entire family were wiped out. She told about the older two boys she considered brothers travelling to America for they could find no work in England.

'They prospered though,' she said. 'And so when Sean and Gerry, the two younger boys were struggling to find work they said to join them in America, but they travelled on the *Titanic* and so drowned at sea. Barry and I no longer felt for each other as brother and sister but as lovers and we decided to marry young to give Barry's mother in particular something to look forward to. Good job we did too,' she went on, 'because Barry's father became very ill shortly afterwards. You see, I'm the daughter he never had and he did so want to walk me down the aisle and he got to do it.'

'What a mercy that you got married when you did then,' Phyllis said. 'Is your husband in the army now?'

Angela nodded. 'And we have a little girl of four who has a nursery place because I do war work, but we also live with my mother-in-law, which isn't difficult as she is the one who brought me up from when I was a baby.'

'Have you been able to tell her what happened to, you?'

'Oh yes,' Angela said. 'She saw the state of me when I arrived home. I was attacked you see and the men made quite a mess of my face.'

'I see,' Phyllis said. 'So tell me exactly what

happened to get you into this situation?'

'Well,' Angela said, 'usually Maggie, your niece, and I come home from work together, but that day I was asked to take an urgent consignment of shells to the docks.'

'That's some distance,' Phyllis said. 'How did you do that?'

'I drove the lorry.'

'You mean you can drive?'

'Yes and that day it was a big truck too,' Angela said. 'I'd never before driven one as big as that, though I have driven it a lot since. We had an old man used to do the big runs like to the docks, brought out of retirement specially, but he'd had a heart attack the night before and though he didn't die the doctor said he couldn't do it any more.'

'You know,' said Phyllis, 'sorry for butting in, but I have to say that while this war should never have been fought and it is a tragedy that so many young lives have been lost, yet, in another way it has opened up new lives for many young women, like you driving for example. Won't be able to deny us the vote when this little lot is over.'

'I'm not that interested in politics,' Angela said, 'though I know all about the Suffragettes. But I do know what you mean about the war, though personally I would rather have Barry by my side and had never learned to drive, but now I can, I must use that skill to help in any way possible, including driving down to the docks. But that day I was late getting back to the factory and Maggie had gone. The Boss offered to call me a taxi, but I thought the people in the street might take the mickey and think I was getting above myself.

Anyway my house was not far from the town and I had made the journey every day for months and wasn't the slightest bit nervous and so stupidly I refused his offer. I was assaulted by three drink-sodden soldiers just yards from my home.'

As Angela began to relate her ordeal, Phyllis felt enormous sympathy for the young woman for she wasn't just telling the tale, but reliving it again and she heard the shame in her low voice, saw the crimson flush redden her cheeks and watched her face contort as if remembering the pain and her eyes fill with anguish. As the tale drew to a close she was enraged that the brutal thugs who assaulted her so were allowed to walk free to do it to someone else.

The result of this was that Phyllis was very impressed with Angela and was quite prepared to help her. 'I will leave it up to you to decide when to come,' she said. 'Just don't leave it too late.'

'No I won't,' Angela assured Phyllis. 'But with my little girl I wasn't showing until about seven months or so.'

'It may be the case again,' Phyllis said. 'And then it may not be. Every pregnancy is different.'

Angela knew this, but sincerely hoped it was later rather than sooner for when she went to live with Phyllis she would have to leave Connie with Mary for secrecy was everything and four-year-olds weren't that good at keeping secrets. Anyway, she was settled in the nursery and might lose her place if she left and Angela fully intended to return to work when this was all over. It broke her heart to have to leave Connie for so long, though she knew it was the only thing to do.

She blessed the shapeless all-enveloping boiler suit they had to wear that would conceal a number of sins, including an expanding waistline. It also helped that she wasn't with the girls much as I she had taken on Bert's driving duties as well so was on her own in one of the trucks most of the time.

Mass at St Catherine's was the point where her pregnancy was in danger of being spotted. Angela would rather have popped along to St Chad's where no one knew her, but that would have been remarked upon and even worse, if Father Brannigan didn't see her at Mass he might come to the house to find out why not and that would never do. So as summer ended and an autumn nip was in the air she took herself off to the Rag Market one Saturday afternoon and came home with a baggy winter coat and a tight corset and every Sunday morning she would lace herself into the corset in an effort to pull in her stomach.

She felt so differently about this pregnancy. She had so looked forward to Connie's birth. She'd longed to see what she looked like and hold her in her arms, but this pregnancy she viewed dispassionately, as an unwelcome intrusion into her life. Even when she felt the baby quicken she couldn't think of it as a human child, but as a bit of rubbish she had to get rid of.

The baby was due mid December and so in mid September Angela wrote to Phyllis and suggested moving in with her on Monday 8th October. Phyllis wrote back by return and said she was looking forward to seeing her again and asked if she could come after dark so the neighbours wouldn't see

her arriving.

Angela was just glad she had another evening with Connie and that night she gave her a piggy-back up the stairs and Connie was giggling as she slid off her mother's back on to the bed. She supervised Connie's prayers when she blessed everyone and for a moment Angela considered telling Connie she was going away for a few days. But she knew she would probably be upset and would certainly ask twenty questions and might be difficult to settle and Phyllis was expecting Angela that night and she didn't want to arrive too late. So as she tucked her into bed she gave her a kiss and looked at that dear little face she wouldn't see for some time and she gave a sigh as she said, 'I love you my darling girl.'

Connie sat up in bed and wound her arms around her mother's neck and said, 'Don't be sad, Mammy. I love you too. Lots and lots I do.' She kissed Angela's cheek and then snuggled down in bed looking absolutely angelic.

Angela almost stumbled from the room blinded by tears. Mary knew she would be upset when the time came to leave and she said, 'Don't fret about the child for don't I love the very bones of her? And I will look after her as well as I can.'

'Oh Mary, I know that,' Angela said. 'It's not that that I'm worried about.'

Mary had hold of Angela's hands and was look-ing directly into her eyes as she said, 'Darling girl, you are doing the only thing you could do that's better for everyone. As for Connie she will undoubtedly miss you, but I am at least familiar and her routine will not be disrupted and the

time will soon pass.'

Angela knew that for Connie a week was a long time, but there was nothing else she could have done and she knew it wouldn't help to delay any more. She remembered to take her wedding ring for she would need to wear it at Phyllis's and now she was no longer at work she put the locket around her neck and then she kissed Mary, and stepped out into the night.

Phyllis was really pleased to see Angela and so positive it soothed Angela's soul a great deal and dispelled any lingering doubts she had by her very attitude. She said she had a plan, but didn't elaborate further on what that was until they were sitting down with a cup of tea.

'Now I will have to say something to explain your presence here,' Phyllis said to Angela. 'So from now your name will be Amy Bradley, for Angela is too unusual a name for this area, and you are my niece and also a pregnant war widow. You have come to stay till the baby is born because my house is more suitable than the cramped back-to-back you live in and share with your husband's family, but you intend returning home for Christmas.'

'Goodness you have thought of everything.'

'Yes I have even bought you this to wear to Mass,' Phyllis said and produced a black widow's bonnet from the shopping bag.

The blood drained from Angela's face and she said, 'I ... I can't wear that. Thank you but no. It's like ... like.'

'It's like nothing,' Phyllis said sharply. 'You are

384

not bringing bad luck on your husband by wearing a bonnet to make our story more authentic and believable. You explained to me that you were doing this for him too, to prevent any malicious gossip by someone not in possession of all the facts contacting your husband and saying you'd been carrying on with someone and were having your fancy man's baby. That could happen. It's been done many times before. Some people's life's work is to make trouble for others. How much would such news upset him as he goes to face the German machine guns and shells and sniper fire?'

Angela gave a gasp. 'I couldn't endure that,' she cried. 'Oh, it would hurt him tremendously, desperately,' Angela said and she took the bonnet from Phyllis and said, 'Thank you once again and I will wear it. I was being silly.'

Angela had never lived in such luxury. She had a large, comfortable bed all to herself with a matching wardrobe and a chest of drawers and a bathroom just down the corridor and she told herself not to get too used to it because she'd be back in Bell Barn Road before that long.

Phyllis was right too about the widow's bonnet. It evoked compassion from everyone when she wore it to church that first Sunday morning. They gathered around the church door after the Mass. There again Phyllis had her tale ready. 'Only married five minutes,' she said. 'Married quick because of the call-up and he never even knew he was going to be a father when he was killed.'

Many had similar heart-wrenching stories and the women spoke comforting words of empathy

385

and understanding, but though Angela wasn't the only one wearing such a bonnet, she was so young and she played her part so well as the sorrowful widow that none disbelieved her. It was also quite conceivable too that she came to give birth in her aunt's comfortable home. They all knew how cramped the back-to-back houses were at the best of times and hospitals were bursting at the seams with the war wounded.

Angela was always glad to see Maggie who came every Sunday afternoon. She brought all the gossip from the factory and the streets around, news of Mary and Connie, and brought any letters that had arrived and she would wait while Angela wrote replies and in this way convinced Barry that life was going on as it always had done and nothing untoward had happened.

Despite Maggie's visits the days passed slowly but it was December at last with squally wind and snow and bone-chilling cold and the baby's due date, the fifteenth, slipped past with no sign. Phyllis had asked a friend of hers, Sally Metcalfe, who was a retired nurse, and also discreet and non-judgemental, to help at the birth. She had put her in the picture about what had happened to Angela and Sally agreed that in the circumstances adoption was the only answer. She was not a jot concerned that the birth was delayed. 'Babies come when they are ready and that's all there is to it,' she said complacently.

That was all very well, but Angela had wanted to be home for Christmas. It would be hard for her not to be at home to share Christmas Day with her child, and she imagined harder still for her child to

understand, and also she thought Mary had held the fort on her own for long enough.

She was in an agony of impatience and then eventually in the early morning of the twenty-first, Angela awoke to water gushing out from her and realized her waters had broken. She felt a leap of excitement knowing that soon the foreign unwelcome baby would be expelled from her and she would be free again and could go home.

At first Angela welcomed every contraction knowing each one was bringing the birth closer and she thought it far too early to wake Phyllis, but was very glad to see her when she did pop her head around the door at half past seven to see how she was. By then Angela was in extreme discomfort and Phyllis went straight down for Sally and her calm presence in the room immediately reassured Angela, though the pains were getting stronger.

Angela found labour progressed much quicker than when she was giving birth to Connie and she soon had the urge to push and Sally had only been there a couple of hours when Angela gave birth to a baby girl, and she gazed at Sally who had caught the child up in her arms as newborn wails filled the air, and felt nothing. When she said this however neither Phyllis nor Sally were shocked. 'I think that's quite understandable after the way you were raped,' Sally said. 'And it's far better that you feel nothing for the wee mite if she's going for adoption.'

Angela sighed. 'I suppose and in the circumstances it's all I can do, but I feel sorry for her, being denied her mother's love.'

387

'You can't pretend what isn't there,' Phyllis said. 'And why should you feel love for a child conceived in such a savage way? Every time you looked at her, you would be reminded of that ordeal.'

'I know,' Angela said. 'And even if I could learn to love her, I couldn't expect my husband to feel the same. And the neighbours would draw their own conclusions. I didn't report the rape, you see, because I didn't want Barry to know of it, so they would have no idea I was attacked.'

'Don't feel bad about this,' Sally said for she had seen the tears in Angela's eyes and heard the catch in her voice. 'Your baby will be taken by some couple who cannot have children of their own and I'm sure they will love her dearly.'

Angela remembered Stan staying something similar about Betty. At the time she had said she would never give a child of hers away and could never envisage anything that would change that. But here she was, going through with it. And although Stan had relinquished all rights to Daniel, he knew who his son was going to and knew they would love and care for him, whereas she was abandoning her baby to the unknown.

'Why don't you lie down and have a wee rest while the child sleeps,' Sally suggested and though Angela obediently lay down she knew she wouldn't sleep.

But she was more tired than she realized because though she did toss and turn for quite a while eventually her eyes closed. She slept for three whole hours and when she awoke she was hungry but less emotional about the decision made about

the baby's future. Both Phyllis and Sally kept the child away from her as much as possible. 'You mustn't feed her,' Sally said. 'We have that all in hand and will feed her from the bottle for the short time we have her, for Phyllis will take her in tomorrow.'

'I would like to send a letter with the baby,' Angela said.

'I don't think it would be appropriate to say what happened to you.'

'No I wouldn't do that,' Angela said. 'I just wanted to tell the child that I love her and though I actually feel nothing for her, that isn't her fault and it might help her a little if I write that I love her, but am unable to care for her properly.'

'I think that's a nice thing to do and it may well be a comfort to her when she's older,' Sally said. 'I'd get that written in plenty of time for Phyllis will take the child early tomorrow morning and have her installed by Christmas.'

'And I can go home.' Angela didn't say it, but that suited her down to the ground.

The next morning, Phyllis set off with the baby wrapped up warm against the winter chill in the basket bought for the purpose. 'You will be all right won't you?' she asked Angela because Sally had returned home.

'I will be perfectly fine,' Angela said. 'But you had better be on your way. Yesterday Sally said something about the children taken to early Mass.'

'Yes,' Phyllis said, 'it would be better to get there before that happens.'

As soon as Phyllis had gone Angela went upstairs and pulled her case from the top of the

wardrobe in the room she had been using and began to fill it with all the things she had brought with her all those weeks ago. She hadn't quite finished when she heard Phyllis returning and she went out to greet her and was astounded to find she had brought the baby back with her.

'What happened?'

'They were full,' Phyllis said. 'Chock-a-block they said they were. Apparently with the war and everything, adoptions have dropped off quite a lot and they couldn't squeeze in another child and certainly not a baby at the moment.'

Angela glanced at the baby still slumbering peacefully in the basket and she looked so small and vulnerable and she had a sudden longing to hold her in her arms. She clenched her fists and held her arms stiffly at her sides to prevent herself from doing that and said, 'Did they suggest anywhere else?'

'The only place left,' Phyllis said flatly. 'The workhouse.'

Angela gave a shiver for just the thought of that place struck terror into the hearts of all working-class people. 'What if they are also full?'

'They're never full,' Phyllis said. 'I mean do you ever see any queue of people waiting to go inside?'

'No,' Angela said. 'And the thought of leaving her in an orphanage is bad enough, though I know they do everything they can to find good, Catholic couples to adopt the babies and young children, but some people never come out of the workhouse. It's rare for anyone to adopt a child from the workhouse. I've never heard of it happening. They might on the other hand send a girl of twelve

or thirteen into service to labour from dawn to dusk twelve hours or more each and every day. You see the poor scrawny and exhausted young girls at the shops sometimes and they look as if they've never had a decent meal in the whole of their lives. How could I subject this poor little helpless baby to that?'

'Everything you say is right,' Phyllis said. 'The baby stands little chance of being adopted from the workhouse. People have to be on their uppers before they seek help from the parish. Most children in the workhouse are not available for adoption anyway because they are not officially orphans. They are looked after so their mothers can work and not be too much of a drain on the parish coffers. And even though we know this and recognize it is not ideal, we are still not burdened with options or alternatives.'

Angela knew that only too well and she nodded mutely and Phyllis, catching sight of her sorrowful face, felt very sorry for her. 'Look,' she said, 'I must get ready for eleven o'clock Mass. I'll see to the baby first and she should sleep till I'm back.'

Again Angela nodded and watched as Phyllis fed and changed the baby and laid her in the cradle by the fire where she would be nice and warm.

'You should be all right now,' she said as she prepared to leave herself. 'I'll be straight back. And after dinner when Maggie comes she might be able to think of something that hasn't occurred to either of us.' She didn't believe it for a moment, but she wanted to take a little of that intense sadness from Angela's face, let her hope a little longer.

Angela grasped that thought like a life-line though, knowing how resourceful Maggie was.

However soon she had more to think about, because Phyllis wouldn't have got right to the end of the road when the baby began fidgeting and making the little mewling noises many babies make before waking up properly.

Angela tried rocking the cradle with her foot, but the baby continued to whimper and then to wail. Angela's breasts began to ache and she felt milk seep from her nipples in response to the baby's distress and this was despite the tight binding cloth Sally had bound round Angela's breasts to give her some ease until the milk had dried up.

Angela had a sudden longing to put the baby to her breast, feel her tug at those swollen nipples and swallow the milk that should have been her birthright. But she resisted the temptation and anyway knew the child could not be hungry for she had just been fed and it must be wind causing her pain, and almost gingerly she picked her up, laid her against her shoulder and began to rock her gently while she rubbed her back.

And as she did so, she felt the shell she'd put around her heart to try and prevent her from loving this child, shatter and break apart and she knew her love for this child, regardless of her conception, was as deep as the love she had for Connie and, had the circumstances been different, she would take her home without hesitation.

However, the circumstances weren't different and privately admitting her love for the baby did not change the situation one bit, except feeling as she did now, it would cause further heartache to

walk away from her.

When Phyllis returned from Mass she saw at once that Angela's attitude towards the child had changed. She was still holding her for Angela hadn't wanted to put her down, though any pain she'd had was eased and she had fallen into a deep sleep. Phyllis felt her heart constrict with pity for Angela. She had planned to get the child away to the orphanage before any bond was formed between them like she had done with Maggie's mother all those years ago, but in this case it looked very much as if she was too late. 'Oh, Angela,' she cried. 'You shouldn't have touched her.'

'I had to,' Angela said in her own defence, 'she was crying.'

'And now you feel differently about her?'

'Yes I do,' Angela said. 'And I can't help how I feel, but I know it changes nothing.'

'No,' said Phyllis, 'it doesn't and we can't let it and that's the pity of it.'

When Maggie arrived, she was enchanted by the baby but she was careful not to go overboard, as she would usually, for these were not usual times and the future for the child was very uncertain. She was quite shocked that the orphanage was full and though she thought hard she could come up with no solution but the workhouse. 'The only thing is,' Maggie said, 'I think if you just turn up with the baby in your arms they'd insist on taking you in as well.'

'They couldn't do that,' Angela said. 'Anyway I wouldn't go.'

'I don't think you would have much of a choice,' Phyllis said. 'Maggie is right, they look after the

393

child and put the woman to work to pay for their keep because you are living off the parish.'

Angela glanced from one woman to the other in panic. 'What shall I do then because I can't do that?'

'There is only one thing to be done,' Phyllis said. 'It is a terrible thing to do and I never ever thought I would be advocating it, but in the circumstances it is all I can think of and that is to leave her on the steps of the workhouse.'

Both Angela and Maggie gasped and Angela said in horrified tones, 'What a dreadful thing to even contemplate.'

'Agreed,' said Phyllis. 'Give me an alternative and I will gladly take it.'

Angela could think of nothing, but she did say, 'Are you sure they'd want me to go into that dreadful place as well?'

'They might not if you tell them everything and I mean everything,' Phyllis said. 'And they may not believe you were attacked at all, as you didn't report it to the police. What I'm saying is there would be a hue and cry and there would be no way to keep it secret and it's almost certain one of your neighbours will get to hear of it and then you cannot really protect your husband from hearing about it either.'

'Oh what am I to do?' Angela cried. 'Maggie what would you do if you were me?'

Maggie took a deep breath and said, 'Though it goes against my conscience and tears, the heart out of me to say it, I believe to leave her on the workhouse steps is the only thing to do.'

Phyllis gave a gasp at the anguish in Angela's

beautiful eyes. There were tear trails on her face too and Angela felt as if her heart was breaking as she said in a voice husky with distress, 'That's what must be done then.'

'Not you,' Phyllis said. 'If you're sure, I will take her.'

'No,' Angela said. 'I will take her.'

'You are not fit,' Phyllis protested. 'You are just days from giving birth. By rights you should still be in your bed, never mind gallivanting all over the place.'

'If this heinous thing has to be done, it must be me that does it,' Angela said. 'She is my daughter and this is the last service I can do for her. I will be able for it, don't worry.'

There was nothing further Phyllis could say, but she thought Angela looked very white and strained. She owned that the worry about what would happen to the child would undoubtedly have contributed to that strain and yet still Phyllis thought that she was doing too much and too soon.

She knew Angela wanted to be back home as soon as possible for the sake of the young daughter she had been separated from for many weeks. She could quite understand her impatience to be back with her, especially as the child was only four and a firm believer in the powers of Santa, and when Maggie had asked her what she wanted Santa to bring her she said she was going to ask Santa to bring her Mammy back home, that was all she wanted.

Such earnest and heartfelt words from such a young child brought tears to Phyllis's eyes and

Angela had been broken up completely, so Phyllis knew, come what may, Angela intended to make it home by Christmas Day.

'It's how to do it bothers me,' Maggie said.

'What d'you mean?'

'Well you can't just walk up to the main gates if you're trying to get in unseen. Chances are they'd be locked anyway and there's a high wall around the rest of it.'

'Then how am I going to do it?'

'It's a problem all right,' said Phyllis. 'They have very high walls at the front, but maybe they are not as high all around. Only thing to do is reccy in daylight. I'll go into the town tomorrow and take a look.'

'Tomorrow is Christmas Eve,' Angela said quietly.

'I know.'

'Well what if I can't find a way in tomorrow?'

'Angela, let's cross that bridge when we come to it,' Phyllis advised. 'And in the meantime, pray hard tonight before you sleep.'

TWENTY-SIX

Phyllis was in a more positive mood when she arrived home from town the following morning. She was a little disconcerted though to see the baby in Angela's arms, especially as she had said to Angela before she went that she had already changed her and given her a bottle of milk as well.

'Angela,' Phyllis said warningly, 'you are only making it harder for yourself.'

Angela tossed her head and said, 'D'you know, I don't much care how hard it is for me, because I deserve it to be hard. I can see from your face you have good news as regards getting into the workhouse grounds so these memories will have to last a lifetime.'

'Oh Angela, I feel sorry for you and I wish there was a better outcome for both you and the child, but it isn't your fault.'

'Up until now it hasn't been my fault, I agree,' Angela said. 'But getting rid of my child will be my fault, because it will be my decision and it's wrong and quite possibly a sin.'

'And the alternative is?'

'That's the devil of it, Phyllis,' Angela admitted. 'There isn't one, but I'll never forgive myself for what I am forced to do this night, not till the end of my days.' She glanced at Phyllis and said, 'You've found a way in haven't you?'

Phyllis nodded. 'In Whittal Street,' she said, 'the road that runs alongside the workhouse down to St Chad's.' Angela nodded and Phyllis went on, 'Part of the way down that road there's an entry and at the bottom of the entry is a gate. It was fastened in some way though I couldn't take too much of a look at it in case I was spotted. But even if you couldn't open it, you could climb over it and lift the basket over because it isn't a big gate. From what I could see it leads on to the place where a load of bins are stored at the side of the house. If you go after dark, and that's four o'clock these winter days, you should get in with-

out being seen. It's important that you get away as soon as the door is opened because they might search for you and might work out how you got in, so get out as soon as you can and make for St Chad's, for it's unlikely that they'll think of you making for a church, so you'll probably be safe there. And if there is a hue and cry, and there might well be, wait until it has died down before you make your way home.'

Angela knew that Phyllis spoke sense. The workhouse, she imagined, would take a very dim view of people dumping children on their steps and if she lingered in the yard and they gave chase she could be caught and that would never do.

Never had a day seemed to drag like that one and while one part of her wanted to get the dreadful thing she had to do over and done with, another part of her wanted to hold back time, for after that day she would never again see the child she had given birth to, who was already entwined into her heart.

Eventually the sky began to darken and Angela gave the last bottle she would ever give to the child and then changed her. They had planned this with care for the December day was raw. The basket was padded out with a soft, woollen blanket and she was dressed in a little vest and a winceyette nightdress and a thick woollen matinee jacket. She had bootees on her feet and mittens on her hands and a bonnet covering the black down on her head. More blankets covered her and Phyllis had even cut a piece of thin rubber that she had bought at the Bull Ring to go on top because she said, 'Even if it isn't actually raining the nights

could very damp.'

Then Angela was ready in the hall with her small case in one hand and the basket with its precious load in the other. She was very pale and her stomach growled for she hadn't been able to eat all day through nerves and she was feeling light-headed. But when Phyllis said, 'Are you sure you are well enough to do this?' she answered her heartily enough, that she was.

And then she said to Phyllis, 'There are no words to thank you enough for what you have done for me. I don't know what I would have done if you hadn't agreed to help me. I know the outcome would have been totally different.'

Phyllis shrugged. 'You have been dealt one bad hand in life and yours might have been ruined, though you had done nothing wrong. So bless you my dear. Let's hope and pray your young man comes home safe from this unholy war and you are able to settle down in peace and raise your daughter.'

'Oh, yes,' Angela cried. 'Please God.'

'Please God indeed,' Phyllis said and though she wasn't a demonstrative woman generally, she put her arms around Angela and held her tight for a few moments. She knew she would miss Angela because she was good company and she was glad she had been able to help her and she said, 'I do hope it goes all right for you this evening. Will you let me know?'

'Of course,' Angela said. 'I intended doing that anyway. I'm not going straight back to work. I want to spend a few days with Connie and Mary.'

'I should think you won't be rushing back to

work,' Phyllis said. 'You have just had a baby. You should be resting.'

'Well it's true, not much rest is to be had in a munition works,' Angela said. 'So I'm having a break, so I'll come up and see you the day after Boxing Day. Connie's nursery opens then and we'll be able to talk more freely.'

'Oh I shall look forward to that.'

Suddenly at the door, Angela leant forward and kissed Phyllis's cheek. Phyllis gave a little gasp and put a hand to her cheek which was reddening into a blush. Angela went into the night carrying a case in one hand and the basket over the other arm. She knew both would get heavier with every step she took, but she couldn't risk taking a tram for no one must see her abroad with a newborn baby on a bleak December night.

If there was a bit of commotion about a child left on the workhouse steps and made the news, they might put two and two together.

She continued to put one foot before the other while her aching arms began to throb with pain. She was taking the side roads to avoid meeting people and they were not that well lit, but now and again she would pass a hissing gaslight and the pool of light showed her the sleeping baby and her heart would constrict with love for the child she had to give away. She was immensely relieved that she didn't have to go far because the workhouse was this side of town.

It was on a road called Steelhouse Lane, the road named because of the large police station across the road from the workhouse and Angela imagined there would be few people about in

that area at night.

She was right, there wasn't a soul about. She passed the front of the workhouse and thought what a grim and forbidding building it was. It was large with many floors, built of pale brick but looking dark, unwelcoming.

A high brick wall surrounded it apart from the firmly locked gates in the centre which led to a short gravel path and then three steps to the heavy solid studded door. It almost broke Angela's heart to think of her daughter spending her first Christmas in that miserable place, especially as she knew it was just one of many Christmases she would spend there.

Angela averted her eyes from the edifice and made her way to Whittal Street which ran down to the right side of the workhouse. At the end of that short road was St Chad's, which was Birmingham's Roman Catholic Cathedral, where she might run for sanctuary if she was pursued. The nearer she got to the place where she must relinquish her child the worse Angela felt. Her whole body felt heavy and cumbersome and there was an agonising pain in her heart and it was only the thought of soon seeing Connie that sustained her.

She found the entry easily enough, but it was like a big black hole for there was no light at all and the darkness was intense. But she couldn't dither on the pavement and so she went in, shuffling along uneven cobbles cautiously, hearing her heart thumping in her breast and her mouth suddenly so dry she had trouble swallowing.

When she came to the gate she laid down the case in order to have one hand free to feel all over

the gate and try and work out how it was fastened and eventually on the other side of the gate she felt bolts, one at the top and one further down and they didn't seem to be held fast in any way, but they were stiff.

She put the basket on the ground beside her and tried to ease the first bolt out slowly, worried that it might suddenly shoot out with a bang if she was too firm, or open with a penetrating screech.

And then the baby began to whimper. She had slumbered beautifully while she had been carried, but now she was registering her discontent.

It was the very worst time for her to cry, or make any noise at all, and Angela had slid open the first bolt, and as she reached for the second the baby's whimpers became louder, and she threw caution to the wind and drew the bolt free with haste. The gate opened without a creak of any sort and as soon as she picked up the basket again the baby stopped crying.

The way was open for Angela to do what she had come to do and yet suddenly she couldn't move, it was as if she was rooted to the spot.

She couldn't do it, she decided. It was inhuman to expect her to put the child she had just given birth to on the steps of that vile-looking place and never ever know what happened to her. It was too cruel to ask a mother to do that and hot scalding tears fell from her eyes at the thought of it.

And even while the tears rained down her face she thought of the practicalities of keeping the child, as she had done before. She thought she could just about stand the condemnation and

disdain she knew would be shown by many of the neighbours if she brought home a newborn baby when her husband had been away two years.

It would be harder to bear if their contempt impinged on Mary and even little Connie as she knew it might well. But how could she risk word getting to Barry and what if he was so upset he failed to keep his wits about him and was killed because of it? Could she ever live with herself if that happened? She knew she couldn't.

And how would they live if she couldn't work? Mary wasn't up to the care of a newborn baby and the nursery only took children from six months and might not take her at all if they knew the circumstances of her birth. In fact Connie might lose her place too. That would be disastrous for them all for the savings she had accrued wouldn't last for ever. And what would happen when Barry came home and said he wasn't prepared to care for a child forced on his wife in that violent way. He might even think the child had bad blood.

She couldn't blame Barry for feeling that way if he did, nor could she disobey him and so she would lose the child anyway, which would upset them both more than if she left her now.

She faced the fact that that small child's life was going to be sacrificed for the good of everyone else and that thought was hard to bear. If only she had something to give her to show how much she was loved. The letter was stowed in the basket where it would be found, but she would have liked to have given her something of her own, something she valued. And then she remembered

the locket, her most treasured possession.

It should have gone to Connie on her wedding day, but all her life she would have the love of a mother and this little mite would have nothing. She took the locket from around her neck and eased one of the baby's hands from the covers and took off the mitten. When she touched the baby's palm with the locket her little fingers folded over it and Angela replaced the mitten and put the little hand under the covers again.

She went through the gate for it was no good delaying this any longer and she crossed the small yard and walked against the wall so she wouldn't be seen by anyone looking out of the windows, which was highly unlikely because the yard was as dark as the entry. When she reached the corner of the house she peeped around furtively to check there was no one about and then before she could lose her nerve altogether she placed the basket on the top step, pulled the bell rope on the wall and heard it jangle in the house.

They took a long time to answer the door and Angela was getting so chilled, her teeth had begun to chatter. And yet she kept her eyes focused on that door and when it began to open, she was off like a hare. The person who had opened the door gave a bellow, probably on realizing that there was a baby in the basket, and as Angela raced across the yard she heard the sound of many boots pounding through the house towards the door.

Then she was in the entry, showing no caution now nor panic, remembering to pick up her case, and with it bumping against the side of her legs, she was out and tearing down Whittal Street

towards St Chad's.

She barely took time to get her breath back in the porch, but in the church she saw there were a good few people praying already and lighting candles and so she made sure to dip her hand in the font as she entered the church and genuflect before the altar because people would think it odd if she didn't. She didn't skulk at the back of the church either, but made her way into the main body of the church and entered a pew beside two other women for she thought that was safer if she was pursued. She stowed her case under the pew and she knelt with head in her hands and tried to still her pounding heart as she prayed for the child she had just abandoned and Barry and Stan and all the fighting soldiers and their families.

Phyllis had said that even if she were chased they wouldn't think of St Chad's and she would be safe in there. But people did come from the House looking for her. She heard the Commotion at the back of the church and though many looked round, she kept her eyes firmly on the altar. The priest was a man called John Hennessy who people said was a kindly soul. He had not seen Angela come in but he had attended Catholics at the House and it always upset him to see how many were treated, especially the ones they called fallen women. A fair few were mere girls and forced into the sex that resulted in a child. So he had little time for those working at the House and he frowned as he asked the two men what they wanted.

They said they were looking for a girl who had left a baby on the workhouse steps and run away.

'And did you see her come in here?'

'Well, no, Father. Not exactly,' one of the men said. 'Fact is we don't know where she went. She like disappeared into thin air. We thought we'd try here on the off chance.'

'Well as you can see,' the priest said, 'there are no runaway girls here, just respectable men and women saying a few prayers before the greatest event in the Christian Calendar, the birth of our Lord Jesus Christ and I'm sure they do not welcome this intrusion.'

The priest said this with such authority that the men from the House were apologetic. 'Sorry, Father.'

'Yes, well, I suggest you look for that unfortunate young woman some other place for she is not here.'

They went on their way and Angela breathed a sigh of relief and Father Hennessy made a mental note to pray for the poor girl they were searching for. She must have been desperate altogether to leave her baby in the indifferent care of the workhouse and he was sorry for her, whoever she was.

Angela had the urge to leap up and follow the men out but she controlled that urge and waited till half an hour had passed and then she set off for the Bull Ring and home.

Anxious now to be home as soon as possible, she took a tram along Bristol Street. As she alighted and went up Bristol Passage she gave a shudder remembering her ordeal at the hands of three drunken soldiers who weren't worthy to wear their uniform. She had never walked this way in the

dark and alone since that night because she was usually with Maggie and if she had to work late, she took up Mr Potter's offer of a taxi home. It always caused a bit of a stir in the street but better that, Angela thought, than risk being violated.

She mustn't think of it again, she told herself firmly. All sad thoughts must be shelved. She hadn't seen Connie for two long months and the last thing the child wanted was a Mammy with a doleful face, especially with it being Christmas Eve too.

Maggie had told Mary Angela was making for home Christmas Eve if everything went to plan and so Mary was half expecting her, but said nothing to Connie just in case she didn't make it.

Angela opened the door with a smile nailed to her face to see Mary and Connie at the table eating a meal. She set the case down as Connie turned her head. When she saw her mother framed in the doorway, her mouth dropped open and the blood drained from her face.

Angela shut the door with her foot and said, 'Hello Connie.'

Her words seemed to galvanize the child, who leapt from her chair into her mother's waiting arms, and then she burrowed her face into her mother's neck and burst into tears.

TWENTY-SEVEN

Connie had longed for her mother's return and asked Santa to bring her home for Christmas, and he had, and she was very happy about it. But, the Mammy who came home was not the same as the one who left. She looked the same and sounded the same, more or less, but...

Connie hadn't the words to say to show how she felt and she didn't understand the innate sadness and guilt that clung to her mother. However she knew something wasn't quite right and that unnerved her and so she didn't want to let her mother out of her sight. So when she learned her mother didn't intend going straight back to work after Christmas, she refused to go back to the nursery when it opened the day after Boxing Day.

Angela didn't mind spending some time with the child she had missed so much but when she refused to go to nursery she thought she might leave her with Mary while she returned to Phyllis's to tell her how things had gone. However, Connie became so distressed when she suggested this, she knew she had to take her. 'You must come too, Mammy,' she said to Mary as they washed up the breakfast things. 'You know Connie has ears on her like a donkey and there are things to be said that I definitely don't want her to hear.'

Mary could quite see that and anyway she had

408

a great desire herself to see this lady who had looked after Angela so well when they had no idea where to turn and thought all was lost.

Phyllis was delighted to see them and be introduced to Mary whom Angela had always spoken of so warmly and she had a special smile for Connie. 'Did Santa come and bring you nice things?' she asked.

Connie nodded, thinking of the paint box and a pad with lots of paper to paint on, a beautiful white teddy from one uncle and soft leather boots from the other and a jigsaw from her Auntie Maggie.

'And what was your favourite present?' Phyllis asked.

'Mammy,' Connie said without hesitation and then went on, 'I asked Santa to bring her and he did, before the other presents because she's special.'

Angela felt a lump form in her throat as she realized Connie was deadly serious. She had no idea that was what she thought but Phyllis didn't turn a hair. She just nodded sagely and said, 'That must have been the way of it all right.'

'Yes,' Connie agreed happily.

'And do you think you could eat some biscuits with a glass of milk?'

Connie decided she liked this lady, whoever she was, and she nodded her head eagerly. 'Yes please.'

'I have the kettle on for us too,' Phyllis said. 'It won't take me a jiffy.'

'And I have some Christmas cake and a few mince pies,' Mary said.

'Oh we'll have ourselves a little feast,' Phyllis

said as she got to her feet.

'I'll give you a hand,' Angela said and immediately Connie slid off the seat beside her. 'I'm only going as far as the kitchen. Stay here and I'll be back in a moment.'

Connie had her mutinous face on and for a moment Angela thought she was going to argue with her. Mary knew that too and said, 'Bold girls who don't do as they're told don't deserve milk and biscuits in my book.'

Connie looked at her Granny who could be stern when she chose and she decided to not risk her getting angry and so she sat back down on the chair.

'You see how she is,' Angela said to Phyllis as she reached the relative safety of the kitchen.

'I see a very unhappy girl,' Phyllis said.

'She won't let me out of her sight,' Angela said. 'When she realized I wasn't going to work straight away she refused to go to nursery and then when I suggested coming here without her she got really upset. I had to bring her.'

'Of course you did,' Phyllis said. 'She is a confused girl at present and there is a shadow behind her eyes and that's distrust. She loves you very much and she doesn't want you to disappear again. You must be very gentle with her. Shall we go back now? I think we have it all organized.'

As Angela followed Phyllis down the corridor she thought that though she had had no children herself she had seen straight away what ailed Connie. And she was so right, making Angela feel ashamed that her actions had caused Connie's unhappiness.

When Phyllis handed Connie the plate with the biscuits on she looked at her mother straight away because there were four of the most delicious-looking biscuits on that plate. They didn't have that many biscuits and even then she was never allowed four straight off. Mammy always said that was greedy, but she didn't seem to see and so Connie polished them off quickly in case she should suddenly take notice.

They tasted as good as they looked and she sighed in contentment and took a gulp of milk before saying to Phyllis, 'Did Santa come to you?'

'Sadly no,' Phyllis said, with a smile. 'It wasn't that I was a naughty girl or anything, Santa just doesn't come to adults.'

Connie looked a little sad about that and so Phyllis said, 'I have got toys here in my house, just in case I might want to play with them.'

Connie wrinkled her forehead. She didn't think adults played with toys but this lady might for all she knew so she just said, 'Where?'

Phyllis said, 'They're right here in the cupboard.' Then she went on to ask Connie, 'You know Maggie don't you?'

'Auntie Maggie,' Connie confirmed.

'Well she has lots of young brothers and when they were small they would come for a visit and they would get very loud and unruly if they got bored.'

Connie didn't know the word unruly, but she knew the word loud very well, especially when referring to boys. There were plenty of loud boys at her nursery and they didn't have to be bored or anything, it was just the way they were and so

411

she nodded and said, 'I know.'

'So I bought some toys and stored them in this cupboard by the fireplace. There's a Noah's Ark they seemed to play with a lot and a spinning top they all liked. There's a box of lead soldiers somewhere and some books. Would you like to play with them now?'

'Ooh yes please.'

Phyllis opened the cupboard and Connie dived happily into it pulling out one thing after the other. She thought it an unexpected treasure trove for toys weren't that plentiful in her house either. Mary took the seat nearby and Angela and Phyllis sat on the other side of the room so that as long as they kept their voices low they could talk with ease and Angela told Phyllis how dreadful she felt about actually leaving her child on the steps of the workhouse. 'I gave her my locket,' she said quietly.

Mary's head shot up at that, though they were speaking quietly, and she walked across to Angela. 'I thought that was going to be given to her ladyship,' she almost hissed indicating the child playing on the floor.

Angela sensed that Mary wasn't happy with her doing that. She understood, for the locket was given into her keeping by her mother, and she would want it to go to Barry's child and she attempted to explain: 'Mammy, through all her growing up Connie will have every ounce of my devotion and attention. I love her far far more than words can say and she is special, because she is part of Barry.

'But the child I gave birth to is still my daughter however she was conceived. She is a child I can

412

never acknowledge and even worse than that, I will never see her again nor know what happens to her, but I am certain she will have a miserable childhood in that place. I wanted to show her that somewhere there was once a mother who loved her and I had nothing to show that but the locket. It was the only thing of value I ever owned and it seemed right I give it to her. It is the only part of me she will ever have.'

Phyllis took Angela's trembling hands. She seemed unaware of the tears coursing down her face and said, 'I fully understand why you gave the little one the locket, but can you be traced by it?' She knew that if they could find out who she was by the locket, she might be in trouble and Phyllis too, for she was sure it was a crime to abandon a child.

It was Mary who answered because she had followed Phyllis's train of thought, but Angela was struggling to control her emotions before the eagle-eyed Connie noticed her mother was upset. 'No,' she assured Phyllis. 'All the locket contains is a miniature of Angela's parents on their wedding day and the other side held two or three of the many white-gold ringlets Angela had as a young child. There is no writing anywhere, not even dates. And Angela,' she went on, turning to face the girl, 'I spoke out of turn. This I know was the hardest thing you have ever had to do and I understand the dilemma you were in and you were right to give the child the locket. In that place it's probably the only thing she'll ever own.'

'I know it was very hard for Angela too,' Phyllis said. 'Believe me, if there had been any alter-

native we would have taken it.'

'I know you would,' Mary said. 'I'm not criticizing you in any way. I think the whole thing is unbelievably tragic and I can only thank you again for what you have done for Angela.'

When they were leaving shortly afterwards Phyllis said, 'If you will be able to carry it you could take the ark home if you like. Connie was very taken with it.'

'Oh I couldn't.'

''Course you could,' Phyllis said firmly.

Angela shook her head, 'No, it's made of wood and painted and everything. It must have been very expensive.'

Phyllis shrugged. 'I really can't remember. I bought it years ago and it isn't as if it's new. It's been well played with over the years. Look,' she went on as Angela still hesitated, 'I don't have small visitors any more. Maggie's brothers are all grown up. And it's unlikely you and I will ever see each other again, for how would the friendship be explained? You were supposed to be my war-widowed pregnant niece. This is the end of the road for us so let your daughter have this as a sort of late Christmas present. I would like to think of her playing with it.'

Angela could no longer refuse, she was too choked up because she knew that Phyllis was right, they would never see each other again and she realized the sacrifice she made for a perfect stranger. It was different for Maggie's mother because she was Phyllis's niece and part of their family.

It was hard for both of them to say a final good-

bye because they had become close, but she had to face the truth that Phyllis was someone she had needed at a certain point in her life, but now that period was over and she had to go back to her old life and Phyllis had to do the same.

With the ark packed away in various bags Phyllis had pressed on them, and Connie in a state of extreme excitement at being allowed to take the ark home with them, it was hard to hold back the tears as Phyllis and Angela hugged for the last time. But it had to be done and as they set off down the road, Angela wiped her eyes surreptitiously lest Connie see that she had been crying.

'You all right?' Mary asked.

Angela nodded. 'Have to be I suppose.'

'And that's the truth right enough,' Mary said. 'Mind you I am surprised you wanted to come home after living in that house for a couple of months with all mod cons.'

'Home is where the heart is, you know that,' Angela said. 'My heart is with you and Connie and Barry in the back-to-back we all live in.'

That night Connie played up about going to bed in the attic on her own. She had always been so good before, but now she said she was frightened. She couldn't explain why she was frightened but Angela, catching sight of her child's ravaged panic-stricken face, knew she was gripped by a real and genuine fear that if she went to bed her mother might disappear again. It tore at Angela's heart strings because it was her fault. She shouldn't have sneaked away without a word to Phyllis's after Connie had gone to bed at night. She should have

415

tried to explain to her.

Realising this, she was gentle and understanding with Connie who ended up sharing her mother's bed. 'There was nothing else I could do,' she said to Mary when Connie had eventually settled down for the night. 'All this all stems from disappearing without a word and then staying away for over two months. That's half a lifetime for a child.'

'This whole business has certainly upset her,' Mary agreed. 'I have never known her like this.'

'I'll have to regain her trust,' Angela said. 'All the time I was away, though I missed Connie, I never knew what it was doing to her. All my energies were on the child I would be abandoning, because you were right, I couldn't help myself, I did learn to love the child after the birth and of course it was even harder to leave her then, unbearably hard. But I can't help her now and so must put any worries about her out of my mind as much as I can and concentrate on Connie, who I can do something about, and do all I can to help her recover her love and trust in me. Connie is my first priority and I owe it to her to be the best mother I can be.'

Angela tried to do that in the next few days as she allowed herself to really recover from the birth and she spent that time with Connie. The weather wasn't kind to them but Connie just enjoyed being with her mother. Despite what she had said to Mary, though, thoughts of the child she had left behind did creep into her mind more often than she would have liked, but she pushed them away and didn't let them spoil her times with her young daughter.

Those thoughts did return at night, very often

invading her sleep, and left her lying awake worrying that leaving the child in the way she had done was a sin. She knew she would never be able to admit what she had done to a priest, not even in the partial anonymity of the confessional box. That meant she had done no penance of any sort nor received absolution and she shouldn't receive communion with such a sin staining her soul, but if she didn't go people would think it odd and might even remark on it.

This bothered her so much at the first Sunday home that she prayed more devoutly at Mass than she had done in a long time. She said how sorry she was for what she had been forced to do and asked God to show her some sacrifice she could make in atonement for what she had done. There was no blinding flash of light, nor did God's angry thunderous voice re-echo in her head, but she was confident that he would show her some way that she could make it up to Him without involving the priests at all.

Despite the fact that Maggie had said that Mr Potter would welcome her back with open arms, Angela hadn't been convinced and wrote to him after they returned from seeing Phyllis and he wrote by return saying he was looking forward to seeing her again and suggesting her starting the following Monday.

TWENTY-EIGHT

Mr Potter was pleased to see Angela again and told her as soon as she was changed to go down to the delivery yard. Angela had thought that someone else would have taken on the driving in her absence and she would be back in the factory, but Sylvia, the woman who had covered for her, was quite willing to relinquish the role back to Angela. 'I don't really like driving,' she said. 'I learnt to drive because I thought I should, but I don't enjoy it and some of those trucks are heavy and difficult to manoeuvre, so I'm glad you're back. I will be better in the factory.'

Angela was sorry Sylvia felt that way, but very glad to get her old job back. She just loved the freedom of the open road.

However when she arrived home she found a letter had arrived from a solicitor to discuss 'matters to her advantage'.

'I wonder what it's all about,' Angela said. 'I've never had anything to do with a solicitor. Anyway there is no way I can take time from work after just having three months away. I'll have to write and say so.'

Towards the second week in January the Bank Manager, Mr Higgins, called to see Angela one evening and said that in view of the vital work Angela was engaged in he would open the bank the following Saturday afternoon so that she

418

could view her inheritance and give instructions as to what to do with it.

'There must be some mistake,' Angela said. 'I have no inheritance.'

'This is from Mr Maitland's estate,' Mr Higgins said. 'He left you some jewellery that had belonged to his mother.'

'Jewellery?'

'Yes indeed,' Mr Higgins said. 'Some nice pieces amongst them. And I apologize for the delay in contacting you. These were not part of the will he left with Geoff Rogers and Co. but some private arrangement between him and Geoff Rogers. It's all legal and above board and they were lodged in the bank for safety's sake. Apparently he was adamant his wife should not have any knowledge of them.

'I didn't know George had died, nor that just days later Geoff Rogers heard of the death of three of his four sons, and that the surviving son was critically injured in a hospital on the South Coast, and he went to see him and completely forgot about the jewellery until he returned, which is when I contacted you.'

Angela remembered how Mary and Matt had suffered over the death of two of their sons and could quite understand the man's distraction. She said this to the bank manager and went on to say, 'I didn't know anything about this, nor was I expecting anything.'

'I believe he thought a lot of you.'

'I thought the world of him,' Angela said sincerely. 'He was a lovely and kind man, but I only helped him in the shop and never in the world

would I have expected him to leave me anything. I am just so sorry he is dead.'

'If you come to the bank on Saturday afternoon you can see the items for yourself,' said Mr Higgins.

'Yes I will be there,' Angela said. 'Thank you making special arrangements for me.'

She went with Mary as Maggie offered to look after Connie and she was nervous and bewildered and so was Mary. Angela had never been into a bank before, the same as most working-class people in those days. Banks were not for the likes of them. If they should manage to save anything at all, a very rare occurrence with a great many, money went into a box under the bed or sometimes the Post Office.

Knowing how awkward she was probably feeling, Mr Higgins was kindness itself to both women and Angela was grateful for his understanding and then was overcome with the kindness and generosity of George when she saw the array of beautiful things that now belonged to her: a pendant on a gold chain, a pearl necklace and a diamond one, an array of bracelets and brooches and a diamond ring. Angela was completely overawed and knew that never in a million years would she have an occasion to wear any of it and she said, 'Mr Higgins, I know nothing about jewellery, but is any of this valuable?'

'Oh yes, there are some lovely pieces here,' Mr Higgins said. 'But I couldn't give an accurate value, not being a jeweller. That could be arranged though?'

'That won't be necessary yet,' Angela said. 'For

now I want everything to stay in the bank where it's safe. I don't want to make any decisions until I can speak to my husband and I won't see him until this blessed war is over.'

But she already knew what she wanted to talk to Barry about and that was selling some of the pieces to fund a secondary education for Connie and the rest of the pieces would be given to her on her wedding day in place of the locket.

'As you wish,' Higgins said. 'It is no problem to us to store them for you.'

And so life continued as it always had. Connie got over her fear that her mother might disappear again and returned to the nursery, but not for much longer because she would be starting at St Catherine's School after Easter and Angela was glad because Connie was outgrowing the nursery. Barry wrote that he could scarce believe that the toddler he left behind would soon be at school and it brought it home to him more forcibly how much of her childhood he was missing.

However, just before Easter the Germans launched a Spring Offensive. Angela couldn't believe it. After an icy, blustery winter, she had been looking forward to spring, when the sun might warm her body and heal her soul because she still felt a little battered and bruised. Added to that she was war weary, everyone was war weary and looking forward to a lessening of hostilities and now the Germans seemed to be starting again. So many had already died and the fields of France ran with blood. But the soldiers were tired, both Stan and Barry had mentioned it, and now they must

421

raise their game to counter the German advance. Angela prayed, imploring God to keep her husband safe a little longer.

The German assault began on 21st March and it was called St Michael's Offensive. 'Funny nation the Germans,' Angela remarked when she read this in the papers they scrutinized every evening. 'Fancy calling an Offensive after a Saint.'

'Does seem odd,' Mary said. 'And yet a woman I met shopping was telling me that it's a very Catholic country.'

'Germany is?'

'That's what she said.'

'I never thought that of Germany,' Angela said. 'France certainly, but not Germany.'

'No I have to admit I don't know much about these people our boys are fighting. But this woman seemed to know a lot and she says that the Kaiser is pinning great hope on this new offensive. He's looking for a speedy end to the war, with Germany the victors.'

'Surely she shouldn't be talking that way?'

'Maybe not, but there was only the two of us in the shop,' Mary said, 'and she didn't say that's what she wanted. She had two sons and both enlisted. The eldest was killed last year and she worries greatly for the other one.'

'Oh I bet,' Angela said. 'I worry about Barry as soon as I open my eyes in the morning and when I sleep I dream about him.'

'I know,' Mary said, 'and yet there's no saying Barry is even involved in this.'

'That's true,' Angela said. 'But he must be involved in something for no letters have come this

week, nor from Stan either.'

'Yes,' Mary said. 'But that has happened before.'

It had and the first time there had been no letters Angela had been a nervous wreck and then, three weeks later, a bunch of letters came together. She accepted the fact that if Barry was actually fighting, he would have little time and less inclination to write her an epistle. And even letters written might be difficult to post, but letters were literally her lifeline, letting her know her beloved Barry was alive and well.

'And,' said Angela, 'if that woman you met shopping is even a bit right they may need every man jack over there deployed to fight this Offensive for it's inconceivable that Germany might win. Too many of our boys' bodies litter the fields of France, or arrive home maimed and damaged, to let the Germans win now, or they will have given their lives in vain. If this is the final push they need to give it all we have to repel the German Army. And I am saying that knowing that Barry and Stan may be in the thick of it.'

And they were in the thick of it. They had been told very little but veterans like Barry knew the German surge had to be overcome at all costs and the Germans beaten back, that the outcome of the war might depend on it. The fighting was as fierce as ever, but Barry was an experienced soldier now.

He had often worried for Stan but Angela always assured him that she was still receiving letters from him so he was bound to be all right. But Barry often wondered if she would tell him if anything

had happened to Stan for the women were told not to worry the men at the Front. He had never caught sight of him before now, but he saw him that day because Stan had come looking for him.

He knew the next day Barry was preparing to go into the front trench to lead the second attack and Stan, who'd seen neither hide nor hair of Barry through all the years of war, decided to seek him out and wish him luck. The day was a cold one and Stan squelched through the muddy ground, the smell of cordite hung in the mist of the early morning and the sounds of fierce fighting could be heard, the crack of rifles, the thumping boom of the big guns, the incessant clatter of machine guns and the whistle and whine of shells.

Barry was standing talking to some of the men that he would be sending over first the following day and Michael Malone was amongst them and he was ridiculously pleased to see Stan in the distance. He had lost many friends and comrades and for Stan to have got through so far virtually unscathed was amazing. Barry's face split into a huge grin and he gave Stan a wave. It was as he started to walk towards him that he saw the arc of a shell in the air, but Stan had his back to it. Barry started to run, shouting a warning, but Stan couldn't hear, so Barry launched himself in the air and threw himself on top of Stan as the shell hit the ground and exploded, killing Barry outright and the two soldiers beside Michael and blowing Michael's left leg clean off.

When there had been no letters for five weeks, Angela was frantic. Each day she woke with a

dead feeling inside her and was glad of the job that gave her no time to think and worried about Mary spending hours alone in the house. 'It must be awful not knowing anything,' Maggie said to Angela one morning. Michael's mother had been to see Maggie and told her of Michael's injuries and she had been shocked and saddened and yet glad to know he was alive, but for Angela there was just silence. There was no way of finding out what had happened to him.

'It is awful,' Angela said. 'See, this has happened before, this lack of letters and then two or three come together. But it's never gone on this long and for Stan's letters to stop as well...' Her voice trailed away and her eyes looked very bleak as she said, 'I hope to God nothing has happened to him Maggie. I don't think I could bear it.'

Maggie was very much afraid the unthinkable had happened and Barry was already dead, but if she was right she didn't want her friend to go under and so she spoke quite briskly, ''Course you'll be able to bear it. You'll have to cope because you have a child to see to and she is part of Barry and you owe it to him to bring her up the best way you know.'

'You are right, Maggie, so right,' Angela said. 'And the first thing I must do is try and find out what's happened to Barry. I won't be in tomorrow, at least for the morning and Sylvia can do any deliveries needed.'

'Well I won't blame you,' Maggie said. 'And neither will anyone else, but I don't know what Mr Potter will make of it.'

'Well if he doesn't like it he'll have to lump it,'

425

Angela said almost fiercely. 'To me this is more important than making shells.'

She didn't say that to Mr Potter, but she did say she was fed up living with uncertainty. 'Barry wrote to me two days before the Germans started their Spring Offensive and that's over five weeks ago. Since then I have heard nothing, I don't know whether he is alive or dead and I need to try and find out and I intend to have tomorrow off to do that.'

Mr Potter realized Angela was coiled tight as a spring, her voice too betrayed just how anxious she was and he knew he was looking at a young woman at the end of her tether. So all he said was, 'Are you going to the Barracks at Thorp Street?'

Angela nodded. 'I wouldn't know anywhere else to try.'

'Nor I,' Mr Potter said. 'Take tomorrow off and find out all you can about that young husband of yours and I really hope the news is good.'

'So do I Mr Potter,' Angela said. 'Oh so do I.'

Mary approved of what Angela was doing but all Connie heard was that her mother wasn't going to work the following day and she was ecstatic because Mammy promised her that they would have breakfast together and then she would take her to school and meet her teacher Mrs Cleary.

Connie had begun at St Catherine's School just over a fortnight ago when it re-opened after the Easter holidays and according to Mary, possibly helped by going to nursery, she had settled to it as if she had been going all the days of her life.

The next morning Angela woke with knots of apprehension in her stomach while Connie was

still fizzing with excitement. She had no appetite, she hadn't had any for days, but having breakfast together mattered to Connie so she forced herself to eat the bowl of porridge Mary insisted on before school and they walked hand in hand along Bristol Street and Angela remembered going the same route hand in hand with eight-year-old Barry when she was Connie's age, for all the McCluskys had gone to St Catherine's.

She stood in the playground and let the memories flow, her and Maggie skipping or throwing a ball up the wall or joining with others to play cops and robbers or tag. The bell was rung by an older child as it had been in her day and when the teachers came into the playground the children lined up in front of them and Connie went up to the teacher who was obviously Mrs Cleary and pointed her mother out and the teacher approached her smiling. 'Connie didn't really need to point you out for she is the image of you,' she said to Angela.

'I know, but she's excited I'm here. I don't usually make it because I work long hours in a shell factory. I'm playing hookey today.'

'She told me what you do. You have a bright girl there, Mrs McClusky. She says her father is a soldier.'

'He is,' Angela said. She bit her lip anxiously and then because the teacher was so approachable, she went on, 'He's missing, not officially, but we have heard nothing for more than five weeks. I've had the day off to see if I can find out more.'

'Oh good luck,' Mrs Cleary said. 'I must get the children back to the classroom before they break

ranks and run amok in the playground, but I do hope you find all is well.'

'Thank you,' said Angela and watched Mrs. Cleary leading her class in, with Connie giving her a surreptitious little wave as she turned the corner, which caused a smile to tug at Angela's mouth.

The women in the office at Thorp Street Barracks couldn't really help. 'I thought you might have casualty lists or something,' Angela said.

'We will have,' said the young woman behind the desk. 'You must understand they are difficult to compile when the conflict is still going on.'

'And you must understand that Barry is my husband, the father of our daughter, and I am desperate to know what has happened to him.'

'I know,' the girl said more sympathetically. 'You're not the first to ask, believe me.'

'Maybe that's because we are told nothing,' Angela said ironically. 'See, these are not numbers on a page, or percentages, they are people, sons, fathers, sweethearts and uncles and these people need to know and as soon as possible what has happened to their loved ones. Has anyone even made an educated guess how many have died in this Offensive to date?'

The girl shook her head. 'They may have done that, but I have no figures given to me.'

Angela felt suddenly so helpless and downhearted. She felt her shoulders sag and she had the desire to lie on the floor and weep.

'Look,' the girl said. 'All I can advise is to try to be patient for if anything has happened to your husband you will be informed in due course.'

'And that's all the help you can give me?'

'Yes I'm afraid it is.'

'Thank you,' said Angela, wondering what she was thanking her for.

She thought of going back to work, but she was too dispirited. They had all known in the factory why she'd had the time off and would be asking questions she couldn't answer and it would make her feel worse than ever.

On the other hand, going home to Mary to tell her she knew no more than when she had set out that morning was not a great prospect either. But she could hardly walk the streets all day and she supposed Mary had to know how it went regardless and so she turned for home and arrived in tears.

Mary cried too when Angela told her what had happened at the Barracks with the girl in the office. Later, when she was calmer she said, 'I was so cross with the girl behind the desk and it really wasn't her fault. She was only young and if she hasn't been given the information there is nothing she can do about it.'

'I suppose not,' Mary said. 'We just have to wait then?'

'Fraid so.'

'Bloody hard isn't it?'

'It is bloody hard. I think it's the hardest thing in the world.'

Angela was glad when it was time to collect Connie. Connie had not known whether she would or not, so she was delighted to see her mother and all the way home she chuntered on about her day and how good it had been. They were going to go in the front door, but there was something stopping

it from opening so they went in the entry door. They found the body of Mary slumped against the front door, blocking it, and there was a crumpled telegram in her hand.

With a cry Angela was on her knees beside her. Mary wasn't dead, as she had feared, but she needed help and Angela went out of the entry where the children were playing and sent Freddie Webster for the doctor for she knew him to be a sensible boy who lived down the yard. The doctor had a surgery on Bristol Street, which was no distance, and Angela watched Freddie's legs pounding as he tore down the street and knew he would be there in no time and gave a sigh of relief.

Connie was sitting on the floor patting Mary's face gently and as her mother came in the entry door she turned with troubled eyes and said, 'Why won't Granny wake up?'

Angela got down on the floor beside her daughter and held her close as she said, 'Granny is very tired and needs the doctor to help her wake up.'

'Oh. Is he coming then?'

'Yes he's on his way,' Angela said. 'So soon Granny will be as right as rain again.'

'Yes,' said Connie, happier now for she knew doctors were very clever people, not that she ever went to the doctor's because they cost money and anyway she was never sick, not that sick to need a doctor. But if there was something wrong with Granny that needed a doctor he would fix her in no time, she was sure.

'Now we need to make Granny more comfortable,' Angela said. 'We need a pillow and a blanket.'

'I'll get them, Mammy.'

'You get the pillow from my bed,' Angela suggested, getting to her feet. 'I'll fetch the blanket, it's too big for you and you might fall down the stairs.'

When they returned to the room Angela moved Mary a little away from the door and placed the pillow beneath her head and tucked the blanket around her as Freddie's mother, Nancy put her head around the entry door and said, 'Our Freddie's just come in and said you sent him for the doctor.' She came into the room as she spoke and saw Mary comatose on the floor. 'Oh my God! What's happened to Mary?'

'This happened,' Angela said, indicating the crumpled telegram she had prised from Mary's grasp and put on the mantelpiece.

'Barry?' Nancy asked and Angela just gave a brief nod because Connie was watching her and she knew who Barry was.

'Ah poor soul,' Nancy said sympathetically. 'And poor you.'

Nancy's words caused tears to prickle behind Angela's eyes because she hadn't even begun yet to deal with the enormity of her loss.

Then Nancy turned to Connie and said, 'Would you like to come and play with our Jenny?'

Jenny was a big girl of eight, but Connie shook her head. 'I need to stay with Mammy. I want to see my Granny wake up.'

'The doctor might send her to hospital so they can help her,' Nancy said. 'And you wouldn't want her to go on her own would you?'

Connie shook her head and Nancy said, 'Well

I'm sure your Mom would like to go with her and when your Granny wakes up she'll like it if your Mom is there, but she can't take you with her because they don't let children into hospitals.'

Connie turned to her mother and said, 'Don't they?'

Angela shook her head for tears were too close to risk speaking. Nancy was aware of this and knew it was important to get the child away because Angela was holding herself together with difficulty.

Nancy bent down on her hunkers and said, 'So d'you want to come home with me then? I'm sure I have a spare thruppenny bit in my purse and you could go down Bristol Street with our Jen and buy some sweets.'

Connie smiled and Nancy stood up and held out her hand and Connie took it and as they passed Angela Nancy said quietly, 'Don't worry about tonight, she can stop with us if it makes life easier.'

'Thank you,' Angela said brokenly. 'You are very kind.'

The door had barely shut behind Nancy and Connie when Angela sank to her knees as her legs refused to hold her up and, as the tears flowed, anguished sobs came from deep within her. She cried in deep sadness and despair at the loss of her lovely Barry. It was as if a deep black hole had opened up in front of her for she couldn't visualize a future without him.

Angela had got a grip on herself by the time the doctor arrived minutes later. He said that Mary had suffered a heart attack, which Angela had

thought it was and said she had to go to hospital immediately. He asked Angela if she knew what might have caused it and she showed him the telegram. 'Her son?'

'Is he also your husband?' the doctor asked and Angela nodded mutely and he understood her distress and saw that she was barely coping with it.

She travelled in the ambulance with Mary holding her hand and then she sat for hours on a hard chair in a bleak corridor with paint peeling from the walls and illuminated by small high and very dirty windows and she thought about Barry. She wondered how he died and hoped it had been a quick death. She would hate to think of him suffering and thought she would never know.

And she suddenly knew what it was all about. God had enacted his revenge and Barry had paid the ultimate price for her transgression. Mary might pay as well for she wasn't out of the woods yet and they said the next twenty-four hours would be critical and if she pulled through, she had a chance.

Mary made it through the night and as soon as Angela knew that, she went off to the factory and gave in her notice. News of what had happened to Barry and Mary McClusky had flown around the area as it tended to, especially in those cramped streets and so Maggie had heard all about it and told all her workmates as soon as she arrived at the factory and they all felt sorry for Angela.

'Shame about her old man copping it like that,' one girl remarked. 'But I bet she weren't so bothered about her mother-in law. I wouldn't mind a bit if mine popped her clogs 'cos she's a

right pain in the neck.'

'Oh it isn't a bit like that for Angela,' Maggie said. 'Her mother-in-law Mary brought her up.'

'How come?'

Maggie found herself telling the whole tale of Angela's childhood, engendering even more sympathy for her. So when she arrived to give notice everyone, including Mrs Paget, made a fuss of her and said how sorry they were about Barry and his mother and Mr Potter expressed his deepest condolences. He quite understood why she had to leave and said so as he shook her by the hand and said she was one of the best drivers he'd ever had working for him. She left feeling she had been greatly liked and appreciated and though it didn't change what had happened, it made her better able to cope.

Despite how her workmates felt about her though, she knew if Mary died it would be her fault, like Barry's death was, and it caused an ache in her heart every time she thought of this. Overlying it all though was a feeling of guilt that she knew she would always feel and she deserved to. That was her punishment.

Mary didn't die, though they said her heart was very weak and another heart attack would probably kill her. But if she had a stress-free life and no heavy physical exertion she might live some years yet.

Mary wasn't impressed and said she wished they hadn't fought so hard to save her, and this upset Angela for she wasn't sure what she would have done if she had lost Mary too, and she prayed hard for her to pull through, and she said she needn't

have bothered, but of course she couldn't argue with Mary and risk upsetting her.

A week later Mary was much better physically so they were getting ready to release her from hospital and the doctor asked her if she had any pain in the chest area. 'I have a throbbing, almost unbearable ache constantly in my heart,' she said. 'There's nothing you can do about it for there's not a physical cause. It's just the tearing pain I have with the loss of another son. I am more than ready to go home. There's worse than me might need this bed.'

Angela knew exactly how Mary felt for her pain too was sometimes agonizing and she got through it, one day at a time. She had told Connie her daddy wouldn't be coming home, but she didn't seem that bothered and Angela tried not to let that upset her. After all she was too young when he left for her to remember him and lots of her friends' daddies were away too. In fact there were few men about generally. In contrast to Connie's reaction, Finbarr and Colm were totally devastated by news of their young brother's death. They sent heartfelt condolences and Mass cards for Masses to be said for the repose of his soul. Even Father Brannigan sounded sincere for a change when he said how sorry he was.

A fortnight after the telegram, a letter came. It was from Barry's commanding officer expressing his condolences. He described Barry as an outstanding young man he had been proud to know for he proved to be honest, reliable and brave, and saying the loss of him must be a grievous one

for them to bear. He went on to describe him as a first-rate soldier too and completely fearless in battle. He put his life on the line many times to save comrades and, stalwart to the end, he eventually gave his life to save another and he would be recommending him for a military medal.

When Angela finished reading the letter out to Mary and folded it up she had tears in her eyes, but they were tears of pride. 'Thought a lot of our Barry obviously.'

'And why wouldn't he be?' Angela asked. 'Barry is a son and husband we can both be proud of.'

'He is that,' Mary said. 'Now I wish I could find out what had happened to Stan.'

'Stan must be dead, Mammy,' said Angela. 'I wrote to his sister after we got the telegram to see if she'd news of him and in her reply she said that the deal she made with Stan was for no contact.'

'I know that but surely the war changed all that?'

'Not as far as Betty was concerned. Stan wrote to her once to explain he was enlisting and telling her about the money put in trust for Daniel when he is twenty-one, but she didn't reply.'

'So he could be alive or dead and she'd never know?'

'That's about the strength of it,' Angela said. 'We are his point of contact. Any telegram or communication would come here. I don't understand why we haven't had a telegram or anything, but after all this time he must be dead.'

Stan wasn't dead, but he was in hospital, or the loony bin as he preferred to call it. When they collected him up from the battlefield he was un-

conscious and it was some time before he realized it had been Barry McClusky who had saved his life and so lost his own, and he had wanted to weep, for it was the opposite of what he would have wanted to happen.

He had not got away totally unscathed and they were ages putting his insides back together again and then they had to dig shrapnel out of his body, but he knew he would survive physically. Whether he would ever get over the mental anguish he felt when he thought of Barry sacrificing himself for the worthless person he thought he was, was another matter.

Barry had had so much going for him, a lovely wife, an adorable child, a mother who thought the sun shone out of him and a job he had enjoyed and was good at. His own life was sterile in comparison. No one would grieve overmuch if he had died in the war. He more or less expected death and instead he was still here now because of Barry.

Stan knew they were all worried about his mental state and put some of it down to battle fatigue because he had been in it since the beginning, and he couldn't really explain about the black cloud that hung over him. He only knew it would never disappear. It would always be there because he had inadvertently hurt the woman he loved.

He loved Angela with every shred of his being, though he had never shown it. He was an honourable man and wanted Angela to be happy and knew that what would make her happy was if Barry was to return from the war unscathed. It was his fault that Barry wasn't doing that because he would be alive if he hadn't taken the full

force of the exploding shell. Barry sacrificed his own life in an effort to save Stan's miserable skin. However could he face Angela with that on his conscience?

Well he couldn't he decided and he had told the authorities there was no one to inform about his whereabouts, so no one knew where he was, but as soon as he could convince the doctors he was sane enough to be released, he would disappear into the countryside where no one knew him.

Through the late spring and summer of that year Mary and Angela coped with the loss of Barry in their own way and Connie helped a great deal and prevented them sinking into serious depression and gradually they didn't so much 'get over it' but rather learned to live with the pain. 'Day to day I can cope as long as I keep busy, but odd things catch you out like the other day someone was whistling a tune Barry used to whistle.'

'I know what you mean,' Mary said. 'Mind how the two of us would nag Barry not to take his socks off and throw them down in the room and he would take no notice?'

'I remember.'

'Well I came upon one the other day,' Mary said. 'It was behind a cushion and I cried bucketloads and I thought if he was here now he could throw his socks wherever he wanted to.'

Angela smiled ruefully. 'Seems irrelevant now,' she said. 'I crossed the road the other day to avoid the hurdy-gurdy man because the memories of the last time we saw him were too painful.'

The summer drew to a close and the schools

reopened and Connie was as keen as ever to go back, especially as Angela drew money out of the savings to buy her some serviceable clothes for school, a thick coat, woolly stockings and stout boots for the winter and when she was all dressed up in her new things to show her Granny she said she was as smart as paint.

Angela hated the slide into the dark nights of winter for since the attack she'd been afraid of the dark. And she hated the way sometimes the mornings seemed reluctant to start the day and it was often murky and grey and sometimes that continued into the day. And that's how it was on Monday 11th November when the church bells began to peal. All the churches around were chiming out the joyful news that the war, which had near annihilated all their menfolk was over at last. The bells had been silent for four years and everyone knew what it meant when they were chiming now.

Factory hooters joined in as people were released from their places of work and thronged the streets, some people singing and a few banging dustbin lids together, adding to the general cacophony. Connie arrived home with Jennifer Webster for the schools had been closed and Jennifer thought her too young to come home on her own.

Even Connie, catching the atmosphere, was excited though she wasn't sure why. Euphoria gripped the crowd and Angela would have liked to have joined them, but Mary had a bad cold and she wouldn't leave her that day of all days, but Connie was allowed to go with Nancy Webster and her children who promised to look after her. 'You shouldn't be staying here with an old woman

either,' Mary said. 'You should be off with the rest.'

'I am not staying with an old woman,' Angela retorted. 'I am staying with a mother I love with all my heart. I'd prefer to be nowhere else and I want to remember the man we have lost and Stan too. The end of the war has come too late for us and many more like us.'

'Yes,' said Mary, 'but not for Connie.'

'What d'you mean?'

'Well that's the legacy her father has assured for her because they say this has been the war to end all wars.'

'It's true; they do say that, yes.'

'Well she will grow up without a father, but the carnage has been such that there will be lots of fatherless children and all those fathers will have died so that Connie and the rest might marry and have sons of their own, safe in the knowledge they will not be snatched away to fight in a war. Her generation will not be blighted by war as this generation has been.'

What sense Mary spoke, Angela thought. She'd been feeling so downhearted. She knew that Barry would have gladly given his life to secure a better future for his daughter and in the same spirit she must live with his loss and deal with the guilty feelings that nagged at her almost constantly. Each night she prayed earnestly for the little winter waif she had left behind on the workhouse steps, the baby she still grieved for. And each night she also thanked God that she had Connie and Mary hopefully for a good few years yet, so she was almost content.

ACKNOWLEDGEMENTS

I had trouble with my eyes as I was attempting to write this book and as eyes are extremely important, particularly for a writer, I was very worried indeed. The problem was, almost seven years ago, I had the lenses in both eyes changed as I was growing cataracts behind them. The consultant assured me I would have almost A1 vision after the operations and would never develop cataracts and sure enough, just as he said, I could for the first time read, watch television, work on the computer etc. without glasses. It was wonderful.

Four years down the line, I noticed a slight deterioration in my sight and put it down to natural ageing, but this deterioration continued and I thought that I must have Macular Degeneration. I said nothing, but over the years bought a daylight lamp and stronger and stronger reading glasses. By the time I was writing *The Forget-Me-Not Child*, my eyesight suddenly deteriorated further to the extent I could see very little – including the keyboard, which was a blur – or what I was writing.

I eventually took myself off to the optician expecting to hear her say that I was losing my sight and there was nothing that could be done and I

was delighted to hear that that was not the case at all. The fact was, that though the cataracts had been removed, the debris that would have grown behind the cataracts had continued to increase and the best news of all was it was treatable. I had to wait more than three weeks to see a surgeon for laser treatment but apart from daily eye drops and a few floaters, afterwards I was able to see again.

I am always grateful to have such a strong team behind me at HarperCollins but never more than then, for they were so understanding and supportive, particularly my editor Kate Bradley and my agent Judith Murdoch. My heartfelt thanks go to them and also Charlotte Brabbin, my publicist Hayley Camis and to Rhian McKay who did such a sterling job on the second copy edits. Writers usually work alone and it is sometimes a relief to know I have a comfort blanket of such reassuring people at my back and I owe a debt of gratitude to you all.

I am also grateful I can rely on the support of the family too: my husband, Denis; my three daughters – Nikki and her husband Steve; Tamsin and her husband Mark; my daughter Beth; my son Simon and his wife Carol and of course the five grandchildren – all of you are immensely dear to me.

But the most important people of all are you, the readers, for without you there would be no point in doing what I do. I value every single one of you, so thank you from the bottom of my heart and I sincerely hope you enjoy this book, it is the start of a trilogy. I love it when you write and tell me what you think.

The publishers hope that this book has given you enjoyable reading. Large Print Books are especially designed to be as easy to see and hold as possible. If you wish a complete list of our books please ask at your local library or write directly to:

Magna Large Print Books
Magna House, Long Preston,
Skipton, North Yorkshire.
BD23 4ND